Forever Never Dies

Also by

Trudie-Pearl Sturgess

*The
Silent Sisterhood*

Forever Never Dies

Trudie-Pearl Sturgess

AuthorHouse™
1663 Liberty Drive
Bloomington, IN 47403
www.authorhouse.com
Phone: 1-800-839-8640

© 2010, 2011 by Trudie-Pearl Sturgess. All rights reserved.

No part of this book may be reproduced, stored in a retrieval system, or transmitted by any means without the written permission of the author.

First published by AuthorHouse   05/14/2011

ISBN: 978-1-4490-7558-3 (sc)
ISBN: 978-1-4490-7559-0 (dj)
ISBN: 978-1-4490-7560-6 (ebk)

Library of Congress Control Number: 2011907949

Printed in the United States of America

Any people depicted in stock imagery provided by Thinkstock are models, and such images are being used for illustrative purposes only.
Certain stock imagery © Thinkstock.

This book is printed on acid-free paper.

Because of the dynamic nature of the Internet, any web addresses or links contained in this book may have changed since publication and may no longer be valid. The views expressed in this work are solely those of the author and do not necessarily reflect the views of the publisher, and the publisher hereby disclaims any responsibility for them.

To my wonderful family,
Nana Sarpong Naana Konadu-Yiadam
Mama Joyce Micheal Aseidu
Nana Kessie Papa Yaw and their children and grandchildren.
Chrissel and Torian Sturgess,
I love you all with all my heart and soul.
Hope lives. TS

Thank you, Dr. Sally Braun-Jackson for editing the book.

Jacket Photo by
Chris Rhodes/Dream sound Canada.

Visit the Trudie Sturgess Web Site at
WWW.trudiesturgessgroup.com

Chapter 1

Brooke has learned over the years that her mother is a wonderful warmhearted woman just like the mothers of her two best friends, Kate and Tia. As a teenager, she always wished that her mother could be a lot more like them, but the twenty-six-year-old woman understands her mother much better now than she did growing up. Her own marriage to Jason Gray has been tested with betrayal and public humiliation, but somehow she and Jason have managed to put their marriage back on track. She does wish, though, that her mother would stop grieving and love again.

Working with her mother has also proven to be fulfilling, though a couple of years ago, Brooke shared her concern with her mother about starting her own real estate brokerage. Sarah admitted that she was thinking about retiring and enjoying what's left of her life before it's too late, so there was no need for Brooke to open another brokerage of Gemini Real Estate Inc.

"It's yours, B.B. I was just a caretaker until you knew what you wanted. Now that you love the business, it is all yours to do as you wish," Sarah says.

Brooke replies, "Gee, thanks, Mum, but I have something different in mind. I'd like to do something that Jason and I could build together for our children someday." Brooke chuckles, "You know, I tried to share my idea with Jason two years ago when we were in Holland, but the poor darling though I wanted us to start a family!"

"Jaden is thinking of starting his own law firm," Brooke continued, "and he asked me to find him a commercial space to lease." Brooke sat down next to her mother with her laptop open and logged on to the MLS website. "Mother, I want you to take a look at this property for me. I was thinking we could buy it and develop it. We can rent out the main floors. Jaden could have his new law firm there, too. He does real estate law, you know. I'm thinking Jason could start his own mortgage firm and he could have space on the second floor, and we—Gemini, that is—could move our office up to the top floor. The building is selling "as is" and I have already had the market evaluation done on it. I'd like your approval so I can make an offer on the property."

Sarah didn't have to think about it because she loved the idea, so she told Brooke to go for it. Privately, she has been worried that Brooke has put her life and marriage aside for Tia. Tia's illness made everyone uneasy not knowing the outcome. They all thank God she is well now. Sarah loves how Brooke feels overly protective of Tia and her children, but Sarah is glad she is now thinking about her own life with Jason. Jason is enthusiastic about the idea, and he asked if they could sell the loft since they hardly live there, and he could use the money for his start-up costs, putting the rest away so they could buy a home later. Brooke replies, "Tia's younger sister, Lisa, has visited the loft and wants to buy it. However, if Lisa want it, I'm sure she'll want to close it as soon as possible. Can we move that quickly?"

"That will not be a problem for me. It's all on you, sweetheart. I know how much you love the loft."

"Okay. I will call Lisa soon, then. Tia has already designed a web site for you. She wants you to give her the name so we can get going at the same time," Brooke tells Jason.

While lunching with Kate and Jaden, Brooke and Jason told them about the proposed move to the new building. Unhappy with her career trajectory at Bankers Trust and needing a new challenge, Kate said, "I'm thinking of leaving Bankers Trust. Jason, will you need a partner in this new venture?" Jason was too happy to have her as a partner because Kate knows the London financial market inside out. She told Jason many of the Asian community find it difficult to obtain a mortgage from the banks. Brooke agreed, adding that she and her mother were thinking about that market niche, too, as many of their Asian clients can't meet their closing costs simply because the banks will not lend them enough money.

Naana Konadu-Sharp has a lot of her private money tied up in mortgages that she has lent to people who had difficulty obtaining enough mortgage funds. "Lisa tells me that they are looking to expand their company African Mortgage Funds. I am meeting with Naana and Lisa next week to see if they want to buy the lower level of our building. If it works out the way that I think it should, we all will be making money in a full-service Real Estate Services building!" Brooke enthused.

They all sat back to listen and to watch Brooke explain the concept and collectively thought, "What a brilliant idea!" Later, when Naana and Brooke met to discuss the details of African Mortgage Funds acquiring space in the building, Naana suggested that Brooke lease some part of the lower level to Dr Freedom Washington, as he had just returned from Liberia and he was looking for a space in that neighborhood to set up a private practice. Brooke recalls that Dr. Washington's sister, Lock, is one of Tia's close friends and next-door neighbor to her mother. Lisa agreed that such an arrangement would be a good idea since her mother's company does a lot of business with the African businesses in the area. Within six months, Brooke, Jason, Kate and Jaden had turned the nasty old building into a sleek five-story commercial building.

Tony Blair, the British Prime Minister for the past fives years, has urged the residents of southeast London to clean up the area. Naturally, Brooke did not have any problems getting the permit to rebuild the Sky Line, as Brooke called the building in Greenwich. Overall, Brooke attempted to accommodate everyone's needs and wishes. They added underground parking as well as parking at the back for the staff; state of the art security protected access to individual offices as well as client and patient computer records; and ergonomic office furniture enhanced the functionality of the work space. Brooke hired a contractor to paint soothing colors on the walls and to install a water feature in the lobby of the building. The whole building conveyed a sense of unity and harmony. Naana Konadu-Sharp is very impressed. She was not too sure about the project to beginning with, as she seldom mixes business with friends and family. Lisa, her middle child, is now twenty-two years old and attending the University of London. She also works for the African Mortgage Funds. She helped sell the idea to her mother to move their offices to the Sky Line. As predicted by Brooke, they were all doing very well. She and Jason have now bought a home in Thames Mead, a four bedroom back split, a beautiful open-concept home with a cathedral ceiling. Brooke and her mother tastefully decorated the gorgeous home. Jaden and Kate have welcomed another son whom they named Thomas. His older brother, James, has been staying with Jason and Brooke while Kate is in hospital. The Sharp's and Sarah Williams came to welcome the new baby home. Jason, James and Brooke were the last to arrive at the party. Mrs Lee couldn't help asking when will Jason and Brooke start a family, and everyone laughed. Jason could not keep the secret anymore, so he blurted out that Brooke was already five months pregnant, but that she didn't want anyone to know yet. Just at that moment, Brooke returned from the kitchen with a plate full of food and everyone stared at her.

"If you all stop looking at how much I'm eating, I can tell you all that I'm expecting twins in four months," Brooke sassed.

Jason passed out. Later, he confided to Jaden, "I hope the twins are boys because I don't think I can handle three Brookes!" Overhearing the remark, Bobby Sharp told Jason, "Welcome to my world! Just wait until they become teenagers with loud music and boys calling all hours of night. Then you will wish they were babies again. I don't envy you young kids," Bobby patted them both on the back as he took his wife by the hand. "We'll say good-bye, now, and leave you to your party."

Brooke was spending the weekend with her mother when the babies begin to kick harder then usual. She began to panic thinking there was something wrong. Sarah assured Brooke she would be okay. "I was not planning to have kids this early. It's a lot harder done," she thought. She has gained more weight and been told to watch her weight and cut her work load. There are two things that Brooke Williams is known for other than looking good: food and work. Her feet swell often, so she has to massage them frequently. She feels happier than she has been in a long time she tells her mother. Despite the current discomfort, Brooke is looking forward to the twins being born. She didn't want to know the sex of the babies when she had her ultrasound. Sarah is also looking forward to being a grandmother. She hopes the twins will give her the opportunity to really bond with her daughter and the grandchildren.

Sarah rubbed Brooke's feet while she talks on the phone with Naana Konadu-Sharp. They have been very close friends because of the girls. She really admires Naana's strength; not too many women in her position will have the courage to do what she has done over the past ten years with Bobby. "Bobby Sharp is one lucky son of a bitch," Sarah thought.

Bobby Sharp has realized during the past year, since his wife has been in Canada helping Nathan with his grandchildren, what a lucky man he is to have a wife like Naana. They have been married for twenty-five years.

Not once has his wife ever complained about their life, or his inability to be faithful to her. She has single-handed raised the girls and kept them out of everyday trouble most families face. He has noticed that his wife has moved to Tia's old room since her return from Canada and works longer hours. She seldom talks to him these days. He hates it, and realizes he has been taking her for granted over the years. Now it looks like she doesn't care what he does anymore. As Bobby opens the car door for her, Naana asks him to drop her off at her office.

"Darling, I was hoping we could spend the afternoon alone. I wanted to go to W.H. Smith, so I can buy you a book and go home. While you read, I can order some take-out food for us," Bobby offered.

"That's sounds good, but I have a lot of work to do at the office and lots of phone calls to Ghana," she said with her eyes closed, head leaned back against the seat.

Bobby didn't push. He knows his wife runs her other company in Ghana over the phone when she is in England. He has not been to her new offices, so he got out of the car and followed her into the building. It was very different from her old offices.

Naana turned and said, "You must go home, Bobby. I will call a cab home when I'm done."

Both her cell phone and her private phone in her office were ringing. Nathan was on the land line. "Nathan, darling! Can you hold for one moment, please?" she said as she reached for the cell phone. It was the girls calling to say they had arrived safely in Holland. "I'll call you right back. I've got a call on the other line."

Picking up the land line again, Naana said, "I am sorry, darling. The girls drove to Holland today and they just arrived. How are you? How are Tia and the children?"

Nathan told her they were all fine and everyone was good. She told him that Bobby was here with her so she put the phone on speaker. Nathan told them that he and Tia are going to get re-married, and that they wanted to come to Holland and get married in the house so everyone can be a part of it. "Would grandmother Gertrude mind, do you think?" asked Nathan.

"Oh, Nathan! That's great news! I'll call mother and then we can chat next week and arrange everything," replied Naana with tears of happiness in her eyes.

"Father, Steven and Jackie are coming too, Mother," said Nathan.

Tia came on the phone, "Mother, why are you in the office on the weekend? Don't you have better things to do?"

"Just a few things to finish up. That's all, darling," assured Naana.

Tia felt her mother's loneliness and she was not too pleased about it. "I hate how you let Daddy abandon you like this, Mother. This is not right!" Tia exclaimed.

Naana laughed. Bobby knew Tia was right.

"I'm sorry, Tia. You're right. Mother will not let me make it up to her. You know. I've been an old fool, darling. Perhaps, you can put in a good word for me?" Bobby pleaded.

His wife is smiling at him which relieved his anxiety a little bit.

"You don't get to hide behind me, Daddy. I am very disappointed with you. Nathan is mad at me for hogging the phone, so I will call you later. I love you!" Tia hung up the phone.

Naana assured Bobby that she really does have a lot to do at the office and that she will be home soon. Bobby told her to hire him for the day, so that the work would be finished faster and he can take his wife home sooner. Naana realizes that she has missed him, too, and frankly, she could do with the help. Between the two of them they finished the work in no time and headed home together. They ordered a take-out and a movie. Bobby could not remember the last time he laid on the sofa with his wife to watch a movie. It felt good just like when they were in college. "Hmmm. She still wears the same perfume," he noticed as he rubbed her back. Naana nodded off to sleep.

Bobby carried Naana up to their room, gently lay her on their bed and covered her. He came back downstairs to tidy up the take-out food. On his way back upstairs, he heard the shower running in their bathroom. Naana was awake and out of the bed. He quickly took of his clothes and joined her. She told him that she was too tired for his nonsense. He kissed her on the neck and gently washed her back. She moaned with pleasure and asked what he's up to. He assured her that he has not been up to anything. He has realized what an idiot he's been while she was in Canada. He asked himself why she has stayed with him all these years. Any other woman would have dumped him by now.

She gently brushed the hair from his face and said, "You've always had my heart, and it's locked with a key. I've been waiting for you to grow up, darling."

"I am still in love with you, just like the first day of enrollment at college," he murmured. "I miss holding you at night, your soft kisses in the morning, Princess. Please, come back to our bedroom," he begged.

Naana gently kissed him on the nose, knowing she also has missed him. He said, "I am so proud of what you have done with your company. I didn't realize just how much it has grown in the last few years." Naana was no different from most Africans: she did not want to work for any company when she graduated from college. She decided to run her own business using her family's private money to lend to those to whom the banks often don't lend. Twenty two years later she was making more than her husband makes in a year as president of Bankers Trust. She has opened a foreign exchange bank in Ghana and it is doing very well, too. She tells her husband that Lisa is doing well in university in both business and law. She hopes that when Lisa graduates, she will want to take over the business.

Bobby loves listening to her telling him about the girls. He has had breakfast with the girls every morning since they were babies, but Naana has been the mother as well as the father to them. He still takes his two younger girls to church every Sunday, and they will meet up at his parents with Naana for lunch or sometimes the elder Sharps will come to their house for lunch. Bobby has had numerous affairs since they've been married, some he managed to hide, but the last resulted in a child, a ten-year-old boy. His mother used to be Bobby's assistant and they had an affair for two years. It was one of the things Bobby regrets most. He refused to leave his family for her, so one day he came home from work to discover Brenda in his home with his wife. She has brought the newborn and threatened to leave the child, which she did for six months.

Naana took care of the baby day and night. Bobby refused to go near the boy. She would take the child to her office and come home and make dinner for the girls and Bobby. The girls also loved the little boy, but Naana never told them that he was Bobby's illegitimate child. After a while, Brenda came to her senses and came for the baby. Bobby still refused to see the boy, although he provided handsomely for him. Naana has often encouraged Bobby to see the little boy, maybe let the girls knows about him, but Bobby refuses. She made it clear to him not to come near her in private, and half of Bobby died the day his wife found out. She told him he can have a divorce anytime he wishes. So, holding her, kissing her, and talking to her tonight is so relaxing.

Naana asks "Are you okay?"

Shamefaced, Bobby replies, "I miss you, so much. Please forgive me. I have been ashamed for everything. I have never really apologized for my actions," he murmured.

Brenda and BJ is a subject that Naana often doesn't want to think about. She stands up, sweeping her hair over one shoulder.

"A white man married to an African woman with three children—all girls—the man having an affair with a white woman with a son and naming the child after himself; the child being dropped off for the wife to take care of her husband's love child is not something any woman can forget!" Naana muttered. She left the room. Bobby has never really thought of it as his wife puts it. His children will never forgive him when it comes out. He has never thought of his wife as an African, or himself as a white man. He runs his hands through his hair and opens his eyes to what his wife had said. He runs downstairs after her with only a towel wrapped around his waist, his heart racing. Bobby thought the whole thing was out of sight and out of mind, but this was worse then he expected. Bobby was on his knees, holding on to Naana, telling her that he was sorry.

Tears in her eyes, Naana says, "Bobby, please get up." Her voice is kind. "I'm not upset about your betrayal or my humiliation. Think about poor, sweet BJ and the girls. They loved him, Bobby. Instead of you coming clean and telling them that was their brother, you wanted to hide it. I also . . . love him," she cried. "BJ deserves better than this. Every child deserves to have a father. You may have abandoned him, but I haven't. I see him every weekend that I'm in London."

Shocked, Bobby let go of his wife, enraged that his wife would go behind his back. He asks, "Why would you do that?"

"Why not? Your lover made it clear she didn't want B.J, just like you did. I am sorry, but someone had to be there for my children's brother if their father wouldn't." She lashed out. "I am going to bed. I have to drive him to his football game in the morning and I don't want to be late."

"I forbid you to see that boy again, Naana." Bobby shouted up the stairs.

She laughed, and said "good night."

Naana was asleep by the time her head hit the pillow. Bobby didn't sleep all night. He has never thought of Brenda and the boy. He had no idea that his wife has a relationship with the boy all these years. "What the hell is Brenda playing at?" he asked himself. "How am I going to put a stop to it? I am not going to lose my wife over one mistake. I have paid the biggest price there is. I cannot allow this to continue."

When Naana opened her eyes, it was two in the morning. Bobby was still up, looking more upset with each passing minute. She opened the comforter and told him to come to bed. He did, so she cuddled up to him and said, "please come with me tomorrow to watch BJ play football. He is in the finals, Bobby, and he is really good." She kissed him and went back to sleep.

Bobby was still sleeping at six in the morning. Naana has not told him that she has agreed that BJ should come and stay with them. Brenda is getting married and moving to America next month. BJ doesn't listen to his mother. Brenda has no plans to take the boy with her to her new life. Brenda's fiance has made it clear that BJ is not part of the package. BJ loves and respects Naana, and in return Naana adores the boy. Brenda knows it. Bobby has been afraid to open his heart to the little guy—that much Naana knows, but she doesn't see BJ the same way as her husband does.

Sarah Williams has advised her to let the boy go before it tears her family apart, but Naana's heart and sense of duty will not let her. She finishes all her baking and makes assorted sandwiches for the boys after the game. She takes her mug of tea upstairs to the bedroom and slips back in bed. Bobby reaches for her as he normally does in the morning. For half a second, she thinks about pushing his hands away like she usually does, but instead, she slips her hands between his legs and feels his hardness as a rock. She firmly grasps his penis and slides her hands from top to bottom as he moans to her not to stop. She stops and rolls her body on top of him, kissing him on the full lips. Bobby has always found his wife sexually irresistible, he was instantly aroused. He runs his hands on his wife's lower back and felt her sexiest lingerie. He was shocked to see Naana wearing a thong. He stopped to catch his breath and said, "I didn't know you wear thong panties?"

She kisses him affectionately and asks, "Don't you like me wearing thong underwear?"

He pauses, "No . . . ooh . . . Um . . .It's very sexy on you. I thought . . . um . . . only young people wear that."

"Are you saying I'm old?"

"Darling, I . . . um . . . don't know, what I'm saying. I miss you . . . I want you . . . You're gorgeous."

Naana smiles and kisses him. It was a phenomenal love-making session for the both of them, more so for Bobby. It was uninterrupted, completely relaxed. Naana was still massaging him with her mouth and her fingertips. She went all the way down with her tongue, and Bobby eyes almost popped out as she nibbles and sucks with various kisses, on highly sensitive areas. He has forgotten his wife was so sensuous. He was tickled pink by the time she ran off to the bathroom to take a shower. When she returned, Naana was all dressed up in Banana Republic jeans and high-heels boots. She put on over-sized sunglasses on top of her hair, and suddenly she looked like one of his children. He asked where she was going this early in the morning dressed like a teenager.

Naana smiled. "I'm taking BJ to his game. I told you last night, darling," she said innocently. "You change your mind about coming too? I can wait for you, darling, can you help me put the cooler in the car, please?"

Bobby was speechless as he got out of the bed and put on a golf shirt and jogging pants. "Why are you so stubborn? Princess, the boy may not even be mine. Please, can you not just forget about this and come back to bed? I miss snogging you."

Naana chuckles and kisses him. "BJ is yours. He is a lefty just like you and Tia. He has sexy blue eyes just like yours, darling." She smiles, savoring the best part, "and he calls me Princess, just like you do. I know how you feel, darling. That's the only reason why I have not pushed the issue of you getting to know him. I love him. Please, don't ask me to give him up. We have all weekend to snog." She winks at him.

Bobby can see how much his wife loves the boy. He just doesn't understand why any woman would. Any woman would have his head by now. He hugs her and they walk downstairs. He puts all the food and drinks in his wife's car and watches her drive off. In an instant he dashes inside the house, grabs his car keys and tries to follow her to the football pitch.

Meanwhile, BJ is waiting in the kitchen of his Mom's apartment with a bowl of Coco Pops. He wears his football jersey, though he wishes with all his heart that his sisters would love him just as much as Princess loves him. He wonders what kind of a home they live in, as he has often wished that maybe Princess will one day adopt him as her son. Brenda comes to the kitchen with her newly blonde hair tied up in a pony tail. B.J hands her a cup of tea and asks if she is all right.

"I'm well chuffed for you, BJ," Brenda says.

"Yeah, me too. I love Princess and she loves me. You don't give a toss about me and that's okay. I'm not mad at you. Princess is not a tosser, you know? I'm going to get my trainers," BJ says as he leaves the kitchen.

When Naana arrives, he saw her park her car. He runs out of the flat with his bags, rushing into her arms. Bobby was parked on a far corner watching them, as Naana kisses and hugs the boy. "He is tall, almost five feet tall," Bobby thinks. Naana brushes his hair away from his face and kisses his cheek again. It looks like he is telling her something interesting. Bobby wishes he could hear what they are talking about. He sees Brenda throwing the boy's bag down by the car. She has not changed much. BJ gets into the front of the car with Naana and they drive away. Bobby follows them, almost losing them at one point. She ties back his hair and pats him on the back as she cheers him on. There's a crowd of parents avidly watching the game, so Bobby gets out of his car and joins them. He can't tell which one is BJ because all of them wear their hair in the same style until he saw the back of BJ's jersey with his name on it.

During a corner kick BJ stood less than a few feet away from Bobby, who was watching his son with mixed emotions in his heart. BJ scores both goals for his team and runs to Naana for hugs at the end of the game. All the kids gravitated to Naana's car where she took out the snacks and the drinks and passed them around. BJ was not eating because he was busy hugging Naana. The other kids eat their sandwiches and laugh, sharing their favorite moments of the game. Chelsea FC midfielder Ashton Wentworth is there with his wife, Lock, and their two boys. The Wentworth's boys are younger and play in a younger league than BJ, but they know each other well. Naana has been friends with Ashton Wentworth and Lock Washington for a long time. She has been investing their money wisely for them over the years. They talk and laugh, and she gives them an invitation from Nathan and Tia for their Christmas wedding in Holland. Ashton and Lock are happy that Tia is well again, and that she and Nathan are getting re-married. All the kids depart with their parents afterward, and while Naana was saying good bye to the Wentworth boys, BJ shouted that he was coming. Bobby did not see him standing in front of his car, so he almost ran him down. BJ goes to the door and demands that he come out of the car. Bobby opens his door and nervously steps out of the car.

"I saw you at my flat. I saw you in the car mirror trying to follow us then we lost you. Why are you following us?" BJ demanded.

Bobby did not know what to say to the boy, and with some relief, he noted his wife walking towards them. BJ was not happy that the man was not answering his questions.

"Mister, I will not ask you so nicely again!!!" BJ said with a commanding voice. "Why are you following us?"

Looking at the youngster, it was like looking at himself when Bobby was the same age. Striding toward the brewing conflict between BJ and Bobby, Naana slipped and almost lost her balance. Bobby rushed to help her, but BJ quickly pushed him away and took Naana's hands, "Princess! He's a pervert! He's been stalking us. I want you to go to the car, Princess and call the Old Bill. I'll make sure the pervert doesn't run off okay?"

Naana thought the boy's earnestness was funny, but she didn't laugh. Instead, she smiled and said "Darling, the pervert is my husband!"

BJ kicked Bobby in the nuts. "That's for taking the piss out of my mom and being a twat for cheating on Princess with my mum, you pervert! I thought you would be more handsome, but you are an old geezer and a prat who likes to pull pretty girls, aren't you?" BJ gives Bobby a bollocking. He is about to kick him again when Naana picks him up.

Sitting again in his car, Bobby feels so much pain throughout his body as he leans his head against the headrest. "The little son of a bitch" he thought. Naana asked if he is okay. He managed to smile and kissed his wife. BJ thought the kiss was yucky.

"We will see you at home. Are you sure you are okay?" Naana asked again.

She placed BJ on the front seat and snapped his seat belt in place. Bobby had his head down on his steering wheel when they drove past him. Back at the house, Naana put BJ in Tia's old room: "This was your sister's room before she left home, so it's yours now. I will help you decorate during the week, okay? Come on, let's go give you a bath," Naana said gently.

"I'm ten years old now. I know how to take a shower by myself," BJ assured her. "My daddy is not a regular punter, is he?"

"Daddy is a regular person, darling. Why do you ask?"

"I thought he looked pretty swish."

Naana chuckled, "You are right, darling. Daddy is swanky."

BJ laughs. "Brill," he thought.

Naana showed him where the towels were kept and demonstrated how to adjust the hot water in the shower. "I'll be downstairs if you need me,"

Naana called out as she descended the stairs. Bobby came home, feeling a little better." Naana teased, "How is the pervert doing?"

"That was not funny at all! Being taken down by a ten-year-old for cheating on my wife is just too much," Bobby muttered, shaking his head in disbelief.

"The little brat has no discipline," Bobby remarked, and then, noticing splashing sounds coming from upstairs, he inquired "Who is in the girls' bath room?" Naana begin kissing him.

"Yuck! Ew, you too snog all the time, too?" BJ asked. He had a towel wrapped around his waist and was standing on top of the stairs.

Naana laughed. "Go and get dressed, then bring your schedule down here, okay?" Naana instructed him.

"Why is that boy in our home?" Bobby demanded.

"He will be staying with us," Naana whispered in his ears.

Bobby went weak in the knees and dashed off to the kitchen to sit down. He pondered the situation: "Why is my wife punishing me this way? What if the girls come home early . . . then what?"

Seeming to read his mind, Naana explained, "BJ is their baby brother whom they will love just like I do."

BJ heard her and added, "I love you lots and lots, Princess. I love Tia's room. I am so chuffed she is alright now. I used to wait up so I could go on line and chat with you when you were in Canada. Isn't Trey cute?" He says enthusiastically.

"He sure is," Naana agreed.

"I am sorry I hit you. I don't like people who tell lies," he said to Bobby.

Bobby felt like a stranger in his own home. Not only has the little brat kicked him in the nuts, but he has also taken his wife away from him too. "Pay back is a bitch," he thinks. He can't wait for the mid-term to be over, so the kid can go home. BJ helped Naana make lunch, and when he pulled out a chair for Naana to sit at the table, Bobby noticed that he was a well-mannered boy. When the meal was finished, BJ helped clean up the dishes and then politely asked to watch television. Naana told him he could watch telly and that he should fix himself some snacks if he got hungry again later. "I will be in the living room with Daddy." She pointed to Bobby.

Bobby felt uneasy with the boy in the house. "I was looking forward to having the house and my wife to myself for the whole week," he said petulantly. "I cannot cope with him in the house with us," he whispered to Naana.

Naana decided to come clean on the subject of BJ: "Brenda is leaving for America in the morning. She is getting married next week."

Bobby thought, "Good riddance!" Naana continued, "She wants BJ to stay with us till she can come for him."

Bobby blurted, "No! It's been almost ten years since I made love to my wife. God, I didn't even know you wear thongs. I can't do it. One mistake," he paused, "I've been punished enough. My kids are going to be heart broken." He was in tears now, "I can't do it to them, what I have done to you. They'll hate me, Princess."

Naana threw her arms around him and whispered, "No . . . they'll not hate you. We will be alright. We'll get through this as a family together. It will be okay. You'll see!"

Bobby sobbed and said, "Tia will not forgive me. I will lose my grandchildren. Naana, please, let's rethink this. Lisa will have my head for abandoning BJ and I'll go and talk to Brenda. I'll offer her money."

"Bobby, please don't make this hard for yourself. It will be alright. It will all work out."

They went to their room. Naana fell asleep right after they made love. Bobby came downstairs and noticed BJ had put his schedule on the fridge. BJ asked "Are you okay, Dad?"

Bobby smiled, "Yes."

BJ runs out of the kitchen before Bobby could asked what he was up to, or whether he needed anything. A moment later, BJ returned with a sheet of paper in his hand and a serious expression on his face. He place the paper on the counter top and turned to Bobby, "Make yourself useful!" Bobby didn't like the boy already. "How dare he talk to me like this?" Turning toward BJ, Bobby asked, "What do you need?"

"I got this recipe from our Tia's computer." BJ pointed to the paper. "Princess likes pasta and broccoli. She always gets that when we go to dinner. I am going to make it for her. You can set the table, quietly! Don't make noise, okay?"

"Yes, sir! I like being told what my wife likes to eat by a ten-year-old." Bobby watched him, and thought "it looks likes he knows what he's doing in the kitchen." BJ asked Bobby what he likes to eat. Bobby found himself saying that he was a fish and chips man.

"Me, too. You can bring the chips from the freezer. There's a chip pan behind that cupboard," BJ pointed to Bobby.

Bobby has never cooked for his wife or the kids. He thought, "Hmmm . . . . working in the kitchen with my son is not so bad. It's relaxing, even." He dropped the pan and BJ reminded him to keep the noise down. Naana opened her eyes. It was almost six, and she has been sleeping the whole afternoon. "How could Bobby let me sleep, this is BJ's first day home?" She quickly ran downstairs and found her husband in the kitchen with BJ doing dishes.

"I am so sorry I over slept," Naana said.

BJ dropped what he was doing, and pulled a chair for her to sit and gave Naana a mug of tea.

"We made you dinner. Princess, it's your favorite!" he said.

"Daddy doesn't cook," Naana observed.

"Why did you marry a geezer who can't cook and who cheats on you, Princess? That's not good. A man should be able to cook for those he loves. You're a pretty girl. You could find a good man on the computer, you know? Like my mom did."

Naana thought he was adorable. She giggled giddily and laughed girlishly. Bobby didn't like him, as he felt somehow BJ was there to remind him of his biggest mistake.

Naana squeezed Bobby hand. She winked and smiled, seductively shrugged her shoulders, "Sorry, Bobby! I fell in love with him."

Bobby stood tall by the sink. "Mmm . . . This is delicious! BJ, where did you learn how to cook?"

"The old bag! When I go to her flat, she says, a man should know how to cook and clean," he screeched in imitation of his grandmother's voice. "I did all her chores!"

"How is your grandmother doing?" Naana asked.

"I called her this morning. I told her I was coming to live with you instead of with her. She said you are probably the only folks that love me and want me. She said that she was well chuffed for me. I told the old bag, that suits me fine . . . 'Course, I only love you, my sisters, Jayzel and Trey. I don't like that Nathan much though, he sounds more like him." he pointed to Bobby. "Is he a prat like him?"

Bobby dropped his fork in amazement. He may have kept BJ from his daughters, but it sure looks to him that BJ knows plenty about the Sharp family, and with a temper just like Tia's, that's for sure!

"No, Nathan is a sweetheart, darling," Naana assures him.

"Well, he'd better be good to my sister, or else!"

Naana laughed hysterically. She put some of the pasta in Bobby's mouth. BJ was not a big eater, so he finished his plate of food quickly and went to bed after dinner. Bobby finally found himself alone in bed with his wife. A good time, he thought, to talk to his wife about how much he doesn't want the boy with them. All of a sudden, BJ comes into their room saying he can't sleep. Before Bobby can tell him "too bad," the boy was in their bed, cuddled up to Naana. Bobby was surprised how relaxed his wife was with BJ—just like the day Brenda dumped the baby on their door step. He managed to take his wife affection from him then, and it looks like he is doing it again. The boy was sound asleep. Bobby picked him up and placed him back in Tia's old room and covered him. Naana Konadu-Sharp is not the type of woman to wait for her husband to lead. In her early fifties, she was not more than one hundred and twenty-five pounds, five foot six inches tall. She goes to the gym three times a week, and has been taking kick-boxing with BJ the last four years, that her husband doesn't know about. She hates routine sex. She has always made an effort to stir things up with Bobby because he is prone to distracting himself with worries. Tonight, he was distracted by her sexy French lace underwear, but he couldn't say what he wanted to because of BJ. Naana casually took his golf shirt off, and guided him into the bed. Bobby could not take his eyes off the lacy push-up bra she wore, she looked stunning, her body was like a teenager . . . Bobby felt like an old fart, looking at her. He was very surprised that she still found him attractive.

"I want to relieve some of the tension you have." She flirted with him, teasing him with her lips and fingertips. She whispered in his ears. His wife's seductive powers turned him on, the sensation was so overwhelming he was actually trembling and growing weak at the knees. His wife was like this sexy vixen, doing thing out of his imagination. After twenty-five years of married life, she was still wild in bed. He thought, "how am I going to keep up with her?"

Chapter 2

Tia Sharp has managed once again to turn on television viewers to CTV Monday nights. Viewers simply cannot get enough of *THE SAGA* because of the story lines and the new cast members, and once again it is the number one show on prime time. Everyone expected Elizabeth Starr to turn heads because she's so gorgeous, but it has been the little five year old girl and her brother who played Elizabeth Starr's children on the show who have drawn attention. The two children are naturally adorable on the screen. It's hard for the viewers to tell that they are acting as their emotions about their mother's illness translate so realistically on the screen. The story line this week focuses on the effects cancer has on young children at that age. Despite rave reviews for the young actors, CTV has been very tight-lipped about the children on the show. They are not even named in the cast and crew credits. The executive producer and the writers did give a press conference where the usually camera-shy writer-producer sat down with the cast members and answered some questions about the show.

"Rumor has it that you're married to the attorney, Nathan Carter?" one of the associate press members asked Tia.

She simply smiled. She told the press there was more surprises yet to come on the show. She thanked them and left.

"Miss Sharp is a star!" Amy crowed.

Tia put her arms around her. She has come to love and respect Amy over the past three years they've been working together. "None of this success would have been possible without you, Amy. My mother was so disappointed the day I mentioned that I had taken a job with software giant Nortel Networks. She had a cow. She said I was lazy and that I don't apply myself, and that writing for a television show has always been my passion. I thought the old fart was nuts and she should mind her own business," Tia told Amy.

"Of course! You thought I was nuts, too," Amy added.

"Of course. Thank you, Amy, for helping me realize my dreams, and for being my business partner. I been thinking though . . ." Tia murmured.

Amy raised an eyebrow, "What have you been thinking?" Amy asked nervously.

"Well . . . you know the television business in and out. Not just in Canada, but also in Europe, too. Would you consider forming a production company with me?" Tia asked.

Amy Hall dropped in the nearest chair she was so surprised by the suggestion. As Tia waited for her answer, Amy pointed out, "We can't. We have a noncompeting clause in our contract with CTV."

Tia sat back in her chair, "I'm not so sure that our contract can prevent us from branching out. Amy. I don't know about you, but I like to call my own shots when it comes to my life and everything I do. You should be the head of a studio in my opinion. I can't work my butt off for these pigs, like you do. I am going to take a look at our contract and see if there is anything that could prevent us from forming our own independent production company. *THE SAGA* is our show, Miss Hall! I want CTV to run it like they have been, but I will not write and produce another show in the CTV studio after this season ends. I want everything we do under the auspices of our own company, Amy." Tia said emphatically.

Amy loves how this kid thinks. "Tia, honey. Even if we could, we can't raise the kind of money one needs to have a production company, and the banks will take all the profit just like the studio takes all our money. It will still be the same thing. We will still be working for someone. Let's face it. We need big fucking dicks beside moneys to have our own production company. We need balls!" Amy points out.

Tia stood up. She had this wicked grin on her face. Amy wondered what was going on in her head. "Amy, I am leaving for Holland to spend Christmas with my family," she paused. "Nathan and I going to get remarried on New Year's Eve."

Amy didn't let her finish before throwing her arms around Tia in a congratulatory hug. Amy said, "No divorce this time, I hope?"

Tia smiled. "I'd love it if you and Mrs Hall would come and joins us in Europe. I can introduce you to our bankers for our company. I'm hoping by then we will have the balls or the dicks as you put it to make television history. We are in this together, Miss Hall! I'm branching out and you are coming with me,"Tia declared.

Amy was speechless. After a moment of silence, Amy blurted, "Well, you certainly are full of fucking surprises, ain't you?" Moving closer to Tia's desk, Amy leaned over it and looked her in the eye: "Tia, it takes more than what you and I have to form a production company." Amy reminded her again.

Tia tossed a file on her desk, "Walk me to my car, Miss Hall. When you have time, read through the file, please. We are going to do this and I am not going to do it without you," Tia insisted.

Nathan was at home with his father and the children. They're very close these days. It was not as bad as he thought it might be when Tia suggest they should all live under one roof. He enjoyed the family life they have built, though he wishes his mother could be with them. It brings tears to his eyes when he thinks of her. Anthony can see that.

"I miss her too, son. She knew it, you know? That you and Tia would be this magical together, so did I, son," Anthony cried. "You have no idea what a void you and Angel have filled since my Heather died. Seeing what kind of a man you have become makes me so proud of you, son."

"What are my two sexy men crying about now?" Tia comes and kisses them both on the cheeks. She knows them both so well. "I miss mother, too, you know. If I come home and find you two lads crying one more time in the house, I'll get my belt out," she teased. "Remember what Trey said: No crying in the house!" Tia hugs them both.

They were both so relieved to see her doing so well and back to her old self again. "I saw you on the TV. So . . ., are you seeing Nathan Carter, or are you his wife?" Nathan asks with a silly grin on his face.

"Why don't you take me upstairs and I'll tell you, after I have my wicked way with you, Mr. Carter." She teases.

Tia has tried her very best to seduce Nathan, but he has not given in to her attempts. The sexual tension between them has built its own cocoon around them, and being around each other day to day is a challenge that Nathan feels he is about to lose. He sweeps her into his arms and takes her into their bedroom.

Tia asks, "Is this sweet surrender?"

Nathan replies, "Ah, sadly, no. I want to talk about Kevin Peters." Tia is on the verge of getting upset. To mask her feelings, she states assertively, "I am leaving!" Nathan stands in front of the bedroom door and quietly locks it. "Tia, father is out with the children for the rest of the day. No more jokes. No more avoiding the topic. I need to know whether you have feelings for Mr Peters and if you're still in contact with him. I need to know what happened before you got sick and I need to know before we get married again." Nathan demands.

Tia is pushing back tears. She has been dreading this moment since she came home from rehab. Calming herself, Tia knew that the Kevin Peters topic had to be discussed. Things had to be out in the open. "No, I am not in contact with Mr. Peters. I don't have any feelings for him. I did not have any feelings for him when I was with him . . . Nathan, I have not spoken to Mr. Peters in quite some time—long before I came to Canada, in fact. When he turned up at my doorstep the afternoon Trey was born, I was just as surprised as you were. Afterward, Daddy and I found him in the bathroom after you," she paused, pursing her lips, "after you demanded a DNA test on our son."

Nathan tightens up his jaw.

"I asked him why he was in my home and in the labor ward with me. He told us Brooke had sent him."

Nathan began to kick the door, he felt so enraged. Tia told him, "Nathan! Please, stop bashing the door." She took his hands and sat down on the floor with him. Nathan said, "I thought you wanted me home . . . when we made love . . . the night before Trey was born, I assumed you had forgiven me for our divorce and that I was coming home." He turned and looked at her then leaned his head back against the door. Tia could see the anguish in his face as he closed his eyes, remembering the past.

"I did want you home. Jayzel and I both missed you so much. I told Daddy, you would be back in an hour with flowers crying and begging . . . . I would be all over you kissing you. I didn't think . . . You would give us up so easily . . . I tried to make you . . . see so many times, Nathan, what we shared, but you were so set on destroying everything we were. Sweetie, I thought," she sighs, "I thought leaving you would make you see what we have is real. I was wrong . . . I'm sorry. Mother's death was the last straw for me. I couldn't get the image of you and Nicole in our home out of my head."

"I did not have sex with Nicole in our home. I was not having an affair with her as you thought. I did become too dependent on her, but I couldn't see what my dependency was doing to you and our marriage—not until your mother pointed out a few things to me after my mother's death. I did come back to the hospital to apologize. When I got there, Kevin was in the nursery feeding Trey and telling you how much he still loved you. What was I supposed to think?"

Tia said, "he didn't say anything to me about his feelings until the night I came by the condo to ask you to come home. Nathan, you wouldn't come home, then. I told you I was still in love with you and I missed you. Kevin thought I was afraid because of the children. Anyway, nothing happened between us. He left and went back to England. You were the one sleeping with everyone . . . and didn't care if I knew about it, so when Kevin called and said he wanted to spend the holidays with me and the kids," Tia paused and then pushed on, "I still didn't think it was appropriate for me to have my ex-lover with me and our children, especially at the holidays that means so much to *us*."

"Then, why did you, Tia! Why was Kevin Peters at the cottage?"

"Sweetie, you refused to talk to me. It had already been over ten months, close to a year. Nathan, you weren't just my husband. You and I were very good friends for a long time. I felt we had built a trust and respect long before I fell in love with you. When I saw you at Christmas with Santa at the cottage, I wanted to tell you to come home. Ask Steven, if you don't believe me. Nathan I have . . . I have missed you . . . but I knew you were happy with Elizabeth. It was Elizabeth who told me that you were still in love with me. I was on my way to England to end things with Kevin and come back and do whatever I could to win you back. I told Daddy, I had no idea I was carrying his child when I was told that I lost the baby . . . Actually, I was relieved. I'm sorry to say but I was because it would have complicated matters so much . . . I took out my anger on you when I had the leukemia because of my own disappointment with myself, not with you. Nathan, I was lost without you. The book of poems you gave me on our first anniversary and the children were the only things that kept me from losing it all the time."

Nathan responded, "First, I thought that you were seeing him and then I thought you had been having an affair with him behind my back. Mother told me you loved me and you would never do that. Nicole drove me to the hospital to plead with you but I just couldn't do it, Tia. I thought

I had lost you anyway, until I saw you and the children at the studio with him acting like the children were his. It was then that I knew you still loved me, and the children loved me. I broke down and Elizabeth told me to man up and come home, so did Nicole and Ian. Amy hit me a few times for being a bastard. Steven, Jackie and Daddy all hated me. Only your mother spoke to me. No one else did. It was like I didn't exist." He paused and moved away from her. "When Amy called and said you were ill, I couldn't breathe, Tia. I was crying at the hospital . . . I didn't care who saw me crying. I was walking in the rain one day, and I remember the story mother used to tell to me . . . when I was a boy about God." Tears are streaming down Nathan's face: "I asked God to help me and my family, and that I couldn't lose you a second time. The children made it easy for me to cope . . . They didn't hate me for abandoning them. They hugged and kissed me all the time. I lied to them: I told them you were working in Europe. Lisa would write to them from you, and she would send them all kinds of gifts on your behalf. They didn't know it was from Auntie Lisa. She would also call every morning to talk to them before we go down for breakfast. Your mother . . . is an amazing woman, Tia. If anyone ever did to Jayzel what I did to you and the children, God help that person. Your mother would always tell me that I am not rotten, and she loves me."

Tia is crying now, listening to what her younger sister did for her children and the role she played in their lives during her absence. It was heart-warming and the pain behind Nathan's voice is evident, and it is clear that he has suffered more than anyone could know. He let everyone think that it was all fun and games for him. He wiped his face.

"When your mother arrived to help, I was a mess, Tia. She gave me the strength and hope that I didn't have. I've never known anyone like her. She sees the good in everyone. Looking at her was like having you home except that Naana was not as mean to me as you are."

Tia hit him, then she put her head down on his lap. Tia too has tears rolling down her face. He picks her up and helps her into the bed where they hold each other. "Grandmother Gertrude told me that you will take me back and that you couldn't resist my charm and that I'm so cute." Nathan smiled at the recollection.

"Did she? Huh!"

"Yes, she did."

"I think that old fart has a crush on you. She and I should have a little chat about what's mine."

"I am so glad you are here to make me more miserable for the next hundred years, Tia. You have no idea how much I have missed you, Baby." He leaned his forehead against hers with his eyes closed.

"I've missed you too, very much, Nathan." Tia gazed into his eyes and kissed the backs of his hands. She chuckled, "I shouldn't have gone from one situation to the next. I was still your wife, even though we were divorced. I felt that you were still my husband. I resented Brooke, you know?" She sighed. "But in a way, I loved her for opening my eyes to your imperfections. I love you, Mr. Hot. More than ever, I do." Tia leaned over and passionately kissed him.

He rolled Tia on top of him and brushed her hair off her face. "I have dreamed of this moment when I have you in my arms all alone in the house looking at your beautiful face. I don't want to lose you again. I can't. Let's try to discuss things between us instead of assuming things." Nathan sighs. "I missed you, too. I especially miss the way you feel. You taste different from any other women that I know. I can't help but be jealous whenever I see you close with anyone."

Tia gently kissed him. She wanted to ask if Nathan had an affair with Brooke, or it was just a kiss they shared the night before their wedding, but it is one of those secrets she didn't really want to know. If it's true, it will hurt her and if it's not, it will hurt Nathan. She takes his hand and guides it between her legs. He kissed her on the neck between her breasts. Her body felt warm and cold at the same time.

What he has with Tia is perfect, and beautiful, and still blossoming into something even more amazing. Nathan told her so. He felt very steamy, very sensual. He cuddled and snuggled up to her, vowing "I will not break any promises this time. We are going to wait till we are married. We agreed. You said if I let the children come on your TV show you would wait, Tia. Now stop making me go crazy." He quickly got out of the bed.

Tia put a Celine Dion CD on the stereo and turned it down low. She smiled and said, "Ooo, sorry Nathan. I lied. Nathan Carter, you get back in here and make love to me before I scream the whole countryside down," Tia threatened.

"Go ahead, go right ahead, Miss Sharp! No one will hear you!" Nathan chuckled. "I am going downstairs to my office to get away from you."

A few minutes later, Nathan is on the phone with his mother-in-law when Tia walks in half-naked. She sports sexy black over-the-elbows French lace gloves and a long, long strand of pearls. High-heeled pumps, a lacy push-up bra, her hair flows down her back. Nathan sucked in his breath for a second, the glimpse of her sexy well-toned body is enough to weaken any man. Nathan is aroused by the sight of Tia in stockings and garters with thong panties. He tells his mother-in-law that they will be in Holland in two days and hangs up the phone.

"You . . . um . . . didn't have those . . . um . . . on when you came home from the studio," he said softly.

"Mmm, ha! You like, Mr. Hot?" she teased. Nathan lifted her up against the wall, her breast was warm in his mouth, and she wrapped her legs around his waist and moaned, "Mmm. I missed you, Nathan."

"I've missed your sexual confidence, and your afternoon seductions, baby."

"Mmm . . . you adore my naughty seductions, sweetie."

"Mm—ha! I . . ."

By the time Anthony returned with the children, they were still making love on the floor in their bedroom. Trey asked them why they were sleeping on the floor. Nathan was so embarrassed after Trey left, he quickly ran to lock the door. Tia thought the look on Nathan's face was priceless.

"I see somebody has to be the adult in this relationship," Nathan observed. "I am not coming down to dinner. Trey has probably told father what we were up to. I'm not coming down to get the third degree from father about my responsibilities."

"How about you come here and kiss me? That is one of your responsibilities," Tia teased.

"Tia, our son just caught us making love, and you still won't leave me alone! Well, too bad, Daddy's Angel! You have caused enough trouble for one afternoon, Tia Carter."

Tia has his penis in her mouth as he stands with his back to the door, both hands pressing against the wood of the door. By the time she is through with him, Nathan is the one who does not want to leave Tia alone.

"Did you discuss your idea about a studio with Miss Hall?"

"Yes. She is a little skeptical about it. I was thinking of getting together with Lock while we are in Europe."

"Of course! I'll make sure I call Ashton before we leave. He told me the last time we spoke that mother had given them the invitation, but they're going to Africa."

"I want to make a movie about their lives. Lock loves the idea. What do think?"

"I think it's an interesting idea. I did discuss with Chase about the lot for you. I think he may have found one already that will suit your purposes. I think we will be able to raise the money ourselves without going to mother for a loan. I left some things for you to look at in your office, baby. I want an answer before we leave. Do you still want to get re-married?" Nathan asked with a gift-wrapped box in his hand.

"Join me in the shower and I'll let you know." He smiled.

Anthony had made dinner by the time they both came downstairs. Nathan's prediction was correct. When Tia and Nathan sat down to eat, Trey asked, "Why did you not have any clothes on in your room, Daddy?"

Jayzel commented, "That's why you must knock before you go into people's rooms, silly baby. Aunt Brooke says she sleeps naked, so we must always knock before we go into grown-ups' rooms. Their skin gets wrinkles, you know. Old people can't go to bed with clothes on. Daddy is old and he will get more wrinkles, and that's not a good thing to have wrinkles, silly baby!"

"I am not a silly baby! I know more about the digestive system than you do, huh! huh!" Trey teases.

Poor Nathan is so embarrassed, he hardly knows how to respond to his son's question. Tia begins her naughty ways under the table and he quickly runs to the fridge and when he returns to the table, he switches seats.

Chapter 3

Everyone is in Amsterdam except the Carter's. Gertrude loves the twins, and of course, they all know about BJ now. She adores him just like her other grandchildren. The girls are mad at their father for abandoning their brother. They love BJ, and in return, he, too, is overly protective of his sisters. He has just turned eleven. He asked for a bike for himself and one for Naana as his birthday present. He is a good boy. Bobby still insists that he is not his son. He has cut down his work load because he didn't like BJ taking so much of Naana's time away from him. Bobby joins them for kick-boxing, although his body feels so sore when he returns home, but the rewards from his wife make up for all of the pain. His jealousy over BJ has brought out his romantic side. He and the little guy always fight about who is going to rub Naana's feet after gym. Lisa and Claire think it is so funny that their father is fighting over their mother with an eleven-year-old.

Brooke is not taking to motherhood with quite the same enthusiasm as Kate and Tia. The twins have a full-time nanny, and of course, she named them Morgan and Jackson after her father and grandfather. Jason liked that idea. In contrast to Brooke's arm's length relationship with the twins, Sarah can't stay away from them. She told Jason no more babies.

Guntar announced that the Carter's have arrived. Jackie was able to get time off and came as well. Jayzel and Trey have grown since the last time Brooke saw them, and they wasted no time jumping into her arms and kissing her. They love Brooke the best of all their aunts. Steven will be coming from New York on Boxing Day.

Anthony and Jackie were greeted by Kate. Trey informs everyone that his mummy and daddy are outside kissing. That's all they do everyday. In fact, Bobby came to the hallway and saw the couple were at it just like how their son described. He gave Nathan a hug. Tia walked passed him just like he expected. Once everyone was settled, Nathan strode across the living room to sit next to Gertrude. The two of them were sitting on the chesterfield holding hands when Jackie whispered to Anthony and Tia, "Why does everyone make such fuss over Nate everywhere we go? I mean, look at him with Gertrude. It is like mother all over again," Jackie complained.

"Wait till you see him with my mum," said Tia. "It is the same thing. What can I say? My husband has that effect on women who love him," Tia said proudly. "Come Daddy, come meet grandfather. Nathan and grandmother are going to be here awhile."

Tia's grandfather gave Anthony a hug and turned the charm on Jackie. "I see Getty is with her favorite grandson. It's been Nathan this and Nathan that for the past two days. Come, my dear. Sit with me. I hear you're the young doctor in the family. I'm so happy to have you all with us for Christmas." He called Rose, the maid, to bring them tea, and she informed them that dinner would be ready in ten minutes.

Claire and Lisa entered the room to greet everyone, and before Tia could say hello to her sisters, Lisa was gone and had taken Jackie with her. Naana and Sarah were holding the twins, so Tia sat down and took them both in one arm each. "They look so much like Brooke," she thought. Sarah was in tears as she has thought of nothing but Tia's struggle with illness over the last year and half. She was relieved to see Tia back to herself again. Rose came in with the tea for everyone. Tia noticed BJ was almost as tall as her mother with nicely blow-dried hair like a model. He had their father's beautiful blues eyes. He was holding Trey's hands, while laughing and talking with Brooke. Tia heart beat faster as she looked at her mother. Naana smiled and called BJ to come and meet his big sister. He hugged her and whispered, "I'm so happy you didn't die. I was so sad when you got sick." Tia couldn't help crying as he let go of his embrace. "Please, don't cry," BJ fussed.

"I'm sorry. BJ, you have grown! You are so handsome, sweetie. I love your hair," said Tia as she ran her hands through his hair.

"Claire likes to blow-dry my hair everyday. I hate it, but it makes her happy to do it, so I let her," he shrugged. Tia took him in her arms again.

Bobby was ashamed even more now. Everyone has embraced BJ. Bobby sure wished he could turn back the clock and do a few things differently.

As promised, the dinner was ready and laid out buffet-style for everyone to help themselves. As usual, the three young girls didn't come to dinner. Rose told Tia that they had gone out. "When did we become old?" quipped Brooke. "We used to do that."

Kate giggled, "We got old, silly, when we all decided to have two children each."

Nathan was still holding Gertrude's hands, talking and laughing. Naana told Anthony that it was so good to see him happy again.

Anthony said wistfully, "He really couldn't have done it without you, you know." Then noticing Naana seemed tired, he asked "What about you? Are you alright?"

She sighed and smiled, "I have been busy at work with a heavy workload right now, but other than that, I'm great. I leave for Ghana in two months. There are a lot of things to do before I go. You may see me and BJ in Canada throughout the summer, though."

"Oh, yes? Why?"

"BJ will be in a soccer camp outside Toronto for six weeks. Nathan wants to take Tia on vacation, so if you don't mind some company, BJ and I would love to spend some time with you and the children."

"Oh! I'd love to have you and BJ. He looks like a fine boy," Anthony said.

"He sure is," Naana replied. Anthony has never really understood why some men find the need to cheat on their wives. He was not brought up that way. It broke his heart when Nathan tom-catted. Anthony thanked God everyday that his son has come back to his senses. His heart really goes out to Naana. The lady has a big heart to love the little boy the way that she does. Anthony has always thought that Nathan was specially blessed. Meeting the rest of Tia's family really does show why Tia has so much love for others, too. Anthony wished Heather was alive to have met them all. He knows she would have loved them.

Tia quickly went to him and said, "You look tired, Daddy. Let me show you to your room, so you can have a rest. I'll tell Rose to bring you some tea later."

Antony said good-night to everyone and left with Tia. The children were all in one room except the twins who were bunking in a room next door to Brooke's room. The kids bedroom door was open and BJ was reading to Jayzel. Both Anthony and Tia thought that was sweet. By the time Tia was heading back to re-join the party, the kids were all sleeping. "I can't sleep. I sleep better when I sleep with my mummy and daddy," BJ told Tia.

"Can I make you a hot chocolate?" Tia asked.

"It's okay. I have to try and sleep. I want to show Trey a new trick on my video game in the morning. If I don't sleep now, I won't be able to get up on time and get my mummy her tea and daddy will try and make it for her," he said. Leaning confidentially toward Tia, BJ remarked, "He doesn't make it the way Princess likes it."

Tia thought BJ was sweet. "Do you want me to stay with you until you fall asleep?"

When she left the room, Bobby was standing by the children's door. Bobby tried to initiate conversation, but Tia walked past him again. Discovering Nathan already asleep in their room, Tia went to her grandfather's study to check on her emails. She couldn't find her laptop and found Brooke already in the study with a glass of wine working on the computer.

"Some things never change!" Tia exclaimed.

Brooke looked up and waved at her to come sit by her.

"You look great for someone who just gave birth to twins a month ago," Tia said with a twinge of envy in her voice.

"Actually, they cut me up and took the little darlings out. I wish you and Kate would have told me that babies are a pain. Jayzel was a good baby, but all these boys do is cry, cry, cry." Brooke complained.

Tia asked, "Are you okay?"

Brooke sipped some of her wine, "I'm afraid of being a bad mother to the boys. I've been trying not to get too close to them, but it's not easy. I'm going upstairs, now. They should be waking up for their bottle in ten minutes."

Tia went upstairs with her. Sarah was up with one of them already. Brooke made the bottles for them. It was nice watching Brooke with the twins. Tia smiled, "Brooke, you are crazy about them! Look at yourself! You can't put them down."

"They are adorable, aren't they? Listen, I think I have found the property you wanted for your company. Let me show you after breakfast when the boys are having their mid-morning nap," Brooke suggested.

Tia said good-night and headed to her room. She took a quick shower and found her laptop on the bedside table, so she wrote until four in the morning. She hardly sleeps more than four hours a night causing Nathan to worry excessively that something else might be wrong with her. When he opened his eyes, it was well after four and Tia was still up.

"Baby, I want you in bed now before we wake up the whole house. Tia you told me you'd be right back to bed three hours ago. Baby, please come to bed now."

Tia smiled at him, logged off her laptop and jumped into bed, cuddling up to Nathan's toasty-warm body.

"I know you are afraid of sleep and the nightmares. It will get better. I promise you, Baby," Nathan mumbled. He rubbed her back until she fell asleep and then he held her tightly.

Bobby has been uncomfortable since BJ came to live with them. The more he protested that he disliked the boy, the more he likes him. He is a fine young boy, although after three months of living with him, all their friends and family have learned about his infidelity. Bobby recalls Naana saying that Brenda wanted the arrangement to be temporary, but somehow Bobby finds himself wishing that BJ could stay longer so that he could get to know him better. He knows how much Naana loves him, so he wonders whether it will be possible to negotiate a longer stay. He decides he'd better wander downstairs to the kitchen to make tea for his wife, but when he steps into the hall, Bobby discovers he is already too late. BJ and Trey were up and they were standing at their door with her tea. Bobby tried to take the tea away from him.

Trey told him, "Go and pick on someone your own size, buddy."

BJ tells Trey, "He's my Daddy. We both like to do nice things for my mummy. He doesn't like it when I beat him, though."

Trey gives BJ a high five. Bobby felt humiliated by the boys. He let them in the room and the two boys got on the bed with Naana. BJ tells Trey they have to go downstairs for breakfast and that Naana doesn't ever eat breakfast. Trey comes back and takes Bobby's hands to come with them. Bobby didn't want to go at first, but he went with them anyway. Jayzel was eating by herself when she saw Bobby, so she ran to hug him.

Trey asked Jayzel, "Did you know he is BJ's Daddy?"

Jayzel nodded affirmatively, "Yes, and our grandpa, too."

Trey replied, "We have lots of grandpas, eh?"

Jayzel told Bobby that Trey is a baby and doesn't know much. Bobby noticed that the children like to eat and watch cartoons just like BJ does at home. Bobby has not really spent any time with Tia's kids, either, so he asked if they would like to spend the morning with him doing something.

Jayzel declined the invitation saying, "I don't like to do things boys do. They are very dirty and I like things to be nice and neat."

They two boys were laughing at Jayzel when James, Kate's son, joined them. BJ said that he needed to go and find gifts for his sisters. Jayzel said, "I love shopping! Can I come, too?" Bobby told them to eat quickly and they all could go shopping. Anthony was up and Bobby asked if he wanted to join them when they went out to the shops. He said, "Sure!" Jayzel and BJ had a list, but the others did not. They just wanted to go to McDonald's and get hamburgers. They got all their shopping done and they went to McDonald's. They put all the gifts under the huge Christmas tree. Bobby saw BJ looked angry as he ran and dashed off to the pool. He was screaming for help. Nathan and Jason were the first to get to the pool area, and once there, Nathan jumped into the pool. They pulled out Claire and Nathan began to perform CPR.

BJ remarked, "I don't want my sister getting your germs. You can put your hands and push on her chest, while I count up to five. I know CPR, okay?"

The rest of the household stood and watched him give his sister mouth-to-mouth and tell Nathan to push down on her chest.

"Don't touch her boobies, okay? It's rude to touch a girl's boobies. You can go to jail if you do."

Nathan nodded and nervously glanced up at Bobby. After three attempts at CPR, Claire threw up and tried to sit up. BJ asked Nathan to help him turn her on her side, so she wouldn't choke. He put his forehead against Claire's, and brushed her hair away. She sat up and asked what happened.

BJ said, "You were walking funny and I saw you fall in the pool. Tia's husband helped save your life. Are you alright? How do you feel?" He looked up and saw a drunk boy sitting on a patio chair and asked, "Who is that lad?"

"I'm not sure," Claire replied.

Turning to Nathan, BJ asked, "Can you help me take my sister upstairs, please?"

"Sure, Buddy," Nathan says.

Before going upstairs with Claire, BJ went to his father and asked him, "Daddy, make sure that lad doesn't leave. Okay? I will be right back."

A very nervous Bobby Sharp managed to say yes to his son. A few minutes later, BJ came back and he hit the boy sitting on the patio chair across the face. The boy was awake.

"What did you give my sister, mate?" BJ yelled at the boy.

The boy was hysterically laughing.

BJ turned to his father, "You see the lad is laughing at me. He gives my sister drugs or alcohol and he is laughing at *me*?" BJ points to himself.

He was heartbroken. He told the boy to stand up. The rest of the household, including his father, were all shocked by BJ's handling of the incident. He began kicking and hitting the boy. Because the boy kept laughing, BJ dragged the boy into the pool, "You're not laughing now, are you, mate?"

Nathan jumped in the pool and dragged the boy out. BJ kicked the boy one more time to send his point home. "If I find you giving my sister anything illegal, I will beat the crap out of you!" BJ looked exasperated. He told Nathan to throw the boy out, which he was only too happy to do. Quickly dashing inside, BJ said, "I'm going to see if Claire is alright."

Sarah, Anthony, Jason, and Kate had watched the whole incident in shock. By the time Nathan and Bobby got upstairs to the girl's room, BJ had a towel and was trying to dry Claire's face. Bobby stood there helplessly, watching his son telling his sister about the dangers of drugs and alcohol. He tells Claire that she should always say no to drugs and alcohol, no matter who she's with.

Bobby left them and thanked Nathan. Naana was still sleeping when Bobby went into their bedroom. He went to the bathroom and cried. He couldn't understand Claire's behavior: seventeen years old and drinking or doing drugs? God knows what. He may live in the same house with his children, but he doesn't really know them.

Meanwhile, down the hall, Tia woke up and found Nathan soaked and wet. She asked if he fell in the pool with his clothes on.

"Yes, baby, I did. In a manner of speaking, that is. Claire fell in the pool. She was intoxicated, so BJ and I pulled her out. You should have seen the beating BJ gave Claire's boyfriend." Nathan mused.

Tia jumped out of bed, shrieking, "What the hell was Claire thinking?" She stumbled into a pair of track pants and pulled a t-shirt over her untidy hair. Tia was heading out of their room, when Nathan told her that Bobby was with BJ and Claire. Tia chuckled. "My dad is not the kind of father who tells kids off. He saves that job for me 'cause I'm the oldest. I have to go and check on them. This will be too much for my mum."

Nathan trails behind Tia as she charges down the hall to Claire's room where BJ was still trying to dry Claire's hair. Tia hugged them both and asked if they were okay. Claire was crying and said she was sorry for all the trouble she had caused. BJ pleaded with her not to cry. Tia told BJ to go get changed.

"I have to go and see if Daddy is okay. He looked knackered," BJ said.

"How about you get changed first? Claire can blow-dry your hair afterward and I'll go and see if Daddy is okay," Tia suggested.

She told Nathan that she would be right back. Her mother was sleeping, but their bathroom door was open. Tia stood by the window with her hands in her pocket. Bobby thought Tia was his wife. "I'm sorry, I woke you up, Princess."

Tia turned and faced him and point to the bed. She asked if her father was alright. Bobby was looking momentarily stunned, as Tia could see. She looked at him sympathetically and suggested her father meet her in grandfather's study in ten minutes. Before leaving the room, she told Bobby the children were both fine. She hated knowing how uncomfortable her father was. Nathan, too, had a serious look on his face when he reminded Tia how shocked Bobby was. He didn't know what else to say but to hold her.

"Baby, that is inexcusable. I still have to talk to him. Claire could be heading for worse. I know first hand with Jaden when Brooke and I tried to cover his alcohol and drug abuse. Claire's behavior is not acceptable. BJ has taken on the responsibility that my dad should have shouldered. It's not right for a boy his age." Tia explained.

Nathan agreed. "He was exasperated. The boyfriend would not say what Claire had taken or what they had been drinking. He turned to your father before he began to give the boy a beating and dragged him back into the pool for a taste of what he felt the boy had done to his sister."

Tia was in tears now as Nathan shared with her what had happened down by the pool. "You see, baby, that is my point with BJ: imagine if it was not an enclosed pool. With this weather, Claire would have been dead by the time BJ or you got to her," Tia muttered. Nathan held his wife, thinking the same thoughts. "BJ didn't want me to give Claire CPR." He chuckled.

"Why?"

"Oh, baby, get this: your little brother didn't want me to give his sister my germs!" Nathan and Tia laughed.

"Are you serious?" Tia asked, with a look of disbelief.

"Yep! Not only did he not want me to give his sister mouth-to-mouth, he also told me flat out to make sure not to push or touch his sister's breasts, or—I believe the word the little brat used was 'my sister's boobies'. Babe, did you know, you can go to jail for touching a girl's boobies?—according to your brother, that is," Nathan said.

Tia was on their bed laughing helplessly. She couldn't believe how bold BJ could be. He kind of reminds her of herself. "I'm glad you can laugh, babe. Mother is not going to be laughing when she learns about this, Tia."

Tia sighed. "I know, sweetie. I'm meeting my dad downstairs to talk to him about the children. Brooke also wanted to show me a property she may have found for me for the studio."

"Baby, I have Chase looking into properties all over Ontario for you. I don't want Brooke meddling in your business affairs."

"Sweetie, I fully agree with you. She went to a lot of trouble to get the information for me, though. I owe her a look, at least. I'll not commit to anything without discussing it with you first."

"Tia, I know how important this to you. As your husband, it is my duty to take some of the stress away."

Tia kissed him and teased that he should join her in the shower, "You know . . . it takes some of the stress away!"

Chapter 4

Gertrude was showing Anthony her newest art collection and telling him how wonderful Nathan is. "He has called every Saturday morning since his last visit with, Tia and Jayzel, you know? We'll talk on the phone for hours!" She pointed to a heart sharped box for Anthony to pass to her. She, too, called him Tony just like Heather used to do. She took out some hand-written cards on which Anthony right away noticed Nathan's hand-writing. "This is my favorite," said Gertrude as she gave it to Anthony. "Go ahead. You can read it." Anthony noticed that the card had been written two days after Trey was born.

> Dear Grandma Gertrude,
> Two days ago my Angel gave birth to our son, a beautiful baby boy, six pounds seven ounces, Trey Anthony Carter. I wish with all my heart that you and my sweet mother were here to hold him. I feel like somehow without you two lovely ladies, I will not have the family that God has blessed me with today. Since my sweet mother is not here today, I want to thank you and Naana for the love that is Tia and the children. I love you. Please tell Grandfather the good news for me.
> All my love,
> Nathan

Anthony didn't know that Nathan was this close to his wife's family, and that through all the madness of their divorce, he had kept in touch with his wife's grandmother.

"Nathan is a good boy, Tony. It warms my heart to see that he and Tia have found their way back to each other," Gertrude murmured. The old lady took Anthony's hands and showed him more cards that Nathan had sent her. He felt like he was in the cottage sitting in the family room with Heather. Naana Konadu-Sharp has just come downstairs accompanied by her father, Sarah Williams, and of course, BJ. When they walked into the family room, BJ lead her over to Gertrude and they both greeted her with a kiss.

"Don't you look so handsome!" exclaimed Gertrude. "I hear you and Nathan are heroes the way you saved your sister and gave that boy a good beating." Gertrude was proud of BJ. BJ was trying to signal to the old lady that he didn't want his mother to know about it. "Oh, Grandma, my mummy don't know. My sister and I didn't want her to know," whispered BJ as he let go of Naana's hands to speak confidentially to Gertrude.

Gertrude and everyone laughed as they watched the expression on BJ's face change from confidence to fear when Naana told him he was in trouble. "BJ, go get your sister and your father, and tell them to meet me in your grandfather's study."

"Now, Naana, don't be too hard on the boy," advised Sarah. "He's just trying to look out for his sister, do the right thing, you know. I heard BJ was quite the young man standing up to that boy on behalf of his sister."

"That's what I'm afraid of," Naana said.

Gertrude was still laughing about the look on BJ's face. Her husband asked what was so funny.

"My dear, BJ does not strike as me as the easily scared type. Did you all notice his face when his mother told him he was in trouble? The poor boy is about to cry. I hope Naana will go easy on him." Gertrude began to laugh again. This is going to be the best Christmas. She shared her plans with Sarah and Anthony that she was making all the food this year. She has asked Guntar and Rose to take the Christmas holidays off. "They will return to help me with the wedding." Anthony added that he and Nathan would help, too.

"Is Nathan as good a cook as you?" Sarah asked.

"He's getting there," Anthony said.

Sarah still remembers that lovely New Years they all spent with Anthony and Heather when Tia and Nathan first got married.

Tia was in the study talking to her father when BJ and Claire entered the room. Bobby stood up and and went to them. He hugged them both and said, "It will be okay, kids. You'll see." Tia put her mug down and said, "No . . . it is not okay. Sit down, you two!" Naana joined them all in the study and closed the door. Tia has had enough of her father's laid back attitude and her mother's tendency to over-look things.

"I want you two kids to listen to me," Tia said.

Claire begin to cry and BJ pleaded that they were sorry. Bobby reassured them,"It's okay. No harm done."

"What happened this morning was not okay," Tia said as she got up from her chair. "You both are going be to punished. Claire, your drinking and drugging days are over."

Claire tried to talk, but Tia yelled at her to be quiet. BJ sat beside her and put his arms around her. Tia continued, "You are not setting an example for your little brother! Claire, while you are here, you are not allowed to leave the house and you are not allowed to see or to talk to your friends on the phone."

Claire tried to protest and their father interjected, "Tia, please. The kids have learned their lesson."

"What lesson, Daddy?" Tia asked. "You lost that privilege, Claire, when you put your life and BJ's life at risk. You embarrassed Mum and Dad in front of our families and friends. You go to your room and think about your actions."

BJ tried to leave with Claire, but Tia told him, "Come back here, young man. I'm not done with you yet." BJ ran to Naana, "I'm sorry, Mummy! Really, I am!" Naana's heart broke, "I know, sweetie. I want you to listen to your sister, okay?" Naana wiped his tears away.

Tia sat BJ on her lap, and brushed his hair away from his face. She spoke in a soft voice, "I was so proud to hear how you save Claire's life today. It's good that you stood up for her, sweetie. I don't know if Mum and Dad have told you how much we all love you. I'm not mad at you. I think you did the right thing for your sister."

BJ immediately hugged Tia and said, "I will always protect my sisters."

Tia, Bobby, and Naana smiled. Tia replied, "I know, sweetie. I want you to promise me that you'll enjoy being my baby brother, not too much like a grown up, okay?"

"I've turned eleven now. Mummy says I'm her little man, now," BJ whispered in Tia's ear.

Tia laughed and said "he can go and tell Jayzel and Trey that she will see them soon."

After BJ had left the room, Bobby thanked Tia, but Tia turned to him and lashed out, "Thank you for what? Daddy, you need to start being a good father to these children and a good husband to your wife. Stop hiding behind your wife and let her raise *your* children by herself."

"That's enough! Tia, you can't speak to your father in that tone," her mother snapped.

"I can, Mother. I did the same with Nathan when we were first married just like you're doing for Daddy. You love him unconditionally. Well! It's not just the two of you anymore," she points to them and sat behind the desk. "There's an eleven-year-old boy who loves you and Claire so much that he puts his own needs aside to go back and forth to make sure you're happy because our father doesn't have the ability to stop being selfish and lazy."

Bobby fully understood what Tia has said, but he didn't want to face it, and he felt ashamed, too. Naana was enraged that Tia would dare to talk to them in that manner. Bobby took his wife's hands and said, "She's right, Naana. She's totally right. I need to step up and be a better man."

"You agree with our daughter being rude?!" Naana exclaimed, surprised.

Bobby ran his hands in his hair, sighed, "Yes, I do."

Tia got up to leave, but her father asked that she stay for a few more minutes.

"You know, the past twenty years of our marriage, Naana, you have raised the children alone and done homework, after-school activities and solved problems."

Naana objected, "No, darling. That's not true."

Bobby shook his head, "It is, Princess. I don't know when Tia became this wise woman. Lisa is in university doing well and working for you, but I didn't know she was working for you until you were away in Canada and Lisa asked my advice on a loan that she needed to approve for one of your clients. She's brilliant, you know! Claire is seventeen years old. I don't even know which school she attends. Her friends are all in college and Gertrude tells me Claire is a great artist, that she really has some talent," Bobby paused. "And now BJ comes into our lives. I have come to love the boy. I can see how much he loves you and that's why he looks after you and the girls. At first, I didn't like the boy. I told his mother to get rid of him."

Tia looked at her mother as tears rolled down their faces. "When she dropped him off at our door when he was a baby, I hated him more. When you told me that you had been seeing him all this time, remember, I told you that I forbid you to see him and you laughed at me." Bobby smiled. Tia could not believe what her mother had endured all these years. "I have to take some of the responsibility and start being a father, a good role model for the kids and for you, Naana. I have been a real bastard. BJ was right: you can have any handsome man of your choice. I don't know why you're with a prat and an old geezer like me"

Naana walked up to him and put her hands on his cheeks, "I love you. I've been waiting for you to grow up." She begin kissing him. They forgot Tia was in the study with them, and Tia wished they would not embrace so heartily in front of her.

Chapter 5

Kate and Brooke had just finished giving the twins their lunch when Tia walked into the kitchen and suggested a girls' night out. "Amy will be arriving in two days, and I thought I should run the idea by you two."

Brooke replied, "I can't go. I don't want to leave the boys alone at night." Just at that moment, Jason entered, coffee cup in hand, and crossing to the sink, he rinsed his cup and remarked, "You should go, darling. One night is not going to kill them!" Then nuzzling her neck, he joked, "I'm a competent mum. Hmmm?"

Kate rolls her eyes and Tia examines her fingernails, waiting for Jason to leave so they can continue their plans.

Jason added, "Anyway, I was talking to Gertrude . . . she is trying to book a private room at the casino for Tia and Nathan's pre-wedding party. She tells me that she has a Nanny coming to help her with all the children and she has all kind of DVDs and games planned for them. I want you to go out on a girls night out, so that we can go to the casino. Please?" Jason pleads with Brooke.

"You see girls? You have twins for a man, and he becomes soft," Brooke said. "I'll think about it. Right now, I need to go down to Grandfather's office and show Tia and Kate something. The boys are all yours, Handsome!" she kissed him and departed with the girls.

Jackie and Lisa have just awakened at two in the afternoon. They were by the pool eating their breakfast when Nathan joined them with Jayzel. Trey is taking a nap. Lisa can't believe how much Jayzel has grown. She is wearing her swimsuit, and informs her aunties, "The house my Daddy made for us in Canada has a pool just like this one, only my pool has a fireplace."

"Wow! That sounds awesome! Would you like me to come and swim with you?" Lisa asked.

"No, thank you. This is my special time with my Daddy. After, he is going to help me learn about the brain so next time I can beat my brother when we do the test." Jayzel said matter-of-factly.

Both Lisa and Jackie asked Nathan why he is teaching his children about the brain.

"My Daddy knows about the human body. My brother and I are going to be doctors just like Grandpa and you Aunt Jackie." Jayzel replied before Nathan could respond.

"My brother has always been wired," Jackie noted.

"My mother says that Nathan has been through hell since his divorce." Lisa commented.

"Well, he only have his stupid self to blame. I hope he learned his lesson this time. 'Cause if he screws up this time, he is going to be by himself, for sure." Jackie said emphatically.

Lisa plays with the kaneta bracelet with a heart shape on her wrist and gasps, "Men are trouble."

Jackie scoffs, "You say that now. Wait until you fall in love . . . then you'll know how much trouble they can be if they are anything like Nathan."

"Falling in love, eh? If there is such thing. Nathan is all right: we love him."

Lisa has not said much about BJ, but she loves him, too. Like everyone else, she finds her father's infidelity humiliating. Her mother's forgiveness astonished both Lisa and Claire. Lisa has been thinking of leaving home since the whole thing came out. She bought Jason and Brooke's loft apartment from them, but has not moved in, yet. Once she is done with her finals, she would be out of the house before her father could say she is too young to leave home. Lisa and Jackie had formed a friendship on their first meeting in Canada almost six years ago. Jackie has never been to Europe before and she loves it. Lisa is a health freak just like Jackie. The two girls are both vegetarians and don't drink alcohol. They managed to have fun at the night club last night with Lisa's boyfriend Vidal and his cousin Patrick. Jackie liked how cool and calm Lisa is. Most of the rich kids at UCLA are snobs, so she doesn't talk to any of them. It's been cool hanging with Lisa, since they both have to study for their final exams. Lisa has promised that they will have more fun once they are done studying. Even though Jackie is not much of a party person, she loves hanging around with Lisa, Vidal and Patrick. They watched Nathan do the back flip in the pool for Jayzel. She clapped her hands and gave her father the towel, as she waved at the girls. As Jayzel and Nathan walked past the study, Jayzel saw her mother with her aunties, so she went inside.

"Aunt Brooke, my Daddy did a new back flip in the pool. He promised to show me how when we go home to our own pool." Jayzel said.

Nathan smiled at his wife, picked up his daughter and left.

"Your husband is a freak! Jayzel tells me he is teaching them how to be a doctor. Who teaches their children how to be doctors at that age?" Brooke asked.

"Brooke, why do you dislike Nathan? You two were once the best of friends. What happened?" Tia asked.

Kate suddenly wished she could be invisible because she knew how this conversation would end.

"I don't dislike Nathan. I've always thought that he's a sweetheart, but he really got on my bad side when Jayzel was born and he tried to push me away from my baby. It's all forgiven now. Although, I think he hates how Jayzel loves me more than him." Brooke said with a big smile on her face.

Tia shook her head and Kate thought that Brooke would never change.

Deftly changing the subject, Tia asked, "What are we going to with Urban Style?" They have four shops now and all are doing well. Kate doesn't design their clothes anymore because they have a good supplier from China now.

"I was thinking that since Lola has been doing a good job overseeing things the past four years that we should make her a part of it. She is family and we've been paying her the same as the other managers. I don't know about you two, but I want to hold on to our little company," Brooke said.

"I feel the same way," Kate added.

Tia did not respond right away. The girls asked what she's thinking. "It sounds cool. We *should* think about making Lola a big part of Urban

Style. In the short term, I think I need an arm's length relationship with the company. I am going to be super busy when we return home. I haven't spent any time with the children in the past year and a half, and Nathan has assumed all the responsibility for everything. Jayzel will be starting school next fall, and I'm planning to have my production company up and running by then."

"Right!" said Brooke. "Then, let's talk production company." She showed Tia the property she found for Tia's production company. "You said you needed something the size of two schools. The schools in England are not as big as the Canadian schools. Also, Claire and I went to London's Pine Wood Studio to visit, just to get a feel of what you had in mind. An old friend from college was shooting a movie there, so he showed us around some of the studio—well, their sound stage, anyway—I think the lot that I found will do very nicely for what you have in mind. The property is not far from Hamilton. It used to be a hobby farm."

"What's a hobby farm?" Kate asked.

"A very small farm, usually set up for the owner's particular interests, but not especially intended to generate a large income," Brooke explained. "It's big enough to build a small studio. Here. Take a look at this 3D image that Claire did on the computer for you. I have been watching *THE SAGA* the last three months. Here are the houses you have in the show . . . The city building where the stockbrokers are . . . the hospital . . . the school . . . and the coffee shop. You will also have more than sixty good acres of land for outdoor scenes if you need to blow things up or whatever you TV people do. The price is surprisingly cheaper, too."

Tia was quiet. Brooke could not read her expression. Kate is fascinated with what she has seen on the computer. It looks so real. Tia finally said, "This could work. It's not far from Toronto." Brooke replied, "I was looking into your finances in England. I came across this." She handed a report to Tia, which she read.

"Is this a joke?"

Brooke said firmly, "No, Tia. It is not. I called the bank and I told a little white lie that you were thinking of buying a property and that I was doing a credit check on you. I asked your mother about it, and she was not too pleased about me digging into your finances. She told me to mind my own business."

Tia showed it to Kate. Kate's jaw drops open with astonishment. Tia said, "No, it can't be. It's impossible. I would have known if I had that kind of money. In fact, Amy and I were going to ask my Mom for a loan from her bank in Ghana, but this changes everything."

"Let's ask her now. I for one would like to know. I could tell your Mum was hiding something the way she was so uptight about my snooping," Brooke remarked. Tia nodded affirmatively. Brooke was out of the room and back with Naana in the study in no time. She picked up the report and said, "We want to know how you got all this money put away for Tia that she doesn't know about. Tia also wants to know if she can borrow money from you for her new production company."

Nathan happened to be in the study, too, and overheard the whole conversation. "Brooke, I'm fed up with you interfering in my family's personal business. I want you to stop right now!" Turning to Naana, he said "I am sorry for Brooke's rude behavior."

"But I'm not interfering!" Brooke protested.

"Good! Then you will not mind leaving me and my wife alone?" Nathan replied.

"Baby, please. It's okay. I want to know where all that money came from. Mother?" Tia asked.

Nathan felt exasperated when Tia asked her mother about the money.

"Mother doesn't have to disclose anything to any of you. Tia, can we discuss this in private?" Nathan said.

Mrs Sharp spoke to Nathan and Tia in French. She explained that the British government gives each child money. It's call the Child Benefit, and every child gets it until the age of eighteen. I put my children's money in a trust fund for university education or for their first mortgage, or a car or if one day they get married. I sometimes used the money in my company or on the stock market. Tia went to university in Canada and paid for it herself. Nathan paid for your wedding and he bought you a home. I did tell him about the funds, but he said he wanted me to keep investing it for you and that you two have enough money to start your production company without it. I have no idea how Brooke got her hands on these records. I have someone investigating how she obtained this information. I intend to press charges."

Nathan ask Brooke, "How did you obtain Tia's financial information?"

"I ran a credit check on Tia and the trust fund showed up." Brooke admitted.

"That much I believe. Banks don't release this kind of information you have on paper to just anyone. I've been a banker for twenty-five years, Brooke. I know. I don't lend money to friends or family, Tia. This is something you should discuss with your husband, not your busybody friends. Grow up! I will press charges if you stick your nose in my business, Miss Williams." Naana Konadu-Sharp left the study in a huff.

The girls were laughing. Nathan didn't think it was funny. He picked up Tia and carried her out of the room as the other girls shouted "boo". He dropped her roughly on their bed and locked their door. Tia was still laughing. "Do you want to get married to me next week or this is all a joke to you? Tia, you're not a teenager with your gal pals that you can do anything you want and have a good laugh about it. Mother didn't deserve that rudeness from you or Brooke." Nathan was serious.

Tia suddenly stopped laughing. "You look so sexy when you are angry."

Nathan unlocked the bedroom door and left. Tia was still laughing, but by the time she stopped, tears were streaming down her cheeks. Pondering her first marriage to Nathan and Brooke's propensity to interfere, Tia realized that her suspicions about Brooke and Nathan were probably true. Simultaneously, the notion that Kate had known all along also struck Tia, and a further idea came to her that Kate must have known that it was Brooke who slept with Nathan the night before their wedding. Tia also knew that if she wanted her man back, she would have to be strong, wipe the tears from her face and go downstairs to join everyone at dinner. When Tia entered the dining room, everyone was already seated and had begun eating. Nathan rose from his chair and crossed the room to meet her by the door.

"I want you to tell everyone that the wedding is off," he said. "I have booked a flight and I'll be leaving tomorrow night."

As Nathan left the room, Tia's knees weakened. She grabbed hold of his arm as the tears began to roll down her face. She saw that he was upset, too.

"Tia, please don't touch me," he mumbled.

Kate witnessed the whole conversation between Tia and Nathan, and she could see what was about to happen. As the couple conversed intensely in the dining room doorway, Kate nudged Brooke and motioned toward Tia and Nathan. "See what comes of your meddling?" Brooke shrugged.

Kate excused herself and as she passed Naana's chair, she leaned down and whispered, "Will you help me help Nathan and Tia?"

Naana replied, "I think Tia needs to decide whether she wants a marriage or a best friend who sleeps with her husband."

Kate was shocked to learn that Naana knew about the night before Tia's wedding. "How did you know?"

"I was in Canada when Jayzel was born. I guess they turned to each other when they thought Tia was going to die."

"Oh, no! This is worse than I thought!" Kate exclaimed.

"Come on, Kate. You can't fix this for her. Tia needs to do this alone," Naana advised.

Kate stood there feeling helpless and betrayed. She decided something decisive had to be done. Tia and Nathan belonged together. They couldn't give up so easily. Kate followed them to their bedroom. Nathan was sitting on the bed, taking off his shoes. He looked up as Kate entered the room.

She shouted angrily, "You can't let Brooke break up your marriage just like that! Not like the last time!" Kate hugged Tia and Nathan, "You're not going to break Tia's heart because of Brooke! You hear me?"

"Listen, Tia. I'll put the children to sleep, but you need to fix this. Okay?"

Tia nodded and closed the door. Nathan laid on the bed looking up the ceiling, thinking "what if she really does go downstairs and tells everyone that the wedding is off?" He put his hands out and Tia ran to him.

"I am so sorry, Nathan. Please don't leave me a second time. You promised. Baby, you can't break your promise. I'm your wife, the mother of your children and the best lover you ever had," she teased. Nathan smiled. He was running his hands in her hair. He was quiet, letting Tia do all the talking.

"I need you. I got a little carried away. I didn't mean to embarrass you and mother like that. I was curious to know where all that money came from. I swear, I wasn't going to ask for the loan after we discussed doing it ourselves. Please baby, believe that I want the same things we talked about. You can't leave me again, Nathan. Please, say something!" Tia cried out.

There was a knock on the door. It is Jayzel asking if she can come in. Nathan quickly wiped Tia's tears and said, "Yes, baby, please do come in."

"Grandma Gertrude wanted Rose to come and see if you was alright. I told her I would come and see, Daddy. Are you alright, Daddy?" Jayzel asked.

"Yes, baby. Please tell Grandma I'm with Mummy. I'll join her later for tea, okay? I want to spend some time with Mummy alone, baby," he told his daughter.

"Okay, Daddy," Jayzel said as she closed the door behind her.

Nathan asked, "How about you let me take you out to dinner?"

"Only if you promise not to leave me," Tia responded happily.

"Tia, you and I are forever, baby. Forever never dies. I told Jason Gray to keep his wife away from mine, or I tell everyone that his wife sleeps around. I'll not play any games with my family. It's unfair for me to ask you to choose, Tia, but we need to keep certain things separate from your relationship with Brooke," he said solemnly.

Tia didn't think it was funny, so she asked, "Are you attracted to Brooke?"

"No. I'm not attracted to Brooke. Maybe once a upon a time, but I'm attracted to my wife and only my wife. Tia, I know the kind of marriage that I want with you. We had it for a while before . . . Mother died. I didn't know what . . . I had until I lost you. I missed you everyday and what we had together. I can't trade you for anything less. Unless you have a twin out there. I want to meet her, so you can go off with Brooke."

"Very funny, you just lost yourself a dinner date," Tia said tartly.

She picks the up the phone, spoke to someone in Netherlands, and by the time she was done, Tia had a naughty smile on her face. Nathan knew that look very well.

"You'd better not be having phone sex, Mrs Carter. I'm going to have tea with Grandma. Let me know if we are going to dinner soon." He kissed her and she said "will do." Tia loves Nathan and whenever he lies to her it hurts her more than he knows. She was not sure about his affair with Brooke until now. Although,it hurt that they had an affair, it doesn't hurt as much as when she first learned about their dirty little sick affair. She is enjoying seeing them twist in their lies.

Naana was happy to see Nathan happily walking down the hall. Bobby was carrying BJ back to his bed like he normally does. He asked Nathan how he got his children to sleep by themselves. Nathan said that Jayzel and Trey had always shared a room. They talk a bit and they will sleep after. He tapped Bobby on the back for good luck. Anthony, too, enjoys

Gertrude's company. They watched Tia's mother, Naana with her head on her father's shoulder and thought they looked like Nathan and Jayzel, they are so very close.

Gertrude told Nathan she was glad they only had Naana because she didn't think he would have time to spoil another girl the way he spoils Naana.

"I wish Steven could have joined us for Christmas. He is going to miss the the big family photo," Gertrude said.

Just at that moment, Rose came in and handed a note to Nathan. "I have to go, Grandma. I think my wife is mad at me." He kissed and hugged everyone as Anthony and Naana laughed.

"I wish Tia would take it easy on him. He is such a good boy," Gertrude said.

Nathan stopped by the family room to read the note Tia had sent him.

> *Baby, I miss you. You know, I was watching you all day, and I thought I should send you a note to let you know how much I love your ass . . . uh-huh, you have this sensuous kind of ass. I'm thinking I would like to see you undress right now! I could touch you. Would you like that? Are you getting a hard-on just thinking about it? Dinner for two by the pool.*
>
> *Mrs Nathan Carter*

Tia is waiting by the pool surrounded with candle lights. Nathan is relieved she still has her clothes on.

"I was afraid you wanted to go skinny dipping," he smirked.

"Oh, yes! We'll do that later," she teased. She pulled out a chair for him to sit down. "I was thinking a table for two. Afterward, I can show you how our married sex life is going to be upstairs. Unless you want me to show you right here, Mr. Hot?" she suggested.

She has not called him that for a long time now, but he loves the nick-name. He noticed that she had made a smoothie for him. He leaned forward and kissed her softly on the lips. "I like this . . . this is nice, baby," Nathan said.

Tia is not eating her food, though she is smiling. She takes his hands and begins to suck on his fingers, while her foot is all over his legs under the table. He puts down his fork and says "that's it! We are going upstairs before someone walks in on us like horny teenagers."

"Oh! You are no fun, sweetie!" she said.

"I will show you fun upstairs," he promised.

"I think you are right about us waiting till we are married," Tia said, as she began to eat her meal.

Nathan raised his eye brows. "Baby, you are like a powerful aphrodisiac." He squirmed, "A man could go to jail just looking at your fine ass. This is not going to be easy for either of us. Our friends and family know we can't keep our hands off each other. Are you trying to get me killed before we get married?" he asked seriously.

Tia is laughing. "Those unmentionable, dirty words. I am shocked . . . Mr Hot!" Tia teased. "I want to thank you."

"For what?"

"I have written a script. It's a beautiful love story. I didn't have a name for it till you gave me one tonight."

"What name did I give you?"

"*FOREVER NEVER DIES*: Steven is the director. It will feature Elizabeth Starr and Kelly Powers. We are hoping to cast Jayzel in with your permission, of course."

"Would you and Steven listen if I said I didn't want my baby girl in your TV movie?"

"I would try . . . but, of course, there's always the romantic treats for my ever-so-understanding, sexy husband." She has her feet all over him under the table again.

Nathan stands up and begins to undress, "You have issued a challenge that I intend to win hands down, Mrs Carter." He did a double back flip into the heated pool. Naturally, Tia, being a competitive nature, did even better one.

Chapter 6

Brooke was preparing the twin's bottles when she heard the romantic music and laughter coming from the solarium. Curious, she opened the door and stood watching Tia and Nathan playing in the pool like a pair of love birds. She couldn't help it: she watched them surreptitiously from her vantage point in the kitchen. She heard Naana and Kate chatting behind her, but paid no attention to their conversation. In the morning, Naana Konadu-Sharp would be going to Paris with her father. She wants to take her grandchildren and BJ to Euro-Disney. She'd like to include James and Thomas, Kate's children, so she asks her if they can come too. Bobby, Nathan and Claire are also accompanying Naana and the grandkids. It will be a fun day for all of the children, even though it is Christmas Eve day. Naana knew Jaden would be arriving in the morning, so she thought it might be nice if Kate and Jaden could have some time together without the children.

"What do you say Kate?" she asked.

"Oh, I really couldn't do that, but thanks anyway. The boys are not well-behaved like Jayzel and Trey. They fight a lot and can make you barmy," Kate said.

"Well, I raised three girls. Tell me about fights! I think I can handle your boys. Besides, Lola has agreed to meet us in Paris, so come on, say yes," Naana pleaded.

They noticed Brooke staring, with rapt attention, at something outside in the solarium, and wondered what had grabbed her attention. Kate walked across the room to stand next to Brooke. She, too, saw Tia and Nathan cavorting in the pool. Kate had just about had it with

Brooke's spying on Tia and Nathan, so she pushed the door closed and said, "Brooke! Your kids are fussing." Then with ill-concealed anger in her tone, Kate muttered, "Can you not leave them alone, for God sakes! Brooke why are you so interested in what they do?"

Brooke felt insulted by Kate's outburst. "What's got your knickers in a twist?" Brooke snapped at Kate as she headed upstairs with the twins bottles.

"You and I need to have a little chat—unless you want me to tell Jason about your affair with Tia's husband!" Kate blurted out loud.

Sarah Williams was up with one of the twins and overheard what Kate had just said about her daughter's inappropriate behavior. She opened her door and asked the two girls to come in. Kate can not control her anger. She is enraged and took it out on poor Sarah for doing such a bang up job on raising Brooke. On her side, Brooke did her best to deny Kate's accusations.

"Why don't you ask your daughter about sleeping with Nathan the night before his wedding to Tia! Ask about her affair with him when Jayzel was born and Tia was fighting for her life!" Kate shouted.

Brooke dropped the bottles on the floor. The shocked look on Sarah Williams face said much.

"Ask Brooke for the real reason why Nathan was so determined to have poor Jason sent to jail for a so-called rape! Nathan has had it with Brooke's interference in his family's life. He almost walked out on Tia and the kids tonight, thanks to Brooke! We've been friends—no, we've been sisters—the three of us for forever, but this is going to tear us all apart!" Kate left, slamming the door.

Sarah is embarrassed. She had no idea that Brooke could have been capable of such mayhem. "Why could she not have shown some restraint?" Sarah wondered. She put the twins down to attend to Brooke sitting on the floor, sobbing. Sarah had no idea how to console her daughter. Tia is at the door, knocking and asking whether everything is okay. Sarah doesn't want to let her in, but Tia and Nathan have let themselves in already.

"Brooke, why are you crying?" Tia asked. She turned to Nathan, spoke to him in French, and he left.

Tia joined Brooke and Sarah on the floor, cuddling up to Brooke and murmuring comforting words. Sarah knew that Brooke's behavior was going to drive a wedge between the girls. Later, Nathan returned with Kate, who has now calmed down. When the three girls were tucked into the queen-sized bed, Nathan closed the door and left. Sarah felt like a fifth wheel, so she grabbed her bathrobe and left the room, too.

Naana could not sleep after she put BJ back into his own bed. Bobby is fast asleep, so she went downstairs to make herself some tea. She sees Sarah by the fireplace. Christmas has always been difficult for Sarah because it brings back the memories of Jackson. Naana sets down her mug and throws her arms around Sarah. "Did you know?" asked Sarah. Naana realizes that Sarah has just found out about Nathan's and Brooke's indiscretions.

"The kids will sort out their own mess. There is nothing we can say or do, Sarah. They are grown-ups. As sad is this is, the girls do love one another, regardless of who's been doing what . . . You know Brooke as well as Tia. We can't be drawn into their affairs . . . We see this as adulterous, but they may see it as something else." Naana observed.

Sarah can not understand how Naana can be so calm about Brooke's behavior. "What a kick in the guts! When Tia learns the devastating truth about Nathan and Brooke, it will kill her." Sarah worried. Sarah Williams is embarrassed, angry and hurt. She is more shocked that Tia's mother knew about Brook's affair with Nathan and kept quiet about it. A reeling Sarah warned Naana that this incident could drive a wedge in their families. "You don't know the half of Tia and Brooke's shenanigans!" Naana said.

"Do I need to know anymore, right now? I can't even look at Brooke. I'm so disgusted and they're all over her in my bed after what she has done. I wish she was a little girl so I can ground her," Sarah told Naana. Naana laughs.

"Welcome to my world! I don't think it was planned. They will be okay. I threaten to have Tia and Brooke put in jail for snooping in my business today. The two of them had the nerve to asked me for a loan for Tia's new company and laughed right out at me in my father's office. Let's face it, our kids are nothing like us. I don't believe this will drive a wedge between them because their relationship is stronger than that." The two ladies laugh. Naana walked Sarah to her room and by the time they got there, all three girls were sleeping.

Naana said to Sarah, "I don't want to be here when Nathan comes for his wife." She had hardly finished the sentence when Nathan appeared, extricated Tia from the pile of female limbs and briskly carried her in his arms down the hall to their own room. The two older women snickered and giggled like teenage girls.

Over his shoulder Nathan called out humorously, "I am glad I am a source of amusement, ladies! Good night!"

Sarah thought, "What a sleaze ball," though she actually did like him—sort of—but then . . . she thought "Adulterous jerk!" Glancing at her daughter sound asleep in the bed with Kate, Sarah sank into a chair thinking "What a mess!"

Nathan knew why Brooke was crying and losing her self-control. He had seen her peeping though the door, spying on him and Tia in the pool. He made sure he put on a good show for the slut, so she could see that this time he was not playing any stupid games with his relationship with Tia. He was also certain that Kate knew something about his affairs with Brooke and he thought of confessing to Tia before one of the girls does, but then again, the fall out from the confession might leave him without a family this time. He worried that learning about his affairs with her best friend might be more devastating to Tia than the knowledge of his flings with other women.

Tia had one of her nightmares and woke up crying. Nathan reached over and held her close, his hands caressing her hair and the back of her neck until she relaxed and fell asleep again. As he held his wife in his arms, Nathan couldn't help crying over the truth of his affairs with Brooke, and he realized that getting mixed up with her had been stupidly dangerous. He hardly slept afterward, so he continued to hold Tia and to watch over her through the night. He rarely sleeps after one of Tia's nightmares, a remnant of last year's cancer. He was fed up with her constant pain from the nightmares. He slipped out of the bed and headed straight into Sarah Williams' room.

Sarah Williams looked sophisticated and glamorous even at five in the morning, even without any make up on her face. She had just finished feeding the twins when there was a knock on her door. Her visitor did not wait for her permission to enter. Nathan swung open the door and closed it behind him. Kate and Brooke were both sitting on Sarah's bed. They felt themselves weakening when they saw Nathan in Sarah's room. "What arrogance," Sarah thought.

"Mr. Carter, I know most people find you irresistibly charming. Unfortunately, I'm not one of them. To what do I owe this visit?" Sarah asked as she put her grandson in the crib. Nathan glanced at Brooke and Kate smiled and said, "Good morning!" With his hands in his pockets, he looked sheepish, like a little boy caught with his hand in the cookie jar.

"Mrs Williams, I sensed last night that you may have learned about affairs you, Kate, and my mother-in-law seem to think that I had with your daughter." Sarah and Kate tried to respond, but Nathan silenced them. "Two people sharing a kiss in a weak moment is not an affair. With Brooke, well . . . well, she is a very beautiful woman. I saw no harm in giving her a kiss. I'm sure in Britain, that's how you British do."

Sarah Williams is more enraged by his suave urbanity. "You are out of control, young man." Sarah snapped.

"No, I am not! You and your daughter are the ones that are out of control, ma'am." Nathan raised his voice.

Brooke pleaded, "Nathan, stop! Just stop it!" Nathan went and stood by the twins crib, "I cannot believe that you will sit still and let your family start a rumor that is not true about me and you, Brooke. Why do you hate me so much?" He turned to Sarah, "You have no idea how much your daughter hates me. I equally feel the same about her. I will not stand by and let you two," he points to Sarah and Kate, "put ideas in my wife's head like Brooke has done in the past."

Brooke stood and said angrily, "You wait a minute here, you jerk. I will not have you threaten my mother and Kate. I have not defended myself because I felt sick of kissing you."

Nathan laughs in response. "you enjoyed kissing me, Brooke."

Kate got out of bed, intending to leave. She didn't know who to believe and didn't much care, either.

"Oh, Kate . . . speaking of affairs, how is yours with Brendon Chan?" Nathan asked.

One of the twins began crying, so Nathan picked him up and placed the baby on his shoulder, rubbing the baby's back until he quieted. The women all watched in amazement as Nathan, now not being hateful, gently soothed the baby to sleep.

Kate's knees buckled at the mention of Brendon Chan. Nathan asked again, "Are you still sleeping with Chan?"

Brooke snapped, "Put my son down and get out!"

"Oh, I am not done with you yet, Brooke. I see that you'd rather tell a lie than tell the truth. Okay, we never had an affair, but you don't want me with Tia. Well, here's some news for you: I am in love with Tia and she's in love with me, so get over it! I'll not lose my wife and children like the last time you all conspired against my marriage!" Nathan threatened.

"Mr. Carter, you have made your point, young man. You may leave now." Sarah demanded.

"Get off your English high horse, Mrs Williams! How long did you wait when your husband died before you whored yourself to his best pal, Doctor Michael Doyle? Is that why you stuck your brat of a daughter in a boarding school instead of raising her yourself? Tell us. Are you still sleeping with your husband's old pal?" Nathan shouted at Sarah.

Everyone felt the awkwardness in the room when Nathan mentioned Dr Doyle. Brooke pulled herself together and slapped him across the face. "Leave now, while you still can," she suggested as she opened the door for Nathan.

"I will not lose my family over your lies this time. Why don't we just get Tia and Jason in here and get this over and see who loses whom?" Nathan shouted. "Kate, tell your junkie of a husband when he decides to tear himself of away from the good Doctor Vroom and join you and your boys, he is no longer my wife's lawyer. I'll tear each of you apart, bit by bit, if you don't stay out of my marriage. Your British gossip doesn't extend to me and my family. You all disgust me!"

Nathan left the room. Before Brooke closed the door, she winked at him. Nathan is proud of himself. The son of a bitch was crinkling up quietly inside. He returns to his room and slips into bed next to Tia. When needed, Nathan can persuade anything and anyone to believe him. That's why he's a good attorney. He is no stranger to telling lies and turning things around on others. Occupational hazard, he calls it. Tia can always tell when he is lying. Usually, he tries not to look her in the eye when he lies.

"Nathan Carter is pure evil. This is all my fault," Brooked claimed.

Sarah Williams is exhausted and astonished by Nathan Carter's outburst, especially the accusation about herself and Dr. Doyle. Kate was inconsolable. She never had an affair with Brendon Chan. How could Nathan have known about her crush on Brendon? Who is this Doctor Vroom person that Jaden can't keep away from? Brooke forgot about the fact that she has stood by and watched Nathan snipe his lies and humiliate her mother in front of Kate like that. She turned, shamefaced, to Kate and tried her best to console her.

"Kate, don't let it get to you. Nathan knows Tia will leave him one day and he just likes to take it out on people who can't stand up to him. He is a master manipulator," Brooke reassured her.

Kate was in tears as she confessed that she had feelings for Brendon. "There's been no affair. That's why I quit my job at Bankers Trust."

"I'm sorry, girls," said Sarah, "but I think I've had enough for one morning. You're on your own with this one. I'm going to get dressed, put on my make-up and go downstairs to help Gertrude plan the Christmas dinner."

Brooke asks, "Are you seeing Dr Doyle?"

Sarah raised her eyebrows, "You and I are not going to talk about that. Michael and I are old friends, BB. I don't buy Nathan's lies. My guess is that you did have an affair with him and that your are still at it or you two would not have put on such a performance. If this becomes public, Brooke, you will be on the outside looking in. Not Nathan. Jason and the boys don't deserve this, BB. End it now before it is too late."

As she applied her make-up, Sarah advised her daughter "Naana Konadu-Sharp is a very warm, kind-hearted woman, but if you snoop in her business, you will definitely end up in jail. I can only offer you very limited protection. I just don't have the kinds of money to go up against her, and quite frankly, BB, I would not want to. I am very disappointed with you. Get control of yourself, BB.!"

Brooke didn't know how to respond. She simply closed her eyes and turned her focus on distraught Kate.

"Who is Brendon Chan?" Brooke asked.

Kate wiped her face and replied, "My former boss at Bankers Trust."

"I thought you said he was mean and would not even look at you. When did this all happen, Kate?" Brooke asked softly, almost whispering.

"Brendon drove me to the airport when I was going to visit Tia before she got married the first time. Jaden and I were not together. We began spending more time outside work as friends, and continued to hang out after Jaden and I got back to together. He asked me out on a date, but the attraction ended when I realized that Jaden had changed and that I was still in love with him. Things had been very uncomfortable for me and Brendon. That was why I quit my job. He felt I was using him. I don't know who could have told Nathan because I never told Tia. Nothing happened! He's being telling me he has feelings for me, but we never even kissed. Who is this Doctor Vroom that Nathan is talking about?" Kate cried.

"Nathan was insinuating."

"No, he damn right said I had an affair with Brendon."

"This is rubbish! I am going to wipe that smile off his face. You wait and see."

Kate grabbed Brooke by her scrawny arm and mustering as much menace in her voice as possible said, "I wouldn't start anything to cause a rift between him and Tia. You can not handle this. I can't either. I will talk to Jaden when he arrives tonight."

Chapter 7

Nathan accompanied his children to Disneyland-Paris on Christmas Eve morning. Before he left, Nathan gave Tia a surprise gift, something she wanted very badly. Tia is shocked to find the gift on her bedside table. She called Amy and told her the good news. Amy advised her that starting a studio is a lot harder than she thinks.

"Well, then, make sure you read the file I gave you three weeks ago. Remember? We were chatting in my office and I gave you a file folder and told you to read it. I will want to know what you think when I pick you up at Amsterdam Airport three days from now."

Anthony came into the study, bringing Tia her morning tea. He can't help it, but Anthony Carter has not stopped worrying about Tia since she came home from the hospital eight months ago. He knows his daughter-in-law is a workaholic.

He says, "I wish you would slow down Angel."

"Daddy, you would not believe what Nathan did!" Tia turned her laptop so her father-in-law could see the screen. She beamed with excitement as she said, "This is Sunlight Studios. Daddy, this is my Christmas and wedding gift from my sweet husband!" Tears course down Tia's cheeks as she explains to Anthony, "I wanted to form a production company with Amy Hall. Nathan didn't like the idea of me going into business with Amy and wanted something for the family."

Anthony asked, "Did Nathan buy you a whole town?"

Wiping her face, Tia laughed. "No, Daddy! He bought me a huge piece of land, the size of two schools! I used the computer to simulate sets, office buildings, a gift shop, and still have a huge lot left to play with. It is located close to home and to Toronto. Do you know where Waterdown is? That's where the studio is going to be." She hugged Anthony, practically smothering him, Tia was so excited.

Tia continued, "who would have thought that we would be here, about to get re-married and still so much love in him? Half of the time, I still want to kill him . . . You know, Daddy, this means we will see more of Steven. He will not have any excuses about how expensive it is to make films in Canada!"

"Angel, you are supposed to be slowing down, not speeding up," said Anthony with concern. He has watched Tia work non-stop since coming to Holland. He is worried about her, worried that she might have a relapse.

"I was talking to Lisa and Jackie before they ran off to God-know-where about my wedding. Nathan and I want Jackie, Lisa and Claire as my bridesmaids. Steven is going to be the best man, and my brother is going to give me away. What do you think, Daddy?"

"I think it would be nice if Jayzel and Trey had some responsibilities, too," Anthony observed.

"Oh, they will! I want this wedding to be a happy occasion for all of us. My grandfather always wanted me to get married in this mansion. That's why he kept this house all this time. Come, I want to show you the gym he built for my mum when she was a teenager. That's where we are going to have the reception."

When they arrive at the gym, Kate and Brooke are working out.

"Where have you been all day?" Brooke asked.

"I had a lot of work to do. I was locked up in the study. Kate, I thought you went to Paris with the children?" Tia asked.

Anthony thought that the gym was a good size. He asked if there was anyone coming apart from Amy.

"Yes. Doctor Michael Doyle is in Paris," she paused and said, "Also, Ian and Nicole will be arriving with Amy in the same flight with their little boy."

"Tia, why would you want Nicole here?" Brooke asked sarcastically.

Tia glanced at Brooke, and there was an awkward silence in the gym.

"I find your comment about my husband's friend to be very distasteful, Brooke. I am exhausted with your constant interference in private matters between me and my husband." Tia held out her manicured hand to her father-in-law and they trailed off.

Kate gave Brooke a withering look, "Girlfriend, why can't you just leave them be? People will start to think you are in love with Nathan yourself. He will stop at nothing to keep his family. Has Tia shown you the big piece of land he has bought for her production company?"

Brooke was quiet. Tia has not told her about the studio lot. She wondered if it was the one that she found for her.

Meanwhile, the children have returned from Paris worn out and ready for naps. BJ, for once, went and slept in his own bed. Because Tia has been working all day in her grandfather's office, she made plans to spend a romantic evening away from the mansion, just her and Nathan, at the Regency Hotel at five o'clock. She informed her grandmother that she will not join them for dinner, but the old lady is in tears since she is looking forward to having Christmas Eve dinner with all their family and friends.

Tia canceled her plans and move them to Boxing Day and planned an even bigger event for some of her guests as well. That evening Tia was the last to come down to dinner. For Nathan, it was just like his last visit to Holland with her. She has done her hair in pin curls, and is wearing a printed sleeveless dress with silver, copper and gold brushed-metal hoop earrings. Everyone held their breath as she walked into the dining room. Tia said to Nathan, "I have not seen you all day . . . Are you going to come and give me a kiss, or do I have wait till we are married?"

Everyone laughed. The young couple were openly locking lips in front of their family and friends. Anthony covered Jackie's face with his hands. Gertrude said, "now that's what I call romance!"

Jaden, who has arrived early and is already seated at the table, whispered in Kate's ear, "How come you don't dress like that?" Kate hits him on the head and tells him to shut up and eat his dinner before he ends up on the sofa for the night. Throughout dinner, Nathan and Tia fed each other food and kissed non-stop.

Naana shakes her head and remarks, "One day apart and look at them! I wonder how they were able to get a divorce. Kids these days are too horny." Naana tells her husband. Bobby can't stop laughing.

"You are just as naughty as Tia. The only difference is you are a lot more private than our daughter is." Bobby proclaimed.

"How about you meet me in our room in ten minutes and I will show you naughty. I'm going to check on the children," Naana teased.

After twenty-five years of marriage, Naana Konadu-Sharp still knows how to keep their sex life hot. Bobby has been enjoying his wife a lot more even though BJ has been taking all her attention away from him. He is happy that the boy is sleeping in his own room tonight. Tia's and Nathan's open affection with each other was infectious to everyone in the house. Everyone can see how much they love each other. Seeing how Nathan couldn't keep his hands off Tia, Jason carried Brooke upstairs, and Jaden, likewise, escorted Kate to their room like there is something in the food making everyone romantic. After dinner, Nathan took tea with Gertrude. He reads to her since her eye-sight is not as good as it used to be. At seventy-six years old, Gertrude enjoys her evening routine with Nathan. Tia returns to the study to play with her computerized mock-up of her new production studio.

He grandfather quietly steps into the living room where Nathan and Gertrude are having tea. "My dear, I told Tia to come for her husband before he and I start a fight over you," her grandfather said.

Gertrude kissed Nathan and said, "good-night, my handsome Prince. Daddy has always been jealous whenever you to come to visit, you know?"

"Who can blame him, Grandma?" Tia teased.

Tia thought about putting an end to Nathan's and Brooke's lies. It is affecting people she cares about and she didn't want that to fester. She sat Nathan down and told him she knew about his affair with Brooke all along. Nathan did not try to lie about it this time. He wanted to explain, but Tia said she didn't want to hear it. Tia told Nathan that right now she is more concern about how it is tearing everyone apart. She kissed him and left the room. He followed her into the study. Sarah Williams, Kate and Brooke were in the study waiting for Tia as she had asked them to do. None of them has any idea why she wants them there. They thought it may be something to do with her wedding.

"I am so sorry for keeping you all waiting."

"I can't stay long. I have to go and see to the boys," Brooke said anxiously. She is still upset about Tia's outburst with her in the gym earlier today, and the fact that she has not said anything about the studio lot Nathan has bought for her made Brooke more uncomfortable. Tia pulls Brooke into a chair, and she puts one arm around her. She loves Brooke very much, so this meeting is not intended to humiliate any one, but it is something that needs to be done before it ruins relationships.

"Nathan and I are getting married in less than a week," she tells them.

"We know!" they all yelled.

Tia smiled. "I wanted to apologize on behalf of my idiot husband and Brooke. You all know they can be a pain in my rear end, but I love them both very much."

Brooke interrupted, "I swear we have not done anything wrong for Tia to apologized for us."

Tia sat on the edge of the desk and informed them that she has always known about Nathan's affair with Brooke, since way back when she was pregnant with Trey. The awkwardness in the room was unbelievable.

"I'd hate to see what this is doing to all of you, especially Nathan's inability to stop and think of the consequences of his actions. Enough people have been hurt over Nathan and Brooke's inappropriate behavior," Tia said.

Nathan rubbed an already tense jaw as he stood stiffly in front of the French windows thinking, "It is all over," as tears roll down his face. Sarah and Kate were glaring at Brooke. Sarah sat up straight in her chair with a sophisticated demeanor. She glanced in Brooke's direction with ill-disguised contempt. Sarah is exasperated, Tia can see, as is Kate.

"It is not my intention to humiliate anyone, please," said Tia. "But I am not naive about this either. I have felt what you and Kate are feeling right now, Sarah. We are family—not a perfect one—but we are a close, loving one. I am *so sorry* for all the pain this must be causing you all. I thought that by not confronting it, it would go away, that the affair would fizzle out," Tia paused. "I am sorry for Nathan's rude behavior to you this morning, Sarah. I was coming to tell off Nathan and Brooke, but I ran into Jason first and I needed to distract him from coming into your room. I had to run back to bed before Nathan caught me spying on him." Tia chuckled and then continued. "Sarah, you have been like a mother to me. I will not lose you over my husband's rudeness. You all mean more to me than you ever know, but it seems to me that we don't always behave the way that you, Lola and my Mom want us to do, Sarah. Even so, we love each other very dearly. Please, Sarah . . . Kate, please . . . . This was all a long time ago."

"If anyone should be sorry, it ought to be BB and *him*," Sarah said, pointing to Nathan. "Tia, I cannot sit back and let you marry someone like Nathan Carter a second time around." Nathan feels enraged by Sarah's comment and flexes his hands and rubs his jaw as he continues to stare out the window.

"Me, too, Tia," Kate said softly.

"Why can't you two just leave them alone? They are *in love*. Nathan Carter is an arrogant jerk and a first class bully, but he adores Tia and their children, and Tia adores him, too. Good luck trying to stop something God has blessed!" Brooke remarked as she pulled herself together.

Tia and Kate began to laugh, and Brooke joined them. Nathan and Sarah walked out of the study. They passed Naana in the hall, who asked "What's upsetting Nathan, Sarah?"

Sarah replied, "Tia just exposed the affair he was having with Brooke. Mr Carter's ego is hurt that Tia had know all along about his lies and his cheating ways with Brooke. All this was, apparently, a long time ago before Trey's birth."

With her heart in her hands, Naana asked, "Is the wedding over?"

Sarah raised her eyebrows, "One would think so. I told them that I cannot sit back and let Tia get married to a man like Mr Carter and the kids laughed me out of the study . . . Whoever they are, those are not our kids!"

Naana began laughing, "I am so relieved that it's over. This could have been a major mess."

"Tell me about it! I think Mr Carter has realized just how much trouble he's in with Tia. I almost feel sorry for him!" Sarah laughed.

"We all hate to confront that disturbing thought, but Nathan will do what he always does . . . He'll send constant flowers and little gifts, drop love notes on her desk professing eternal love. She will soon forgive and forget," said Naana reassuringly.

Kate said good night and left the room. When they were left alone in the study, Brooke didn't know what to say to Tia. "I am going to bed, too, so I can open gifts with the children in the morning," Brooke said. Tia didn't take her eyes off her laptop, "Okay, Sweetie. I'll stop by later on my way to bed and kiss the boys when they wake up for their midnight feed."

Brooke is embarrassed about her affair with Nathan, more so now that it is out in the open. After all the lies she has spun, she now wishes that she could have come clean a long time ago. She hates the awkwardness between them. She has been worried about Tia and how she has been doing since her recovery from cancer. Brooke knew Tia wasn't sleeping well because she always looked exhausted.

Attempting to bridge the gap between them, Brooke said, "Okay, Tia. I have been a right cow for sleeping with Nathan. I should have spoken up about it a long time ago. But just because I've been stupid doesn't mean you get to be stupid, too. I'm not letting you stay up until all hours working yourself to exhaustion. Let's go!" She pulled a willing Tia out of her chair.

"You just can't stop being my big sister, can you?" said Tia through her tears as she hugged Brooke.

Sarah Williams is in her room with Naana. They have just put the twins down for the night when Brooke and Tia entered in hand in hand. Tia looked exhausted. She gets into Sarah's bed and Brooke is about to cover her when Sarah asked what they were doing in her bed. "Do you two really think you can do whatever you please and the rest of us are just going to accept your behavior?" Naana asked. "Get out of Sarah's bed! Go to your own rooms and your own husbands!"

"Yeah, but Tia needs a proper sleep. She is not able to sleep well." Brooke pleaded with her mother.

Sarah looked at Naana and the two ladies began to laugh out loud. The girls didn't not share their mothers' humor.

"You two lost the privilege of sleeping in Sarah's bed when you decided to sleep with your sister's husband, like how you wear each other's clothes. How dare you? You both have put us through a lot of sleepless nights. Do you think we're just going to stand for it?" Naana asked scornfully.

Tia is already asleep. Brooke is amazed by Naana's anger because she is usually so reasonable, not like her own mother who always over-reacts.

"I am sorry. None of this is Tia's fault. She not able to sleep through the night and Nathan, too, is exhausted, even though he won't say so. Mother, it's just for one night. Besides, she is already asleep. I can't move her to another room. It will disrupt her sleep," Brooke declared.

"BB, go and call Mr Carter to come for his wife," Sarah muttered.

"Mother, please! Tia needs me."

Sarah goes to the bed where Tia is sound asleep and turns to Naana. Naana said to Sarah, "Don't even think about it! They are adults now. If they are going to be disobedient, then we must treat them as such." Both women can see how much the girls care for one another. Nathan is at the door looking for his wife.

Brooke told Nathan, "You know, there is a guest room downstairs. Why don't you take Tia there? She can sleep there tonight and you can get a good night's sleep."

Nathan replied, "Thanks, but no. I sleep much better with Tia next to me. Good night, Brooke."

Brooke was beginning to feel a rising irritability toward her own mother as well as toward Tia's mother. She turned and began to smart-mouth them when Naana opened the door and said, "Brooke, why don't you go to your own husband before you wake up the twins? It's not just Nathan and Tia who need their sleep, you know!"

Finding herself in the hall, Brooke yelled, "you are utterly and completely crazy! I hate you two!"

Both ladies replied, with amusement, "Thank you! Good night!"

Meanwhile, in the Carter's room, Nathan snuggled behind Tia and buried his face on her back. "Tia, baby, are you sleeping?"

"No, Sweetie. I'm not and I don't want to hear how my husband slept with my best friend the night before our wedding. It's over."

"Baby, I'm not trying to justify my . . . Tia, I love you! I was truly sorry the moment it happened. Um . . . I can't lose you over this, please, baby."

Tia replied, "I'm here and I'm not going anywhere. The next time you cheat on me I will do a lot more than divorcing you and taking your children away from you! I will not have our family torn apart because of your poor judgment!"

Nathan felt worse knowing full well that Tia didn't joke about things like that. "Please, forgive me. I wanted to tell you. I knew it was one thing you could never forgive."

"Well, I have. Otherwise, we would not be here. I love you, Nathan, but you know there are certain things I will not stand for—no matter how much I love you."

"I know, baby . . . I'll never cross that line again, Tia. I wanted to tell you so many times, but I was afraid you would leave me again."

"I did leave you, mainly because I didn't like the man you had become. I believed in the saying that if something belongs to you, it will come back to you. I can't share you, Nathan."

"Yeah, I know. I won't. I'm not the same man that I was when we married. Life without you was not a life. It was hell, an everyday hell. I am so very sorry for everything that I didn't say sorry for all the pain that I put you and the kids through, because of my selfishness. I didn't deal with a lot of the fallout from my break-up with Ellen . . . I brought all that bad stuff into our marriage and took it out on you. Tia, I'm not just in love with you and our children. I love our whole entire family. I would never do anything to hurt all of you. Believe me, baby, please. I mean it! All the pain that I have put you all through . . .," he turned Tia over and discovered she was already asleep. "I will not lose my family again, not again."

Brooke could not sleep, so she went to see the twins at six in the morning. Naana and her mother were up feeding the boys already. "Can I come in?" Brooke asked.

"I'm going downstairs to help mother with breakfast," said Naana.

Since it was Christmas Day, Sarah had dressed the twins in green and red outfits. Brooke apologized again for everything on the previous night. "I have no excuses. I'm supposed to be looking out for Tia, but I'm not doing a very good job of it, am I?"

"Actually, Brooke, you are doing an extremely good job," Naana affirmed. "I was there when Tia had Jayzel, and I was there when the cancer started. You left your business and your husband to go take care of her both times. We all know how much you love her, but you need to ease up a little and give some of that love and attention to other people in your life. Tia is not the only one who needs you, darling." Naana hugged the young woman and left Sarah and Brooke alone.

Sarah agrees with Naana's assessment. "Today is the first Christmas with my grandsons! BB, I am so proud of you! I'm also sorry for having a go at you last night. Merry Christmas, my sweetheart. I was afraid of losing you all on account of Mr Carter. I love you so much, BB! You shouldn't do things on impulse, sweetheart, and you do need to put the same effort on Jason and the children that you put on Tia. You girls are grown up now. Everyone can see how the three of you will go to any length to make each other happy—more so now that you all have your own children. I do hope that whatever it was with you and Mr Carter is truly over."

Lisa and Jackie spent Christmas Eve at the guest house. Vidal had plans for them, but Lisa has said she still needs to do a lot of studying. Vidal and Patrick arrived just before seven with dinner and DVDs for them to watch. Naana asked Rose to make popcorn for them. They stayed up half the night watching movies, before the boys left. Vidal wanted to spend the night with Lisa, but she refused, explaining that she still had some studying to do. Jackie went to sleep right after the boys left. Lisa couldn't sleep, so she spent the rest of the night talking on the phone with Vidal. So much for the studying she had to do! Jackie found her on the sofa still on the phone with him when she woke up later that morning. Lisa told him she was not able to sleep, and within minutes there was a knock at the door. Lisa shouted "Come in!", but the person kept knocking, so she told Vidal that she had to answer the door and hung up on him.

Opening the door, Lisa discovered Vidal on her doorstep. "I forgot to give you your gift last night," he explained.

Lisa put the gift bag down on the island, sat down, leaned her head back and kissed him softly on the lips. "Merry Christmas, baby." She took both his arms and wrapped them around herself and closed her eyes to sleep. Later, when she opened her eyes, she saw a UPS parcel had arrived from Ghana. She is anxious to open it, but it has been so long since she last lounged in Vidal's arms that she doesn't want to break the magic. She also didn't want to spoil things by thinking about lost love and broken hearts. The past was never meant to be she told herself as she raised her hands to rub her nose and glanced at the kanete bracelet on her wrist and he is all she can think about—his voice, his laughter, his sexy smile that melts her heart. She gasps as she feels Vidal's hands rubbing her butt, so she gets up and puts a Backstreet Boys CD on the stereo. "I want it that way" was playing while they both fell asleep.

For Christmas morning, Anthony Carter and Gertrude have cooked and baked a feast for their families and friends. They were all in the family room with each of the children busy opening gifts. Jaden and Bobby were busy making a video tape of the festivities. Tia was barely awake, drinking tea that her brother made while Nathan rubbed her back. BJ loved all his gifts, and he early waited for his mother and sisters to open their gifts that he got them. He had patiently made each of them a circle of love, a beautiful silhouette circle in sterling sliver, custom hand-stamped with the names of his sisters on them, a very charming gift. Naana begin to cry when she beheld her gift, but BJ hushed her, told her not to cry.

Trey said, "Grandma, did you know that BJ said that you are the best mummy in the whole world? My Grandpa, not your husband," he went and took Anthony's hand and exclaimed, "My mummy is the best mummy in the whole world, too!" Everyone laughed. They all enjoyed breakfast and opening gifts together.

Chapter 8

Tia headed back to the study. Since Amy and Steven were expected to arrive the next day, she wanted to be ready to unveil her plans for the studio. She worked intensely all day and when ten o'clock rolled around, she was still in her pajamas. Nathan has had it with Tia's exhausting work ethic. He barged into the study and without warning carried off his wife, took her upstairs and placed her in a warm bubble bath. Before she could protest, he slipped into the tub behind her. Tia drank fruit cocktail while Nathan washed her. Later, he helped her out of the tub, led her over to their bed where he massaged her skin with rich oil until she sleeps. It is quite possibly the first night since Tia came home from the hospital that she has been able to sleep through the night. Nathan had a huge smile on his face when she finally opened her eyes the next morning.

"Why are you so happy" she asked softly.

"Baby, you slept through the night without any nightmares!" He threw his arms around her and said, "It's over, Baby!"

Tia felt so relieved she began to cry. "There is something I must tell you. Nicole will be arriving today. I invited her and her family since she is your oldest and dearest friend. I knew you would want her here."

"Uh-huh. Not if it is going to upset you. I want to make you happy, Tia. I want to earn your love and trust again. I will not lie to you again. I promise," Nathan asserted.

"Don't make promises you can't keep, Nathan. Who the hell is Dr Vroom?"

Nathan nervously rubbed his jaw, "She's an ex-girlfriend. We were done the summer you and I met. Why?"

Tia was quiet. "You just promised me a moment ago no more lies." Tia raised her voice.

"I'm not trying to hide anything. I was through with her months before you and I met. Baby, I had no idea you knew about my relationship with her. I am sick of everyday seeing you in tears. Ellen cheated with a guy. They were seeing each other casually when she and I were together. The guy later ended up in her rehab, and she was very embarrassed about it, especially once she found out that she was carrying a child. It is not what you think. Tia, I am telling you the truth. If you want, I can take you there now to ask her. I have not been with anyone since you got sick. The thought has not even crossed my mind to sleep around and cheat on you. Tia, I had it all with you before you left me. Elizabeth tried to fill the void . . . but she knew that I was lost without you. I swear! Please, believe me, Baby. I am telling you the truth!"

"Yeah? Well, I want to meet this Dr Vroom. I have someone standing by to have a DNA test done before we go to the airport. I am not like my mother, Nathan. You'd better be telling the truth!" Tia said emphatically.

Nathan let go of her. "Damn! Baby, you don't believe me? Fine! I will take you to her." Nathan stormed out of the room, slamming the door.

Tia has always thought that if you are going to a war to fight for something you love, you must always look your best. With that thought in mind, she put on a Cartier diamond bracelet and earrings, a pair of Banana Republic jeans, a Ralph Lauren shirt, a black bomber jacket and black high heels to complete the ensemble. She looked elegant. She kissed her children, saying, "Daddy and I are going out, and we will bring back a surprise for you."

Tia slipped into the back of the limo, crossed her legs and put on her sunglasses to avoid Nathan's questioning stare.

"Perhaps you want me to beg before you'll condescend to talk to me. I won't do it, Tia. Not this time. I am telling you the truth," Nathan said softly.

He hated not being close to her. Tia moved to sit opposite him, and Nathan wished he could put his arms around her. Tia refused to rely upon Nathan's word as she had done in the past. She, too, wanted to reach out to him, kiss him, and tell him that she believed him. She knows he has changed, but when it comes to Nathan, Tia knows she has been humiliated enough by his actions. She knows that no matter how much she loves him, if the Vroom child turns out to be his and he has lied about it all along, it will be very hard to forgive this one. The limousine pulls into a driveway of a gorgeous doll house on the south end of Amsterdam. A little boy with a mushroom hair cut is playing outside. He kicks a soccer ball against the side of the house, and it looks to Tia that the boy has a lot of energy for his age. He is not using his words, but he is screaming so loud that when a middle-aged woman tells him in Netherlands that he needs a break, and that his mother has visitors in the house, the boy hits the woman, and with a kick and a shriek, he returns to kicking the ball. The woman shouts that he's crazy, and Tia felt the woman was unkind. The boy kicks the ball toward the limousine and almost hits Tia as she gets out of the car. Nathan isn't very happy about this boy's behavior. Instead, Tia kicks the ball back to the boy, and they share a few minutes of kicking the ball together. Tia says in Netherlands, "Thank you! No more, now." Without acknowledging Tia, the boy kept kicking his ball and returned to the game he was playing earlier.

Nathan grabbed the ball. "Sally, can you ask your grandson to stop kicking his ball to my wife. We are here to see Ellen. Is she around?" Nathan asked rudely.

"Ya! Ya! Come, come," the woman said, motioning to Tia and Nathan. "I go get Ellen. Ya!" Turning to the boy, the woman said in Netherlands, "Make sure you don't run onto the street! These people will watch you while I go get your mother." Tia kicked the ball back to the little boy.

Nathan thought, "What a freak! And what's up with all the yelling?"

A few moments later, the woman returned, "You must come, Nathan, with your wife, ya?"

Nathan wasted no time to kick the ball far away so that the boy would have to chase it. He grabbed his wife's hand and led her into the house. They entered a small kitchen, passed through it to the living room, where, to their surprise, Jaden and Kate were seated. Tia can see that Jaden is extremely upset.

Tia asked, "Kate, what are you two doing here?"

Kate replied, "It seems Jaden knew the Doctor when he was in Amsterdam years ago." Kate is also visibly upset, though she does her best to put on a brave face for Tia. She continued, "Jaden has just found out that they have a child. Jaden only remembers the Doctor from the rehab center. He thinks she is trying to pin the child on him."

The implications of Kate's statement cause Tia's stomach to knot, though she feels relieved that Nathan has been telling the truth.

Kate asked, "What are you guys doing here?"

Tia replied, "The doctor is an old friend of Nathan's. Is she sure the baby is not another man's child?" Feeling overwhelmed, Nathan left the house and returned to the limousine. He was sure he had lost his wife's trust regardless of the outcome of this visit.

Kate said, "No . . . the doctor has DNA evidence to prove that Jaden is the father. Jaden doesn't remember sleeping with her or knowing her before he was in rehab."

Tia said, "Well, I hate to leave you in the lurch like this, but Nathan and I can visit some other time . . . unless you need me to stay, Kate. Do you?"

Kate responds, "Oh, no, Tia! It's really not necessary. We'll see you later."

Tia graciously leaves the house. As she walks down the path toward the parked limousine, she sees Nathan leaning against the limo talking to a woman whom Tia thought might be Dr Vroom. The woman stared at Tia with raging hostility. Tia simply smiled and slipped into the back of the limousine. It soon became apparent to Dr Vroom that Tia thought the little boy playing outside was Nathan's and that she had some connection to Jaden.

"I don't like your wife's insinuation that I'm a slut," Ellen said smugly.

Nathan sneered, "She didn't call you that. You take your anger elsewhere."

There has been nothing but mutual loathing between Ellen and Nathan since the night Nathan found her in a hotel room having sex with a stranger. Learning that the stranger was, in fact, Jaden, made Nathan loathe her even more.

"You know, Ellen, I just bet the reason why your son has so much difficulty talking is because he ingested so many drugs as a fetus."

Ellen tried to slap Nathan, but he pushed her hands away and got into the limousine. As Ellen stood in her driveway and watched the limousine disappear down the street, she realized that she still loved Nathan. She mused that it had been a strange relationship that ended in an even stranger way. After two and half years of a long-distance relationship, Nathan came to spend the summer with her. Ellen was so sure he would have married her. One careless mistake cost her future. Kurt is a pretty boy: he has brown hair and Ellen's delicate features. At six years old, he is not able to say more than two words at a time despite all the love that Ellen has lavished on her son.

Ellen Vroom met Nathan Carter many years ago in California while visiting a cousin in America who had an internship at the same law firm where Nathan was working at the time. Ellen and Nathan would meet for a brief moment at a party, thrown by a mutual friend. The next day, Ellen was surprised to receive a phone call from Nathan because they hadn't had much to say to each other at the party. Ellen remembered Nathan and how charming he had been with one woman in particular, a beautiful red-head, Nicole Brightman. Nathan told Ellen that Nicole was both his best friend and his co-worker. Ellen was relieved to learn that Nicole was married. Ellen agreed to a date with Nathan, and afterward, for weeks, Nathan romanced Ellen. After two months of fairly steady dating, Nathan brought Ellen to Toronto where they spent the weekend in a luxury hotel making love and ordering room service. Ellen was head over heels in love with her man, and privately, she hoped the weekend would result in something more, so when Nathan declared his love for her, it was like a dream come true. At the end of three delicious months, Ellen had to return to Holland. Nathan had decided to open his own law firm in Toronto, and since both Ellen and Nathan were leaving California at the same time, Nathan thought he would take the scenic route and accompany Ellen to Holland. Nathan loved Amsterdam and its environs, and the two lovers enjoyed touring the sights before Nathan had to return to Canada. The following two years saw the long-distance relationship develop through a series of phone calls and long-weekends. Despite the challenges of establishing a new law firm in Toronto, Nathan decided he needed to take the summer off to visit Ellen. He needed to get to know her better, to meet her parents, and to determine whether she might be "the one". Leaving the law practice in Nicole's capable hands, Nathan went to Holland. He bought a nice doll house-style house for Ellen and her mother. During his visited they talked often about their feelings and their hopes as a couple. Nathan also told Ellen he had been thinking about her often and that he wanted her to meet his parents. Ellen was over-joyed. Even though they didn't live in the same country, she felt strongly that they had been able to make their relationship work. But there was something about Ellen which Nathan did not know: she has a dark side to her personality which, so far, she has managed to keep hidden.

One aspect of life in Holland that Ellen enjoys most is the opportunity to explore her sexuality, particularly having sex with random men periodically. In fact, Ellen uses an agency who caters to every sexual need any individual might have. Seven years ago, Ellen was at a club that organized sex parties. Customers paid a lot of money to participate, but they got the pick of any man or woman for sex games, no strings attached. At the time, Jaden Blake was working as a male escort at this same club, so it was inevitable that he and Ellen might meet. The good thing about this kind of party is that you don't have a conversation with your partner, and the chances are good that you will never see that person again at the next sex party. The club host arranges to have sexy young men and women from all over Europe to attend these events. Customers pay in advance to attend and tickets are mailed to customers well before the date of the party. During Nathan's visit, Ellen misplaced a ticket, so she has ordered a second one, knowing the party would take place long after Nathan had returned to Canada. In actuality, Nathan did not leave Holland as planned, but stayed on for another month. Ellen went to her sex party anyway. Nathan arrived at her home to have dinner with Mrs Vroom. While he sat in the kitchen talking to Mrs Vroom while she finished the dinner preparations, Nathan noticed a piece of paper tucked under the cookie jar on the table. Curious, he extracted the paper and discovered that it was a ticket to one of Ellen's "events". Nathan knew Ellen attended a lot of "events", so he thought it might be romantic to surprise her by showing up at her event to support her. Nathan was surprised to discover that tonight's event was being held in the night club of the Imperial Hotel rather than in the hotel's ballroom. He spoke with one of the hotel workers, who spoke very good English, and inquired whether he was at the wrong event. The worker was only too happy to apprise Nathan of the purpose of the event. Disgusted, Nathan was about to leave when he saw Ellen in the lift with a white man wearing a dark suit, so he decided to follow them. Nathan frowned, thinking about how to find out what Ellen was doing without having to confront her directly. Hmmm . . . . Suddenly making up his mind, Nathan strode across the lobby to speak to a hotel clerk. "Yes, sir! I can escort you to the same floor where that lady is going. Yes, sir! We can go right now!"

Together, Nathan and the hotel clerk ascended in the lift. When the lift stopped, Nathan stepped out into the hall just in time to see Ellen go into a room with her date. Turning around, Nathan gave the clerk a generous tip, "That's all. Thank you, very much, young man," he said as he strode down the hall toward Ellen's room. "No problem, sir! Glad to be of service!" the young man said as he closed the elevator doors.

Nathan is hurt. Usually, he does the cheating and the manipulating in a relationship, so he feels jealous of Ellen's behavior and also jealous of the man she's with. There is a small lounge adjacent to the elevator area, so Nathan sits down to contemplate his next move. Ensuring no one is in the hallway, Nathan strolls down the hall to Ellen's room and pauses in front of the door. The door is on the latch, not completely shut and Nathan can hear raucous laughter coming from the room. The temptation is great to nudge open the door, but Nathan knew that even greater problems could arise if he simply walked into the room.

"Hey, come here! It's ready!" shouted the man from the bathroom.

"Now, here is an interesting possibility," thought Nathan. He nudged the door open a little bit more. His new angle of vision allowed him to see the whole room, but not the bathroom. Both Ellen and her escort were in the bathroom together. Thinking an open door is a tacit invitation, Nathan decided to step into the room. He was mildly surprised to see Ellen openly snorting some white stuff with some blond man. He has stripped himself to the waist and loosened the fastenings of his trousers. The man and the girl begin having sex in the bathroom. Nathan notices that the guy has a tattoo of a hawk on his upper left shoulder. Disgusted, Nathan swiftly leaves the room before they notice his presence. "How could I have made such a mistake with Ellen?" wonders Nathan as he leaves the hotel.

Nathan did not go back to Ellen's house that night. He briefly thought about leaving Holland the next day and forgetting about her and the whole evening, but instead, he got a room at the same hotel and spent the night there with two beautiful blondes. It was the first time that Nathan had been with two women at the same time and he loved it! He woke up after lunch and called the front desk to ask them to upgrade his room to a suite. Something had snapped inside Nathan Carter's psyche, and he was enjoying every bit of his darker side. Ellen was at work when Nathan returned home, so he left her a note saying he had something to do in Paris and that he would call her soon. For two weeks, Nathan enjoyed sleeping with the most beautiful women that Europe has to offer. He was not overly upset with Ellen. He actually felt rather relieved and thankful, in a way. He sent Ellen a sexy evening dress and the sexiest underwear with a note to meet him for dinner. Having received these gifts, Ellen was certain Nathan was going to propose to her that evening. The dozen white rose sent to her workplace clinched the notion that a proposal was immanent. She arrived at the hotel and was told to go to Mr Carter's suite. Ellen was not surprised to find Nathan in the penthouse suite. He has always been very romantic. He opened the door and greeted her with a kiss on each cheek. Even though they have been apart for two weeks, he doesn't give her their usual long, sexy kiss that he likes so much. She noticed that he has ordered a lavish dinner with a bottle of champagne in an ice bucket. Nathan pulled out a chair for her to sit down. Suddenly, inexplicably, Ellen felt very nervous. She smiled, and said, "Thank you." A knock on the door interrupted the moment. Nathan said, "Would you please excuse me for a moment?" as he opened the door. Nathan re-appeared in the dining room chuckling, with his arms around two sexy women. He didn't introduce them to Ellen, though her poured a glass of champagne for each of the girls. As he sat down in one of the dining chairs across the table from Ellen, one of the girls tried to kiss him. "No kissing!" he told them. Ellen's heart began to pant when the girls began undressing Nathan right in front of her. Nathan never took his eyes off Ellen while he had sex with the two girls. As the tears rolled down her face, Ellen wondered, "Why would Nathan do this to hurt me and humiliate me? Nathan is the sweetest, kindest man I know. What is happening?" Ellen wanted to tell him to stop. She wanted to get up and leave, but she couldn't. She felt compelled to stay and see through the whole sordid event. When the girls had finished with Nathan, he escorted them and Ellen out of his suite at the same time, like nothing had happened between them. He didn't offer a word of explanation to Ellen. When she returned home, Ellen didn't look herself. Her mother was in their living room watching TV.

"How's Nathan, love?"

In response, Ellen fell on her mother's lap and sobbed broken-heartedly for the rest of the evening. When she returned to work the next day, the first person she saw was the English man with whom she'd had sex three weeks ago at one of her events. Luckily, the man didn't seem to remember her. She requested some time off work. She had no idea whether Nathan was still in Holland, but she suspected he must have known something about that last event. After almost three years together, he dumps her this way? It didn't make much sense. During the last few days, Ellen has been stomach-sick. When it didn't stop, she went to the doctor and was told she is pregnant. It's not what she wants right now, but she hopes that if Nathan knew they were going to have a child, all might be forgiven. After all, it seems they both have cheated on each other. He is a man with needs. She understands that. She called Nathan's office in Canada and was told he was still in Europe. She called his hotel, but couldn't get any information, so she drove to see him the next day, only to learn that Nathan has found out about her other lifestyle when she told him she was pregnant.

Nathan's response was, "I hope you and your junkie Englishman with the hawk tattoo will be very happy!"

Jaden has had nightmares almost continually since the morning he found himself in Dr Vroom's office in the rehab center. At first, he thought his mind was playing tricks as those were dark times for Jaden. However, if this is the truth, then all of those nightmares are things he did while living in Holland. He felt nauseous and asked to use the bathroom. As he closed the door, Jaden began to vomit. Meanwhile, Kate was left in the living room with Ellen. Kate can sense that her attitude has changed, and it makes Kate uncomfortable. Kate excuses herself saying, "I'll be outside in the car. I need to make a phone call." Finally, Jaden came out of the bathroom and rejoined the women. He was beginning to have an anxiety attack when Dr Vroom shifted her gaze from Nathan to the man who changed her future with Nathan simply by sleeping with her. She recalled for Jaden the night they met. She told Jaden about it and explained why she had asked to be replaced by a different doctor at the rehab center. Jaden explains that he doesn't remember much from those times, but assures Ellen that he will take on any responsibilities that their son needs and play whatever part she want him to play in their son's life.

Jaden has no idea how he will explain this one to Kate, nor how he will make her understand and forgive him. He has often wondered why he had so much money when he was in Holland years ago. It never occurred to him that he might have been working as a male escort, going from party to party and getting paid for sex. He used the money for a down payment on their first home. It was money he received for having sex with women he hardly knew while he was on drugs. Kate is a forgiving woman, but no woman is going to forgive him for this. He told Ellen he would keep in touch. Mrs Vroom brought Kurt inside and Jaden asked, "Can I hug you, Kurt?" Kurt nodded, so they hugged and kissed. Jaden apologized to Ellen before he left. As he walked to the car, Jaden ran his fingers through his hair and closed his eyes. He was not able to fight back the tension as his whole body began to feel like he had been hit by a truck.

At the curb, Jaden saw a stressed-out Kate standing by the car. As he looked up, Jaden vomited once again, so Kate ran to his side, exclaiming, "Are you all right?" Jaden nodded affirmatively, panting with relief, then muttered, "I don't remember sleeping with her, Kate."

Kate didn't immediately respond. Instead, she got in the car and started it before Jaden took his seat. "Can we go somewhere to talk about things, love?" Jaden asked.

"There is no need," responded Kate. "It is in the past. It happened when we were not together."

Jaden was both relieved and alarmed by Kate's reaction to his past with drugs, alcohol and sex. "Oh, boy! Kate's mum is going to love this tale!" Jaden thought ruefully.

Ironically, at the same time, Kate was thinking, "Mum's going to give me her I-told-you-so speech." Kate sighed and continued to drive even though it was not easy. Jaden also noticed Kate trembling with restrained anger and asked her to stop and park the car.

"Kate, I know you said it was in the past and that it doesn't matter, but I think it does. I think it matters to you a great deal. When I wrote to Dr Vroom years ago, it was only to thank her for helping me get back my life and you, Kate."

Kate didn't say a word. Jaden continued, "My intention was not to instigate something. You and the boys mean everything to me, Kate. I didn't plan for Kurt, but I can't walk away from him either."

Despite her misgivings, Kate murmured, "of course!"

"Thank you for understanding. I love you and the boys. You're my first priority, but any time you want to discuss Dr Vroom and Kurt, just let me know . . . and we'll talk about it. Kate, please, I don't want this to come between us. I have everything a man could possibly want with you and the boys. I don't want to lose it again, love." Tears were trickling down Jaden's face, now.

"Oh, no! I feel the same way, too! Even though it's shocking, the revelation of you sleeping with a woman you don't remember and her son you've never thought about until now will not come between us."

Tia and Nathan arrived at the airport in Amsterdam each with their own thoughts. Tia wondered why Nathan had never said anything about

Jaden and the doctor to her years ago. Nathan said when he met Jaden on their first visit to Europe when Jayzel was born he wasn't sure how he knew Jaden even though he recognized him. Later, on their second visit, he saw the hawk tattoo and asked Jaden about it, but as they were divorced, it wasn't really the right time to mention it to Tia. "Actually, I thought Kate already knew about Kurt. I just assumed they wanted to keep it private." Tia rummaged in her purse, took out a couple of painkillers and swallowed them. She drank some of her tea and looked up at the Arrivals screen. Amy and Nicole's plane has already landed. They are going to get their luggage. Steven's plane is twenty minutes late. Tia asks, "Is Dr Vroom still in love with you, Nathan?"

"Damn it, Goddess! I don't like this! You're my wife. I'm in love with you. I don't care about anyone else. I need to know that you're not going to run off and leave me again like the last time." He muttered something inaudible under his breath. "Goddess, I don't need to remind you my relationship with you is special—different from the others. Baby, if you want me to bombard you with flowers every day and extravagant presents that will make us broke, I will! But, please, don't punish me for my past mistakes."

"What really happened between you and her?" asked Tia.

"Well . . . It was like this. Ellen had a whole other life that I didn't know about, and when I learned what kind of person she really was I had to end the relationship." Nathan told Tia everything. "When I went to Holland, I didn't know people like that really existed. I mean, characters like that make a good story or an entertaining movie, but they're not for real, you know? Anyhow, the hotel clerk really opened my eyes to the sex trade in Europe. According to him, it doesn't matter which part of the world you come from, all you need is a hotel room and the right web site, and your every sexual need will be fulfilled at any hour of the day."

Tia began to understand why Nathan had been so casual when they first met, and why he continued to entertain casual relationships when they were first married. Nathan took Tia by the hand and cradled her small hand in his larger hand. "I remember the moment we first made eye contact. It was in this airport when our eyes met. We held the gaze for a moment before we both smiled and gasped at the same time."

Tia remembers the same moment, too. "I was also hurt and humiliated by someone that I thought I knew. I didn't want to believe the emotions I felt . . . when you looked at me and smiled," Tia said softly as tears rolled down both of their faces. They leaned toward each other, pressing their foreheads together.

Nathan said, "I was just on the point of running far away from you when Brooke was standing next to me talking to me and introducing us. Tia, what I felt at that moment was just like the day I felt Jayzel kick my hands. I love you. And if I can take back everything that I did to hurt and . . . Brooke, I will. You are the only one for me. Please . . . I need to know you're not going to leave me again."

Tia gently kissed him. He looked like a little boy lost to her, and she smiled at him. "Life without you was an everyday hell, too, Baby."

Tia sat on his lap and they were in full lip lock when Amy said in a loud voice, "Do you two ever stop? This is an airport, for crying out loud! Get a room!"

Nicole and Ian assure Amy that this is typical Tia and Nathan behavior. Steven's flight has just landed. It won't be long now before they'll all be together at the mansion.

Gertrude welcomed them all, and Nathan lost his crown as Gertrude's favorite grandson, as the two Carter boys sat side by side with Gertrude during lunch. Tia was back in the study with Amy telling her about the plans for Sunlight Studio and the projects she has been working on since they last saw each other. Amy asks, "How do you get the time to do all this? I went to the lot and saw Chase Page and the contractors. The weather has not stopped them from pushing ahead with the work."

"Yes, that is just our office they are building right now. The studio itself will be re-built once City Hall approves the plans. But I'm told that won't be a problem. Now, Amy, your job as the head of Sunlight Studio is to recruit the best in the business. I was not able to get the loan that I needed. Between Nathan and I, we have enough cash to finish our offices and four small studios. I was able to get most of our equipment from a production company that my brother-in-law used on his last film in Canada. They filed for bankruptcy, so we were able to get a deal on the equipment. I have set up an appointment with some of their production team members so that you can interview them. I am thinking, though, that we need our own in-house casting directors and talent scouts," Tia gushed with excitement.

She continued before Amy could get in a word, "I have assembled some young writers, producers, publicists and videographers from all over to come and compete to be a part of Sunlight Studio Media Group. The response has been amazing. I'm still getting more responses every day. There are two new shows that I have been working on. One is a comedy and the other one is a two-part drama. CTV is still going to be our partner, but all the shows will be filmed at Sunlight Studio. So tell me what you think," she paused and turned the laptop toward Amy for a look.

Amy is quiet, digesting everything. Tia has never known Amy to be quiet, not this quiet, and she is beginning to panic. Suddenly, Amy let out a loud scream that got the whole household running to the study. "Tia Sharp! You are a fucking genius! I don't know what to say about you . . . but honey, you're a dream come true! I love it, love it, *love it!*"

Tia told Amy that the television world today produces a lot of reality shows. "I've hired a web-site specialist to help us create the edge we're going to need."

"Tia, I love the way that you have used your knowledge to tap into this industry! By this time next year, we will be producing all kinds of shows and having all the up-coming young people in broadcasting working for Sunlight Studio without breaking the bank. Fuck! As a studio head, honey, I won't have to pay for sex!" Amy added with a wink. "You are a genius!" Amy raised her martini glass up high and toasted Tia.

Tia winked at Nathan, who was standing by the door looking on and feeling very proud of her.

"CTV is hoping we can finish filming "Forever Never Dies" before Valentine's Day, but Steven said he would be busy for the next six weeks, so I'm guessing filming will begin on the first week of March. I have all the contracts with me except Kelly Powers's. I wasn't able to reach her agent before I left. I'll also meet with Lock and Ashton Wentworth when we go to England about the movie that Sunlight Studio wants to do about their lives. I'll be spending more time in England, then, if everything goes as we planned. Liz Starr will be arriving in two days for the promotion of "The Saga". Miss Hall, there is no turning back now! Sunlight Studio Media Group is ready! My question is . . . are you?"

"Hell, yeah!" Amy exclaimed enthusiastically.

Tia threw her arms around Amy and hugged and thanked her again and again. Tia knows that none of this would have been possible without Amy Hall's advice and encouragement for Tia to pursue her dreams.

Tia felt like no one had done anything fun since they arrived in Holland. In actuality, Tia herself had not had much fun since her arrival, just work,

work, work on the new studio. Feeling frivolous, Tia rented a boat for the whole family to get out of the house for the afternoon. They had their lunch and went to watch a football game. Ajax played against Liverpool FC. It was just four days before Tia and Nathan's wedding. In the midst of all the laughter and shouting at the football teams, Tia announced that she would be moving to the Regency Hotel. Nathan snorted and declared, "You're forbidden to stay in a hotel before our wedding." A lively argument ensued, so Steven suggested, "Let's play a game of basketball—boys against the girls. If Tia's team wins, she and the girls can move to a hotel and do as they wish. If Nathan's team wins, the girls must do as their husbands wish and stay at the mansion. What do you say?" Of course, Tia accepted the challenge. Her grandfather has a huge indoor basketball court, which was built originally for Naana when she was growing up. The guys recruit BJ for their team, to even the numbers. Nathan joked, "No, the boy will want his sisters to win."

Naana is offended by Nathan's comment, so she told the girls that if they want one more player, she will play for them. Nathan laughs and gives his brother and Jason a high-five. "It's on! The girls are going *down*! This game isn't about the girls staying in the hotel. We need our wives to know we are *men*."

Chapter 9

Kevin spent the Christmas holidays with his sister, Ola, who has managed to get Tia's address in Holland and has two plane tickets for her and Kevin to go and visit Tia and the kids. Kevin had some misgivings. He did not think it was such a good idea, but went with his sister anyway. They have just arrived in Holland and Ola gave the address to the taxi driver. They arrive just as Gertrude's staff return to their duties after their holiday break. Rose announces two more of Tia's guests have arrived. Gertrude told the maid to bring them into the family room and to take their bags to the guest house. Kevin was as nervous as hell as he entered the family room. Gertrude immediately welcomed them and the maid brought them tea.

"I am so happy you can join us! Tia will be so happy you came," Gertrude told Kevin and Ola. Kevin felt a little more at ease to hear it. Gertrude continued, "They're all at the gym playing basketball. It's the boys against the girls. Let's go see. My daughter is playing, too. She used to play as a teenager, you know."

Kevin and Ola have never been inside such a big house before. Kevin remembered that Tia had invited him a long time ago to come and meet her grandparents. With sadness in his heart, he realized that he had made all the bad choice, then. Meanwhile, in the gym, there were a lot of cheers and screams. Kevin couldn't see Tia, but he could see her father-in-law and he did not seem very happy. Brooke saw Kevin first, but she didn't recognize him right away because he has gained so much weight. Brooke pulled Kate aside to ask, "Did you tell him about the wedding?" as she pointed at Kevin and Ola. "Why are they here?" Kate shrugged, "No, I didn't tell him about it, and I've no idea why they're here."

The basketball game was so physical that Nathan was beginning to regret his challenge to Tia and her sisters. He could see that both Tia and her Mother are very good players and in good shape, too. They are capably to shout from various spots around the court and block the guy's shots from different angles. Tia is left-handed, so it is difficult for Steven to guard her. She is fast as are her teammates. Nathan and Steven are both shocked to hear the girls talk trash as they play. Everyone saw Kevin except Tia and Nathan.

The girls were leading by four points when Anthony said, "C'mon fellas, let's shut the girls down!" On the opposite end of the court Tia's grandfather was also telling his daughter and granddaughter that he wants to see them wipe those handsome smiles off the faces of the Carter boys. Nathan has the ball when he looks up and sees Kevin talking and laughing with Gertrude. Tia dashed over to him and stole the ball, throwing it to her mother, who fired the three-pointer to finish off the boys. Tia ran to the study to confirm her reservation. She has no idea that Kevin and Ola are in the house. Nathan picks up his ego with a little help from his mother-in-law. She advised him not to lose his cool and to be the better man here—whatever the situation may be. They both go and greet Kevin and his sister. Gertrude adds that Rose has put them in the guest house. Privately, Naana and Nathan both wish that Gertrude would have checked with them first. After saying hello, Nathan informs everyone that Tia is in the study. "Grandmother, will you excuse us? I am sure Tia will be eager to see Kevin and Ola."

Ola couldn't help noticing how beautiful the mansion is. Nathan escorted them to the study and knocked on the door. "Come in!" called Tia. At the sound of her voice, Kevin felt close to tears. Nathan also shared his feelings as he opened the door, though for different reasons.

On the subject of Tia and Kevin, Nathan is over-tired. He recalls the day Trey was born when he walked into Tia's room and saw Kevin there. He also remembers just how humiliated he felt that day and didn't know what to think today as Kevin's arrival is completely unexpected.

Knocking on the door and pushing it open, Nathan said, "Sorry to interrupt, babe. You have visitors." He ushered Kevin and Ola into the room and closed the door as he left. Tia is on the phone and asks them to sit down. She puts the phone on hold and steps out of the study. In French, she said, "Baby, don't leave. I need you."

Nathan paused and said, "I'm okay. We will talk later. Go and see to your visitors."

"Nathan, this can't wait. Please?" she pleaded.

Tia is shocked to see Kevin and Ola. She knew Nathan well enough to suspect that he is probably feeling jealous. "He probably thinks I dreamed this up to hurt him," Tia thought.

"Nathan, we are husband and wife," she reminded him. "We do things together, not alone. Kevin is married and has a family, and you *know* that my heart has always been with you—even long before someone started sending photographs of Kevin and his family to us."

"Sure, sweetie. Finish your phone call. I'll be right behind you."

Tia returned to the study. She paused before picking up the phone again. "Ola, how long are you two in town?"

Ola looked at Kevin, "I'm not sure."

Tia put one hand on the phone, "My husband and I are throwing a party tonight. Can you two join us?"

Ola seemed to need convincing. "Please? It will be nice to spend some time and catch up properly," added Tia.

Kevin couldn't believe it when Tia said "my husband". He felt like he had been stabbed with a knife all over again. It took every emotional strength not to cry right there. Tia hung up the phone and turned to talk to Ola.

"Where are you staying?"

"We have a hotel booked, but your grandmother asked us to stay and your husband said you would love it if we stay."

Tia flashed a smile and said, "My husband is right. I'll not take no for an answer."

Ola is beaming. Tia points her pen at Nathan, "Baby, you need to reclaim your manhood. We beat you fair and square out there in the gym," she teased.

"Uh huh," Nathan moved and stood by Tia, smiling, "you two saw the game? You see . . . . Tia and my mother laid down a challenge knowing full well that they had an advantage of playing basketball better than my team. Now, she wants me to pay up. Now, does that sound fair to you guys at all?" Nathan asked.

Kevin has never seen Tia and Nathan up close like this talking and laughing with each other. They seem very close, and he hates Nathan more than ever now that he knows the man has been pretending to be Jayzel's father. Kevin thinks, "He must know that Jayzel is my daughter."

"Rose will be here soon to put these boxes in the limousine for me. I want you to charm grandmother into the limousine along with mother and Sarah, too. Grandfather is with her, so good luck getting past him!" Tia chuckled.

Momentarily, Nathan forgot they had company and were not alone in the room. "You are setting me up again. Well, this time I'm not going to fall for it. Grandfather encouraged you girls to kick our rear ends. I heard him. You know what, baby? I will go and put the old Carter charm on grandmother and mother, and give grandfather a taste of the Big Daddy Carter," he said with a smug smile on his face. Turning toward Kevin, he said, "Can I escort your sister to the limousine?" Ola has forgotten why they came to Holland and she is enjoying herself already. Tia has always been a fun person to be around, so she took Nathan's hand and left the study.

"Does Nathan have an ego bigger than Canada, or what?" Tia thought, smiling. Turning to Kevin, Tia says, "you can go with them, too, Kevin. I'll see you later. It's really nice of you and Ola to come and visit. I hope everything is okay with your family. Your wife is very close to giving birth to your son soon, right?"

Kevin's heart rate escalated as soon as he heard her say that. He didn't get a chance to respond as she was out the door and gone.

Nathan has ordered a dozen colossal baskets of Tia's favorite roses, and they could not have arrived at a more perfect time. He tells the maid to put down the basket she's carrying on the coffee table. He was still holding Ola's hand as they joined the rest of the household in the family room.

"May I please have every one's attention?" Nathan said. "All of you lovely people witnessed my wife and my beautiful mother-in-law here kick my butt off at the gym." Everyone laughed. Nathan was as charming as ever. Even Kevin thought so, loathing him more now seeing how much everyone likes Nathan.

"Well, this is for you for a job well done, mother." He gave Naana one of the baskets of the white roses and kissed her on the cheek. "Rose, please give that basket to Mrs Williams." Rose nodded and passed a second basket of roses to Sarah. Gertrude was standing by her husband as Nathan boldly goes and sweeps the old lady off her feet into his arms, just like they all have seen him do to Tia dozens of times. The old lady was blushing as Nathan sat her on his lap. He said, "You all know that grandfather was a good coach, and he coached the ladies very well in the game. I couldn't possibly buy you some flowers, grandfather," he signaled the maid to bring one of the baskets. "This is for my beautiful grandmother."

Gertrude beamed as she received the basket of flowers, "Oh, my dearest . . . you sure know how to spoil a girl! Look, darling! Isn't Nathan a sweetheart?" Gertrude turned to her husband.

"Yep! Yep! He most certainly is, my dear," her husband said.

"There's a limousine outside for all you ladies to get in. Tia has a very special day planned for all of you." Nathan tells them.

Nathan carried Gertrude into the limousine. Amy, Nicole, Kate and Brooke already were in the limousine drinking when Nathan placed Gertrude beside Brooke. They were all thinking "How does he do it?" Tia was leaving the house with Ola, Jackie and Lisa in the second limousine with her mother and Sarah Williams.

As the car door closed, Tia said, "I have something for you upstairs, Mr Hot." She winked at Nathan and slid into the back of the limo. He watched it drive off. The men were still in the family room when Nathan returned and told them that it wouldn't be just the ladies having fun. "Gentlemen, I will meet you all downstairs in an hour dressed for dinner. All of you! No exceptions!"

Nathan was going up stairs when, Kevin picked up his courage to ask if he could have a quick word.

"Mr Peters, you are my wife's friend and our house guest. Tia is expecting you in an hour. You and I have nothing to discuss, sir. I will see you downstairs in an hour, Mr Peters," Nathan said smugly.

Nathan was at the top of the stairs by the time Kevin caught his breath and thought of a rejoinder. "How rude!" he thought. "I am not going to let him steal my child," Kevin said to himself.

Anthony and Steven did not want anything going wrong with Nathan and Tia's wedding this time. They both warmly greeted Kevin. Steven gave him a hug as he said, "it's very good of you to come." Anthony similarly hugged Kevin and said, "You're a good man, Kevin."

Anthony tapped Kevin on the shoulders and said, "Let's go get ready, son. The girls are waiting for us and we had better be just as dolled up as they will be!"

Kevin has always found Anthony to be a kind gentleman. He wondered whether Anthony knew that he is Jayzel's biological father. Kevin asked about Jayzel and Trey.

"They are at an outing. We will see them later, son. Go get ready." Anthony reassured Kevin.

Kevin felt a little better. If Tia is waiting for him, then that's a good sign. He decided to tell her everything. He's certain she will forgive him everything and take him back. He thought, "I am here to re-claim my daughter and Nathan Carter had better be ready for the fight of his life! I plan to win this battle, hands down!"

Tia has booked a whole floor of the Regency Hotel for her family and friends. When the women got to the hotel, they hit the spa first. A hotel staff person brought a gift-wrapped box for all of them. Tia told them to get changed and not to drink too much champagne. "This is going to be a night to remember! I am getting married in four days," Tia exclaimed.

Meanwhile, at the mansion, Nathan finds a suit laid out on the bed with a hand-written love-note from Tia. It makes him smile to think she took time to do these things before leaving the house. The not read:

> Baby,
> In four days, my dream will come true. I have carried your heart with me all my life—even before I met you. I've always believed that you would find me, my love. I cannot put to words how at peace my heart feels. You're my everything, Nathan. Forever never dies. My love . . .
>
> Tia Carter

Nathan cried when he read the note. To calm himself, he took a shower, and though he was dressed in no time, he was the last to arrive downstairs. In the limo he sat between his father-in-law and Tia's grandfather. He could see Kevin's expression has changed. He looks more relaxed. Such things did not bother Nathan. He told the gathered men that the girls would meet them in the casino of the hotel. They exchanged their money for casino chips and the staff told them to enjoy the open bar. Dr Michael Doyle was there already, so Nathan greeted him and introduced Bobby, Steven, Kevin and Tia's grandfather. "Everyone, this is the good Doctor who saved Tia's life. He is also a very good friend of my father and also of Mrs Williams."

Nathan and Steven sat down with Jason and Jaden to play a card game. Once again Kevin felt like an outsider who doesn't belong with them. He went to the bar and ordered lots of drinks, starting with a martini and moving across the spectrum towards the Greek Ouzo and the Scotch Drambuie. Nathan noticed Kevin's behavior, so he went to the bar and asked the server to bring Kevin a cup of strong coffee.

"Piss off, man, and leave me alone!" said Kevin aggressively.

"Mr Peters, I am a very peaceful man. Be advised to carry yourself with dignity and respect tonight—for your own sake as well as your sister's. I don't wish you any embarrassment, sir, but I will not permit you to tear apart my family like you did when my son was born," said Nathan in a warning tone.

Kevin is already drunk and there is no reasoning with him. He raised his voice toward Nathan and could not be placated, so two big black men came, lifted him up and threw him outside the hotel.

Jason, who saw the whole thing, spoke as Tia would have, "I hate the son-of-a-bitch too, Nathan, but if you allow the man to make a scene he will win. I think we should do what Tia would do: we will show him kindness. Let him understand that he can't just come in here and work up our family like he has done in the past."

Jaden added, "You have three brothers here to support you, Nathan."

Nathan turned to look at his brother. Steven nodded in agreement, "They are right, Nate. Please listen." Nathan nodded and gestured for them to proceed. Steven went and picked up Kevin, took him to a room upstairs and did his best to sober up the man. Somewhat embarrassed, Kevin thanked him on their way back to the casino. In the hallway, near the lounge next to the elevators Jason came at Kevin out of nowhere and pinned him against the wall: "I don't know what right you think you have to barge in on our family. I'm warning you . . . your law degree means nothing to us. You're still a low-life just like you were when you whored yourself to get a British passport. Understand this: this is our family and we all protect one another, mate!"

Shaken, Kevin pulled himself together and continued downstairs with Steven to meet the others for more pre-dinner gambling. Once inside the casino, Kevin asked a server to bring him a cup of coffee.

Amy, Sarah and Gertrude entered the casino wearing beautiful evening dresses and more diamonds than the Queen of England. Nathan tried to pull up a chair for Gertrude, but Osei Kofi said, "Young man, you and I are very close to a duel if you don't leave my wife alone!" Anthony and Dr Doyle both laughed heartily.

"You know, Tony, if your boys were our ages, I'd have serious worries about my Getty. It's been nothing about how charming Nathan and Steven are. Getty used to think that I was charming, and then these young upstarts showed up at the house," he said jokingly to them.

"Well, they do take after their mother," Anthony said in return.

Ola arrived at the casino wearing a black chiffon dress with spaghetti straps and pearl drops in her ears. Kevin did not recognize her. "You look like a Princess," Kevin complimented her.

"She sure does!" said Anthony from behind and turning to Kevin, he asked "Are you okay?"

Kevin smiled. Ola, not noticing the tense undercurrent, bubbled, "Tia hooked me up. I had my nails and everything done." She flashed her nails at Kevin. "We just have to wait for the right time and we can both talk to her. Tia loves you and once she knows what's happened, she will not marry that show-off," Ola pointed to Nathan, who was winning more money than he needs.

Nathan wore a midnight blue suit, a lime green shirt and a lime green tie that Tia had picked out for him before she left the mansion. He gave his dices to Gertrude to kiss and threw it on the table. He called for two fours: two sets of fours turned up. The casino manager said, "Mr Carter! Sir, I am afraid if I let you play one more game you and your girlfriend here," he pointed to Gertrude, "will close down my casino!"

Grinning, Nathan took his winnings, and arm-in-arm with Gertrude left for dinner. Tia and her mother had still not arrived. Brooke said, "They're having dinner together in Tia's room. They'll join us later." Nevertheless, everyone else enjoyed a lovely dinner at the hotel. Brooke played hostess and asked them all to follower her into the ballroom. On Tia's request, the hotel staff have turned their ballroom into a night club with a live band and karaoke, too. Lisa started the festivities by getting up on the stage and belting out a love song. Bobby Sharp had no idea his daughter could sing. In no time at all, everyone was up dancing and having fun together. Tia and Naana arrived together, fashionably late, and dressed to kill. Tia wore a pink dress that Kate had designed which featured a silk duchesse satin bodice with a silk taffeta skirt—very glamorous—her hair in an up-do of curls piled on her head held together with a diamante hair band, and of course, diamond drop earrings and a diamante bracelet on her wrist. Naana, more modestly dressed as befitted the mother of the bride, wore an elegant, white silk crepe skirt and jacket. Her hair was curled so that it emphasized the shape of her face, and pearls adorned her ears and throat.

When they entered the ballroom, the young men were in a corner drooling over some strippers. Jaden tapped Nathan on the shoulder. "She looks dazzling," he said. Steven added, "I feel like I'm at a Hollywood party." Nathan turned to see his bride and gasped with pleasure.

"I've been missing you terribly," he said as he cupped her face in his hands and kissed her on the nose.

Nathan's hands caressed her hair and the back of her neck as they embraced again. In the dimmed light of the night club, he whispered, "You've totally bewitched me. Would you like to dance with me?"

Nodding agreement, Tia allowed Nathan to lead her onto the dance floor. They danced to a song called "This I Promise You", a song Tia loved, written by Richard Max. The popular boy-band Nsync sang it. As they danced, Tia thought that the words of the song seemed very fitting for how they felt for one another and for the journey they were about to take four days from now.

For Kevin, the song evoked different memories. He recalled making love to Tia the Christmas he spent with her and the kids. That same song had been playing in the background. He felt an unpleasant stab of envy as he always did when he thought of Nathan and Tia together. "He loves her," thought Kevin as he drank some more red wine. "He loves her, and I love her, too." Kevin snapped at a waiter to bring whiskey and keep it coming. Kevin stared in fascination as Tia and Nathan danced and kissed. He couldn't help shivering with rage and emotions he had never experienced before. When the song ended, Nathan went and sat down with Gertrude. The old lady looked exhausted. Osei Kofi decided to be just as charming as Nathan. "Tonight, I am going to be the irresistibly charming young man that Getty fell madly in love with and wipe that smug smile off your boy's face, Tony." All eyes were on Osei as he went to the table, hugged Nathan, and carried Gertrude out of the club. Despite the loud music, they all started to whistle and call out encouragement as the grandparents exited the room. A few minutes later, Bobby and Naana, and also Tony left the party, returning to the mansion in the same limousine as Osei and Gertrude. Even though the music seemed to get a bit louder, everyone continued to enjoy themselves as they danced into the wee hours of the night.

Nathan was right about Sarah Williams and Dr Doyle. There was an unspoken romance between them that everyone could see but Sarah. Brooke encouraged her mother to stop grieving for her father and try to live life—if not for herself, then for the twins. Michael overheard Brooke talking to Nathan about Sarah. He loved Brooke's way of coming out and speaking her mind.

"She has grown to be just as beautiful as you Sarah. When I met her in Canada years ago, I told Tony and Heather how I felt about you all this time. They encouraged me to open up and tell you. I am sorry if I make you uncomfortable, Sarah," Michael said.

Sarah has also had some feelings for Michael over the years. She felt it was not appropriate to say anything, even though he has always been there for her since Jackson's death. Six years ago, he moved back to England when Sarah thought she might have cancer. Despite their close friendship, Sarah has gotten used to being alone, so much so that she didn't know how not to be alone. However, She missed Michael while he was in Canada. Sarah is afraid of betraying Jackson's memory for having thoughts about his best man. Naana Konadu-Sharp has often told her that Jack would want Sarah to love again, but it made her sad to think of Michael each day more often than she thought of Jack. She winked at him, and said, "Are you going to ask me to dance with you, or do you want me to ask you?"

Dr Doyle looked very dashing as he placed his martini glass on the table and bowed his head, holding out his hand, he said, "Will the lovely lady dance with me?"

Sarah put her hands in his, and his arms went around her waist, holding her tightly. She tried to wriggle free from his embrace, but that strange melting feeling in her stomach prevented her. She liked the comforting feel of his arms around her. Brooke watched them gazing into each other's eyes as they danced. Jason asked, "Are you okay, love?" Brooke nodded, "Mmm . . ."

Jaden joined them at the table and asked, "Where is Kevin? Has anyone seen him? For that matter, where is Tia?"

A glance around the room indicated that neither Kevin nor Tia were anywhere to be found. Nathan was alarmed, as was everyone else. They had all been watching Dr Doyle romance Sarah, so they didn't see Tia leave with Kevin. Ola saw them go, but she wanted them to be left alone so Kevin could say his piece, convince Tia not to marry Nathan.

Jaden grabbed Ola's wrist, "Listen, love . . . This is not high school play-time. I want to know if my sister is with your prat of a brother before I lose my temper!"

Ola ignored him, wrenching her wrist out of his grasp at the same moment Brooke noticed Ola didn't have her room key.

"Hey! They're in her room!" Brooke yelled. "Come on!"

Nathan was sitting down watching Sarah dance and refused to go running up and down stairs over what might turn out to be nothing at all. "Tia's just gone to fix her make-up. I'm sure that's all it is."

Meanwhile, Ola was closely following the others, fussing and telling them "Leave my brother alone! He has suffered enough. Leave him be!"

Jaden snarled, "Shut your trap, wench, before I shut it for you!"

As it happened, Ola's room was not locked and as they raced down the hall, they could plainly hear Tia screaming, "Stop it!"

Steven said to Kate, "Go downstairs and get Nathan. Move!" Kate hustled down the stairs.

As Jaden and Steven entered the room, Kevin threw a bottle of whiskey against the wall. Tia began to head for the open door, but he grabbed her forcefully and brutally tossed her onto the bed. His eyes were full of fire and rage. He attempted to kiss her, but she moved her head at the last second.

"If you lay your filthy hands on me again, my husband will kill you!" she said with authority.

Kevin laughed. "You're fucking dead-beat of a husband does not have the balls. He fucking left you when his son was born, and now he's trying to steal my daughter from me? I'd like to see him try!"

Kevin ripped off Tia's skirt and slapped her across the face. He told her to shut up. Like an animal, he undid his zipper and was almost on top of her when Tia managed to get off the bed and into Steven's arms. The look of horror on all their faces was unimaginable. They all thought that Kevin had raped Tia. Her nose was bleeding and she was half-naked. Steven's body began to shake with the horror of it all as he held Tia protectively. They all stood watching helplessly. Kevin laughed again and told them not to feel sorry for her, that Tia enjoyed every minute of it.

Wiping tears away from her face, Brooke said, "I'm taking Tia to her room. Jaden, don't let Kevin out of this room until I come back. Do you hear me?"

Jaden nodded.

Jason, Kate and Nathan heard Kevin screaming at the departing Tia, "Nathan is not a real man. You need me! You need a real man!"

Jaden and Ola saw Nathan's expression as he approached the room and saw his wife's skirt on the floor. He also saw a camera on the table. Nathan asked his brother to wait outside and close the door. Jason tried to say something, but Nathan closed the door on him. They could still hear Kevin dishing out insults to Nathan. It's how they all knew he was still alive.

Jason asked, "What happened?"

"The wanker raped our Tia," Jaden said. He turned to Steven, "I told you guys that we should throw him out earlier."

Kate asked, "What happened earlier?"

"That asshole tried to hit Nathan, but we thought-" he stop he couldn't get his words out and Kate was also in tears.

Meanwhile, inside the room, Nathan viewed what was on the camera and opened the door. "Lets go guys." They were all surprised.

Kevin said, "Yeah, that's right. Run like a pussy. I told you all that Nathan Cater was not a man. He is fucking wanker! Yeah, run like the pussy hole that you are!" Kevin tried to stand up, but he fell.

Nathan said to Ola, "You need to go take care of your brother." Nathan was kind rather than scornful towards Ola. Poor Ola was not only confused and embarrassed but also rather ashamed of what she has witnessed her brother do to Tia, and then laughing about it. She tried to apologize.

Nathan told her, "Go make sure your brother is okay," and then he closed the door.

The hotel security had arrived at the room. Nathan said to the security chief, "I want someone to be placed on this door till my brothers and I return in the morning. There is a man and a woman in there. I don't want them to leave this room or this hotel."

"Yes, sir!" the security guards said.

He asked where Tia was and was told Brooke had taken her to her room. Jason said, "I will go and ask Dr Doyle to have a look at Tia."

Nathan replied, "No, man. It's okay."

Jaden said, "It is not okay. I want to go and kick the living daylights out of Kevin."

Nathan hugged Kate and said, "Why don't you go and say good night to your sister. Please tell her I'm on my way, sweetie. Okay?"

Kate could not understand how calm Nathan was. She left nervously.

Nathan gave the camera to Steven and said "I want you to guard this with your life." Jaden said sarcastically, "That fucking asshole raped the woman you love, the mother of your children, and you want your brother to guard some stupid camera with his life? I'm calling the old Bell. I want to see him pay, locked up so he will never practice law again. I don't know why you all are so calm. Tia has been like my little sister, way before you all met her. I will not stand by and let Kevin Peters get away with this."

Nathan put his arm around Jaden and told him, "Please calm down, Jaden." Jason and Steven chimed in their agreement with Jaden. They, too, could not understand Nathan's reaction to the situation.

"Steven is my little brother, and now you and Jason are my brothers, too. I want you all to listen to me," he spoke very softly and calmly. Nathan asked them to go to Steven's room with him. His arms still around Jaden, trying calm him down, he resumed, "Mr. Peters did not do what we all thought he did. Take a look at what's on that camera." He pointed to the camera. Nathan went to the bathroom to wash his face. The whole thing was captured on film. Steven thought it was without a doubt the most brutal assault he has ever seen filmed. It was so real it sent chills down their spines. The three men all had tears rolling down their faces when Nathan emerged from the bathroom.

Jaden wiped his face and exclaimed, "You little beauty! We got the asshole. He is going to be put away like the animal he is."

Nathan was quiet. Jason asked if he should called the police now.

Nathan said, "No, Jay."

"Why not? Nathan, it is all on that tape, mate," Jaden points out.

Nathan loosened his tie and told them to sit down. "Jaden, you are a good lawyer." Jaden smiled because coming from Nathan, that meant a lot. "This tape will not be allowed into an evidence. I don't know the laws in Europe, but I am certain that I don't want to bring in the cops. I want you to hear me out, please, all of you. The man knows that he is Jayzel's biological father. Tia has always wanted to keep that to ourselves, but somehow he has found out."

Jaden stamped his foot. "This is all my fault. I may have told him a couple of weeks ago when we ran into each other at the court house in England."

"Tia is about to own one of the biggest studios in Canada in a few months. We can not afford the press all over this. They will eat us alive. Kevin Peters knows that I am a high profile lawyer. His attack on Tia was against me. His lawyers will spin this to humiliate my family. I cannot allow that, gentlemen. You were all there. You saw the look on his sister's face. She believed her brother had raped Tia. The girls needs us. Mr. Peters is been handled as we speak, and I will not lose my daughter. I want you all to sleep and think about what I said. We will talk and we will all find a way together as brothers to make Mr. Peters pay for his actions for tonight. I'll retaliate on Mr. Peters' action against my wife . . . The man is not remorseful for what he has done to my wife. I will retaliate, gentlemen . . . Lets go and see the girls."

Jaden still wanted to go and beat the crap out of Kevin, but Nathan tapped his shoulders, "Me too, little brother."

Jaden has been blessed since he met Kate. Although his drug and alcohol abuse almost cost him everything, he is very happy and feels lucky. Even though he has done the unthinkable once again, fathering a child he can't even remember sleeping with the mother. Kate still loves him and forgives him. Kate and Brooke have now been told by Tia that Kevin did not rape her, but he knows about Jayzel. She doesn't know who told him. Nathan is going to kill him once he finds out what Kevin has done. Kate told her, Nathan already knows he wants—Kevin to be left alone. Brooke glanced at Tia with fear. Kate asked what is going on.

"Nathan will never let this go. I am sure he's planning his retaliation as we speak. Nathan is up to something," said Brooke.

"Nathan is always up to something!" Nathan said with a smile as he opened the door.

Steven went and took Tia in his arms again and said, "We should have been there to protect you, Angel." He kissed her on the nose.

Brooke told Jason that she would be spending the night with Tia. True to form, she was already in an argument with Nathan about how Kevin should be horse-whipped. When Jason dragged her out of the room, Nathan stood behind the closed door and wanted to cry when he saw Tia's face. He thanked God that Kevin had not raped her. He closed his eyes to fight back the tears and took off his jacket. Tia was standing in front of him when he opened his eyes. He put his arm around her and stared into her tear-filled eyes.

"Can you ever forgive me? I should have kept my eyes on you, Baby." He brushed a hair away from her face and wiped her tears away with his thumb.

"This is not your fault, I should not have gone off with him without telling you, Sweetie. I am so sorry. I wasn't thinking," she murmured.

"I want Dr Doyle to take a look at you," Nathan said. Tia's mind whirled with doubt that Nathan doesn't believe her.

"No, sweetie, please! I just want to forget about—Baby, he did not rape me!" Tia cried out. "He did not raped me! I did not kissed him . . . or anything." She was crying and in a panic at the same time. "I know you don't believe me, Baby, but I'm telling you . . . the truth. He did not . . . rape me!"

Nathan wanted to hug her and tell her that he knows and that he believes her, but he couldn't get the words out. He was now upset and crying, too. He started to kick the walls. Brooke burst into their room with Jason. It wasn't long before Kate and Jaden followed. It was heart-breaking seeing both Tia and Nathan in such a state.

Brooke said, "You know what? I want you men to go and kick in the bastard's head before I do!" Nathan wiped his tears and began to laugh. It was infectious, and they all joined in. The girls stopped and were looking at their husbands as if there was something different about them, but not sure exactly what it could be.

"We didn't marry you boys for your good looks. Are you going to sort the son of a bitch out, or do you want me to show you how?" Brooke demanded.

"We will sweetheart, please." Jason pleaded.

"This is not right. If Naana sees Tia all bruised up tomorrow there will be hell to pay," Brooke hissed at the men. They all glanced at Nathan. Nathan took Brooke's hand and walked to the back of the room, "Let me re-assure you, Brooke, that we are handling the matter."

"Darling, look at her," Brooke pointed to Tia. "This is nothing that we haven't dealt with before. The man put his hands on my sister . . . and what about my Jayzel, ha? I don't want Kevin Peters near my Jayzel or Tia ever again, Nathan."

"He won't. I promise you, Brooke."

"Well, your promise don't mean a damn thing to me, darling. Sort it out." Brooke walked off to the bed and shot the men a nasty look.

"Why the hell did we marry these men?" Brooke snapped.

"We fell in love with them. What are we going to do about Jayzel?" Kate asked.

Tia's eyes were even darker when she picked up her blackberry and pushed a few numbers and said, "By this time tomorrow, Mr. Peters will know that he made a huge mistake coming to Holland," Tia said softly.

"Listen . . . Darling . . . We need to talk to your mum," Brooke suggested.

"She knows. I will not lose my husband this time, nor Jayzel."

There were tears in their eyes as Kate, Brooke and Tia put their foreheads against each other. It broke Jaden's heart seeing the girls that way. Jaden wanted Nathan to take Tia back to the mansion. He said, "It may not be very good for her to be at the hotel."

"It will be running away. I can't let everyone see my wife like this. Naana knows what Kevin did and she asked that we all stay calm. I don't know how I'm going to get her through this. This is more than I can handle," Nathan confided to the guys.

"Why did she go to the room with him?" Jaden wondered aloud.

"I don't know. I should have been there. I wouldn't have thought Kevin would go to this length, but this is over-the-top. I will take from him what he . . ." Nathan paused.

Chapter 10

Sarah was back in the mansion and just putting the twins to sleep. She tried to adjust her clothes and smooth her hair, but kept being distracted by the memory of Micheal's embrace. Naana Konadu-Sharp has come to the nursery to check on the twins, so she stood and watched Sarah.

"I see someone is back in the romance game, and it's about time, too!" she exclaimed.

Sarah was shivering with emotion. She brushed her blonde hair away from one shoulder to the next. Naana frowned, smiled at her, "I think I've taken a shine to Micheal." Sarah was shaking uncontrollably as she fell onto the sofa to calm herself down. "I am too old for romance. Don't you feel too old for romance, darling?"

Naana frowned and replied, "I just got back into romance after eleven years of no sex, so speak for yourself!"

Sarah raised an eyebrow, "That's how long you kept Bobby out of your bed?"

"Oh, no, good heavens! He was in my bed alright. I made it abundantly clear if he laid a finger on me I would snap it off." They both laughed.

"Oh, no! I left him in the family room by himself," she cried.

"Sarah, you left *who* in the family room by himself?"

"Micheal brought me home. I wanted to check on the boys. He might be there still—I think."

Naana told her, "Go see to your guest. I will stay with the twins until they sleep."

When Sarah returned to the family room, Michael was gazing intently into the fire. Nonchalantly, he reached down and toss more wood onto the blaze.

"Michael, darling! Forgive me. The boys are so adorable it's hard for me to tear myself away from them."

Micheal thought it was the best compliment she has given him the whole night. She fixed him a martini just the way he likes it—dry with an olive. He put the glass down and leaned against the marble mantelpiece, his pale green eyes bored into hers. She had a dazzlingly innocent smile that caused Micheal to grin back at her. As their eyes connected, he noticed the curve of her hips and the swell of her breasts in the tightly fitting dress she wore. He put his arm around her tiny waist and glanced at his watch, "I would very much like to take you to lunch tomorrow, Sarah, if you could tear yourself away from the boys." He smiled dashingly.

She moved away from the fireplace, but his arms went around her waist and he held her tightly. Gazing into his eyes, they both felt the irresistible urge not to let go. He bent towards her. She had that strange melting feeling in her stomach again, just like when they were dancing at the hotel. Sarah looked up into Micheal's candid green-eyes gaze. His warm lips against her lips, she knew she wanted to kiss him as his arms held her closer and his hands stroked the nape of her neck and his lips drew nearer. She didn't want him to stop. She has forgotten passion and anything to do with it. His kisses were full and firm; so perfect was her response, they did not feel the need to breathe; they drew breath from each other.

"Is that a "yes" you will have lunch with me?" he whispered.

"Yes, Micheal."

He didn't let her finished before he kissed her again. "Good night, Sarah. I will send a car for you at noon." Sarah didn't want him to leave so soon after their kiss. "What does this mean?" she wondered as she stared into the fire, smiling and softly crying. Micheal has awakened her passion and she did not know whether she was ready.

Back in the hotel Ola was still in shock. She didn't know what to do, or what to expect from Tia's family. They all saw Kevin and how he had behaved. How long before the police come and arrest him for rape? He was sound asleep like he had no cares in the world. How could he have raped Tia? Ola wondered whether she should get a lawyer for him before the police show up or go and talk to Tia. Ola called her brother Aaron in England and informed him about the night's events. Aaron suggested that she stay calm, and told her he would be in Holland with their younger brother tomorrow to help sort out everything. Aaron hoped to God that Tia's family would not call the Old Bell before he arrived. For Ola, what began as a wonderful evening has turned into her worst nightmare. She is relieved that her brother will come to Holland to see Tia. "Why would Kevin rape her? It makes no sense. This is terrible! Only an animal would do what Kevin has done and laugh about it afterward. Poor Tia . . . How is she going to cope with this?" Even though she felt fatigued, Ola could not sleep a wink, so she lay in her bed dozing. Some time in the middle of the night, Kevin woke up and began to vomit. He wondered how much he'd had to drink and whether he had also made a fool of himself. He got up to wash his face and rinse his mouth in the bathroom and found Ola asleep in the chair. He was tempted to wake her up to find out how the rest of the evening went, but thought better of it. Realizing that he was in Holland, that he had attended Tia's pre-wedding party, he went back to sleep happily think how beautiful she looked last night. "I've utterly lost her. Anyone can see how much Tia loves Nathan. I wonder if they have told Jayzel about me and if they have . . . what does Jayzel think of me?" Feeling a mixture of anger and hope, Kevin drifted off to sleep. Later, there was a knock on the door. Ola startled awake, feeling like she had almost had a heart attack since she was expecting the police to arrive at any moment. To her immense relief, it was only Steven at the door.

"Good morning, Ola. Are you alright?" Steven inquired.

Breaking down in tears, Ola replied, "Oh, yes. Yes, I think so. Aaron and my younger brother will be arriving in Amsterdam this afternoon to help me before Kevin is arrested for assaulting Tia. Has Nathan called the police, yet?"

"I don't really know. Nathan is busy consoling Tia. I haven't heard what they plan to do." Surreptitiously, Steven placed the camera by the door when Ola wasn't looking. "Did Kevin say anything about what happened last night?"

Ola is too upset to reply. She can't get her words out, and she is amazed to see two security guards standing by the door of Tia's suite. Steven followed her eyes and offered the observation, "Nathan just wants his wife to be safe."

"Oh, yes, of course!" replied Ola. "But I am sure Kevin didn't mean to hurt Tia."

"Nate asked me to tell you to call room service if either of you needs anything." Steven said. He told Ola to let him know when her brothers arrive so he can send a car to the airport for them. Having done his duty, Steven left. Ola felt more relaxed, but at the same time was confused. Why is Nathan being so kind to them after everything Kevin has done? Taking Steven at his word, Ola called room service and ordered breakfast for herself and Kevin. While she waited for her order to arrive, Aaron called to say he was unable to get a flight to Holland and that they are on a stand-by ticket. If everything works out, they will be in Holland in a few hours.

"Oh, Aaron! It's going to feel like ages and ages until you're here!"

Ola ate her breakfast, and since Kevin was still sleeping like a baby, she picked at his food. A newspaper had come with the order, so she scanned it while she waited for Aaron. Feeling antsy, it was difficult to pass the time. Ola felt bored. Noticing the camera, she picked it up and viewed the pictures on it from the party. Suddenly, the phone rang. It was the front desk calling to say her brothers have arrived. It is the middle of the afternoon and Kevin is still sleeping. Aaron is enraged, demands to know what really happened.

Ola does her best to recount last night's horror. "I don't know all the details. All of us were dancing downstairs when suddenly someone asked 'where's Tia?' and then someone else noticed Kevin was gone. We all rushed up here to the rooms. Tia was shouting. The men burst in on Kevin and Tia. Their clothes were all messed up. Tia was crying, and her face was bruised. After that I don't really know, but Tia's whole family know that Kevin raped Tia. According to her brother-in-law, Nathan has been consoling her all night. They have not called the police yet, and I can't seem to find out what they are going to do about all this."

The expression of horror on Paul and Aaron's faces matched the horror Ola felt in her heart. "What could prompt Kevin to behave in such a way toward any woman? Especially Tia. He loved her!"

Paul moved a chair to sit down and the camera fell down on the floor. It was playing the video of what Ola had recorded. Aaron's eyes caught what Paul was watching.

"What the hell is this?" asked Paul, shocked.

Ola buried her face in her hands, sobbing. Kevin is now awake. Ola sits on the foot of the bed and Kevin reaches out to touch his sister.

Ola screams, "Don't touch me!"

Kevin's body begins to shake as he asks, "Why are Aaron and Paul here?" He notices the camera and takes it out of Paul's hands. "Who filmed this?" asked Kevin, pointing to the camera. Ola turned her head, would not look at the camera. She closed her eyes, afraid to watch any more of it.

"Ola . . . There is some very incriminating evidence here of someone who looks like me assaulting Tia," Kevin paused. "I want to know who filmed this. I'd also like to know why Aaron and Paul are here."

Ola would not respond. The phone rang, and thinking it might be the police, Ola nervously answered it. It was room service calling to say Mrs Carter had ordered food to be sent to them, but as she didn't order any drinks, they wanted to know what should be sent up. Ola replied that anything would be fine and hung up.

Kevin was frantic now and asked again, this time grabbing his sister, why Aaron and Paul were there. Aaron and Paul restrained Kevin. Of course, Kevin thought the worst about his sister, assuming that she had helped Tia and her family to set him up with a look-a-like actor assaulting Tia on video. Aaron couldn't believe that Tia or any member of her family would do something like that.

Kevin remarked, "They *would do* something just like that. They are stuck up rich people and they think they can do whatever they want and get away with it. I'm going to file a law suit against them. I'll take away my daughter from them."

"Ola," Aaron got his sister's attention. "Tell me again what happened last night."

Ola didn't feel like re-hashing last night, but her brothers made it difficult for her to ignore everything. "We came to see Tia. She is in Holland visiting her family and going to get married in three days to her ex-husband. Her family asked Kevin and I to stay with them. Tia had a party last night in this hotel. She rented a room for all the ladies staying at the hotel with her. I told Kevin that her family are always with her, but that we might find a time to talk to her so that she knows how much we all love her and the kids. Kevin was drinking way too much. I gave him my room card so he could come up here and sober up. I said I would meet him here with Tia later. Tia's family could not find her after the party and there were looking for her. They asked me whether she was with Kevin. I didn't say anything. I suppose I hoped that either she was with Kevin, or that they had run away together."

Kevin shouted, "Liar!"

Aaron motioned for Ola to continue. "They all started to have a go at me . . . and Tia's husband said for them to leave me alone, that Tia was okay." Ola said.

Kevin stood up and threw a magazine at Ola, almost hitting her, "You see! She sat there and let him set me up!"

All of the brothers looked at Ola with disgust.

"That is not what happened!" she cried. "Tia's brother-in-law and two of Tia's sisters were running to my room. I followed them with one of Tia's brothers-in-law. We all heard Tia screaming 'stop, stop' when the lift door opened."

Kevin started to laugh, "You see . . . I told you!" The camera was on a desk, so Ola moved across the room and picked it up. "Aaron, this is your camera that I borrowed from you." Pressing some buttons, Ola played everything on the tape. Some of it was erased, but they could all see Kevin throwing Tia against the wall and pushing her onto the bed, ripping off her skirt and slapping her. There was nothing after the next frame, but the whole tape made everyone think they saw a very drunk Kevin sitting on the bed, yelling, screaming, and boasting that Tia wanted it, that she love it rough, and that Nathan was not a man. Without a doubt, it was Kevin on the video, not an actor as he has always maintained. There were tears rolling down their faces when Aaron asked why it was filmed. Ola said that she was making a film of everything when she got to Holland, so she could give it to Kevin and Tia as a gift when they reunite.

"I must have left the camera turned on when I went to the party."

"Have you shown this to anyone else?" asked Aaron.

"I saw it for the first time, same as you," affirmed Ola. "I didn't know about it before this."

Kevin is extremely angry with all of them. He yelled, "How could you all think it was me? I love her! You all know how much I love her! I could never do that to any woman. She and I have a beautiful daughter. This is all Nathan. He wants to steal my child! Only, I am going back to show this to her parents," Kevin asserted.

"Shut your mouth, Kevin! This is you on the video. It's your face, your voice, and you still have the same suit on. You call yourself a lawyer? What's wrong with you? Kevin, why?" Aaron cried out.

Paul asked softly, "Do you have any proof that Tia's little girl is yours?"

"I don't need any proof that she's mine. They all think that I abandoned her." Shaking his head, Kevin muttered, "If I did what that video is showing, then God help me!"

"Tia's husband is a very rich, powerful lawyer in Canada. Her family are rich and powerful. If Kevin really raped her and if it was witnessed by members of her family, as you said Ola, how come they have not called the Old Bell?" Aaron asked, very suspicious of the events. Then, incredulously he said, "Tia wants us to join them for dinner tonight!"

Kevin says, "They will not report this, don't intend to . . ."

"Why the hell not?" Aaron asked.

"Tia is a TV producer and the ex-husband is always on the telly. The kids are on one of her shows. They are opening a new studio. Amy Hall told me all about it. She is the head of their new studio," Kevin explained. "They will not report this to the police. Nathan and Tia will not want the press all over this. I have to go and see her. I am so sorry, Ola, for being a twat. I did not rape Tia." He strode to the door and stepped out into the hallway.

"Well, whether you did or didn't, I'm coming with you." Said Ola.

They have a couple of security guards covering the suite. "Mrs Carter's suite is for invited guests only!" The security guard says.

Kevin tried to interject.

Nathan heard the noise in the hall and opened the door to see what's happening. He instructs the security guard, "I'd like to see the Peters family return to their suite, please." Nathan closed the door. Kevin felt like a nobody. The guard shrugs and says to Kevin and Ola, "You heard him. You can go to your room or I can have you thrown out of the hotel."

"Let's go," says Kevin to Ola, and they return to their room.

A short while later, the Peters family hear Tia's voice in the hall. Aaron opened the door. With an exclamation of delight, Tia hugs Aaron and Paul. "What are you guys doing here? What brings you to Holland?"

While Aaron explains their presence, Ola taps Tia on the shoulder and they hug affectionately.

"We heard you were in Holland, and we really wanted to see you," said Aaron.

"Oh! That's so sweet of you guys." Tia was a little teary. "Where are you staying?"

Aaron replied, "We've not booked a hotel yet. We're not planning to stay that long."

Tia insists on calling the front desk and requesting two more rooms for them. "I am taking everyone out, and you two must join us."

Throughout this conversation, Kevin was in the bathroom. He froze when he heard Tia's voice, and then he began to panic. He decided it might be best to come out and face her now rather than later. Tia smiled and walked toward the door. The Peters brothers thought Tia was behaving strangely for someone who was raped and assaulted by Kevin. Aaron wanted to find out what was going on. Tia was almost out the door when Kevin called out, "Wait! Please tell me what I did to you last night," he asked frantically.

Tia saw the same expression on the faces of his brothers and his sister, so she decided to put them all out of their misery. "You assaulted me and attempted to rape me, but you did not rape me," she murmured without looking directly at Kevin.

"I am so sorry!" Kevin moved to touch her hands, but Tia moved away. The tears finally came as she strolled down the hall toward her own room.

Kevin sank to his knees on the floor, his brothers and sister relieved that he had not raped Tia. Kevin wasn't sure of his own emotions. "I'm finished. We should not have come here. This is a lot worse than I thought. Why did I beat her?" Kevin was crying and seemed remorseful for his actions.

Paul said, "It's okay. Tia knows you had too much to drink. She doesn't hold anything against you, Kevin. Tia has class."

Ola added, "She's not a vengeful person like a lot of people. I think that under the circumstances, Tia kind of took away the awkwardness. That's not an easy thing to do, not under these circumstances."

Aaron expressed his rage that Tia's face was so badly bruised. "Why would Kevin put his hands on her in this way?" he wondered.

"Tia has always been like a sister to us, not just one of Kevin's many ex-girlfriends," Ola pointed out to her brothers. "We just want to make sure she is alright. Why would Kevin want to hurt her?"

Nevertheless, Aaron was not as relaxed as the rest of them. He didn't want to make a big deal about it, so he tried to console Kevin. The image in his mind of Tia's bruised face made Aaron feel even more ashamed and disgusted with his brother's actions.

Tia's extended family stayed in her room until six o'clock in the morning, venting their amazement at Kevin's behavior, dissecting the many possible reasons motivating him, and supporting Tia as she came to terms with the shock of being abused by a long-time friend. Even Nathan could not have wish for the sight of Kevin Peters assaulting Tia on video. When the last well-wisher departed, Nathan tried to put his anger on a leash as he slipped into bed next to the sleeping Tia. As he began to doze, he thought about Tia's plans for her guests the next day—well, actually today. The weather in Holland has been very good. Even though it is winter, it has not snowed yet. Tia and Nathan rented a yacht for the evening so their guests might enjoy a lovely dinner cruise. Jackie and Lisa joined them. It is fully staffed and they enjoyed a lovely dinner. Steven wasn't very happy to see Ola and her brothers on the yacht. The rest of them did their best as Nathan has asked them to do for Tia's sake.

"Let show them we have more class than the Peters family," suggested Nathan, though he is determined not to let Tia out of his sight.

This evening, Nathan looks as sophisticated as ever, and Tia is her usual glamorous self. Brooke and Jason have not had a night off like this for a long, long time; neither have Kate and Jaden. The grandkids are happily enjoying their own festivities back at the mansion under the watchful supervision of Sarah and Naana. Nicole has never been to Europe or experienced anything like this before, so she can see why Nathan fell in love with Tia. She is dazzling. Amy Hall, also, is amazed to be part of it, and so are the Peters. They could not help but enjoy themselves. Tia has strings of strippers, both men and women, parading on the yacht. Everyone dances and drinks champagne. Kevin disappeared because he felt sick watching Tia and Nathan all over each other. Aaron was worried about Kevin, so he thanked Tia for her hospitality and said he wanted to go back to the hotel. Nathan and Tia escorted the Peters family back to the hotel in the limousine. Tia thanked them all for coming to Holland to see her. "I doubt we'll see each other again since Nathan and I have something to do out of town before we return to Canada."

"Is there any chance we could speak in private, Tia?" Aaron asked.

"It will save me time explaining everything to my husband later if we talk now. You can say what you wish to me now."

Nathan's face crinkles up in a smile.

Nervously, Aaron decides to plunge into the delicate topic: "We just want to know if you are okay, and if your daughter may be Kevin's?"

Nathan felt insulted. He lifted Tia off his lap. "I want you all to listen to me very clearly and understand me very well. I don't know who the hell you Peters family think you are. How dare you insult me and my wife? Your brother assaulted and attempted to rape my wife last night. I suppose you all think he's a big man, am I right? So now the rest of you want your share and my daughter is the target? I believe your brother is a lawyer. You know, last night's nightmare experience I put down to him having too much to drink. I wasn't planning to involve the police, but in view of what you just imply, please be advised that I will do whatever is necessary under the law to protect my family from any harm."

Ola began to sob noisily. Paul and Aaron were shaking with fear.

"Mr Peters, my daughter is on television all over the world. Do you know how many men have claimed to be her father since she began appearing on television? My wife was assaulted and your brother attempted to rape her and now you are targeting my child? Is this about money? Who the hell are you people?" Nathan raised his voice, demanding an accounting.

"No, sir," Aaron replied. "We just wanted to make sure that . . . that Tia is all right."

"Sir, I promise you, we are not here to add to the grief our brother has put on your family," Paul added, pleading.

"Do either one of you have families? Children?" Nathan asked, lowering his voice.

"Yes, sir. I have a small child," Aaron said.

"Well, then, Mr Peters . . . put your wife and child in my wife's position. Imagine, as a father and a husband, who adores his wife and child, and let's put your brother and all of you and whatever it is you're after with my family into the mix. What measures would you take in my position to protect your family?"

Ola looked devastated. She looked like she might cry some more.

"I am so sorry, Tia. I didn't mean . . . we didn't . . ."

Tia did not let Aaron finish his thought. "So that is why Kevin assaulted me and put me and my family through one of the worst nights of my life. As much as I want this to be over, I can't, Aaron."

Aaron knew there was more pain than Tia would admit. He could see it in her eyes as she fought back the pain. He wanted to hug her and tell her how sorry he was. Nathan got out of the limousine and said to the Peters family, "Your brother will pay dearly for what he did to my wife last night and the nightmare that he unleashed on my family. I advise you all not ever to come near my wife again. Next time, I will not show such restraint," and taking Tia by the hand, they left.

Outside the hotel, standing on the curb, Ola said, "I wish we had not come here. If that little girl wasn't his, there is no way that he would be this upset. Remember what Kevin said about Tia's little boy? He left her when he thought she was having an affair with Kevin. All of this is Angela's doing. I told Kevin not to marry her and now look what's happened. Tia is not okay at all. A person she loved and trusted beat her up and tried to rape her. I feel just humiliated for asking her about her daughter."

Aaron added, "Her husband is going to seek revenge. I just know it. I would if I were in his place, if someone tried to do all that to Ola or to my wife. I don't think I could be as calm as Mr Carter. I would hurt anyone and everyone the person loves. We have made an enemy tonight by going where we had no business and by asking stupid questions for which we have no proof. That pair put on an act for us tonight. I work with people who are traumatized, and there is no way Tia is all right about Kevin's violence. Mr Carter will seek revenge now that he feels his family is in danger from us. That little girl is not Kevin's and we have just given Tia's husband a good reason to go to the police about all this. The child is on TV. Everyone will think we are blackmailing them for money. How could Kevin put us in this situation? I tell you, I'm sure Mr Carter is that kind of man . . . You just don't say I'm sorry and it's all forgotten."

"This is Kevin's mess. He can clean it up himself. I'm going home first thing in the morning," Paul said.

Upon returning to their room, they found Kevin sound asleep. "Look at him! Sleeping like he hasn't a care in the world! After everything he's done, how can he sleep so soundly?" Aaron asked.

"We are going home," Paul said firmly. Turning to Ola, he added, "You've always had a friendship with Tia, you saw how hurt she was. She did not want to embarrass us or shame us. That's why she has not called the Old Bell. Not that rubbish Kevin told us about the press. Did you even see the email that Adam sent him to begin all of this?" Paul shook his head in disbelief. "Rich people take it very seriously when it comes to threats to their family. Mr Carter now thinks that we are after his wife and child, not simply an ex-boyfriend attacking his wife. If he goes to the police, it doesn't matter where we are because they will make this a big deal." He pointed at Kevin, "Look at him! How can Kevin put us all in this mess?"

"We must make a formal apology to Tia and her family in the morning before we leave," Aaron advised his brother and sister.

"What if the husband doesn't accept our apology?" asked Paul.

"Then, the man is truly an arrogant, sophisticated bastard. His pride might not want him to let this go. Ola, you met Tia's other family. Her mother and grandparents are Africans. Our traditions are the same as the Ghanaians. If worse comes to worst, I will go and apologize to them first thing before Mr Carter does what he needs to do to protect his wife and children. Tia and Kevin didn't break up in a bad way. Tia has always been good to us—even after she and Kevin broke up. If they share a child, she would definitely have told him or us. Whatever game Kevin is playing, our brother has hurt this family in a way they don't deserve," Aaron said calmly.

"That may be," said Paul "But I'm not too sure that Kevin didn't know about Tia's illness. He was going to get married to her. If they share a child, Tia would have told him."

They all glance at Kevin who is now awake and listening intently to the conversation.

"Yeah, I left the party early. The press had arrived and I knew that Tia has always been camera shy. She's not accustomed to the press like Nathan is. I offered to bring her upstairs until the press had left. She agreed to come. I leaked to the Dutch press that the producers, writers and some of the cast member of 'The Saga' are in town and staying at the Regency Hotel."

"Okay, Kevin, what gives? Why do you want to hurt Tia like that, especially without any proof that the little girl is yours?" asked Ola.

"I just wanted ten minutes to be alone with her, just to talk and explain why I haven't kept in touch. I want her to know that I hadn't abandoned her and the kids. I will apologize for the incident."

"I don't know," said Aaron doubtfully. "I don't like it."

"I for one cannot be a part of all this. I'll be leaving as soon as I thank Tia for her hospitality. You can do whatever you want. Let's not forget how our brother savagely, violently beat this girl in front of her family." Paul says.

"It was not intentional!" shouted Kevin defensively.

"Not intentional! How can you say that? Attempting rape, selling someone you claim to love to the tabloids knowing full well she is not used to them. How far are you willing to go to hurt this girl?" Aaron asked with a loathing look at Kevin.

"Tia has been hurt enough," Paul said firmly.

Kevin jumped up, shouting, "No! I cannot lose Jayzel to Nathan Carter. I'll not let him raise her as his child!"

"Oh, get over yourself! That little girl is not your child. If she was yours, Tia would never hide it from us. Oh, we asked Tia and her husband about your claim, Kevin. They now know why you attacked Tia. The man is not going to let go! I'll not be a party to you and your wife's sick games, Kevin. Tia had cancer, Kevin. *Cancer.* If she had a child with you, do you really think she would keep it from us? I don't know you! I wish to God that Mr Carter would go to the police about you. No father would put his child's mother through such a nightmare. And you try to justify it! You hurt people and say you love them and that's supposed to make it all okay? Not this time, Kevin. Would you treat Tia's husband the way the man has treated us if it was he who did these things to your wife?" Aaron snapped at him.

"Aaron is right, Kevin. This has gone too far. You've got to stop. They are kind people, but this is not something one easily forgets," Ola said.

"Nathan doesn't have the balls to go to the police. He *knows* I'm Jayzel's father."

"Sure you are Kevin. Now that the little girl is on TV, she's yours. You are a lawyer, do the maths! Where were you when Tia was pregnant with the child if the child is yours? Where have you been all this time? Beating and raping? That's really going to get her to love and respect you, oh yeah! Any judge would let you near the child, Kevin. I'm a man. I would not raise the spawn of a man I hate. Mr Carter hates you, Kevin. You do the math. I'm going home," Aaron lashed out at his brother.

Kevin couldn't believe the attitudes of his brothers and sisters, but he can't give up either.

Chapter 11

Tia couldn't hold it in any longer, and she broke down and began to cry. When Nathan tried to calm her, she screamed at him not to touch her. Burying her face in her hands, Tia had a good cry, and then suddenly she stood up and snapped at Nathan, "How can you stand there and do nothing when an animal, a bastard like Kevin Peters puts his filthy, fucking hands on me?"

Nathan can see that Kevin's behavior has finally triggered Tia's anger.

"Baby, I am handling the matter. I have not stood by. I will not stand by and let this matter go unpunished," he said softly.

"That's not good enough for me! He fucking tried to rape me, Nathan!" she yelled.

Tia reached for the phone. Her brown eyes were dark with anger. She spoke in an even tone in Netherlands and then hung up the phone. A few minutes later, someone knocked on the door. Tia wiped her face and went to open the door. A man handed her a small envelope. They spoke in Netherlands. Tia paused, walked to the bed, took out an envelope and threw it at the man. She said something in Netherlands and made a shooing hand gesture. The man nervously shook his head and closed the door. Tia frowned, looking slightly annoyed. She adjusted her clothes and smoothed her hair back. She walked to the bar and made herself and Nathan margaritas. Raising her glass, she said, "This is to you, baby, my irresistible, charming, sophisticated husband, who cannot stand up and fight for the woman he loves. Not to worry. Kevin Peters is going to know how it feels." She threw the drink against the wall and is almost out of the room when Nathan frantically caught her hands.

"Please tell me that's not a gun in the little package your Dutch friend just brought you?" he demanded.

Tia did not respond. Nathan kicked the door closed with one foot and leaned Tia against the door with one hand on her waist and the other clasping her hands. He released her hands and brushed her hair off her forehead. Putting his hands together like he is saying a prayer, and pressing them to his lips, Nathan said gently, "I cannot afford to have you arrested and charged with a felony three days before our wedding."

Tia has no expression on her face. "Baby, I am handling this matter as delicately as I know how," Nathan continued.

Tia cried out, "I know that Kevin has been selling information about us to the press!"

Nathan stared at Tia with fascination, suddenly seeing something in Tia he had not previously noticed. He began to laugh hysterically. "You are definitely my other half, Tia Sharp! You have had them watched the whole time! Baby, Baby, why did you not tell me?"

Tears rolled down Tia's face as she threw the envelope down on the bed. "You didn't believe me when . . . when I told you he did not rape me. You thought . . . I wanted to . . . cheat on you . . . that I was trying to make it look like . . . he raped me when Steven and Brooke barged in on us."

Nathan's heart is breaking. "I never thought that. There was a camera in Ola's room that recorded the whole incident. I found it when I went to beat the crap out of him. I viewed its contents. That's why I didn't lay a finger on him. I will not let him get away with this, but I never thought of what you're saying. Not once. It never crossed my mind. I was so numb, Baby. I didn't know how best to comfort you and make it go away, Goddess. I called mother for help. Why did you not tell me?"

"I saw the camera when I went to the room with Kevin. He mentioned that Jayzel is his and that he was going to take her away . . . so I turned it on and attached this to it and filmed it."

"What is that device?" asked Nathan.

"It's a zip drive. It is used to download films. I did not think he was going to . . ." she paused, and Nathan takes her in his arms as their pain turns into numbness.

"Baby, you are tougher and more resilient than you appear to be. We are fighting for our child, our family. Goddess, please don't doubt that. I will not sit and let anyone put their hands on you and hurt you like Kevin has. Please, let me handle this." Nathan pleaded with her. He hated seeing her distress.

Tia cried out, "I can't wait, sweetie. He came to my hotel and threatened my life. I will not hide behind you or Brooke to fight my battles for me. This is my town. I have handled things and there is more in store for Mr Peters."

She turned on her laptop and positioned it so Nathan could see the screen. Tia fixed herself another margarita at the bar and put a CD of Mozart's music on her MP3 player. Stripping off her clothes, Tia filled the bath tub with bubbles and got into it. Meanwhile, Nathan's jaw dropped when he saw what was on Tia's computer. His whole body is weakened, numbed. He couldn't watch anymore, so he turned it off. Feeling helpless, he looked at the woman lounging in the tub and realized what Tia meant about Amsterdam being her town and handling things her way. Tia has definitely revealed her darker side, a side which Nathan greeted with enormous sympathy as he dashed to the bathroom.

"There is no other way to say it, Baby. When you retaliated, you do it up well! An eye for an eye, whoa!"

"Nathan, my family are very wealthy. We may live a very simple life, but there is nothing simple about the world we live in. I will not let that confident brute, Kevin Peters, get away with raising his hand to me." Tia smiled coldly. "Around these parts, money buys everything and that's exactly what I did!" she exclaimed with a hardness behind her eyes.

Nathan is afraid to ask how Tia managed to orchestrate . . . .

"No one but my mom and Lisa knows what you just saw on the laptop. Only the four of us. I will protect myself from those who would hurt me. Kevin Peters will wish he was a dead man by the time I'm done with him," she sighed.

"So, who was that guy who came to the suite a while ago?" asked Nathan.

"Oh, him. He's hired to make sure that no harm comes to me and my loved ones while we are in Holland. My mum and Lisa will handle the rest."

"Tia, this makes me feel less than a man—like I can't protect you and the children. I can't let mother and Lisa get involved in this. You're my wife! I called mother last night to seek her advice on how to handle things."

"Oh, don't worry. I'm not overriding your authority as head of our family, Baby. Mother has the resources that I need to bring the Peters family to its collective knees. If you wish it, Mother will not do anything further." Tia paused, reflecting on her conversation with her mother. "Sweetie, can you honestly say that you want me to forgive and forget? I cannot forgive something like this. Baby, I won't!"

"What Mr Peters did to you was savagely violent. I cannot let him get away with it whatever your heart's desire," Nathan promised.

"Why don't you come in the tub and I will show you my heart's desire," Tia winked.

The Saga was also being shown on Holland's RTLV station. Like everywhere else, it was a big hit. Tia invited Elizabeth Starr, the model-turned-actress to Holland. Elizabeth was also staying at the Regency Hotel and the tabloids in Europe have no boundaries when it comes to taking photographs and printing trashy gossip. Tia is having breakfast in her suite with her guests—except the Peters, Lisa and Jackie. When Elizabeth Starr arrived, she brought a tabloid newspaper with her. Offering it to Tia, she said, "The press know we are in town. They know you and Nathan are getting re-married in two days."

Amy Hall is displeased that the buzz around *the Saga* has shifted from the show to Tia's wedding. There was a photograph at Tia's party, taken on the previous night. Tia's attitude is surprisingly calm. She tells Amy not to worry. "I know who has been leaking the story to the press. It's all been handled."

Amy finds the word "handled" disturbing, so she avoids asking for details.

Tia adds, "We have a press conference in an hour in the hotel media room. I plan to answer all their questions and get as much publicity to promote "The Saga." This is a good thing, Amy! Relax!" Tia winks. Tia has been on the phone for the better part of the morning. Kevin has managed to get inside the media room with his brothers and sister. Most of the questions were directed to Elizabeth Starr, though one of the reporters asked about Tia's wedding.

Tia responded, "Actually, Nathan Carter and I are already married and the sex could not be better." Everyone laughs.

The same reporter asks, "Are the children who play Ms Starr's children on the show really yours?"

Tia smiled, winked, and asked, "What do you think?"

"Well, I notice that their names are not on the credits," pursued the reporter. "Is that because Jayzel is not Mr Carter's biological daughter?"

Tia smiles broadly, "Mr Carter and I met in Amsterdam years ago, and we fell in love. We have two beautiful babies. I have never been in love with any other man, other than my husband." Tia points to Nathan and says, "Hey Baby, I didn't know I had a child by another man?"

The cameras shift to Nathan. Someone shouts, "Can we get a picture of the two of you?"

Tia is happy to oblige by locking lips with her leading man in front of the cameras. The press loved them as they shutter-bugged while Nathan and Tia kissed passionately. The press conference ended and the members of the press were escorted out. The security guards told the Peters family to wait, that Mrs Carter wants to speak to them alone. Kevin said smugly, "I told you guys . . . There is nothing to be frightened about."

Aaron asked anxiously, "Is everything all right?"

Tia sports a dress with a short hemline and flirty pumps, looking sexy from head to toe. From her seat on the small stage, Tia spoke to the security guard in Netherlands, who left her alone with the Peters family, closing the door of the conference room behind him as he left. She didn't look up as she told the Peters family to have a seat. Standing up, Tia pointed a remote control at the TV.

"I want to share something with all of you before you leave," Tia shot a disgusted look at them.

Kevin glanced at his brothers and sister as they all gazed at the screen. Aaron smiled coolly at Kevin, but Kevin was not able to withstand the expressions of shock on his sibling's faces.

"It is illegal to record people without their consent," Kevin stammered.

"Oh! Uh, well, I am so sorry for the intrusion, but under the circumstance I felt the need to protect myself and my family. Don't you think? Since I felt my life was in danger, Mr Peters," Tia said with an even tone.

"This is entrapment, Tia. I can have you put behind bars," said Kevin, angry.

Tia became extremely agitated. She slapped her hands on the desk and said, "Shut the hell up, Kevin! You can have *me* charged? That's sweet! Why don't we call the cops right now Mr Peters and see who gets charged with what? Do you really think you can come into my life and rip my family apart?"

Kevin is quiet. Ola couldn't watch, so she looked up at the ceiling. Paul and Aaron looked on in shock. Kevin is trembling when the security guard returned with the tabloid report Kevin had met last night. They were talking in Netherlands. The man pointed to Kevin and left.

Aaron asked in a shaking voice, "Why Kevin? What is all this about?"

"I will tell you why your brother has no respect for himself or for anyone whom he claims to love. You see, for more than a year now he has been sending me and my husband photos of his wife and child as if we give a damn who Kevin is married to. Oh, you want to know the latest one is an ultrasound picture of his unborn son." Tia threw an envelope full of photographs.

"Why Kevin?" Aaron asked again.

Suddenly everything falls into place for Kevin. He has no idea who has been sending photos to Tia, but he realizes that the whole thing has been a set-up from the beginning. Jayzel can't be his because Tia would have told him. "Oh, my God," he thought.

Tia continues, "My family are off limits to you all. I will have the security guard come and escort you all out. I thought of all of you as family once. I'm just not too sure any more. I had nothing but love and respect for all of you. Every time your brother goes out of his way to hurt me, I make excuses for him. I let you near my family because I trusted you, my children trusted you and you sell me out to the tabloids for money, attempt to rape me and put my marriage in jeopardy. The last time you showed up on my doorstep in Canada, you tore my family apart, Kevin, and this time you beat me black and blue because you think I took something from you. What the hell did I take from you? What kind of a man are you? You guys sit there when he tells you what he has done to me and my family. You still stand by him and help him destroy my family! What kind of a family are you? I thank God for my cancer because it prevented me from doing something foolish. I cannot believe I almost gave up everything for you, Kevin. My family doesn't go out of their way to hurt people like you do. Even those who have hurt us are always treated kindly. If we reacted the way you do, we would all be behind bars by now. I wish you all a safe journey back to England," Tia said softly.

Tia left behind her laptop in the conference room, so Nathan returned to retrieve it and met the Peters sitting there looking like someone has just died. He picks up the laptop and is heading toward the door when Kevin makes an attempt to apologize to him. Nathan smiled and turned away. At that moment, Aaron is certain that Nathan Carter will seek revenge on his brother, or maybe he already has and they don't even know it.

Realizing nothing else could be done to bring Tia back to him, Kevin decided to leave the hotel. He got to the front door just in time to watch Tia and Nathan get into their limousine and drive off.

"I have lost her now and forever! What am I going to do?" he thought. He wondered whether Tia had a video of the incident. He couldn't believe she was so afraid of him that she would have security cameras everywhere. "I love her. I would never have hurt her if it wasn't for Angela. Angela has taken away everything from me," Kevin said to Ola. "She will never forgive me, now, Ola. She thinks I'm after her money. It was never about the money. I really believed that Jayzel could be mine. I can't explained how it felt when I think of Tia and the kids. I didn't get a chance to apologize. I did not think about the kids when I talked to that reporter. I have lost them all and I still love them all!" Kevin cried out.

Paul and Aaron have a lot more respect for Tia for what she did. They were all disgusted listening to Kevin rationalize his behavior toward Tia and her family. They felt themselves losing respect for him. They all thought Kevin and Angela ought to be on their own and not drag the rest of the family into their own mess.

Aaron told Paul and Ola, "Kevin knew about Tia's illness. He did abandon her and the children. Why else would he send photographs of him and his own family to her and her husband? He savagely beat her up. We all saw the tape. This is not over! He has dragged us into his mess, making us all part of it now. All this time, he never once mentioned that he has been sending them photographs. That is stalking and harassment! I am sure he never loved her. I would never treat anyone I love like this, no matter what, especially a woman for that matter!"

Both Paul and Ola were thinking the same thoughts.

"Why would Kevin do this to Tia?" wondered Paul. "She is a sweetheart."

Meanwhile, out on the street in front of the hotel, Kevin managed to convince his brothers and sister not to leave Amsterdam right away. "I need to speak to Tia's mother before we leave. I've arranged to meet Mrs Sharp at her mother's art gallery."

Doubtfully, Aaron, Paul and Ola agreed to accompany Kevin.

Meanwhile, Naana described Kevin's assault and attempted rape of Tia to Sarah, who advised her to report him to the police.

"Tia would not let me," Naana told Sarah.

Gertrude's gallery manager came in to say that Mr Peters is here, so Naana told her to send them in.

"Would you like any refreshments?" asked Naana.

"No," they all chorused nervously.

Despite her growing irritation, Naana spoke in a calm tone, "I sent you a message informing you that my day was fully booked today, Kevin. I thought you and Ola were staying at the guest house. Are you not comfortable?"

"Oh, no. Um . . . we are. Thank you. My brothers Aaron and Paul arrived so we didn't want to impose."

"I hope you are comfortable where you are?"

"Yes."

"So, Kevin. What can I do for you?" Naana inquired.

"I want to apologize to you and Tia."

Naana was not ready to deal with him yet. Instead, she told Kevin, "You and Tia are adults. In life, we sometimes make decisions that hurt people we love. Whatever happened between you and Tia, it's time for you two kids to forgive and forget. You didn't really have to come all this way to apologize. There is no need. This is not Africa," Naana chuckled. "Now, I have a very busy day ahead of me. It was very nice of you to come, since you're here, why don't you guys check out some of our African history in the gallery before you leave?"

Kevin tried to respond, but at that moment Gertrude's manager stepped into the office.

Naana said, "These are very good friends of Tia. Why don't you show them around for me?" She turned to Paul and Aaron, "It was very nice meeting you all."

Later that afternoon as Naana and Sarah were getting into their car, a young man approached, passing an enveloped to Naana. He pointed to something. Mrs Sharp gave the boy a big tip and rubbed his hair. He flashed a big smile as Naana instructs the boy to return the envelope to the man who sent it. The boy is happy to oblige.

From his vantage point at the entrance to the gallery, Kevin watched the women climb into the black BMW SUV and drive away. She did not expect his letter. Kevin was feeling hopeful when he awakened New Year's Eve morning back in England in his sister's home. Their brief meeting with Tia's mother helped put things in perspective for him. He realized that he didn't need to convince his siblings to stick around with him in Holland when he went to plead his case with Tia's mother. He wished she would have expected the letter as it would have made things easier for him.

Ola said, "The Sharps are very kind-hearted people. If Tia's little girl is yours, there is no way that her family would keep you away from her."

"What do you mean if she is mine, Ola?"

"You were there when the reporter asked about the little girl at the press conference."

Kevin stood up and made a dismissive hand gesture. "You know there were trying to save face. Jayzel is my child and that is one thing Nathan Carter is not going to take away from me."

"I am saying this because I am a nurse. Tia had leukemia. If that little one was yours, they would have told you by now. You must go home and sort things out with Angela before it is too late."

Kevin smiled. "You know, Ola. I wish that I did go back to Canada—even for Tia to say to my face that she didn't love me anymore. If I had, I would not be in this situation. I can't leave Angela with two kids. My kids."

"So what are you going to do?" asked Ola.

"I called her, told her that I was sorry about Christmas. I had a business meeting and I will be home tonight."

"Are you sure?"

"If I leave her, she will take away the kids. I can't let my son be born and not be a part of his life. Besides, I want to find out who has been sending photos of me and Angela to Tia. Aaron is right. Tia and the kids deserve better. I have caused her more hurt than I care to admit. Everything she said was the truth about me. Ola, I've loved her from the moment I met her, and I made all wrong choices. Her family and even the Carters are very kind people. I've brought shame to all of us."

"I'm worried about what her husband said."

"Let him do his worst. I would if I was in his position. Although, I doubt that he is a vengeful man. Nathan loves Tia and the kids. He will not want them to be unhappy. A vendetta with me will not serve any purpose. The man knows that I'm finished and that's a victory for him."

"What about Angela? Kevin, you can't stay married to someone like her. You have no idea what she is capable of."

"I do now. I'll do what I can and I will take my children with me and her to Lagos. Then we will see how much she wants me. She will have me all to herself now. It's going to be a big ocean for her to swim. I'll give her more than she wanted, I promise you. I have to go and apologized to Aaron and Paul before it is too late."

Chapter 12

Sarah looked ravishing in a black pants suit when she entered the family room. Gertrude had all the children with her, who were watching a man do a magic tricks. The twins were downstairs with Brooke and Jason when Guntar came in and told Sarah that Dr. Doyle has sent a car for her. Brooke walked her mother to the car before she could change her mind. "Relax, mother!" Brooke said encouragingly. "Enjoy your lunch. And no kissing on the first date!"

"Yeah, right!" added Naana, "just flirt outrageously with him!"

Michael Doyle was in the private dining room of the hotel waiting anxiously for Sarah. He greeted her with a huskily voice, "I've missed you terribly. I am sorry I didn't come and pick you up. I thought you may not want to come."

Sarah found herself embracing him. Michael's hands were caressing her hair and her back. She enjoyed it. He drank martini while Sarah drank tea. Periodically, he would reach across the table and touch her hands during lunch. Since the weather was nice, they took a walk after lunch and talked about how Sarah was spending her retirement.

"Oh, I do a little painting, and for the last couple of months I have been enjoying looking after the twins."

Michael chuckled, "They sure are cute little boys!"

"Mmm, yes, they are. This fall Naana and I have been taking a kick-boxing class, and we love it."

They pause in their stroll and Michael wraps Sarah in his arms and kisses her.

Giggling, Sarah says, "Brooke said I'm not allowed to kiss you on the first date."

"I see. It seems she has inherited Jack's stubborn streak!" Michael said, enjoying the moment. "She looks so much like you, Sarah. She gave me a right going over when I first met her in Canada years ago. Tony and I were both put in our places. Do you think I should have asked her permission before kissing you?" He has this concerned look on his face that Sarah thinks is very sweet. She kisses him with passion. A young man passing by tapped Michael on the back and said in Netherlands, "Your woman is a babe," but as neither spoke the language, they assumed he meant for them to get a room.

Surfacing, Michael suggests, "Let's go see Gertrude's art gallery."

"Yes! Let's do that." said Sarah, glad for something to do besides kissing.

Unbeknownst to Sarah, Naana has played matchmaker. When Michael confided to her his feelings for Sarah, Naana knew Sarah shared those feelings. Even though Sarah tried to stay true to Jack's memory all these years, it was difficult not to think about Michael, and Naana knew she could not bury her feelings for forever. Nevertheless, Naana thought Michael and Sarah needed a little shove in the right direction, so she asked Tia to invite Michael to her wedding. She also used her influence to land him a job at London's Kings College Hospital. Naana would like to see Sarah happy again.

Michael didn't want the afternoon to end, but as the afternoon light began to fade, he signaled a cab and directed the driver to the mansion. Michael confessed that he didn't want the day to be over. Though Sarah agrees, the day has been full of unaccustomed emotions and a little overwhelming, too.

"Will you join us for the rehearsal dinner at the mansion, Michael?" Michael beamed like a teenage boy in response. He gave her a kiss on the cheek just as Brooke and Jason were walking on the grounds and saw her mother and Micheal embracing.

"Dr. Doyle, she is not your sister, you know?" Brooke yelled in a humorous tone. The expressions on their faces were priceless. Jason's face was crinkling up with a laugh, too. Sarah is about to tell her daughter to grow up when Brooke approached them and pulled Michael aside to say, "The lady has not been on a date for twenty-one years, now. I think she expected a little bit of tongue action, if you know what I mean?" Brooke winked and slapped a kiss on his cheek, and taking Jason by the hand, they returned to the mansion.

"Well . . . I'll not be a gentleman if I don't do what am told," Michael said with a grin. He slowly placed his lips on Sarah's for a kiss that was more delicious than their previous kisses.

Bobby Sharp has not had a moment alone with his wife since they arrived in Holland, mainly because of wedding details, but now BJ threatens to occupy her attention, too. He told his son to take a bath and to sleep in his own bed.

"Yes, Daddy," BJ said. He kisses his mother and Gertrude goodnight. BJ didn't insist that his mother come with him like he normally does.

"I'll take him upstairs and see that he takes a good bath," said Naana.

"No, I'll do it," said Bobby. "You should spend some time with your mother."

Gertrude smiled, "You know, I just love it when the girls visit. The house is alive when they're here, but I wish they'd leave their taste in music at the door."

Naana laughed, "I hear you! It is pretty deafening, isn't it?"

Since the first night he jokingly retrieved Gertrude from Nathan's flirting and carried her upstairs, Osei Kofi now carries his wife to bed every night. Clearly, he adores his wife and daughter, and it's plain when he comes into the family room and kisses Naana on the cheek and carries his wife upstairs, that he has learned a thing or two from Nathan. Gertrude's cheeks are slightly flushed, and Naana and Sarah can't help but laugh at the old man trying to be thirty years younger.

"It's official! My father is trying to be like my son-in-law," quipped Naana.

"Nathan Carter is a very charming young man," agreed Sarah.

At that moment Brooke's voice drifted out of a partially opened door. Sarah relaxed visibly, "Sounds like I should brace myself for a million questions about Michael."

"Oh, she wouldn't dare, would she?"

Sarah raised an eyebrow, "Oh, yes indeed, she would!"

Tia and Brooke came into the family room. "So . . . I hear someone had a hot date today with the handsome Dr Doyle?" Tia prompted.

"Well, mother, tell us about the kiss! Did the good Doctor use his tongue?" Brooke put her arm around Tia as they giggled.

Sarah glanced at Naana in embarrassment and shock. "You don't have to tell us all the details about your date with the good Doctor—just the kiss will do very nicely," Tia teased.

"I am going to give you two a minute to leave before I have your husbands in here and tell them about little drooling you two were doing over two sexy strippers at your party. I'm sure Nathan and Jason are men enough to deal with you two and your carrying-on," Naana threatened.

"We didn't do anything of the sort that your girl pal here didn't do with her date. Jason and I saw them with our own eyes. They were worse than Tia and Nathan, the way they were carrying on," Brooke announced.

Sarah buried her face in her hands in embarrassment. The girls giggled and left.

"Do tell, darling! What exactly did you and Michael *do* on your date?"

"I think Bobby has put BJ to bed by now. It's your turn to go up and let your husband put you to bed, Darling. I have phone calls to make. Good night, and do take it easy on Bobby. Poor darling, he looked worn out."

"You are going to tell me about that kiss, Sarah," Naana winked at her.

When Naana got upstairs, BJ was sound asleep in his own bed. Jayzel and Trey were still up with their father.

"Did you know, Grandma, that we are sleeping in the same bed with our daddy?" Trey said.

"Wow! That is so neat guys," Naana smiled at them. "Good night, my sweethearts. You be good to Daddy."

"Thanks for the extra security, mother. I appreciate it," Nathan said.

"You enjoy your evening with your kids, darling."

Bobby is holding a bottle of champagne when Naana came into their bedroom. "Your father warned me today that if I don't put a smile on your face, he will have my guts for garters."

"Darling, champagne is not going to put a smile on my face."

"Oh, no! Good heavens, no. I wasn't planning to get you drunk, Princess. I was going to go down to the guest house to chat with our Tia. I told Rose that I would take this to the girls." He motioned to the bottle in his hands. Naana reached for the phone and called the maid to take some champagne to the guest house for the girls.

"I think you'd better put that bottle of champagne down, and come put a smile on my face like my father told you to do, darling."

When it comes to romance Naana Konadu-Sharp is one romantic woman. She loves all things romantic. She sits on the sofa with her legs crossed and is giving her husband sexy come-hither looks. Bobby puts some soft crooner music on the stereo and lights up some of his wife's candles. He leaves the room and comes back with a coffee mug. Naana laughs, "Most men I know bring roses."

"Most men you know? Princess, I am a jealous man! Come and dance with me! You can tell me all about most men that you know and the roses while your tea cools down."

She walks straight into his arms. He still makes her heart beat fast.

"I still find you irresistibly sexy," she says. He loves it when she tells him that. After all these years she still desires him and finds him sexy, even though he has put on some weight and looks more like a sixty-year-old instead of forty-nine. Naana looks more like a twenty-year-old, not someone who is about to turn forty-six in a few months.

"Sexier than the man that brought you roses?"

She kisses Bobby on the nose, "Way sexier." She slips her hands and gently squeezes his bottom. He loves that. The candlelights soften the ambiance of their bedroom. They dance slowly toward the canopy bed where Bobby has prepared a surprise for her—a bowl of strawberries wait on the nightstand. He slowly removes all her clothes except her high heels, then seating Naana on the side of the bed, and kneeling before her, he slowly feeds the berries to her. She licks his fingers, savoring the juice. Bobby parts her legs, finding her most sensitive part with his tongue. Her legs tremble as she moan softly, rubbing his neck as he continues to stimulate her. Another surprise is waiting on the nightstand, a bottle of rose-scented oil. Reaching for the oil, Bobby pours a little into the palm of his hand to warm it, then reaches up to massage Naana's breasts, still feeding the strawberries and letting the juice run over her lips. Bobby has never intensely excited Naana like this before. She finds her own temperature rising with his. As his sexual excitement rose, Bobby stood up, he is hard and throbbing. He grasped Naana's legs, causing her to lean back a little and tilt her pelvis toward him. Wrapping her legs around his hips, Bobby thrust forward into her. Suddenly, he was making fiercely passionate love to her and Naana squeezed hard and stroked his back.

The real magic for Bobby was when his wife climbed on top of him. The most awesome, incredibly concentrated stimulation of his life brought him to a mind-numbing climax in minutes as if his blue eyes almost popped out of their sockets. Rocking with emotion, feeling the endorphins coursing through his veins, Bobby tightly held his wife afterward.

"Promise you'll never leave me," he whispered.

She cried, "You are my soul mate, the father of my four children."

Bobby realized that she just said four children instead of three. "We only have three kids, Princess."

"BJ makes it four kids between us."

Bobby did not say anything. She lead Bobby to believe that BJ was with them for a short time, until his mother settled down in America. Naana has not found the right time to break the news to him that BJ's stay is permanent. She was hoping that Bobby would have bond with the boy by now.

"Princess, I was thinking that BJ maybe could stay a bit longer with us if it is possible."

"How long do you have in mind, darling?" she asked softly, hopeful he would make it a long time.

"I think he is a fine boy. I see how he makes you happy. It's up to you really, but if you think it's a bad idea I will understand."

Naana was sobbing, she was so happy. She knew her husband has fallen in love with his son, but was too afraid to say it. "I am so sorry, my love. Please don't cry. This is very selfish of me to suggest the boy stay with us."

"No, Bobby. I am utterly and completely happy."

Bobby and Naana have been together more than twenty-six years, but he still doesn't understand her sometimes, or women in general for that matter. "So why are you crying? It can't be the sex. Darling, you told me you love it," he said, mystified. Bobby had this serious look on his face and was sitting up in the bed, consternated.

"Sex was excellent. I really enjoyed it more than—" She paused.

"Talk to me."

"What about, Bobby? I love BJ. I confess I have been manipulating you so you will fall in love with him and let him stay."

"You can't manipulate me to let him stay. I love him and the girls do, too. I asked them . . . if it would be okay for him to stay. We all just worry about you. I am more concerned about our sex life. I spend days on the Internet doing research about how to sustain romance in a long marriage. If you are not happy, I'd like to know now, so I can fix it—before your old man kill me, Naana. Unless you want to be a widow so you can run off with a young man with a six pack chest?"

"What I meant is BJ was always staying with us indefinitely. I lied about how long he was staying."

"I am very happy you lie to me, but don't lie to me about our sex life."

She sat up and pulled the sheet up to cover herself. "Bobby our sex life could not be better, darling. I love the fact that you know how to be an old-fashioned lover, and tonight . . . I don't who that man was! I enjoyed making love to you more and couldn't get enough of you. When you said BJ could stay, I was happy. Bobby I don't like this talk of me running off with a young man. I am still in love with you just as much as I was in college. Bobby, I love you more than ever now, darling. You're a good father, and a good grandfather to Jayzel and Trey. You have been a good husband to me, too. Even more in every way."

He was staring at his wife incredulously. She looked so sexy that he was aroused by talk of him being a good father and a husband. He started to kiss her on the neck and he told her she was delicious, thrilling and that he wanted her more and more as he kissed her endlessly. They made love again, more slowly this time, and when it was over, Bobby sat up and watched Naana sleep. She has been his priority since his talk with Tia. He has tried to make a lot more effort and not to be too old-fashioned. They are doing more things together, like they used to do in college. He chuckled when he remembered what she had said about manipulating him to let BJ stay. He slid out of the bed and went downstairs. In the kitchen, the boys were hanging out without their wives. Nathan was making a milkshake and he asked if Bobby wanted some.

"Son, what I need is youth and energy to keep up with my wife."

They laughed and Steven suggested Viagra.

"My problem is not nature. My wife has the body of a teenager and I'm an old fart!"

The boys laughed. "Oh, yeah. Sure. Go ahead and laugh. In ten years, you guys are going to be just as fat as I am now," said Bobby as he made himself a tower of a sandwich.

"Then, you should give me that," smirked Steven as he took Bobby's sandwich away from him and began to eat it. "After all, you've got to watch your waistline. Me . . . I don't have one!"

Nathan gave Bobby a smoothie, who complained that he didn't like healthy drinks. The boys laughed, and with a grin, Nathan said, "Try this one, papa."

Feeling the object of their laughter, Bobby took the offered smoothie and high-tailed it out of the kitchen. The guys watched him go, then sat down to watch Steven's new movie. Later, they discussed crashing the girls' hen party in the guest house.

"I can't," said Nathan. "Tia would kill me. Besides, the kids are sleeping in my bed, and I'd better go check on them."

"Me, too," said Jaden.

Not yet ready to turn in for the night, Steven and Jason jumped into the pool. Steven wanted Jason to help him plan a bachelor party for Nathan. They remembered that the next night was the rehearsal dinner.

"I hear grandfather has something planned for after breakfast. He said the men will want to go up against the girls when we see what he has planned," said Steven. "I just hope it's not a game of basketball."

"Not likely. He loves the casino and motor racing, so either way, we will win," Jason bragged.

Amy and Tia were able to convince Steven to shoot his new TV movie at the Sunlight Studio lot in Canada. Tia likes to have her hands in everything to do with the studio. She has learned much about the business in a short time. The contract she has drawn up for the studio staff contained an iron-clad clause: if any of the staff are fired or quit, they will be unable to work for any of Sunlight's competitors for the next five years; a confidentiality clause is also included in every contract.

"This contract is impressive," commented Nicole. "Did Nathan write it?"

"No. That's all Tia," said Amy.

"Wow! She is very good. Not many attorneys know about this clause."

"The kid is a genius. She didn't just do broadcasting, she studied business and media law, too."

"Nate never said."

"Tia Carter is more than a pretty face. One day, she is going make it big in this business," asserted Amy.

Nicole thought, "Amy is right. Nate always wanted to marry someone like her." Nicole felt partly responsible for their divorce. She was surprised when Tia sent them a ticket to come to Europe and join them for the New Year celebrations and for their wedding. She didn't really want to come, but Ian saw the ticket and said it would be nice to come. She's glad that they have come.

"Her family are very nice, eh?" Amy said.

"They all are. Tia and Nathan's first wedding was such an extravagant event," Nicole said.

Tia entered the room. "We are all set to start production in three weeks at Sunlight Studio. I just got off the phone with Mr. Page. Our offices are now completely finished. They will begin building the sets in three days," Tia said, updating Amy on the project.

"Tia you are on vacation, honey. Work can wait, please. I will make you a margarita if you promise not to talk about work," Amy offers as Nicole laughs.

"I'm with her . . . Tia, from what I've heard, you have not stopped working since you got here. It's time to relax! Your sisters are waiting for us in the hot tub."

"Nathan is going to flip. I promised him and my parents no wild party, and my grandmother needs her rest. Guys, please not tonight," Tia pleaded with them.

Amy and Nicole have to drag her to the poolside. Already, there were men in the hot tub with Kate and Brooke sandwiched in between them. Tia said, "Here we go, again!"

"Boy, do I feel old!" Nicole remarked.

"Speak for yourself, Nicole." Amy didn't waste anytime. She was in the hot tub before Nicole could respond.

"Nate is going to do a double back flip if he finds you anywhere near these hot guys," Nicole whispered to Tia.

"You think?! Oh, my goodness, they are so fine!" Tia exclaimed.

"I would think twice before you two get in that tub." Nathan said.

"I second that," said Ian.

Surprised to see Nathan and Ian, Tia whispered to Nicole, "What the hell are they doing here? This is supposed to be our party without our husbands."

"I know . . . this sucks," Nicole said, clearly disappointed.

Jaden and Jason were nervously watching their wives. Nathan walked over to the poolside and said, "You fellas have ten seconds to leave the property."

"But we were paid for the whole night!" objected one of the young men.

"Amy, which two of these boys do want to stay behind?" Nathan asked. Amy pointed. "Okay . . . the rest of you, beat it!" Turning to the security guards, he added, "Do the job you were paid to do. I don't want to have to come out of the house with my brothers again!"

Both Kate and Brooke were already drunk. Steven and Nathan picked them up and took them to the guest house to sober them up.

"In case, you two forgot, you are married! What the hell were you thinking?" Nathan yelled at them.

"Yes sir!" they said, laughing hysterically.

Jason looked at Jaden and burst into laughter. They also thought their wives were funny.

"You know, you English people are nuts! I am going to talk to my wife," Nathan told them as he left the guest house.

"Baby, please. This was not my idea," Tia told Nathan.

"I don't doubt that. Tia, you should have told them the noise was too loud. Papa couldn't sleep, my brother and Jason were behaving like children earlier in the pool. Gertrude needs her rest and I don't want strippers near you."

"I will come home now, sweetie."

"No, baby, you are missing my point. Come here." Nathan took her by the waist and sat her on his lap. "Baby, you have missed your sisters. This is your time with them. I want you to enjoy yourself for the next two days without any worries."

"I'd rather come home with you."

"Baby, you are safe here with your sisters. If you like, I will stay for while, okay?"

"I want you to stay," Tia said.

Tia laid her head on his shoulder. Nathan knew that she was trying her best to cope with what Kevin Peters did to her. They have not talked about it much. It angers him whenever he thinks about it. Brooke is a little more sober than she was. Jason has refused to leave the guest house, so have Ian and Jaden. Tia and Nathan join them in the living room. Nicole has made popcorn and they watch movies all night. Nathan has been so happy since Tia came home from rehab, but what Kevin Peters has done to Tia frightens him to the depths of his soul. He has no idea how he is going to protect his family from the threat that Kevin Peters represents. He hates to hide behind his mother-in-law to protect his family.

Tia called her grandfather and told him his gift would have to wait and that they were just going to sleep. Tia has not been able to sleep at all and it is often the early hours of the morning before she can relax enough to get some rest.

Brooke asked Nathan, "What are you going to do about Kevin?"

"Relax, Brooke," Jason said. "I'm sure Nathan will handle it."

"Listen. Tia has not been able to sleep a wink. She only just managed to get to sleep after Kate and I took turns holding her. I'm not going to sit around and see her in such distress," Brooke cried.

"I promise she will be okay," Nathan reassured Brooke.

"Right. Just remember that she is looking to you to do something about Kevin. I'll not stand by and let just anyone hurt Tia. Nathan, I won't!" Brooke insisted.

Nathan tried to convince her, but Brooke lashed into him about his responsibilities. Jason attempted to intervene, "Sweetheart, this is not easy for Nathan. He will handle it in his own way and in his own time."

"You know," remarked Brooke. "I liked it better when you two hated each other." Turning to point at Nathan, she said, "You'd better handle it—and soon—or I will!"

Nathan grinned appreciatively, "I love your wife, man, but sometimes I just want to ring her neck!"

"I hear you. She can't stop worrying about Tia. Listen, Nathan. I hate to agree with Brooke, but we can't let the Peters get away with this. We have sworn to protect each other. I'm not proud of the way that we stood by and let Kevin Peters walk away from what he did. I know my wife well enough to know that she will not let this go—and in a way, I don't want her to. We all have children, but for our girls, Tia has always been the baby. Brooke is going to make my life, Jaden's life and yours pure hell until we sort it out."

Nathan replied, "If she was a man, I would be worried. I feel Tia loves Brooke more than anything. Well, Mr Peters has already been 'handled'. This is as much as I can tell you right now."

"Nathan . . . . Please . . . . For the sake of our families. Brooke is never happy when Tia is miserable," Jason added.

Nathan laughed. "You are a lucky man, Jason. Brooke is stubborn, but a loving woman. I hear you. I hate to see what she would do to me if I didn't handle this matter to her liking. She was so good to me and the children when Tia was sick. You have a good wife, there," Nathan said.

Jason replied, "I'm hoping she will take it easy on all of us!"

The men we all dressed for dinner and gathering downstairs. As usual, the girls were late.

"Oh, Dad. Jackie won't be here tonight because she and Lisa finished studying, so they took off. They will be here for the wedding, though," Steven told his father.

"Darn! I've not spent any time with her at all," Anthony complained. "Maybe once we are in England."

"I still need to find a perfect gift for Gertrude before Jackie and I leave. I will not be coming to London with you this time, Dad. I will take the children shopping before everyone leaves, but I have a lot of re-writes to do, or Tia will have my head. Please talk to Nate, Dad. No more screw ups with his family this time," Steven advised his father.

"Nate is a good boy. Your brother understands the meaning of fatherhood and of being a husband."

"I hope you're right, Dad," said Steven.

Anthony smiled, "I am sure he will do just fine. We are all looking out for them."

The rehearsal dinner was an extravagant event. Gertrude was more excited than anyone in the house about the wedding. The Carter boys both charmed her. The women all looked dazzling. Tia looked very exhausted when the girls left to go to the guest house. They promised not to play anymore loud music for the night. Naana had a meeting in town the next day, so she could not go to the zoo with the kids as planned. Bobby wanted her to cancel her meeting, but she couldn't. "I promise, we'll all do something together next week when we're back in England." BJ wanted to accompany Naana to her meeting.

"BJ, sweetie, you can best help me by staying here and making sure Daddy doesn't eat any junk food."

"I will, mummy," BJ promised.

"Gee, thanks Princess. That boy is going to watch me like a hawk!" Bobby squirmed.

"Good! I want my husband around for the next fifty years, not dying on me of clogged arteries. Come here and give me a kiss."

Claire and BJ hate it when their parents kiss. They are both at an age when intimacy is perceived as disgusting. BJ yelled to Guntar "Quickly! Open the car door for my mother!"

Bobby voiced his objections. "I have not said a proper good-bye to my wife yet," Bobby snapped at BJ. Naana kissed BJ on the cheek and reminded him to keep his eyes on his father for her. Climbing into the car, Naana rested her head against the seat and closed her eyes, smiling.

"I see that Bobby did put the smile back on your face," said Sarah, who had been waiting patiently in the car all this time.

"The old fool has been watching porn on the internet."

Sarah couldn't help but laugh. Then, with a straight face, asked, "I'm assuming you two tried it out?"

Naana was noncommittal. Their conversation was interrupted while they visited the hair salon, but as they returned to the car, Sarah observed, "It was a completely surreal experience watching that boy on video assaulting Tia."

"Tell me about it! Now, I want you to go and have a surreal experience with Michael!"

Sarah noticed the car had stopped in front of Michael's hotel. "You are nuts, Naana! He is a virtual stranger, darling. My feelings for him are inappropriate."

Naana insisted, "the man has been in love with you for years. He's not a virtual stranger. I want you to go and turn matters into an appropriate afternoon of passionate, steamy, hot sex. Darling, you'd better have a bloody smile on your face by dinner!" Naana chuckled.

"I certainly will not! *Darling.*" Sarah retorted.

It occurs to Naana that Sarah may not be ready for romance. She didn't want to push her friend into a relationship she wasn't ready to have. "Okay, darling. Michael will be staying with us from tonight. Mother has sent him an invitation and he has accepted. I was thinking maybe you need to spend more time alone with him before he arrives at the mansion. I just want to see you two get comfortable." Naana tried to reason with Sarah.

"You sound just like my late father when he married me off to one of his chums."

Naana laughed at the back-handed complement. "Was it a good marriage?" she asked cautiously.

Sarah raised an eyebrow and laughed loudly. "I thought you needed me to help you with something today?"

"No . . . we are done. I want to go home and get some work finished while the kids are still sleeping. Mother is also taking a nap, so I will have the whole house to myself. I tell you what . . . if you get bored, call me and I will come pick you up."

"I am not a very sentimental romantic type," Sarah admits, her expression serious as she attempts to make a profound decision. She hesitates, digging in her heels. "I have my doubts. Thank you, Naana, but I don't think I want to."

"That's okay," said Naana.

"Oh, bloody hell! What have I got to lose? I will see you later!" Sarah says impetuously as she dashes out of the car. Naana has a big smile on her faces as she returns to the mansion.

Sarah enjoyed her afternoon of romance with Michael. As he opened the door of his room, he exclaimed, "I was thinking about calling Brooke just now!"

"Oh? Why?"

"I am going to be moving back to England to work at Kings College Hospital. I was hoping she could find a flat for me."

"That's a big move."

"No, not really. I have been coming and going between England and Canada for years now. It's just too much. I've always wanted to retire back home, and now it looks like it's going to work out for me."

"I am very happy for you, Michael."

"Would it be too bold if I kiss you?"

Sarah planted one on him and said, "Now you can kiss me!"

The afternoon went by quickly for them.

Chapter 13

Lisa and Jackie were alone in the main house when Naana returned. Both girls had their faces glued to their text books, studying for up-coming final exams. Lisa lifted her head and smiled at her mother.

"You didn't go to the Zoo?"

"No, I have some work to do. This is the only time I can do it," Naana told Lisa.

"Grandmother is sleeping. Rose tells me the dining room is set and the caterers will be here at two. Jackie and I will not be joining you guys for dinner, Mother."

"Lisa, sweetie, do you remember our deal?" Naana reminded her.

"Mother, we have hit the books since we arrived in Holland. I am all studied out! So is Jacks," Lisa cried.

Naana knows what it's like. She has not forgotten. She bit the side of her mouth, deciding what might be best for the girls. "I'll be back in a minute or two with a reward for both of you."

Jackie asked, "Do you guys always get rewards for studying for exams?"

Lisa laughed. "I want us to go out and just enjoy ourselves without my sister and her entourage . . . before our lives pass us by! My mum has no idea what university is like these days."

Jackie laughed hysterically when she saw Naana standing behind Lisa with raised eyebrows and a silly expression on her face. She hit Lisa lovingly on the back of her hair.

"Thanks a lot, Jacks," said Lisa sardonically.

"Oh, you are welcome!" Jackie replied, still amused.

"Here, your mum does have an idea. I'm proud of you two for your hard work. Priscilla helped plan this for you. I want you home no later than three tomorrow for your sister's wedding. Afterward you can go back. Lisa, I don't want the hotel manager calling me for any embarrassment. Guntar will drop you off as soon as you are done. Priscilla is already at the hotel adding the finishing touches to your New Year's Eve party from me."

"Wow! Your mom rocks, Lisa!" said Jackie with admiration.

All the Sharp girls are very different, but the one thing they have in common is that they all enjoy a good party. At twenty-two, Lisa Sharp has eclectic taste compared to her sister Tia whose taste is more glamorous. Lisa was born with a silver spoon in her mouth, and whatever Lisa wants, Lisa gets. She has been friends with Priscilla Gates since they were fifteen. Heck, the two girls practiced learning to French kiss with each other. Lisa has been trying to avoid Priscilla since her return to Holland this time. She cannot believe her mother enlisted Priscilla's help to plan a New Year's Eve party for her and Jackie. Lisa sank into a nearby sofa looking miserable.

"Why are you so sad?" asked Jackie.

"Priscilla is one of my exes that I have been trying to avoid this whole time."

"Your ex has a girl's name? Europeans are strange," commented Jackie.

"No . . . she is a girl. I date both girls and boys. You know . . . the best of both worlds!" Lisa blurted it out.

Jackie has never known a lesbian, and she is shocked to learn Lisa swings both ways. Lisa notices the expression on Jackie's face.

"Jacks, relax! Kissing a family member would be incest. My mum has no idea what she has done. I don't need this kind of disruption. I have my New Year's Eve planned, and it doesn't include Priscilla and a bloody party."

Jackie sighed. "Wow! So, what are you going to do?"

"We are going to have a bloody good night tonight at one of Tia's old hang-outs, Amsterdam spot and we can chill back at the hotel with Amsterdam's sexy young men. I will deal with Priscilla tomorrow."

"My brothers are still sleeping, so I will leave a note for them and my Dad."

Lisa put an arm around Jackie, "I am so happy you are here." Lisa had a silly grin on her face. She reached for a nearby phone and said to Jackie, "Vidal and Patrick are going to join us tonight. I hope you don't mind?"

"Yeah, that's cool. I enjoy their company. I'm just going to relax and not think about up-coming exams."

"You need to get your leg over. It's a New Year's Eve tradition, Jacks."

"My leg over what?"

"It means a bloody good sex, Jacks."

Jackie is not used to being so open about sexuality. She is not a prude. And it's true that she's had two or three boyfriends in her twenty-two year-old life, but Lisa's frankness about sex and sexuality is a bit disconcerting for Jackie.

When they entered Lisa's favorite beauty salon, the girls rushed over to kiss Lisa on the lips. Jackie has no idea what they are talking about since they all spoke in Netherlands and they all talk so fast, she can't make it out. Jackie had her hair braided, while Lisa had hers set in glorious bouncy waves of curls. By the time they both left, Lisa was locking lips with Vidal Collins.

"I thought you didn't fancy him that much," observed Jackie, confused.

"Truth be told, I may get married to him one day soon," said Lisa, chuckling. Lisa and Vidal are from the same social background. Their parents are good friends. Vidal has always been crazy in love with Lisa since they met three years ago, but all he ever got from her was a kiss. She will not let him tell anyone that they are together. More or less, she has told him to see whoever he wants, but if she ever finds him with any girl, it's over. Vidal has threatened to end the relationship many times, but he just can't. He is head over heels in love with her. Patrick Collins Junior and Vidal are first cousins. They are also the very best of friends, and they are both in the banking business. Lisa has instructed Guntar to go home, telling him that the boys will escort her and Jackie to the hotel once they are done with their hair and nails.

"Of course, Miss Lisa. You call if you need me," said Guntar as he retreated to the limousine.

They chatted and giggled with the hair stylists until they were done. Lisa gave them a big tip and told them that it was from Jackie. Jackie was a little flushed with the sheer extravagance of it all. Lisa laughed, "Jacks, we can go back home if you are not up for this."

Jackie's voice sounded muffled with emotion, "My mom always used to tell me to enjoy life. Well, damn it! This is it, baby!" Jackie exclaimed.

"That's what I'm talking about, Jacks!"

Jackie loves how Lisa lives her life because she seems to know what she does and does not want. Lisa is not afraid of what life has to offer. On top of it all, she's smart, beautiful, and very gutsy.

"After we get back to the hotel, we'll get changed, call up the boys and go to the race car track."

"To watch the races? That sounds boring for New Year's Eve," commented Jackie.

"No, silly. We're going to drive the race cars!" exclaimed Lisa.

Jackie had no idea Lisa could drive a race car.

At the track, Vidal suggested, "Look, Lisa. If I beat you, there will be no more games."

"You're on!" responded Lisa. "The first one to complete three laps around the track wins."

Vidal tried to shake her hand on the deal, but instead, Lisa slowly kissed him and jumped into her car. Vidal, is completely in shocked, he watches Lisa take off, jaw hanging open.

Jackie asked, "What did you say to him?"

"Oh . . . I told him if he beats me, we both are going to give him the best blow job in his life. If I beat him, he was going to get the best blow job in his life. Look at him! He bought it!" She winked at Jackie and drove off. Jackie couldn't believe it. She didn't want to give anyone a blow job. "Lisa is nuts," she thought, "although, the Collins cousins are both very sexy."

Patrick and Vidal were both about one hundred and fifty pounds, six feet tall, and Vidal had sexy green eyes like Lisa, a shaved head, and muscular shoulders. Of course, Vidal couldn't concentrate, so he lost the race. Lisa rewarded him with another slow, sexy kiss. The boys wanted to come to the hotel but Lisa said no because she wanted them to join her and Jackie for dinner tonight.

The Carlton hotel luxury penthouse suite was not like any hotel suite that Jackie had seen. The suite had two bedrooms, an open-concept living room and dining room, with a fireplace in each of the rooms as well as the living room. It was very elegant. "The view was incredibly fabulous," Jackie thought.

Lisa is on the phone, less impressed with her surroundings than Jackie.

"Who are you talking to?" asked Jackie.

"Oh, just a girlfriend," said Lisa noncommittally.

"Just how many girl friends do you have?"

Lisa was chuckling and said that she would never kiss and tell.

"Hey, Jacks, what do want to do tonight?"

"I am comfortable. I'm just happy to be here."

"How about a late lunch? I want to take nap before Vidal and Patrick arrive," Lisa suggested. She ordered lunch from room service. There was a knock on the door. Lisa was in one of the bedrooms getting changed, so Jackie asked, "Did you tip the guy from room service?" Jackie opened the door to find a sexy girl standing in the hall.

"Hello," said Jackie.

The girl responded in English, "I'm here to see Lisa."

Jackie thought, "how rude," but then she stood aside and motioned for the girl to enter the suite.

"Someone's here to see you," hollered Jackie, and turning to the girl, she said, "Please have a seat."

Priscilla is a beautiful blonde with blue eyes and sexy full lips. She wore Apple-Bottom jeans with fur-trimmed boots.

"Very sexy and sophisticated just like Lisa," Jackie thought enviously.

Lisa comes out of the bedroom sporting sexy white bikini underwear and matching bra. She is not surprised to see Priscilla. Lisa leans over to kiss her on the cheek, clearly frustrated by this unexpected visit. To cover her emotions, Lisa pours a glass of orange juice for everyone, passing one glass to Jackie and another to Priscilla. Despite the emotional turmoil, Lisa is comfortable in her underwear. Both girls admired her body, but only Priscilla voiced her thoughts, "You look beautiful, baby."

"What can I do for you?" Lisa asked softly.

Jackie felt uncomfortable, so she took her juice into one of the other rooms, but Lisa intervened, taking her by the hand and saying, "Please, Jacks. Sit down." Lisa is running her hands through her silky hair.

Priscilla asked, glancing in Jackie's direction, "Can we talk privately? Please, Lisa? There is so much I need to say."

"We have nothing to say, baby. We are finished. I have moved on. I'll not give up Vidal for you like I did with Chance. I won't." Lisa said firmly.

"Lisa, I think about you every day. I miss you. We can't be finished! Please! I am sorry for all that jealousy and other stuff. I promise, baby, please . . . I've missed you so much," whispered Priscilla.

Lisa hugs Priscilla and says softly, "I've missed you, too, but we can't go back." Lisa walks the distraught young woman to the door and opens it for her.

Priscilla is pleading with Lisa now, knowing how much Lisa hates to see her cry. Using her fingertips to wipe the tears from Priscilla's face, Lisa pulls her gently into her arms and closes her eyes. She has missed Priscilla more than she cares to admit. Jackie watches them intently, finding it a huge turn-on to see Lisa sensually kissing and caressing Priscilla's hair. It is the sexiest thing Jackie has ever seen. She is burning with curiosity and found herself getting wet just by watching them. It seemed like they might never come up for air. She knew just how Lisa liked to be kissed. Happily, Priscilla reminds Lisa what she'll be giving up. Lisa pulls away.

"Oh, don't stop, Lisa!" Priscilla begs.

"Sorry. I can't do it."

Priscilla assumes that because Lisa's mother enlisted her to help throw a New Year's Eve party for Lisa that all has been forgiven. Lisa has not returned any of her calls over the last six months, and she knows that Lisa is not seeing anyone.

Priscilla whispered, "I miss you, baby. Please, don't say it's over. Have dinner with me tonight, just the two of us, so we can talk."

Lisa sighed. "I can't give you what you want, baby, as much as I am tempted." She paused, closed her eyes to fight back tears and to collect her thoughts. "You have no idea what you have put me through all these months. I can't throw away my future for you. I love you. I still do. I can't go back. The risk as a whole is too much for me. I was never enough for you, Priscilla."

Priscilla tries to touch Lisa, but she moves away, "Not now. I can't do this now." Lisa kisses her on the cheek. Stepping back from their embrace, Priscilla takes Lisa's hands in her own, kisses the backs of them, and leaves. Priscilla didn't want to leave because she can tell that Lisa is still hurt. For half a second, Lisa thought about going after her. Kissing Priscilla has awakened something inside her, but she told herself firmly that it is over. Priscilla is certain that Lisa is not over her and she intends to do whatever she can to win back Lisa. On her side, Lisa feels torn. She has been doing so well for almost seven months without Priscilla. Her future is with Vidal. Nothing and no one is going to come between them!

Closing the door behind Priscilla, Lisa crosses to the stereo and puts a Destiny's Child CD on the player.

"I'm sorry, Jacks. How is your lunch?" Lisa sat down beside her and bites into her tofu sandwiches. She looks at Jackie in time to see her blushing deeply. Lisa put her sandwich back on the plate and placed her hands on Jackie's forehead. She did not have a temperature.

"Jacks, sweetheart, are you alright?" Lisa asked with concern. "Are you coming down with something?"

"That was *so* sexy."

"What was so sexy? Are you alright? Why did you space-out like that?"

Jackie realized that Lisa did not understand what Jackie referred.

"Can I ask you something?"

"Sure, anything, Jacks."

"How does it feel?"

"How does what feel, Jacks?"

Jackie is blushing again, unable to take her eyes off Lisa. She desired her and Lisa knew it, but Lisa's mind is on Priscilla. Lisa has thought about her, too, but she was now certain, without a doubt, that the relationship was over. They had shared moments like this in the past: Priscilla would tell Lisa she was sorry, they would make love, and it would be the same thing all over again a few days later.

"It's over," Lisa told herself.

"Stop looking at me like that and eat your lunch, Jacks! You can just get that thought out of your head."

"Oh, get over yourself! I don't have inappropriate thoughts in my head."

"Well, that's good! I love you, Jackie, but it would be inappropriate for us to . . ." Lisa paused, closing her eyes. Lisa enjoyed sexual games, though at heart she is an incurable romantic. She has a reputation for having seduced many young women, and for breaking a few hearts, too. With Jackie, it is different. Lisa loves her like a sister. It would be wrong for them to sleep together. Lisa was aware Jackie felt hurt, but Lisa knew they should not go any further. Anyway, Lisa wasn't completely certain that Jackie would be receptive to her as a lover. To test matters, Lisa kissed Jackie ever so softly on her upper lip, then the lower lip, and finally on the full lips with her tongue tickling Jackie's tongue, while gently rubbing her back. Surprisingly, it was Lisa who pulled away. Jackie begged her not to stop. Secretly, Lisa loves it when her lovers tell her not to stop, but with Jackie she felt bad. Lisa confessed that she doesn't want to stop either, they are practically sisters, and sisters kissing sisters would be wrong.

Jackie kissed Lisa. "It's not wrong," she said as she kissed Lisa again and again. Lisa wanted to stop but couldn't. She needed to take her mind off Priscilla. Besides, she has not been with a girl in a while and she has missed the feminine style of lovemaking.

"Are you sure, Jacks?" Lisa murmured.

Jackie moans, "Yes. *Yes.*"

Lisa kissed Jackie on her lips, on her neck, then pulled Jackie on top of her so that they lay together on the sofa. She stroked Jackie's back. A wave of desire Jackie has never felt before passed through her. It was beyond what she thought might be possible. Lisa knew how to kiss, how to touch her, and it was like nothing Jackie had known. It was like the romance books her mother used to read to her and her brothers. They were now entwined on the floor by the fireplace. Lisa was faster than any lover whom Jackie had known. She had her clothes off, was nibbling her neck, squeezing her breasts. Jackie moaned as she enjoyed the sensations of the best oral stimulation ever. Her body shook as the level of sexual intensity rose. Lisa moved Jackie onto her side and began to kiss her back. Jackie's wetness told Lisa how much she anticipated Lisa's fingers on her clitoris. Lisa rubbed the clit until it was erect and hard, then she slipped the vibrator into Jackie's vagina, just far enough to tease the G-spot. Jackie gasped and gushed more wetness. Lisa used the vibrator to stimulate the clitoris again, and then she inserted it a little further into Jackie's throbbing vagina. It was not long before she came with a body-wracking orgasm. Lisa held her close, passed her hand through Jackie's hair.

"Are you cold?"

Lisa helped Jackie into one of the bedrooms where they lay on the bed wrapped in a soft comforter.

"Oh, I loved that!" exclaimed Jackie.

"What did you love, Jacks?" Lisa asked, softly. Jackie wanted to say that she loved Lisa, but she knew Lisa well enough not to say that. It saddened her that she could not tell Lisa how much she loved her and that this was not a curiosity thing, an experimenting thing, for her.

"I love the way you make me feel," said Jackie.

Lisa closed her eyes. She has fought her feelings for Jackie. She has been behaving like she doesn't share those feelings because they are family, nothing more. She kissed the back of Jackie's neck and moved her hands up onto her breast.

"Don't stop touching me," Jackie begged.

Lisa turned Jackie to face her, "Are you sure you can handle this, Jacks?"

"Lisa, this is not a curiosity for me. I want you, Lisa."

"You just had me, Jacks," Lisa chuckled.

"I want to be with you. I don't care what anyone thinks. I want you," Jackie said bluntly.

Lisa closed her eyes and didn't say anything.

"Please tell me you are feeling this too," Jackie said. "Lisa! Tell me what you're feeling. We just shared a beautiful thing together!"

Lisa knew what Jackie wanted her to say. "Jacks, I'm just worried about you. It's a big leap to go from what we were. I don't have any regrets."

"I don't want to go out. I want to stay in, just the two of us," Jackie said.

"I'm sorry, Jacks. I can't. Vidal and Patrick are going to be joining us for dinner. I also made a date with . . . I was planning to spend the night with Diamond. That I can cancel, but not dinner with Vidal."

Lisa reached for the phone while still caressing Jackie's hair and the back of her neck. She tells the front desk not to send up anyone, except for room service and the Collins cousins. Jackie knew she was being selfish, but she didn't want to share Lisa with anyone.

Lisa has always made her feel special, even before they made love. Now, she feels that their friendship has deepened. Jackie softly kissed Lisa on the cheek and held her tightly. The phone rang. It was the front desk announcing Priscilla.

Noticing the expression on Lisa's face, Jackie asked, "What's wrong?"

"Priscilla is downstairs insisting that I'm expecting her."

"Why don't you want to see her?"

"It's over, Jacks," Lisa said tearfully.

"Are you okay?" asked Jackie. "I mean, are you okay with it being over?"

"I thought it would be easier by now. I guess I was wrong about that."

Jackie felt she had been used because she has just begun to see that Lisa slept with her because she was hurt. She was not fully over Priscilla.

"Jacks, I was not in love with Priscilla. We've been friends and lovers on and off for almost four years."

"It's okay. You don't have to explain to me."

"Jacks, please . . . I think I do. We have not been together since last summer. She and I are over. I kissed her when she was here and it brought back feelings I've been trying to get away from. I felt bad about it."

"You seemed to be enjoying her," Jackie spat, feeling hurt, too.

Lisa had no idea that Jackie had been watching them. "I didn't know you saw everything."

"It's got nothing to do with me," said Jackie as she moved from their embrace.

"Jacks, don't be like this. We just made love. How can you say it has nothing to do with you?"

"I just don't want to be hurt. That's all. I don't like games."

"Hey . . . I will never hurt you, Jacks," Lisa whispered. She kissed her on the back of her neck, slipped her hands under Jackie's arms and caressed her breasts. She was sitting in between Lisa's legs, with her back facing Lisa. Jackie lifted her head and tilted it back for a kiss. Lisa slipped the vibrator between Jackie's legs and felt the wetness pouring from her. As she drew near to orgasm, Lisa let her fingers find their way inside Jackie, who moaned and whispered, "I love you."

"I know you're going to be mad at me for saying that, but I do love you, Lisa. Please don't be mad," she pleaded.

"I'm not mad. I love you, too, Jacks. Did you enjoy it? Or is there something else you want?"

Jackie was a little embarrassed. She wished she knew how to please Lisa. This was her first time making love to a woman and she felt a little lost, like she didn't know what to do. It was also her first time experiencing an orgasm this way. It dawned on her that she would be returning to the States in a few days. "What am I going to do without her?" wondered Jackie. During the past two weeks, they have shared a lot of laughter, Lisa has made incredible love to her, the way she kisses, her smell, her touch . . . Jackie wanted to cry when she thought about going home. What if Lisa forgets her?

"Don't think that," said Lisa.

"What?"

"What you are thinking. I won't forget you, Jacks. I just can't."

"Are you sure?"

"Come here," she took her hands and guided her to her body and kissed her. Jackie loves how Lisa kisses.

"Don't be afraid to touch me, Jacks," Lisa moaned softly, their tongues exploring each other's bodies. They spent the whole afternoon tasting each other, sharing the passion between them. Lisa ordered a lavish dinner from room service, and there were candlelights everywhere in the room. She wore a cream braided sleeveless top, black draped tie pants. She was bare foot when she opened the door for the Collins cousins, who both kissed her on the cheek. She told them to be quiet, that Jackie was sleeping. Patrick points to Jackie standing there half asleep wearing a hotel bathrobe. He and Vidal crossed the room to give her a kiss on the cheek.

"Hey, Lisa, why didn't you wake me up?"

"Because you looked like you needed the rest," smirked Lisa.

Jackie did look tired, so Patrick and Lisa took turns feeding Jackie morsels from the room service tray. Jackie felt spoiled, and she told them so. Vidal smiled and said, "You should get used to that!"

The four of them enjoyed their dinner together. The boys left at midnight with assurances that they would see the girls at Tia and Nathan's wedding. Now that the boys are gone, Lisa has filled the Jacuzzi tub with bubble bath, and invited Jackie into it. When Jackie begged her for more, Lisa took her right there in the tub. Jackie lost count of the number of time she orgasmed. It wasn't difficult to feel spoiled by Lisa's affection. Jackie wondered whether Lisa treated all her lovers in this way.

"Is it always like this?"

"How do you mean, Jacks?"

"Are you always this romantic with your lovers?"

"Yes, except with you. It's more lovemaking not sex."

"What is the difference?"

Lisa set aside her glass of water. "With you I don't have to think about it. I know what you want, how you want it, and" she kissed Jackie's hands, "others in the past were . . . just just to fill my needs, really. Once that need is met, I just move on to the next girl."

"Was it like that with you and Priscilla?"

"Yes. Sort of . . . We were lovers for a long time. We had a relationship until I met Vidal almost two years ago."

"So, it's safe to say you are in love with Vidal?"

"No . . . not 'in love' Love. We are going to get married soon."

"Why do you want to get married to someone you don't love?" Jackie wondered.

"But I do! I fell in love a long time ago . . . before I knew what love really is, and . . . well, Vidal understands me as I do him. We both don't like being hurt by people we care about. We know each other's needs and respect each other. We are very good together. Our goals in life are more or less the same. Most importantly, we have fun together and know what kind of life we want."

"How is it with him?"

"How is what with him?"

"The sex. The lovemaking."

"We have not slept together, but we make love all the time. Today on the race track was making love. Rubbing his thigh while he drove us to the hotel was making love. Kissing him is making love. Sex is not making love. It's just fucking," Lisa explained.

"Wow! You have not had sex with him and he is so much in love with you? That's nuts!"

"Does it turn you on, Jacks?"

"Very much so, honey. You are one strange girl."

"My mother thinks I am strange, too," Lisa chuckled.

"You and your mother are very close?"

Lisa smiles. "She is a phenomenal woman. She sets goals for us and we do our best to achieve them. She is a very savvy business woman, that's one of the things I love about her. It's like you with medicine, Jacks. You are passionate about it. I think that is so sexy. You are sexy, very sexy."

Lisa has ordered breakfast for Jackie from room service, but she didn't order any for herself since she doesn't like to eat in the morning. Jackie is sleeping so peacefully that Lisa doesn't want to wake her up. Lisa pulled off the covers to expose Jackie's naked body. Her creamy skin was such a turn-on that Lisa began to caress Jackie's back with her tongue. Jackie rolled over. The phone rang. It was the front desk again. Priscilla was downstairs, so Lisa told the front desk to send her up and to deliver a breakfast for Priscilla *pronto*. Lisa grabbed one of the hotel bath robes and wrapped it around Jackie as she shook her awake.

Sitting up, Jackie murmured, "What time is it?" as she grabbed a hotel bath robe and wrapped it around herself. Lisa handed her a glass of orange juice, "It's seven in the morning."

"I thought we were not going back to the house until three?"

"Yes, sweetheart, but don't you want breakfast?"

Jackie looked at the breakfast tray. It looked delicious. Even so, she would rather stay in bed with Lisa without interruptions from her army of ex-lovers, she thought.

"Mmm . . . You are spoiling me, you know. I'm not used to this," Jackie commented.

Lisa leaned over and kissed her gently on the lips, "Well, get used to it!"

Jackie went into the bathroom while Lisa answered the door. When Jackie returned to her breakfast, Priscilla was sitting with Lisa, eating and talking. She sees Lisa pick up the napkin and wipe Priscilla's mouth and couldn't help feeling a little jealous. Jackie decided to get her laptop and check her email while Lisa and Priscilla were talking. From her vantage point, Jackie could see them laughing and talking, evidently still close despite the break-up, and another little stab of jealousy hit Jackie's heart.

"Come and eat, Jacks!" invited Lisa.

Jackie walked nervously to the table thinking, "what if Priscilla notices that we've made love."

"Jacks, meet Priscilla."

"You are Tia's little sister-in-law, am I right?" Priscilla asked.

"Yes," Jackie replied dully.

"Lisa told me about you when she visited Canada." Jackie wondered what Lisa had said about her. Priscilla was not worried about Jackie because she was certain Lisa would never sleep with her. Besides, Jackie is not really Lisa's type and they are more or less family.

"Jacks, the massage therapist is on his way to give you a massage. You must hurry up and eat your breakfast."

Jackie is not eating, so Lisa picked up the fork and put some food in Jackie's mouth. The gesture is so loving that Priscilla instantly concludes that Lisa likes Jackie. She wants to ask Lisa whether they are lovers. If they are, Priscilla is certain Lisa will not let her come to the New Year's Eve bash tonight, and Priscilla is determined to win Lisa's heart tonight. The rejection hurt so much that she felt like crying. Deliberate, or not, being pushed away by Lisa hurt tremendously.

"I have to go to the gym," Priscilla said as she stood up to leave. "I'll see you tonight. Thanks for the flowers you sent yesterday. They are lovely." She kissed Lisa on the lips and crossed to the door.

Lisa reached for Priscilla's hand, "Listen, baby. I may not come to the party tonight. I'll let you know, okay?"

Priscilla tried to be understanding. "Aw, come on! I understand you need to work, but it's New Year's Eve! We always spend New Year's Eve together! Have spent it together since we were sixteen!"

Lisa shrugs.

Priscilla hugs Lisa and says, "Well, okay. Whatever you want."

Lisa immediately felt guilty, so she pulled Priscilla into her arms again and hugged her. She smiled and replied noncommittally, "I'll see you later."

Their eyes met and held before Priscilla opened the door and stepped into the hall. Jackie can't believe Lisa sent her ex flowers yesterday. How could she? They had just made love. They belonged to each other, now. Suddenly, Jackie lost her appetite. Lisa tried to feed her, but she would not respond.

"What's the matter, sweetheart?"

The massage therapist was in the room, having arrived just as Lisa was closing the door on Priscilla.

"I don't think I want a massage."

"But, I'd like to see you relaxed," objected Lisa. "It's not for me, so I can get my kicks watching you being massaged. I have some work I need to finish. Besides, I'm not good at giving massages. Sweetheart, you are tense, but by the time he is finished, I'll be done my work. I promise. I'll be all yours until we go to the wedding, Jacks."

"I want to go back to bed."

"After you get a massage, we can go back to bed. I promise, Jacks. Do it for me," Lisa kissed her on the cheek.

Jackie relented despite her misgivings. The masseur had magic hands. As he worked on her body, Jackie felt relaxed and horny simultaneously. Part of her wanted the man to stop, but she was enjoying herself immensely. When Jackie commented on how loose she felt, it was like Lisa knew. She paid the masseur and told him to close the door behind himself as he left. Lisa began kissing Jackie in front of the guy. Jackie felt embarrassed, especially since the guy seemed to enjoy watching them. Lisa didn't seem to care as she ripped off Jackie's bath robe and began sucking on her breast.

"Okay, fella. You can leave!" said Lisa. The man takes his time exiting the suite.

Jackie ran her hands down Lisa's slender, silky body. She bent her head and traced Lisa's neck with her tongue, nibbles her breasts with her lips. It felt nice sucking Lisa's breasts, and Jackie didn't want to stop until she found her fingers in Lisa's most private place. She was glad when Lisa began to respond to her touches, running her hand in Jackie's hair.

"Please tell me how you like it," Jackie whispered.

"Mmm, you are doing . . . just great . . . Jacks," Lisa moaned. Jackie feels satisfied when Lisa comes. They didn't want to let go of each other. Jackie watched the fire as they lay on the rug caressing each other and kissing. Jackie knew Lisa would not leave her now and move on to the next girl, especially now that she was able to satisfy Lisa. Jackie loves the taste of Lisa. She has never before tasted a woman. "She smells and tastes like vanilla," Jackie thought.

"I think I'm in love with you, Lisa." Lisa did not respond.

Jackie thought she was mad, but actually Lisa had fallen sound asleep. When Jackie tried to relinquish her, Lisa said, "Ooooh, hold me, Jacks," with such a sleepy voice that she sounded irresistibly sexy. It was a different kind of intimacy—one that Jackie loves and is afraid to lose. Lisa has awakened something in her that she didn't know existed. Over the past four years, going to UCLA, she has seen lots of women kissing and embracing in public, and she usually thought of them as freaks. But the sex she and Shawn have is nothing like this, not at all. It is always the same. He never does anything new and when they are done—or rather, once they have both orgasmed—Shawn rolls over and falls asleep, or he leaves, or he goes into the living room to watch TV. There is no cuddle time. They don't laugh or talk like she and Lisa do. There is just no excitement with Shawn. Jackie realizes that for some time now, she has put up with Shawn's inexperience and never really enjoyed their intimacy.

Lisa rolled on top of her, opened her eyes and asked, "Are you okay?"

Jackie, feeling overwhelmed, over emotional, blurted out, "I think I have fallen madly in love with you. I've just realized the consequence of our relationship. That is, my father and my brothers will not expect it. I feel really lonely in California and I'm dreading going back there in a few days."

It broke Lisa's heart to hear the distress in Jackie's voice. Hearing Jackie talk about her life in the States made Lisa wish there was something she could do to help.

"Jacks, you only have one semester left until graduation. It will go fast, sweetheart."

"Not without you, it won't," cried Jackie.

Lisa is accustomed to dealing with problems that money can fix. With Jackie, the problem neither could not be solved simply by writing a cheque, nor by calling someone to take care of it—like the detritus of her relationship with Priscilla. Lisa knew she would be finished school in three weeks and that her mother would be going to Africa for two months. It was her responsibility to take care of the business while Naana was away.

"What can I do to make this easier for Jacks?" Lisa mused, then she said aloud, "My exams begin on Monday. Why don't you come to England with me tomorrow afternoon?"

"I can't. Steven and I leave in two days. He has some re-writes to do for Tia."

"Steven can still leave in two days, but you don't have to, Jacks. You still have two more weeks left before your first exams. I'll get you a flight from London to LA. Once I'm done with my exams, I will fly to LA to spend some time with you before my mom travels to Africa."

"You would do that for me?" Jackie asked, incredulously.

Lisa sat up with a dazzling smile on her face. Whatever Lisa wants, Lisa always gets. Jackie Carter was no different: two girls who always get their own way. Lisa understands Jackie's concern about their relationship, but it doesn't bother her nearly as much as it does Jackie.

Naana Konadu-Sharp knows Lisa is into girls and plans to marry Vidal Collins. Lisa doesn't give a toss what her Dad thinks. She will never do anything to embarrass or to hurt her mother, though she can't see how sleeping with Jackie would affect her mother. She whispered, "Tell me what you think about coming to England with me."

Jackie found herself saying she would. As they showered together, Lisa made passionate love to her under the shower. They both felt nothing could go wrong with their new-found love. Lisa has drawn the line against falling in love with anyone, although Vidal has come close, but nothing can compare with the love she and Chance shared. Lisa hopes she will love Vidal more every passing day. How can her destiny be wrong? She blames it all on jealousy. Deep in thought, she rolls the bracelet on her wrist and feels like crying. Jackie can see that Lisa is deep in thought. She has noticed that every time Lisa seems to become introspective, she rolls her bracelet. Recalling Lisa wearing the same bracelet when they first met in Canada years ago, Jackie assumed that Priscilla must have given it to her. Jackie was reluctant to ask about the bracelet, so she asked, "Are you okay, Lisa?"

"I'm thinking about how Nathan and Tia were able to find their way back to each other after Nathan's betrayal. Not may true loves are able to do it," Lisa says.

"That's true, but Nate and Tia had your mom helping them find their way back. Not many soul mates have that," observed Jackie.

"Well . . . being in love is too stressful, I say. Life is about living it and enjoying it to the fullest." She puts her arms around Jackie's waist and pulls her toward her. "Are you ready to go back to the mansion?"

Jackie giggled, "I wish we could stay here—in the hotel!"

Chapter 14

"Tia had another sleepless night," Brooke told Nathan.

"Let me see her. She needs me," insisted Nathan.

"You can not go to the guest house before the wedding. It's tradition. You can't see the bride before the wedding! Besides . . . Naana is with Tia and they are both sleeping now."

"I can't wait until four o'clock," whined Nathan. "It's only ten now, and I'm a mess with worry. I've got to see my wife."

"Not on my watch, Mr Carter. You're not going to bully your way out of this one. That's the tradition," interjected Sarah.

"I am not going to sit here helplessly when my wife needs me," Nathan snapped.

"You won't. Gertrude needs you. She is in her studio waiting for you," Sarah calmly told him.

"I will attend to her later. Right now, I am going to the guest house to be with my wife. Mrs Williams, tradition will have to wait," said Nathan in a snap tone.

Sarah knew Nathan could be stubborn, so she came prepared. She called the security guard to escort Nathan to Gertrude's studio. "If he tries to go to the guest house, you boys have my permission to hurt him. Not on his face, though . . . Mr Carter is a handsome lad, wouldn't you say?" Turning to Nathan, she whispered, "I don't want to be responsible for you getting your butt kicked on your wedding day, darling!"

Nathan tightened up his jaw and stood up. His father, brother and Dr Doyle were all laughing at his predicament.

"Well, then . . . Brooke, you keep your eyes on Tia."

Brooke pulled her mother aside to say, "Would it kill you to give him a break?"

"Yes, darling. It will kill me. Naana is taking care of her daughter. You should go and take care of your husband and children."

"What has gotten into you mother?" Brooke asked.

Gertrude has done a sketch of Nathan, Tia, and the children as a wedding present. The likeness was unbelievable.

"I knew you loved art, but I didn't know you could draw this well. Grandmother, this is awesome! When did you find the time?" Nathan asked.

Gertrude beamed, "It was done over the summer and I was going to give it to UPS to bring to you and Tia. When you called and said you wanted to come home to get married, I was so happy you found your way back to each other." She kissed Nathan on the cheek, bringing tears to his eyes. Nathan has always wanted a family and love like this as long as he can remember. His only regret is that his mother didn't live to see it.

"Now my dear, this is your wedding gift. You can open it now. Sit right here, so I can finish the painting. Tia paid me to do this for her," she said.

"Tia retained you to do a painting?"

The old lady smiled again, "I love spending so much time with you, and Tia wants me to paint you today, so that she can put it in her new office that you are building for her. She wants me to keep you out of the guest house until the wedding." Gertrude winked.

Nathan smiled. "The Sharp women know me too well," he thought.

"Go, now. Open your gift while I set up," said Gertrude.

Nathan is overcome with emotion when he opens the gift-wrapped painting that Gertrude has given him as a wedding gift. It is just like a photograph his father took of his mother at a charity fashion show in Ottawa the night Anthony proposed to her. Nathan has always loved that photograph of Heather. She looked so beautiful—just like the painting Gertrude has done. His knees weaken, so he sits down and glances up at Gertrude who is too busy setting up her equipment to notice his expression. Nathan wipes away his tears he doesn't want Gertrude to see, but it is already too late. She has seen him crying.

"Oh, my dear. It's okay to cry. Your dear mother would have been so proud of you, Tony tells me."

"I am not so sure, Grandmother," Nathan says softly.

"Listen, my dear. You're not only cute." Nathan laughs because he has not been called cute for a long time. Gertrude continues, "But you also have a good heart. You're a good boy, Nathan and that's why we all adore you. Heather is watching over you. I'm sure she is proud of you, too. Now, come let me sketch you before Kofi comes and gets all jealous again. My husband doesn't like me keeping company with charming young men, you know?"

Nathan flashed a big smile. He was not worried about Tia as much any more. Over in the guest house, Tia was also restless. She wanted to see Nathan, but her mother told her she could not go to the main house until her brother brought her later. Jayzel was there and Brooke was painting her nails for her. Brooke always likes to make a fuss over the little girl, and Jayzel loves her Auntie Brooke. Elizabeth Starr and Amy Hall are chatting about Tia's new TV movie. Elizabeth couldn't believe Tia has cast her in the movie and that Steven will direct it.

"Is Steven seeing anyone?" asked Elizabeth.

With a warning tone, Tia replied, "Read your contract very carefully."

"Oh, there is no need. I trust you," Elizabeth said childishly.

"Rehearsing is going to be grueling, Liz. Amy and I will not tolerate any lateness, and none of the shenanigans typical of CTV's studios will be condoned at Sunlight. Amy and I just won't stand for it," Tia warned her.

Amy raised her eyebrows and seconded Tia's comment, adding, "Honey, read your contract very carefully."

The whole mansion was transformed into a wedding wonderland, bursting with white hydrangeas, roses, daisies, baby's breathe, and all manner of white flowers arranged in effusive bouquets and placed artfully throughout the main floor of the house. Candles were lit and classical music was playing. Nathan and Trey were dressed in their tuxedos when Anthony came to check on them. Nathan was more nervous than he had been before his first marriage to Tia. His hands were trembling when he tried to fix his tie. Chuckling, Anthony came to his aid and fixed the tie for his son.

"You look so handsome, just like when you were a little boy, son."

"Do I look handsome, too, Grandpa?" Trey asked, looking up at his father and grandfather.

"Of course you do!"

Together, they went downstairs to the family room. Gertrude had arranged for the photographer to take family photos. She instructed him to take one of Nathan, Anthony and Trey. Then, she told Steven to join them, so there would be a picture of all the Carter men gathered together.

"That is going to be my favorite picture!" exclaimed Gertrude. "Don't they look handsome?"

Next, Gertrude asked Bobby and Kofi to stand next to the Carters so that Gertrude could have a photo of all her favorite men. BJ arrived and asked, "Are you all ready?" He, too, looked handsome in his tuxedo. Trey gives him a high-five. "Make sure you don't lose the rings, Trey!" instructs BJ. "My mummy wants everyone to go sit and stay in their places like we practiced yesterday. I am going to bring my sister, now. Okay?" BJ was bossier than ever.

Nathan took a deep breath. Jaden, Jason, and Steven were standing beside him. Gertrude told the photographer to make sure he takes pictures of the girls coming down the stairs. The double French doors to the family room were opened as Gertrude began to play the piano. Trey came down the stairs first, followed by his father. Jayzel followed in a pink gown. Nathan bent and kissed her on the cheeks as she moved to stand opposite her father. Kate stepped down the stairs, followed by Brooke, Jackie, Claire and Lisa. They were all dressed in pink, sleeveless taffeta gowns with plunging necklines and beaded A-line skirts, echoing Jayzel's dress. They all looked lovely standing next to Jayzel, opposite the men. Nathan was holding Trey's hand while they waiting for the women to come into the room. It was the longest wait of his life. Trey was told he couldn't talk until his father and mother kiss, but he could not restrain himself.

"Wow! Doesn't my mummy look like a princess?" he exclaimed aloud.

Nathan turned to see Tia and BJ at the top of the stairs. He watched them slowly descend and when Tia finally looked up, their eyes met with a wave of heat they often felt in each other's arms. Tia stopped and gazed into Nathan's eyes. She couldn't take her eyes off him until BJ stepped forward and asked if she was all right. She smiled at BJ and fixed his tie. BJ hates his sisters making a fuss about him, but he is beginning to get used to them now—even their kisses, hugs, and their remarks about his cuteness.

"You are going to be the prettiest girl there," BJ insists.

Tia wore a white Casablanca wedding gown. She looked stunning. Her mother was her maid of honor. As she adjusted Tia's veil, Naana said, "Darling, you look lovely today." Naana turned and sat down next to Bobby. All the guests turned their heads to watch as BJ and Tia made their way toward Nathan. BJ could not contain himself.

"I give our Tia's hands to be married to Nate," he shouted.

Everyone laughed as he and Trey high-five each other like they normally do. Nathan and Tia were already locking lips, when the priest coughed to get their attention. He raised his hand, then suddenly dropped it to his side. Naana Konadu-Sharp walked down the aisle and took the microphone, "Are you two getting married today, or have we all come here to watch you two make out?"

They exchanged their vows without further commotion, then moved to the gym for the reception. Gertrude's artistic talents really shone in the decoration of the reception room. One would never know the room had recently been a gym and the site of a recent boys-against-the-girls basketball game. White and gold draperies hung on the walls, bouquets of white hydrangeas and white roses were placed on the tables covered in white tablecloths. Their guests feasted on a lavish meal prepared by one of Holland's top catering companies. It was an extravagance of fairy-tale proportions that Gertrude had dreamed for her granddaughter. After the meal, everyone danced. The reception was magical. Nathan took the microphone to thank everyone for coming and to thank Gertrude for giving him and Tia the wedding of their dreams.

"Being Tia's husband is an honor, I sure hope she doesn't leave me this time!" Everyone laughed, and Nathan continued, "This is the most unbelievably loving family you will ever meet."

Nathan and Steven did their best to charm Gertrude. Jackie asked her father if she could visit England before returning to California. Anthony raised no objection. Jackie did not see Lisa after the wedding. Vidal came to the wedding, but he, too, seems to have disappeared at the same time as Lisa. Guntar came to tell Jackie, "Miss Lisa is waiting for you in the car." For a moment, Jackie wanted to tell the poor driver to go and tell Lisa to get lost. She couldn't believe Lisa had forgotten about her already. Steven noticed that his little sister was sad. Steven hates to see Jackie upset and he feels that he hasn't done a good job of looking out for her. Even though they live together, Jackie is always busy studying, and Steven is always in and out of LA so frequently that it is difficult to track Jackie's activities.

"Are you okay?" Steven asked.

"Yes," Jackie replied curtly, and walked away, deciding at the last second to go out to the waiting limo.

Lisa walked to the parked limousine and slid into the back. "Are you all right, Jacks?"

Jackie did not respond right away. "I don't want to go back to the hotel," she said petulantly.

"It okay, sweetheart, we are not going back to the hotel. I want to give you a New Year's Eve to remember," Lisa said as she logged on to her laptop.

Jackie wanted to say that she doesn't like sharing and that she wanted to spend her New Year's at the mansion, but the car is already in motion and Lisa is on the cell phone throughout the trip to the airport.

"Come on, Jacks, we have ten minutes to board our plane," Lisa told her.

"What do you mean?" she asked quizzically.

Lisa hugged her and whispered "In an hour we will be in London Gatwick airport." Jackie is crying and asks, "Why didn't you tell me we were going to England?"

"I wanted to surprise you, Jacks. Come on!"

Just like Lisa predicted, they were in London an hour later. They took a taxi to the Sharp home in Croydon. Lisa transferred their luggage to the trunk of her car. Jackie asked, "Is that your car?" and Lisa just smiled. "Wait for me in the car, please, Jacks!" They drove in silence, and when Lisa finally parked the car, she asked Jackie again to wait for her in the car. Lisa took their belongings inside and returned to open the door for Jackie. Jackie was upset.

"I want to wait in the car," she said childishly.

"You look so sexy when you are angry."

"Thanks a lot!" Jackie hissed angrily, frustrated.

"Stop bugging me, Jacks. Let's bounce. It's cold out here. You can tell me what you are angry about once we are inside. Okay?"

Lisa opened the door to the loft. She had candlelight setting the mood and Usher playing on the stereo system. Jackie smiled when she realized that Lisa wanted the loft to be more romantic. She turned and faced Lisa with a smile.

"Does this mean I get a kiss for effort?"

"Wow! You, honey, are so romantic," she whispered.

Lisa took her coat off and got down on her knees, removed her boots and told her to go inside.

"Wow! I love your loft!" Jackie exclaimed.

"This used to be Jason and Brooke's. They didn't need any of the furniture. I've always loved this place, so Vidal bought everything inside the loft from them. I'm still living at home with my parents, but I often stay here when I have exams or when Vidal comes to visit."

Vidal . . . Jackie is beginning to resent him now.

"So, what did Vidal think about you leaving?"

"I need to get ready for my exams. That comes before anything. Vidal understands," Lisa said, as she kissed Jackie. "I will make it up to him when comes to visit me in two weeks."

Jackie is jealous, knowing that once she leaves, her replacement will be filling her shoes. She has been very emotional, particularly over her feelings for Lisa. Even though being with a girl is new to her, Jackie doesn't like to think of herself as possessive or jealous because it's a turn-off for Lisa.

"So . . . Do you have a bathroom in this fabulous place, or what?"

"Second door on the left, Jacks."

Jackie is in the bathroom for so long that Lisa didn't know what to expect. She has been on the phone planning more surprises for her.

"Hey, Jacks! Hey, what do you fancy? A night in alone, or do you want to go to a New Year's Eve party?"

"Can we stay in, please?"

"Okay. I want to go out and pick up some stuff before the stores close. Wanna come?"

Lisa hates cooking. If truth be told, Lisa Sharp can cook like a chef, but leads everyone to believe she can't boil water. Jackie, however, enjoys cooking and isn't so much into eating out like Lisa does. Lisa tells her that there is a restaurant that makes delicious vegetarian food. She is going to call in an order.

Jackie says, "Show me your kitchen." There is nothing in the cupboards and very little in the fridge but water, soy milk and orange juice. Jackie makes a list and they drive to the nearest supermarket. When they return to the loft, Jackie makes seared sesame tuna, stir-fry with shitake noodles, red beet salad, and pineapple kabobs for dessert. Lisa enjoys watching her cook even though Jackie wouldn't let Lisa help in the kitchen.

"My mum once tried to make the pineapple thing you made. It was horrible."

Jackie laughed heartily. "It's hard to picture your mum and horrible together. It just doesn't go well together."

"Yeah! Thank you, Jacks."

"For what?"

"This . . . this is delicious." Lisa sighs. "I really appreciate you coming to England with me. I didn't think you would want to leave your brothers and your dad."

"You didn't?"

"No."

"I was not happy when we returned to the mansion. I felt a little . . ." She paused. Lisa finished her sentences for her, "You felt uncomfortable when I took off with Vidal." Jackie was a little teary. She tried to fight the tears, so Lisa took her by the arm and guided her to the living room and they sat down together on the sofa. She hates to see Jackie crying. Lisa put her forehead against Jackie's and told her, "It will get better, I promise."

"I think so. What are the rules and the regulations of this? I don't understand," Jackie cried.

Lisa leaned back in the sofa and surveyed her well with her eyes. She put her hands out for her to come to her embrace, and with hesitation Jackie does.

"Tell me what is it you want, Jacks," she asks quizzically.

"I don't know."

Lisa is caressing her back, and whispers, "when you know, you tell me, Jacks. I love you. I don't know where this is going. I will do anything to make you happy. Don't asked me to give up, Vidal. I do love him. He's my future, and that is one thing I can never do, give him up."

Jackie pulls out of her embrace.

"Jacks, listen to me. It was very selfish of me to bring you with me."

Lisa is in tears now, too. "You know, after everything that Priscilla put me through, I promised myself never again will I let any woman get close to my heart."

"Why did you let me?" Jackie murmured.

"I didn't . . . Jacks, you took me by surprise, and I don't want to give you up."

"That's nice of you," Jackie hissed sarcastically.

"What do you think if you go and tell our family that we are lovers . . . and we want to be together?" Lisa asked.

"My Dad will not see anything wrong as long as I am happy," Jackie responded.

"So will my mom. My mother knows I see girls. She also knows that I plan to be married one day and have a family. You and I go out in the open and we tell everyone and believe me they will support us—until we break up and we tear up our family, Jacks! Is this what you want?"

Jackie is quiet.

"Jacks! I know this is all new to you. We really don't have to rush."

Jackie has not been able to think of anything but Lisa since they made love. Lisa is perfect for her in every way except that she is Tia's sister and a girl. Jackie runs into Lisa's arms and cries "I am sorry."

"Don't be sorry."

They spend the evening in bed watching movies until Lisa slept. The phone rang, but Jackie didn't know if she should answer it. It kept ringing, so Lisa reached over and pushed the speaker button. Priscilla's voice is on the other end.

Her voice full of recriminations, she asks, "Why did you leave without telling me? Why are you trying to hurt me this way?"

Lisa hates it when she does this, so she replies, "Well, it was okay when we were together. Baby, you chose drugs and sleeping around over me. Baby, we have been over for months. You have yourself a happy new year. I have exams to worry about." Lisa hung up and put down her head without realizing Jackie was there. When Jackie reached out and touched Lisa, she almost jumped up to the ceiling. Jackie laughed. Lisa looked at the clock to see it was almost midnight.

"I'm going to make a call in my office. Is there anyone you want to call to wish a happy new year?" she said pointing to a phone. "Call whomever you like. I'll see you in ten minutes." Lisa slipped out of the bed still in her underwear.

Jackie had no idea what the time difference between London and LA might be, but she decided she would call Shawn just to tell him they were finished and to let him know that her email to Stephanie was sent to him. Jackie has been on cloud nine since she slept with Lisa, so she sent a long, descriptive email to Stephanie about Lisa's lovemaking and how romantic she is. Jackie couldn't believe that she had wasted almost two years of her life in a loveless relationship with Shawn. Jackie feels liberated now that the relationship is over. She knows she has not lived her life as most girls her age have done, Jackie is now beginning to enjoy what life has to offer, as Lisa often puts it. She calls Holland to wish her father and her brothers happy new year, then decides not to wait for Lisa to return to the bedroom before taking off her own clothes and grabbing one of Lisa's silk robes to wear. Jackie strolled through the apartment, looking for Lisa's office and found her on the phone, talking with the phone on speaker, as usual.

Jackie strides over to the desk, swings Lisa's chair around to face her, and slips off her robe. "Are you going to spend all your time on the phone with your lovers, or are you going to hang up and come give this lover a kiss?" she says provocatively.

Turned on by Jackie's sudden bold attitude, Lisa promptly hung up the phone, sat Jackie on her desk and took her there. They made love all over the loft until the early hours in the morning. Lisa couldn't figure out what had gotten into Jackie because she seems more relaxed and a lot less emotional, more fun. Much different from the girls Lisa normally sleeps with, Jackie has learned her needs in a relatively short time and knows how to please her in and out of bed. Also, Jackie has bewitched Lisa. There won't be any worries about drugs or cheating. Lisa fell asleep in Jackie's arms.

The next day they drove to Southend in the afternoon and walked around the pebble beach. Jackie enjoys the English weather because it feels like spring even though winter has hardly started. It's nothing like the freezing cold Canadian winters. Lisa's first exams are in two days. She wants to show Jackie around, but Jackie wants Lisa to study.

"You can show me around on the weekend," Jackie insists.

Feeling the stress of the exams, Lisa is intense and nervous about them. Back at the loft, Jackie got an idea of how to relieve Lisa's exam stress. She boiled water and poured it into a bucket, undressed Lisa and told her to lay down on the bed. She poured body oil in the warm water and threw in three hand towels. When the hand towels were sodden, Jackie wrapped Lisa in the towels. By the time Jackie had completed her ministrations, Lisa was so relaxed, she almost had an orgasm. However, the warmth of the towels and the scent of the oil lulled Lisa into a restful sleep. For the next few until, until the day of the exams, Jackie prepared her scented towel wrap for Lisa to help her relax and get much needed sleep. The first two exams were done on Thursday. Feeling frisky, Lisa told Jackie, "I'd like to take you to one of the clubs I own."

"You own a night club?" asked Jackie in disbelief.

Lisa grinned. "Yeah. Two of them, actually. Technically, my mother owns them. I used her money to invest wisely in things that will bring in more money."

"Wow! You are smart. So . . . what's it called?"

"The Vibe. It's mostly for late teens and people who are in their early twenties who are gay or bisexual, a place to hang out and be themselves. England has a very conservative attitudes toward the homosexual lifestyle. English people have not embraced it in quite the same way as the rest of Europe has, even though it is the twenty-first century! There is an internet cafe and a non-smoking, private area. Tia, Brooke and Kate have a shop there, too. There's a hair salon. I have a penthouse on top of the building. I was thinking you could go and get your hair done, see Kate's mom at the store. She will be at Urban Style, and you could get some shopping done while I look at the books and approve some up-coming events that the club manager has booked."

"Do you think my wardrobe is wack?"

Lisa laughed. "No, sweetheart. I have a lot of work to do, and I don't want you to get bored. Kate's mom will take care of you. I will be in the penthouse with Corey," Lisa reasoned with her.

"Who is Corey?"

"Corey is my details guy. We have been having problems with drugs in our clubs. My mom wants me to put a stop to it ASAP. Corey is the man to help me do that."

Lisa and Mrs Lee were talking in Cantonese, while Jackie watched, increasingly impressed with Lisa. At the hair dressers, Jackie told the stylist to give her a different look, one that she can manage as she doesn't often go to a hair salon. By the time she went back to the boutique, Mrs Lee hardly recognized Jackie. Jackie asked for a medium length cut, so the stylist gave her an Eastern edge, Chinese bangs cut just above the eyebrow at both an symmetric and asymmetric angle. She straightened Jackie's usually wavy black hair and put some burgundy high lights and copper low lights to complete the look. Jackie looked gorgeous. Afterward, at Urban Style, Mrs Lee and the sales associates presented their own fashion show. Enthralled with all the great clothes, Jackie soon lost track of time. Worried, Lisa called the boutique to ask what was happening, and Mrs Lee replied, "I'm just bringing her upstairs, Miss Sharp."

Lisa's penthouse, is more simply furnished than the loft, sported a colorful Ikea style, with three bedrooms and a spacious living room-dining room area. One of the bedrooms had been converted into an office, Lisa was working at the computer and barking orders at someone on the phone. She did not immediately recognize Jackie.

"This is a private flat. Go back to the kitchen. I will be down soon to talk to you about the menu. I told Simon that I will be done soon. If you are going to be my new chef, you can't just show up unannounced whenever you feel like it."

Jackie started to laugh uncontrollably. "Who is this Simon?" she asked between bursts of laughter.

"Simon is my club manager. You look fabulous, Jacks," Lisa complemented her.

"I told her she looked sexy," Mrs Lee remarked, winking at Jackie, before she left.

"I did it!" she said exuberantly. Lisa gets up and kisses her on the cheek. She loved Jackie's new look.

"I am almost done here. There is a new house band playing in the club. We are also trying out a new chef. If you like, I will ask her to make us something to eat so we can stay and listen to the band, or we can go back to the loft—whatever you want, Jacks." Lisa is happy to see Jackie coming out of her shell. She has been like a new person since New Year's Eve. She wonders if Jackie is okay.

Chapter 15

Simon is very flamboyant, so much so that most people suspect he is gay, despite his assertions that he is not. Clean shaven, long blond hair like a rock star, happy-go-lucky bubbling personality, fabulous fashion sense—it's all a bit too much. Simon used to drive a limousine and double as a bodyguard for Frank Bruno's children. Frank Bruno was a British heavy-weight boxing champion in the eighties. Consequently, Simon knows who's who in British celebrity circles. Drop a name . . . Simon can tell you who has slept with whom, whose career is not going nowhere, and who just signed a pre-nup. With Simon around, one needn't read the tabloid or watch the entertainment news on TV. Simon knows it all. He is in his early fifties but looks like a twenty-year-old. He is Lisa's right-hand man. He was drowning in debt two years ago when Lisa, who was given the unlikely task of foreclosing on Simon's mortgage held by her mother's company, fell in love with Simon's out-going personality, though she wasn't so crazy about his lack of business sense. The man can put together an event faster then anyone she knows. Lisa has nick-named him Uncle Sam. Simon brought the new chef to the penthouse to meet Lisa. Jackie is checking her email in the office, so they have lots of time to talk about menus, staff, and so on. The new chef is a girl Lisa met at one of her clubs two weeks before she left for Holland. She was eager to spend the night, but Lisa begged off saying she had an early meeting in the morning, so they have been unable to re-connect until now. Lisa remembered her saying it was her nineteenth birthday that night, so Lisa sent Corey over to her table with a bottle of their in-house cheap wine for the girl and her friends. The girl later approached her after Corey had left and thanked her. Lisa was not expecting that kind of thank you, but it has been a while for her. Since all that mess with Priscilla, hooking up with girls she hardly knows is not something she does regularly. They talked and laughed together, so when the girl pulled Lisa to the floor, she couldn't say no—after all, it was her birthday. Lisa kissed her on the cheek and wished her happy birthday and left. Lisa was about to get in her car, when the girl re-appeared and smacked her with a kiss and invited Lisa to her place. Lisa declined. The girl pressed her number into Lisa's hands. Lisa thought she was sweet and was going to call her the next day, but she lost the chit of paper.

"This is the beautiful Miss Sharp. Boss lady, meet Debbie, my new chef," Simon introduced them.

"We met—almost a month ago. You said you were in catering," Lisa recalled.

"Yes, you remembered?"

"Now, now kids. Remember our deal . . . we don't fuck in our house! If you kids have been shagging, I need to know, boss lady. You have always said, no fucking with the staff." He blurted it out, outrageously loud. Jackie heard and came out of the office to see what was going on. Lisa gave him a silencing look, but then she was very painfully honest.

"No, Daddy dearest. We have not been shagging, as you put it! If you must know, I lost her number before I went to Holland. We did kiss and it was a bloody good one, too!" Lisa told him.

"Wow! Don't you just love her!" Simon says facetiously. He turns to the chef and says, wagging his finger at her, "No more snogging the boss."

Debbie was a little embarrassed. She has been thinking about Lisa and their kiss and why she never called. She smiled.

"Please, do sit down." Lisa pointed to a chair. "I have nothing to do with the hiring and firing of Simon's staff. I wanted to meet with you because I was hoping you could make me some meals I can take home. I do have a very special house guest and we are both vegetarians," Lisa explained.

"Oh, love. I thought you and Miss Jackie were staying to have dinner with me? I asked Corey and my new bride to join us. I wanted to show Miss Jackie how we do it in England. Come on." Simon interjected.

"I'll ask Jackie, if we can stay and enjoy Debbie's food tonight, since Simon is paying," Lisa smirked. Jackie went back into the office when she heard what Lisa had said. She didn't want to eavesdrop any more.

"I am also throwing a party here next weekend. Simon said you have the menu already. I'd like to go over it with you, if you don't mind?" Lisa asked. "Would you excuse us a moment, Debbie. Simon, come with me." Lisa goes into her office, turns to face Simon and says, "You're over budget—again. I don't want to be checking up on your spending all the time. From now on, if we're going to have a live band on Friday and Saturday nights, you should charge a cover." Simon protested, claiming the kids can't afford more than what the club is charging already. "Well, if they can afford to buy drugs, they can afford to spend more coming to the club." Jackie is very impressed how Lisa talks business.

"One more thing . . . there's been talk about drugs in our clubs. You don't need me to tell you how bad it is for our business! Corey has not come up with anything for us on that. We have installed four cameras. I am hoping they will see something our boys are not seeing."

"I am trying, Lisa. The punters are not making it easy to find these cats. They always find a way in! You might consider having an undercover cop here to flush out these cats, boss lady. The situation that we talked about before you went to Holland . . . I hope you had time to think about it? I'm well chuffed about Debbie taking the job. She comes from some posh hotel in the west end," he tells Lisa.

"Yes, I did discuss the issue with my mother. She feels the same as you do, so you get someone here immediately and I want all the staff watched too, no exceptions! If ever Priscilla is here they must not allow her into any of our clubs. Simon, I mean it. Let's be diligent about it. My mother was alarmed, she will shut us down if we can't get rid of this problem," Lisa warned.

"Okay, love. I am on it. I will see you later, Miss Jackie," he says.

"Jacks, sweetheart, I won't be long." Lisa left with Simon and joined Debbie in the living room.

"I'm sorry for keeping you waiting, and for that bit of awkwardness earlier."

Debbie smiled at her. Lisa felt awkward again because she really did want to call to ask Debbie on a date for New Year's Eve, but if Debbie is going to work at the club, any hanky panky is a no-go. Debbie wore her hair in an up-do, the same style she wore when Lisa met her at the club. Lisa recalls Debbie boldly approaching her for a slow dance and trying to slip her tongue in her mouth. Lisa wrote on the menu and handed it to Debbie. Their eyes met, held for a moment, Debbie sighed. She hoped Lisa had written down her number, or at least a naughty message, but she was disappointed. Lisa had simply made a few changes to the menu. Debbie was hoping they could mix business with a little something. Something!

"This looks good, Debbie. I hope you will enjoy working for Simon. The old bastard is a sweetheart, though he can be a right plunker sometimes, but a sweetheart just the same." Lisa says.

Debbie smiles. She has a sexy smile. Lisa wanted to say so, but knew she shouldn't. Lisa was walking Debbie back downstairs when Jackie came out of the office asking if they could go back to the loft.

Lisa hates to bring her private life to work, so she turned to Jackie and said firmly, "Debbie here has gone to a lot of trouble to make dinner for us. Simon and his girlfriend are expecting us to join them in the dining room in ten minutes. We'll go after dinner."

Jackie wanted to say something, but Lisa kissed her on the cheek and said, "I'll be right back."

She went and opened the door for Debbie. Debbie paused on the threshold, "Did you really lose my number?"

"Yes, I did. I wanted to call and thank you for the dance before I left town and em . . . asked . . . It is good to see you again, Debbie," Lisa whispered.

"Will it be possible for us to talk sometime?" Debbie asked as she wrote down her number.

Jackie couldn't hear what they were saying, but she was sure that the Chef had just given her number to Lisa. Lisa gave it back to her and the girl didn't look happy. Jackie smiled.

"Sure. Any time. My numbers are by the phone in the office downstairs. You can call anytime, okay?"

"I wasn't talking about work."

Lisa smiled. "It will be a bad idea for me to . . . um . . . I don't have romantic relationships with my staff. I can't afford a law suit."

"That's good. I'll give my two weeks notice, now, then."

She has made her intentions known, so she winked as she smiled.

"I am sorry. I have fallen in love with a very special man. I think it will work out well for the both of us this time. You don't have to give up your job for me."

"He's a very lucky man," said Debbie.

Lisa sighed as she watched Debbie go downstairs. She closed her eyes to clear her mind and when she opened them, Jackie had changed into a stunning black cocktail dress. She looked fabulous.

"Do you still want to take me to dinner?"

Grinning, Lisa said, "Hell no! I want you, here, right now! No, I want to have dinner alone with you. Let me grab my stuff, so I don't have to come up here after."

Lisa called the kitchen and told Debbie that she would not be joining Simon and Corey for dinner. Debbie was a little disappointed. She yelled at the waitress to bring back the food, "Miss Sharp is not staying. We need to make this to go. Now!"

Debbie did her best to get Lisa's order for her and brought it to her by her car. Lisa and Jackie were just outside by the club when she met them. Lisa told her she shouldn't have and she would have come and picked up the food herself, but Debbie demurred. Lisa opened the door for Jackie and she put Jackie's shopping on the back seat of the car. She opened the trunk of the car, so Debbie could place the food in it. Lisa lead over to fix one of the bags, brushing hands with Debbie. They found it difficult to let go of each other's hands, but Lisa pulled away first.

"Thank you, again," Lisa said.

Debbie smiled and walked away.

Vidal had called that morning while Lisa was writing her exam at college. He told Jackie that he would be coming to England in two days to surprise Lisa. He told Jackie that Lisa hardly sleeps during exams because of the stress and he wants to come and be with her. Jackie was a little jealous, but she knows that Lisa loves him and she just wants to spend the next two days alone with her before Vidal comes. She has promised to spend more time with her father when he arrives in the morning. It won't be long before Jackie leaves for California and her own exam schedule.

"Vidal called while you were at school today."

"I will call him in the morning."

"He is coming to see you in two days. I was thinking that I will stay back at your parents place and spend time with my Dad, so you and Vidal can have more time together—what do you think?"

"You don't have to stay at my parents to spend time with your Dad, Jacks. Anthony can come and have dinner with us at the loft. We'll be in and out of my parents house most of the time anyway. This is our time together, we only have a week left before you go home, and then we will not see each other for another two months, Jacks. Why would you not want to be with me?" She pulled the car into her parking spot and turned toward Jackie. Jackie did not respond.

"Jacks, what is going on?"

"How do you mean?"

"Why do you want to move in with my parents? Don't tell me it's because Vidal is coming. You know very well that he and I can't live alone until we are married. He is not coming to stay with me. I know you've spend most of this week alone. I've not even shown you around the city. I plan to to do all that with you next week," Lisa told her.

Jackie asked "Can we go inside? I'm getting cold." She was being evasive and not answering Lisa's questions. Lisa felt angry, so she got out of the car and left her there, well fed up with Jackie. Inside, Lisa went to the fridge and poured soy milk in a glass and went into her bedroom. She was in the bathroom by the time Jackie made it into the loft with all the shopping and the food. She hates seeing Lisa upset, but she needs to wean herself slowly from her before she returns to California. Otherwise, she will not be able to cope with her life there without her. Jackie has never known this side of Lisa. She has always seemed strong and understanding. Jackie joined Lisa in the tub and tried to touch her.

"Don't, Jacks." Lisa got out of the tub.

"Lisa, please. We need to talk about this."

Lisa ignored her and got under the shower to rinse herself. Jackie figured she would have a better chance talking to her there, but Lisa had locked the door. Jackie left her alone and warmed up some of the food they had brought from the club. She set a table, lit some candles and chose some soft music. Lisa was dressed and almost out of the loft when Jackie begged her to let her explain.

"You don't have to explain anything! Jacks, I am going out and you don't need to wait up for me."

Jackie let go of her. She was not going to beg Lisa to stay, but she found herself saying, "I don't want you to go out, Lisa, please. I just needed to wean myself of you before I go home."

There were tears rolling down Lisa's face. "Has it been so terrible with me that you need to get over me before you go home to Shawn?"

"No! Shawn and I are done. He broke off things with me a week ago. Actually, I couldn't be happier. You seem to put me before anything and I don't want to be in the way when Vidal comes. It was only a suggestion,

Lisa. You left him at New Year's Eve for me. I just don't . . ." she paused. "I am not used to us, as you are. The truth is when I'm with you it is like the outside world doesn't exist. Next week, I will be back in LA living my boring life. I won't have you with me, and part of me still thinks this is all a dream, this forbidden love affair that you and I have. Lisa, loving someone, for me, is not being selfish. I have been selfish keeping you away from the man that you love, Lisa. He misses you. I could hear it in his voice," Jackie explained.

"I've been worried out of my mind about you. How you are going to cope with everything once you go back to LA?" Lisa wondered aloud.

Jackie hugged her and said that she would be fine. "I will miss you terribly, but I will be fine." They were both relieved. They sat down and talked and ate. Jackie asked where Lisa was going all dressed up. Lisa replied, "One of my clubs has a ladies night tonight. I was going there to drown my sorrows."

"Will you give me a minute to get dressed? We can go together," offered Jackie.

The Empire was very different from the clubs in Amsterdam where Jackie and Lisa partied. They got a corner booth in the non-smoking section and the waitress brought them smoothies.

"Take them back," Lisa said. "Bring us bottled water, please."

"Why? What's wrong with smoothies?" Jackie asked.

"We are not in Amsterdam. There are a lot more drugs in England than in Holland. You just have to be careful of what people give you to drink, that's all."

The waitress returned moments later with a bottle of house wine, "A complement from a customer at the bar."

Lisa said, "Ask the customer to join us."

"Do people always send you drinks when you come here?" asked Jackie.

"Sometimes. Do you want to dance?"

"No. I feel weird being on a date with a girl. I don't think . . . . um . . . I don't think I can dance with you," Jackie murmured shyly.

"It's okay, Jacks. Do you want to go back to the loft? Sleeping with a girl in private and being out in public for all eyes to see is different. I should have known you weren't quite ready for this. I just want to thank the person who sent us the wine and then we're out of here, okay?" Lisa wanted to kiss her, but she wasn't sure how Jackie would respond to being kissed in public by a girl. Instead, Lisa rubbed her knee under the table and re-assured Jackie that she understood her feelings.

"No, I'm sorry," Jackie sighed.

"What are you sorry about Jackie? Your name is Jackie, am I right?" Priscilla asked. She leaned over and kissed Jackie on both cheeks. She tried to kiss Lisa, but she moved aside. "Baby, why did you not show up for your party?"

Lisa frowned. "I came here to be alone, so if you don't mind, I'd like to be alone."

Priscilla turned to Jackie and asked, "Are you a lesbian?"

Jackie said vehemently, "No way!"

"Then you won't mind if I borrow my lover here, do you?" Priscilla said.

Jackie thought this was a nightmare. "Yes, I do mind if you borrow your ex-lover. Why can't you just leave her be? Lisa has suffered enough, get lost!" Jackie demanded.

"Baby, are you going to sit there and let her talk to me like this?" Priscilla asked.

"Your evil little seductress act has not worked. She told you in Holland that you two are finished. Why don't you get lost?" Jackie said rudely. Lisa sighed with anger. She had enough of this catty exchange. She asked Jackie to excuse them, then she pulled Priscilla to the dance floor for a slow song.

"You're pathetic! I have indulged your bad behavior for too long. I told you it was over, but you refuse to accept it. I have fallen in love with Vidal. Your desperate attempt to split us apart did not work. You are out of control, so don't count on me to bail you out of anything from now on," Lisa warned her.

"Does Vidal know that you still have feelings for me?" Priscilla asked.

Lisa let go of her. "I no longer torture myself about you and things you do. I'm done with you. Good night," Lisa said coolly.

"He tastes different from what you are use to, baby. Do you really want want us to be over?" Priscilla asked.

It had occurred to Jackie that Lisa may not be over Priscilla as much she claimed. She recognized that Lisa was still hurt by whatever Priscilla had done. Debbie and Corey were at the table talking and laughing with

Jackie when Lisa returned. "I am sorry. I didn't know you don't drink." Debbie smiled, "The waitress said you wanted to see me."

"Oh! I just want to thank you for the bottle of wine."

"Hey, Jackie," said Corey. "Will you dance with me?"

"I will if Lisa and Debbie join us."

Lisa smiled. "Maybe later, Jacks. I want to talk to Debbie for a minute." Turning to Debbie, she said, "I'm sorry. Jackie worries too much about me. Why aren't you out there dancing away the night?"

Debbie's response was unexpected, "Are you in love with her?"

"No. She is my ex-girlfriend."

"Damn! You have one sexy ex." Lisa smiled.

Debbie observed, "It's nice to see you smile. Your sister-in-law doesn't like to see you so sad, nor do I."

Lisa doesn't like to show her emotions too much around outsiders. It's a weakness she often tries to hide. It was nice seeing Jackie enjoy herself with Corey.

"You look very beautiful, tonight, Debbie. I'll be fine once my exams are finished." Debbie felt fluttery when Lisa told her she was beautiful.

"What are you studying?"

Lisa turned to look at her and Debbie saw Lisa's unabashed desire. They caressed each other's hands under the table. Lisa loved the secrecy. She saw Priscilla on the dance floor and realized she had missed her. Lisa also acknowledged the two of them have some unfinished business. Priscilla was drinking too much, again, so Lisa asked the waitress to send Priscilla over to her table. Finally, she returned her attention to Debbie's question.

"I am studying business law and finance. Do you enjoy being in catering?"

Just then Priscilla arrived and fell into Lisa's lap. "Waitress, bring some coffee, please," ordered Lisa.

"Don't need coffee," slurred Priscilla. "Want you to take me home. Miss you."

"Come on, baby. Drink some coffee for me and then I'll take you home." Lisa caresses her back.

Debbie was about to leave, but Lisa slipped her hands onto her knee and asked her to stay. "Talk to me," she said.

Debbie felt she couldn't say no, even though her heart told her not to stay, not to get embroiled in Lisa's drama. Jackie was enjoying herself with

Corey on the dance floor. Marc Anthony's "You sing to me" was playing on the sound system and Corey was holding her tightly as they danced. Jackie saw Priscilla sitting on Lisa's lap slurping some coffee. Jackie anxiously tried not to appear jealous. After all, Lisa had asked Priscilla to dance and she had told Jackie to enjoy herself with Corey. For her part, Debbie has had enough of Lisa and her so-called ex's histrionics.

"I have to be on my way home now," said Debbie. "Enjoy the rest of your night, ladies."

"Wait a minute," said Lisa.

Debbie thanked Corey for the drinks and reiterated her intent to leave.

"We're leaving, too," said Jackie. "Can we drop you off somewhere?"

Debbie accepted the ride. She thought Jackie was leaving with Corey. They met Lisa outside putting Priscilla into a taxi, who was adamantly refusing to go in the vehicle. Priscilla gestured to Debbie, "Hey! She will leave you and come to me once she fucks you. She always does."

Jackie hugged Debbie, "I'm sorry! That was completely uncalled for." Debbie stepped forward and helped Lisa put Priscilla into the back seat of Lisa's car.

"I'm sorry, Debbie. Listen, come with me. You're not having fun here," Lisa suggested. "We'll drop Priscilla at her home and go back to my place, later."

Priscilla lives in southwest London, Kew Gardens, with her parents. Lisa pulled up in front of the house and opened the door for Priscilla, who vomited all over Lisa at the curb side.

"I'm so sorry, baby. Please, don't leave me," Priscilla cried.

Lisa took her hand and reached for Debbie with her other hand. She opened the door with Priscilla's keys. The home has an awesome layout, a grand foyer with two staircases. Lisa takes Priscilla into a room on the main floor. It is beautifully decorated all in white. Priscilla sees Lisa holding hands with Debbie and smiles lasciviously.

"Are we going to have a threesome?" she asks excitedly. Lisa shook her head in disbelief.

"Have a seat, Debbie," said Lisa, motioning to the sofa. Lisa ran to the bathroom and returned for Priscilla. Lisa reappeared moments later and began to undress in front of Debbie. Lisa is aware that Debbie is staring at her, so she takes the time to strip right down to her underwear, even though she didn't really need to. She opened Priscilla's closet door and took out a pair of Apple Bottom jeans, slipped them on, and grabbed a T-shirt. She walked over to Debbie and asked, "Do you want anything to drink?"

"I'm good," said Debbie nonchalantly. "I'm not into threesomes, just to let you know." She grinned.

Lisa gasps, then broke into a big smile. "Wait just a minute while I check on Priscilla."

Debbie watched Lisa turn back the bed before re-entering the bathroom. Moments later, she returned with Priscilla, all cleaned up and sobered up.

"Priscilla looks even more beautiful," thought Debbie.

As Priscilla gets into bed, she and Lisa are talking in a language that Debbie can't understand. Lisa lays on the bed with Priscilla until she falls asleep. Debbie watches them thinking "classic case of emotional abuse" and she wonders why Lisa lets Priscilla do this to her.

It was close to midnight before Debbie and Lisa left the Gates mansion. Lisa thanked Debbie and apologized for dragging her out of the club. Debbie said she didn't mind, "I'm enjoying myself. It was an eye-opening experience to have a glimpse into your life, Lisa." Debbie thought Lisa was thoughtful and compassionate, the way she took care of her ex-lover. Priscilla sure had an irritating way of playing mind games with Lisa.

"Why did you drag me with you, or does this sort of thing turn you on?" Debbie asked.

"To stop me from temptation. *You* turn me on," Lisa said with a smile.

"That is pretty sexy temptation. Are you and Priscilla finished, or is this a game you two like to play to spice up your relationship?"

Lisa couldn't read Debbie's expression in the dark night. Her tone was one of concern, though, Lisa thought. She replied, "We are though, and I am not into games—unless they are romantic games. What about you?" Lisa asks softly. She momentarily takes her eyes off the road to glance at Debbie. The silence deepens. Lisa pulls into the drive-through of a coffee bar and buys two green teas, and gives one to Debbie.

"Thank you. Mmm . . . this is delicious. You really don't have to take me home, Lisa. Jackie must be worried about you by now. I will take a cab home. Thanks for the tea." Debbie said as she sipped the hot beverage. Lisa parked the car, "Jackie is fine and Corey will be taking her home, so you see, I am not in a rush. I'll drive you home."

Lisa's cell phone rang. It is Jackie.

"I'll be there in ten minutes to pick you up," said Lisa.

"No. I'll meet you at the loft in an hour," replied Jackie.

Lisa leaned her head back against the seat, closing her eyes for a second to clear her mind. When she opened her eyes, Debbie had also leaned back with her eyes closed. Lisa couldn't help wondering what Debbie could be thinking. Debbie's lips were inviting, and in a heartbeat Lisa tilts back her seat and pulls Debbie on top of her. Debbie tries to touch Lisa, but Lisa braids her fingers into Debbie's. Lisa runs her fingers on Debbie's lips, then sucks on them. Debbie's mouth is soft when Lisa caress her lips with her own fingertips, and the rest of Debbie's body begins to tremble as she aches with a burning desire to touch Lisa, who is kissing her softly and roughly at the same time. Pulling out Debbie's pony-tail, Lisa runs her hands through Debbie's beautiful blonde hair. The steam begins to build in the car as Lisa leans forward to cup Debbie's breasts, sucking the nipples to a ripe hardness. Debbie notices that every time she tries to touch Lisa, she maneuvers Debbie's hands behind her back or places them on top of the steering wheel. Debbie's heart beats even faster as Lisa hikes up her skirt, open her thighs to discover Debbie's wetness, and Lisa begins to massage her buttocks, stroke her thighs and stimulate the anterior wall of her vagina. Thrusting her fingers inside, Lisa stimulates Debbie's vagina, so that she rides it like a penis, only it is way better than any penis she has ever ridden. Debbie is dying to touch Lisa, but wary Lisa pulls Debbie's hands back. Lisa never once stops kissing her, and she didn't let Debbie's clit get lonely. She teased it with a finger tip until Debbie climaxed. When the orgasm subsided, Lisa began to dress Debbie all the while continuing to kiss her. Lisa has eyes everywhere. She puts the car into drive while Debbie is still sitting on her lap with her other hand gently caressing her legs. Lisa drove so slowly to her flat that Debbie did not know what to make of Lisa Sharp. It was a wild and crazy seduction. Lisa has got Debbie's attention now! Later, when Debbie lay in her solitary bed, musing over the events of the last hour, her cell phone rang. It was Lisa: "I forgot to ask if you were okay."

With tears in her eyes, Debbie replied, "Yes."

"I was wondering then, if I could take you to lunch tomorrow?"

Lisa has never slept with any of her staff before, but there was something about Debbie that keeps Lisa off-balance. Nevertheless, she has not been able to get Debbie out of her mind since the night they met.

Tonight, she felt a kind of connection with her that she has never felt with any woman—not ever. "Only if you tell me that you are okay?" Debbie asks.

"I will be, once you say yes to lunch," Lisa replies.

"Yes. Miss Sharp, I'll have lunch with you."

Lisa gasps and says, "I don't want to say goodnight, but I know you're tired." Debbie murmurs agreement. "Well, then, I will pick you up at eleven!"

As she hung up the phone, Debbie instinctively heard an echo of Priscilla's words. She really had not expected Lisa to call after a shagging like that. "Huh, huh. I guess I was wrong," Debbie said to herself. Lisa was on the phone by the time Corey brought Jackie home. Jackie could not tell whether Lisa was upset. Lisa put out her hands and beckoned for Jackie to come to her. Jackie sat on Lisa's lap while she worked on her computer.

"Talk to me, Jacks."

"What do you want to talk about?"

"Anything, sweetheart. I like listening to you talk. It's relaxing." Lisa stops typing for a moment to kiss Jackie. "Mmm, I've been wanting to do that all night. You looked beautiful tonight, Jacks." They kiss again. Lisa continues, "Anyway, since I didn't get to dance with you at the club, would you dance with me now?" Jackie smiled. Lisa looked into her eyes and said, "I'd like to dance really slowly with you, take your clothes off before you go falling in love with Patrick."

"You're jealous? You do care? I was worried for a bit," Jackie said, laughing.

Lisa did not let her talk as she kept kissing her. Jackie spend the rest of night the talking. Lisa realized just how strong-minded Jackie could be. She told Lisa that she didn't recognize Debbie until after Priscilla laid into her that she was the chef. "She is very nice. I like her. I think she may have a crush on you," Jackie said.

"Me, too," Lisa says, half asleep as she held tightly to Jackie.

Jackie brushed her hair off her face and kissed her, and whispered, "I love you, Lisa", before she closed her own eyes and fell asleep.

Chapter 16

No one was sadder to leave Amsterdam than Nathan. He loved being there with all his family around night and day. The trip to England poses difficulties for Nathan because he does not have good memories of England, especially his last two visits there with Tia. Both were not worth repeating. Although, to be fair, at the time, he didn't have the strong family support and the friendship he now has with Jason and Jaden. This trip has already been fraught with tension. Brooke fought with everyone over where Tia, Nathan and the children would stay for the two weeks they were going to be in England. In the end, she won. Tia loves their new home. It is reminiscent of her and Nathan's first home in Ottawa, very comfortable. Amy Hall and Elizabeth Starr will also be in England to do some publicity work for *The Saga*, and Sarah Williams is happy to have them and Dr. Doyle as her house guests. The relaxed atmosphere of the three weeks spent in Holland dissolves into the workaday world of English city life. As they arrive in London, Nathan recognizes that the festivities related to his marriage are coming to a close. The exigencies of everyday life are returning.

Lisa has asked Naana, Tia and Nathan to meet her Saturday morning at the African Mortgage Funds offices in the Skyline Building. Everyone is curious about the meeting. Why does Lisa want to meet on Saturday? What is so urgent that the meeting can't wait until the next business day? Just as they arrive at the Skyline, Jaden also pulls into the parking lot. They congregate outside the offices of African Mortgage Funds.

"What are you doing here?" asks Jaden.

"Lisa insisted on a meeting here," replies Tia.

"You told her about Kevin?" probes Jaden.

Tia raises her eyebrows in response, but there is no time to talk further as Lisa comes to the door.

"You're late! Come in! Come in! Let's get started!" Lisa encourages everyone to settle into chairs. She takes a file folder from Jaden and suggests he keep Jackie company in her office. He nods agreement and slips out of the meeting room as Lisa passes the file to her mother, who skims it and forwards the file to Nathan.

Lisa sits in her own chair and plays with a pen while the file makes the rounds of the table. When everyone has had a chance to peruse the documents, Lisa begins the meeting by presenting some background information.

"Six months ago, I was going to foreclose on Mr Kevin Peters home and place of business. As you can see, it is well documented that representatives of African Mortgage Funds have made every effort to contact Mr Peters and make arrangements concerning his outstanding mortgage payments. Mother, I know how you do business, and how you pride yourself on not foreclosing on your clients. Unfortunately for Mr Peters, I don't share the same views," Lisa said with authority. Naana glances at Nathan and Tia. "Sweetheart, you are the Vice President of this company. I trust your judgment fully, though I do sense something personal about this particular file."

"Well, no. Not exactly. Though there are some interesting connections with this file. That's why I called you guys here. I know when Friday comes and Mr Peters and his so-called family are on the street, you and Tia are going to be on my back saying that is not how we do things. I asked Nathan to join us because he is part of the family and because our business affects his children's trust funds." Lisa paused to gather her thoughts, then with growing momentum, she resumed her presentation. "We ought to learn something from the banks and the way they handle outstanding debt payments. Since you will not let me foreclose on any of our clients, I had to think hard about what to do with the Peters family. I didn't have time to offer the Peters options like you usually do, Mother, because of my exam schedule and also because of the time away in Holland. However, Mr Peters and his family have been treated in the same way as all our other clients. We hold the mortgages of his two brothers and their sister. The sister's loan is up to date. Kevin Peters and his brothers, though, are all behind in their payments. So . . . on Friday, the Peters brothers will be served with eviction notices at the same time."

Tia tightly clasped Nathan's hand. Inwardly, Nathan chuckled. He could not have wished for a better revenge. He glanced at his mother-in-law, assessing her reaction to Lisa's news. Still, it did not take all of the hurt away knowing that the Peters were getting exactly what they deserved.

"I don't like paying lawyers to do my dirty work for me," Lisa told them.

"Whatever do you mean, Lisa?" Nathan asked, slightly affronted by her apparent slight of his profession.

Lisa stood up and passed another file to her mother. Naana read it and passed it to Nathan. Nathan examined the papers, thinking, "So Lisa is going to foreclose on the Peters. How will she manage that without the lawyers processing the paperwork?" Then his expression changed. In fact, Tia and Naana had wondered the same thing, too. Lisa studied their body language, saw them stiffen with discomfort as they read the documents.

"Look, Mother, you're still the President of this company, and I will abide by your policies, even if I don't fully agree with them, but I'd like your approval on this file."

"So, did you find the Peters another lender?" Nathan asked.

Lisa smiled as Naana responded, "Well, that's not really how we do things here, but I can see that Lisa has thoroughly investigated our options and I give her my full support on whatever she decides to do." Naana turned toward Nathan and Tia with tears in her eyes. She couldn't hold them back any longer after everything Kevin Peters had done to Tia. She never suspected that her own company held the loans of all of his family members. It was ironic. The man who beat and attempted to rape her daughter is finally going to know what pain is. Tia is also thinking along the same lines as her mother, while sobbing quietly on her husband's shoulders.

"Okay. I want to know why you two are so emotional about this," Lisa demanded.

"I assure you, Lisa. There is nothing much to tell."

Lisa moves to the window and looks out at the city below. "I have not found the Peters a new lender as you might think. That would imply a decision on our part to foreclose. I don't want their homes or businesses. We always have a clause in our loan agreements with all our clients that protect us should we need to recover our loans. In fact, we ask clients to initial the clause so they are aware of it. I decided to exercise the clause and sold their loans to another company. That company has decided to foreclose on the Peters, and they will lose their homes on Friday. Our company is free of the association. I dislike being put in the position of listening to the falsehoods of people I love. You want to keep secrets? Fine! You do that! But when someone comes into our homes to hurt one of use, Mother, then we will need all our strength to hit back!"

Lisa paused, out of breath.

"Mother, do you remember giving me a little investigative task while we were in Holland?" Her mother nodded. "And do you remember me wondering why such drastic measures were required?" Her mother nodded again. "You refused to tell me. Well, the people I hired to do what you wanted . . ." Lisa paused. She sat on the edge of the table. "I'm just surprised that you would sit there and let Kevin Peters get away with what he did to my sister! Nathan, I don't take kindly to people who go out of their way to hurt my family!" Lisa exclaimed.

Nathan was encouraged by Lisa's attitude. She smiled and sighed.

"Okay. Now, listen to me very carefully all of you. Kevin Peters is going to regret the day he put his hands on my sister and tried to rape her." Lisa's tone cut through them like thunder. None of them could respond.

"Mother, next time you want to hide something from me, don't put it on your computer! I'm sorry, but your little pulp fiction-style revenge just wasn't good enough for me. You have to have more money to build an army. A son of a bitch like Kevin Peters is not going to get away from what he did to Tia! The mother-fucker is going to get a lot more than a fuck up the ass. Did you guys really think you could hide this from me?" Lisa turned to Tia. "You know how close you and Brooke and Kate are, but they are not family." Lisa turned to Nathan. "That fucking busy-body will come after your child."

"What are you talking about, Lisa?" asked Tia.

"You all know what I'm talking about! Mother is very kind and sentimental—too kind. The threat that Kevin Peters presents is extremely serious. I can't emphasize that enough. I'm surprised at you, Nathan, that you would be so relaxed about this animal. I want him and his family far away from my sister and the children at all costs!"

"What makes you think that I don't?" responds Nathan coolly.

Lisa huffed in exasperation. Tia and Nathan continued to hold each other's hands as Lisa described what she had done to prevent Kevin Peters from getting close to the family. Tia is sobbing, while Nathan is sucking the inside of his cheek, contemplating his feelings about Kevin Peters getting his just desserts.

"I strongly advise everyone here not to discuss this meeting with anyone outside this room." Lisa affectionately put her arm around Tia. "I know you have your own family now, Tia. Brooke and Kate are always there for you, but I want you to know that I am always here, too, if you and the children need me." Lisa pulls Tia into her arms and hugs here. When they let go of each other, Lisa says, "You are a lot stronger than you think, Princess. You are going to be alright."

Lisa handed Tia a bottle of water. As she sipped the water, Tia thought, "I can't believe my little sister has grown up to be this strong, powerful woman."

Lisa spoke to the group again. "Kevin Peters is finished, and just as well, too. A so-called lawyer who can't read a simple loan agreement, and who behaves brutally toward my sisters, is an idiot. Mother has built a dynasty that I will protect at whatever cost. I especially don't want the Peters family perceiving us as their enemy. Rather, we are their savior."

Lisa Sharp is not a forgiving person. She thought of her family's safety and how best to protect them all. Lisa is not done with Kevin Peters. Her sister, brother-in-law, and mother may feel that justice has been served, but in the course of her investigations, Lisa has learned that there is someone else who wants to bring down Kevin Peters. This individual wants to take him down hard. Lisa has learned that Kevin plans to go into African politics.

"Kevin Peters will regret the day he assaulted my sister." Everyone glance at one another, wondering what is about to be revealed. "I'd like to see him try to recover from the storm he and his brothers are about to face." Lisa laughed derisively. Suddenly, she sat down and changed the subject. "Anthony wants to have a surprise birthday party for Jackie. It's all arranged to take place at one of my clubs next weekend. I won't be able to join you for lunch tomorrow because I have some things to do."

Tia asked, eyebrows raised, "Do you own a night club?"

"Yep! Your sister is a little Peter Stringfellow in the making!" her mother confirmed proudly.

Jackie and Jaden entered the room. Everyone hardly recognized Jackie with her new hair cut and make-over.

"Sweetie, I love your hair!" exclaimed Tia as she hugs her sister-in-law. "You know, I can't believe how grown up you girls all are."

Naana spoke to Jackie, "Anthony and I are taking the children to the London Zoo at Regent Park. Do you want to come, too?"

Jackie beamed, "Oh, yes! We can go to the famous London toy store after."

"With six children in the toy store?" Naana asked doubtfully.

"Mother, you mean seven children," said Lisa as she hit Jackie on the head with one of her files.

"Good luck getting Jacks out of Hamley's, never mind BJ and the rest of the children," Lisa warned her mother. They all laughed. Jackie protested that she was not that terrible in the toy store.

Nathan responded, "No. You're worse!"

Tia stood up to leave, and Nathan followed her signal by gathering up the files and passing them back to Lisa. As they walked to their car, Jaden caught up with them. "Sorry guys," he said. "I thought it was you who put Lisa up to taking action against the Peters family. Your sister is very good at what she does. Very disciplined for her age."

Nathan didn't want to say anything, even though he loved Lisa's idea of revenge. "The kid is nothing like Tia. Thank God," Nathan thought. Tia had her own private thoughts about her little sister. She was reminded of one of the characters she had created for her new show.

Jaden pointed out Carlton Stadium to Nathan, "That where we are coming this afternoon to watch the game."

A long-time friend of Tia and Kate, Ashton Wentworth is now the Head Coach of Chelsea FC. He sent tickets to Nathan and Tia, inviting them to see a game while they are visiting England. Since Sarah lives next door to Ashton and his wife Lock, Tia will stop by their house to thank them for the football tickets before she meets Amy to finish up some work. She also wants to invite them to dinner.

"I just found out that my sister owns a night club. Want to go check it out?" Tia asks everyone.

"Why not? The twins are spending the weekend with my mum. Naana has your boys, Kate, as well as Trey and Jayzel. We can pick up the children when we go to dinner at the Sharp's on Sunday," Brooke suggested.

"Then, it's settled," said Tia. "I will call Lisa and let her know we're coming."

As Lisa hung up the phone, she said, "That was Tia. They want to hang out tonight. I'm leaving to visit the clubs to make sure everything is alright. I'll reserve a table for them. Lock and Ashton Wentworth will be joining them, so I'll have to make sure security is very tight. I will see you later, after I pick up Vidal, and then we'll come by the house to pick up you, Jacks." Lisa grabbed her bag and headed toward the front door.

Jackie asked, "Who are the Wentworth's?"

"Ashton is a footballer. Lock Washington is his wife. They are friends of Tia's and they happen to live next door to Brooke's mom. The press can't get enough of them because they are so chic. I have to make sure they will have their privacy and enjoy themselves tonight," Lisa explains.

Naana remarked, "Your father is not happy that you left home, Sweetheart. Neither am I with Vidal moving to London. I don't want you two kids living together. I want to discuss Chance with you, when you have time. Lisa you can't run from things." Naana made her feelings known.

"You are so old-fashioned mother. You need not worry. Vidal and I are not doing anything of the sort. I will be at home once I'm done with my exams. I will be leaving home one day anyway, and Vidal and I will be living together as man and wife, so you and Papa need to get used to that idea. There is nothing going on between Chance and I. I need him to do what is needed. He understands what we are dealing with. I will not worry about anything, mother. It's done." Lisa kissed her mother and Jackie and drove off.

Naana smiles. She is so proud of her daughter. By the time they reach the Sharp home, Bobby and Anthony are ready with all the children. They drive to the Victoria and Albert Museum. Afterward, they got on a London Sightseeing bus tour which took them to the Tower of London, Tower Bridge, Millennium Bridge, and Big Ben. The children didn't really like visiting all the famous London landmarks, but Jackie and Anthony did. They had a fish and chips lunch before going to London Zoo. On their return, they went to Hamley's toy store. Before they went into the shop, Naana told the children they were allowed two toys each. Jackie, just like Lisa and Nathan, had told Naana that morning that she would be the difficult one to get out of the store. Anthony loves the fact that his little girl is going to be a Doctor in a few months but still likes toys. Vidal is in the house with Lisa and Corey Jeffrey, the police detective working for Lisa at the club. He came by to ask Jackie out on a date. Politely, Corey asks

Anthony whether he minds if he takes Jackie out tonight? Bobby thought he was brave and well mannered. Anthony and Naana both teased him and said "Well, we really don't know anything about you, but we find you in the house alone with Lisa and now you want to take Jackie out on a date." Corey's white face turned even whiter as they started to laugh at his discomfort. When he stuttered, "I am not—I mean, we are not completely alone in the house. Lisa's boyfriend is around here somewhere. I work for Lisa. She's my boss. I wouldn't dream of—" Lisa looked at her parents and Anthony and they all started to laugh. Jackie liked him, but she was worried about Lisa's reaction if she dated him.

"Will you give us a minute, Corey?" Jackie asked.

Corey nodded.

Lisa was upstairs in her old bedroom, gathering more stuff to take to her loft. Jackie closed the door and gave her long kiss, whispering, "I miss you." They kissed again. Jackie couldn't bring herself to tell Lisa about Corey's date.

"So where is Corey taking you tonight?"

"I didn't exactly say I would go. I'm supposed to be going out with Patrick tonight. He's making a special trip to London this weekend. I can't go out with Corey."

"Do you fancy Corey?" Lisa asked.

"I am going home next week, Lisa. Did you forget? I also made a date with Patrick. He had something to do in Holland this week, which is why he didn't come with Vidal. I don't want to hurt anyone's feelings."

Lisa chuckled, "I didn't forget about you going home—and it is only one dinner with Corey." Lisa opened the door and walked downstairs with Jackie.

"Hey, Corey! Jackie will go out with you tonight. You can pick her up from my loft. Just don't do anything I would do!" and she winked at them.

"Are you sure, Jackie?" Corey asked.

Jackie smiled in reply.

"For God's sake, Jacks, put the man out of his misery," Lisa yelled.

"Sounds good, Corey," Jackie said. "Thank you."

After the football game, Jason and Jaden took Nathan to the pub for lunch. Nathan had immensely enjoyed the game. "Thank you so much, guys. I don't know how Tia and I would have coped without your support the last few weeks."

"I wouldn't worry, mate, about Kevin. By the time Lisa is done with him, he will wish he knew God," Jaden remarked.

Jason hinted, "You know the kid knows the mafia, right?"

"Come on, fellows!" Nathan joshed with his pals.

"No shit! He's right." Jaden affirmed. "About two years ago a lad from Lisa's college went on a date with her and the lad tried it on after the date. Rumor has it that Lisa got some of her thugs to beat him up badly. Jason said his wife told him."

"You know . . . Her club manager used to work for Frank Bruno," Jaden told him.

"No, way!" Jason exclaimed.

Nathan laughed. "Listen, Lisa is not your average rich brat. She is very intelligent. Besides, I think my mother-in-law is the lady mafia, not the kid. I thank God that she did not blow my dick off when I fooled around on Tia."

Jaden was laughing out of control. The girls were late meeting them in the club. Jason, Nathan, and Jaden felt like old men getting in line to enter Club Vibe. When they got to the front of the line, the bouncer said, "I can't let you in."

Jaden objected, "But we know Lisa."

The big black man chuckled and said, "Yeah? My mum knows the Queen."

Nathan called Tia who had just pulled into the parking lot with Liz Starr and Amy Hall. The bouncer recognized Liz from *The Saga* and said, "Miss Starr can go in, but the rest of you just piss off."

Lisa steps out of her Italian spots car with Vidal just in time to see the bouncer turn away her relatives from the club. She yelled out to the bouncer, "Hey, Jordan! Mate, you put your hands on my sister again, I'll blow your fucking dick off, mate." She winked.

"Sorry, boss lady," the bouncer said as he let them inside.

Jaden leaned over and whispered into Nathan's ear, "See? I told you so. Now do you believe me?"

They were escorted by Simon to the VIP lounge in the upper level of the club. Ashton and Lock were already there with her brother, Freedom, and his new wife, Sharon, who is also a doctor. Lisa disappeared somewhere and came back with three of the hostesses.

"Listen, guys. Whatever you need, these women will get it for you."

"Where's Jackie?" asked Nathan.

"Jacks is on a date with Corey. They'll meet us here later," replied Lisa. "Enjoy your evening!"

"You're not going to join us?" Tia asked.

"I'm having dinner with Vidal at the penthouse. We'll come down later to meet Jacks and Corey."

"You have a penthouse?" Tia asked incredulously.

Lisa smiled, ignoring Tia's prying question. "We have a new chef. She is on her way to see you. Oh! Here she is. Debbie, this is my sister, Tia." Tia shook Debbie's hand.

"Your dinner is ready, Miss Sharp," Debbie said.

"Call me Lisa." Lisa took Debbie aside and asked her to make sure that Tia and her friends have a great time at the club. "Make sure they are well pampered. You know . . . the works: lots of your special appetizers, beautiful cocktails, shooters, whatever they want. Let's show them a really good time!"

Lisa hugs Tia and leaves the party. Tia watches Lisa as she walks through the club, marveling how she accepts people's good wishes like a celebrity. People Lisa couldn't possibly know were approaching her to shake her hand; some hugged and kissed her, too.

"You know, your sister is a star in the making," Liz observed. Amy raised her glass, "I second that. She definitely has the 'it' factor."

Tia threw back her head and laughed heartily in agreement. "Yes," she thought. "Lisa does have that 'it' factor, for sure."

They all enjoyed a lovely meal. Tia did not eat much and Nathan watched her pick at her food, worrying about her health, worrying about a possible relapse. Her mother seems to think that the worst is over, but Nathan is not too sure. He took Tia to the dance floor along side of Ashton and Lock. As they danced, he asked, "Baby, are you okay?"

"I am, now that I have my husband all to myself. I am anxious to go home, baby," she confessed.

"Well, we leave a day after Jackie's birthday. How about that?" Nathan reminded her. Nathan saw a good-looking white boy dancing with Jackie. Nathan couldn't help getting upset. "She is too young to be out this late with a guy," he said.

"Oh, baby! Leave them alone. It's nice to see Jackie letting her hair down."

Nathan couldn't stop looking at them. Lisa and Vidal joined them on the dance floor. Tia and Nathan watched them dance and kiss. Nathan commented, "My God, these kids are hornier than we are!"

Tia laughed. Nathan was happy to see Tia relaxed and enjoying herself. "I am going to tell that boy if his hands drop any lower to my sister's ass, I will break every British bone in his body," Nathan threatened.

"How about we go say good-night and you can take me home," Tia said with a smile. She began kissing him.

"I'm sorry, baby. I'm going to take Jackie home. I'm not leaving my sister here with all these horny boys. I know what they want, believe me, baby," Nathan told Tia.

"They are having a good time. Baby, please. Can't you just let her be for one night?" Tia pleaded.

"No!" Nathan left and got Jackie just like he said he would.

"You know darling, when my Jayzel grows up, I'll not have to worry about her dates," Brooke said, chuckling.

Tia looked at Jason and they both laughed. It was nice just the four of them without the children at Brooke and Jason's home. At the back of the house, Tia and Brooke sat in the hot tub drinking wine just like they used to do when they were teenagers. Jason was telling Nathan how they have not changed since the day he first met all of them.

"I knew they were close when I met you guys at the airport years ago. It's amazing looking at them now as parents. Eh?" Nathan said softly before he turned his attention back to the TV. This has been an experience that Nathan is not going to forget. He wishes his mother could have lived to see the family that he has married into. Heather Carter thought they were wonderful, when she met them on his first wedding to Tia. He turned and looked at Brooke and Tia. This time Tia also turned and their eyes held each other. Tia knew what Nathan was thinking about at that moment. Tia has been thinking about her late mother-in-law too. Heather Carter was a romantic lady who thought that Nathan and Tia were pure magic together. Tia sighed and told Brooke that it is going to be difficult going back to Canada this time.

"It's been good having all of us together," Tia said.

Brooke assures her that it will be okay. "Jason and I plan to spend the summer with you folks. Who knows? Kate and Jaden may come, too. If you get homesick, Tia, you can always come home."

"Hear, hear!" exclaimed Tia as she raised her glass.

Chapter 17

Friday and Saturday nights are very busy at the club. Both the bar and the kitchen are busy with wait staff passing in and out with orders for their tables. Lisa keeps a watchful eye on the operations of the club. She walks through, pausing to ask customers how the appetisers and finger-foods taste, chats with regulars and walks behind the bar to ensure an adequate stock of liquors and liqueurs. By the time she completes her rounds, it takes about ninety minutes. She returns to her penthouse after saying good-night to Tia, Nathan and the Wentworth's. Jackie intends to spend the night with Tia and Nathan, so Lisa reviews some files on her desk before turning in herself. Earlier that evening, Corey had brought Lisa a file, which she now read with interest. She smiled to herself. Later, as Lisa got into her car, she saw the new chef getting into a taxi. Lisa paid off the taxi driver saying, "I'll drive you home, Debbie."

"No, Miss Sharp. It's okay."

"Miss Sharp, hmmm?" Lisa opens her car door for her. Debbie thanks her as Lisa turns to inquire where she is going. Debbie gets into the car, leans her head against the headrest and closes her eyes. It is so dark, Lisa can not see Debbie's expression. Lisa asks, "If you don't have any plans, would you like to spend the rest of the night with me?"

"I have to work in the morning." Debbie says, excusing herself.

"I happen to know you're not working until Thursday. I'll take you home now, but if you change your mind, call me." Lisa shifts the car into drive and pulls away from the curb. Five minutes later her cell phone rings. "Please excuse me," Lisa says to Debbie, thinking it might be Jacks. It is Debbie.

"Well, you did say I should call."

Lisa glances at herself in the rear view mirror and smiles as she puts her foot down on the gas.

All of Lisa's friends, lovers and acquaintances love the loft, and Debbie is no exception as the space has significant caché. Telling Debbie to make herself comfortable, Lisa disappears into the kitchen for a moment. She locates a bottle of wine and two glasses. Behind her, Debbie follows, slipping her hands around Lisa's waist and kissing the back of her neck. It feels so good. Lisa places the bottle of wine on the counter and turns her head slightly to kiss Debbie softly on the cheek. Lisa pours some wine for her, and together, they walk to far end of the loft where Lisa has a hot tub and a flat screen television mounted on the wall. A gas fire place adds ambiance and a pile of soft towels languish on a nearby chair. Lisa undresses Debbie and tells her to get in the tub. Debbie smiles, and tries to say something but Lisa presses her fingertips against Debbie's lips, "Please, get in." Debbie dips her toes and the water feels just right. In less than five minutes she is fully relaxed, giving up herself to the pleasure of the hot water. Lisa sits in the chair drinking water and watching her. Debbie asks, "Are you going to join me in here?"

Lisa smiles, "No, I don't like hot tubs very much."

Frowning, Debbie asks, "Well, then, why did you buy one?"

Lisa says, "It kinda came with the loft."

Debbie wishes that Lisa could get in the tub with her because she thinks it will allow for a more relaxed conversation and she is just dying to ask about Priscilla, to get all the 'dirt' on the girl, but there's plenty of time to snoop on that topic. Lisa Sharp is not what she expected. Debbie tries not to think.

"What are you thinking about?" Lisa asks softly.

Debbie sighs deeply and closes her eyes, thinking, "now or never." She stands up slowly. Lisa meets her with a gigantic bath towel. While drying Debbie, Lisa asks "Are you okay?" Slipping on a bath robe, Debbie does not immediately respond. She realizes she is in a different world now.

"Where were you?" asks Lisa gently. Debbie simply smiles.

"Come on, I'll show the spare room. You must be tired—unless you want to stay up and watch some movies with me?"

Debbie pulls her hands gently. Smirking, she says, "You brought me here to spend the night in your spare room?"

"What is it you want from me?" Lisa asks.

Lisa retreats into her office. Debbie follows. "Look, if this is one of your rich-girl games that you like to play, I don't like it, Lisa."

"What *do* you like Miss Read? . . . Gina Read is your real name, isn't it?" Lisa coldly flings out the accusation.

Gina closes her eyes and realizes that possibly Lisa's mom must have told her secret. Debbie holds her breath for a second. Gina Read, aged twenty-six, is a member of the Leeds police force. She grew up in London, left home at sixteen, leaving behind a younger sister and a grandmother. Gina joined the Police Academy when she was just eighteen. In the intervening years, she has worked her way through the ranks to Detective Sergeant. Because family life was harsh, Gina has not often kept in touch with her younger sister or her grandmother, so she was devastated to hear the news of her younger sister's death by drug overdose. For two days, Gina stayed in her small townhouse and drank whiskey. When the bottle was empty and there was nothing left in the fridge to eat and the grieving was over, Gina did not recognize herself when she looked in the mirror. The sister to whom she had barely spoken to over the last ten years was all she could think about. Gina was even more upset when the autopsy revealed that Dana had been almost four months pregnant at the time of her death. Nevertheless, Gina could not bring herself to attend her sister's funeral, but Dana's memory is never far from Gina's mind. She wants to put the person behind bars who sold her sister the drugs that killed her. Gina tried to investigate her sister's death, but as she became immersed in the case, she realized she needed more time than the little bits she could get during the work day—a few minutes at lunch, a working coffee break, just didn't allow for progress on Dana's case. Gina decided to take a leave of absence from work and moved back to London. That was five months ago. Coming back to the present, the loft is suddenly colder than an iceberg. The only sound is Alicia Keys voice on the CD player. Lisa sat behind her desk and stared at Gina, loathing in her eyes. Finally, Lisa says, "Dana was my only friend since primary school. We were like sisters . . . I abandoned her when she started taking drugs two years ago. I refused to have anything to do with her. Little did I know that she was buying more drugs with the money I kept giving her. I was in Amsterdam, by a poolside watching . . .," she paused. "Watching my girlfriend's stomach being pumped."

Gina is in tears as she listens to Lisa. Gina couldn't look at her. She has been wrong about Lisa.

"Once again . . . drugs have found their way into my life. I stood there helplessly, not knowing someone that I loved was already dead. While Priscilla was being transferred to the hospital, your grandmother called and told me that Dana had died."

Lisa gets up and leaves her office. She can't hold back her tears. Lisa didn't cry when Dana died, so her tears for Dana have been bottled up and deeply buried in her heart of hearts. When Chance called and revealed Debbie's actual identity, Lisa felt like a truck had hit her. She told Corey to confirm Chance's information, but instinctively Lisa knew that Debbie, her new chef, was actually Dana's sister. Lisa's whole body broke down when Corey called to confirm the ID. She shook, thinking about the passionate afternoon she had just spent with Debbie.

"Dana's sister?" she asked Corey. Of course, it all made sense. Corey would know Gina was a police detective and deliberately failed to mention the fact when she was hired. Lisa dislikes people lying to her. She also dislikes feeling a fool, so she spent the rest of the afternoon doing her own investigation on Gina Read. Since Lisa felt she could not trust her own employees, she turned to her mother and confided the situation. Naana Konadu-Sharp admitted that Gina was working undercover for her to ensure the drug trafficking in Lisa's clubs got cleaned up.

"Lisa, I am tremendously proud of you, but your carelessness over your romance with Priscilla has caused a lot of problems. I don't like scandal, and you certainly don't need me to tell you about the dangers of drugs. You must not reveal Gina's identity to Simon or to anyone else. I want your relationship with Priscilla to end. You're twenty-two years old, an adult. I do not support this silly romance because she will put your life in danger. I, for one, cannot afford to lose you, darling." Naana firmly expressed her expectations of Lisa's behavior.

By the time Gina comes into the living room, Lisa has calmed down. "Are you okay, Gina?"

Gina is surprised by Lisa's sudden attitude change and her apparent concern.

"I am. Lisa, there are some things I need to explain to you."

"It's not necessary. My mother already told me this evening," Lisa is enraged now. "The spare room is the second door on the left. I am going to bed."

Gina grabbed Lisa's waist. "Lisa, when I met you the first night at the club, I hadn't even spoken to your mother. She called me on Christmas

Eve with her concerns about your club. I didn't know who you were until Simon introduced us. And by then, it was too late."

Lisa is not buying it. "Too late for what? Before we slept together the first time? The second time? I have lost count! Well, was it a good fuck—Gina or Debbie, whichever one I fucked? Was it part of your job to sleep with me?"

Gina dropped her hands. "How can you say that, Lisa? I didn't mean to lie to you. Things just happen." She paused.

Lisa was beside herself with anger. "Things just happened? Not with me, they don't!"

Lisa turned and with two strides, crossed the hall into her own room. Gina stood on the spot in stunned silence. She hardly knew what to do next. Meanwhile, Lisa had retreated to the shower in her en suite bathroom. Gina, taking a daring decision, followed Lisa into the shower. They exchanged more bitter words when suddenly Gina took Lisa's face in both hands and kissed her fully on the lips, preventing any further sass. It wasn't long before they were locked in a passionate kiss under the shower. Lisa is not in control anymore. Gina's fingers are exploring her body, touching her in places Lisa usually touches other girls.

"Stop!" exclaims Lisa.

"You're not enjoying this?" Gina asks.

"I hate you." Lisa says softly to her, breathlessly.

Gina smiles. "I hate you too, Lisa."

Lisa kisses her again, smothering Gina with kisses. Gina responded unreservedly. Lisa could tell that Gina Read was experienced. She intuitively knew what Lisa wanted, knew how to please a woman just like Lisa did. Gina's sexual appetite was prodigious and quite a match for Lisa. Afterward, Lisa lay breathlessly on top of Gina, whose fingers were still inside Lisa.

Lisa confides, "You know, I haven't cried for Dana until today."

"Why not, Lisa?" Gina asks softly.

"Growing up, Chance and Dana were my only friends. She was wild at times. I was devastated when Chance and I broke up. We have always known that we are soul mates. We grew up liking—," she paused. "When we went to college, I decided that I wanted to take over my mother's business someday. It comes with a lot more responsibilities than people think. I had lost my first love and I wasn't going to lose that, too. I go to school and I have worked full-time since I was sixteen," Lisa says.

"Wow! It must be hard work," Gina teases.

"It's not as easy as it looks. Everything that I have, I have worked my butt off for it. Sure, my mother has opened doors for me to which most people my age don't have access to. But I still have to work just as hard to get ahead. Dana didn't understand. She used to until she began taking drugs and no, she was not into girls and we never slept together. I loved her. I *loved* her."

"When did you learn about my sister's drug habit?"

"When she failed her exams during our sophomore year. I found out that she owed some thugs a large amount of money. I sent Simon to go and pay them off. A few days later, she came to my parents home and tried taking drugs in the house . . . so I kicked her out."

"Did you talk to her after that?"

"No, every now and then she would call and ask for money. I told Simon to find something for her to do at the club. I never used to go to the clubs like I do now. But I was told by Simon that she was good at whatever it is that she does. I was shocked and ashamed when she died . . . That's the only reason why I've put up with Priscilla and her foolishness."

"So what do you plan to do about your so-called ex?"

"There is nothing I can do about her. I put her in a rehab home last summer and she still has not changed. I'm not going to get fired for her. My mother is reasonable, but I work for her and she will not tolerate very much of Priscilla's shenanigans. This much I know. Not many people my age like to work with their family. I do. I have a very good working relationship with my mother. She knows how much Priscilla means to me. I cannot disobey my mother, either. My problem is I'd be walking away from someone I love who needs me, too. It's just not that simple. Our relationship is over, but I can't stop worrying about Priscilla. I just don't know what to do for her at this point, but I won't lose my business the way I lost Chance for her. I just can't."

Gina thought she had Lisa all figured out. It broke her heart hearing Lisa talk and it is obvious she still loves Priscilla and this Chance person very much. Gina wondered what really happened.

"Are you in love with them?"

"Not in love, I do love her, but not in love . . . but lust. Chance has my—" Lisa stopped and rolled the bracelet on her wrist and smiled.

"In lust . . .ha? But love her . . . You are not going tell me about this Chance. Are you in love with your man or just to please your mother?"

"Did my mother ask you to ask me this?"

"Nope! I'm just being nosy."

"Somewhat. We are good for one another, Vidal and I. As you can see, I also . . . um . . . well, I do enjoy being with beautiful women, too. Priscilla and I have not made love since Dana died. I kissed her a few weeks ago in Holland. The next day I left and came to England. She was so pissed off because she had helped my mother plan a New Year's Eve party that I didn't attend. I guess things changed when I slept with . . . There's no going back now. Priscilla and I are done. My mom is right. She will put my life in danger. I can't . . .," Lisa sighs, trailing off lost in her own thoughts.

Gina tried to ask her more questions, but Lisa began kissing her and making love to her again. Inevitably, she found herself weakening to Lisa's touches and kisses. Gina lost all sense of the reality of the consequences of sleeping with Lisa Sharp. Lisa Sharp is one naughty girl when it comes to seduction. Gina Read loved every bit of the excitement of Lisa's lovemaking. Lisa massaged her entire body and traced her fingers on Gina's body. Lisa let her suck on her fingers every now and then as she watched Gina gasps, moans and begs Lisa not to stop. Lisa didn't want to stop. She parted Gina's legs and used her tongue to create stream everywhere she touched. Gina dug her fingers in Lisa's back. When the orgasm came, Lisa held Gina, stroking her body, helping her come down from the adrenaline high.

Her phone begin ringing. Gina asks, "Why don't you pick up your phone?"

Lisa smiles, "Is there anything you want? Any little thing I can get you?"

"I'm fine," replies Gina. "Please, answer your phone."

Gina picks up the phone and hands it to Lisa, who refuses to take it. Instead, she begins to nibble on Gina's neck and she is about to hang up when she hears Priscilla's voice on the voice mail crying and sounding very distressed. Lisa closes her eyes, "I'm sorry, Gina."

Gina disentangles herself, "Well, I do need to use the bathroom."

Lisa lets go of her, pointing the direction to the bathroom.

"You look totally exhausted. Why don't you call her and see if she is okay?" Gina asks.

Lisa is startled by the tone of concern for Priscilla in Gina's voice. Lisa bites her bottom lip thinking about how to respond. Lisa puts her arm around Gina's neck and studies her for a long moment.

"Are you always this reasonable, or do you not care that we just made incredible love after love, we are still in bed, and I'm fighting every urge in me not to kiss you. It's inappropriate for me to be here with you and talking to my ex-lover on the phone, don't you think?"

"Bollocks! She needs you, Lisa. Like it or not, you are worried about her, so why don't you call her and put both our minds to rest so we can both relax."

Lisa put her lips on her neck and softly nuzzles. "I need you, too," Lisa whispers. Gina pulls away and runs to the bathroom. Lisa wraps a bathrobe around herself, and walks barefoot to the kitchen to make tuna sandwiches. She grabs two bottles of water with a yogurt and heads back to the bedroom. Gina is in bed checking her messages on her cell phone. She takes a sandwich from Lisa and bites it. "Mmm . . . this is delicious. Mmm." She puts down her cell phone and asks if Lisa is okay.

"I will be if you stop eating my sandwiches! Come, I'll show you the kitchen, so you can make your own," Lisa chuckles.

"Wow! So it's going to be like that, ha? What happened to you, your ex upset you? I mean, is she all right?"

"I don't know,why? . . . You fancy a threesome?"

Gina thought Lisa has some nerve. She chuckles. "Thanks, I'll pass on that. I'm too old for a threesome. One of you is quite enough." Gina takes the sandwiches away from Lisa because Lisa is laughing hysterically. She stops and drinks some water, "you are funny, Gina. I like that, but don't lie to me again if you want to keep seeing me."

Gina leaves the bed and go to stand by the window with her back turned to Lisa.

"I don't like it when people I care about lie to me. I don't like games—only the romantic kinds, Lisa."

Lisa is standing behind her when she turns. "I want to play all kinds of romantic games with you if you let me. Promise that there will be no more talks about the past, or about present relationships?" Lisa was insistent. Gina threw her arms around her as Lisa hugged and caressed her back. It was nice for both of them to stand and hold each other. Lisa is not thinking of Jackie, or of Vidal or Priscilla, and not even of Chance at that very moment. All she wanted was Gina Read. Being Dana's older sister has not changed anything. They walk back to bed where they kiss tenderly. Gina, too, is not thinking of anything at that moment but the feel of Lisa's touch on her skin, the softness of her lips and the way she kisses. It is a new kind of excitement for Gina as they cuddle up together and sleep.

Chapter 18

Just like Lisa said, Kevin Peters and his two brothers had their homes repossessed for non-payment by order of the mortgage company that holds their loans. It was ironic: when the bailiffs arrived at Paul's house with the eviction order, Kevin was there and read the eviction notice.

"Why didn't you respond to the mortgage company?" Kevin asked Paul.

"I sent all of the letters to you, Kevin," he replied. "When I got the last one that said if the arrears are not paid within forty day, they would repossess my house, I sent you the letter. You told me that you would sort it out. That was two weeks before Christmas."

Meanwhile, on the other side of town, Kevin's middle brother, Aaron, has also suffered the same fate by the same mortgage company. Aaron's wife drove to Kevin's law office to ask for help because Aaron was out of town. She found bailiffs at Kevin's office, closing the premises.

"No! It cannot be!" exclaimed Kevin. "I have just two months of mortgage payments left on the business and on my house."

At that moment, Kevin's wife called to tell him their home has been repossessed by the mortgage company.

Kevin laughed, and said, "I think someone is playing games with us. We can't all have a repossession order against us and get evicted all on the same day. It takes time. The mortgage company will have to petition the court and the mortgage company's solicitors will send letters to us pending the foreclosures, guys."

The bailiffs asked them to leave, threatening to call the police. Kevin felt insulted and replied, "Enough is enough! This isn't funny!" Kevin lightly shoved the guy on his left shoulder. The guy lost his balance and fell. Kevin, thinking it all darkly funny, stood there laughing while his brother Paul looked on with dismay. They all thought it was funny when the guy fell, but within minutes the police had arrived, who arrested and charged both Kevin and Paul with assaulting an officer of the law. Kevin used his phone call to contact Ola, who informed him that it was not a joke. In fact, Paul's and Aaron's homes were also foreclosed, and that his wife and daughter were staying with his in-laws. Ola informed him that his wife had asked Kevin's former boss to arrange bail for them.

"No, don't use him," said Kevin. "There a lawyer I know who is very good, Jennifer Haywood," he told Ola. "Give her a call."

Jennifer Haywood is the same lawyer that Nathan Carter used, a few years back, to put Jason Gray in jail for allegedly raping Brooke. Jennifer was having lunch with Nathan and his mother-in-law at one of Lisa's clubs when Ola Peters called her cell phone. Jennifer assured Ola that she would have her brothers out of jail in no time.

Miss Haywood turned to Nathan, "You'll not believe who is in jail, requesting my service."

Nathan raised his eyebrows and frowning, asked, "Who?"

"Our friend, Mr Kevin Peters," Miss Haywood said with a smirk.

Nathan turned to his mother-in-law and spoke in French, "No, I thought Lisa said she was not going to strike against the Peters just yet, mother?"

"Are you not going to ask why Mr Peters and his brother are in jail?" asked Miss Haywood.

Nathan was speechless.

"Mr Peters and two of his brothers had their homes foreclosed this morning. They allegedly assaulted one of the bailiffs. Well, it's the weekend. It looks like our friend is going to spend the weekend in the nick," Jennifer says sardonically before leaving.

Jennifer Haywood arrived at the Collingwood Police Station with Ola Peters to see her brothers. Miss Haywood informed them that she was able to get bail and that they would be released in a couple of hours.

Kevin thanked her and announced, "I'm going to file a law suit against the mortgage company."

"I advise you not to do that, Mr Peters, since you don't have solid grounds for a law suit," interjected Miss Haywood. "Mr Peters, I spent half of the day with your sister looking at your mortgages. The mortgage company has been requesting their money from your brother, from you and from your wife for the last six months."

"That's not possible," Kevin insisted.

"It is, indeed. Your first lender requested a meeting with you and your brothers, but you declined and went with a different lender." Jennifer showed Kevin the letters.

Kevin took the papers and read through them. Kevin said, "But all our mortgages were obtained from African Mortgage Funds."

"No. That's not so. Last summer your wife said we should switch because the rate was too high. Remember?" said Paul.

"No. I don't remember," Kevin snapped at his brother. "It still doesn't add up that they would send all these letters over the past last six months and I never saw one of them until today."

Ola bent her head down and she and the lawyer exchanged glances.

Kevin, exasperated, demanded, "Well . . . What is it?"

"Your wife did, Kevin. In fact, she confirmed that you and your brothers chose to ignore the demands of your lenders."

"She is a liar!" Kevin exclaimed.

"Well, that is something for you to discuss with your wife. My work here is done," Miss Haywood said as she stood up. "I'll send you my bill."

Ola told them all to calm down. "Let's get you guys out of jail before we talk about everything."

Ola waited outside in her car while Kevin and Paul collected their personal property and were given a court date. As soon as Kevin and his brother stepped outside there was an army of photographers and news cameras on them.

The first word Kevin could hear was, "Is it true that you assaulted your pregnant wife and busted up your television before leaving her and your child to go to Amsterdam for a gay orgy?"

Kevin lost his temper and assault the reporter who asked the question. The others got it all on camera. He made his way to Ola's car, and as he jumped in, he demanded that she take him to his in-laws home. Ola flatly refused to take him there.

"Stop the car! I want to get out!" Kevin yelled.

Ola pulled over, and replied, "Kevin, your wife has taken out a restraining order against you. You're not to go near her or your daughter."

"That's rubbish. I spoke to her this morning and told her I would be coming home tonight."

Ola was confused. She didn't know what was happening, and couldn't understand why they were all suffering in the same way. She drove to her own home, instead. When they arrived at Ola's house, Aaron's wife was there, crying.

"I promise, I will fix everything for all of us," Kevin said.

He pick up the phone and made a call. When he hung up the phone, he said, "By this time, Tuesday morning, we'll have all our homes back."

Kevin Peters made the early evening news on all the television stations in the UK. It was a lot worse than Ola thought. Kevin assured them that they would have the last laugh when they sue the media for defamation. He told them not to worry.

It was a long night for Kevin, his brothers and his sister. They all have one question in mind: "Why would Kevin's wife do this to them?" They don't like her in the same way they've always liked Tia, but they have been consistently kind and respectful to her. Privately, Ola has always known she was a bad apple, but she didn't want to say anything negative to Kevin. Kevin, himself, was beyond devastation. He did all he could to keep his anger and his emotions in control. The embarrassment and the shame is nothing he could ever contemplate. He wanted to call his father and seek his advice, but was reluctant to do so. His father had always advised him to marry a Nigerian woman from his own tribe. Someone from a good home. Kevin wishes to God that he had listened to his father's advice. It broke his heart to see his brothers and their wives lose their homes because of his own wife's hatred for him. "How could I have married such a woman," Kevin asked himself.

Before he meets the loan officer on Tuesday, Kevin needs to do some research, but the TV clip or his arrest is featured on YouTube, so he couldn't bring himself to use the computer. He didn't want to read about himself or think about his situation until he knew he could return his brothers homes to them. Kevin was certain that Angela's accusations would be proven to be lies, so he didn't worry much since he trusted the law. He thought about her and her reactions to recent events. What would Tia say about his arrest and his assault on the reporter? With a shock, Kevin realized that the reporter might also file charges against him. He has not thought about the Law Society and the consequences of his actions. He has been a good husband to Angela and Angela has also been a good wife to him. He couldn't fault her for anything up until the time his former boss sent him that poison email. "This is all his doing, the bastard! I am going to make him pay for everything I have lost and more," thought Kevin vengefully. He called his father.

"It will all be okay, son. Come home once you have sorted out the mess up with your brother's loans. You know, the elections are coming up. By this time next year you could be a state governor, son. There is more money and power in African politics than being a solicitor in the UK."

Kevin felt better hearing that. He thought about Jayzel and Trey. He didn't get the chance to see them when he was in Holland. Kevin wondered whether they had returned to Canada yet. "Hmmm. Once I get back to Lagos, I will sent an apology letter to Tia. Yes, that will mend some of the damage I have done."

Kevin didn't think he would lose his law licenses over the assault charges, but even if he does, he doesn't care about that anymore. He has no desire to live in the UK now. He has not thought about his daughter or his unborn son since he left for Holland. In fact, he was going to go home and tell his wife he wanted a divorce. "She can have everything and the kids, too, if she wants," thinks Kevin.

Feeling relieved now that he has a plan in place, Kevin sighs deeply and turns on the television. There is Tia Sharp-Carter at a press conference on *Entertainment Now*!

Chapter 18

Nathan and his mother-in-law couldn't believe what they were hearing. They had gone to Lisa's penthouse for a mid-morning meeting and overheard her talking on the phone. "Kevin Peters was arrested this morning for assaulting a bailiff. He is going to make the early evening news as well as *The Panorama* on Monday night. Did know you that he assaulted his pregnant wife and threw a bottle into their television just days before Christmas?" Lisa gushed.

Naana interrupted the call, forcing Lisa to hang up the phone. "How do you know this?" her mother asked curiously.

"Did you know that Kevin Peters was married to a white girl just to get his immigration papers?" Lisa asked.

"Yes," her mother admitted.

"Well. There was some abuse during the marriage. Anyway, the ex-wife is going to be on *Panorama* with a home video as evidence of his abusive behavior towards women. There's a pornography website, which allows people to post home videos. There's a video of Kevin Peters taking it up the ass, posted by his wife." Lisa winked. "Isn't pay back a b . . . . h?" she added.

Nathan wondered aloud, "How did you manage all this, Lisa?"

"I'd like to take credit for this, but I'm sorry to say Mr. Peters wife, Angela, did it all. She was his brothers lawyer. I spoke with Mrs Peters a few months ago regarding their loans. She was very quick to point out to me how we could foreclose on them. In fact, when I initially refused to do it, it was she who suggested a new lender for them. Long before I realized that Kevin was Tia's ex-boyfriend, she approached an associate of mine for help. I overheard the conversation in which she described her plan to take down the Peters boys. I have no idea why. Instead, I did my own investigation on Mr Peters. Chance advised me to take out my own insurance on Mr Peters before he put his hands on Tia."

"You confided in Chance about this?" Mrs Sharp asked.

Lisa smiled.

Nathan asked, "Who's Chance?"

Lisa quickly changed the subject, "No mother. I'm not really sure why Angela had that much hate for Kevin Peters. I was intrigued by the intensity of it. Anyway, I sent her a copy of the video of her husband taking it up the ass. I also edited some of the footage of him assaulting Tia and lashing out at Nathan, and sent them both to Angela a few weeks ago. I was told that his wife had hired his former boss—the man he sued for unpaid wages—to get him out of jail. I'd like to see the outcome of it." Lisa laughed. "I think more people will tune into *Panorama* this week than the week they interviewed the Princess of Wales."

Lisa turned to Nathan. "How much pain do you want to see Kevin Peters suffer?"

"What are you up to now, Lisa?" asked Nathan. "Come on! Tell me!" he demanded.

"It looks like Mr Peters got bail. He wants to meet with me on Monday morning to discuss a loan. I told my assistant to tell him that I'd be happy to meet with him on Tuesday morning. I'm thinking you should buy me breakfast Tuesday morning. What do you think?"

"Lisa Sharp, I would not want to hurt your sister. God help me if I ever do, 'cos you are one *bad* girl," Nathan kissed Lisa on the cheek.

Vidal walks in and punches Nathan on the mouth. "The next time you ask before you put your hands on my lady. How dare you, Mr Carter?" Vidal asserted.

"Oh, my baby is jealous," Lisa begins to laugh as she kisses Vidal.

Nathan is shocked. "You," he points to Vidal, "and your girlfriend here are both crazy. Damn it! I will let this one go this time," Nathan warns him.

Lisa is still laughing. Vidal frowns and says, "I don't like other men putting their hands on you. I don't care if he is your sister's husband. He looks like a pervert to me."

"Oh, baby. I love how you all man. Come here, give me kiss."

"My wife is not going to be happy about this, Lisa!" Nathan spat at them.

Lisa is still laughing. Nathan shakes his head and slams the door behind himself as he leaves.

It is Jackie's birthday. She has spent the last two days with her father at the Sharp home. After Nathan broke up her date with Corey, the other night and took her home like a little girl, Jackie was so embarrassed by Nathan's over-protective behavior. She missed Lisa so much. She wondered whether Lisa missed her just as much. Nathan and Tia dropped her off at the loft and Lisa asked them to join her for dinner. As it turned out, Lisa spent most of the evening playing video games with Trey. Nathan watched television with Jayzel while Jackie helped Tia cook. They enjoyed a lovely dinner together, but no one was happier to see them leave than Jackie. She is leaving in two days and Lisa is acting like she doesn't even care. Jackie took the toys Lisa bought for the kids to the car for them.

There was a small gift-wrapped box taped to the back of the door with Jackie's name on it. She opened it to find a gold and diamond charm bracelet with a heart shape and the letter 'L' in the middle. Jackie burst into tears when she saw it. It was the most expensive, the most beautiful gift she had ever received in her life. A note attached to the box said "in the living room sofa". Jackie thought that Lisa was in the living room, but actually, there was another, slightly bigger gift in the sofa. She opened it to discover a digital camera and another note that said "in my office chair". Just like last time, Lisa was not in the office, but another gift sat on the chair. Jackie opened it. An i-pod with a note said, "I'm waiting in bed for you. Happy birthday, Jacks!" Jackie had tears rolling down her face as she entered the bedroom. Her heart beat faster with every step. She had to stop and lean against the wall to pinch herself just to make sure she wasn't dreaming. In a sexy black Victoria's Secret underwear, Lisa lounged on the bed. She smiled and presented one more box to Jackie. "Happy Valentine's Day!" Lisa grinned mischievously, "Jacks, put it on, so I can take it off you, later!"

"You didn't have to buy me all these gifts. It is too much, Lisa."

"Put it on, Jacks! For me." Lisa winks. Jackie sits down on the bed. "I lose all sense when I think of you, nothing else matters. What have you done to me?"

Jackie slowly undresses and puts on the underwear. Lisa bites the side of her bottom lips and puts her hands out to Jackie. She sits in between

Lisa's legs as she wrap her legs around her. She points to the bracelet and says, "so you know that you're always in my heart. I want you to take pictures and send me each day. All the songs that we've made love to are on this i-pod, and the ones that we'll make love to in the future are on it, too. Lastly, just in case I'm not with you on Valentine's Day, know that I'll be thinking of you and only you, Jacks." Lisa begins to kiss the back of her neck. Jackie moans and cries at the same time. They have made love every day now for the past four weeks. The two days they spent apart was hell. Patrick has been calling Jackie everyday now, too. They will talk for an hour on the phone. Patrick and Vidal are different from the rich kids who attend UCLA with her. She is going to miss everyone, but she didn't want to think about leaving all this behind in two days, and not just Lisa. She has been thinking of Patrick a lot—the more she talks to him, the more she likes him. She share this thought with Lisa.

Nathan and his family were spending their last weekend with his in-laws. Jayzel and Trey were sleeping in the loft. They were so happy at the loft with Lisa they didn't want to leave. Tia is telling her mother about the loft while Claire and BJ both sit on either side of their mother. Naana rubs their backs while listening to Tia re-count Jayzel's and Trey's adventures. Naana tells the children to go and brush their teeth and tuck themselves into bed; she will come up and say good night later. Claire protests that she is the oldest, so why does she have to go to bed the same time as BJ?

Tia reminds her, "No baby, you're not the oldest, I am." Bobby carried Claire upstairs. Nathan and his father said good-night and left Tia to enjoy some alone time with her mother.

"Mother have you been to Lisa's loft?" Tia asked.

"Yes, why do you ask?"

"Mother, don't you think you've spoiled Lisa?"

Naana laughs. "Mother, the kid lives more or less like your average Hollywood royalty. Doesn't that worry you?" Tia ask quizzically.

"Spoiled Lisa? Tia, your sister has been working and bring in more clients in the last five and half years than any of my employees. She is doing a double degree, sweetheart, and let me tell you that's a lot of hard work. Lisa has earned everything that she owns all by herself—with my guidance, of course. She does live a very different lifestyle, like you said, but I couldn't be more proud of her. I wish she would end her romance with Priscilla Gates before I do. The young lady is trouble and the sooner your sister end things with her the better I'll sleep."

"Don't tell me . . ." Tia raised an eyebrow, but couldn't bring herself to say it.

"Don't tell me *what*, Tia?"

"Oh, my God! She is . . . No wonder!" Tia exclaimed.

"Tia your sister is what?" Naana is almost alarmed thinking about what might have Lisa done now.

"Mother, it doesn't bother you that Lisa is gay?"

Naana is chuckling at the expression on Tia's face. Her mother gasps, "Oh, sweetheart! Homosexuality has been around before mother and father's time. Young girls like Lisa's age like to discover their sexuality in different ways from your traditional Adam and Eve. Lisa is no different. Don't tell me you never thought of being with a woman or imagining such things?" Tia can not believe her mother dares ask her that. "I most certainly have not, Mother!"

"Lisa tells me she has fallen in love with the Collins boy and they plan to get marry—regardless of her feelings for Chance."

"Come on, give me a break, Mother. Lisa is gay. My guess is she has had more romances, as you call them, and broken more hearts than Nathan Carter! It explains why she and Chance are not together," Tia told her mother. Naana thought Tia's comment was funny. "I'm sure she hasn't. Your sister has a good heart and cares about other's feelings. She will not discuss Chance with me."

It dawns on Tia that Jackie may have a crush on Lisa, or that they might have a thing going on. The thought frightens her. There was something about Jackie today. Tia thought maybe Nathan's over-protective behavior the other day was the cause of it. Now she is not too sure. Her mother asks if she is okay. Tia nods, "Speaking of Chance . . . did you know that he stills wears the promise bracelet that he and Lisa had since they were kids?"

"Yes, his father tells me that he doesn't date at all. He just works, works, works. I think—I think he was the one who helped Lisa set up Mr Peters. I'm more worried about young Mr Collins. Vidal and Lisa have nothing in common, and she still lives in the loft that she and Chance bought together. She hates my interference in her private life, so I try to stay away from it."

"Soul mates are known to find each other. I'm sure Chance and Lisa will come back to each other. What time is BJ's game in the morning?"

"It's at ten. After we take the kids out to McDonald's we can drop them off at Lola's. Jackie's party's begins at six and we can all have dinner at the club. Why do you ask?"

"I need to run an errand after BJ's game, but before we go to the club. I also have to go and thank Sarah for having the children over as well as having Amy and Liz as her house guests. Amy has not stopped talking about her little vacation. I sure hope she has everything done by the time I get home next week. Nathan, too, has a trial in two weeks, but he wants to go and visit grandmother before we go home."

"You keep your husband away from my mother! Father is too old for Nathan's charms," Naana warns her daughter. They both begin to laugh.

Chance-Michael Benson, the third, is a twenty-four year old. His father is a Conservative MP for London South Kensington, who comes from a long line of Ghanaian politicians. Just like Lisa, Chance works alongside his mother at the MB & B Bank. Lisa and Chance met on her first visit to Ghana when she was eleven years old. Legend has it that the Bensons possess spiritual powers, and that if their loved one is in pain, they can feel it and somehow take away this pain. It is a power that Chance's father has and which Chance will also discover he can feel the pain of others when he meets Lisa Sharp.

Chance's sister, Meg, invited Lisa to a sleepover. In the middle of the night, Lisa suddenly became very ill. Chance told Lisa to wait calmly until his father and grandfather got the car to take her to the ER. Lisa's pain became so great that when Chance held her in his arms, he also passed out. Lisa was taken to the hospital where doctors discovered her appendix about to rupture. Since that day, Lisa and Chance have been inseparable and their destiny set sail. They are both vegetarians and enjoy charity work since their early childhood. They attended the same secondary school in London and they shared their very first kiss in a hot tub in Chance's family country home in Brighton. They pledged their hearts and souls to one another with an identical bracelet made out of kanete cloth, swearing an oath that whenever they were apart, all they would have to do is to rub on the bracelet for all to be well. On Lisa's sixteenth birthday, Chance found her in bed having sex with Priscilla. He was devastated beyond belief. He could not understand why Lisa would betray their relationship, so he was

Forever Never Dies

unable to forgive her while he continued to love her. Chance asked his father if he could go and study in the US where his mother's family live. His parents agreed, deciding Chance could spend his vacations doing an internship in Asia just like his father did at the same age. Lisa wrote to him often, telling Chance how much she loves him and misses him. Chance wrote back, but he never did tell Lisa that he had seen her in bed with Priscilla three years ago. When Chance returned to London to work with his mother, it was Lisa who suggested that they buy Brooke and Jason Gray's loft. They both agreed to raise half of the money. Lisa proposes living together, but Chance says he will only on the condition that Lisa end her relationship with Priscilla. Surprised that he knew about it, Lisa refuses, so Chance ends the relationship. They discuss business every now and then, but nothing else. He misses Lisa terribly, but cannot forgive her, and watching Lisa date Vidal Collins has not helped matters either. They all move about in the same circle of friends. The only way not to see Lisa is not to socialize. Right now, Chance feels like he has no life.

Tia has given Chance an invitation to join her at a birthday party tonight at one of Lisa's clubs. She and Brooke have delivered it personally and they insist they won't take no for an answer. Chance smiles and walks them to their car, assuring them he will be there. Back in the house, Chance glances at a photograph of him and Lisa walking on the shore of Brighton Beach. He feels like crying. Looking for relief, Chance tries to meditate, but finds himself easily distracted by worries of Lisa's careless lifestyle. She is pig-headed, he thinks, and won't listen to advice about her life. For the past week he has been having nightmares about Lisa and her mother bleeding to death. He shares his worries with his father who advises him to put his feelings aside and talk to Lisa. His father suspects Lisa may be in real danger. Last night, Chance work up in a bloody nightmare of Lisa and her mother, like other dreams, being shot to death in his arms. Chance cries in his bed as his whole body trembles. In other dreams Chance sees his late grandmother—his father's mother—and as he walks with her, he sees himself marrying Lisa with their family and friends in attendance. Lisa wraps her arms around him, kissing him, telling him she has never slept with any man, not even Vidal. She has been waiting for him to forgive her so they can be together. In other dream, her body was very cold as Chance watched her give birth to their child, but there was something present that made Lisa cry with unimaginable pain after they go home with their child. He cannot make out what it might be. He holds their baby in his arms as Lisa wraps her arms around both of them. The sensations were so real. Chance felt relaxed when he opened his eyes. He reached for the phone and called Tia to say he would be at Club Vibe with his sister and Uncle Curtis, who is very close in age to his sister. "Fantastic!" was Tia's response. Chance spent the rest of the morning reading a report about Lisa's club manager, Simon. He concentrated on the report until he found what he expected to see. And smiled.

Chapter 19

Sarah Williams has been a widow for almost twenty-two years. The last time she made love was with her late husband, Jack. She lay in Michael Doyle's arms and sobbed. Nonplussed, Micheal did not know how to console her. He is a little embarrassed too because since his divorce six years ago, he has not made love to a woman until today. Although his ex-wife never did once complain about his lovemaking abilities, in fact, no woman has ever complained about his sexual prowess since secondary school.

"Sarah, darling. I am a doctor. If you're hurt, um, I'd like to know, darling," Michael whispered tenderly.

Sarah realized what an embarrassment this is for both of them. She lifts her head off his chest, and brushes her hair back with one hand. She can't read his eyes, except they are full of love and understanding.

"You were brilliant, darling," she said in a whispering tone. "Brilliant."

She wanted to run to her bathroom to call Naana, but it is after midnight when she glanced at the clock on her nightstand. Michael is a little relieved, and he begins to relax as she softly kisses him. She puts her head down on his chest and smiles.

"Thank you, why are you crying? Are you having second thoughts about us?"

Sarah's expression is puzzled. He felt no impatience, though he has long been wanting for them to make love. Sarah pulls herself up and with her hands on his face draws him close to kiss him.

"I have inadvertently disappointed you. I am sorry. It's been close to twenty-two years for me, Michael. I was overwhelming happy. I did not think about your needs, Michael."

"What a delightful surprise," Micheal thought, "she has not been with anyone since Jack's death."

"No, Sarah. I wish . . ." he paused, then said, "I wish I took my time to please you more. I couldn't wait any longer. I'm surprised I lasted this long all this time, in the same house with you sleeping down the hall from me."

Sarah thought, "he is romantic and sweet." She has forgotten about passion and how its feels to have an orgasm. Her body is still shaken just thinking about it. She wonders if Michael will think it's unladylike if she tells him that. She, too, has been having all kinds of sexual thoughts about him. "Where the bloody hell is Naana when I need her? This is absolutely awful," she thought. Michael took her hands and placed them on his already rock-hard penis.

"My goodness, the man is a beast!"

She gently squeezes it, as she lifts one of her legs up over his hip. She also took his hands and placed them between her legs. She closes her eyes and bites one side of her upper lips. Michael is gazing intently at her as he tries to discover her every sexual need. Sarah's hands are wrapped around the head of his penis, slowly stroking it. Wanting to slow down a little bit, Michael lay Sarah comfortably on her back. She felt a sensual rush like a wind throughout her whole body as his tongue found her sensitive spots. Michael aggressively sucks and squeezes her butt cheeks at the same time. Sarah feels her humanness all at once and knows she has been sexually starved. The erotic pleasure Michael is giving her is nothing like anything she knew with Jack, and nothing like any of her fantasies. Michael continues to nibble her earlobes and to ravish her nipples while his penis began to sing a different song in her vagina. Sarah is so relaxed that she feels herself responding intuitively to his body. Their sexual union was like beautiful, well-composed music, a symphony of sensation. Sarah thought, "now, I know how Bobby Sharp feels." And moments later, Sarah asked herself, "How am I going to keep up with him?"

Lovemaking has changed—it is like a delicious Swiss chocolate that never completely melts. When Sarah finally got to talk to Naana, that was how she described Michael's lovemaking.

Since meeting BJ, Trey also wakes up early and the first thing he does is make tea for his mom, just like BJ does for Naana. The two boys were in the kitchen with Anthony, Jayzel and Claire when Tia came down and asked whether they had eaten breakfast yet.

"Good morning, Mummy! BJ made me and Auntie Claire breakfast. He said girls are not allowed in the kitchen," Jayzel reported.

"That's right, dude!" Trey said and gave BJ a high-five.

"Well, I have to bake and make sandwiches for BJ's team mates, Sweetie, so this girl has to be allowed into the kitchen! We have a few hours before the game starts. Why don't you kids go and watch some cartoons?"

Claire did not go with the children. She looked so serious doing something on her laptop that Tia asked what she was doing.

"Just playing around," said Claire evasively. Claire is seventeen years old, and a first-year art student in College. "Hey, Tia! Your new studio . . . do you guys have a logo designed yet?"

"No, I'm not that far yet. Why do you ask?"

"Did Brooke show you the designs I did for her presentation?" Claire asked.

"You did that?"

"Yeah!"

Tia closes the oven door. Nathan has come to the dining room. He kisses Claire on the forehead and looks at what Claire is doing on the laptop. He calls to his wife to come and see.

"Claire, honey, what is that you are doing?" Nathan asks.

"I'm hoping Steven will want to build this and shoot his TV movie on my set. He said he is making this movie next month—*Forever never dies*. I'm trying to finish it, so I can give it to Jackie to take to him. You see, if Steven likes it and if I pass my driving test on Monday, he will buy a car for me. He promised." Claire exclaims.

"Who promised to buy you a car?" Naana asks with authority.

"Steven. If he likes my designs and if I pass my driving test on Monday." Claire explains.

"I'm going to ring Steven's neck!" Naana says. Everyone is puzzled with Naana's reaction.

Nathan intervenes, "It sounds like a good deal, Mother. I mean . . . don't you think?"

"It is a good deal for you and your wife. Nathan, Claire's designs are worth a lot more than a new car. I don't like people trying to take advantage of my baby. Brooke did that with Claire's design and almost got away with it. Well, I'm gonna have Lisa all over this," she says with determination.

"Steven is not taking advantage of me! He's my brother! He loves me, and Daddy will not buy me a car because he's afraid of you. I'm not going to let you spoil this for me! You are mean!" Claire tries to run out of the room, but Nathan picks her up and sits her on his lap. There were tears rolling down her face.

"Claire honey, Mother and I will go and buy a car for you if you pass your driving test on Monday. Sweetie, please don't cry," Nathan cajoles Claire.

"No, we'll not go and buy a car for her. Nathan, your sister knows the rules. We cannot change them to suit one child. She has been drinking and smoking pot and that takes away all that she is entitled to, Nathan." Naana firmly says.

"I know, Mother. But she has stopped all that. The rules say that everyone has to earn things. Claire will earn her car. She can baby sit Jayzel and Trey while I take Tia on a honeymoon in the summer and she can also work part-time as a production designer at the studio. I will ask Tia and Amy about it. Mother, please . . ." Nathan begs his mother-in-law.

Naana doubts very much that Tia and Amy will hire Claire. Claire is very lazy. She will have to discuss it with Bobby. Mulling over the idea, Naana didn't respond right away. Claire cried that she hates work and doesn't want to spend her summer at Tia's stupid Studio. She is going to California to work for Steven.

"Honey, if you want your car on Monday, you'll work at the studio. Listen Claire, your work is good and Mother is right. I'm not going to let my brother and my wife ripe you off, sweetie. Okay?"

"Excuse me!" Tia interrupted.

"I'm sorry, Baby. Mother is right. Claire's design is worth a lot more than a car. I'm going to talk to Steven. If you two want Claire's designs, you are going to pay the market rate and I want her name on the credits as the set designer. I'll have a contract for mother to sign for Claire. You guys knew the kid has talent. That's why Steven made that deal with her. I don't want Mother suing you and your studio, Baby," Nathan said smugly.

Anthony, Bobby, Naana and Claire has left the couple in the dining room while they fight over Claire's designs.

"Now, you listen to me, Mr. Carter. Don't you dare threaten me. I did not know anything about Claire's designs. I thought the kid was watching pornography on the laptop when you called me to come and see. Amy and I are not going to hire Claire at our studio. The kid is lazy and spoiled. I have you! I don't need another spoiled brat at my place of work!" Tia spat.

"Damn! Baby, you are so sexy when you are mad."

The couple were all over each other when Anthony and Naana returned.

"Do you two ever stop? This is a family dining room. Take it up to your room. My Goodness! The children are waiting in the car for you. Tony is riding with us."

Anthony and Nathan help put all the snacks in the car. Trey is wearing one of BJ's jerseys and is kicking the ball with him. Naana takes photographs of the boys. The game begins as Trey runs on the sideline cheering on BJ. When BJ scores a goal, Trey is on the field with the rest of the kids. Trey didn't want to leave the field, so Nathan put Jayzel down to go and get him off the field. They all spent the afternoon with Kate's mother. Nathan and Tia left, saying they would see everyone at the club for Jackie's party.

Chapter 20

Lisa is studying when Tia and Nathan arrive. Vidal lets them into the loft. When he hugs and kisses Tia, Nathan asks him to give him a reason why he should not punch his lights out.

"You put your hands on my baby, you have me to deal with," Lisa hollers from the office. "I'm in the office. Come in! Mother called me about Claire's designs. She will not expect anything less than this." Lisa gives a paper to Tia.

"You guys are outrageous. I'll not pay Claire this much money, and to a seventeen-year-old kid!" Tia said handing the paper back to her husband.

"Look, Tia. I've been on the phone since mother called checking facts and numbers. That is the going rate. If you and your lawyer-husband think that I'm going to roll over because your family, well, you're wrong. That is the going rate for the work that Claire has produced. I'll have someone buy the designs by Monday if Sunlight Media Group doesn't want them," Lisa threatened.

Nathan can't believe Lisa. "How about Tia thinks about it and I'll have a contract drawn?" Nathan suggested.

"I have already drawn up a contract." Lisa picks up a file and hands it to Nathan.

"Tia will not agree to this. Come on, Lisa, be reasonable." Nathan hands the contract to Tia, who skim-reads it.

"This is very good, Lisa," Tia says, chucking.

"Well, thank you. What do you say? My boss doesn't like to be kept waiting. Tia, this is a good opportunity for Claire to grow up. She will abide by this contract, I promise you. It's a good deal for you and your studio. Tia, as a businesswoman starting in a competitive business, you'll want to cut costs and the middle man. With Claire, you have your very own in-house designer at a fraction of the cost for the next five years. Claire designed all my clubs. Did Brooke tell you that the Skylight Building is one of her designs?" Lisa asked.

"No, way!"

Lisa shakes her head yes, and tells Tia that their little sister has talent but she has no focus.

"I'll discuss it with Steven and Amy, but you'll have to come down on price," Tia demanded.

"No can do. Tia, it's the going rate for young, unproven designers. Here, call the competition. Find out what their starting salaries are. Please, excuse me." Lisa said as she left her office, giving Nathan and Tia time to confer.

"What do you think, sweetie?"

"I think your mother and sister are *mafiosas*, they're so damn good in business. It makes sense, too. I think Steven will agree. I mean, Steven knows talent when he sees it, so does Amy. But Baby, it's your company. You have to decide who you want on your payroll. I also think Claire will be an asset to your up-coming venture that we talked about." Nathan advised his wife.

A few moments later, Lisa returned and asked, "Do we have a deal?" Tia thought she would play her little sister's game. "No, I'm sorry, Lisa. I don't think our little sister has what it takes to be a set designer in this business. Nathan and I have discussed it, and um . . . we are willing to give Claire a try." Tia winks.

"You guys are good. I hate you two," Lisa says affectionately. "Come on! Jacks is in the living room with Patrick. I'll go get changed and we can go to the tracks. Does Nathan like motor racing?"

"Yes. But he can't drive like us, though," Tia says.

"Thank you! Baby, I'm good in everything!" Nathan brags.

"Well, that's good to know. I told the Collins boys that if they win we will give them a blow job. Since your husband can't drive and those two can't drive, I guess Mother will be happy that we are not out there giving men blow jobs," Lisa chuckles.

"I don't find it funny. My wife is not going to give anyone . . ."

Tia did not let Nathan finish. She told her sister to go and get changed.

Jackie didn't know that her brother and sister-in-law were in the loft. Patrick came from Holland to surprise her on her birthday, but Jackie wasn't even thinking of Patrick in that way. They spent half of the night on the same bed talking until morning, when Lisa fell asleep. Jackie spent the rest of the night in the spare room with Patrick. It was nice waking up in his arms. He finally kissed her at lunch, even though Jackie wasn't expecting a kiss from him. She liked Patrick. Lisa seems to be okay about it, too. They were in the living room locking lips when Tia and Nathan entered. They did not see them standing there watching them. "Why is it that every time I turn around my sister is with some white guy?" Nathan asked his wife.

Tia is relieved because she thought Lisa and Jackie were sleeping together. She told Nathan to relax and that Patrick is a good boy. "Look at them! They've not even come up for breath. You two need to come out for air!" Nathan shouted.

"This is not your average motor racing. This is Silverstone. Michael Schumacher, Damon Hill and Canada's own Jacques Villeneuve have won Formula One races here. Today, the Sharp sisters are going to win," Lisa crowed.

Patrick said, "I'm not going to race. Jackie is going to drive us both in one car." Vidal and Nathan began clucking like chickens. Jackie said, "Oh, no, my man. You're going to race and like it. You'll be beaten just like the rest of them."

Of course, Tia and Lisa took the first and second places respectively. Surprisingly, Nathan was last, even his little sister beat him. They lost track of time and forgot about the dinner at the club. By the time they arrived Naana was not impressed with her children at all, as they were both giddy with laughter. Jackie can't believe it: by far, this is the best birthday party ever for her.

Little did they know that Priscilla had crashed the party. Sarah, Michael, and Naana are about to leave when Priscilla pulls a gun and points it at Naana's head. The rest of the children were in the club dancing the evening away when one of the security guards came and whispered in Lisa's ear. Despite the dim light, Tia sees the distress on Lisa's face, so she taps Nathan on his knee to get his attention. They all see the sudden fear Lisa reflected in her face. Tia can also see Lisa's eyes, which are filled with rage. Then a stunning, smashing pain exploded in Lisa's whole body. Lisa is falling even though she is still sitting down. The security guard is standing over her. Lisa says hoarsely, "Find Corey and Chef Debbie. Tell them the situation. Make it clear to them not to call the police. I want them to meet by the private dining room door. Now!!"

"What is going on?" Nathan and Tia ask with concern.

"I want you to get Jacks and do something for me, please, Tia."

Tia notices Lisa's expression has changed. She is smiling. Lisa wrote down what she wanted her sister to do for her. Tia is ever a romantic herself, so she knew exactly what to do.

"I will be right behind you with Nathan. I just have to talk to Vidal. Please excuse me," Lisa said.

Vidal is dancing with Jackie and Patrick. Whatever Lisa said to him must have made his night. He lifted her up in the air in the middle of the night club sensually kissing Lisa, with all eyes on them. When they finally stopped and he let go of her, Lisa pulls him towards her and passionately embraces him. Jackie has shared passion with Lisa countless of time, but this is like magic, one you see on a movie screen. Tia and Nathan shared Jackie's feelings as well as everyone in the dimly-lit club who saw the couple kiss and embrace. Wow! Tia thought. Tia quickly kissed Nathan and left with Jackie.

Lisa told Nathan that their mother is being held at gun point in the private dining room by her ex-lover. Nathan's heart couldn't take it. Why is it that every time something beautiful happens in his family, something tragic also comes? He couldn't think.

"I need your help, Nathan," Lisa cried hopelessly.

Nathan looked and saw Brooke dancing with Jason. Lisa followed his eyes. "We can't involve them. This is our family matter, Nathan," Lisa says as she takes Nathans hands and steers him downstairs to the private room. Brooke sees them go. She looks around for Tia but can't see her.

"Not again!" she screams and tells Kate and Jaden to come with her. Nathan Carter will never change. "Well, he is not going to do to Lisa what he did to me," she thinks to herself, assuming the worst of Nathan.

Priscilla is out of her mind, drunk and high. She has dragged Naana Konadu-Sharp at gunpoint to the penthouse above the club. The two gunmen who came with her are standing nervously next to the door of the private dining room. Their instructions are to watch Sarah Williams and Dr Doyle. They were told by Priscilla to watch Sarah Williams and Dr. Doyle. Anthony and Bobby lift early to go and pick up the children from

Kate's mother's. Sarah has gone into shock as Michael holds her tightly in his arms and prays that the police gets there in time.

Lisa and Nathan meet Corey. Chance is with him. Lisa can not hide her emotions from Chance when their eyes meet. She falls into his arms. He speaks softly, "Everything is going to be alright, Princess. I want you to draw on the Princess's positive energy, okay?" Chance says and they embrace again. They are informed that Mrs Sharp is with Priscilla in the penthouse. Priscilla demands that Lisa come up in five minutes or she will shoot Mrs Sharp. Brooke and the rest overheard the conversation between Chance, Lisa, and Nathan. She demands to know what is going on.

Lisa takes them all into Simon's office. To Lisa's surprise, Simon is getting a blow job while sitting in his chair. Lisa can tell that he, too, is high.

"Security!" Lisa called out.

"Yes, ma'am?" responded one of the security guards.

"Please, escort this young woman and Uncle Sam off the premises. Do it immediately!" Lisa said in a cruel, harsh voice. Turning to Corey, she asked, "Can you bring the private dining room up on the screen?"

"I can if it is within range of the camera." Corey zooms in and out with the lens. The pictures are very clear as the system is state of the art.

"Why are we standing here playing detective? Has anyone called the police?" Brooke asked. Brooke grabbed the phone, intending to dial 9-9-9. Preempting the call, Lisa put her hand over Brooke's, adding, "Brooke Williams, you may have Tia and the rest of the people in this room wrapped around your spoiled little fingers, but I strongly advise you not to say or do anything stupid." Lisa spoke softly and calmly to her.

"How dare you speak to me this way, Lisa?"

"She dares, Miss Williams, because she is the owner of this club. She dares because she will call the situation the way she sees it. Now, I suggest we all calm down and not get overly excited," says Chance.

Just then, Gina Read appeared with two bullet-proof vests. Chance removed Lisa's jacket and put one of the vests on her. He took off his own shirt and donned the other vest. Nathan and Brooke exchanged a glance when they saw the portrait of Lisa on Chance's forearm as he put his shirt and jacket back on.

Lisa conducts an impromptu conference with two of her security guards. "I want you to make sure none of these people leave this room or use the phone," says Lisa, gesturing to indicate everyone around her.

"Take away their cell phones if necessary. If any of them gives you trouble, you know what to do."

They were all silent for fear of not knowing what was happening or what game Lisa might be playing.

Lisa and Chance left hand in hand with Corey and Nathan. The rest sat down on the sofa in the office holding their hearts in their hands. None of them has ever been in such a situation, but they all hear the echo of Lisa's words reminding them not to do anything, not to be a hero.

As Lisa, Chance, Corey and Nathan walk toward the private dining room, she says, "I want to talk to these guys alone. I know them well because they've been to my club frequently. If I need your help, Corey, I'll call out."

"Absolutely not!" objects Nathan.

Corey replies, "Yah, boss. She'll be fine. Every regular knows Lisa is tough, deals with the shit herself. She's ruthless. There'll be no fuss."

Gina adds, "Corey and I are cops, working undercover to clean up the illegal drugs circulating in her clubs. We need Lisa to approach these guys before we barge in there."

"I know all that," Chance says, "but I want you to handle the situation they way we discussed it before. I'll not put the Princess's life in your hands. The objective is to bring her out safely."

While Chance spoke to Corey and Gina, Lisa took the opportunity to pull Nathan aside. This is the first time Nathan has seen his sister-in-law show real fear. It broke his heart.

"Nathan, if I . . . If I don't make it through the night," Lisa fought back her tears, "Let my mother know . . . that I am very sorry, sorry for all this, and . . . I love you all very much."

Nathan nodded, choked up himself with intense emotions, but he knew exactly what Lisa meant. He didn't know what to say in return, but he suspected she didn't really need him to respond. He can't help feeling frozen, helplessly immobile with fear and anxiety. Nathan would like to be able to put his fears aside to help Lisa, but he is unable to think clearly. Time seems to slow down, passing second by second, frame by frame, like a slow-motion replay film. Lisa and Chance have gone inside the private dining room, while Corey and Nathan stand outside in the hall. Corey is holding what looks like a phone. He exclaims to Gina, "They done it!"

"What?" Nathan asks, his heart beating rapidly, "They've done what?"

Corey is holding a remote camera. Inside the dining room, Lisa is wearing a small camera attached to her watch. Miss Williams and her boyfriend are okay. Corey shows the footage to Nathan. Together, they open the door and went into the room. Corey and the Chef handcuff the two thugs.

Diplomatically, Lisa says, "Brooke is in the Club Manager's office with her husband, as well as Kate and Jaden. They have no idea that you and your friend were being held at gunpoint. Mrs Williams, I do apologize for everything you and your friend have been through tonight because of me. I am so very sorry."

Sarah asked, "Where is your mother, Lisa?"

Lisa replied, "I am going to bring Mother downstairs soon. Nathan will take you home."

"I cannot go home without knowing that my friend is safe," Sarah cried.

Putting her arms around Sarah, Lisa said, "I cannot put you in any more danger tonight. Brooke . . . we all could have lost you tonight. You have no reason to trust me . . . I'll not lose Mother."

"Naana is going to be alright, darling, but I am coming with you. Lisa dear, you just did something miraculous to save me and Michael," Mrs Williams pleaded with Lisa.

"Mrs Williams, please! I have to go and get my mother. I promise Mother is all right," Lisa said firmly.

Sara is in tears. "I think you have risked your life enough already tonight, Lisa, darling." Sarah felt a little lightheaded and sat down suddenly.

"Mrs Williams, you have been like a sister to my mother. You have grieved enough in your life time. Right now, I am trying to find a way for all of us not to grieve again. Please let Nathan take you home." Lisa's voice was full of emotion. Nathan marveled at her ability to handle crisis situations. Lisa has carried a huge burden tonight. Nathan thought, "the kid has put everyone she loves first. That's why she sent Tia and Jackie on an errand. Lisa didn't want them here to feel what she is feeling."

Lisa used the pause in the conversation to dash off to the penthouse. She knows she cannot afford to be emotional at this time. Sarah persisted in her intent to help rescue her friend, so Nathan and Michael tagged along behind the two determined women. Unaware of their presence, Lisa paused outside the penthouse door to wipe away her tears and to straighten up her clothes. Feeling confident again, she opened the door but did not close it. Priscilla is holding a gun and a bottle of wine. Chance is sitting on the sofa holding Mrs Sharp's hands, talking to her in their native Twi. Priscilla is not as high or as drunk as Lisa thought. Noticing Lisa's arrival, Priscilla puts the bottle of wine on the coffee table and points the gun directly at Naana's head, "You left me because of her!"

Lisa stops in her tracks in the middle of the room. She has told herself she isn't going to lose her mother tonight. She's not so sure any more. Nevertheless, the thought frightens her. For the last twenty minutes, Lisa's whole body has felt unimaginable pain—pain unknown to any of her closest friends and family. She also feels exhausted by the intense emotional ups and downs of the whole evening. Despite these challenges, Lisa is in control of her emotions, but inwardly her anger boils over the pain caused by the one woman whom she has loved all her adult life. Lisa thought about her life, her choices, her dreams to one day marry and have a family. Everything important to Lisa flashes before her. She is panting. Instinctively, she knows not to do anything drastic. Pulling up a chair from the small dining room set, she sits herself down in the middle of the room. She positions herself so that Priscilla can see she is unarmed, not wearing a wire, and not shielding her body in any way. Lisa does not want to do anything that will escalate Priscilla's desperation, at least not so that she will start shooting.

Chapter 21

Meanwhile, outside the penthouse, Brooke holds her mother and her husband as they pray that Naana and Lisa will be safe. They can only hear Priscilla's voice. Nathan has also gone inside the penthouse.

"Why is Chance and your brother-in-law here?" demands Priscilla.

Lisa turns to see Nathan coming into the room. "They are here to take Mother home, sweetheart. Come! There's a party downstairs. I want you to come with me. Come, give me a hug. I've missed you," Lisa says. "I didn't mean to screw things up between us the way that I did," she adds.

The rest of Lisa's family wait outside, exchanging glances.

"You said we are over. I know. *She* took you away from me," Priscilla says petulantly, pointing the gun at Naana. "She will not let you love me. That's why I want to kill her!"

"I'm right here, sweetheart. Come! Come to me. I was afraid when Dana died. I didn't want to lose you the same way. I gave up my soul mate for you, sweetheart. Don't take my mother away the way you took Chance away." Lisa extends her hands. She hates to beg for anything, and playing Priscilla's game makes Lisa feel nauseous because she knows Priscilla will assume Lisa still cares for her.

"You said we are over," repeats Priscilla.

Lisa continues to offer her hands. She smiles. "I was hurt, sweetheart. I've been afraid, watching you kill yourself a little bit every day with drugs. I didn't know what else to do. I don't know what to do to help you. I still love you, sweetie. Please, come to me," Lisa smiles.

All of their friends wait anxiously outside the door, listening, quivering in fear. They can all feel the rhythm of their collective heartbeats. Priscilla puts the gun down on the table with a clatter. She wipes her face, stammering that she promises she has stopped taking drugs, that she's sorry.

"I'm not going to hurt Mrs Sharp."

Nathan, Chance and Mrs Sharp watch as Priscilla runs into Lisa's arms. Nathan strides across the room to hug his mother-in-law, crying into her shoulder and thanking God that he didn't lose her tonight. Letting go of Naana, Nathan stepped back to see Lisa hugging the girl who held his mother-in-law at gunpoint. He feels more enraged, nauseated and disgusted over this situation than he has ever felt over any other crisis. He pulls Priscilla out of Lisa's arms.

"Do you think you can point a gun at my mother and get away with it? You are going to be locked up!" Nathan yells.

It took everything to restrain himself from hitting Priscilla.

Lisa gathers Priscilla into her arms again. They all watch with a mixture of disgust and astonishment. By the time Lisa lets go of Priscilla, she is upset again and screaming, "You love me! You love me! You can't marry Vidal tonight!" Priscilla grabs the gun and points it toward Naana.

Chance and Lisa immediately throw themselves on Mrs Sharp as Priscilla pulls the trigger, shooting at them multiple times before Gina is able to take away the gun. Naana's mind goes blank as her daughter throws herself on top of her at the same moment Chance does. She fights hard to roll Lisa and Chance over to shield them from the gun, but they are too strong and she is not able to move them. She cries in an agony of pain for them as she lays helplessly underneath them. Nathan and Gina manage to restrain Priscilla. Across the room, the rest of their friends scream and cry for Naana, Chance and Lisa. Gina pulls Lisa and Chance away from Mrs Sharp. She is not sure whether Chance is dead or alive.

"Are you all right, Mrs Sharp?" Gina asks.

Naana doesn't immediately respond as she is dazed with shock. Gina can't get a response from her. They all hold their breath in fear. She raises her own hand to Corey to let him know they are okay. There is blood on the floor, but it is not coming from either one of them. Lisa and Chance took most of the shots. Lisa, too, is in shock. Gina put a bullet-proof vest on her earlier in the evening, so she is hoping that Lisa is not hurt. Gina tries to stay calm and not show any emotion. Corey comes to say he is going downstairs to meet the police. He takes Priscilla with him. Sarah sees the blood and asks, trembling, "Is everyone all right?"

Gina replies, shaking her head to clear her thoughts, "One of them got hit, but I'm not sure who. Lisa is not dead. She has a strong pulse."

Hearing her name, Lisa opened her eyes. She didn't feel any pain. Next to her, Chance lies in a pool of blood. She places her ear close to his chest. She hears his heart beating very fast. Whispering, Lisa says, "You cannot leave me again, my Prince. I need you now more than words can say."

Chance is in so much pain. He holds her hand and slowly opens his eyes. The love is still there. He wants to tell her that he, too, needs her, misses her and wants to be with her. Everyone in the room felt their love for each other. It was pure magic to watch them. Chance sat up. "Princess . . . Are you? Is your mother alright?" he asked Lisa as they embraced. Lisa let go of him to ask Nathan whether her mother was okay. Nathan managed a dismissive smile. He picks up and places Naana on the sofa, becoming nervous and distracted when he realized the blood could be Lisa's or Chance's. He felt a wild sense of impatience as he squatted to talk to Lisa.

"Are you okay, sweetie?" Nathan asks.

"I feel great! Is everyone all right? I think mother is in shock. Chance is hurt." Lisa didn't want to show emotions. "Dr Doyle, can you please help my mother and Chance?" Lisa asked.

Lisa is outrageously upset, but she manages to control her emotions, staying calm and focused.

Nathan says gently, "Lisa, sweetie. I think you've been shot. Are you in any pain at all?"

"No. I'm fine. I think Chance is hurt."

"I'm fine Princess. Let the Doctor take a look at you, please," Chance says. He stands up and Lisa sees the blood dripping through his arms. She begins to take off his jacket with shaking hands. Wincing, she closes her eyes when she sees the wound. Suddenly, she is also feeling pain in her arms. Naana cried out for someone to call 9-9-9. Chance and Lisa objected.

"I'm wearing a bullet-proof vest. I can't be hurt," says Lisa.

Gina and Nathan help Lisa remove her blazer. "I do feel a lot of pain in my left shoulder," she says. Naana squeezes her hands and begins to sob. Lisa casually glances at her watch and comments, "I'm getting married in an hour."

Everyone thought she was in shock. Lisa takes off her shirt. There is a lot of blood streaming down her back, all the way to her jeans. Naana screams, "Call an ambulance! Someone call an ambulance!"

"No, mother! Get some towels. Dr Doyle can fix us up right now. I don't want to be late." Gina hands Dr Doyle a first-aid kit. She is trembling as she observes the wound. "Um . . . I'm sorry, Miss Sharp. You must let us take you to the hospital. You are bleeding too much." Gina stammers, quivering in fear as she looks on.

"I'm fine, Gina. Please tell Corey not to let the police know I'm here. Remember what we discussed before. I'm going to get cleaned up and go home. I will be here at ten to find out why my mother was held at gunpoint. Thanks, Gina. Thank you for saving my life and my mother's life."

Gina glances at Mrs Sharp before she leaves them. Lisa's mother pleaded with her to let her take Lisa to the hospital, but Lisa firmly negated the idea. "It will affect not just my business, but yours. The hospital will notify the police of a gunshot wound. They will want to investigate. The whole sordid mess will come out in the papers, and the paparazzi will hound us for weeks. No, mother. I'm fine. It looks worse than it feels. Are you alright, Mother?"

"I am, Lisa." Mrs Sharp hugs her daughter for a long time. Lisa whispers to her mother not to cry. Both of them are still shivering with shock, as is everyone else in the room. Dr Doyle affirms it is just a scratch wound. "It needs to be cleaned, Lisa, and might need some stitches, too. Chance has the identical scratch wound on his arm, too."

"Brooke," says Lisa, "There's an emergency medical case in my office. Would you be so kind as to retrieve it for us? Thanks." Brooke returned a few moments later with the medical case.

Lisa felt a lot more pain that she lead everyone to believe. She went into the bathroom and ran a shower while everyone waited for her. Chance hugged Mrs Sharp and left. Nathan sighs with relief, deeply grateful not to have lost both of them tonight. Everyone comments on how unbelievable tonight's events have been.

The phone is ringing. Naana picks up the receiver to discover Tia on the other end.

"What are you still doing in the club?" demands Tia. "Daddy and I have been calling everywhere for you and Sarah. We were beginning to get worried. Lisa and Vidal are getting married tonight, Mother. Did you know that?"

Naana stared at the phone in shock. Suddenly, Lisa's comment made perfect sense.

"Mother! I have no idea where Lisa is, or why they are getting married tonight. The priest is here in the loft, waiting."

"I'll be at the loft shortly with everyone in tow," Naana replied as she disconnected the call. Naana has had a lot on her shoulder's tonight. She asks Brooke and Kate, "Did you know that Lisa had plans to get married tonight?"

Both women answer simultaneously, "No."

Lisa re-entered the room dressed in a black pants suit and realizes they are all looking at her.

"Listen! I am sorry for everything. You can all have a go at me tomorrow at lunch, but right now I am going to the loft to get married. I would love for all of you to come—if you want. I do need one of you to give me a ride."

"You can ride with me and mummy, darling," offers Sarah.

Lisa and Naana sit in the back of the car, holding hands. Mrs Sharp gently rubs her daughter's hands as Mrs Williams drives toward the loft. At the curb, they all pile out. As they walk toward the building, Naana turns to Sarah and says, "She can't get married! What am I going to do? You saw her with Chance." Sarah throws her arm around her friend as they go into the loft together. The loft is decorated exactly as Lisa asked Tia to do. There are candlelights everywhere. Joe Cocker "All I Know" is playing softly on the stereo. Lisa hugs Father Thomas and thanks him for coming. Naana approaches Father Thomas, "I cannot allow Lisa to get married tonight." Vidal, who has been waiting two years for this day, looks at Lisa wondering whether this is one of her jokes. Instead, Lisa intervenes, "Mother, Vidal and I want to thank you for coming tonight. We are getting married tonight, Mother. We have been taking the marriage preparation course at the church with Father Thomas for the last six months. I would love for all of my family members to stay, but anyone who feels the same way as mother does can leave now." Lisa points to the door. Naana looks desperately at her husband.

Tia asks, "Lisa, can we talk in private for a moment?"

Lisa replies, "There is no need. Anything you have to say, you can say in front of these people."

"Why don't you two wait so we can plan a nice wedding for you?" Tia suggests.

"No. My life flashed right in front of my eyes a few hours ago. I'm afraid I can't wait. Mother, I just cannot wait. I don't mean to be disrespectful, Mother, but I can't wait any longer."

"Are you pregnant?" pipes up Brooke.

"Not that it is any of your business, Brooke, but Vidal and I don't believe in pre-marital sex. Mother, I cannot do this without your blessing," Lisa pleads with her mother.

"I'm so sorry, Lisa," says Naana, then turning toward Vidal she continues. "Vidal, you should know that something happened about two hours ago at the club. Why don't you and Lisa go and talk about it in her office? I cannot allow you two to marry tonight because it seems too hasty." Naana paused, gathering her thoughts. "It seems to me that tonight's wedding is a knee-jerk reaction to events at the club earlier tonight. Vidal, you need to talk it all over with Lisa so that you fully understand what's going on here."

Lisa made no move to take her fiance into the office. Vidal looked at her questioningly, but Lisa avoided his gaze. Sighing, Naana decided to precipitate matters. "Tonight has been most horrendous for all of Lisa's family. Lisa's ex-lover, Priscilla, held us—held me and Sarah and Michael—at gunpoint at the club. She shot at us. Both Lisa and Chance were shot on the arm."

Vidal was stunned. He listened to Naana describe the events of the shooting at the club, and then he got up and slowly undid Lisa's jacket. She begged him to stop, but when the jacket was removed and the bandage revealed on Lisa's arm, Vidal closed his eyes and said a quiet prayer of thanks that his beloved still stood before him. He enfolded Lisa in his arms, gently kissing and hugging her. Tears rolled down his face. It was an intensely private moment, one in which Naana felt like an intruder. With a nod to the others, she walked toward the front door of the loft apartment and stepped out. As Bobby got to the door, Vidal addressed him.

"Mr Sharp! Mrs Sharp! I would like your permission to marry your daughter. Please, you know how much Lisa and I love each other. We cannot get married without your permission. We are both adults, but we would appreciate your approval."

Bobby looked at his wife, saw her distress and knew exactly what to say. "I'm sorry, Vidal, but we can't. Not tonight, at any rate."

Vidal shook hands with Bobby, "It's okay."

Turning back, Naana moves across the room to Lisa to hug her. "I love you, my darling. I am so glad you are safe!" The two women embrace once more before Naana leaves to join Bobby.

Vidal shook hands with Father Thomas and saw them all to the door. Closing the door, Vidal turned to Lisa and carried her to her bedroom where he undressed her, took off his own jacket and got into bed next to her, carefully cuddling her. Lisa began to tremble and sob, not knowing where to begin or what to say to Vidal. Like Naana, Vidal had begged Lisa to end her relationship with Priscilla. It had been a topic of discussion for over a year and once Vidal had threatened to leave Lisa if she did not end the relationship with Priscilla.

"Lisa . . . Please talk to me. I feel helpless. I don't know what to say to make it all better. I don't know how to make your pain go away. I have so many questions, and yet . . . and yet I know now is probably not the best time to be asking everything I want to know."

Lisa sobbed softly into his shoulder. She knew what he wanted to ask, so she turned to face him despite the sharp pain in her shoulder. She closed her eyes, though she could not hide the emotions and the anger she was feeling at that moment. Then, Lisa suddenly sat up on the bed and ran her fingers through her hair. Sighing, she plunged into the conversation she knew had to happen.

"I have not been seeing her. It's been over between Priscilla and I since the last time we fought about it."

Vidal didn't know what to believe. He loves Lisa, but she doesn't seem to understand how much he loves her. Vidal also knows that many of Lisa's closest relationships with friends and family operate on a need-to-know basis. She does not reveal much of her inner self to anyone, and Vidal fears that his relationship with Lisa may be slipping into the need-to-know category, too.

"Do you still have feelings for her?" he probes gently, half dreading the answer.

Lisa leans her head back, contemplating. "No. I don't. I am sure about that. I fell in love with you . . . I . . . I . . . I've been running away from the fact that you love me. I've been afraid of you leaving me for someone else. Priscilla was my way of not thinking about . . . um . . . of not thinking about how much you mean to me."

"Did you want to get married tonight because of her, or because of Chance?" It was a risky question, but it did need to be asked.

Lisa wishes Vidal didn't need to know the answer to that question. She looked at him for a second. "No! How can you ask me that? I've been waiting for us to get married for the past seven months. Tonight, when I was told about my mother, all I could think about was how much I love her and you. The thought of not . . . I'm sorry, Vidal. I just can't be going on the way we have been. I want us to be married. I want to wake up next to you for the rest of our lives. Priscilla made it clear for me tonight. I knew in my heart of hearts that I wasn't going to lose you or mother. I had no idea Chance was in the club."

Vidal sits up, and leans forward to kiss Lisa. It was a warm, sweet, loving kiss, like the kind they shared on the dance floor when she told him she wanted to get married tonight. The kiss deepened and Lisa put her arms around Vidal. They drew apart and Lisa rested her head on Vidal's shoulder.

"Don't worry, babe. I'll get permission for us to marry soon. We won't be apart very long," Vidal reassures Lisa. He knew she was still in pain and wished there was a way for him to take it away. He wanted very much to spend the night with her, just to hold her. Lisa wanted to go and spend the night at her parents home with Jackie. Jackie is leaving in the morning, but Lisa was sure Vidal didn't know that. Vidal knew Lisa was worrying about her mother even though she didn't say it in so many words.

"None of this was your fault, Lisa. I am so thankful I didn't lose you tonight."

Not knowing how to respond, Lisa leaned forward and kissed Vidal again, this time very slowly. Vidal didn't want her to stop. Lisa stops, pulling away because she suddenly felt cold. She felt confused because she was sure she had seen Chance in her room asking how could she break her word. Vidal had his own thoughts about Chance and the potential threat of him coming in between Vidal and Lisa. He was so close to marrying her tonight! Vidal wanted to do his very best to console Lisa without showing any jealousy. He is enjoying just holding Lisa. For her part, Lisa couldn't stop thinking about Gina Read and Chance, what they did for her tonight. Feeling drowsy, she smiles as she cuddles with Vidal.

Chapter 22

Meanwhile, in the living room of the loft, Tia admits to her mother that she feels a little hashed.

Naana chuckles, "Put Jayzel in Lisa's shoes twenty years from now and tell me that you and Nathan would have done anything different!"

"Well, I don't think Lisa will disobey her mother, no matter what Lisa wants," Jackie asserts.

Tia nodded, "Well, I'm beginning to see that. My sister has suffered enough. I can only imagine how she must feel about everything she has been through tonight. Brooke told me how Lisa threw herself in front of my mum to shield her while her ex fired multiple shots at them." Tia can't help bursting into tears.

"Oh! I didn't know that!" Jackie replied. Privately, Jackie wished she could hold Lisa and make sure she is feeling okay, but added, "Lisa is very selfless when it comes to assisting the people she loves."

"Oh, yes! But experiences like this change you. I know this very well. I wish for once my mum and dad would have thought of Lisa's feelings first." Patrick suggests to Jackie that they should give Lisa a call, just to check on them. They leave the room to look for a phone. Nathan is in the home office talking to his father when Tia comes in and sits on his lap. Lately, he has been out of his mind with worry over her, but Tia seems to be doing well with everything. Today could have been a tragedy.

"Are you okay, Baby?" asks Tia.

"I don't know. You should talk to Mother, Tia. I don't think it was just Lisa who was hurt tonight. That girl would have killed Mother without a second thought. A little something of mother has died tonight," Nathan observes.

Tia loves how caring Nathan has become these days. "You know, sweetie, I want to thank you for your support. These last few months, it's been one thing after another. I can't remember the last time I did anything romantic for us. I was thinking . . . we should leave the children with Mrs Hall the weekend when we go home and we should take some time together before your murder trial begins. What do you say?"

"We can't," Nathan says simply.

Tia responds with one of her looks causing Nathan to laugh. She hits him with a throw-cushion from the chair, which only serves to make Nathan laugh more uproariously.

"Seriously, we can't," says Nathan as he struggles to get his laughter under control. "We can't because I have something else planned for our first weekend back home as man and wife. I will not be there for the trial. I have arranged for someone else to do it. I was just discussing with father if he minds . . ." Nathan pauses for effect, "if we stay in Europe a bit longer."

"How long did you have in mind?" asks Tia.

"I'm not sure. Can we discuss it with father?"

"Of course, Baby," says Tia, throwing her arms around him. She was thinking of staying a little bit longer, too.

"Come on! Let's go. I want to go and hold my children. I was thinking that after you have spent some time with Mother, you can come downstairs and we can do all kinds of naughty things all night. I miss you, Baby."

"Mm . . . Me, too," Tia kisses Nathan on the lips.

Sarah Williams has never been as scared in her whole life as she was tonight. After she left Lisa's loft, she and Michael asked Brooke and Jason to spend the night at her house. The twins were already at Sarah's house with their nanny. Brooke didn't want to leave her mother alone after her ordeal. Their thoughts never left the Sharps. Sarah told them how Lisa had privately reassured Sarah that she would bring Naana downstairs to safety. Lisa's words were overwhelmingly powerful and honest, resonating with Sarah's life. Everything Lisa said was the truth: "From now on, I want to enjoy life with my family and the man that . . ." Sarah was a little emotional as she stopped and looked at Brooke who was lovingly held in her husband's arms in the sofa across from her mother. She reached for

Michael's hand and affectionately rubbed his cheeks. She said, "I want to enjoy life with my dear friend Michael with whom I have fallen very much in love with, and you," Sarah points to Brooke and Jason, "I am going to spend a lot more time with Morgan and Jackson."

Brooke runs to hug her. "Oh, BB. We have spent a lifetime grieving. Let's spend the next years of our lives being a family, all of us."

Jason also went and hugged his mother-in-law. Jason was so worried about his wife and mother-in-law this evening that they were all he could think about. He wanted to ring Lisa's neck for putting them both in such danger. Thinking he could have lost both women, Jason decides to have a good talk with Lisa in the morning. "I am not afraid of her and her mob," Jason thinks, "though it is nice seeing Sarah so happy after all these years."

Naana Konadu-Sharp checks on her children and grandchildren, giving them all kisses and hugs before retiring to her own bedroom. Bobby Sharp is not a man who deals with emotions very well.

He knows that his wife and his middle child almost died at the hand of his daughter's crazy ex-lover. He looked into his wife's eyes, but he couldn't see the glorious combinations of youthful exhilaration he often saw when he looked into her eyes. He immediately rushed to her and held her. She was weeping softly as he kissed her cheeks and caressed her back. Moments later Naana was struggling again, resisting the horrifying feeling of Priscilla putting a gun to her head. She began trembling violently, but could only manage to nod when her husband asked whether she felt alright. Instantly, Naana became irritated at the thought that Bobby might be using sex to deal with what she is suffering. The realization made her pull herself out of his embrace. Bobby went over to his wife and put her arms around his neck.

He pulled her close. "I love you, Princess. Always remember that."

"I have to go downstairs to the study to make a phone call, darling. Don't wait up for me."

She turned from him and moved to the door. As it closed behind her, Bobby thought that he heard her whisper, "I'm sorry." Naana went to the window, saw that it was raining. She twisted her long hair into a knot, pinned it up, and pulled the curtains open to see outside. She knew it would be difficult to deal with everything that has happened. The realization that Bobby was unable to comfort her brought tears to

Naana's eyes. She suspects she is on the verge of a nervous breakdown, but her father's advice thunders through her thoughts: "My Princess, it is difficult for a marriage if one spouse takes and takes and gives not an ounce of support back." She certainly understood what her father meant at this moment. Unfortunately for her, that is what marriage to Bobby has been for many years.

It was Nathan who described tonight's events at the club to Anthony Carter. He is waiting for Jackie to come home. She called to say she would be coming home with Lisa to spend the night with her. Anthony has just squeezed fresh orange juice for the girls. He pours some into a glass and goes into the Sharp's study. Naana looks preoccupied. He hurried to the window when he saw her crying. He swept her into his arms. It is impossible to ignore the fact that Bobby neglects his wife at this time of need, but Anthony knows full well the burden Naana holds to keep her family together. He has nothing but admiration for his son's mother-in-law. It hurt him terribly to see her this way. She felt comfortable in Anthony's arms, hearing his steady breathing as he holds her, knowing he has a genuine interest in her well-being when he asks how she is holding up, followed by a second searching glance, as if to make sure that everything is all right with her.

"I don't know, Tony. I don't know how I'm going to get through this one," She murmurs.

They stared at each other in silence, holding hands.

"Tony, I can't tell you how terrified I was. I still can't believe any of it. It's just inconceivable! Lisa is heart-broken, though she is putting on a brave face. All of this could have been avoided if I left them to figure out their own mess, you know? Of all my children, Lisa has always been the most sensible. I have been a selfish parent, and I've never listened to what she wants. Not really. I'll tell Lisa to do something and with no questions she does, hmm."

Anthony Carter was seated opposite Naana in the study. Half of her face is bruised, but she looks genuinely shaken. He felt great empathy for her.

Chapter 23

Lisa has just pulled into the drive way of the Sharp's home. She sees Chance and Curtis getting into Chance's car. Curtis greets Lisa with a kiss and asks if she is okay. She replies she's fine and they make small talk for a few moments before Curtis gets in the car. Chance does not make eye contact with Lisa as he pulls out of the driveway.

"Who's that?" asks Jackie.

"My past," Lisa says wistfully.

Lisa thinks about Jackie often—not so much as a lover, but as a sister. She knows Jackie has strong feelings for her, and also for Patrick, but she's afraid to confront them. Patrick is a good man. His intentions for Jackie are genuine. Jackie leans over toward Lisa, kisses her. Lisa responds by kissing her back. As she pulls away from Jackie, Lisa opens the car door, jumps out and runs around the car to meet Jackie on the passenger side. They hug. Since BJ came to live with the Sharp family, Lisa has moved into the addition part of the house to have some privacy. She needs to have some space apart from her parents down the hall, and her two younger siblings.

"I'm going to check on my Mom. Why don't you go and see your Dad? I'll see you soon."

"Not just now, Lisa. Please . . . My dad can wait," replies Jackie.

Lisa knows what Jackie wants. She hugs her and says, "I'm sorry, Jacks. My Mom needs me more than ever right now. She is my priority. I'll be with you as soon as I know she is alright. I promise!"

Jackie knows that the whole Priscilla experience has frightened Lisa, but Jackie is determined not to lose what she shares with Lisa. Still . . . she is not so sure about it anymore. They see Anthony comforting Naana in the study, making Lisa loathe her father more.

"One would think that for once he would be there for her," thinks Lisa venomously.

Lisa wears dark shades, which when she removes them, her green eyes are full of tears. She sits on the sofa next to her mother, puts her head on Naana's lap and closes her eyes.

Anthony asks, "Are you alright, dear?"

Lisa opens her eyes and smiles, "I'm fine. I appreciate you looking after my mother. Thank you."

Anthony felt an overwhelming need to hug them. "It will get better, you know. This will all pass." He took both of their hands, reassuring Lisa and Naana, "I'm here for you if you need me. Now, excuse me. I'd like to spend a little time with Jackie."

Lisa has not been able to get the image of Priscilla holding a gun out of her mind. Neither can Naana get the picture of Lisa shielding her from the bullets out of her own mind.

Lisa says dully, "I had to come home and make sure that you were not alone." She puts one arm around her mother's waist and buries her face in Naana's lap. Naana gently rubs Lisa's back and tells her none of this mess is her fault.

"I love you, darling. I hope you can forgive me. I suspect I'm too hard on you," Naana sighs. "I think my interference in your personal affairs has caused this terrible incident tonight."

"I disagree, Mother."

"It's not easy being a lone parent. Sometimes I make the wrong decision about you and your sisters, darling."

"I've never know you to be wrong about anything, Mother. We may not like how you punish us, sometimes, but we do love you. We know you'll always be here for us." Lisa felt a lump in her throat as she sat up to look her mother in the eye. "Mother, I'm impatient with . . . things in my life, but with your guidance I've learned to be a little more patient. When I was told by my security guard that you were being held at gunpoint by Priscilla, I wanted to hit him with a bottle of wine for letting it happen. I felt enormous pain in my whole body at that moment. I looked out on the dance floor and saw Vidal dancing with Jacks and Patrick. They looked so happy, Mother." Lisa took a deep breath and ran her fingers through her hair. "Tia was there, too, with Jacks. I knew I had to get them out of the club. I couldn't let them see my pain or my rage . . . whichever one you want to call it. Chance told me to think of you and how you're always so calm about life. I drew on your strength since I could not get my words out." Lisa and Naana were sobbing. "I just . . .," Lisa paused, "I just don't go around sleeping with girls, you know? Falling in love, sleeping with someone is the ultimate intimacy for me, Mother. I have to establish trust, first. The blah, blah, blah of the romantic stuff that we do has to be all about trust. I loved her, Mother. God help me, part of me still does. She knew! She knew that I'd be broken without you. She knew!"

Naana nodded as she listened to Lisa re-count the events from her point of view.

"I felt physically ill that someone I loved wanted to hurt you. My relationship with Priscilla has been one hell of a storm, but every storms runs its course sooner or later. I could have lost you and Chance tonight, Mother." Lisa is in tears as her mother stood up and hugged her.

"Come, now, darling. You'll never really lose me," says Naana, reassuringly.

"I fear the nightmares that Priscilla has unleashed on you and Mrs Williams are not going to be as easy to get over as everyone seems to think. I was getting over Chance before all this. I hate to break my promise, but maybe he is better off without me. He knows me better than I know myself. I lost him—"

Naana wants to tell Lisa to talk to Chance. She hopes that they might find each other on their own.

Lisa calls Sarah to see how she is. She passes the phone to her mother, so they can catch up and leaves the room to find Jackie. Jackie is determined to take Lisa's mind off everything that has happened tonight. She lights a single candle and puts Kenny G's instrumental album on the stereo.

Naana wants to finish her talk with her daughter, wants to learn more about her relationship with Vidal. Father Thomas did, in fact, speak to her and Bobby about the young couple's faith, their beliefs and the kind of marriage they both want. It makes Naana think about her own marriage and how proud she is of Lisa and her choices. Learning that Lisa and Vidal always go to church and work with the youth is one thing she didn't know about her daughter. Naana heads to her room on the other side of the house. There are no lights on in the playroom as she passes. She can see Lisa standing with her back to the door. Naana cannot hear the music playing softly on the stereo, but Lisa sways to it. Jackie is half-naked in her underwear as she takes off Lisa's jacket. Lisa seems to be in pain and Jackie tries to comfort her.

Suddenly, Jackie stops her ministrations. "I want to make sure that you are fully relaxed, Lisa. You've been through a lot tonight. I feel bad that I'm leaving in the morning, because I'd like to stay a few more days just to make sure you're okay."

This is not at all what Lisa has in mind, but she can't bring herself to tell Jacks that she wants to be alone. Instead, Lisa smiles encouragingly. From her vantage point, Naana can see the girls as they move together. She can see that Jackie is doing all the talking, while Lisa sits down. It appears to Naana that Lisa is crying, and may be in shock. She watches as Jackie passionately kisses Lisa. They stop. Lisa stands with a half smile on her face. Suddenly, a wave of realization washes over Naana as she comes to a full understanding of what she has just witnessed. With an infinite weariness, Naana returns to the living room where she takes refuge in an easy chair. She leans back in the large, comfortable chair and closes her eyes. Tears well up as she thinks about watching the girls.

Meanwhile, back in Lisa's room, Jackie kisses the wound on Lisa's arm. Lisa shivers with pleasure. On her way to bed, Naana passes the room where the girls are busy feeling each other up. She watches for a moment as they lay on the rug in front of the fireplace, kissing and exploring each other's bodies. Naana's heart beats rapidly as she closes the door on them and goes upstairs to check on her grandchildren sleeping soundly.

Afterward, Naana gets under the shower and finds herself crying again. As she slips into bed next to Bobby, Naana marvels at how he seems not to have a care in the world. She wonders how he can sleep so well with everything that has happened.

Naana thinks of Chance and the heartache that Lisa is causing him and Vidal. She wishes Lisa would have the courage to trust her instincts and see what everyone else can see—that she and Chance are one in a million.

Tia and Nathan love the surprise that Lisa has left them. It is what they have been missing. They have not made love since Kevin Peters attempted to rape Tia—not even on their wedding night. The hot tub temperature is just right. They undress each other and climb into the hot tub. The sensation of slippery, hot, naked skin is a bit overwhelming. They find themselves laughing less and moaning more. There is something indescribably erotic about Tia's touch that Nathan cannot resist. He finds her sexy beyond words. The touch of her slick cheeks as she slides into her husband's lap in the tub is a huge turn-on. Nathan feels warm. He watches her drink champagne and place her glass on his lips to drink. "No, baby. I'm going to be driving us home. I shouldn't be drinking at all."

"Nathan, this is the most private time we've had since we've been in Europe. Don't you want to be with me?"

Nathan watches her expression as he caresses and strokes her. "Baby, no man on this planet can turn you down for anything. This is incredibly romantic. Just the elegance of it makes me want to stay here all night, making love to you in every room in this loft."

Tia smiles, mischievously. They did make love all over the loft just as Nathan had said. Nathan told Tia that it is imperative that he keep his promise to God. "I can't never forget that I've been given a second chance with you. Not just you, baby, all our family. Right now." He paused, then kissed her and rolled over on the bed. Nathan got out of bed and began getting dressed. "Half of our family needs us," he remarked.

Tia knew what Nathan meant. She didn't want him getting caught up in what happened tonight. Their divorce and her cancer has changed her husband to be the man she wished he would be when they were first married. Tia wishes that tonight it could be just the two of them, but she felt the same way as him that her mother and sister needed them. She asked why they have to go back to her parents house now, not in the morning. Nathan zipped up his pants. "I love your father, but I feel he neglects Mother and the family a lot. Just like I did with you and Jayzel years ago."

"So you want us to go home because of that?"

He signed. "No, baby. We are family and when one is in trouble, we all are. Mother has always been there for us and our children. She needs us now to be there for her and her child. There is also a legal issue here too. Lisa and I discussed some of it earlier and with Chance's help we took some preventive steps, but we don't want anything that will perceived as threats on our family again. We still have a lot of things to take care of. Baby. If we spend the night here I may never want to leave. I'll forget about my other responsibilities. I want to get back in the bed and not let go of you. I am going to the bathroom to get cleaned up. How about you get dressed?"

Tia thought about following Nathan into the bathroom and seducing him there one more time, but she knows that their experience has helped them to have a physical and emotional bond with one another, so that they don't have to say to each other what their needs are. She also has been thinking about her mother and Lisa and felt the same as her husband about her father. She was hoping that this time, it would be different.

The kettle is whistling. Naana quickly turns it off. The usual comforting sound of the steam had become a mournful wail in the early hours of the morning. Naana was only able to sleep for two hours. It had become obvious to her last night why Lisa and Jackie had been inseparable since Holland. Lying awake in bed, staring into the darkness, Naana slipped out of bed before her husband reached for her. She was in no mood for sex this morning. She had not realized, until now, how alone she always felt. Usually the children have filled the void, but that was in the past and now it is not enough. She picked up the kettle and began to shake. Lost in her own thoughts, Naana did not hear Lisa's approach until her daughter placed her own hands around her mother's and guided the heavy kettle back to the stove-top. Naana falls into Lisa's arms, weeping, "I'm sorry. I feel like everything is falling apart and . . . I . . . can't fix it. I have no one to turn to for help." Her mother looks dazed and disoriented. It broke Lisa's heart to see her mother this way.

Nathan and Tia had just come into the Sharp home, and they overheard Naana. It enraged both of them that Naana would feel she could not confide her worries to Bobby. They both went and threw their arms around Lisa and Naana. Tia is the first to pull away from the group embrace.

"I'll not stand for this! Mother, you and Lisa should not be dealing with this alone!"

"Baby, please!" Nathan pleaded with his wife. He turned to Lisa to ask, "Were you able to sleep?"

Lisa replies, "Yes. Even though my cell phone keeps ringing, I need to study, and I want to go to the club to speak with my staff before the police get there."

"I'll accompany you," offers Nathan.

"Like hell, you will!" exclaims Lisa. "We discussed this last night, Nathan. This is not the glaring spotlight of celebrity that you are used to in Canada as a high profile defense lawyer. I'm going to talk with the police and answer whatever questions they might have for me."

Tia and Naana ask, "Why don't you want Nathan with you?"

"The police arrested the two thugs who held Mrs Williams and her friend, along with Priscilla last night. If I show up with my brother-in-law, a well-known, high-powered defense lawyer, then some idiot, starstruck police officer will start nosing around in my business. I'm not going to give them the opportunity to entrap me and my staff. The use of an illegal firearm is ten to twenty-five years behind bars in the UK."

"Hmm, the prosecution would still have to prove criminal intent here, Lisa. There is no evidence that any of your employees had a gun at your club or fired a gun last night. The shot could have come from anywhere," Nathan argued.

"It's very easy for a prosecutor to get a conviction in this country, especially once you are charged or implicated in any crime. People in England are especially dazzled by wealthy defendants. Someone like me would be tried on every television screen in the country before the truth could come out. Everything that Mother and I have worked for would be gone."

"So what do you plan to do? Are you going to press charges?" Tia asks.

"No. I am not going to press charges."

"Why not, Lisa? Priscilla attempted to kill you as well as Mother. And Chance. Why would you let this go? Don't you think you and Chance have suffered enough?"

"Chance left me. Not the other way around. Tia, the police don't know what happened at the club. I'm not letting this go. It's being handled as we speak."

"So are you going to tell us why they were arrested?" Naana asks nervously.

"We found a lot of drugs in my club manager's office last night. I didn't know who to trust. Nathan, Chance and I discussed the implications of it. We put all the drugs in Simon's car. It seems he has been using the club to sell his drugs. After Priscilla shot us, Gina wanted to arrest her."

"Did she?"

"No, Mother. She did not. Priscilla ran a traffic light and was pulled over by a cop. She was driving under the influence. That's why she was arrested. It has nothing to do with me."

"Lisa, Gina Read is an undercover police officer. She will not lie and cover up this mess for you. Please go with Nathan. Explain things to the police and forget about our business," her mother insisted.

"I can't have Priscilla behind bars for something like this. She needs help, Mother. That was not her last night: it was the drugs. Gina will not mention the incident to the police because she has no proof. No evidence."

"How can you be so sure?"

"You might as well know now because it will probably come out anyway: I have been . . . um . . . sleeping with Gina Read."

"What?!" exclaimed Nathan and Naana simultaneously. Lisa smiled at them.

"C'mon guys. Don't be so naive. I met her in one of my clubs weeks before I left for Holland. She claimed it was her nineteenth birthday, so I sent her a bottle of wine, and let's just say she was *very* appreciative in the way she thanked me." Lisa chuckled. She sits down, drinks some orange juice like nothing unusual has happened, but Naana, Tia and Nathan were looking at her in shock.

"Well? What do you expect?" demanded Lisa. "When I got back from Holland, Simon told me a new chef had been hired, so I asked him to send her up to make a meal for Jackie and I. A few minutes later, Simon introduced Gina Read to me as the new Chef. I did some digging and discovered that she also was Dana's sister. Boy, was I pissed about that!"

"Who's Dana?" asked Tia.

Naana supplies the answer, "Dana was one of Lisa's friends who died of a drug overdose. I was worried about Lisa, so I hired Gina to help me clean up Lisa's club."

"What Mother really means," said Lisa with sarcastic emphasis, "is that she hired Gina to spy on me. Anyway, I left Jackie with Corey to take her home one day at the club, and I took Gina in my car for a ride—just to give her something to think about." Lisa winked meaningfully.

"You paid off a police officer?" asked Naana in disbelief. Both Tia and Nathan were laughing.

"I'm glad you two think this is funny, but in England, bribing a police officer is still a crime," said Naana pointedly to Nathan. "You should know that your sister is going to jail."

"No, Mother! I don't pay for sex!" Lisa blurted out. "Come on! Look at me! I'm Lisa Sharp for God's sakes! Women are dying to give me what they won't give their lovers and husbands. It will be a cold day in hell when I pay for sex."

Naana has had it with both daughters: Lisa's casual attitude dismays Naana and Tia's propensity for finding Lisa' sordid situation amusing is just too much for Naana. "Well, be that as it may, I still want you to take Nathan with you, please."

"Mother, if I show up with my brother-in-law, the police will assume I'm guilty of something and in need of Nathan's services. To top it off, my staff will think I've gone soft. I pay those idiots good money to watch my back and this happened? No, Nathan cannot be there. I am going to fire Simon for bringing drugs into my club and for putting your life in harm's way. Nathan cannot come because the staff will think I'm hiding behind my attorney-brother-in-law. Lisa Sharp doesn't run out of fear, and no one threats my mother, and no one shoots at me and gets away with it."

"Lisa, I am coming with you," insisted Nathan.

Lisa laughs. "No, you are not. I have to go and study before Vidal comes for me."

Holding both of Lisa's hands and looking directly into her eyes, Nathan says, "No, Lisa. You don't seem to get it. I am coming with you and that's final. You cannot handle this alone."

Lisa wiggles out of Nathan's hands, "Fine! You keep your pants on, you can come. I'll talk to you later!" She left with a big jug of orange juice.

Naana covers her mouth with her hands and whispers to Tia and Nathan, "Is there any young woman out there with whom your sister has not slept with?"

Chuckling, Tia says, "Let's face it, Mother. Lisa has probably slept with more girls than my Baby here has."

"Oh! Oh! My wounded heart!" says Nathan mockingly, clasping his hands over his heart. "That's not funny, Baby!" objects Nathan.

Tia and her mother are now laughing at Nathan. He grabs his wife by the waist, saying, "Mother, Tia and father and I want to know if you would mind us staying until the middle of next month before we go back to Canada?"

"Of course, darling! This is your home. May I ask why? I mean . . . I though you have a trial coming up. And Tia and Steven have a movie, too."

Tia and Nathan are quiet for a moment. "I do, Mother, but all the groundwork is done. One of my associates has already taken over some of the workload, so I can be here with my family."

"You kids really don't have to stay because of last night."

"No, Mother. All we do is work, work, work. We hardly have time to see the rest of our family other than through phone calls. I want to stay so I can go to Holland every weekend with the children and spend more time with Grandmother and Grandfather. I'm hoping they will miss us and agree to come to Canada so we can all spend the Easter holiday together as a family. I'm not ready to leave yet. I enjoy having all my family around me, you know?"

Naana smiles, tears coming to her eyes, "I was hoping you could stay a bit longer, too. It's been good having you all home. Maybe we can all go to the cottage next weekend? I know Mother and Father will love that!" She smiles again.

BJ and Trey appeared to say they were coming downstairs to make tea for their mums. Nathan gave both boys 'high-fives'. BJ has been a good role model for Trey. Naana looks at the two boys. It warms her heart to see them thinking of others before themselves. Jayzel is still sleeping. Upstairs in their room, Tia and Nathan get into bed. Tia rolls on top of Nathan and he rubs her back. Soon, they both sleep soundly. It has been a long night for all of the Sharps, the Carters, and their friends. Nathan and Tia are relieved that their Mother and Lisa are coping and that Priscilla and her thugs are going to be put away. Nathan thought, "That Lisa is a genius the way she set up her ex-lover without having to press charges." Lisa wouldn't want her mother having to testify in court.

Lisa gives Jackie the orange juice and tells her that she won't be coming to the airport to see her off.

"Why not?"

"Vidal is picking me up and we're going to the church for a meeting that will take most of the day. I'm sorry, Jacks."

"No, don't be. I hate saying good-byes anyway." Jackie wants to talk about last night's events and how Lisa is feeling. Instead, Lisa is kissing her between the thighs.

"I will call you once you are in LA. We can talk then. I won't be able to do this to you over the phone or the internet, though, Jacks!"

When Jackie woke up later that morning, Lisa was already gone, leaving a note saying, "I love you, Jacks."

Anthony is glad that the Carter family is staying a bit longer in Europe. He thought it would be best under the circumstances. Now, he is not so sure anymore. He suspects that his feelings for Tia's mother aren't so much those of a concerned in-law, but perhaps something deeper. He needs to fight those feelings because they are not appropriate to have for his son's mother-in-law.

Tia drove Jackie to the airport with Anthony and her children. Jackie is very quiet, almost tearful, as she boards the plane that will take her back to her boring life in LA. She listens to the songs on her iPod, the songs to which she and Lisa made love and feels the heartache grow for Lisa's touch. On the aircraft was airborne, Jackie feel asleep and remained asleep until the plane touched down the runway of LAX Airport. Steven forgot to meet her. After waiting for almost an hour, she decided to take a cab home. As she pulls her suitcase toward the taxi stand, Jackie feels a depression coming on since everywhere she looks people are making out. She feels terrible. She sees a man in a black suit holding a big card with her name on it.

"I am Jackie Carter," she says to the man.

He passes her a note, which says, "I took a Concord plane from London Heathrow Airport just to be with you. I miss you already, Baby. Have dinner with me tonight at eight!"

The driver sees tears rolling down Jackie's face as he opens the car door for her. He says gently, "My employer wishes me to take you home and to return for you at seven, tonight."

Jackie didn't bother to ask who his employer might be. Lisa is so romantic that this would be typical of her. Still... considering that Lisa has two more exams to write and one of them first thing tomorrow morning, this escapade would be a little over the top for Lisa. Jackie ignored her personal misgivings and relaxed into the soft leather seat of the limo. It is afternoon in California. The weather seems hot compared to the cooler weather in Europe. Jackie has forgotten how hot it is in LA. Steven's home is located in Pomona. He doesn't live in Malibu or Beverly Hills like most of the people in the film industry do. Instead, he lives in a five-bedroom ranch home, sitting on five acres of land fully fenced with wrought iron and beautifully landscaped. There are some out buildings, one of them a small carriage house in which his housekeeper lives, a young, single mother of two, originally from Cuba.

The housekeeper greets Jackie and helps her carry the suit case into the main house. As usual, the house is dead quiet.

"You wants something to eat?" asks the housekeeper.

"No . . . No, thank you."

Jackie retreats to her room upstairs and throws herself on her bed. She wants to call her lab partner, Stephine, to say that she is back and ask her to join her for dinner, then thought she should not. "Lisa is probably staying at some fabulous hotel and just wants to be alone with me." Jackie slept again and when she awakened, it was almost five o'clock. She rushed to the shower and couldn't help masturbating under the warm water. Jackie was not into fashion like Tia and Lisa, but since spending so much time with the Sharp sisters, she has picked up some of their style tips. She chose a black micro-mini dress, crystal strands drop earrings, and repaired stray wisps of the finger waves she'd had when she left Europe that morning.

Steven was in the living room with actor-rapper Ice Cube when he saw a girl coming down the stairs.

"Hey! How come you didn't say you have a shorty in the crib, dog?" Ice Cube asked.

Steven turned his head. Initially, he thought it was Tia, or maybe Lisa. He certainly didn't recognize Jackie.

"Damn! Jackie, does Dad know you had a make-over?"

Jackie grins broadly at her brother. "I miss you too, big brother. Thanks for picking me up!"

"I'm sorry! I forgot you were coming home today, sweetie."

"I'm going to dinner."

Steven was amused that she was going out on a date with Shawn the first night back. "I thought you were Tia or Lisa coming down the stair, for a second."

Jackie graciously accepted the compliment. "It's nice being compared to Tia and Lisa because they are so beautiful," thought Jackie.

Steven watched her get into the limousine.

"She looked like Lenny Kravitz daughter, didn't she?" he asked Ice Cube.

"No, dog. Your baby sister is banging! Man, she looks way sexier than Zoe Kravitz!"

Meanwhile, in the limousine, Jackie closed her eyes and enjoyed the ride. She didn't notice the driver exit onto the freeway towards Malibu Beach. When the door opened, someone helped her out. The person's hands felt different, less feminine, not so soft, firmer. It was Patrick Collins. He looked so sexy in a white polo shirt and shorts. Jackie was surprised, a bit disappointed, but she managed a smile and reached out to hug him. When he finally let go of her, she was happy to see him and relieved, too, that it was not Lisa. Naana Konadu-Sharp would have killed the girls if she thought they were entertaining themselves on the night before an exam. Patrick slowly kissed her. Jackie realized she liked how he kisses with his tongue. It was like kissing Lisa, but different. She brushes her fingers across his lips to wipe off her lipstick. He sucked on her fingers until her knees weakened. When he finally stopped, Patrick put his arms around her and said, "Come and meet my mother before we go to dinner." Patrick's mother is an actress. In fact, Jackie knows her very well since she used to date Steven. Kelly Powers was delighted to see Jackie again, coming forward to give her a big hug and kiss.

"Damn! Baby, Jackie-girl, you look hot!" Kelly exclaimed. Jackie smiled.

"She meets your approval, Mother?" Patrick asked with both of his hands folded on his chest, smiling broadly.

"You know, honey, Jackie's brother, Steven, is a close personal friend of mine. In fact, I'm shooting a TV movie with him at the end of next month in Canada. I'll be staying with Nathan and Tia while I'm there. How is Tia?" Kelly asked as she hugged Jackie.

"No way! They cast you in *Forever never dies*?"

"Yes! Tia called just before she left for Europe. She faxed me a script. I couldn't put it down, and when she said Steven was directing, well, that just clinched the deal. I told her I'd be there in a heartbeat! My agent just stopped by with the contract a few minutes ago."

Patrick interrupted, "We'll have to go now, Mother, if we don't want to miss our reservation."

"Well, you kids enjoy yourselves! It's so nice to see you again, Jackie." Kelly waved good-bye as Jackie and Patrick got back into the limousine.

"Why didn't you tell me that Kelly Powers is you mom? I'm almost half in love with you and now I'm gonna have to break up with you."

Patrick smiled when he heard that Jackie was half in love with him. "I'm also half in love with you, too, Jackie. I don't want you to break up with me—at least, not until we have kids and our kids have kids. I figure that by then, I won't be able to get it up, and *then* you can break up with me. But on one condition: I get to pick the stud you leave me for."

Jackie thought Patrick was hysterically funny. By the time she stopped laughing, she was sitting on his lap kissing him.

"She had me when she was in her teens. It didn't work out with my father. My mother was determined to fulfill a long-held desire for a career in show business. My father had to go back to Europe to take up the reigns of my Grandfather's business. Mother and Father didn't want me to grow up like the rest of the Hollywood brats. They agreed to protect me from the gossip and the privacy invasions that most celebrities and their kids have to contend with."

"Wow!"

"She is a good mother. I think my father is still in love with her even though he says that he is not. They still share an extraordinary friendship."

"They also share you." Patrick nodded in agreement. Then, changing the subject, he said, "There is this new restaurant opening in West Hollywood. I thought we could go there for dinner. It is called The Soulless."

"I want the driver to take us to Pomona. I want to cook for us, instead. I don't like eating out like Lisa and you guys do."

"Actually, I don't like eating out either. Vidal loves eating out and when we're together, that's what we spend most of our time doing." Patrick smiled with pleasure. He told the driver to take them to Steven's house. Jackie cooked a lavished meal fit for a king, making pesto chicken with steamed artichokes and fresh figs. She couldn't find anything to make for dessert, but she found a large carton of ice cream in the freezer, so they took it to Jackie's room.

"Haven't you unpacked, yet?" asked Patrick.

"No, I took a nap and I woke just in time for our date," she smiled.

"You look so sexy, Jackie," Patrick whispered.

Jackie blushed. She is not accustomed to men telling her she looks sexy. Patrick put a big chunk of ice cream in her mouth, and inadvertently spilled some on her dress.

"Oops! I guess that dress had better come off so it can be washed right away!" smirked Patrick.

Jackie laughed as he unzipped her dress and lifted it over her head. He put more ice cream on her neck, and lapped it up. Jackie turned to face him and put some ice cream on his nose. Patrick took a step backward, leaving the ice cream carton on Jackie's desk. He removed her panties, then picked her up and sat her on the desk, spreading her legs apart. He put some of the ice cream directly between her legs. She instantly felt the cold, and sucking in her breathe, Jackie closed her eyes and leaned her head back. Patrick watched her facial expression. Her nipples popped out hard, her back arched reacting to the cold ice cream just before he delicately flicked his tongue against her ice-cream-soaked clit, tasting her, tasting the frozen treat. He carried her to the bed where they caressed each other lightly as they kissed. Jackie removed Patrick's shirt. She trailed her tongue on his chest as she unzipped his pants. He was fully aroused, straining against the fabric as she released his penis and took him in her warm mouth. Patrick moaned and pulled her up so he could study her body. He felt the way her body responded to his touch. He listened for her sighs and then at the optimal moment, he entered her. Jackie rubbed his back. Any thoughts she may have had for Lisa disappeared by the time she felt the power of his throbbing orgasm inside her.

A few days later, Jackie had her first exams and afterward she went to the free clinic where she works. Patrick sent her flowers—lilies, her mother's favorite. She is told that there is a patient in room nine who needs her help. She knock on the door before entering the room and says, "Hello, I'm Dr. Carter. I'm an intern here. There is nothing on your chart. What can I do for you, today?" She looks up to see Patrick on the bed. Jackie is surprised to see him, but also thinks it's not funny. "Are you trying to get me fired?" she demands.

Before she can react, Patrick has her pinned against the door with her legs wrapped around his waist. She drops the chart to hold on to him as he takes her right there in the examination room. When he leaves, Jackie goes to the staff room and signs out, like nothing has happened. They meet at his mother's house. They skinny-dip in the pool before succumbing to their desires again. Standing in the shallow end of the pool, leaning against the deck, Patrick enters Jackie from behind. As they rock in their embrace, the rough tiles on the deck of the pool graze Jackie's nipples, stimulating her further. She clenches Patrick's member in a mind-numbing orgasm. Weakened, she leans back against Patrick's chest and he lowers her body into the water, cooling her tingling senses. Patrick takes Jackie to his room inside the house. Laying her gently on his bed, he massages her body with his mother's body oil. As he makes love to her again, he describes what he is doing as well as his own sensations. He asks often, is she enjoying their lovemaking, is there anything she likes best.

Jackie loves it all, but her favorite moment happens when she is on the brink of orgasm and he stops thrusting. Begging him to begin thrusting again is her most luscious moment, pushes her into a madness for gratification.

At the end of their afternoon session, Patrick slips his hands under the pillow and comes out with a small box. Jackie's eyes are closed, resting, coming down from the high of repeated orgasm. He places the box on her belly, kisses her eyelids and whispers, "Jackie, Baby, open your eyes for me, please." Jackie opens her eyes and her heart begins to beat faster. There were tears in her eyes when she said, "Yes, I will marry you."

It was like everything stopped at that moment. Patrick's hands shook when he slipped the ring on her finger and continued making love to her. They both cried when they came. He held her as Jackie lay on top of him admiring the ring on her finger, gasping with surprise.

Chapter 24

Back in England, Gina Read has mixed emotions about Lisa Sharp. From the first night they met at the Club Empire, she was as folks said she was: sitting at her table with her spoiled rich friends having dinner, laughing, but Gina could tell there was more to Miss Sharp than met the eye. Gina found Lisa intriguing. Lisa didn't waste any time: when she found out it was Gina's birthday, she sent over a bottle of wine. Lisa was almost out of the club when Gina boldly followed her and grabbed her hand.

"I hope you enjoyed your birthday," said Lisa.

"No," replied Gina.

Lisa smiled and asked, "Is there anything I can do to make it a happier birthday?"

"How about a dance with the sexiest girl in the club?" ventured Gina.

Lisa, who had been holding hands with her dinner partner, suddenly kissed the girl good-night and put her in the waiting taxi. Taking Gina by the hand, Lisa returned to the club and escorted Gina to the dance floor. Gina remembered that night as if it were yesterday. The song was by the Backstreet Boys, "The Call". They danced and shared a kiss, which lead inexorably to many more kisses. Gina continued to marvel that even though Lisa knew she was actually Dana's older sister, and that she had been hired to go undercover to help clean up the drug market in Lisa's clubs, it didn't stop Lisa from spending the most incredible night with her. She has been sending Gina flowers almost every day now. Gina has slept with many women in her time, but never anyone like Lisa Sharp. Lisa has it all: money, power, sophistication, sex appeal and a romantic spirit to top it all off. Last night Gina cried herself to sleep think about how Lisa almost died. It was surreal: the crazed ex-lover, the hostages, the gun shots. It all made her heart rate escalate. Lisa called to ensure that Gina was alright. Gina is tempted to ask whether Lisa—for real—got married last night, but opted not to ask at the last moment.

"Want to come by and spend the evening with me?" invites Lisa. She knows Gina doesn't work on Sundays.

"Sure!" exclaims Gina, fully expecting the evening to be anything but tame. She remembered how Lisa had called to ask after her well-being following that wild ride in her car. It was like something out of a romantic movie. It could not have been real, but it was the most exciting experience of Gina's life.

The door to Lisa's loft is wide open. Gina enters, closing the door behind her. Tia and Nathan are still there.

"Thank you for saving my mother's and my sister's lives last night, Miss Read," Tia says as she hugs Gina.

Lisa comes out of her office holding some files. She is bare-foot, sporting gym clothes and remarks to Tia, "We may be sisters, but I don't like to share my lovers with anyone!" The expression on Tia's face was screamingly funny. Lisa openly, slow-kisses Gina as Tia and Nathan watched. After the long, slow, sensual kiss, Lisa held Gina in her arms and whispered, "I miss you." Gina forgets that they are not alone and puts her own arms around Lisa's waist.

"I am going to walk my brother and sister to their car. Make yourself comfortable." Lisa kisses Gina again before taking Tia and Nathan by the hand and heading toward the front door. As Tia gets into the car, she asks her little sister, "Just how many girls are you planning to fuck before you get married, Lisa?"

"Baby, please!" objects Nathan. Lisa grins.

"Baby, please! Mother cannot handle Lisa and her whorish lifestyle. All you can say is 'Baby, please'.' Lisa is getting to be worse than you were, Nathan. I suppose you think it's okay for her to carry on this way? You know? You two are alike! Baby, please!" Tia says mockingly with a dismissive gesture of her hands.

"I think Mother is about to cave. She will give me permission to get married to Vidal by the end of the week, I promise you. Then, I'll stop my whorish ways," Lisa said with a wink at her brother-in-law, who is still laughing.

"Lisa, why do you need Mother's permission? And what is up with all this sleeping around with all these sexy women? Father Thomas told us all about the love affair you and Vidal shared. I have seen it with my own eyes. You are crazy about him and possibly still madly in love with Chance, and you're going to marry Vidal? You're too much like Daddy—can't keep it in his pants."

Nathan and Lisa laugh again as Tia rolls her eyes at them.

Nathan and Lisa laugh again.

"She is my mother, Tia. You have no idea how luck you are. Mother is not as hard on you as she is on me. You and Claire are more like Mother. Me . . . I'm the wild card. I love her and I need her blessing in everything I do in my life . . . Just like you do . . . as I'm sure Nathan does with Anthony. This is about my magazine idea. We'll discuss it in more detail tomorrow because I can't keep a beautiful woman waiting."

"Bollocks! You are one weird kid, Lisa! Promise me you'll stop and think of what you and Chance share. I have learned that much from my own experience with my baby here," Tia points to Nathan, sighs contently and hugs her.

Lisa shakes her head, "Nuh-uh. Chance and I are over. I will see you tomorrow after my exams. I have to take Claire to her driving test in the afternoon." Lisa blows them both a kiss as they drive off.

Gina is sitting in the living room. Lisa sits behind her so she can position Gina between her legs. Cupping a breast beneath Gina's shirt, Lisa squeezes gently. Gina smiles and closes her eyes as she lightly rubs Lisa's legs. Lisa, on the other hand, dials a number on the phone. She begins kissing the back of Gina's neck while the phone rings. Finally, Jackie's voice comes on the phone.

"Hi sweetie!" Lisa says.

Jackie knows that Lisa always uses the speaker phone.

"Are you okay?"

"Oh, yes! I'm doing well. Did you like your surprise, Jacks?"

"Of course! You knew about it the whole time that Patrick was coming to LA! Why didn't you tell me?"

"I didn't want to spoil the surprise."

"We had dinner. He's sleeping now" Jackie tells her.

Lisa is kissing Gina, then she stops to ask, "How was the sex, Jacks?" with a throaty laugh. Jackie is embarrassed and didn't respond right away.

"Did you make love to him?" Lisa prompts. She is kissing Gina behind the ears with her other hand slowly running through her hair.

"Speaking of making love . . . Who are you spending your time with?" asks Jackie.

"Someone very special. I'll call you tomorrow night. I love you, Jacks." Lisa hangs up the phone.

"I've missed you, Gina. Let's get into the hot tub."

"I thought you hated hot tubs," queries Gina.

Lisa sighs and smiles, "Yeah, I do . . . I feel tense, I need to relax. I want to relax with you tonight. I didn't get the chance to thank you last night for saving my life and my mother's life." Lisa pressed her forehead against Gina's. She shivers. She knows that once she marries Vidal, she and Gina will be over. Lisa hates the thought of losing Gina. She has come to love her in the short time they've known each other. Gina, too, is thinking about Lisa, and she shares her feelings. Gina does not want to think about Lisa's pending marriage. Instead, she wants to enjoy the moment with Lisa.

"I hate to see you do something you dislike, Lisa. Why don't we do something else to relax you, instead of the hot tub you hate?"

"Holding you is relaxing, Gina. I don't want to take my hands off you. How is your wine?" Lisa turns to face her. Lisa knew what Gina was thinking. She asks if there is anything—anything at all—that Gina wants before dinner. Gina sets down her wine glass and says, "I want you to tell me why you look so sad."

Lisa replies with a sigh, "I'm not unhappy. I very happy you're here. I'm going to be getting married soon, Gina. You're all I think about. I wanted to be with you more than anything last night. But I was needed at home . . . I . . . um . . ." Lisa trailed off, lost in her thoughts.

Gina managed a smile, "We all have to make lifestyle changes sometimes. Lisa, it's a part of growing up. You will make a lovely wife to Chance."

"I'm not getting married to Chance! He and I are done."

"But you're so in love with Chance! You two are definitely not 'done'—as you say. Why are you so afraid to admit that you love him?" Lisa began kissing Gina. "Okay, I'll change the subject. I was thinking about you and your mother. I went to see her. She seems to be copying. I'm more worried about you—mostly." Gina gazes into her eyes and kisses her. She can't help wondering why Lisa puts on a brave face all the time. Lisa immediately changes the subject, "I feel comfortable with you. I feel better that you are here with me now. I've missed you terribly, Gina."

Lisa slowly kisses Gina as she massages the girl's buttocks. Gina moans with pleasure and tells Lisa that she has been thinking about her, too. Lisa looks deep into her eyes and kisses her on each cheek. Because Lisa is wearing a vest, Gina can't take her eye off the gunshot wound on Lisa's shoulder. She closes her eyes thinking how close Lisa came to dying last night. There were tears in Gina's eyes as Lisa gently ran her hands through Gina's hair. They kissed, while Lisa murmured re-assuring little nothings, telling Gina she is alright, even though Gina could not understand how Lisa might be alright.

"Lisa, how can you be alright? It was not a stranger who tried to kill you and your mom. It was someone you love!"

Lisa sighed and closed her eyes. "Let me ask you something: Your job as a policewoman is to put criminals behind bars. Did you ever have to arrest someone you love and see that person go to jail?"

"No . . . but you didn't put your ex behind bars, Lisa. She put herself there. Damn it! If it was up to me, Priscilla would . . . You know? Lisa, it's okay to . . ." Lisa didn't let Gina finish her thought. She hugged her and whispered, "this is our time together. I don't want to think of anything or anyone but you, Gina."

"I'm sorry, Lisa. You don't have to share your feelings about the incident with me—though you probably ought to think about what's going on between your ex and Simon."

Lisa put her lips on Gina's and began kissing her. Gina realized that Lisa didn't want to hear what she knows about Priscilla, so she gave up trying to pass along the information. They made love on the floor. As Lisa kissed her behind the ears, Gina thought, "That Lisa is amazing the way she handles herself." On the other hand, Gina is heart broken that it will soon be over between them. She is more upset that Lisa did not trust her to share her feelings. Gina understands the huge burden Lisa carries. It is evident that she will go far to protect the people she loves, just like last night. Gina rested her head on Lisa's chest, while exploring Lisa's body with her hands. Lisa breaks up the moment with the observation that dinner is almost ready.

"I can't wait until dinner is over. I want you now," objects Gina.

"You do, huh? I'm all yours. I'm hungry, though. I . . . um . . . I can cook for us," Lisa suggests as they kiss again and again.

"You can cook?" asks Gina, frowning.

"Yeah! Sure! I can cook. I like to cook for my . . . Well, let's just say that my family doesn't know that I can cook. Shh . . . shh . . . If they find out, they will have me cooking for them all the time!"

"Wow! You're really not going to make this easy for me, huh? I can't talk to you about your ex. I can't make love to you. What can I do to relax you?"

Lisa brushes her hair away from her face. She smiles and jokes, "You're already doing that!"

"Excuse me?" asks Gina.

When Gina returned, Lisa was already busy in the kitchen. "Can I help?" she asked.

"No, thanks! Everything is just about done. I got it all ready before you came over, and I'm just putting the salad together," replied Lisa.

Together, they carried everything to the table. "I thought I'd introduce you to tofu," said Lisa as she popped a morsel into Gina's mouth.

"Mmm, mmm, this is very good, Lisa."

Lisa leaned over and kissed Gina. Gina has enjoyed lunches and dinners with Lisa in the past, but they usually happen in a restaurant. This meal is extra-special because it was made just for her. Gina takes a sip of her white wine while Lisa sits across the table, smiling, and watching her eat. Lisa is not a big eater. In fact, she is more of a snacker, one who nibbles at a little of this and a bit of that throughout the day. Lisa gets up from the table to change the music on the CD player. She puts Nat King Cole on the stereo and returns to Gina's side, kissing her on the back of her neck. For dessert, Lisa presents Gina with apple pie and whipped cream.

"Did you make this?" says Gina as she fills her mouth with pastry and cream.

"No . . . my mother made the pie," Lisa explains.

"Mmm . . . mmm . . . I love! This is good!" Gina says with a smile.

As Gina licks her finger and picks up the last few crumbs of pastry from the plate, she takes Lisa's hand and says, "Come with me! I have a treat for you." Gina has already filled the bath tub with bubble bath. "I figure this will be a much better way for you to relax. Don't say no, Lisa! I want to spoil you just like you have spoiled me. What do you say?"

Lisa smiles as she undresses in record time. She lowers herself into the steamy, frothy bubbles and Gina slides in behind her. Gina pins up Lisa's hair and as the steam eases some of Lisa's cares and her body begins to relax, she leans back to kiss Gina. "Thank you," says Lisa.

"So . . . not to be too subtle, but what's on your mind?" asks Gina.

"You are. You are the only thing on my mind right now," replies Lisa. In her heart of hearts, Lisa knows that she still loves Priscilla, even though she feels sick thinking about Priscilla's actions last night. She wants to cry whenever she thinks about it. However, Lisa doesn't want Gina to see how vulnerable she feels, so she covers up her feelings by kissing Gina passionately on the lips and then stepping out of the tub.

Gina follows Lisa into the bedroom. As they lay together on the bed, Lisa closes her eyes and tries hard not to think of Priscilla's touch, her kiss, the feel of her skin. As Gina makes love to Lisa, she cries silently for Priscilla and hopes with all her heart that putting Priscilla behind bars was the right thing to do. Later, while Gina sleeps, Lisa calls Vidal and they talk for awhile before she calls her mother. Sensing some sadness in her voice, Naana asks Lisa if she's okay. Lisa insists she's fine.

"When are you going to come home, darling? I know you like to be alone during exams, but it's not good to be alone too much."

Lisa smiles and looks at the sleeping Gina. "Mother, I'm fine. And I'm not alone. Good-night, Mother." Lisa ends the call and cuddles up to the sleeping Gina.

Chapter 25

When Tia and Nathan arrive at the Sharp house, Naana is alone in her study. She informs them that she will be flying to Holland in the morning to meet with Vidal and his parents to talk about the proposed marriage between Vidal and Lisa.

"So Lisa was right," teased Tia, "you caved in!"

"No . . . I know that Lisa is not going to marry Vidal. In fact, I would put money on it. She hates my interference, but that is exactly what Bobby and I plan to do until your sister grows up and faces things. It's either that or I watch my baby sleep with every beautiful young girl there is. Who knows? She might even be sleeping with the children of half of my friends just to get me to see things her way!"

"She wouldn't do that, would she?" asks Nathan.

Naana raises her eyebrows, "Never underestimate Lisa! I'm afraid she would do exactly that. Your sister's sexual appetite is worse than yours and Tia's put together!"

"Gee, thanks, Mother. We happen to be married and in love," remarks Tia.

"Darling, I know that. So should Chance and Lisa. Lisa is usually sensible, but when it comes to beautiful girls, she is a different Lisa all together. You know, Vidal and Chance have been lavishing their attentions on her with expensive gifts. Not just the luxury loft that she and Chance bought together. They have so much in common it is unbelievable. Lisa also adores Vidal and spoils him rotten. I just don't get what she is afraid of. Vidal loves and spoils Lisa just like Nathan spoils you. Chance challenges Lisa and doesn't put up with her Princess ways."

"Wow! You know, Mother, I've been thinking of buying a loft just like Lisa's for my wife," Nathan says. "I guess it's not something you'd approve, eh? Mother?"

Naana affectionately hit Nathan on the shoulder, "Darling, I'm serious! You and Tia were intimate before you married. Your sister has not slept with the opposite sex. Everywhere we go, Lisa is locking lips with a beautiful girl. Bobby and I are fed up. Those two boys are going to get hurt, or she is going to end up losing both of them."

"Mother, sex does not make a marriage last," observes Nathan.

"No, but it sure does make it fun!" interrupts Tia.

"Nevertheless, Vidal and Lisa are passionately in love, but she and Chance are also madly in love, too. Tia and I have witness it." Nathan re-assures his mother-in-law.

"I know Lisa loves Vidal. I'm not so sure Lisa trusts the love that she shares with Vidal to stop romancing these girls." Naana murmurs.

"Mother, Lisa is still very young. You have instilled pretty good principles and manners in her. I know because my wife has the same qualities. That's why I keep falling in love with her everyday."

"Oh, Baby! That is so sweet," Tia says.

"Gina Read stopped by to see how we were coping with everything. She plans to have Lisa's club manager, Simon, arrested and charged with the murder of her sister within the next twenty-four hours. She wants me to keep my eye on Lisa," Naana says.

"Why does she want you to do that?" Nathan asks.

"She is worried that Lisa is keeping things inside and hiding at work. I'd rather she hide at work than start another romance with this girl. I believe Gina Read and Lisa may be a lot closer than Lisa says. I don't know how to protect her. She hates my meddling in her private life. I'm thinking of planning a wedding for Valentine's Day evening." Naana sighs.

"That is so romantic, Mother!" Tia exclaims.

"It will be if Vidal's best man can be here. I'm hoping it will force Lisa to make a choice between Chance and Vidal, once and for all. I'm leaving for Ghana at the end of next month. I don't want Lisa running around during my absence and getting up to all sorts of trouble. I want her married and under the watchful eyes of her husband before I leave," Naana declared.

"Where is the best man?" Tia asks.

"He is in LA supposedly visiting Kelly, but I know that Kelly is probably in Canada now getting ready to shoot your movie."

Tia says, "You've lost me, Mother."

"Kelly Powers is Patrick's mother. Nick Collins and Kelly Powers had a romance just like you and Nathan. It broke Nick's heart when Kelly refused to marry him and give up show business."

"Wow! I didn't know that! All this time I thought Kelly was just one of Steven's many exes," Tia says.

"Well, I bet you any money that Patrick went to California to be with Jackie and is just using Kelly as an excuse to go," Naana adds. "Enough about Lisa. How is Tony? I have not seen him all day."

"I think he's spending the evening with Dr Doyle and Mrs Williams," says Nathan. "He should be home soon. I'm going upstairs to check on the children while you two have your special time together."

Tia and Naana were silent until Nathan had left the room and the door closed behind him.

"Mother, I thought we agreed that Nathan and I would buy Claire her car?"

"Yes, as far as I know. Why?"

"I'm going to ring her neck," Tia says venomously. "Trust me, Mother. I pray that Claire doesn't pass her driving test tomorrow because if she does, you will have trouble on your hands between Nathan and Lisa," Tia warns her mother.

"Well, we'll not have trouble anywhere. Claire will pass her test, but Lisa will just have to take back that car. It's not safe for a young, inexperienced, driver like Claire."

"Yes, but Mother, Nathan is really upset about it."

"What has Lisa done now, or do I dare ask?"

Tia explained that Lisa had already bought a car for Claire. Nathan thinks it is unsuitable and defeats the purpose of teaching Claire responsibility for money and how to spend it. Lisa doesn't share that idea and she wants only the best for Claire.

"Nathan was livid, Mother. You should have heard him rant about it!" says Tia. She continues, mocking Nathan's tone of voice, "I'm married to one Sharp woman who bosses me around and has me wrapped around her pinkie finger. Lisa is mistaken if she thinks I'm going to let her buy my seventeen-year-old sister an expensive sports car. The insurance on that car will cost a fortune!"

Mother and daughter dissolve in laughter.

"But seriously, I wish I could hear how you all resolve the issue, but I leave first thing in the morning. I wanted to take Jayzel and Trey with me to Holland. Do you mind?" asks Naana.

"No, Mother. Tell Grandmother that Nathan and I will be there on Friday," Tia agreed and then changing the subject, she asks, "How are you doing, Mother?"

"I'm feeling a lot better knowing that Priscilla is behind bars. You know, Lisa did love her. I can't believe she has been sleeping with Gina Read. In fact, I'd not be surprised if they were in bed together as we speak."

"Lisa sure has a way with women," Tia adds. "You know, when you see her with Vidal and Chance, Mother, it's magical. It's like a romantic love affair in the movies. Nathan's right, you know, about the principles you have instilled in us. Lisa is weird, Mother, but she's a good kid and knows what she wants from life. So what can I do about this wedding you are planning for my terrible sister? I may have some ideas about how to get Chance and Lisa together . . ." Tia offers with a twinkle in her eye.

"Oh, Tia! Sometimes I wonder where I went wrong with you kids," worries Naana.

"Whatever do you mean, Mother?"

Naana was about to confess that she had witness Jackie and Lisa together when Anthony walked into the room.

"Daddy! I was thinking that since Mother is going to Holland with the children, you and I could spend some time together this week."

"Are you going away for the whole week?" Anthony asks.

"Yes, but you'll be joining us on the weekend, won't you? Mother loves your company and so do I. I'm going to miss you. I thought I could show you around the English countryside this week, but I have matters in Holland," Naana says.

"Well, I could do that," offers Tia. "You and Daddy can take the children to the chocolate factory in Belgium on the weekend."

"Brilliant!" says Naana, already thinking of the many ways to spoil her grandchildren. Naana was in the living room with Tia and Anthony. Naana said, "I will be leaving in the morning to go to Holland."

"I know, my Princess," replies Bobby. "I will be going with you. I thought I could drive us and I have planned some romantic things for us to do along the way."

"But, Darling, I am taking the plane with Tony, Jayzel, and Trey."

"I tell you what . . . why don't you let Tony take the plane with the children and I'll drive with you. Princess, I have not had any time with you, lately. Please?" Bobby presented Naana with a gift-wrapped parcel. "I have written all kinds of love-notes upstairs, too, to win my Princess's heart and affections, for being such a . . ."

Naana didn't let him finish. She stood up and planted a big kiss on Bobby's lips. "How is a girl supposed to say no to you, looking at your gorgeous blue eyes? Of course, I'll drive with you, my darling."

Bobby swept Naana into his arms and escorted her upstairs.

Tia turned to her father-in-law and said, "I guess we don't have to guess what they are going to be doing tonight!"

Anthony smiled, but couldn't help being a little envious. Tia has often thought about her father-in-law's loneliness after his wife's death. It is one of those things she has never had the courage to discuss with him. Of course, talking about dating would be challenging too since Heather Carter was Anthony's whole life. It would be difficult for him to think of welcoming a new woman into his life.

"Where were you just now, Angel?"

"I was thinking about all of us, the changes and the losses that we have suffered."

"That's just how life is, Angel," Anthony knows his daughter-in-law is leading up to something. He is not ready for it, so he kisses her good-night and goes to bed.

Tia watches Tony depart and thinks, "Well, I guess I'm going to do something about it."

It was a day of tests: Lisa finished her exams on time, and then she met Vidal so they could take Claire to her driving test. They waited outside, hardly speaking, thinking about what to say if Claire should not pass her test. A short while later, Claire came bouncing down the sidewalk to the car.

"I did it! I did it! I passed my test!" she waved the temporary driving license at them. As Vidal drove them all back to the Sharp home, the level of excitement in the car rose substantially. Parked outside the Sharp house was a little red Honda Civic. Feeling confident that Claire would pass her test, Nathan bought it off the lot that morning.

"It's awesome!" enthused Claire as she hugged Nathan.

"It is darling. Congratulations!" Lisa said as she hugged her little sister.

"Come on, Claire! Time for kickboxing lessons! Why don't you drive us?" says Nathan, tossing her the keys to her new car.

Lisa informs them all not to snack too much afterward, "Dinner will be ready by the time you come home. I'm cooking."

BJ and Claire immediately ask Nathan, "Can we have KFC?"

Grinning, Nathan says, "You can have whatever you like—tomorrow. Tonight, we're all eating at home."

"I want to call my Mummy, now," complains BJ.

"You can call Mother after your lesson *and* after you've eaten all your dinner," Nathan told BJ firmly.

"My sister doesn't know how to cook. I have to call my Mummy, now," insisted BJ.

"Is that so? Well, tonight we'll eat whatever your sister cooks for us. Come on, let's go!"

BJ discovers that Lisa can cook very well: she just hates doing it. BJ was impressed with what he saw: beer-battered fish and hand-cut chips.

"You made fish and chips for me?" exclaimed BJ.

"Of course, darling! All for my handsome brother."

BJ loves it when his sisters call him handsome. Claire and BJ eat first and then go upstairs to take their bed-time shower. Lisa is meeting the Peters family in the morning, so she is doing the preparation work with Nathan in the study. Vidal brings her a glass of milk and as he sets down the glass, he informs her that he's returning to Holland tomorrow. Lisa is not happy about that decision and they begin to argue in Netherlands. Suddenly, Lisa leaves the room, angry. Nathan smiles as Vidal turns to him and says, "I don't think you would be laughing if you were in my situation. You have no idea how stubborn Lisa can be when she doesn't get her own way."

"Welcome to my world! My wife is just as stubborn as your girlfriend," Nathan admits.

"How do you and Tia find the balance? I mean . . . do you compromise on everything, or do you give in to her every demand?"

"I tried to forbid her not to do things when we first met."

"I can't forbid Lisa not to do anything. I don't want a relationship like that with the woman I love. Besides, she always wins," Vidal sighs. He leans back in his chair. Tia and Lisa are eavesdropping on the men.

"So . . . Do you still forbid Tia to do things?"

"Hell, yes!"

"Does Tia obey you?"

"Of course, she does! I have given that woman two beautiful babies. How can she not obey me? I'm the man and she is my goddess. Yep! She has me around her pinkie just like Lisa has you. Bro', you are a dead man. The Sharp girls are bad and we love them."

The Sharp girls return to the study. Lisa apologizes to Vidal and admits waiting until after they are married to be intimate together will be alright. "After all, I should learn to obey you," Lisa says.

Vidal stand ups and hugs her. While they embrace, he signals a thumbs-up to Nathan. "I'm sorry, too. It breaks my heart when you're upset."

Lisa glances at her sister and smiles, "Good! Then you won't mind taking me to my room after dinner and making love to me all night long, since you the man!" Nathan tries to leave the study, but Tia blocks the door and won't let him pass.

"Lisa! Please, be reasonable," Vidal pleads. "Baby, please!" Vidal whispers in her ear.

Lisa turns to Nathan, "I'll let your wife deal with *you*."

BJ comes downstairs asking if he can sleep downstairs with Lisa.

"No, sweetheart. You have to try and sleep in your own room, okay? Vidal is going to be sleeping with me."

Vidal was about to say BJ could sleep with them when Tia offered to come and stay with BJ until he fell asleep. "Who cooked for us?" asks Tia.

Vidal says, "Lisa did."

"I love pasta, but only Daddy knows how to make it this good!"

Lisa giggles, "Tony gave me the recipe over the phone and told me how you like it." She puts a fork full of pasta into Vidal's mouth and teases him to eat up. "You're going to need every bit of your strength, man!"

Tia feels bad for the boy, but she starts to smile when she thinks of how Nathan wanted to wait until they were married before having sex.

"You know, Lisa, Nathan wanted to wait until we were married, too. Maybe you should. It's a lot more romantic!" Tia tells her sister. Lisa smiles as she wipes Vidal's mouth with a napkin. This is the first time that Vidal has spent a whole night alone with Lisa. She is unbelievably sexy. He could not sleep a wink for holding her and watching her sleep. Lisa has no idea what she does to him. "She is worth the wait," he tells himself. At six in the morning, he slips out of bed and goes to the gym to work out. Nathan is there, too.

"Thanks for nothing, Nathan! That's the last time I 'll come to you for advice!" Vidal says sarcastically.

"Good morning, to you too. How was the sex?"

Vidal throws a towel at him and says, "There was no sex. I was the one who wanted to make love last night. All Lisa wanted was for me to hold her after she had me aroused. I had no sleep at all."

Nathan laughs heartily, "You'll be alright, man!"

"No I won't," object Vidal. "I'm going to Holland and I'm going to see Grandmother Gertrude. Lisa has given me a week before she cuts my fucking ball off if I don't get her mother's blessing. I'm dying here. It's not just the sex. I don't want to be apart from Lisa, but I feel like I'm competing with Chance—and him hanging around her like a love-sick puppy."

"You really are crazy about her, aren't you?"

"More than life itself. She is unhappy, so am I. We were meant to be married by now, and living in the same country, not apart from each other. I don't want her living in that love nest that another man bought for her."

"So what do you intend to do about it? It sound like what you and Lisa need is romance."

"I'm running out of ideas to keep our romance going with all this stress. What kind of a man am I if i can't make my woman happy? On top of everything, Lisa is just making me hornier than ever. She does things on purpose—just to get me going. Jackie and Patrick just met and they've been shagging every day now."

"Dude! That's my little sister, man!"

BJ leaves for school with Claire in her new car. Lisa makes breakfast in bed for Vidal. She is still wearing her white lace bikini underwear when she wraps both legs around Vidal and begins to kiss him. His tongue feels warm and delicious. She slides her other hand between his legs and feels his ready, raised manhood. Vidal tries to tell her no, but Lisa whispers yes, yes, yes as she continues to kiss him sensuously and to masturbate him. Vidal feels overwhelmed, out of control. He moans, gasps, buries his face in Lisa's breasts as he caresses her back. He has reached a point of no return. His hand is almost inside Lisa's panties when she tells him that she is deliciously wet, but they can't, they shouldn't. She leaves him in the bed and heads to the bathroom, smiling to herself for a job well done. Vidal is left in the bed gasping. He throws a pillow against the wall in anger.

Later that morning, Vidal drove Lisa to her office. It was a tearful good-bye as Lisa repeated her wish for Vidal to stay in England so they could fly to Holland together on the weekend. Vidal wishes he could stay, but he has an important merger in Holland that needs his personal attention. Vidal knows that since the incident with Priscilla, Lisa has been making more of an effort with their relationship. Vidal assures Lisa that the days will pass quickly and they will be together again soon. Lisa says, "Let's elope, if my mother doesn't agree to our marriage!"

Vidal looks at her with shock.

"Everyday without you is torture, Vidal. I can't hold on any longer. Not just making love, Baby, for everything." Lisa has been having nightmares about her and Chance for weeks and weeks now. She's been wanting to call him and talk about it before things get really out of control with Vidal. She loves Vidal but she is madly in love with Chance, too, and then, there's Gina Read. Lisa can't get her out of her mind. Cheating on Vidal is always so easy, but with Chance . . . she has drifted off thinking about them, when Vidal asks if she is okay. There are tars rolling down her face. She wants to say they need a time out, but instead, she hugs him and they begin kissing. When they stop, Lisa says, "I'm gonna miss you a lot, Vidal."

"Yeah, me too. Me too," Vidal replies, his eyes tearing up.

Chapter 26

An assistant pages Lisa to announce the arrival of Mr Peters. "Send him in!" trills Lisa, thinking gleefully about the surprise in store for Kevin Peters.

Kevin arrives accompanied by his brothers and his sister. Collectively, they have no idea that African Mortgage Funds is Tia's mother's company. Naturally, they are shocked to be ushered into Lisa's office.

"There must be some mistake," says Kevin immediately.

"What can I do for you?" asks Lisa.

"I doubt very much there is anything you can do for us. I want to see who owns this company," demands Kevin rudely.

"My mother owns this company, Mr Peters. She is away on business—out of the country, actually—and she doesn't see people just because they demand it. You made an appointment with a loan officer on Friday. I am the person with whom you requested a meeting. Please tell me what you need," Lisa says politely.

Kevin is shocked by the information he has heard from Lisa.

"What can I do for you?" Again, Lisa speaks very politely.

Aaron steps into the fray, "We had a mortgage with your company, Miss Sharp. My home, along with those of my brothers, and Kevin's business premises were foreclosed last week."

"I am sorry to hear that, Mr Peters. I can assure you that we never foreclose on any of our loans. My mother has been in this business for twenty-seven years, sir. Not once has she ever foreclosed on anyone."

"Then, there must be some mistake. Like I said, our mortgages were foreclosed," Arron replies.

"Mr Peters, our loans are strictly for our own Africans so that they can have the opportunity to own their homes and their businesses. That has always been the motivating force behind our business," Lisa explains.

The Peters brothers look at each other. Lisa asks, "Could one of you provide me with a driver's license or a social security number so I can pull your file?"

Kevin, out of sorts, says, "We don't need your help!"

"Just give it to her!" snaps Ola.

Lisa asks her assistant to bring them all something to drink. "I'm sorry. Gathering this information is going to take awhile." Gradually, she finds their files and turns the screen of the computer to face them, so they can follow her explanation. "Yes, we did hold your mortgages, but your solicitor, Mrs Peters, requested we release you seven months ago, claiming that our rates were too high. We still have your sister's loan, as you can see."

Someone knocks on the door. "Please, come in," says Lisa. Tia opens the door. She wears the same sleeveless jumpsuit as Lisa, topped with a jacket. She looks stunning.

"Oops! Sorry! I didn't know you were with a client. I'll be upstairs with Brooke. Call me when you are done," Tia says.

"I am done. We can go now," Lisa says. Tia opens the door wide and sees the Peters sitting around Lisa's desk. "What's going on here?" asks Tia.

"Tia, this is business. It is confidential. I cannot discuss it with you," Lisa says.

Kevin is relieved. He feels enough embarrassment, and knows he doesn't want to be humiliated by Tia's little sister. But before anything could be done, Ola has blurted out the problem and Tia is hugging her and asking what can be done.

"Well, very little can be done at this point," says Lisa, shrugging.

"What does that mean?" asks Tia.

Lisa takes her time explaining the details of the Peters case to Tia. They speak in Netherlands so they can cover the facts and queries more quickly without further embarrassing the family.

"Basically, Tia, Aaron Peters had been away and came home to discover that his home had been taken away and his pregnant wife was living with his sister."

While they talk, Aaron can't help thinking that the woman for whom Kevin has abandoned them all is also the same woman who has taken everything away from them. He loathes his brother even more. Knowing what Kevin had done to Tia almost a month ago makes all of the Peters siblings loathe Kevin. They all watch Tia, as they examine their own misgivings. Tia sits beside her sister behind the desk with her right hand resting on the table top and writing with her left hand. She is speaking on the phone, in French now. Kevin suspects she is talking to Nathan. She puts the phone down and says to the Peters family, "We should be able to have you back in your properties in a couple of hours."

Paul and Aaron are relieved to hear it, and they both profusely thank Tia. Ola is also grateful. Tia leaves the room, telling them all just to sit tight while she makes a few calls. Kevin sits in his chair, alternately fuming and wishing the earth would open up and swallow him. When he made the appointment on Friday, Kevin had wanted to learn more about African Mortgage Funds, but the fear of reading about himself on the internet prevented him from logging on and doing some research. He hates his wife even more now for putting him in this position. Why, of all the mortgage and loan companies in London, did it have to be a company owned by Tia's family that he wanted to use to save his home and business?

Tia and Lisa have moved to the conference room. While Tia talks on the phone, Lisa asks her assistant to fetch the Peters family. When they come to the door, Tia waves at them to come into the room. Lisa motions for them to sit down. "I'm waiting for the lawyer to come. His office is in this building. He is with a client right now, but he will be here shortly."

"I'm a lawyer. We don't need a lawyer," Kevin says shortly.

"Mr Peters, you have been very rude since you set foot in my company offices. Out of respect for my sister, I have put up with your behavior, but I'd like to know what kind of a lawyer sits around and lets his home and business get foreclosed? I advise you to sit down and shut the hell up! For God's sake, have some self-respect. Respect your brothers and your sister, if you can't respect me. By the look of things, it is they who have suffered, not you. You are very lucky that the bank is willing to sell us your loans because it is not something they would ordinarily do. For a change, think of your family's needs instead of the gigantic chip on your shoulder!" Lisa snaps at him.

Kevin can't believe Tia's kid sister is speaking to him this way. He has been humiliated enough. He isn't going to take it anymore. Just at that moment, Jaden Blake enters the conference room and for a second, Kevin wishes to God that Jaden is not the lawyer they are waiting for.

"Sorry to keep you waiting, Lisa. What can I do for you?" asks Jaden.

"I need you to close this deal for me," she says as she passes the file to him. Jaden is about to take the file from Lisa when he notices the Peters sitting there expectantly.

"What the hell are you people doing in our building?" Jaden demands.

"Calm down! It's okay! Really!" Lisa says soothingly. "They are clients."

Jaden begins to laugh. "You folks have five seconds to get out before I throw you out!"

Lisa intervenes, "May I remind you that this is a place of business? Your personal problems have no place in here," she says firmly.

"Sorry, Lisa," says Jaden shaking his head, "You gonna have to get a different lawyer for these people." Jaden is clearly angry that he would be asked to represent people for whom he feels no sympathy for. He is angry with Lisa for even suggesting it. Lisa apologizes to the Peters and asks them to excuse her. She takes Jaden by the hand and they talk outside in the hall. Jaden turns and gives the Peters a withering look as he closes the door.

Not only have Kevin's actions brought shame on himself, but also his brothers and sister feel that since Christmas, Kevin and his estranged wife have caused them and innocent others so much pain, more than all their lives put together. They didn't want to rant and rave at him like Jade Blake did, but they also understood the man's anger towards their brother.

Meanwhile, in Naana Konadu-Sharp's office, the extended family have gathered: Nathan, Jason, Brooke and Kate. When Lisa enters the room with Jaden in tow, she says, "Kate, tell your husband to keep his anger in check. We all agreed that this was the best revenge for Kevin Peters and his family." Jason hates the idea of being told what to do by Lisa. He tries to protest in the same way Jaden does. Brooke says, "I have thought about this, and Lisa is right. Jaden, please, let's do this and get that animal out of our building and our lives for good."

"I agree, too," pipes in Tia from the door.

Feeling the unconditional support of the family, Jaden and Lisa return to the conference room.

Again, relying heavily on his own sense of himself and his status as a lawyer, Kevin Peters does not read any of the documents before signing them. After the copies are distributed, Kevin and Aaron suddenly realize that they have not been given a loan. In fact, Tia has managed, somehow, to buy Aaron and Paul's homes, Kevin's business, and paid off the remaining mortgage on Ola's home. Kevin stands up and says, "We can't expect this. This is not what we came in here for. We need a loan, not charity."

Aaron, grateful for this reprieve, has had enough of his brother's attitude. "Charity! You show some respect to these kind people, Kevin. You have shown no remorse for anything you and your bitch of a wife have done to us all, nor for what you have done to Tia and her family. Whether this is a pity loan or whatever you call it, we thank you kindly, Miss Sharp and Mr Blake, for everything you kind people have done for our family today. I do apologize to you both for my brother's rudeness and everything he has done to your family in the past. We will never forget this and we definitely will pay back the loan, I promise you."

Jaden does not give a toss about Aaron's apologies or thanks, so he leaves as quickly as possible. Lisa explains, "It is not a loan. Mr Peters, I could not guarantee you and your family a loan. Unfortunately, your brother's behavior last week, assaulting a bailiff and a reporter at the court house, made it difficult for me to obtain a loan for you all. I called the MB & B, the bank that currently holds your loans. I know the president personally. That is why, we were able to get back your homes for you . . . Apparently,—again, sir, I'm not saying this to humiliate you and your family in any way—apparently, there was an interview on TV last night with your brother's wife and his former wife on *Panorama*. It was on the BBC. The program has put a cast on all Africans and how our menfolk take advantage of women and their abuse of women."

Kevin screamed, "Liar!"

"You are out of control, Mr Peters. You speak to me one more time in that manner, and you'll find yourself back behind bars. I promise you, I am not a liar. It's all over the news and the internet, along with your gay pornographic video your wife put on the internet. It's the number one download this week!" Lisa avoids looking at their expressions. "Anyway, Tia paid for your loans as a gift for you all. You all own your homes, now. There are no loan payments on your homes. She felt it would be inappropriate to buy back Kevin's home for him, as I'm sure you'll understand. I'll have someone come and escort you out." Lisa left them.

"What the fuck is going on, Kevin? Gay? Are you gay?" Paul asks hysterically.

Aaron says calmly, "This is not the place for this discussion. We must go and thank Tia, let her know that we appreciate her gift and that we will pay her back. Come, Ola." Aaron helps his sister who is in tears, angry about Lisa's revelations concerning her brother and his wife. It is worse than she thinks. "Kevin's wife is pure evil," thinks Ola. They are told that Tia has already left with her sister, but they may still be in the parking lot.

"Well, then, let's hurry, Ola," says Aaron as he guides her out of the building.

Tia was indeed driving off with Lisa by the time Aaron and Ola got to the parking lot. They waited in their car for Kevin who is still sitting in the conference room in disbelief. He could hardly credit Lisa Sharp's assertions that he is abusive toward women, and a participant in a gay pornographic video. "I am going to sue everyone involved in this," he says to himself. As he makes his way toward the exit, Kevin sees Nathan Carter and Jaden. They do not see him, or at least, he thinks they do not. Kevin suddenly realizes that they all work in the same building. He has been so preoccupied that he did not notice when he arrived in the morning. Down the hall, he passes Brooke, hand-in-hand with her husband. They, too, walk past without giving him a second glance. "They all used to like me," he thinks. Kevin opens the main door. The sun is shining, but the weather is very cold. He walks with his head down, so he does not see Tia standing by his brother's car, talking to them. As Kevin gets into the car, he hears the voice that always melts his heart: "It was the least I could do. My sister really deserves all the credit, though. She did the impossible getting your properties back. You take care now. Bye," Tia says. She walks with her arms around her sister into the building.

Kevin watches as his body trembles. Tia's actions give him a reprieve, and his brothers and sister, too. They are all amazed at Tia's generosity. They share the thought that if each of them had been in Tia's shoes, they would have wanted to retaliate. Kevin feels remorseful, but he knows that every time he gets near Tia, his anger just boils over. He feels like he must always prove himself worthy of her. He also feels sorry for everything that's happened, but somehow the words just don't come out properly. On the ride back to the house, Kevin's siblings do not want to talk to him. When they arrive at Ola's house, Kevin is the last to get out of the car.

Since he doesn't have the courage to go into Ola's house, Kevin thinks he will just drive home. As he approaches his car, Kevin sees something taped onto the windshield. Initially, he thinks it might be a parking ticket, until he reaches the car and sees the big envelope. Can it be a bomb? Paul, too, sees the envelope and fears it might be a bomb. He runs out of the house, calling to Kevin not to go near the car, and shouting to Aaron to call the police. Kevin does not hear his brother as he reaches for the envelope and tears it open. Inside, a fistful of photographs of Kevin having sex with a man he does not know, and a copy of the Nigeria Mail newspaper showing Kevin Peters on the front page. A DVD tumbles to the ground as Kevin loses consciousness. Paul thinks his brother has had a heart attack as he and Aaron run to his aid. Within minutes, the paramedics are there. Kevin has had a panic attack, and he will be fine. The stress of the recent events have provoked the attack, but right now, he needs rest. Aaron, Paul and Ola put aside their anger to care for their brother. Aaron Peters prides himself as a good man. He knows very well how the Western world always refers to African men and their abusive behavior toward women. He is familiar with the Western way of describing black men as animals, uneducated and uncivilized. He hates those kinds of stereotypes. Aaron acknowledges that Kevin's attack on Tia made him lose respect for his older brother, but he doesn't believe for an instant that Kevin has also abused his former wife or Angela, for that matter. Aaron also has a hard time believing that Kevin would willingly make a gay pornographic video to put on the internet for the whole world to see. Kevin has always had a dream to go back to Africa, to become a judge or a governor one day, maybe even the President! Aaron wonders whether anyone he knows has seen the video Lisa Sharp was talking about. "Maybe someone taped it," he hopes. He goes outside to pick up the stuff Kevin dropped on the ground by his car. Aaron just scoops it up, pays no attention to the contents of the envelope and carries all of it inside the house. He tosses the material onto the table. It skids across the table and tumbles onto the floor. That is the moment they all understand Kevin's anguish. Aaron, supposing their shame and humiliation was over, sees that these photos represent the beginning of a seemingly, never-ending nightmare. Quickly, he scans the front page of the Nigeria Mail newspaper. He closes his eyes and passes the paper to his younger brother, who reads it and passes it along to Ola. The horrified expressions on their faces reveal much about their inner thoughts. Aaron walks to the television and inserts the DVD into the player. They all begin to retch at the sight of their brother being fucked by different men. They could not tell whether he was laughing or screaming as there is no sound on the tape. It is so horrendous that Ola shouts, "Turn it off! Turn it off! I can't stand to watch!"

While Ola, Aaron and Paul were watching the DVD, Kevin awakened and heard the shocked cries of his siblings. He got out of bed and went into the next room to see what they were doing. He was amazed to see himself on the DVD being repeatedly raped. At first, Kevin was too shocked to respond, but suddenly bile rose up in his throat and he found himself on his knees on the bathroom floor vomiting into the toilet. When it was over, Kevin stood and looked at himself in the mirror. He didn't recognize the man looking back, but he felt so much emotional pain that he couldn't help shouting, "I am going to kill whoever did this to me!"

Ola replied venomously, "Nobody did this to you, Kevin. You did it to yourself. For once, take responsibility for the things that you do and the effects they have on others. How about Dad? Our father is a tribal chief!"

Paul shakes his head in dismay. He, too, has not thought further than his own embarrassment, but what must their father be facing back home in Nigeria?

"Guys, can't you see this is all a set-up? I was probably drugged and raped," Kevin cries.

"Shut up, Kevin! Shut up! I am a counselor, and I know abuse when I see it. If you were drugged and raped as you claim, you would have suffered some injuries, felt pain, even. Shut the fuck up and get out! I don't know what you have become anymore. You beat up a woman you love, that we all loved." Aaron pointed to his siblings. "You tried to rape her, Kevin. My God! What kind of evil are you? You and that wife of yours are the same. You tell her, she is going to regret the day my wife was put on the street in the winter in her nightie. Now, get the fuck out! You are not our brother anymore," Aaron says vehemently.

"I swear to you, guys, this is a set-up," insists Kevin.

"By who?" Ola asks.

"Don't worry! I'll find out who did this to me and make them pay."

"That's nice, Kevin. Please, get out of my house. I don't want anything to do with you, anymore," Ola says as she opens the front door and motions for Kevin to leave.

It has been an overwhelming, devastating, humiliating time for Kevin Peters since the day his former boss called to say that Kevin actually had a child with Tia Sharp. The perfect life that Kevin thought he had, turned instantly into a nightmare. He has done the unthinkable thing to the only woman he has ever truly loved; yet, she has found it in her heart to forgive him and to come to his family's aid. He has been publicly humiliated not only in England, but also all over the world. The Nigerian press is having a field day with the photographs and his father has suffered a heart attack, consequently. His step-mother is refusing to take his calls and his siblings in England have abandoned him. Kevin has been living in his office for almost three weeks, but he has little to do since all of the cases he was working on prior to his arrest have been assumed by his associate. Knowing that Kevin has nowhere to live right now, the associate has invited Kevin to come and stay with him until he sorts himself out. Today, Kevin decided to accept the man's offer. Just as Kevin was closing for the day, Angela and his former boss came by the office to deliver divorce papers. Kevin did not respond as he signed the papers. There was another document attached, a DNA report confirming that his daughter and unborn son are not his biological children. Angela asked Kevin to signed over his rights to the children.

"No! I will never give up my children! Now, you can go. Both of you."

Adam smiles, "DNA doesn't lie, you know. Do you remember insisting that Angela have an abortion?"

Kevin stared at a spot on the wall behind Adam to avoid looking him in the eyes. He did his best to stay calm.

Adam continued, "Do you also recall going to see her father with me and your brother, Aaron, to tell him that you have a family in Canada and that you cannot marry Angela?"

Again, Kevin did not comment.

"Angela did get the abortion as you requested." Adam took a paper from his pocket and put it on Kevin's desk. "This is the medical bill and the receipt of it."

Kevin swallowed, trying not to react. "I think I've heard enough," said Kevin as he grabbed his jacket and left the office. Adam and Angela followed him to his car.

"Oh, by the way," said Adam, clearly enjoying the delivery of his bad news, "both children are mine."

Kevin slammed shut the car door. He wanted to cry, but there were no tears. His whole body shakes and with trembling hands, he put his car into gear and drove off. Blinded by emotion, he did not see the truck coming toward him. The impact caused Kevin's car to flip over the guard rail of London Tower bridge, and push the vehicle into the swirling waters of the Thames River below. His brothers and sister stoically received word of Kevin's crash. Although they have not spoken to each other since Kevin left Ola's house three weeks ago, they insisted that a rescue team search for the body. The divers spent many hours in the water, but Kevin's body was not found. Because of the immanent divorce proceeding, and because Kevin's law practice could not remain suspended indefinitely, Aaron and Paul asked the court to declare Kevin legally dead. After a short deliberation, the judge granted their request and three days after Kevin's disappearance, he was formally declared dead. Feeling honor-bound, the Peters brothers delivered the news to Angela in person. As she is still his wife, and moreover, pregnant, they did not feel it was the sort of news to give over the phone. They knew that Angela was staying with her parents. Ola refused to go with them.

"I can't! She is the cause of all this. I am certain of it!" Ola cried.

"I agree," pleaded Aaron, "but we still owe it to our brother to behave honorably. After all, she is the mother of his children, Ola. Please."

Angela Peters has never forgiven Kevin for insisting that she get an abortion. She did it, but with a great many misgivings. Kevin's former boss, Adam, has liked Angela since the days when she and Kevin both worked for him. She accidentally met Adam a few weeks after she and Kevin got married. She confided to Adam that Kevin has not laid his hands on her since the marriage, and in fact, they have not been sharing a bed. Adam revealed Kevin's secret, that he has an African wife and two children in Canada. He said, "Kevin will never really love you, Angela. Face facts: it is the African way, and only a few of us will marry outside our tribe. The tribe Kevin comes from will have many wives, as much as a man wants and it's not considered adultery in a court of law because the tribe's traditional marriage is different from the Western one."

Angela did not believe Adam, and said as much.

"Do you recall when Kevin sued me for unpaid wages, I mentioned in my witness statement that he has a wife and children in Canada?"

"Yes. I asked him about it at the time, and he told me that it was his ex-girlfriend's kids and that they had nothing to do with him."

Adam stirred restlessly, "Of course, he would tell you that!"

Angela was furious. She thought about everything she had given up for him. She did not tell Kevin that she had the abortion, and she recalls being advised not to have unprotected sex for six weeks since she could easily become pregnant again. Adam is tall, dark, and handsome. He has a lot going for him and he fancies Angela. Kevin cannot stand him. It didn't take much encouragement on Adam's side for Angela to begin sleeping with him. Within a few weeks, just like Angela wanted, she became pregnant again. Angela did her best to make Adam fall in love with her. It wasn't difficult since African men are known for falling in love with educated women. A top-notch solicitor, Angela is also very good at the kinds of things a man likes. Periodically, Adam would insist that she file for a divorce from Kevin so they can be a proper family. Angela has different thoughts. She wants to hurt Kevin Peters so that he will think twice before taking advantage of any woman again. She reminded Adam of his loss, "Kevin was able to set up his own law office because of that massive pay-out from you. Don't you want it back?" They agreed that they would devise a way to take away everything from Kevin that he had originally gained from them. There was an even greater impetus to follow through on their plan when Angela announced she was about to have a son. Adam felt he had no choice but to take action to regain his son's birthright. When Paul and Aaron left after delivering the news about Kevin, Angela did feel a twinge of remorse, but not too much. She went out to pick up her daughter from daycare. When they returned home, Angela put the kettle on the stove to make tea, and turned it on. The phone was ringing. She left the kitchen to answer the phone, not realizing the gas was not lit on the stove. She could not smell the gas leaking into the house, but as soon as she knelt to light the fire in the fireplace, the whole house blew apart in a loud, explosive fire. Angela and her daughter died in the fire. The two of them were buried together at London's Forest Hill Cemetery. For the Peters family, it was much more painful to deal with their sister-in-law's and their niece's deaths than with their brother's death.

"Why would a tragedy like this wipe away a whole family? Where is God when all this happens?" Ola sobbed.

"Oh, God! Everyone knows about Kevin's death but Tia and her family," Paul moaned.

"I think it is too soon. Tia has been though a lot. We cannot impose on her and her family in this way," Aaron observed.

"We have to tell her about Kevin's death. She loved him very much. Otherwise, she would never have helped us the way that she did," Ola pointed out.

Aaron sighed. "I agree with you, Ola, but not now. I've been thinking about her kind gesture. I'll have some money to pay to her on our loans next month. I'll let her sister, or her mother, know about Kevin's death. We all have played a part in Tia getting hurt by Kevin. Only God knows what pain Kevin caused Tia and her family."

Kevin's associate partner, Mr Green, has asked Aaron, Paul and Ola to meet him at Kevin's office to read Kevin's will. Initially, they objected, but he said it was imperative they come. Mr Green informed them that two weeks before Christmas, Kevin changed his will so that everything he owned in England and Nigeria was to be divided equally between his children and their mother, Mrs Tia Carter. Ola looked at her brothers in disbelief.

Mr Green continued his explanation of the circumstances surrounding Kevin's will: "I just spoke to Mrs Carter a little while ago. Mrs Carter insisted that I return everything to you, Aaron. Mrs Carter sends her condolences to you all. She wants you to divide the amount among yourselves, despite the terms of Kevin's will. Mrs Carter also requested the phone numbers of your mother and father so that she and the children can speak to them. Further, she explicitly asked me to tell you how sorry she and her family are to hear about Kevin's death. All their prayers and thoughts are with you all at this sad time. She also instructed me to say that if you ever need anything her numbers remain the same and you must call. Lastly, she said to tell you all that she and the children loved Kevin very much and he will be missed."

Tears flowed freely on all faces as the lawyer read the handwritten letter Tia had faxed to Kevin's office. Mr Green gave the fax to Aaron, who handled it gingerly.

"I'm sorry. There is not an easy way to say this . . ." Mr Green hesitated.

"What is it, man?" asked Aaron, irritated.

Mr Green chuckled awkwardly. "The day Kevin had his accident. I mean, hours before, he left the office, my wife and I invited him to come and stay with us until he sorts things out. Just before we were closing the office, Angela came in with Adam and presented Kevin with a pile of divorce papers to sign—which he did, and they were witnessed by me. I was about to leave when Adam asked me to wait." Green paused again.

"What now? Please, just tell us!" Aaron said.

"Princess and the baby that Angela was carrying were not Kevin's biological children," Green said.

"Liar! Kevin married her because of Princess and he didn't leave her because of the kids. Liar!" Ola blustered.

Green passed a document across his desk toward Aaron. Aaron frowned as he read the DNA report. He closed his eyes and shook his head in dismay as he read the date on the receipt from the abortion clinic and gave the documents back to Green.

Green, an older gentleman with a kind, English face, looked on Kevin's siblings with sympathy. "I was troubled by all the flurry of accusations flung at Kevin, so I hired someone to investigate who put that video about Kevin on the internet. One of the men on the video was arrested in Amsterdam two weeks ago. Kevin went back to Holland and filed a complaint against him, alleging he was raped. The man confessed that he was hired by someone he's never met before and stated that he was paid to come to Holland." Again, Green paused as he fought back his tears.

"Who hired him?" Paul demanded.

"He claims he didn't meet the person face-to-face, but the phone call came from Adam's law office, Kevin's former boss." Green said.

The Peters were enraged and clamored amongst themselves for justice. Kevin had always maintained he had been raped, and they had not believed him.

"When the job was finished, he was told to send a copy of the video to Miss Sharp, but he couldn't as he lost the Sharp's address in Canada. He was paid by Adam in cash, personally. He made a phone call from jail to Adam's cell phone before he hanged himself," Green said.

"I want that man charged," Aaron told Green, referring to Adam.

"Unfortunately, the police do not have enough evidence to charge him. Your father also sent a private letter to you and Paul. He insists that I advise you not to make any threats to Adam."

Aaron chuckled.

"Aaron, if anything happens to Adam, the police will not look at anyone but you as they know that Adam did all this to Kevin."

"Then why the hell is he not in jail?" Paul asked.

"The legal system is not fair sometimes. I have filed a civil law suit against him on behalf of your family as stipulated by your father. The hearing is in a week."

Ola was inconsolable. Aaron was exhausted and devastated by one man's need to seek revenge this way. "I have had nightmares about Tia's husband coming after us for what Kevin did to her. I never once thought Angela was capable of anything so disgusting as this. Why?" Aaron asked.

"They took Tia away from us and managed to take away Kevin, too. They humiliated and shamed our family, and all for what? And now, they are not going to punish Adam for his crime?" Ola asked, incredulous.

"He will be punished, Ola. I promise you. Kevin would want justice if he was here with us today," Green reassured them.

Aaron, Paul and Ola cried for their brother. An envelope of photographs fell off the desk when Aaron slammed his fist on the desk. They were all of Kevin, Tia and the kids in Canada during happier times. He gave them to Ola and they all left Kevin's office. Each had their own thoughts about Kevin, but they all would have agreed that he did not deserve such violence.

Chapter 27

Tia has been working in her sister's office while in Holland. Amy is not very happy that Tia and Nathan have postponed returning to Canada until the Valentine's Day weekend. Nevertheless, Tia has been working hard. She has finished all the re-writes she needs to do. The auditions and rehearsals will begins as soon as she arrives in Canada. Amy is happy to know that at least the scripts are in place. Amy loves Tia's new joint venture with Lisa. Tia's is thrilled to have a new challenge, too: "It will save us a lot of advertising money, which is not cheap. We can reach our target audience with the magazine more effectively."

Lisa's ex-lover, Priscilla, has been calling non-stop for Lisa at her home and at the office. Tia is fed up with the audacity of the girl because her calls interrupt Tia's work. Gina Read assures Tia and Nathan that it is all under control. Even so, Tia is anxious to get back to Amsterdam because she misses her children. Nathan and Jaden are inseparable right now. Together, they are working on a murder trial. Tia laughs inwardly, because they seem like two kids in a candy shop. It looks like they are going to get the conviction they want. Kate and Jaden are joining them for dinner. Tia is under the shower, soaping her body, when Nathan joins her.

"Oh, Sweetie! We don't have time to fool around. Our guests will be here any minute!" Tia protests.

"Speak for yourself, Baby," Nathan replies naughtily. Then, switching topics suddenly, Nathan asks, "Do you mind if we fly to Holland tomorrow afternoon?"

"I was thinking of asking you the same thing, Sweetie," Tia says. "I want to give Lisa a hand with the new Urban Style magazine. I want to make sure that I get more exposure for Sunlight Studios and for our actors. I'm hoping more unknown actors will want to do projects with us now that we own a magazine. We'll be able to position our films in the market since we control the advertising venue."

Nathan chuckles. "I bet Amy is thrilled. Is she still worrying about your advertising costs, Baby?"

"No. She agrees that our partnership with the magazine is a brilliant idea for Sunlight Media Group. I'm just not sure of the launch date. Lisa will not agree to a March launch. Amy and I were hoping that the magazine would be on the newsstands in time for the premier of *Forever Never Dies*. I'm going to talk with her and Vidal about it."

The next day, Tia did not waste time jumping into the warm swimming pool with her children and BJ as soon as she got to Amsterdam. Tia and Nathan have missed their children dearly. The children scream with delight when Nathan does a cannonball leap into the deep end of the pool, splashing everyone with sprays of water. He joins everyone in the shallow end.

"Flip me, Daddy! Flip me!" shouts Jayzel.

Nathan squats in the water and laces his fingers together, forming a stirrup. Jayzel puts her foot into the stirrup and Nathan tosses her over his shoulder to the giggling delight of the little girl.

"Me, too!" demands Trey.

The rest of the afternoon passed to the music of shrieks and giggles as Tia and Nathan played in the pool with the children.

Later that evening, Tia had a quiet moment with her mother. She confesses to her mother, "I don't share the same vindictive feelings toward the Peters that the rest of our family do. In fact, I feel bad about the whole revenge scheme on the Peters."

Naana nods, but wisely does not comment. Instead, she lets Tia open her heart and speak her mind.

"At the time, I didn't say anything because I was afraid of what Nathan would have said. He was so angry, Mother, but I'm so much in love with Nathan now—more than ever—and I'm proud of the man he has become. I just keep thinking that no matter what Kevin has done, I wouldn't have Jayzel if it wasn't for him. How can I have done this?" Tia cries.

"We can't undo the pain we have caused the Peters family. We just have to hope that it's over and God forgives us," Naana says.

Rose, the maid, arrives with the cordless phone, an urgent call for Naana. Gina Read is on the line. "Lisa is in hospital in Epenstraat. She is very sick and the doctors don't know what is wrong with her."

With a cry of anguish, Naana falls into Anthony's arms. Nathan calls out to Guntar to get the car.

"Mother, Lisa is very resilient. She is going to be alright," Nathan assures his mother-in-law as he helps her into the back of the car.

"No, darling. I have to call Vidal."

"It's okay, Mother. Tia is doing that."

Bobby Sharp is on a business call when Tia rushes into the room to tell him that Lisa is sick and that Naana needs him. Bobby tells his daughter to wait while he concludes his call, but Tia is fed up with waiting, so she leaves with Anthony and follows Nathan and her mother to the hospital.

"How can she just be sick? Daddy, she was okay this morning when she left to write her last exam. She said she would take a later flight to come to Holland."

"She will be alright, Angel," says Anthony with a quiet confidence.

Naana has not been inside a hospital since Tia's illness. It seemed like just yesterday that Nathan called to say Tia needed a bone marrow transplant. Naana hesitated. She hates seeing people sick and helpless because it always makes her feel helpless, too.

"I can't go in, darling," Naana whispers to Nathan.

"It's okay, Mother. We'll go whenever you are ready."

Tia arrives with Anthony and when she sees the others outside the main entrance of the hospital, she immediately fears the worst. Instinctively, Tia and Anthony reach for each other's hands as they walk nervously toward Nathan and Naana. Nathan sees them first, and rushes forward to tell them they've not been inside to see Lisa yet.

Anthony puts his arm around Naana, "Come on, honey. Let's go see how your baby is doing."

"Oh, Tony! I can't. I am afraid to know," Naana murmurs.

Nathan looks at Tia, feeling helpless. Anthony stoops to kiss Naana on the forehead, "Yes, you can, honey. We are all here and Lisa needs us." He steps back and gently pulls up Naana and puts his arms around her as they enter the hospital.

Moments later they enter Lisa's room. Gina Read is holding Lisa's hand. She tries to let go, but Lisa is holding her hand tightly. She turns toward the door and sees her mother with Anthony, Nathan and Tia. They are not more than ten feet away from the bedside, but Lisa can't hear a word they say.

"Why can't I hear you?" Lisa says as she sits up and looks at them in confusion. She feels like crying.

Tia approaches Gina, "What happened?"

"I'm not sure," says Gina.

Vidal arrives with his mother and immediately rushes to Lisa's side, putting his arms around her.

"Who are you?" Vidal asks Gina.

"I work for Miss Sharp. She returned to the penthouse this afternoon for the first time after the incident last week. We all heard her scream and we ran to check on her. Miss Sharp seemed to be okay. We all thought she was shocked to be back in the place where her friend had threatened herself and her mother. She felt warm and had a temperature, so Corey asked me to drive her home. She refused, insisting she had to get to Holland to be with her family, so Corey arranged a ticket for me to accompany her."

"Why didn't you guys take her to the hospital and call me?" asked Vidal.

"She refused, sir. She threatened to fire us if she was not in Holland by this evening. She got so ill on the plane that they called the ambulance, and she still would not comply with them. The airline threatened to force her off the plane. She was completely unable to hear when Lisa finally agreed to come to the hospital."

Vidal smiled. "It's true! My Lisa is very stubborn. Thank you for your help, Miss Read."

Lisa is in tears. "Baby, why can't I hear you?"

Vidal strode to the door and shouted down the hall for a nurse. When the nurse came running, he asked, "What is wrong with Miss Sharp? Why can't she hear?"

The nurse explained that some tests were being done, "The doctor wants to rule out certain things before he comes to a diagnosis. As soon as the results of the tests are available, we'll know more and we may have something to tell you."

"Her skin feels very hot. She seems to be burning up with a fever, she can't hear me, and you're standing there telling me you don't know what's wrong with her? Get the doctor, now!" Vidal yelled. Vidal tenderly brushed away Lisa's hair from her face. When the doctor arrived, Vidal demanded to know why the response to Lisa's condition had not been quicker. "Why has she been here over an hour and not yet received any medical care?" The doctor did not respond. Instead, he was about to put his hands on Lisa to examine her, when Vidal said threateningly, "If you put your hands on my fiancée, I'll break your body up in pieces."

His mother pleaded with him to reconsider since Lisa is in so much pain. Vidal took out his PDA and wrote a message on it for Lisa. Lisa wrote something in return. Turning to Anthony, Vidal asked, "Dr Carter, would you please take a look at Lisa for me? I want to have her moved from here to a private clinic, and I need to make sure she is well enough to be moved."

Anthony released Naana and went to stand next to the bed. Lisa has a high temperature. Anthony checks Lisa's ears. He says, "Lisa might have an ear infection and the flight may have made it worse by increasing the pressure in her ear." Everyone sighed with relief. "Can I borrow your PDA, young man?" Anthony asked Vidal, who willingly passed it over. While Anthony was busy typing messages, Lisa began to smile, Naana felt able to breathe again and went to cuddle her. As he finished typing, Anthony looked up and said, "*Barotitis media* is an injury to the middle ear behind the eardrum that results when a blockage develops in the tube that normally equalizes pressure within the ear. Lisa's condition is not serious and will clear up in a few days, though with antibiotics, she'll start to feel better in a few hours."

"Why can't she hear me? Dr Carter, she is very hot," says Vidal frantically.

"Lisa might have had this condition for several days now. The flight, that is, the air pressure changes occurring during the flight caused her hearing loss. She is going to be fine, but she needs medicine for the infection and the pain."

Vidal turns to the hospital doctor, saying, "Why the hell are you still here? Go and get the medication for my fiancée now, before I have you fired!" He frowns.

Nathan tells Vidal to take it easy.

"Sure, Mr I'm-the-man! I'll not take it easy. I'm done taking things easy as far as my relationship with Lisa goes. Would you take it easy if Tia was in pain and no one did anything to help her for hours?"

Tia quickly puts her arms around him and reassures Vidal that Lisa will be fine, "Daddy is a very good doctor. We'll get her medication and we can take her home."

While they all wait for someone to return with Lisa's medication, Naana introduces Anthony to Vidal's mother, Eva Collins. Eva asks, "Where's Bobby?"

"Bobby is at home with our grandchildren," she replies.

Anthony cannot believe Bobby Sharp. What kind of a man would abandon the woman he loves over and over? Anthony is glad Bobby is not here. Naana is still holding Anthony's hand and it felt good just to hold her hand. The doctor returned with Lisa's medication and explained how it should be used. Vidal nodded and said, "Good! Now, I will take Lisa home." Lisa asked everyone to excuse them.

A few minutes later, Vidal emerged from Lisa's room, crying openly. He didn't say anything to anyone, so his mother went into the room to say good-night to Lisa and left.

"Damn it!" wrote Nathan on Lisa's PDA, "What did you do to him?"

Lisa got out of bed and motioned to Gina that she wanted to leave. Nathan caught her by the arm, and said, "Listen to me, you little brat. We've all been worried sick about you. Why are you so upset?"

Lisa fell into Nathan's arms, murmuring something about Vidal breaking his promise. Nathan and Gina looked at each other quizzically.

Naana asked gently, "Lisa, darling. What promise?"

Lisa doesn't answer the question because she cannot hear, but she does say she will be staying at the guest house with Gina.

"No, you'll not," object Naana. "I almost lost you. You are coming home where I can keep my eyes on you."

Lisa didn't let her mother finish before she was out of the room and gone with a very nervous Gina Read. Tia tells her mother that she and Nathan will go after them, and they are able to catch up with Lisa in the hallway. If they hadn't been in a hospital, Nathan would have yelled at Lisa for being such a brat. Instead, he puts his arms around her and carries her to the car while Tia thanks Gina for her help. When they finally arrive at Gertrude's house, there is a flurry of questions and introductions as Gertrude expresses her worry for her daughter and granddaughter, and Tia explains what's happened. Gertrude hugs her granddaughter, reluctant to let Lisa go.

"I'll be at the guest house. Tell Grandfather that I'll see him at breakfast," says Lisa, even though she still couldn't hear anyone, though the pain was a little better.

Gertrude asks Rose to bring something for Gina to eat.

"Oh, no! Don't trouble yourself. I'm okay," says Gina.

"Well, I'm hungry!" says Lisa.

Gertrude kisses Lisa again, "Go with your friend, my darling. Rose will bring you something to eat. I am so happy you are going to be fine."

By the time Naana returned to the house, it was late. Anthony wanted to buy her dinner and she agreed because she didn't want to come home and face her father or deal with Lisa. She enjoyed dinner and a walk with Anthony. She couldn't remember the last time she and Bobby had a dinner-date.

"I don't know what I would have done without you, Tony. Thank you for the dinner-date. I enjoyed it." Naana hugs him.

"Tony, you didn't have my permission to take my baby on a date," Kofi says.

Tia and Nathan laugh. "Daddy has not been on a date for so long, I'm sure he's forgotten how! I'm glad you took mother, though." says Tia. "Tomorrow, you are taking me on a date."

Naana says, "Well, all frivolity aside, I'm going to talk to Lisa about her behavior."

"Do you want me to come with you?" offers Tia.

"Tia, you should stay out of it," says Nathan. "This is mother-daughter stuff."

Tia shrugged her shoulders and sat down again.

When Naana entered the guest house, Lisa was sound asleep on the sofa. Personally, Naana was relieved not to find her daughter sleeping with Gina. Hearing her come in, Gina appeared from the bathroom, drying her hair with a towel. Naana wanted to tell Gina to stop sleeping with Lisa, but instead she thanked Gina for looking after Lisa. "If there's anything you need, Gina, please let me know."

Gina nodded. She felt a little guilty, but she said, "There is no need for thanks. Lisa's been through a lot lately and I'm happy you all are coping well."

"Well, good-night, then. I just wanted to check on Lisa," said Naana as she covered Lisa with an afghan.

Lisa opened her eyes, "I'm sorry if I scared you, Mother. Vidal wanted to take me to the doctor's on Tuesday before he left, but I thought the pain in my ear was nothing."

"I was a little afraid," admitted Naana.

"Why are you with him?"

"Who, darling?"

"Why are you still married to a man who treats you so badly, Mother?"

"Lisa, your father doesn't treat me badly. When you and Vidal get married, you'll learn that it's not always about the other person."

"Chance would always put me before anything, Mother. That's what we are. He would."

"So does your father. It's not easy being married to a woman with a powerful, domineering father, but Bobby does his best. You just said, Chance . . . would always put your first. Is that why you and Vidal fought?"

Lisa sighs, "I can't stand not being with him and he not with me. Chance and I are done, Mother. Can you stay until I fall asleep?"

"Of course, my darling. I'll stay. Your father is on his way. We'll both stay until you sleep."

"Don't tell me somebody is afraid to sleep. I just yelled at BJ to go to his own bed," Bobby jokes as he enters the guest house. "Hello, Princess!" Bobby kisses his wife and daughter. Lisa sits up and lashes out at her father.

"Papa, you'd better start keeping your eyes on your biggest prize, before you lose her. Every time Mother needs you, you're not around. Meantime, Anthony is there to hold her hands."

"I beg your pardon!" Naana asks, shocked.

"Oh, come on, Mother! I have seduced enough girls to know how this works. Papa needs to wake up!"

Bobby Sharp loves his daughter's blunt tone. "Papa is on the case, Lisa. That's why Papa is going to Ghana next month with the Princess. I called my mother to come and look after you, Claire and BJ until we come back."

Naana says tearfully, "You don't have to do that, darling. I'll be working in Ghana. I'll not have time to spend with you."

"I want to watch you work, Princess. I can be there to hold your hands," Bobby smiles.

"Oh, Bobby!" Lisa watches her parents and realizes that they do have a kind of balance that makes their relationship work.

"Whoa! Way to go, Papa! Now, that's how you romance your Princess!" Lisa is holding both her parents hands and smiling broadly when Tia comes into the guest house with Nathan. "What did Daddy do?" she asks.

"Papa has gone romantic on his Princess. How are the children?" Lisa says as her mother giggles girlishly.

"Daddy has put them to bed. We want to see how you are doing," Tia says.

"Oh, I'm on the mend. I just got a text message from Jackie saying she's engaged to Patrick."

"Who the hell is Patrick?" asks Nathan suspiciously. "I thought Jackie was seeing your security guard."

"Patrick is Vidal's cousin. He is also Kelly Power's son," Tia explains.

"Kelly Powers doesn't have a child, Baby. She and Steven only dated," Nathan says.

"Well, it looks like you Carters like to keep it in the family! Patrick is planning to marry her as soon as her exams are over," Lisa says.

"No! They can't get married. Jackie is too young. She needs to play the field a bit more," objects Nathan.

Tia hits him. "Women don't play the field like men do. Baby, Jackie has grown to be a beautiful young woman."

Lisa giggles.

"Steven was supposed to be keeping an eye on her, not letting her go off and get engaged to one of his ex-girlfriend's brats."

Tia and Lisa giggle. "Wow! I'm glad my mother didn't have any boys and that my brother is too young to know about the birds and the bees. Jackie is not a child. She is getting married to Patrick, so you'd better get used to it," warns Lisa.

"I suppose Father knows all about this Hollywood brat that Jackie's marrying?" Nathan chuckles.

"Baby! Relax! Jackie will be fine. Let's go to bed."

Naana called Vidal and asked whether he could meet her for lunch tomorrow, but Vidal said he can't because he's lunching with Gertrude at his parents home.

"Why don't you and your husband join us, Mrs Sharp?" suggests Vidal.

"Thank you! We will."

Bobby Sharp didn't like his wife spending time with Anthony. He shared Lisa's sentiments on that subject, so he took his daughter's advice about keeping his eyes on his biggest prize. He was aware, though, that Tia and Kofi were watching him plan a romantic evening for his wife. They both thought it was about time. It broke Kofi's heart to see his daughter so unhappy.

"I wish my Princess could have married someone like Nate or Lisa's young man."

"Grandpa! That's an awful thing to say!"

"I'm sorry, Tia. I never did like your father. Gerty like to have her way, so I went along."

"I thought you didn't like Nathan."

"I don't! I doubt if any man genuinely likes the Carter boys. I think they are just too smooth. I was smooth once, you know? Gerty still thinks that I am," he smiles.

"I think Mother is going to be alright. I think my Dad is not used to expressing his affections as we do."

"Well, your father had better learn! My little girl deserves more than this. I have stayed out of it because Gerty forbids me."

Tia laughs. "I guess we all know why we are so bossy. So Grandmother is the boss, eh?"

"You damn right! I'd better go and tell Nate to leave my Gerty alone."

"Grandpa!" Tia shakes her head.

Lisa has a nightmare and when she opens her eyes, Vidal is sitting opposite the bed in the comfy chair.

"I thought you were sleeping with your Chef, so I came to spy on you. I didn't believe the story she told about her coming with you because you fell sick," he whispered.

Lisa nervously chuckled, "I love you and only you. You fill the void in my heart, Vidal. I'll wait however long it takes. I will. Sweetie." They hug. There are tears in Vidal's eyes as Lisa rubs his shaved head. "I'm sorry I didn't let you take me to the doctor's before you left England. From now on, you are the man and I'll listen to what my husband-to-be says, okay?"

"I like that. I'm so happy to hear you say it. Why don't we both listen to each other? You are the better part of me, Lisa. Can I kiss you?"

She nods. "You may kiss me."

Tia is not able to sleep and is about to drop in on Lisa when she meets her mother downstairs in the main house, making tea. Naana could not sleep either, worrying about Lisa. She, too, is also going to check on Lisa. They see Vidal sitting next to the bed.

Tia whispers, "They are so devoted to each other." Naana nods her agreement.

"How could I have kept them apart? He is so devoted to her. But I think Lisa is having second thoughts about marrying Vidal. She told me Chance will always put her needs first when they are married."

"You didn't, Mother! They could have eloped and got married without your permission. I think Lisa is going to marry Chance, too. I'm sure Lisa knows you are looking out for her. Mother, Lisa loves you and she appreciates your guidance—we all do—so don't second-guess yourself, Mother, when you point us in the right direction in our lives. You are not just our mother, you know? You have a very unique relationship with each one of us, and you do with BJ as well. Everyone can see it."

Naana is touched by Tia's comments on her parenting skills. Mrs Sharp confesses to Tia that she doesn't remember Lisa becoming the strongest of the family. It worries her that Lisa has taken on the responsibility of carrying all their burdens. She wishes she could let Lisa see that a family is a shared responsibility for all of us. Tia added her thoughts that leaving home early may have contributed to Lisa being so overly protective.

"Oh, no. I don't think so," says Naana. "Lisa was always like that. I just thought that she would have grown out of it by now. Especially now that she has her own life and her own business ventures."

"I guess that is the kind of person Lisa is, Mother. I wish Daddy would stop grieving for Heather and begin dating again. I have been worried about him since Heather's passing. He spends far too much time alone. It would be nice to see him out with someone now and again."

"I have been thinking about Tony, too. Evelyn is in town. You and Nathan have met her. She lost her husband right around the same time Heather died."

"Is she in Holland? She didn't say she would be coming when we visited her."

"She and I are having dinner together, tomorrow."

"You know, Mother, I was thinking of introducing them. She will be a perfect much for daddy."

Naana nodded yes. "I wonder whether Bobby would mind if we all had dinner together."

Bobby slipped his hands under her arms and kissed the back of her neck. "You wonder if Bobby would mind what, Princess?"

"Well . . . Evelyn is in town. I want to set her up on a date with Tony. What do you think?"

"Please do! I feel inadequate enough around your father and my kids. I don't need Tia's warm-hearted father-in-law holding my wife's hands all the time."

"Are you jealous, Daddy?" Tia asks.

"No . . . I think Tony and Evelyn will make a handsome couple. That's all." He took his wife's hands and kissed the back of them.

Naana smiled, "It's settled, then. I will book a table at the Carlton for us."

Tia smiled and hoped that there would be a budding attraction between Anthony and Evelyn. Anthony Carter has not been on a date for thirty-five years. He has been very happily married to Heather, the only woman he has ever kissed. Their love was unlike any other, so it has been a difficult five years without her. This morning, he visited Gertrude's art gallery with Naana, and to introduced him to an old friend, Evelyn White, a pharmacologist from Ghana. Evelyn lives in Canada—Burlington, Ontario, actually. She has been a widow for five years—just like Anthony. She and Naana have been friends since college. Her late husband was one of Bobby Sharp's closest friends. Naana thought she and Tony would be a perfect match. Naana was busy on the phone in Gertrude's office. Trey has wandered off into the gallery. Anthony found him sitting on the floor listening to a story being told about Ghana's independence from the British in 1957. The African woman telling the story spoke English, and Anthony could tell she had a way with children. He adores that quality in women. Anthony stood with his hand behind his back and listened to the story about Dr Kwame Nkrumah, the very first Ghanaian president. The woman pointed to a photograph of Dr Nkrumah. The children all dutifully looked at the photograph before departing to look at other exhibits. Trey stayed behind to study the photograph more closely. Evelyn went and stood beside him. Trey pointed to another painting.

"Did you know my grandmother painted all of these?" asked Trey.

"No, sir. I didn't." Evelyn thought he was a chip off the old block. She has some photographs of Tia's children and has met them all several times. Trey has grown and looks very handsome.

"Let me guess. You must be Mr Trey Carter. Am I right?"

Anthony wondered how the woman knew Trey's name.

"I'm Trey Anthony Carter. Nathan Carter is my father. My mother is Mrs Tia Carter," Trey explained.

"I'm Evelyn." They shook hands.

"You must tell me your mother and father's name, so that I know you're not a weirdo!" Trey demanded.

Evelyn thought he was so cute. She smiled and did as Trey asked. Anthony thought it was time to retrieve Trey, but there was something about Evelyn that Anthony liked. He wanted to ask her to lunch, but felt it might be inappropriate since she is Naana's friend and they have only just met. Bobby informed him that they were all going out to dinner. Anthony had mixed feelings about that. He wanted to spend some more time with them, but he was also hoping for a quiet evening with Jayzel and Trey.

Later that evening, when they arrived at the Carlton Hotel, it wasn't until after they were seated that Naana informed everyone that Evelyn would be joining them. Naana notice that Anthony seemed nervous. She had noticed, too, at the gallery this morning, that he seemed awkwardly nervous. When the big band started, Naana stood up and said to her husband, "Excuse me, sweetie. I want to show Tony that Tia is not the only Sharp woman who can dance."

"She's right, you know, Tony. Princess can dance. Why don't you let her show you," Bobby said encouragingly.

Tony nervously reached for Naana's hand. As they slowly danced to the jazz music, she made small-talk with him. As Tony relaxed, Naana thought she could broach the real subject on her mind. "Heather would understand, you know, Tony."

"No. I don't think she would understand how I could have a little crush on Tia's mother and now one on her best friend. I don't understand it either," he found himself confessing.

Naana Konadu-Sharp has always had men fall at her feet, confessing their love for her. Her marriage to Bobby didn't seem to make any difference to these suitors. Granted, the marriage was not perfect, but Naana firmly believed in "doing unto others as you would like them to do unto you"—just as the Bible says. She has tried to instill that value in her children, too. She hugs Tony. "You have been my strength these past four years, especially these few months that we all have been in Europe together. You alone and the kids have been my biggest support. It is natural that you feel this way about me. I'm happy that you have a little crush on Evelyn."

Tony laughed. "I must say . . . this is the first time a lady has turned me down that I don't feel like running and hiding."

"I find it difficult to believe that you would run from anything," Naana chuckled.

As they walked back to the dining room, Bobby stood up and pulled out a chair for his wife. Evelyn was also nervous when she arrived because the Sharp had not mentioned that Tony would be joining them for dinner. She, too, had a strange feeling about him when they met at the gallery that morning. It turned out to be a very relaxing evening for the four of them. Tony's nervousness slowly dissipated as the evening progressed and Evelyn became more comfortable, too. She was looking forward to having lunch at the mansion the next day. The thought of seeing Tony again added more excitement to her hopes and made her heart flutter in anticipation.

Chapter 28

Jaden Blake has done the impossible and cleaned himself up from a lifestyle of alcohol and drug abuse. He married his high school sweetheart, Kate Lee, with whom he has two sons. He completed his law degree and now has his own law office. He thought his life couldn't get any better until he returned to Holland after a six-year absence to discover that he has fathered a child with a woman he only recalls as a councilor at a rehab center, the one that began his road to recovery. Strangely, it doesn't seem to bother Kate one bit that Jaden doesn't remember sleeping with the boy's mother. Jaden confided his worries to Jason and Brooke.

"Well, Kate could be in shock," suggested Brooke, "or she really doesn't hold it against you."

Jaden added, "I can't get the little tyke out of my head since I found out about him."

Jaden sighed, "His name was Kurt."

"What do you mean his name *was* Kurt?" Brooke asked, mystified.

"I received a fax from his mother today, briefly describing a hit and run accident outside their home."

"Oh, my God. No!" Brooke cried out loud as she reached for Jaden's hands.

"The boy was dead before the paramedics arrived. Of course, the mother is devastated." Jaden felt a lump in his throat. "This is the second time that I have lost a child that I didn't get a chance to know." Jaden was trembling and crying openly. Jason hugged him and Brooke ran out of Jaden's office to go and get Kate.

Kate's trusted assistant was not at her desk. Brooke did not knock as she opened the door to Kate's office and was shocked by the scene before her. Kate was bent over her desk, panties down around her ankles, fucking a man Brooke didn't recognize. Brendon, eyes closed, didn't see Brooke. Brooke slammed the door shut behind her. Kate almost jumped out of her skin as she pulled on her panties and straightened her skirt. Brendon smiled and sighed as he pulled up his trousers and zipped them. He picked up his briefcase and as he left, Brooke slapped him across the face. Brendon laughed, "Your friend was a good fuck. Perhaps we can all get together and fuck our brains out one day. I hear you enjoyed fucking Tia's old man." He chuckled as he strolled down the hall toward the exit. Kate sat in her chair like nothing had happened. Brooke was not her usual self after Brendon mentioned her affair with Nathan.

"Jaden needs you. His son in Holland was struck by a hit and run car. He is dead. Jaden needs you more than ever now. Unless your marriage to him means nothing to you. If it does . . . I suggest you go and see your husband before he turns to drugs and alcohol like the last time he lost a child." Brooke turned on her heel and left Kate's office. Brooke could not believe that Kate would have an affair right under their noses like that. How could she tell a stranger about her and Nathan? What if this man goes and tells her beloved husband about her affair with Nathan?

Since their return from Holland, Kate had confided to Brendon Chan the troubles of her marriage as well as the child that her husband has fathered and claimed he couldn't remember. She was fed up and felt humiliated by Jaden's thoughtless behavior. She couldn't talk to Brooke or Tia about it because they have been preoccupied by the effects of Kevin Peters attempted rape of Tia. She didn't want to worry her friends, but at the same time, she needed a little space for herself. At the time, Brendon seemed like an obvious choice of confidant, calm and self-assured in and out of bed, of Chinese descent. Making love with him was not familiar but exotic. Getting away to spend time together has been difficult, but they would arrange to meet every now and then in a hotel for an afternoon of hot sex. Brendon would invent excuses to come to the Skyline Building and accidentally bump into Kate so they could sneak into Kate's office for a quickie. It's been exciting for Kate, knowing that Jaden is just downstairs, that Jason is across the hall and that her best friends are also nearby. Kate is not one bit sorry that Jaden's son is dead. The repercussions from Jaden's excursions in Holland have amounted to one humiliation after another. How can any man forget about sleeping with a very beautiful woman?

When Jaden and Kate made their fresh start, Jaden had insisted on complete honesty between them. He told her himself all about the beautiful, sexy Ellen Vroom, the doctor from the rehab facility. It was only later that Jaden had discovered he had slept with Ellen back in his druggie days. Ellen enjoyed attending sex parties, and it was at one of them that she had met, and slept with, Jaden. At the time, she had been dating Nathan Carter, so when she discovered her pregnancy, it was natural that she would assume Nathan was the father of the baby. It was only much later that Ellen realized that the gorgeous young man from the sex party must have been the father of her baby. Kate thought the whole sordid story was utterly ridiculous. She went to the bathroom and fixed her make-up and her hair. She grabbed her purse and told her assistant, "I'm going home." On the way out of the building she met Jaden, Brooke and Jason at Jaden's office downstairs. "Jason, I'm taking a personal day off."

"Of course, sweetheart. I will hold down the fort," Jason assures Kate. He hugs her and whispers, "Please call us if you need anything okay? We are family. Brooke and I will come for the boys so that you two can have some time alone." Kate hugs Jaden. She and Brooke exchange such a loathing look with one another that Jason asks if everything is okay.

"Of course, darling. Why don't you go with them and pick up the boys? I'll meet you all at Mother's," Brooke says. Jaden didn't want to go home because he was busy with a case, but Kate insisted, so he reluctantly left with her. Kate drove to London Green Park where they walked around the park without talking.

"I'm sorry . . . I'm sorry that . . . Kurt died."

"Me, too. Kate, I know you never believed me when I said . . . . when I said that I didn't remember being with her. I'll give you a divorce if that's what you want."

Kate is in tears. She couldn't say anything. She has refused to talk about Ellen and Jaden. The two of them have been fighting privately about it since they found out and it's tearing them apart. On New Year's Eve, Jaden desperately wanted to make love to her, but she refused saying she had a headache. A week ago, the boys found a condom in her purse. They thought it was a candy. When Jaden asked why she has condoms in her purse, she said it was her mother's. Jaden lost control and beat her. Kate later apologized and said it was her's and that she had slept with Brendon

Forever Never Dies

Chan. Jaden was so angry he almost hit her again. Instead, he took his children out to the park and sat on a bench crying while they played. Kate wants Jaden to come back to their bedroom, but he won't. He still loves her and feels that it must be all his fault for Kate's involvement with Brendon. Jaden feels less a man, but he doesn't want his boys going through the same turmoil he experienced as a child when his dad left. The thought of leaving his sons and their mother hurts Jaden more than the possibility of returning to drugs and alcohol. Bringing him back to the present moment, Jaden's cell phone rings. He is reluctant to answer it, so Kate answers it for him. It turns out to be Nathan.

"Hi Kate! I want you to look after Jaden. Tia and I are returning to England in two hours."

Kate takes a deep breath and says, "It's Nathan. He wants you to know that he and Tia are coming and he wants you to stay strong for the boys . . . and for me, Jaden. Please forgive me. I lost you once. I can't lose you again. It's been so lonely. I have no excuse for committing adultery."

Without a word, Jaden walked away to the car. He called his mother as soon as they got home and Joyce reminded her son to be strong, that he has a beautiful family. Joyce says, "Whatever pain and sorrow comes, there is always the love of your family. Alcohol will just numb your pain. It will not make it go away."

Needing to talk to an understanding fellow-traveler, Jaden also called his sponsor, who suggested he come pick him up and take him to an AA meeting.

When they arrived in England, Nathan and Tia went straight to Kate and Jaden's home. The sponsor had just arrived, too, to pick up Jaden. Nathan thanked the sponsor for coming, and told him that he would take Jaden to the AA meeting. After the meeting, Jaden and Nathan went the gym where they put themselves through a punishing workout. "Man, lets go to Brooke's and get my boys before you kill me, Nate."

Horsing around, Nathan picked up Jaden in the air, "That's what I'm talking about!"

"You know, I can see why our Tia fell in love with you. You are just as barmy as she is. Thank you, Nate. You have been an awesome mate, after everything . . ."

"Since I'm such a good friend, I want you to listen me. You have suffered a great loss. Go home and hold Kate."

"I don't think I can, mate. Today, I told her she can have a divorce."

"Jaden, take it from a man who has been there, and who knows what you are facing. When I first got married, I cheated on Tia countless times. Hell, you know, I even had an affair with Brooke. The very first time that I met Kevin Peters, he was holding my daughter. I assumed that my wife was sleeping with him. I was so consumed with rage and anger that I almost killed the three of us. My divorce from Tia hurts more than losing my mother. You don't want Brendon Chan raising your sons and sleeping with the woman that you love. I will go and beat the crap out of him and you will end up defending me. We all know how much grief Tia and Brooke will give you—if that happens."

"I'm afraid of losing it all. Kate has always been a good girl, Nate."

Nathan hugs him and says, "You are going to go home and you are going make your wife forget about Brendon Chan, unless you want me to go and sleep with her for you."

Jaden hits him and says, "Man, you are even sicker than I thought. You are barmy, Nate. You're right though. I've been handling this all wrong. The son of a bitch probably shagged her in ways I've never done it before."

"Speaking of sick, dude . . ." The two of them were laughing as they walked into the house.

"Have you two been drinking, or what?" asked Tia. They looked at each other and began to laugh again. Jaden asked where Kate was.

"She is the living room with Brendon." Tia told them. Jaden looked at Nathan and they began to laugh again, but this time Nathan stopped.

"Oh, Mr Chan! Sir, can I have a word with you? Sir!" Nathan called out. Brendon walked into the kitchen with nervous Kate behind him.

Jaden chuckled. "So, tell me love. Did he not give you a good shag today at your office?"

Tia dropped the bottled water she was holding, so surprised was she to hear Jaden's question. Brendon turned to Kate and said something in Cantonese. Suddenly, Jaden stepped forward and grabbed Brendon's balls. He winked at Nathan and said, "You were right bro. His fucking dick is not big enough." Jaden began to laugh as he let go of Brendon's privates. Kate flushed with embarrassment and shame. Once again, she felt humiliated in front of Tia and Nathan.

"Kate, your mother is going to hear about this. You left me for this junkie," Brendon said.

Nathan looked at Jaden who was still laughing. Guiding him toward the door, Nathan said, "It's best you leave, man." Jaden joined Nathan at the front door, grabbing Brendon by the shirt collar and tossing him down the stairs of the front porch. Brendon almost landed on top of his car.

Brushing the dust off his hands, Jaden shouted, "Let's eat!" Kate moved to take Jaden's hand, but he moved away. Tia watched it all from her vantage point in the hall, an expression of disbelief on her face.

Nathan said to Jaden, "I'll call you later. I'm going to take Tia home."

As they leave the house, they find Brendon—still outside, brushing off his clothes—standing beside his car, trying to say something to Tia. Nathan opens the car door for Tia, then goes around to the driver's side, jumps in and drives off.

"Jaden, please!" begs Kate. "It's not what you think. He took my cell phone by accident and he was just returning it."

"Sure, he did. Good-night, love," replies Jaden as he goes into the guest room and closes the door behind himself.

As he sat on the cold floor, Jaden asked himself, "Why?" He took off his gym clothes and did a head stand. He was tired and after a short while, he dropped to the floor. For the first time in a long while, Jaden slept soundly. He has been sleeping with his sons. The boys love it, but they wake often in the middle of the night needing a drink, needing to pee, needing consoling after a dream. Jaden cried for Kurt and prayed that God would help Ellen through this painful time. He knows how much Ellen loved the little boy. Jaden loved him too, even though it hurt him deeply that he couldn't be with Kurt. He wished with all his heart that God had not taken him away like this. Then, he recalled how Nathan had said that things don't make sense when it hurts this much. "How can Kate hurt him this way?" he wonders. "I will not turn to drugs and alcohol this time. My children need me more than ever. And I need them, too."

Kate sat in the dark living room all alone, thinking about how foolish she has been. She thought she had been giving Jaden a taste of his own medicine, but it has not worked out that way. "I cannot lose my family over this," she thinks. "I just cannot. It was one mistake. Jaden will forgive me."

Kate usually gives Jaden his personal space when he refuses to share their bed. Suddenly, it seems fiercely important that she talk to him and make him listen to her. He is in the bathroom of the guest room suite, so she passes through the bedroom and opens the bathroom door and steps inside the steamy room. Jaden has just finished taking a shower and he is concentrating on drying his hair. He sees her there and knows exactly how she is feeling. He loves her still, but this is never what he wanted. He frowns and throws the towel down as he runs his hands through his hair and begins to brush his teeth. He takes her hand and they return to the guest room and sit on the bed.

"Are you alright, Kate?" asks Jaden.

Kate nods affirmatively.

"I'm going to get dressed, Kate. I'm sorry for before . . . Kate, I have always known that your mother would have preferred you be married to . . ." he stops himself from saying it. Jaden continues, "There were a lot of disrespectful things said before. I'm not going to repeat them. I am sorry Tia and Nathan had to see it all. Tia thought Nathan should have told her about the mess our marriage is in."

"I am so sorry, Jaden. *Please.*"

"Kate, you don't have to be sorry. I know how you feel about Kurt. I tried to talk to you about it, love, but you didn't want to know. I don't like this affecting people we care about. I don't like to see you unhappy and upset, Kate."

"Have I lost you?"

"Kate, I'm always going to be around. I cannot force you to forgive me for things I have done in the past to hurt you, Brooke and Tia. If you want to hurt me just like I did, that's fine. I can take it. But you and the kids, our whole family, don't deserve to be hurt by my mistakes. You need to clean up. Tia and Nate are coming back for dinner. They'll be here soon. I'll set the table." He moved to leave the room.

Kate brushed his arm. "I don't . . . Jaden, I don't know how all this began. I love you, our family . . ." she paused. "Jaden, can you let me explain?"

"There is no need, love. I love you, but I have always told you since before we got married and had kids that whatever makes you happy, I will support you. You want to be with Brandon? Go and be with him."

"I don't want to be with Brandon."

"Well, I don't want my kids in this kind of environment, Kate. I hit you. I don't want to be the kind of husband who beats his wife. It's not what I want. I don't want my boys growing up in a single-parent home, or raised by another man."

Kate was crying. She thought she could see where this discussion was going.

Tia made Nathan stop the car on their way home. She didn't want to leave Kate and Jaden in that state. She was upset with Nathan for not telling her that Kate was having an affair with Brendon.

"Sweetie, I thought we were done keeping things to ourselves?"

"I'm sorry. I figured you knew. You girls are so close. Jaden thought you all knew, but he just wanted his wife to forgive the past and didn't want to force her to choose. We cannot solve every problem in our family, though some we can, Baby. They will handle it, as difficult as it is, they will. I don't want you holding this against me. I can't handle not being close to you. Yes, sex is good when we fight and make up, but Baby, it is amazing between us always. I don't want that to change."

Tia smiled and said, "Trust you to bring our sex life into this. I hope you did not advise him to go and sleep with Kate or you will."

"Yep, yep! Baby, you know me. I'm all about love and making love." He said it in a sexy tone and lean over to kiss Tia.

Chapter 29

Lisa was awake at five in the morning just to talk to Jackie in LA. Even though she was still studying for exams, Jackie felt less stressed with Patrick keeping her company. Lisa, too, was improving. Her ears did not hurt so much. Although she hated taking medication, this time she was diligent about taking this medication and it seems to be helping. She locked the front door of the guest house to prevent anyone from dropping by to check on her. Gina was also awake, so Lisa poured some coffee for her and some juice for herself. Together, they walked back to the bedroom. Lisa got back into bed and pulled the covers aside, motioning for Gina to get in the bed with her.

"Lisa, are you alright?"

"I am now that I'm holding you tight."

"This is not what I had in mind," protests Gina. "I thought we were done. That's the only reason I agreed to come here with you." Gina has to fight back tears. She turns her face back on Lisa to hide her tears, but Lisa can tell she is crying.

"Please, don't cry, Gina. Why are you crying? Do you want us to be done?" Lisa pulls her on top of her as Gina stares into Lisa's green eyes.

"I'm an idiot."

Lisa sighs, "You are a very intelligent woman. Don't you ever call yourself an idiot."

"I was worried out of my mind about you and how you have been coping with things. I care a lot about you, you know?"

"That's good to know," Lisa agrees. "I'm crazy about you too. I'm coping with everything as well as I should. Why are you so emotional?

Being with you is not a bad thing for me. Why is it a terrible thing for you?" Lisa asks with a smile.

"No, Lisa. It's not. I'm almost twenty-seven years old. I joined the force because my grandmother refused to accept the fact that I like to sleep with men and women. I have been falling in and out of love. Not once has anyone treated me with respect or cared about me the way that you care about me. I lied to get close to you, Lisa, and you still treated me with respect. I was so worried yesterday when you fell sick. Your fiancée was right about you, though . . . You are a very stubborn girl!"

Lisa smiles as she wipes the tears off Gina's face. Gina continues, "You have a wonderful life and a great family. I don't want to hurt you."

"Oh, I'll be hurt by many people in my life whom I love. You will never hurt me, Gina." Lisa kisses her on the lips.

"I will if I keep sleeping with you. I'll be going back to Leeds at the end of the month."

"No, you won't! You can't leave me! You can't leave the man you've been falling in love with."

Gina raises her eyebrows. "What man? Who have I been falling in love with?"

Lisa is quiet for a moment. "There is one thing that I know best in life: it's women."

"Whoa! Who would have thought?" Gina teases.

"You and Corey belong together. You're not a cop. I've seen you cooking in the kitchen. You have a natural passion about it. Why give it up for a boring job? Come lay down with me. I want to hold you. I'll be having a business meeting this morning with my boyfriend at his home. I want to spend the weekend with you—away from here—so we can do all kinds of naughty, romantic things. Call Corey and tell him how you feel about him. You have nothing to lose!"

"Thanks, Lisa, but I should be going home now that you are safe. I think your mother senses something."

"She is my mother. Mothers always sense things. I love you! That has to be good enough for my mother. You want to know what I sense? Maybe I should show you! You can tell me which you like best. Kissing . . ." Lisa kisses Gina She removes Gina's top to discover she isn't wearing a bra. Gina leans back in the bed. "Sucking your breast, maybe? Mm, Mm, eating your pussy is like delicious chocolate. Or maybe you want me to show you and you can tell me which you enjoy most."

Gina finds herself getting wet as she watches Lisa. Gina knows what she is doing with Lisa is wrong and she believes if Lisa's mother knew of it, it would cause a great deal of trouble—not only for herself but also for Lisa.

Gina needs to fight the attraction, but the kid is so good at seduction, she can't help loving all the attention. Lisa sees Gina blushing. Lisa kisses her neck, whispers "I want you." Gina smiles and begins to relax. Lisa stares into her eyes and tells her again, "I love you." Gina stirs, trying to pull Lisa's head down to the pillow, but Lisa pulls her gently back into her embrace. Gina tries to think of something to say, but she cannot. Her mind is blank. This is not what she hoped for. Lisa tells her to stop thinking, to stop worrying about the things she can't control. It feels good to cuddle, to share the warmth of an embrace without making love. Gina lifts up her head and smiles, "Are you okay?" Lisa smiles back and brushes her hair away from her face as she replies, "I'm with this beautiful, incredibly sexy woman in my arms. Hell, yes! I'm okay."

Gina sits up and looks at Lisa, thinking, "God, this woman is such a turn-on." She wants desperately to kiss Lisa and feels herself weakening as Lisa's hands rub her back.

"I hope you know that what you're doing is pure torture for me?" Gina whispers.

"Uh-huh. Don't you enjoy this kind of love-making? I love you, Gina. I need to put a smile on your face," Lisa whispers.

"What a smile!" thinks Gina.

By the time Lisa was done with her, Gina Read was certain she had done it all. Her body was trembling with new passions. She forgets where she is until Lisa calls the main house to order breakfast.

"Rose," says Lisa, "I have a girlfriend staying with me at the guest house. I'm going to pass the phone to her and she will tell you what she wants for breakfast."

Gina protests, saying, "I can cook for myself."

"No, Rose will bring you breakfast. Just tell her what you want."

"I can go out. There must be a diner nearby."

"Maybe, there is. I don't know. Don't be silly! Let Rose make you something to eat."

Reluctantly, Gina takes the phone from Lisa and talks to Rose about breakfast. While Gina talks, Lisa slips out of bed and kisses her on the cheek. As Gina hangs up, Lisa says, "I'm going to the gym in the main house. I'll see you later in the afternoon. Why don't you call Corey and tell him how you feel?" An hour later, Lisa returns, all dolled up in a Chinese red mini dress with a matching coat. Her hair is pulled up in a French twist. Diamond studs adorn her ears and she carries a black Gucci bag, which she places on the marble center table.

"I'm sorry for leaving you all alone. My sister and brother are in the main house. My mother is wondering whether you would like to join them on an outing this morning?"

"No . . . I'm okay. Really, I don't want to impose."

"I don't want you by yourself. I have asked Guntar to take you all over Amsterdam—show you the sights—for me. He will pick me up later at the Collins and we'll have lunch. I'll see you soon."

Gina watches Lisa get in the back of the car. "Damn! This is going too far," Gina thinks. "How did she know about Corey? Not that it will go anywhere. I've never been able to hold onto anyone for any amount of time." As she dresses, Gina muses that her time with Lisa as been unreal. She is not in love with Lisa, but she does love her a great deal. They both know that their relationship has to end very soon.

The home of the Collins family is located in the south end of the city. They live on an exclusive cul-de-sac in a spectacular South Beach dream bungalow with grand windows and an enormous view of nature. When Guntar pulls the car into the drive-way, Vidal is already standing there with Lucky, his beloved Siberian Husky. Besides Vidal, there is no one the dog loves more than Lisa. The feeling is mutual. When Vidal opens the car door, Lisa steps out and goes down on one knee to greet the dog, "Oooooh, Mummy missed you too," she says as she fondles Lucky, "Missed you so much!" Vidal grins as the dog licks Lisa's face. She takes out a doggie biscuit from her purse and treats Lucky while he wags his tail with delight. Standing up, Lisa hugs Vidal. As she fixes his shirt, Lisa tells Vidal he looks very sexy. In reply, he kisses her on the cheek. Vidal is the only child of Eva Collins, the light of her eyes on whom she has lavished all her love since the day he was born twenty-three years ago. In the 1970s, Eva Collins was a super-model. Over the duration of her career, she has graced the covers of magazines all over the world. Her husband has collected and created a media library of every commercial in which Eva has ever performed. Rumor has it that she used to be close personal friends with Mick Jagger of the Rolling Stones. It has also been said that she introduced Mick to her good friend Jerry Hall after his divorce from Bianca Jagger.

Eva sits in her drawing room drinking tea with her husband, Eric. Eric Collins is in his late fifties, very rich, and like any other rich man, he will be the first to tell anyone that he didn't win his wife's heart with love or charm. It is his little joke. In actuality, it was quite the reverse: Eva won his heart. They met in Hollywood in 1974, introduced by Kelly Powers. Eric's older brother, Nick, was dating Kelly at the time, and it was his first visit to America. Of course, Eric fancied Eva right from the get-go, but didn't pursue it. They met again six months later at Holland's Grand Prix. Eva asked Eric out to dinner, but he turned down the invitation. Eric didn't have time for romance, or partying as everyone called it in the seventies. He didn't want romance, and certainly not with someone in show business. Eric claimed, "They all do drugs and are very sexually charged, so much so that they will sleep with anyone. I want a girl like Mother. We get married and live happily ever after," Eric told his brother.

"Sure you will, little brother. Don't you know they don't make women like that anymore? You dumb-ass snob," Nick laughs as he teases his brother.

Eva was not pretentious. She knew very well about show-biz romances and how long they last. Eva has always had her heart set on becoming the wife of a corporate business man who would cherish her and keep her in the life style to which she has become accustomed. Her agent has said that at the tender age of twenty-nine she will be too old to grace any cover of any magazine. In a daring move, Eva sent a single rose to Eric on Valentine's Day 1974 with a hand-written note attached to it.

> *My dear Eric,*
> *I feel as though my heart has finally found its other half. Be my valentine and have dinner with me tonight at seven.*
>
> *Eva*

Eric's heart melted when he read the note. The rest, as they say, has been happily ever after. Eva always looks stunning. She wears plain black pants with a Versace shirt and belt. She sips her tea and crosses her legs as she listens to Eric tell her about motor racing. They both love motor racing. When Lisa enters the room, Eva exclaims, "Whoa! Now, that's how you rock a Gucci purse, Lisa!" Of course, Vidal and Eric do not see the significance of ladies purses. As far as the men are concerned, purses seem all the same.

"You had us all worried last night, Lisa," Eric says as he greets Lisa. "I was seriously pissed off when Vidal told us about the son-of-a-bitch doctor who left you in pain. Do you think I should ask the hospital to fire him?"

Lisa grinned as she patted Vidal on his shoulder, "Oh, I think my Baby here has beat you to the punch, big-time!"

Eric winks at her. Eric Collins loves Lisa and her business wit. He also likes the fact that she likes spending money at the same time that she knows how to invest money. He was looking forward to retiring, and his personal hope is that Lisa will join Collins Enterprises once she and Vidal marry. Lisa has said that she won't join CE. Eric still hopes she will change her mind. Vidal needs a strong woman like Lisa to help him run Collins Enterprises.

"I was just on-line with Patrick. He and Jackie are going to be married soon. We can all get married at the same time if we get your parents permission," says Vidal.

"I want us to be married alone, in the loft on Valentine's Day. I don't want a double wedding with Jacks and Patrick."

Lisa sits next to Vidal's mother and flips open her laptop. "I have a business proposal for you."

Eva Collins has no business sense whatsoever. Her husband immediately stands up and says, "I have some business to discuss with Vidal. If you two lovely ladies will excuse us . . ."

"Sure you do. Eric, you and I have discussed this topic in the past. I told you I will have what you seek the next time I'm in town," Lisa crosses her legs and puts on her poker face. Eric has discussed many business deals with Lisa in the past. She makes him nervous, but he sits down to listen anyway.

"My sister and her friends started a small fashion outlet in England seven years ago. Their little venture has grown and is bringing in more each month."

"Baby, we are bankers. I'm not going to buy another toy for you to play with. I'll get the permission for us to get married. Please, Lisa. You promised," Vidal reminds her.

"Oh, isn't my Baby so sweet? This is business, Baby, just like I said. Eric, the business that I'm bringing to your attention will bring in money not only for you, but also will cut down Eva's spending by 50% each month. You all know how my Baby likes to spend your money on me."

They all laugh. Lisa continues, "It will also cut down Vidal's spending on me by 50% each month."

"Well, Sweetheart! Between you and my Eva spending all the family money, I am surprised we can still eat each day," Eric observes.

"Father, we are not going to buy them a fashion house. That would be spoiling them. You often tell me that I give into Lisa's whims too much and that she's becoming too much like mother."

Eric frantically motioned for his son to be quiet, but Vidal is turned toward his mother and Lisa as he vents.

"We are the men, father, and we are not going to buy these ladies whatever they want."

His father has moved to the far end of the sofa, putting distance between himself and his son as Vidal continues his opinionated tirade. "I love you two ladies very much, but someone has to think about your pensions. Besides . . . between the two of you, you have more clothes than all the women in a small town in Europe!" Vidal turns to his father, looking for approval and support, notices Eric has moved away. Eric grins, "You're a dead man, son!"

Eva looks at Lisa, shaking her head in disbelief, "Are you going to let my son get away with what he just said?"

Lisa walks over to Vidal and puts her arms around him.

"Vidal and I have discussed this. He is the man. I'm the woman he wants to spend the rest of his life with . . . Whatever he says . . . goes." Lisa winks at Eric and Eva.

Eric loves Lisa's charm and wit. "She's a clever girl," he thinks, "And she's using all her powers of seduction today."

On her side, Eva is not very happy about her son's insinuations concerning her spending habits. After all, as a former world-famous super-model, who gave it all up just to have him, Eva feels entitled to some perks. She still has the scar on her abdomen where the obstetrician cut her open and took out the ten-pound baby. Her body has not been the same since.

"Now, you listen to me, son. If you think you are going to impose on me your little power-trip thing you have going on with Lisa, you are mistaken! I did not raise you to be cave-man and rude!"

"I'm sorry, Mother."

"You'd better be sorry, sweetie. This is the sort of thing that breaks up a good marriage—young men at your age forbidding their young naïve wives to do this or do that. I will spend my husband's money any way I see fit." Eva crosses her long legs and shoots her son a disappointed look.

"Of course, you will, my dear!" chortles Eric. "Now, son. You listen to your mother. She does know more about this marriage thing than you and Lisa." Eric and Lisa exchange a devious smile.

"Baby, may I explain my proposal now?"

"Yes, yes, Lisa. Anything you want, Baby. I'm sorry. Please, go ahead," Vidal says nervously.

"I was on-line doing some research and came across this." Lisa passes her laptop to Eric. He has a proud expression on his face as he looks at the photos on the screen. He exclaims, "I fell in love with her when I finally got up-close to her that evening. She always looks much more beautiful than the photographers on the fashion magazine portray her. She still does."

Eva smiles. It really does turn her on when Eric talks about her that way. Eric is not adept with words, and when she met him, he didn't have any experience with women. Eva has been a very good teacher in all things romantic, and Eric was only too pleased to learn from his wife.

"Lisa, sweetie. I hope your proposal is not about Mother going back to modeling. She has a family now. Looking after me and father is a full-time job, you know," Vidal says with certainty.

"He's right, Lisa!" joins Eric.

Lisa is enraged by the Collins men and their spoiled ways. She does not plan to wait on Vidal like his mother has done for his father. "I know. Eric, Vidal and I are going to be married soon. It will be my job to look after him, but I am thinking more in terms of romance for the four of us as a family—doing something that binds us together," says Lisa deviously. She has the undivided attention of the Collins men, now. "You all know how I love spending money." Eric and Vidal nodded agreement. "Well, I like to make money, too. I hope," she pauses, "I expect Vidal and I will have more than our families have by the time we have our first child. Collins Enterprises and African Mortgage Funds alone are not going to bring in the kind of money that I'm talking about."

"What does that have to do with Mother and clothes?" asks Vidal.

Lisa laughs and gestures to all of them, "Look at us! What do you two see when you look at us?" she asks Vidal and Eric, pointing to herself and

Eva. Vidal hesitates because he doesn't want to put his foot in it this time. He turns to his father.

"We see the women whom we adore," Eric says with a big grin on his face.

"Eva, please come and work with me here. Pretend you are doing a fashion show and you're working the catwalk. Honey, I want you to work the runway for me."

Eva has no idea what Lisa has up her sleeve, but she got up and did as Lisa asked, then stopped and stood side-by-side with Lisa.

"No idea, eh?" says Lisa with a hint of exasperation. "Well, I'm going to tell you two what you have here. It's not just the women you adore . . . No, gentlemen! What you have here is a world-famous super-model. She is still very sexy and gives men hard-ons when they go on the internet to see her. Gay men want to be with her when they see a photograph of Eva Redwood-Collins."

Eva feels aroused by Lisa's conversation. She knows that whatever Lisa suggests, it will be something that will cause trouble in her marriage. Eric is a very shy, private man. They have been married for twenty-four years and not once have they ever fought about anything. This will be the one thing that will drive a wedge between them Even though Eva often thinks of modeling or maybe doing something in fashion, Eric usually discourages her.

Lisa smiles, "Eric liked the little walk you just did, Eva."

"My dear, it brought back a lot of memories. I don't understand what you're saying, though, Lisa. But we can all agree that you two always look very pretty each day," Eric compliments the women.

"To make this short, I want to have a fashion magazine focusing on urban style," Lisa says.

"Sweetie, there is one already—Ebony." Eva points out. She has a copy of the most recent issue on her coffee table. She picks it up and passes it to Lisa. Lisa throws it down and takes Eva's hand.

"I want you all to listen to me first. My sister is opening her own television studio in Canada next month. She has about four movies of the week beginning filming next month at Sunlight Studio and Media Group. In addition, their show *The Saga* features all these up-and-coming young actors. I was at a press conference with them a few weeks ago in England. That's when the idea of a magazine came to mind. All the photographs that were taken by the press at that press conference were not even seen in a single magazine. I checked. I saw the fans going crazy, getting autographs and things. Eric, an urban magazine that I'm talking about will have Eva as my fashion editor. Your wife is a fashion icon. She knows the fashion business. Women, young and old, still look up to her even though she has stayed out of the public eye for the last twenty years. The second most important thing is that Tia wants her studio and all the actors working for her to be huge. Our magazine will give them the exposure they need, but we need to launch the magazine quickly."

"I think the concept will work, Lisa, but I have no experience. Actors doing photo shoots are not free. We would be talking about twenty thousand pounds for a two-hour photo shoot just for the actor alone—not to mention the studio, the crew, and by the time you're done with one spread, you'd be looking at close to one hundred thousand pounds. Just for one shoot. You will not just be doing business with celebrities who are divas, but also with their agents, their publishers and their entourages, all of whom can be a real pain in your rear end. There's art directors, publishers, writers, in-house and field photographers as well as videographers. Not to mention that computer thing you kids like so much . . ."

"A website?" Lisa prompts.

"Yes . . . That's it. A website. A magazine contains a minimum of seventy pages. You'll be looking at a cost of one hundred thousand time twenty just to produce the first issue."

Lisa gushed, "Eva, you just passed an interview with Lisa Sharp!" She looks across the room at Eric, who is equally impressed with his wife's knowledge. It makes him want to take her upstairs.

"No, Lisa. I don't want a job. It's a great idea, but an impossible one. The money involved . . . besides it's not as easy as that. Tia will tell you there is a lot more involved in the media business than what you and Vidal are used to at Collins Enterprises and the African Mortgage Funds. It is a very cut-throat industry at times. You have to be really bitchy to get a simple thing done. It's highly competitive," Eva warns Lisa.

"Is that right, Mother?" asks Vidal.

"Yes, Baby. She is right," interrupts Lisa. "But in our case, the first issue of our magazine is already done by me. All I need is for you and Eric to tell me it's okay for us to go ahead."

"I cannot allow it, Lisa. Baby, I don't have that kind of money for you to start a new venture. I don't want tabloids around us. They are too intrusive in people's personal lives. I'm not used to that kind of lifestyle, like Tia and Nathan. The money alone is just too much. Lisa, please reconsider," Vidal says firmly.

"But I have the money, Baby, and with our partners, I'll have more than enough to get started. I want you all to listen to me. The public around the world has always had a huge fascination with the rich and famous," Lisa makes a circular hand gesture, "an endless curiosity about celebrities and their singular lifestyles. In the fashion industry, image is everything. Tia Sharp-Carter is a well-known name all over the world, and not just for her sense of fashion. Eva Redwood-Collins is also a well-known name world-wide. I have a building that I was going to use as my next night club in London. Instead, I propose to use it for the offices of the Urban Style Magazine, which will be owned by me and my sisters. Our first issue will have a center page which will feature Eva. Tia has this eye-catching advertisement that will create the buzz for our marketing strategies. It will run in magazines and newspapers all over Europe and North America beginning next month. The campaign will be centered around Elizabeth Starr, Kelly Powers, and—" Lisa walked over to Eva and put her hand on Eva's shoulder, "and Eva Redwood-Collins." Lisa sits down and crosses her legs. She surveys their expressions and chuckles. Vidal looks at his father and mother, who both have this amazed expression on their faces.

Lisa continues, "The cover of the magazine will have all the cast member of *The Saga*. The show has had phenomenal success in North America and now in Europe, too. Kelly Powers and Elizabeth Starr are shooting Sunlight Studio's first original TV movie, *Forever Never Dies*. They both have agreed to be in the magazine at no cost to promote their movie. February is a romantic month. Our wedding is going to be featured in that issue, alongside your mother and father talking about their extraordinary glamorous love-affair."

Lisa notices Vidal shaking his head. Whether it's in negative reaction to the idea or amazement, she can't tell. "Baby, listen to me: your parents and our love affair are like the plot-lines of the movies and soap operas that my sister produces. Tia and Eva are not strangers to the celebrity gossip and tabloids rumor mills. We'll be fine. This is who we are! It's our destiny! Like it or not, Eric Collins is your father. Your mother is not only a babe, but also a super-model who at the height of her career gave it all up for the man she loved. *Hello Magazine* will want to do a story about us, once the word gets out that we are engaged. I want that story in our own magazine. This is something that is my sisters, mine, and yours, Baby. We are stepping out of our parents shadow. We want to start our own dynasty, Vidal. You have been my partner and soon will be my husband. I want this so that one day we can tell our children about us and the love that we shared."

Vidal often wonders whether Lisa takes their future seriously. He feels like the girl has taken his soul and he is head over heals in love with her, so it's not been all business and fun.

"I can't Lisa. I *hate* show-biz people. I don't think I can handle it. I *would* like to support you, but I'm a banker. I like being a banker, and magazine stuff, fashion stuff is just *soooooo* outside my comfort zone. I hope you're not mad at me for saying so."

"Of course, not, Baby! Your emotional support is all I need. I love you! We don't have to do the same projects all the time, as long as we support each other's interests."

Eva sits close to her husband now, and she can tell the whole topic has aroused him. He is rubbing her thigh like he does when he wants to make love. Eva has never given up on going back into the fashion business, but she cannot believe that two decades have passed since her last commercial. Eva kisses Eric, "What do you think?"

"About what?" he replies evasively.

"Dear, about Lisa's proposal. Will you let me take a job and help the kids?"

"Yes, yes, my dear. Whatever you like. I think this calls for champagne and orange juice for Lisa. What do you say, son?"

Vidal shakes his head, "You know what? I don't know what to say to you, Babe. I don't even have permission for us to marry yet!"

Lisa pulls him up out of his seat, "We'll get the permission. Trust me. My parents will give us their permission or I'll make things difficult for them."

Naana Konadu-Sharp has just arrived at the Collins home with her mother and husband in tow. They are all looking forward to lunch. Lisa did not know they were in the house as she remarks, "I will not let anyone meddle in our affairs any more."

"Just how are you planning to make me and your father change our minds about your up-coming nuptials?" demands Naana as she enters the room.

"Papa has already said that I can marry Vidal," Lisa says as she turns toward the Collins's, "My father hates seeing me so unhappy." Lisa smiles deviously.

"Yes, Princess. I did say that," then turning toward Naana, Bobby continues, "Darling, Lisa has been very unhappy."

"Since your father let the cat out of the bag, we might as well put them out of their misery so we can plan this wedding." Naana winks at them.

Vidal turns to his parents, "That's a rotten thing to do to your only child!" He walks over to Bobby to shake his hand, "Thank you, sir. I'll look after Lisa. I promise."

"Of course, you will, my darling," says Gertrude as she kisses Vidal and sits down.

"Well, I'd love to stay for lunch, but I have a million things to do. I'll call and email everything to you this evening. I'm going to look at our new offices now. I need to let Tia know that I have an editor. She is looking forward to seeing what you can bring to the table, Eva. I know you can do it!"

Vidal wishes that Lisa could forget about business for an hour and stay for lunch, and he says as much as Lisa moves toward the door.

"Baby, I want all this done before the wedding. Love ya!" Lisa says, pecking him on the cheek as she sails out the front door. Vidal returns to the lunch party feeling that Lisa has come around to his view of things. He sometimes wishes that Lisa were not so independent. He was very worried about her last night when she was hospitalized for a severe ear infection, but to be honest, a bigger worry is the constant presence of Lisa's chef. Vidal thought it rather disturbing that Gina had accompanied Lisa to Holland when there was still a club to run back in London. "Wouldn't Corey have been a better choice?" Vidal shrugged, "Surely, Lisa has her reasons," he thought as he re-joined his parents.

ೀ Chapter 30 ೨

Lisa drove with Gina to her grandparents waterfront cottage an hour outside Amsterdam. It boasted a beautiful view and a park-like setting. Lisa opened the door for Gina to enter the cottage. Gina noticed that the fire was lit and the house seemed very warm. Lisa stood behind her and whispered, "I hope it is to your liking. I stopped by earlier to make sure that everything was in order before I came to pick you up. Do I get a kiss for effort?"

Gina smiles, "Lisa, don't you think your family will be worried about you?"

Lisa didn't want to hear it, so she put her fingers on Gina's lips, shushing her, and lead her to the sunken kitchen-dining room. Lisa pulls out a chair for Gina to sit down. Gina is dazed. In fact, Gina Read seems to lose all logical sense whenever she is around Lisa Sharp. Lisa picked up lunch for them on the way to the cottage, so they ate heartily and afterward, Lisa showed Gina around the cottage. After the tour, they both slept for the rest of the afternoon on the sofa in the family room. Gina has been worried about Lisa's ear infections, especially since Lisa keeps up a break-neck pace every day, refusing to slow down to rest. Lisa insists she is feeling a lot better. Then, quickly changing the subject, she says, "I have an unforgettable weekend planned for us, but first, I have a couple of business calls to make. We are going to dinner in an hour. I want to see you relaxed." She brushed Gina's hair away from her face. "God, you're beautiful, Gina." She kisses Gina on the cheek before disappearing out of the bedroom. When she returns later, Gina is standing by the window thinking, "What the hell am I doing here?" She has no idea where they are going to dinner, so she put on a black ruffle-front dress that she had purchased that morning while shopping with Claire, Lisa's younger sister.

"You look absolutely gorgeous!" Lisa says, taking Gina by the hand. Lisa sports pale-pink slouchy pants and a cream braided sleeveless top. Her hair is in natural ringlets. Gina thinks she looks sexy too.

"Where are we going?" asks Gina.

"Oh! Didn't I tell you? We're going to a club in Rotterdam, twenty minutes away."

In the limo, Gina sits on Lisa's lap for the duration of the trip. Lisa caresses Gina's back, making her even more horny. Club Wave is owned by one of Lisa's associates, so they get the VIP treatment—escorted inside through a private door. The club is full of women, very sexy, well-dressed ladies, most of whom seem to know Lisa well enough to hug and kiss her. She introduces Gina to each of them as her girlfriend. The owner is five-foot, seven inches tall, not more than one hundred and ten pounds with loose, blonde curls, and blue eyes. She wears white shorts and a pink wrapped shirt with thigh-high black high-heeled boots. Gina guesses the woman is in her late twenties. Very sexy, indeed. Lisa lets go of Gina's hand to hug and kiss the owner. Gina watches them as Lisa swings her around, saying something in Netherlands. The woman is blushing as Lisa kisses her again on the cheek. Recovering her manners, Lisa introduces Gina to Diamond, who hugs and kisses Gina on the lips. Diamond and Lisa take Gina's hands and they walk together to a private area in the VIP section. Diamond gives Lisa a bottle of water and a glass of red wine for Gina. Bella is Diamond's girlfriend. She arrives wearing the twin outfit to Diamond's and joins them at their table. Together, they enjoy chicken with fresh herbs, pan-roasted asparagus, baby turnips and potatoes. Lisa has sauteed shrimps accompanied with artichoke salad. Gina feels very relaxed now. From time to time, Lisa picks up her fork and feeds Gina. Diamond asks about Lisa's wedding.

"Hmmm . . . Valentine's Day is the big day," Lisa smiles.

"Be aware that men taste very different from what you're used to, honey," Diamond says as she raises her glass in a toast.

"So I'm told. I'm looking forward to all that," Lisa says with a wink and a smile.

Suddenly, Gina realizes that Lisa has never been with a man. "Oh, my God!" she thinks to herself. "Vidal must love Lisa *so* much to wait for her all this time. So what the hell is Lisa doing with me?"

Lisa can see that all the marriage talk is making Gina uncomfortable, so she pulls Gina onto her lap and kisses her on the cheek. Her fingers find Gina's wet spot between the legs. Gina smiles as Lisa feeds her morsels of orange-vanilla cake. Gina's body trembles as Lisa keeps stimulating her between her legs and feeding her at the same time. Gina, losing control, puts both arms around Lisa, squeezing and stroking her back. Lisa puts down her fork, brushes back her hair and gently kisses Gina on the lips, sliding her tongue into her mouth and sensuously kissing her while Diamond and Bella watch. Finding themselves getting wet just watching Lisa and Gina, Diamond and Bella began kissing, too. Having had the "Lisa experience", Diamond knows first-hand what an amazing lover Lisa can be. She suspects that Lisa is doing more to Gina than just sensuously kissing her. Finally, Lisa stops kissing Gina, who is trying to catch her breath having just been on the brink of orgasm. She didn't want Lisa to stop stimulating her, as it was the sweetest kind of torture. It was not at all like any of Gina's fantasies. That is one thing Lisa has done for her, taken charge of realizing Gina's sexual fantasies. At that moment, Usher's "U got bad" began to play on the sound system.

"Excuse us!" Lisa says to Diamond and Bella as she takes Gina to the dance floor. They dance closely for a few minutes, until Diamond appears behind Lisa and asks if she can cut in. Gina dances with Bella, and later with Diamond.

"Are you spending the night?" asks Diamond.

"No," says Lisa, "We have to be on our way soon."

"Why not? Spend the night and have breakfast with us tomorrow."

"No, this is my time with Gina. I've neglected her lately and I'm trying to make it up to her over the next few days. I promise we'll come back some time soon."

At the end of the dance, Gina returns to Lisa's arms. "You're one lucky girl," says Diamond as Gina puts her arms around Lisa.

Diamond and Bella escort Gina and Lisa back to their limo, and as the girls get into the car, their hostesses wish them both good night.

Back at the cottage, Lisa re-lit the fire and slips off Gina's dress, exposing her delicate flesh. She runs her tongue up and down Gina's back, from her butt cheeks to her ears. Gina's knees almost buckled, she was so turned on. As Lisa kisses the back of Gina's neck, she takes the pins out of her hair and runs her fingers through Gina's hair, smoothing it and straightening the curls until all her hair cascades down her back to her waist. Guiding

Gina into a chair, Lisa steps back, and still holding Ginas hands, Lisa whispers, "You are so sexy, Gina. I'm not sure when it happened . . . I love you. Please, don't be afraid of my feelings for you, Gina." Lisa kisses her on the nose and repeats "I love you" like a mantra. Gina pants as Lisa holds both of her hands behind her back. She tilts back her head, moaning and gasping as Lisa licks Gina's pussy as if it were Swiss chocolate. Letting go of Gina's hands, Lisa guide her into the shower, where kneeling in the shower with the warm water pelting on her back, Lisa took a second helping of Gina. Again, in the bedroom, with damp skin staining the bedsheets, Lisa had Gina for dessert. Finally, they draw apart. Lisa gasps, "Mmm . . . I've missed you, Gina, so very much."

"Same here! I have been thinking about you and the last time . . . we were together," says Gina. She is out of breath. She had been certain it was over between them, but now . . . now she thought differently.

"What have you been thinking? Or shouldn't I ask?" Lisa asks nervously as she gazes into Gina's eyes and caresses her hair.

"I didn't expect us to be together like this again. I love being with you. I had no idea that, um . . ." Gina didn't finish her thoughts. Instead, to disguise her confusion, she grabbed the bottle of water on the bedside table and drank some.

"What? Do you mean that you thought we would not be together like this again?"

"I assumed we were finished, Lisa."

"Are you seeing anyone?"

Gina raises her eyebrows in response to the question. "No! No, I'm not. I have not been . . .," she pauses, upset, confused about the direction this conversation is going.

"I have not been with a woman or a man for almost two years now," Gina finally blurts out.

Lisa laughs hysterically. Gina doesn't find it funny and is almost out of the bed when Lisa grabs her by the waist.

"I find it very hard to believe that. You are an irresistible woman, not to mention incredibly sexy. When we met, I couldn't take my eyes off you."

Gina kisses the back of her hands. Lisa admits, "You should have told me."

"I should have told you what?"

"That it's been a while . . . and that you are not seeing anyone. I would have done things . . ."

"Come on, Lisa. This can't be good for you, too? I should be able to restrain myself. I can't believe that I'm still doing this with you. Your sister and your brother-in-law know that I'm sleeping with you. But what would your mother think if she found out?"

Lisa sits up in the bed frowning slightly. "What we're doing, Gina, is two lovers enjoying each other."

Gina snorts as if the idea is disgusting.

"You looked sad when I said I love you this morning, Gina. Why?"

"I wasn't sad, Lisa. Not exactly. I just wasn't expecting it. I know there is more to us than just the wild sex. I'm worried about you, too," Gina confesses.

"Do you know something? You worry about me more than I worry about me. I have not hidden my relationship with you from my family. My mother knows very well how I feel about you. If she has a problem with us being together, she would have said so. I do love you, Gina. I cannot have you uncomfortable around me or my family," Lisa says.

Gina did not know how to respond. "I'm not completely comfortable around your family. I like them all, I just don't want to." Lisa shushes her by pressing a fingertip to Gina's lips.

"This is brill. I hate it when you do this, Lisa. Why do you find it so difficult to talk to me?"

Lisa knew that Gina also had strong feelings for her, too, but she is afraid of where their relationship is heading. Hurting Gina is the last thing Lisa wants to do. Lisa embraces Gina and tells her not to worry. The expression on Gina's face suggests that she has a long list of questions to ask, so Lisa begins the Q & A by admitting right away that she has been sleeping with Diamond on and off, but not since she met Gina. Lately, Gina has been the only one.

"It's also true that I've not ever slept with a man. Vidal and I want to wait until we are married. He doesn't know I sleep with beautiful girls. He also thinks there's been no one since Priscilla."

Gina is laughing.

"I'm glad you find my whoring ways so funny! Come here!" Lisa is laughing, too. Gina relaxes in Lisa's arms.

"Your family is really nice. Your mothers has so much energy. She was dancing with your brother, Jayzel and Claire this morning. Your brother says Mrs Sharp does that with you guys every morning. Is that an African thing?"

Lisa laughs. "No, it's my Mom's way of relaxing with us in the morning so that we have a smile on our faces before we leave the house. It's like saying a prayer in the morning. It also helps to have us all in the same country! It's our special time with Mom, dancing before breakfast."

"Wow! That's neat! I didn't know your grandmother knew Dana?"

"Oh, yes! I used to come here with Dana when we were in our teens. Dana would often lie to Priscilla for me whenever I cheated on Priscilla. She always covered my rear end for me," Lisa says, chuckling. "Dana would have her boyfriend with her and I'd have Priscilla with me. I wonder what she would say if she were here today."

"About us? Or about your cheating ways?"

"Dana loved me and if she was here, she wouldn't have a problem with us seeing each other. She knew that I didn't just sleep with every beautiful girl that I met. She didn't like my cheating ways at all, but she always covered for me—until I met Vidal. Dana predicted that I would marry Chance. She was just relieved to see me kissing a man when I met Vidal. When Priscilla learned that I had been cheating on her with Vidal, she went ballistic. I spent my whole monthly allowance just to romance Priscilla into believing that I was not into Vidal. Priscilla knew how to keep me in line and I hated to see her sad." Lisa smiles. It was the first time she had ever discussed Vidal and Priscilla with Gina. Gina can see the love that Lisa feels for them. She says, "I sort of figured that out. I mean, the way Priscilla has you wrapped around her pinky, and that night at the club, that was . . . well . . ."

"Oh! Trust me! That was nothing! Priscilla knows me very well. So did Dana. The only difference between them was that Dana was more like a sister to me. I could tell her anything and we had fun growing up together—until drugs separated us."

Lisa laughs. She is enjoying being nostalgic with Gina. She tells Gina about the wonderful relationship she had with Priscilla for three years. "No cheating. I didn't cheat on her. Really. It was a great relationship, you know? When I met Vidal, things changed—a lot—and she couldn't handle it. I should have handled everything better, too. I did what I always did with her—spent money on her. I found that I could not give up Vidal for her. I tried, though, to stop seeing him just to make her happy, like I did with Chance. I'm still in love with him."

Gina is quiet for a moment, thinking things through, deciding how to shape her words. "Lisa, falling in love with someone who loves you back is amazing. It's not something that you give up to make someone else happy. I hate to say this, but why are you so determined to marry your boyfriend when you are so in love with your ex-boyfriend and he, clearly, is in love with you? You still wear his promise bracelet! I'm guessing that is what it is . . . I've seen him with the same thing. He still wears his. Did you know that?"

"Hmmm, yeah, I know. He left me. I'll not go back to him, though. He's seeing some hot girl that I'd like to sleep with . . . I do love Vidal. Things are less stressful with Vidal. Chance and I are too much alike. It's hard to let go of someone I've loved all my adult life. Regardless of what has happened between us, I miss Chance more than ever. I don't understand it."

"Why don't you talk to him?"

"I tried—often—and I just can't do it anymore."

"Well, you do have a hell of a lot of sexy exes. I dare say it would be difficult for anyone to get over someone they love dearly, but I think you will be okay if you and Chance talk, Lisa. Don't settle for second-best, yeah?" Gina smiles.

"I adore sexy women, and *that* would never be okay with Chance. He caught me cheating and he will catch me again. I can't risk losing him over and over. I adore you more than all my lovers. I plan to show you each day how much I adore you—until I'm married. So . . . tell me, do you want us to be over, Gina?" Lisa sits up and gazes into Gina's eyes.

"I think you're barmy, that's what!" exclaims Gina. "I want you to promise me you'll talk to the handsome Chance. And I want you to show me how much you adore me until you get married," Gina says softly.

Lisa sighs and smiles before she kisses Gina.

The next morning Lisa and Gina drove to Belgium, where they visited a chocolate factory and purchased lots of candy. They walked around the small town of Ghent. It was a cold, January morning. Lisa spoke French when she ordered green tea for them in a small cafe. Gina didn't know she spoke French. Lisa smiled and said that her sisters and her mother spoke several languages. They went to a street market where Lisa bought an armload of fruit, vegetables, fish and meats.

"Are you planning to cook for an army?" Gina asks.

"Only for you," came the reply.

"Don't you think you are spoiling me way too much, Lisa?"

"Ooooo, I haven't hardly begun!"

When they get back to the cottage, Lisa makes a fire and insists that Gina stretch out on the couch for a cat-nap. Later, Lisa returns with homemade hot chocolate and wakes Gina.

"Is there anything I can do?" asks Gina.

"No, I'm almost done making lunch and dinner is prepared. Gina, I know how uncomfortable this makes you, please don't be. I've been very selfish when it comes to you and I. I can't help it. I love you and I want to spend this time with you without interference from work or my family. I don't want to think of anything but you. I'm going to be very busy for the next few weeks with the launch of our new magazine, so you won't see me so much, then."

Gina throws her arms around Lisa and hugs her, feeling like lightening has struck her. She knows Lisa was supposed to get married weeks ago, but for some reason, it didn't materialize. "This really is the end of us," she thought. She is happy for Lisa, but sad, too. "I love you, too, Lisa. You're right: we need this time to ourselves. So, why don't you let me help finish making lunch? You're making me horny right now!"

"Hmmm, how horny?" Lisa leans toward her for a kiss. They talk some more about Dana, and also about Lisa's relationships with Chance and Vidal. Lisa finds Gina to be a very good listener, especially since the incident with Priscilla. For Gina, things have been more difficult: Lisa has needed to talk about relationship stuff, and Gina knows she appreciates the willing ear, but as a lover she wishes there was more "us" to talk about and less "them".

"I'm proud of how you dealt with Priscilla. I will also be very proud to see you end up with your soul mate. I'm not surprised that you fell in love with someone like your fiancé. Everyone can see how much he adores you. At the hospital, he broke down when I told him how sick you were. It made me feel guilty." Lisa brushes her hair out of her face and kisses Gina on the nose. They go for a walk along the beach. Gina was cold by the time they returned to the cottage.

"I want to make dinner for us," insists Gina. "Just tell me where everything is and what you've done already."

"Well . . . okay. But only if you cook naked!"

"You're crazy!"

"I'm not joking. I want to see you cook naked. I have already taken care of dinner for us," says Lisa.

Gina laughs. "Promise to talk to Chance one last time?"

This moment out of time is exactly what she needed. It is perfect in every way, even though she really didn't want to come to Holland with Lisa. Gina sighs and smiles, tells Lisa she is happy to be here with her. Lisa braids their fingers together and smiles. Lisa asks, "What do you fancy doing tonight?"

Gina smirks, "I planned our evening while you were cleaning up the kitchen!"

Excusing herself, Gina left the room and came back wearing a black silk bathrobe with her hair pinned up. Underneath, she wore nothing but a smile. As it was raining heavily, Lisa didn't hear her return because she was talking on the phone. She turns and see Gina sitting on the desk and begins flirting with her.

"Um . . . Mother? I'll see you sometime tomorrow." Lisa hung up the phone. Gina leans toward her and whispers in her ear, "Do you like to be kissed like this?" She brushes her lips past Lisa's. "Or do you prefer this?" She kisses Lisa firmly, fully on the lips, and just slightly moist. "Which do you like better?"

"I love it all. Everything. Every naughty, slightly nasty thing that you can do to me and more!"

Lisa tries to kiss her, but Gina moves away, taking Lisa by the hand. She willingly follows Gina to the bedroom where Gina has candles lit and positioned around the room to create a magical ambiance. The bathroom door is open, and there are lit candles in there, too. Celine Dion's moving song, "The Power of Love", is playing softly on the stereo.

"Miss Read! Have I said that I love you?" Lisa asks in a sexy tone.

Gina puts her lips very close to Lisa's ear and whispers, "Mmm. Miss Sharp, I love you, too."

Lisa shivers as she reaches for Gina's hands and they slowly dance toward the bed. Gina undresses her with each step, and they never take their eyes off each other. It is like they know at last what it is they share with one another.

Gina says, "Dessert in bed, love?"

"Mmm, mmm, I love dessert in bed. Want some chocolate?" asks Lisa as Gina nods affirmatively. "Does this mean I get to feed them to you?" Lisa replies with a sexy tone and an inviting smile.

"Uh, um . . . We'll see." Gina teases Lisa with hot kisses. Lisa is burning up with the pleasure of it all. She loves it! Lisa feels relaxed and in the mood for seduction. Gina knows instinctively how to satisfy her. She dips one of the chocolates into a bowl of whipped cream. She holds the chocolate between her lips and brings it very close to Lisa's lips, then with a subtle shift lets the chocolate slip down between her breasts . . . all the way down to her thighs, and only then, does she finally bring the chocolate up to Lisa's mouth, letting her have it. While Lisa enjoys the chocolate, Gina traces her tongue over Lisa's body, giving her bottom a little squeeze as she firmly sucks between her legs. Lisa moans with pleasure . . . gasping as she almost comes to a climax. Gina stops, "Do you want it slow? Or faster?" Lisa is almost delirious. All she can think of is the impending orgasm. She just wants "it", never mind slow or fast. She pants, squeezes Gina's hands, and seconds later her pussy is filled with the throbbing of a vibrator. She is so wet, the vibrator just slips in, and open, so open that Gina can slide her fingers into Lisa's pussy and press on her G-spot, positioning her hand so that her thumb can massage Lisa's pulsing clitoris. Bending over the supine Lisa, Gina gently sucks her nipples until they are hard little cherries. Lisa feels breathless as the wave of orgasm hits like a tidal wave. Tingling with sensation, Lisa enjoys the high of her orgasm while Gina massages her body with scented oil.

"*That* was incredible," says Gina.

"*You* are incredible," replies Lisa with a silly grin on her face.

"Yes, to all of that," giggles Gina. "I hope we're going to do some more naughty, mind-blowing things the next two days."

"I want you to spend the rest of the week here with me. Don't think about it. Just do it!"

"Come on, Lisa. We agreed on spending just the weekend. I have to be at work first thing on Monday. The club, remember?"

Lisa is already kissing and caressing Gina, preventing her from objecting too strenuously. Lisa slept earlier than usual. Gina watched her late sister's friend and thought about how much she has come to love Lisa so dearly. She didn't plan for it to work out this way, but it has and she is enjoying the ride. As she watched Lisa sleep, Gina though that it was inconceivable that she would meet someone so young and yet so sophisticated. Lisa was perfect in every way.

Gina spoke to Corey on the phone that night. He informed her that Priscilla has made bail and come by the club a few times wanting to see Lisa. Her bail conditions prevent her from leaving England.

"I'll let Mrs Sharp know so she can keep Lisa away for a little bit longer. Holland seems to agree with Lisa."

"That's brilliant, Gina. I'll keep an extra eye on Tia and Nathan, too. Priscilla showed up at the Sharp's home while I was there to break the news. It was kind of funny in an ironic sort of way, if you know what I mean."

"Yeah. Okay, well, I have to go over some menus with Lisa's grandmother for Lisa's wedding, but once I'm done I'll be on my way home." She wanted to ask if Corey would have dinner with her, but instead, Corey extended the invitation.

"I don't suppose you'd fancy a dinner and a dance with me tomorrow night?"

She hesitated. "I would but Lisa has a strict rule about her staff sleeping together. Maybe once I leave at the end of next month—if you still fancy the idea."

"I guess she hasn't told you?"

"Who hasn't told me what, Corey?" Gina asks suspiciously.

"Shit! Me and my big mouth!"

"You've stuck your foot in it anyway, so you may as well go for broke. Come on, man! Dish!"

"Alright. You didn't hear this from me. Lisa was telling me that she wants you to take over running the clubs. She asked me to find out whether doing so would affect your cop pension at all. Her mother was sitting right there. I mean, Mrs Sharp was present while we talked about the idea. I thought you knew, Gina."

"I'll see you tomorrow. Please, assign someone to watch over Tia and her husband. Find out the precise details of Priscilla's bail conditions. Please, be as quick as you can!"

"I'm on it! Lisa's brother-in-law and Chance already requested a security detail."

Gina called Mrs Sharp and informed her the news.

"Can you keep Lisa in town a little longer?" asked Gina.

Mrs Sharp knew all about her daughter's affair with Gina, but since the fact was not out in the open, Gina felt a little embarrassed talking to Mrs Sharp. She half expected Mrs Sharp to tell her to stay away from her daughter, but she didn't. Instead, she said, "I know Lisa cares very much about you. She has some high hopes for you, you know."

Gina could not believe that Lisa had been thinking about her future in the police force. It was a wonderful offer, but one she knew she'd have to refuse.

"Mrs Sharp, I know about the offer Lisa wants to make to me. I am certain I will have to pass on it. I'm afraid my feelings for Lisa may harm Lisa's marriage if I accept the job. I plan to return to Leeds soon after Lisa's wedding."

"Well, don't rush into anything," advises Mrs Sharp. "If Lisa wishes to have a relationship with you, she will do it regardless of what I have to say about it. I don't think you'll do anything to harm Lisa."

During the drive to the airport in the morning, Lisa and Gina sat arm-in-arm even though they had made love to each other countless times the night before.

"Did you call Corey?" asked Lisa.

Gina wasn't thinking about Corey and the question took her by surprise.

"Yes! I did."

"Well? Did you tell him how you feel about him?"

Gina laughs. "You are terrible!"

"I want you to think about something for me, okay? I need someone scrupulously honest to manage all the clubs for me. I was thinking you might want to do that."

"Sorry, I have a job already. I can't be bought, Lisa."

Lisa sighed. "Gina, I would never be that disrespectful to someone I love." There were tears in her eyes. "Your sister was close to me just like Brooke and Kate are to Tia. You can never replace her. Her death brought us together, even though you were looking for answers. Dana knew that I needed you. My mother and I would have been dead three weeks ago if it was not for you."

"That's not true. Something different would have happened. Someone else would have intervened."

"Gina, I cannot let you go back to a job that you hate. I just cannot! All that aside, I have come to love you, very much."

"I'll not be your mistress," Gina says bluntly. Lisa laughs, "I don't want you to be my mistress either—as you put it. I love you, Gina. I would never do what you suggest. You deserve a lot more than being my bit on the side and being an undercover police woman, far away from everyone who loves you. I'm not the only one who loves you."

Lisa parked the car and came around to the passenger side to open the door for Gina. Pouting a little, Gina lingers in the car. Lisa is in her gym clothes and wearing a baseball hat to cover her unruly hair. She turns the cap backwards and gets down on her knees beside the car. Looking up at Gina's face, she sees tears rolling down her cheeks. Lisa helps her out of the car and holds her in her arms. "Don't cry," she whispers. "I know you're afraid. Don't be, sweetheart. Please. I love you and I want to see you happy . . . more than anything, I want to see you happy and relaxed, doing something you enjoy. You are always happiest when you're cooking. I'm very much afraid of losing you, but that's not why I want you to take the job. Your grandmother loves you. You can't leave us. I love you, too, Gina." Lisa gives her a tight squeeze before taking her by the hand and walking toward the airport terminal. Gina's plane begins security procedures in twenty minutes, so they don't have much time. Inside the building, they sit down and Lisa pulls Gina onto her lap and puts Gina's head on her shoulder. Lisa wraps both hands around Gina's waist.

Lisa says tearfully, "I can't let go. Three days seems like a life-time before I hold you again. I miss you already. I don't want to let go." The announcement on the PA calls for passengers on Gina's flight to go through security. Giving Gina one last hug, Lisa fans her face and tries to relax her jaw.

"Priscilla made bail," says Gina, deciding at the last moment to warn Lisa about her ex-lover. "Please be very careful. Corey and I want everyone to be diligent about safety."

They kiss softly on the lips and hug gently before Gina gets in line. "I love you, Gina. It's not just because you are the best fuck that I ever had. I really do love you!"

Blushing furiously, Gina says, "Oh Jeez . . . thanks a lot! You are a nut case, Lisa, but I love you, too." Lisa kisses her one last time with her tongue. As she boards the plane, Gina is so full of emotion that she is hardly aware of the British Airways flight to London.

Lisa's mother met her at the gym in the mansion. She thought Lisa looked a bit pale, so she asked, "Are you alright?"

"Oh, yeah. I just said good-bye to Gina. It wasn't as hard as I thought it would be." Lisa sighed, "By the way, Mother. Priscilla has made bail. The judge did impose conditions on her, which I am told she has broken already. There is a warrant out for her arrest as we speak. I don't want you to worry. I know you and Papa are leaving in the morning, but can you give me a week before you leave? Tia and Nathan are being watched closely, and Claire doesn't have to be in college until the week after next."

"Of course, darling. Can I ask what you are doing about her, or should I not know?" Naana quizzed her daughter.

"It's a matter for the police. I promise, everything will be okay. I just don't want you to worry. I'm really very sorry about all this, Mother."

Naana hugs Lisa and says, "My dear, life is about living and enjoying every moment of it. Priscilla has made her own choices and you should stop feeling guilty about your friends' mistakes and their bad choices."

Chapter 31

Eva Collins has always wished to be working for a fashion magazine, even before she began modeling. Over the years, she has listened to Eric talk business with her. You don't get married to a man like Eric Collins and not learn something about business. The man lives and breathes business, except when he's with her and their son, Vidal. Eva has often felt like a fifth wheel these past two years that Vidal and Lisa have been seeing each other because all they talk about is business and how smart Lisa is. Inexplicably, Eva feels jealous of Lisa. Today, she discovered that her husband and son don't take her seriously. They see her as someone who takes care of them and who spends their hard-earned money frivolously. Granted, she loves the lifestyle, but there has to be something more for her. After the Sharps left with Gertrude, Eva went into her husband's study and turned on his computer. She read through all the stuff that Lisa had emailed to her. Lisa really knows what she wants with the magazine. Eva loves the concept already. She was supposed to have dinner with Eric, Vidal and their business associates tonight but she canceled. She tells them, "I have work to do." Eric is understanding, but Vidal is not. Later that evening, Eva is still in the study on the phone when they return from their dinner outing.

"I have found us a fashion photographer. He is an old friend who lives in Germany. He has not worked for the last fifteen years. He will be arriving tomorrow to meet Lisa on Monday. Do you think Lisa will think I'm interfering? I mean, should I have asked first before offering the job to Kojo?"

"No, mother. It shows initiative. That is one of the reasons father and I work well together. I don't wait for him to ask. I do what is needed for the good for the business," Vidal told her.

Eva went and fixed a Manhattan for her husband and poured a glass of wine for her son. She went back and sat down and was at work on the computer again. The maid came in with a package for her and placed it on the table. She didn't think anything of it as it was the usual sort of neatly wrapped gift she often received from Eric. Then again, it could be one of the many fashion magazines to which she subscribes.

Eric asks, "Are you not going to open the box?"

"I will have Mary open it in the morning for me."

Vidal called the maid, "Mary, please be so kind as to open that box for my mother."

"Yes, sir." Mary stepped forward.

"Thank you, Mary. You can go. We will open it in the morning," Eva barked at the maid.

"No, go ahead and open it," says Vidal.

Eva hates it when Vidal overrides her authority in front of the hired help. She raises her head and looks at her husband for support, but he looks excited to see what is in the box.

"Since when do you boys show any interest in my magazine subscriptions?"

They did not answer. Instead, Mary cries out, "It is not a magazine, Madame!"

Eva got up from the desk in time to see it. Her heart beats fast and faster as she puts a hand over her mouth. There are tears in her eyes and her voice is like a child at Christmas morning. She moves slowly toward the box and looks inside. Then, she looks up at her husband and her son. They both have proud expressions on their faces. It was a desk sign, made in black with a gold-plated frame:

EVA COLLINS, Editor-in-chief

Eva read the sign aloud and looked at her men in amazement. Then, she put her hands back into the box to find a very pink Apple laptop. She ran over to her son and hugged him. Vidal lifts her up into the air just like he does with Lisa. Putting her back on her feet, Vidal says, "We are very proud of you, Mother."

Eva is a little bit emotional. Vidal guides her to a seat next to his father. Eric proudly puts his arms around her and kisses her on the cheek. She confesses that she feels nervous and fears she will fail.

"Mother! Lisa would not have hired you if she thought for one second that you would fail. Lisa is a winner. She like to win in everything in life, and in everything she does. You are a winner, Mother. She didn't hire you because you are my mother. She will be very hard on you, but she will also encourage you to reach your full potential as she often does with me. Everyone who works for her will tell you that." Vidal's comments were re-assuring.

"Oh, my goodness! I've gotta go! Lisa sent me some stuff to look at and she will be here after lunch to take me to see the two offices she thinks we may need. I need to get properly dressed!"

Her husband and son laughed. They were both very happy to see her with a new interest, especially since it wasn't shopping.

"I love my gifts, especially the sign that's just like yours at the office, honey," Eva adds.

Claire Sharp is nothing like her two older sisters. The three Sharp girls have been blessed with their own individual talents. Claire has inherited her grandmother's ability to draw and sculpt without any formal training. She is at college studying art and graphic design. Lisa has asked Claire for a digital image for her new magazine. She has hinted that if the new editor likes Claire's work, then she might earn herself a job. Claire doesn't see the need for a job. The idea of a nine-to-five routine gives Claire the shivers. She hates rigid routine so much. Claire was born with a silver spoon in her mouth, the baby of the Sharp girls and spoiled by everyone. Bobby yells up the stairs for Claire to take a shower and be downstairs in fifteen minutes before Lisa arrive. He threatens to take away her privileges. She knows the old bastard she calls her father will do exactly what he threatens, so she tries to shake her tail-feathers and get going. Claire has a unique fashion sense. She comes downstairs to the family room wearing Converse sneakers, a black bucket hat, big baggy pants, a sweat shirt and dragging a dirty art bag, which has obviously seen better days and her laptop scrunched under one arm.

"What the hell are you doing? Go get changed, you little toad!" Lisa yells.

"No, I won't!" Claire says stubbornly.

"What's wrong with the way Claire is dressed?" asks Bobby.

Lisa flashes him a scornful look. "Papa, if a prospective employee showed up at Bankers Trust looking like Claire, would you hire her?" Turning toward Claire, Lisa commanded, "Go get changed!"

Claire refused and sat in the middle of the room.

"You promised I'd have a job," she says petulantly. "I'm an artist. I don't have to dress up like you and Mummy," she spat.

"Okay . . . but you do have to dress appropriately if you want people to take your work seriously. You have talent, Claire. I'm begging you to help me. Claire, please?" Lisa begged.

"Well, okay then, but only until I get the job. I'll not be wearing a bloody suit and high heels all the time."

On his side, Bobby is relieved that the girls are able to work things out without his intervention. He hates having to take sides, and truthfully, both girls are right. Claire should be able to wear what's comfortable for her, and Lisa should not expect Claire to wear a suit when her work involves messing with chalks, pastels, paints and clay.

Finding the middle ground, Claire returns to the kitchen wearing a gray pants suit. She has put up her hair in a pony tail, and she looks very presentable as they go out the door.

At the Collins home, Lisa and Claire are greeted by the maid, Mary. Lisa gives Mary a brown paper bag and says, "This is for Lucky."

"Who is Lucky?"

"He's Vidal's dog."

"Do you always bring a gift for your boyfriend's dog at every meeting? Sheesh! And I can't wear what I want!"

Lisa pushes her little sister into a chair and laughs affectionately. Claire joins in the laughter.

Eva Collins enters her husband's study all dolled up—a smart outfit with coordinating high-heel shoes. Claire thinks she looks like a black Barbie, and suspects that her boobs are not real. She wonders whether Eva has had any plastic surgery done on her breasts. The thought makes Claire laugh. Lisa tells her sister not to be disrespectful and to pay attention. Eva also has the same pink laptop as Lisa. She has cuttings from different magazines spread out on the table. She shows her ideas to Lisa and Claire.

"Hmmm. I don't think I like this. It's looks like child's play," says Lisa. She pulls Eva to one side of the room and explains to her that they cannot afford to look like amateurs. "I don't need to remind you that this is very big business."

"I've got it! Come, check it out!" shouts Claire, waving at the two older women.

"Not now, Claire," says Lisa, clearly irritated.

"Fine! I'm going to get wine."

"You are not allowed to drink wine. This is not your home," Lisa tells her.

Eva and Lisa go over to the big desk. Eva feels like quitting until she sees what Claire has created on the computer. Lisa frowns slightly, "Did you create this just now?"

Claire is not paying attention. She is doing something on Eva's laptop. Lisa is losing patience with her younger sister.

"Go home! Claire, you're not taking this seriously. I don't have time for your games. We are on a deadline here."

"I am! Jesus, Lisa, get off my back! I'm fixing Mrs Collins laptop for her so she can see the layout of the magazine. It will be easier for her to import the real photographs once we get 'em. Stop bossing me around, will you? I know what I'm doing!"

Lisa sighs. She turns Eva's laptop around and there it is . . . just like Claire had said, page by page. She has even created a logo for them and imported photographs of Kelly Powers and Elizabeth Starr for the cover. It looks so real. Eva loves Claire's work, but is nervous to say so. There is some undercurrent here between the siblings that she's not yet grasping. Claire puts some loud music on the computer, and Lisa shuts it off.

"Claire, this is a very good opportunity Eva is giving you to showcase your talent. If you don't take this seriously, you will absolutely not have a job with the magazine."

Claire begins to cry, "I want to go home. You can keep your stinking job! I hate you! I can't believe I wore a suit for this!"

Eva immediately goes to the sobbing girl and puts her arms around her. "Don't worry, Claire. I like your work. You'll have a job, Sweetie. Please, don't cry." Claire hugs Eva back.

"What do you say, Lisa? The kid rocks. She's an artist, a free spirit. We need people like that on our staff."

Lisa sits down and looks closely at the computer screen. She does love the work Claire has done. To keep Claire from distracting her, she tells

Claire to sit down. "Mary will bring you tea. I don't want you to wander off and no . . ."

"I don't like tea! Can I have wine, please?"

"You can have half coffee, half hot chocolate. I mean it, Claire! Don't move from that seat!"

"Yeah, yeah. I won't."

Eva and Lisa retreat to the living room. Lisa admits she does love what her sister has done with her ideas on the computer layout.

"Eva, Claire can be disruptive if you baby her. Are you sure you're up for supervising her?"

"Come on, Lisa. She's great! You saw how she understood my concept right away. I thought you were going to fire me back there! I was about to cry myself," Eva confesses.

Lisa sighs. "I was a bit harsh. I'm sorry about that. You are the best candidate for the job. We need to separate running the business and attending to family. Don't be emotional about things. Family matters can be discussed at another time. Hiring Claire on the spot like this is one of those things. I want you to go in there and make it clear to her that the offer is a conditional offer."

"Oh, Lisa! Please, is this really necessary? She is your sister. This is how all artists in the business behave."

"Claire is a college kid who thinks her parents have money. So that makes her feel entitled to what life has to offer. Eva, your job would be on the line here. Eric tells me you have stayed up half the night putting your ideas together. Do you really want to give it all up for a brat like Claire?"

Eva tried to respond but Lisa cut her off, "I don't doubt that Claire brings talent to the table, and with our budget, we really do need her. You put the idea into her already big head. Eva, you will have a problem on your hands as an editor."

Eva's preference would be to lavish affection on Claire rather than being hard-hearted like Lisa, but she also understands very well that Lisa is not a person who tolerates nepotism in business. They re-join Claire in the study. She has not moved, just like her sister instructed, but she does have an ear-piece on and is shaking her head to the beat of the music and working on her laptop simultaneously. Lisa nods to Eva. Eva takes a deep breath and removes the headset, asking Claire to turn off her music.

"I want to talk to you about your position," Eva says.

"You promised that I had a job!" She looks at her sister angrily. Lisa ignores her.

"You do have the job," Eva confirms. Claire smiles. "Miss Sharp, the job I'm offering is an entry-level position as my assistant and Creative Director."

Claire's face lights up, "Whoa! Creative Director! Sweet!"

"No, Claire, it's not sweet. You will be on probation," Eva says nervously.

"Cool. For how long?"

Eva realizes this conversation is going to be tougher than she anticipated. "Well . . . for as long as I feel it is necessary. One screw-up and you are fired," Eva says seriously.

"Jeez, a minute alone with my sister and you turn out to be just like her and my mum. Well, I'm not going to screw up. I'll show you what a good Creative Director I can be. I want a contract so that my mom and my brother Nathan can look at it before I do any work," Claire demands precociously.

Lisa exhales and says, "I've already discussed with Mother about you working on the magazine, Claire." Turning toward Eva, she says, "Claire will be here first thing in the morning to give you a crash course on how to use your laptop effectively. We need to go and view the place that I told you about. I'll work on getting all the office equipment and furniture for us by the time Kojo arrives, so we should have an office ready fairly quickly. I'm going to see Vidal. You need to talk to Claire." Eva and Lisa hug.

"Thanks, Lisa."

"You did good, Eva. I'll see you shortly."

"Hey, Lisa! Can I come too?" Claire asks.

"Discuss that with your boss. Claire, you don't work for me. I'll not be able to get your job back for you if you mess up. You need to understand that this is business." Lisa warns her little sister.

"I said I wasn't gonna. Stop showing me up already. I like Mrs Collins. Anyway, I think she respects me as an artist more than you and Mummy do. I'm glad I'm gonna work for her. You'll see! I'll show you all!" Clair spat.

Lisa silently said a little prayer thanking God that her sister was taking this job seriously. Eva, too, was glad. She thought Claire might become a huge, raw talent. Eva sits at the desk to make some calls to various distributors while Claire works on the computer. Her son and husband have been eavesdropping on the women's meeting without them knowing it. As the meeting comes to a close, they sit down quietly to read the Financial Times. When Lisa walks into the small dining room off the kitchen, both men stand up and kiss her on the cheek.

"The next time you two want to spy on my private business meeting, do it with style, gentlemen," Lisa tells them. She stands behind Vidal and wraps her arms around him, kissing him on the cheeks. She closes her eyes and murmurs, "I've been missing you."

Eric watches his son and the woman he is about to marry in a few weeks and smiles.

"I've missed you, too, Lisa," Vidal says as he rubs her hands. "I was thinking we should rent a bungalow at Sea Palace since you are going to be in Amsterdam for awhile. What do you think?"

"Great idea! Let's do it tomorrow. I want to spend the night here with you, so I can work with Eva before our meeting with the photographer."

"Sounds good. I'll get Mary to make us a nice dinner."

"No, I'll be making dinner for us."

"Um . . . Baby, you can't be cooking naked here. Father and Mother will have a fit!"

No, we won't!" laughs Eric.

Vidal raises his eyebrows and frowns. He stands up, "I'll help you make dinner for us alone in the guest house, away from dirty old men!"

Lisa chuckles, "Now, boys! Calm down! You can fight over me when I'm old and gray." She winks at Eric. "Right now, I am going to take my Baby with me."

Eric asks, "Where are you heading?"

Lisa says, "We're going to look at some office space downtown. Want to come, Eric?"

"Oh, no. No, thanks! Not me. I'm no good at that kind of thing."

Eric goes to a gentleman's club every second Sunday. He gets a massage and a blow-job, just like most of his business associates who have a lot of stress to relieve outside their homes. He has been taking his son with him for the last year and a half, though no one is the wiser. Vidal hesitates, then says, "I can't go with you, Baby. Father and I have something to do. It's our time together at the club."

"Eric, you're a good father, but Vidal is going to miss his weekend blow-job with you. I need him with me," Lisa blurts out.

Eric couldn't believe that Vidal has told his girlfriend about the club. His face is red and Vidal quickly releases Lisa's hands as he, too, is shocked that Lisa knows about their activities at the club. They stare at her. Vidal nods his head as his nose turns red and tears bleed from his eyes. Lisa stands in the middle of the kitchen and looks at them.

"Come on! We are all adults here. Vidal did not let the cat out of the bag." Lisa wants to go and hug Vidal, but she resists the temptation. Instead, she goes to the fridge and takes out the orange juice. She pours some into a glass and places it on the table. She can see their fear rise when she mentions their activities at the club.

"We all have stress that we like to relieve every now and then. I wanted to open a gentleman's club in England like the one you patronize here. I was there talking to the owner. He was kind enough to show me around the club. That was, oh, two years ago? Vidal and I were just getting to know each other."

Eric clears his throat and asks, "It didn't bother you that Vidal goes there?"

At the time it bothered Lisa a whole lot more that she may have strong feelings for Vidal. She was devastated. Her eyes surveyed Eric and Vidal's expressions before she sighed and said, "There are many stages in relationships, gentlemen. Each one is unique in its own utterly, miserable, dazzling way. Not to say your son and I don't have that, we do. We also respect each other's needs however much we may dislike them or feel about them. We are getting married soon. Vidal's days at the club are coming to an end." Lisa takes Vidal's hand, and he nervously follows her. Vidal turns back for a second and looks at his father's surprised expression. Eric is still in shock that Lisa knows all about the gentleman's club. "I wonder why she kept it to herself all this time," he thinks as he throws down his newspapers and runs his hand through his dirty blond hair. The shock of it has somehow unconsciously paralyzed him. He is seriously pissed off. He puts his hands over his mouth, smothering a profanity. "Will Lisa tell Eva?"

Later, when Lisa and Vidal were alone in the Collins guest house, she waited a minute before saying, "I'm sorry if I embarrassed you. This is our magazine. I cannot do the work alone, and I need you right now, Vidal."

Vidal is nonplussed. It's not often that Lisa needs him or anyone else for that matter. Vidal jams his hands into the pockets of his jeans as he makes eye contact with Lisa. He feels uneasy about her revelations concerning the gentleman's club. Their fingers interlock. "Why did you not say you knew? You let me have a go at you over Priscilla."

"You knew I was sacrificing something good for evil," Lisa has tears in her eyes. "You knew that I would be hurt. I'm so sorry I didn't listen to you, Baby. Please forgive me. I thought I was happy with her," she paused.

"I'm sorry, Lisa. I didn't know that you'd be offended by the club. I won't go there again. I don't really enjoy it the way Dad does. Do you think you can forgive me?"

"I love you, Vidal. All I ask is that we have the relationship that we have promised one another. I don't want to be hurt again and I don't want to hurt you like I have done in the past."

They were both weeping when he hugged her and said, "Part of me died when I saw the gun shot . . ." Vidal paused and sighed. "You mean everything to me, Lisa."

Claire walks in and sees Lisa and Vidal embracing.

"Jeez! You two are worse than Tia and Nathan. Can we go now? Mrs Collins and her husband are waiting. I'm not going to keep my boss waiting for you two." Claire yelled.

"Mother is the boss? I thought we are the bosses." Lisa embraces him once more and says, "We are, Baby."

The first building was already snapped up. Lisa was mad as hell at the realtor because she really liked the space. The second one was too small. In all, they saw six buildings and in the last one, Lisa was distracted as Claire disappeared somewhere into the building. They heard a loud thump. The realtor told them to be careful. The building was being sold "as is" under a power of sale. They entered the main loft and found Claire on the floor. She was not moving. They saw a pile of debris, dust and drywall, on top of her and soon realized that the loud thump they had heard was Claire falling from the second floor. They stood looking on while Vidal called the EMS.

"Oh, wow! You should see all your faces! That was fantastic! I found something upstairs just before I fell. Here, Mrs Collins, check this out!" Claire exclaims.

They are all quietly staring at Claire in various stages of shock and surprise as Claire sits up and folds her legs in the middle of the floor. She scowls at her digital camera, and Eva Collins supposes she has just witnessed what Lisa was warning her about the spoiled little rich brat.

"Miss Sharp! I want a word with you in my car," snaps Eva.

Claire is not laughing anymore. As Vidal shakes hands with the realtor, he says "we'll give you a call later."

As Lisa exits the building, she tells Eric, "I'm not getting into the same car with Claire. I could just kill her, right now!" Lisa is clearly exasperated with her sister's attention-seeking behavior.

Vidal and Lisa retreat to the Collins guest house. They are laying down on the bed relaxing when Claire bursts into the guest house, all cleaned up with her laptop and digital camera in tow. She walks over to the bed and sits in between Vidal and Lisa.

Lisa, completely fed up with her sister, shouts, "Get out, you brat!"

"Jeez, Lisa, can't you take a joke? Mrs Collins and her husband thought that was the bomb!"

Lisa grabs a white silk robe and wraps it around herself. She tells her sister to come with her back to the main house. Eva and Eric are locked in a romantic embrace when Lisa rudely slams the door in their study.

"I'm glad you think the stunt that Claire pulled this afternoon is funny. I don't want to hear anything she has to say. She works for you, Eva. The meeting with Kojo has been moved to the Sea Palace. I'll be staying there with Vidal—away from all of you. It's now your responsibility to find yourselves an office space." Lisa leaves, slamming the door behind her.

Claire giggles and says, "We can get a lot of work done now, without my sister bossing us about."

"We can?" asks Eva, raising an eyebrow.

"Oh, yes!" enthuses Claire. Taking Eva's hand and Eric's hand, Claire leads both of them to the table where she has set up her laptop. "I was snooping around the building. Look!" she points. "I took pictures. I was checking the place out when I fell."

Eric asks, "What is that?"

"It's an enlarger. I think it used to be a photo studio. I got my friend checking it out for me. I don't have to go back to England until next weekend. If you buy this building, I have friends who will restore it for you for free."

"You have friends who can restore a building?" Eric asks, impressed.

"Yes, Mr Collins. A whole bunch of college kids. We will make a video of everything from the beginning to the end. I have three different designs for Mrs Collins to consider. We are going to put everything on the

University of Amsterdam Faculty of Art website. Isn't it cool? It's going to be off the hook!"

"I don't think so, Claire. We are on a deadline here. I need a building that is already finished and clean," says Eva, expressing her reservations about a bunch of college kids restoring an old building.

"You and Lisa are such babies. There is nothing wrong with a girl getting down and dirty. Getting a little bit of dirt on your hands adds to the exhilaration of the finished work." Claire puts her laptop on the table.

"Well, you are the boss. I'm trying to save you money here, too. My Mom says one must always have passion about their work. You'll appreciate your building if you work on it instead of nice and neat. Nice and neat is so yesterday, Mrs Collins. Can't you see? You love this building. I can tell you do. You can't let Lisa boss you around like she does with everyone else."

"I do adore what you have done with the building on the computer. Claire, we are on a deadline here. I don't want to lose any of Lisa's investment before we begin. There will be serious consequences if I do."

"This is the building for the magazine. We can do anything that we dream of, Mrs Collins. Guntar is here . . . Bye! I'll see you in the morning. Although, I don't see why I should bother coming. I wouldn't worry about Lisa and her money. She has more money than she can ever spend anyway!"

"Kid's got a point," says Eric to his wife as he watches Claire get into the Sharp's car.

"Yes," thinks Eva, silently agreeing with her husband, "but at what risk?"

Chapter 32

Kate and Jaden have not managed to put things behind them. Jaden is still sleeping in the guest room. His son's funeral is on Thursday in Amsterdam. Brooke and Jason said that they would go and they can all make a weekend of it. It will be tense because Brooke can not forgive Kate for telling Brendon Chan all about Brooke's affair with Nathan. In a moment of pique, Brooke sold her shares in Urban Style to Lisa Sharp. Wanting a majority share in the business, and thus, more influence over decision-making, Lisa convinced Kate to sell her shares, too. It was an easy decision since Kate wants to stay at home with her boys and work on her marriage. Lisa's offer was just too good to turn down.

Tia has been using her sister's office while in Holland to work on scripts and to make and receive calls. Amy is not thrilled that Tia has once again postponed returning to Canada until after Valentine's Day. Even though Tia has finished all of the re-writes that were needed, Amy wants her present during auditions and rehearsals. Tia described to Amy the new details of the new joint venture with Lisa. Amy loved the idea.

"It will save us a lot of money since advertising is not cheap. We can effectively reach our target audience with the magazine," enthused Amy.

Lisa's ex-lover, Priscilla, has been calling non-stop for Lisa at the Sharp's home and also at Lisa's office. Tia is now fed up with the girl. Gina Read re-assured her and Nathan that everything concerning Priscilla is under control. Tia is also anxious to return to Amsterdam. She misses her children and is happy to learn about Anthony's budding romance with Evelyn White. Tia thinks she couldn't be happier. Nathan and Jaden have been inseparable lately. Nathan is serving as a consultant on a murder trial that Jaden is defending. They think they will get the result they have wanted all along. Tonight, Kate and Jaden are joining them for dinner, so when Nathan joined Tia in the shower, it was with a small amount of anxiety that she protested, "Sweetie, we don't have time to fool around. Our guests will be here any minute!"

"Speak for yourself, Baby," Nathan said in a naughty tone.

They have enjoyed their week alone, though they have both terribly missed the children.

"Do you mind if we fly to Holland tomorrow afternoon?"

"I was thinking of asking you the same thing, Sweetie," Tia replied. "Anyway, I want to give Lisa a hand with the set up of our new Urban Style magazine. I want to make sure that I get more exposure for Sunlight Studios and our actors. I think more unknown actors will be drawn to do projects with us now that we own a magazine to promote them."

Nathan chuckles. "I bet Amy is thrilled. Is she still worried about your advertising costs, Baby?"

"No. She agrees that our partnership with the magazine is a brilliant idea for Sunlight Media Group. I'm just not sure of the launch date. Lisa will not agree to the March launch, and we were hoping that it would be at the same time as the premier of *Forever Never Dies*. I'm going to talk with her about it."

The next day, when they got to Amsterdam, Tia jumped into the warm swimming pool with her children and BJ. Nathan also joined them, as he flipped Jayzel and Trey each one after the other.

Anthony has been on a few dates with Evelyn. They are getting on well, though he has been a little nervous about Tia's reaction to him dating one of her mother's close friends. He asks Naana whether Tia will be terribly disappointed if he invites Evelyn to join them for dinner.

"Tony, Tia adores you. In her eyes, you are the perfect father. All the kids and myself, too, feel the same way. Today, Bobby said something about you that made me think that my husband is not such an insensitive jerk as I've often thought he is. He told my father that you see good in everyone and that having you around has made everyone a better person. Tia loves you, and anyone who makes you happy will make Tia, and all of us, happy."

Evelyn White joins them for dinner and Anthony has been busy in the kitchen with Naana and the cook. When Nathan comes into the kitchen, he remarks, "It's nice to see you out there playing the field again, Father. How's it feel?"

"Um, I don't know, son. Are you and Tia okay about me dating?"

"No, father . . . we are not okay. We are absolutely fine with you dating! We love Evelyn. In fact, I asked Tia the last time we visited her if we could get you two together. I guess your Angel was not ready to share you then. But Tia is very happy for you, Father. Tia worries too much about you being alone. I think Mother would want you to be happy with someone like Evelyn."

"So do I," agrees Anthony.

"I think Trey has a little crush on her, though," Naana teases.

"He has the irresistible Carter charm, Father. You'd better watch out!"

"Well . . . technically, Trey saw her first," Anthony confesses.

"I never thought I'd see my son and father fighting over a beautiful woman," Nathan jokes.

They all join in the laughter.

Trey comes into the kitchen holding Evelyn's hand. He pulls out a chair for her to sit down. Nathan nods at his father and mother-in-law to look at the young man. They all chuckle. Trey is so serious. He stands on a chair to pour coffee in a mug, which he passes to Evelyn. He has a towel wrapped around his waist, and he announces to the other adults, "My Daddy is going to give me my bath now," and turning to Evelyn, Trey says, "You are going to be okay. My Grandpa will fix you a snack."

Evelyn smiles, "Um . . . this is very good coffee, thank you, Trey. It was very nice of you to introduce me to your Mummy and your Aunties."

Trey smiles, "It's okay. They like you, eh? I wanted to have you as my girlfriend so that you can tell me lots more stories about Africa, but BJ says I should give you to my grandpa. He is old, you know? I'm going to get more girlfriends when BJ and I become football players, you know?"

Trey's grandfather and grandmother both chuckle as his father picks him up and takes him upstairs for his bath.

"Whoa!" says Evelyn, giggling. "What a charmer!"

"I guess it's safe to say that young Mr Carter has thrown in the towel," Sarah teases.

Anthony blushes, embarrassed. "If you ladies excuse me, I'll go and see my Angel in the study while you ladies gossip about me," Anthony responds humorously. He caresses Evelyn's hands and leaves the room.

"Where are Lisa and Claire?" asks Sarah.

"Lisa is with Vidal. They are staying at Sea Place guest house. They claim they are sick of me meddling in their private affairs," Naana tells Sarah.

"You, darling? Meddling?" Sarah raises an eyebrow and both women laugh.

"My plan has not worked. Lisa seems to be getting closer to Vidal each day. I did invite Chance to join us, but he, too, has been seeing some girl these days, or so his grandfather tells me. I don't know what to do to get them in the same place at the same time."

Sarah and Naana update Evelyn on the Vidal-Chance-Lisa love-triangle. "It sounds like quite the saga," observes Evelyn. "Am I to assume that you are meddling in their up-coming nuptials in hopes of making Lisa see sense?"

"Of course, darling!" exclaims Naana proud of her mischievousness. "I have not seen Claire the whole of this week. She'd better not be in any sort of trouble," says Naana ominously.

Compared to her sisters, Claire Sharp is undisciplined and lazy. Most people would say she is nothing like her two older sisters. What Claire does have in common with her two siblings is the determination to achieve what she sets her heart on. Right now, Claire's heart's desire is not simply a job with Urban Style Magazine, but also to prove to her new boss, Eva Collins, and also her sisters, that she is capable of keeping up in the game. Claire did her best to convince Eva that a brownstone they visited in the south of downtown Amsterdam will be the best building for the new home of the fledgling magazine. Eva will not hear of it. She has her own pressures, most significantly a need to prove to her son and her soon-to-be daughter-in-law that she is the right person for the job. Claire, characteristically stubborn like all of the Sharp women, refuses to hear it. Acting on her own impulses, Claire took her grandparents to see the building the next morning. She described her plans and showed them her designs. Gertrude, a romantic, implored her husband to buy the building, which is being offered for sale at fifty percent less than its value. Kofi tells Claire to consider the building her eighteenth birthday gift.

"Oh, no! *No!*" protests Claire. "That's not why I brought you here. I need you two to help me convince Mrs Collins that it will be a beautiful home for the magazine. The building does not have any structural damage, though the second floor is in bad shape, but it's not anything that can't be fixed with a little hard work," Claire says.

Kofi replies, "Eva Collins won't set foot in a building like this because she might break a nail, right Gerty?"

Gertrude laughs. "Then, it's settled, my dear. Grandfather will buy the building so you can fix it up. I know you'll show your sisters and Eva that you are not lazy. Grandpa and I will help you as much as we can."

"No, Grandmother. If you buy this building that means, I'll be stuck in Europe forever. I want to go to New York and study art and become BIG! I can't do that here. No . . . I must find another way," Claire says.

The realtor interrupts their chat, "Listen, folks. I have another interested buyer, so the building can easily be sold by the end of today. Are you going to make an offer, or are you just looking?"

Kofi shakes his head, "I will give you two percent more than the asking price of the building if we can close this deal today. My granddaughter wants to restore it. Claire, my Sweetheart, you can still go to New York and study art, but this is your building. Grandma and I know you can do it. We want to see you make it look just like it is on your computer."

"I don't know, Grandpa, you really think I can do it?"

Gertrude and Kofi both nodded their heads yes. Claire wasted no time after the closing. She got the power company to turn on the power. She assembled all her friends, and with their loud music pumping, the kids did what they said they would. Claire filmed everything from start to finish and uploaded it to the University of Amsterdam Faculty of Fine Arts website. People were tuning in to the work-in-progress. Even the media got involved to see what the buzz was all about. At home, no one has seen Claire for days. Her mother is enjoying dinner with her friends when Gertrude and Kofi enter and announce that they are going to be on TV tonight with Claire and her friends.

"Why? Why are you all going to be on television with Claire?"

"It's a surprise," giggles Gertrude, but more than that she and Kofi will not say. Alarm bells start to go off in Naana's mind. She gets up from the table and goes over to her father.

"Come on, Daddy. You can tell your princess."

"Princess, Mother and I thought it would be a very good birthday gift for Claire. She wanted it so badly, so we thought, why not buy if for her?"

"Buy what for Claire, Daddy?" asks Naana suspiciously. She looked at her friends and they all shared the same puzzled expression.

"Um, my dear, you can see it on the university website now, if you can't wait for the news," her mother says.

Naana hates when her parents behave evasively. She turns to Sarah for assistance, who has disappeared from the table with Evelyn and her parents. Naana went to her father's study. Tia is there with Anthony, and they are both engrossed in something on the computer.

"Mom! Come and see this! You'll not believe it!" Tia exclaims. "Claire and a bunch of her weird-o art kids have done this amazing job with some old building downtown! The kids are making headlines all over the world, Mother." Naana feels relieved the situation isn't worse.

"Mother just told me that they are going to be on television tonight with Claire. They bought her something for an early birthday gift, but they won't say what it is. Whatever it is, I'm glad she is not in any sort of trouble. I have not seen her all week. She has exams next week, so I hope she has studied, or I'm going to take away whatever Daddy has bought her." Naana threatens.

"I thought she was supposed to be working with Lisa and Eva on the magazine?" Anthony asked.

"Yes, Tony. She is meant to be. My guess is she probably got bored. Or knowing Claire, she got fired."

"I sure hope not," says Tia.

"What do you mean, Angel?" asks Tony.

"Daddy, Claire has just made her mark right there!" Tia points to the computer screen. "Every advertising agency, every design firm will be out there scouting and recruiting kids with talent. I'm just glad that Lisa has us committed to a five-year contract with Claire, or else we would be screwed. Steven says she has talent beyond her age. I didn't take the kid seriously because she's so lazy and spoiled. We have got to get to Grandmother and Grandfather to tell us where this building is, right now, Mother! Nathan and I need to see Claire before the media rush. Any ideas where Lisa is?"

"I'd better let Lisa know. Whatever is going on, she's not going to be too pleased with this at all," Naana says.

Lisa has enjoyed her time alone with Vidal, staying at the Sea Place Guest House. She walks around their bungalow at Sea Place in red Victoria's Secret underwear and high heels. Vidal has a hard-on just watching her standing in the kitchen pouring milk, half-naked. Lisa knows what she is doing. Vidal wishes he could make love to her right there in that kitchen. He goes and stands behind her as she leans back on him and lets him kiss her. She precociously opens the fridge and bends over to look inside. Lisa smiles to herself, knowing Vidal can't help looking at her shapely rump. She comes back to the table and sits down beside him, taking off her shoes. Vidal watches her every movement. Lisa pretends not to notice. Suddenly, Vidal can't take it any longer. He jumps up from the table saying he is going to take a shower so he can take her out to dinner.

"No, Baby. I want to stay in tonight and order room service so I can feed you." Lisa puts her hands on Vidal's shoulders, drew him in close and kissed him lightly on the lips. As they draw apart, their cellphones begin ringing at the same time. Vidal gets off the phone first and says in a slightly panicked voice, "We got to go, now, Baby!"

"I'm going to murder Claire for this!" Lisa threatens, grinding her teeth.

"I guess there is no need for me to tell you, then?" Vidal chuckles.

Lisa doesn't respond as she throws her cellphone down on the sofa and heads to the bedroom to get dressed.

The building is finished. One of the kids has spilled paint in the room where Claire wanted the photo studio to be. She is yelling and screaming at the kid over an accident anyone could make. The poor guy is almost in tears as her parents, her sisters and Nathan watch with shocked expressions on their faces. They all turn to Lisa and ask what she did to Claire.

"Hey! You little toad. I told you to stay out of trouble. What the hell have you done?" Lisa asks angrily.

"Oops! My bad, Lisa! I thought you didn't want to know. Mrs Collins is responsible for me, remember?"

Claire sits on the floor and begins to clean up the mess the paint has made, drinking wine straight from the bottle. She bites on a pizza slice and passes the wine bottle to one of her friends, who takes a swig and passes it on to the next person. Lisa is disgusted, watching Claire and her weird-o friends sharing their germs, so she tells them to beat it.

"Claire, you tell me what's going on now, or I am going to smack you silly," Lisa yells.

Claire is cracking up as she smiles and says, "I work for Mrs Collins, now, so stop bossing me around." There is a big bag of potato chips on the floor. Claire puts a handful in her mouth, wipes her hands on already dirty pants. Lisa pulls Claire on the earlobe. Naana has had enough of this behavior and decides to step in between the two sisters.

"What is going on here, Claire?" asks Naana.

Both girls are talking at the same time. No one can hear a word. Tia looks at Nathan and nods. He understands her intentions immediately. Stepping into the fray, Tia drags Lisa to one corner of the room while Nathan takes Claire to another corner. Claire tells Nathan everything. He could not be more proud of her, but he tells her to be quiet and let him do all the talking. He re-assures Claire that Mrs Collins is not going to fire her. Claire immediately hugs Nathan in gratitude.

"That's why Mom and Dad should have had boys. You and Steven care about me more than Tia and Lisa."

"That's not true, Sweetie. We all love you. We just don't want anyone to take advantage of your talent," Nathan says soothingly.

Claire asks, "Are you sure Lisa is not going to make Mrs Collins take away my job?"

Nathan puts his arms around her and says, "I'm your brother and I will not let anyone take away something that you love. Come on! Let's go make Mrs Collins and Lisa miserable!" he says in a humorous tone.

"Are you going to tell us what you are up to, Claire?" Lisa asks calmly.

"I thought your editor-in-chief was meeting us here. Where is she?" Nathan asks. He is still holding Claire's hand.

"She is talking to Vidal outside. I'll go get her." Lisa returns with a very nervous Eva Collins and her son. Nathan doesn't wait for Lisa to start ranting and raving. Instead, he steps forward, hand extended, and says, "It's a pleasure to meet you, Mrs Collins. I believe you gave my little sister a task?"

"Well, you see . . ." Eva began, about to explain that she didn't know anything about the building.

Nathan interrupts, "As you can see, the building is almost finished. You and your employees can feel free to walk around later." Nathan points to Tia and Lisa, "Since you didn't have a contract with Claire to work for your magazine, we have a proposal for you all."

Tia knows how her husband works, so she jumps into the negotiation, "Now, you just wait a minute, Mr Carter. You cannot be serious. Your sister-client here has a binding five-year contract with my studio. I own fifty percent of Urban Style Magazine. Do I need to remind you,

Forever Never Dies

counselor, that there is a non-competitive clause in her contract with my studio? I'm not here to negotiate with Claire, but simply to remind her of her contract obligations before talking to the media," Tia fires back at her husband. Nathan loves it when his wife starts talking legal talk with him. He smiles. His mother and father-in-law are standing in one corner of the room looking and listening to their children in amazement.

"You are right, Mrs Carter. This building is fabulous, wouldn't you say? I want twenty-five percent of the magazine shares for Claire," Nathan demands.

Tia and Lisa begin to laugh. Nathan turns to his mother-in-law and whispers, "I will explain on our way home, Mother." Nathan chuckles. "Ladies, I'm glad you find this amusing. You have two hours to agree to my offer or I'll get an injunction on every work that Claire has produced for your magazine. I'll sue and bankrupt Urban Style Magazine before it launches, Ladies," Nathan winks at the girls.

"I don't take threats from anyone when it comes to my business. This is extortion, and I'll not stand for it, Tia. Do something!" Lisa says to Tia.

"Mr Carter, this is extortion. We'll not stand for it. You and your client-sister can get the hell out of my building now. Claire was on probation. You need to explain to your client what it means to be on probation! You may also need to explain to your client very, very carefully about her contract with me before she threatens us with a law suit. Mr Carter, you may also know that my partner and I don't take threats of this nature from anyone! Now . . . get the hell out of my building." Tia demands.

"I see your partners have misinformed you, Mrs Carter. As to who owns this building . . . well, actually, Claire owns this building. Two hours! Feel free to look around." Nathan kisses his wife on the cheek. "I'll see you at home, Baby. Mother, shall we go?" He turns and takes his mother-in-law's hands. Gertrude and Kofi also left with Nathan and Claire.

"What the hell is he talking about?" Lisa asks.

"Hmmm . . . My guess is that this is the birthday gift Grandmother and Grandfather gave Claire. Mother told me about an hour ago that our grandparents had a surprise, but that we'd all find out about it on TV tonight."

"No, no! It cannot be! We viewed this building a week ago. Claire wandered off and fell through the ceiling. I was fed up with her screw ups so I dumped on her . . ." Lisa pauses, thinking. "Eva, is there something that I need to know before I go and kill my sister and brother-in-law?"

"Claire was taking photographs when she fell. She came across a photography studio and a whole bunch of things left behind by previous tenants. She wanted us to buy this building and restore it the way we would want it. She came to show you and Vidal on her laptop, but you two wouldn't listen. I had no idea that she has the kind of money to buy this place. She was certainly passionate about it. Eric and I thought she was right. You and Vidal wanted to be left alone, so I didn't want to bother you," Eva says.

"She is very passionate about it, alright. Claire has documented everything on video. I have been watching the college kids working day and night, getting the building the way that it is now. I'll not give up any of my shares in this magazine, but I don't want to be in a legal battle with my husband over this. Nathan will use whatever means he can to get what he wants for Claire," Tia warns them.

"Well, that's too bad! I don't get taken down so easily. He and Claire have themselves a fight," Lisa declares.

"No, Lisa. You can't. Why don't you and Tia give Claire twenty-five percent of the shares," Vidal suggests.

Lisa's expression is unreadable. "Giving Claire twenty-five percent is not a problem here. Claire is spoiled though very talented and wants to work in this line of business. I'm not sure our little sister knows we work to earn things in this family. Claire doesn't understand that having a share could cause huge problems. We need to keep Claire in line, not spoil her," Tia explains.

Lisa hugs Vidal. She sighs. "Claire already owns twenty-five percent of the magazine. Mother asked me to put it in trust until she is twenty-one and can be trusted. I'll not roll over for Nathan and his need to give into our sister's spoiled ways. Claire has to work for this as Tia said. Nathan doesn't have the grounds to sue for the work that Claire did. Claire works for me, and as her employer, I'll ask her to do what she is told to do. Nathan is just going to have to accept it. If your husband wants to play games, I'm ready for him. I need to know that we all stand together on this. Mother wants Claire to make it and so do I. I know I'm hard on Claire, but I see her as a CEO of this venture one day. Mother doesn't want Claire falling into the stereotypical artist's life with a wild druggie lifestyle. Claire needs to work her way up from the bottoms. There is no other way about it," Lisa says firmly.

"So you can't tell her she already owns a piece of the company?" Vidal asks, incredulous.

"No, you can't. I'm sorry, Lisa. I should have kept a close eye on her like you told me to. She really is serious about this magazine. She told Eric and I that when you work hard for something you learn to appreciate it more. If you let Nathan hand this to her, she will throw it away. Mrs Carter, please . . . can we not find another way to work out some kind of deal? Lisa is right about Claire being a CEO one day. I see real leadership qualities in her, too, but she lacks focus and polish. Claire does have raw talent, not just with her computer, she is a creative thinker. Certainly, she can be a handful at times, especially when people don't grasp the ideas she brings to the table. I've met a lot of great creative people like her before. They're very good at what they do, but they are just a little strange compared to other people. Claire is like that. I don't think she knows how great a talent she holds because it's normal for her. I'd like to help mentor her—if I still have my job—please? The kid is awesome when we are not yelling at her. She can do it, Lisa," Eva says.

"I agree, Mrs Collins. Lisa and I have different work ethics and we can't afford to spoil our little sister like everyone else does. Nathan is not going to back down, unless we put our heads together to take him down," Tia says.

"I disagree. Sorry, Tia, but I think my Baby can take on your husband over this. Claire does work for Lisa. You guys have not done anything wrong. You can lease this place from Claire and Claire can keep her existing job with mother. Nathan wins and you can tell him later that Claire did already have shares, but it is for you to tell her at the appropriate time. I don't like the stress she causes Lisa, though," Vidal offers.

Lisa smiles. It warms her heart when she hears Vidal talk about her like that. They all agree that Vidal's suggestion is the best solution for the present situation and that Naana should be the one to talk to Nathan.

Naana took a deep breath as she approached Nathan. "Well, here is what's been decided. We all agree that Claire is not yet ready to handle the responsibility of having a share in her sister's magazine."

Nathan interrupts, "But Mother, the shares could be put in trust for Claire. Her sisters could be appointed to act for her until the proper time."

Naana is suddenly very quiet. She has to work hard to keep her poker face.

"Mother, you have a share in the girl's company already in trust for Claire, don't you?"

Naana sighs. "I am not getting involved with you in your battles with your wife and her sisters. You kids will have to find a way out and do what is right for Claire. Darling, we all know that Claire is talented. I'm not sure whether you and Steven can see how spoiled and lazy she actually is, but she is young and you boys want to give her everything. Lisa wants to see her do well. The whole point of the magazine is for Claire to find her own way in this business with the guidance of all of you. As older brothers and sisters, you all have to put your heads together on this one, darling, to guide Claire. I have no doubt that you and Lisa will find something else to fight about. That's what you two do, but it doesn't have to be over this. Nathan, you are going to have to work with the girls if you want a job for Claire. She was on probation and messed up. Let's not forget that, darling. In most other organizations, she would have been asked to clear out her desk and would have been escorted out the front door. We're not going to do that, but we are going to help Claire realize that she must learn how to balance her artistic excess with the demands of holding down a job in the business world."

Nathan smiles. "You do know that my wife and Lisa will probably want to skin me alive by now. Mother, did you observe the look on Lisa's face?"

"Yes, I did. She was proud of Claire, but she will not hand over the magazine to her like you want them to do, Nathan. Lisa wants her sister to be successful. She is going to have your head. You might as well know that Lisa is just as stubborn, if not more so, as her sister."

"Well, thank you very much, Mother. I'm the man and I intend to manipulate the beautiful Sharp women and win a job for Claire. She is going to be successful, Mother. She just needs a little gentle handling. Tia and Lisa can be so mean when it comes to business matters. Right now, I need to win this one. I'm afraid I'm about to be crushed by Lisa." Nathan knits his brows together, thinking through the points of the case. Then, to help himself see his way to a solution, Nathan begins to think aloud: "I don't have any legal grounds to use to sue for wrongful dismissal or to ask for reinstated employment for Claire. Mrs Collins did make Claire a conditional offer. Lisa probably thinks she has this in the bag . . . She and Tia together are going to be difficult opponents to beat. I'm gonna need to bring in the big guns . . . I can't let Claire down . . . With a few manipulative, well-chosen words, and Claire crying in the background, Mrs Collins will certainly re-hire her."

"Darling, I don't know what to say to you. You are one manipulative man!" Naana chuckles. As Nathan and his mother-in-law laugh, he winks and says to her that it's not over.

Chapter 33

They walk around the building. They all agree that Claire and her friends have done an amazing job in a very short time. The building still needs more work. Tia tells the group that she is thinking of having the magazine launch moved up since the buzz is around Claire and the building. They must work fast so they can use the free media press to launch it."

"Oh, yes! This is the sort of publicity that money can't buy," Eva adds.

"There is one problem: Claire and Grandmother are going on television tonight," Tia points out.

"Lisa put a stop to that before we arrived here, but you have to work fast, though. I don't trust your husband and his competitiveness with Lisa. He likes the media and I don't want him using them against her. That is the main reason why I didn't want to get involved with this venture. I'm not used to the media like you guys are. I just want my lady to be happy and stress-free," Vidal says to Tia.

"Vidal, here's something you're going to have to get used to if you're going to be part of our family: Nathan and Lisa will never stop trying to put one over on the other. It is one of those things that you and I must avoid—for our own well-being. We are family first and that comes before anything. Nathan knows that. All of this could have been avoided if Lisa had trusted Eva to do the job that she is hired to do. It doesn't matter about how much business experience Lisa has. The media and the rest of the world won't give a damn about that. When it come to the rich taking advantage, I know how it works and so does Eva, the more sensational the story is, the better for selling papers. This is our story and we must take control of it ASAP! I don't doubt Lisa's ability to handle things with Claire. They just rub each other the wrong way, always have done. But we do need to set ourselves apart from many families who go into business together. We are going to have disagreements and we always need to find a simple solution to every disagreement that we may encounter in the future; otherwise, we will fall, all of us." Tia asserts.

"You know, Baby? Tia is right. We are bound by love. I know you like to win in everything and I want you to do it, too. But just this once, can you and Nate not fight?" Vidal pleads with Lisa.

Lisa hates to argue with Vidal in front of people. She hugs him and whispers that she will think about it. Tia is proud of Lisa and how she handles herself and Vidal in public. Tia smiles and takes Lisa's hand.

Nathan was planning his strategy when Claire entered the study and closed the door behind her. He pauses in his work and asked, "Are you okay, Claire?"

"Oh, yeah . . . you promise you won't be mad at me?" she asks, looking sad.

"Of course not, Sweetie. I won't be mad. What's wrong?"

"I don't want a share in my sister's magazine. I'll not be able to go to art school in New York or go to California to work with Steven. Lisa says working for the magazine will help my art and open doors for me that Mummy can't buy with her money or Steven with his Hollywood connections. I enjoy doing creative things. I just get bored sometimes. I don't mean to mess up. I think my sisters will not want me working with them because I'm not a business person like them. I can try to be, I promise, Nate. I just don't want my sisters to tell Mrs Collins to fire me. Mrs Collins is nice. She's not as mean as my sisters."

"Why the hell should we trust you when you go behind our backs?" Lisa asks as she slams the door open wide. Eva, Tia, and Vidal stand behind her. Claire quickly runs and stands next to Nathan, who tells her to sit down.

"Vidal, would you close the door?" asks Nathan politely.

"Claire, Sweetie, you know that Lisa is right. Mother can't buy you a career in this business with all our money put together. If it were that easy, we would. Steven and Tia can open some doors for you because they have special connections. Tell me something. Do you really enjoy working for Mrs Collins?" Nathan asks Claire while looking at Eva to determine her body language. Claire nods an affirmation. Nathan continues his questions, "Claire, you do know that I cannot force Mrs Collins to give you your job back. She made you a conditional offer and you broke it within twenty-four hours. I need to know you really want this job. Okay, Sweetie?"

Claire begins to cry, and through her sobs she says, "Yes! Yes I do want the job!"

"Claire still has her job," Eva blurts out.

"Claire," says Nathan, helping the girl to dry her tears. "Will you wait in the kitchen for us?"

Claire nods and on her way out of the room, she thanks Eva and promises no more screw ups. The second the door closed, Nathan began shouting, "Mrs Collins, ma'am. I don't give a damn who you are, but in the future don't interfere when I'm dealing with my sister."

Vidal butts in and tells Nathan, "Don't you dare speak to my mother in that manner!"

"Vidal, Claire is my younger sister and I want what is best for her. I may come across in a way that suggests I like to spoil her, and yes, to some extent, I do . . ."

"Oh, and you think I don't? I'm part of the family, too!" Vidal shouts in reply.

"I want you two stop this right now!" Lisa shouts. "What Nathan is trying to say, Baby, is that your mother cannot give in to Claire's tantrums the way she did just now. Eva and I have discussed this issue already. Claire doesn't appreciate anything, but she is our sister whether we like it or not. Ideally, I'd like to give Claire whatever she wants, if I could. The magazine is our family business. Claire needs to earn her place in it and follow the rules like all of us do. If Claire wants to be a part of this magazine, she will have to prove herself to me and to Tia, and convince us that she is up for the game. This is big money we are talking about. We are playing with the big boys now and we don't need the added stress of an unpredictable teen. Tia and I have our primary jobs, too, let's not forget," Lisa explains.

"Mrs Collins, I do apologize for my tone. We just don't want Claire going wild and pulling a stunt like this again," Nathan says sheepishly.

"She won't, Mr Carter. I just don't like to see her cry like that. The kid is just misunderstood. Mr Carter, she is very passionate about her art. Can't you and your sisters give her a break?" Eva pleads.

Nathan looks at his wife and sister-in-law. "No! We can't! Mrs Collins, if you can't handle Claire, that's fine, but in the future, you must run thing past Lisa or Tia first. They need you on this project, but I want you to understand that I don't like to fight over business with my wife and Lisa. As you can see . . . two against one is hardly fair," Nathan chuckles.

"I don't believe you, sometimes. You are more manipulative than I thought. Mother must have told you, didn't she?" Lisa asks accusingly.

"Mother didn't tell me anything," says Nathan emphatically. "Look, Lisa . . . I know that you are proud of Claire. I saw the look on your face when we learned what she did. You like to handle our little sister with discipline. I don't like to see her cry. I got a little carried away earlier, at the building, and I'm sorry. Hey! Lisa, I'm always going to be one step ahead of you, just like I beat you with the car for Claire. I'd say it's two-zero now, wouldn't you?" Nathan begins to laugh heartily.

"Let me give you something to think about, Big Brother! If Claire gets fired from Urban Style Magazine, she will not be able to retain employment with any of our competitors for a very long time. I would say that scores are now even." Lisa smiles.

"Damn! Lisa, where did you go to law school?" Nathan asks.

Tia and Vidal begin laughing. "I'll be at the Collins guest house with Vidal. I will meet you at the building in the morning. I want to run something by you. If I stay here, you are going to be a widow, Tia." Lisa kisses her sister and hits Nathan with her purse as she leaves.

Nathan says, "Baby, Jaden needs us in the morning. It's Kurt's funeral."

"Hey! Lisa, wait up! How about tomorrow afternoon? I'll bring some help," Tia says.

"Okay. Sounds good. Good-night, Tia."

"That was not a very good gift for Claire. I'm not impressed, Grandfather. The next time I'll not be so kind to you and Grandma," Lisa winks at them.

"I told Gerty that you would be utterly mad, Lisa," her grandfather says.

"Lisa knows how these things work, my dear. You do like what your sister has done, eh?" Gertrude smiles. Lisa shakes her head, "Somewhat, Grandmother." Lisa and Vidal told them good-night. Being alone is a lot harder for Lisa and Vidal since they both want a lot more than kiss and a cuddle they often share. Lisa spends the night working and thinking about Gina, sex with her, and hoping they will wrap up things quickly here in Holland so she can fly to England and spend some time with Gina. Lisa finally slips into the bed next to Vidal. As she cuddles up with him, thinking of Gina, Chance has been on her mind lately—a lot. They have not spoken since the night Priscilla shot at them. She closes her eyes to sleep, thinking about Chance. In the middle of the night, Lisa has a nightmare and wakes screaming that her love for Chance is forever, that it will never die. Her whole body shakes as she cries in the dark bedroom. She has forgotten where she is and is surprised to see Vidal standing by the window with his hand folded over his chest. He pants, angry that Lisa still loves Chance. They have never discussed Chance in all the time that they have been together. He knows that Lisa left Chance for Priscilla, and in his book, if a woman leaves a man for a woman then the man must be half a man. He makes this point to Patrick when they learned that Priscilla shot at Lisa and Chance. That Lisa loves him, not Chance, Vidal is not so certain anymore. This is not the first time that Lisa has had a nightmare and called out Chance's name and declared how much she loves him. Vidal has been happy because Lisa is in Holland for the next few weeks. Their relationship has changed in subtle ways over the past few weeks, and he can't afford to lose her after all these years. Vidal is very close to marrying her—in less than three weeks. As he wipes away his tears, Vidal returns to bed and holds Lisa in his arms.

Kojo arrives from Germany with his own equipment and is pleased with the photography studio in Claire's renovated building. Lisa told him that her wedding will be in three weeks. It's going to be a small affair. "I want photographs taken this weekend of my family at my grandparents home as well as the Collins, especially Eva and Eric. By Monday we will have the photographs of Kelly Powers and Elizabeth Starr for our cover as well as some of the cast members of *The Saga* and *Forever Never Dies*. Sunlight Studio wants to see our magazine before we send it to print."

"I will get on it, Lisa," Kojo says.

"I have all the flowers and the cake sent to Gertrude. She says we can shoot the wedding photographs by the pool. Claire and I have been working on the rest of the props that we need and all the wardrobe is already for the photo shoots," Eva tells her.

"Our office equipment will be here this afternoon before Tia arrives. Have you decided where your office is going to be?" Lisa asks them.

"No, I thought you and Tia would decide that," says Eva.

"I want you and Claire to pick your offices now, and we'll decide the rest once Tia gets here. I have our distributor coming to meet us soon. I was able to land us an ad. There is an African cosmetics and fashion company. They want us to run their ads in our magazine. I was also thinking of placing a few free ads for some of Claire's friends who helped with the building. We'll be meeting them next week. You and Claire must be very diligent about everything now, please. We cannot afford to make mistakes now," Lisa advises.

Claire asks if she can wear her own clothes instead of suits all the time. Lisa says she can, except for important meetings. Claire seems satisfied with the arrangement. Lisa calls Gina. Lisa has been calling her everyday since she left Holland. She has managed to convince Gina to take over management of Club Vibe. She has moved into the penthouse above the club anyway. She misses Lisa terribly, but tries not to mention it. Priscilla was found dead at a night club in east London, a possible drug overdose. Corey heard the news and told Gina. Gina has broken the news to Lisa's mum. Lisa asks whether there is any news on Priscilla yet. Judging by the question, Gina assumes Mrs Sharp has not shared the news of Priscilla's death, so she hangs up the phone. Lisa calls her back. Gina asks whether she can call her back in a few minutes. Lisa says, "No, I will wait." Gina puts her on hold, and using the other line, calls Mrs Sharp. Permission is granted to share the news.

Gina re-connects her call with Lisa. "I don't know what to say, Lisa . . . Priscilla is . . . um . . . dead. I'm so sorry, Lisa."

"How? What happened?" Lisa's tone is even though she sounds exhausted.

"Tell me you're not alone, Lisa. Please!" Gina pleads with her.

Lisa lies, "I'm not alone, Gina." Her voice is soft, fatigued.

"What was the cause of death?" asks Lisa.

"Um . . . um . . . Drugs, a drug overdose." As soon as Gina said the word drugs, Lisa dropped the phone and leaned back in her chair, closing her eyes in a faint. A few minutes later, Naana and Bobby arrived at The Building. Her father picked up Lisa in his arms and helped her to the car. He hold his daughter in his arms until she began to feel well enough to sit up. Naana told Eva that Lisa was not feeling well and that she would take her home, nothing to worry about, just exhaustion. Vidal knows and will meet them at the house.

Eva can't help worrying about Lisa as she watches the Sharps drive away. She tells Claire that Lisa has gone home, but we need to review all of these photos before Tia arrives for our meeting.

"Did you know, Eva, that Tia used young kids like me from colleges and universities all of Canada to work for her at her new studio? Maybe we could do something like that here, too," suggests Claire.

Eva replies, privately thinking it's a good idea, "I'll check with Tia first, but we'll see if we can arrange some internships."

Just at that moment some bumping in the hallway attracts their attention. The new furniture for the offices have arrived. Lisa has taken care to order furniture in fabrics that reflect each of their personalities. Eva's furniture has animal prints. Claire asked for a sofa, and Lisa added a cool sound system, knowing that Claire likes to work to music. Gertrude has contributed a box of her paintings. At the main reception, three huge photographs are the focal point of the room: there is one of Eva during her modeling days, and one also of Elizabeth Starr and another of Kelly Powers. They are positioned side-by-side on the wall, creating a very dramatic effect as one enters the reception area. Eva recognizes her photo and wonders how Lisa got her hands on *that*?

Kojo beams with pride, "That was my first assignment. She wanted it big."

When she arrives at The Building, Tia is impressed with how the office set-up is proceeding quickly. She agrees with Eva that some internships might be useful and suggests she go ahead and invite some of the college kids who helped Claire to come to an interview. They also posted an ad in the Amsterdam Journal indicating the day and time next week for open interviews for all positions. Tia reconstructs Urban Style's website to include a tab for the new magazine and decides to feature photographs of Eva Collins and Claire Sharp.

"This is the bomb, Tia!" exclaims Claire when she previews the new website.

Meanwhile, an electronics technician has just finished installing a huge flat-screen TV on a wall in the reception area. He switches it on and it begins showing a slide show of all the advertisements Kelly Powers, Elizabeth Starr and Eva Collins have ever done during their respective careers. It runs on a loop, repeating the shots endlessly.

Tia says, "This was Claire's idea. She saw a similar concept at my studio. I hope you like the surprise."

"Would it be okay to hug Claire and tell her I'm so proud of her and her work" "Eva asks.

Nathan says, "Go right ahead!"

Claire enjoys the praise, knowing she'll have to keep up the good work in the future.

Bobby Sharp has never been able to console his wife or his children when they need him. This time, it's going to be different. He tells himself he must make an effort.

"I'll go and check on the grandchildren and BJ, too," Bobby tells Naana. He takes off Lisa's shoes and places them next to the sofa in the living room of the guest house. He calls Rose to bring some orange juice, and by the time Tia, Nathan and Vidal arrive, Lisa is asleep. Tia and Naana cannot believe that Bobby has managed to calm down Lisa. Later that night, when Bobby and Naana were making love, she began to cry.

Bobby asks, "Why are you upset, my love?"

Naana replies, sniffling, "I'm not. I'm proud of how you got Lisa through today. Myself, I had no idea how to console her."

Bobby strokes her back as he holds Naana in his arms. Then he says thoughtfully, "I have neglected the girls so much over the years I'm surprised they love and respect me."

"How can you say that? You're their father! We all love you, Bobby, so much."

"I had a different up-bringing as a child. I want to try to make time for all of you, Princess, from now on, especially before they all go off and start their own families. I must say, though, that I didn't like your manipulative plan to get Chance back together with Lisa." He chuckles, enjoying the deviousness of his wife's plan. "I agree with you, though. Lisa is too much in love with Chance to let him go. I hate to see her marrying someone she doesn't really love. She will be so upset when she learns what we all have been doing to set her up with Chance. Won't you please reconsider? She has been through an awful lot with Priscilla and her death is going to be hard on her, Princess."

"You are right, but the Bensons arrive tomorrow. It's too late now. Plans have been set in motion, so we're just gonna have to wait it all out, darling," Naana says.

Meanwhile, at the guest house, Lisa awakened from a nightmare about Priscilla and Chance. Vidal is there with her. She wraps her legs and arms around Vidal and switches on the TV, tuning in to MTV. Vidal's heart beats rapidly as he lays his head in between Lisa's breasts. She begins to kiss and rub his head with one and while the other hand caresses his chest. They are enjoying their time alone, away from everyone.

"You know, Baby, I'm a little worried about moving to England after we're married," Vidal confesses. "I've become used to everything my mother does for me, though it's been nice living here at the bungalow, just the two of us, doing things together like we are married already. I like how you take care of me. I told my father so, today."

"We will be alright, Baby. Amsterdam is only an hour away. I intend to spoil you rotten in every way," Lisa declares.

"Me, too," Vidal promises as he nuzzles Lisa's breasts.

"I'll be leaving for England today, after the photo shoots. I have to go to Priscilla's funeral. Please, don't forbid me to go. I need to say good-bye. I'll not go without your blessing, no matter how I feel."

Vidal thinks about it for a moment, then says, "Of course, you must go!" He pauses, thinking how to ask his next question, then decides just to say it, "Are you still in love with Chance?" He closes his eyes, dreading the answer.

Lisa replies, "I don't know what I feel for Chance. I do know that I love you, very much. I just don't think that I'm ready to get married. I've enjoyed spending time alone with you. I think marriage to you will be good for me. I don't know what else to tell you. Please, believe that. A lot of things changed for me when Priscilla . . . We will be fine."

"Are you going to be okay?"

"Yes. It was a little bit overwhelming to hear of her death. I loved her once, you know. Not as much as I love you, but I did love her."

Tia has also kept the death of Kevin and those of his family to herself. She has nightmares about it. When Nathan confronts her about them, she finally shares the news with him. "You should have told me, Tia. We agreed, no more keeping secrets from each other. How can I know what's on your mind if you don't tell me, Goddess?"

"I wanted to. I tried to push it out of my head, especially the part that I played in bringing him down. I was more than ashamed when his lawyer called me. I tried to tell you, but there was never a right moment, Sweetie."

"Do you think," Nathan sighs, and sits up in bed, "Do you think we should go to therapy?"

"No! Baby, please! I have not dealt with what he did to me. I thought I would be okay, but every time I close my eyes, I'm back at the Regency Hotel and he has his hands on me. I find myself fighting for breath. I'm afraid that one day, I'll not be able to wake up," Tia cries.

Nathan holds her and assures her that she will be alright. "I want us to talk to someone when we go home. I don't want to lose you to a nightmare, Goddess. I love you too much to see you go through this pain. I should have kept my eyes on you that night."

"No, no. It was not your fault, Sweetie. I never should have left the party with him."

"Well, I feel bad that I couldn't protect you. And I feel bad that I have to hide behind my sister-in-law to seek my revenge. What kind of a husband am I?"

"You're a good man, the man I loved before I even met you, Nathan. Baby, please . . . we are on the same page. We can't let the past hurt us like before." Tia kisses him and is about to slip her hands between his legs when Trey and BJ open their door, bringing Tia her tea.

"Are you going to come downstairs? Auntie Brooke is there. She made the tea for you, Mummy," Trey informs her. He is cute as a button in his Batman bathrobe.

"Yes, Baby. Tell Auntie Brooke that I"ll be down soon," Tia instructs them. "Close the door behind you!" She puts down her tea and rests her head on Nathan's chest. In a few minutes, she has fallen asleep again. Nathan sighs as he quietly slips out of bed. He goes to his father's room. Anthony is in the shower, singing. He looks so happy when he comes out of the bathroom that Nathan did not want to trouble him.

"What's wrong, Nate?" asks Anthony.

"Tia needs your help, Dad. I don't know how to help her. In fact, I feel rather helpless."

"Is she still having nightmares?"

"Yes. Why don't they go away?"

"Someone whom she once loved did a terrible thing to her. It's not easy for any woman to recover from that kind of thing, especially now that he has died so suddenly."

"You knew about Kevin's death?"

"Yes. Naana and I saw it on the BBC news about his wife and child, how his wife did all those awful things to him and his family. It was so sad. He was very good to Tia and the children, you know?"

"Yeah, Dad. I know he loved Tia and the children. What can I do to help my wife?"

"You are doing all the things that she needs. Angel will be fine, son, she will."

"Dad, I'm not so sure anymore. I want to try to get help for her when we go home. I mean, for all of us. What do you think?"

"I know someone. I will call her when we get home."

Anthony hugs his son, thinking "It's not fair for Nathan and Tia to be going through all this."

Jackie has finished her last exams and Patrick is waiting in the car for her. He doesn't look himself at all, but he smiles and kisses Jackie.

"How did it go?"

"I think I aced it. Are you okay?"

"Vidal just called. Priscilla's dead. She died of a drug overdose and Lisa is not taking it very well. Vidal is with her, but she is returning to England today. I just wish Vidal would forbid her to go to that funeral."

Jackie wishes she could be there with Lisa. "I agree. I don't think she should be alone. She loves Vidal. I wish she would stop being afraid and let him see the vulnerable side of herself. Knowing Lisa, she is just going to work herself into exhaustion. I'm sorry, Patrick. I know I said I was going to wait and fly to Europe with you, but I may have to leave as early as next week. Naana is going to need help consoling Lisa."

"It's okay. I'll join you once my mother leaves for Canada; otherwise, I'll not see her until the summer. Jackie, I'm so sorry."

"No! Don't be. I'll miss you more. This will give me an opportunity to talk to my Dad about us getting married."

Chapter 34

Back in London, Farrah Benson encourages her son, Chance, to accept Mrs Sharp's offer to visit her in Holland. His father's advice is similar: "Mrs Sharp is a princess, and in our culture if a princess sends you an invitation, you don't reject it like this." Chance is aware of the implications of not visiting Mrs Sharp, but he is worried about the impact of Priscilla's actions against Mrs Sharp and Lisa. He tells his father, "I just don't know how to face Grandma Gertrude after all these years. She sends me birthday cards, Christmas cards, every year. Not once have I called to thank her."

Farrah adds, "Daddy and I are going to Amsterdam tonight. We will be Gertrude's guests. Naana is going to Ghana at the end of the month. Her company is Grandpa's primary sponsor in the up-coming Ghanaian elections. Gertrude and Kofi can't go, so Naana thought we should come to Holland. We can have some photos done for Grandpa's campaign. Why don't you join us for the weekend?"

Chance sighs and looks up at his parents. "Why not? I'll call Yolanda and we can make a weekend of it."

Farrah swept her blonde hair over her shoulders in disbelief. She whispers to Chance Senior, "That's *not* what I had in mind."

Her husband laughs, "It's okay to manipulate me into doing this and that for you, but I guess it's safe to say that you and the Princess have your hands full with Chance and Lisa."

Farrah throws a pillow at him and they both laugh. Farrah calls Naana to tell her the good news. Naana is eager to meet Chance's girlfriend, hoping she will be the fire the two mothers need to bring their kids together.

Yolanda Heart is twenty years old, a web designer, and has been dating Chance for four months. They've had an up and down relationship, and right now it's in the dumps. The night that Priscilla shot at Chance and Lisa, their relationship hit a new low. Yolanda knows that Chance thinks about Lisa often, so much so that a few days after the incident, while they were making love, Chance accidentally called her Lisa. All this time, Chance has never said he loves Yolanda. Then, all of a sudden, Chance says, "God, I love you, Lisa." Yolanda pushed him off her, hoping that Chance would deny saying what she knew she heard. Instead, he got dressed and went home. Yolanda thinks Chance has always been the perfect gentleman, and she especially likes how he sends her flowers every time they make love, accompanied with a note saying how much he loves her. This is the first time that he hasn't sent flowers. She loves Chance and doesn't want to lose him, but she may not have a choice about that. They have never talked about any of Chance's previous girlfriends, so everything Yolanda knows about Lisa has been gleaned from their circle of friends. Yolanda is the same age as Chance's best friend, Curtis, who is also Chance's uncle. Curtis says that Lisa is Lisa Sharp, who dated Chance for years until Chance went to college and they suddenly broke up. Curtis doesn't know what caused the break. Yolanda asks, "Does Chance love Lisa?"

Curtis replies flippantly, "We all love Lisa, why?"

Yolanda keeps her thoughts to herself. Tonight, Yolanda is in her South London flat, getting ready for bed, trying to block Chance from her thoughts, missing him anyway, when the doorbell rings. She looks through the peep hole to see Chance. Opening the door, she lets him into the flat. He raises his hands up in submission. He is holding a take-out bag and a bottle of wine, clutching a single white rose between his teeth. There is a note taped to his forehead, which reads "the world's biggest ass-hole. I'm sorry." Grinning broadly, Yolanda plants a big kiss on his forehead and pulls him inside. They have sex on her living room floor. Afterward, he tells her that he has been calling her at home and also at work to apologize, but she won't take his calls.

"I was hurt," she says simply. Yolanda sits on top of him, her blue eyes filled with tears. Chance wipes the tears from her face with his finger-tips.

"I know, honey. I am very sorry. I had a weekend away planned for us, but there is this family thing . . . in Amsterdam and I was hoping you'd want to spend the weekend there with me."

Yolanda did not let Chance finish, "I'd love to!" and then they were making love again.

Naana meets the Benson's at the Shicpol airport with her son and her grandchildren. Just like everyone who meets them, the Bensons think Jayzel is adorable, and of course, BJ and Trey are madly in love with the Benson's daughter, Meg. They both take one of her hands and do their best to charm the sixteen-year-old. Chance also cannot put Jayzel down, like Nathan does. At the mansion, Guntar takes their luggage into their rooms. Osei Kofi disappears with Chance, Sr, to talk politics. The children also manage to get Chance, Meg and Yolanda into the pool with them. Yolanda is not in the least bit troubled by the fact that they are spending the weekend with Chance's ex-girlfriend's family. Chance hates jealousy, and he is certain he has never given Yolanda cause to be jealous.

The photo shoots took longer than Lisa expected. It took a whole day at the Collins home because Eric had the same problems with the cameras that Vidal did. One would think someone had thrown a bucket of ice water on him. Eva, as a model, was not the same as the loving mother. Tia and Lisa agreed that Eva was the biggest diva they had ever worked with, and Tia can say that she has worked with the best of them when it comes to celebrities and their tantrums. Tia knows how to soothe wounded egos, but Eva complained about everything. She refused to wear the clothes from the Urban Style store. Tia put her foot down and told her to put on the clothes or forget about her and Eric having an exclusive full-page spread. It took some work, but Tia convinced Eva to model different types of jeans from the Urban Style collection, and she put those photos on their website to increase sales in their stores. Brooke was a little jealous. She began to wish she had not sold her shares in the clothing store to Lisa. Kojo told Lisa that he hoped he would never have to photograph Vidal and his father, not ever again. Lisa chuckled because she knew how wooden the two men could be. They were scheduled to go to the mansion the next day to shoot more photographs, but Vidal was relieved to learn that he would not be needed. Lisa, also reprieved from the photo shoot, stayed in her office, proof-reading and editing. She was not completely happy with the material that is ready for the first issue of the magazine. Something is missing, an edge, something to set Urban Style Magazine apart from all other fashion mags. But what? "Perhaps, I'll talk it over with Vidal tonight at the guest house," thinks Lisa as she peruses the layouts on her desk. She and Vidal are always together like glue these days.

Anthony was barbeque-ing with Bobby, and Evelyn lounged by the pool. Jayzel was sitting on Chance's lap, learning her lines for *The Saga*. Yolanda is a huge fan of the show, so she was star-struck by the little girl. Meg also loved the attention that the two young boys were giving her. They have spent the whole afternoon playing video games with her, which she loves too, and they vie for her attention.

Claire was the first of the Sharp sisters to arrive and to meet the Bensons. She told her mother and her house guests that she had an idea for the magazine's first issue. She blurted it out to the ladies sitting in the family room. Grandma Gertrude winked at Farrah Benson, who exchanged a devious smile with Naana. Claire said she was sure Tia would go for it, but Lisa might not like it at all. Claire expressed her wish that Nathan might be home so he could help her manipulate Lisa into adopting her idea.

"Can we invite the Collins family for dinner?" Claire asks.

"What a splendid idea, Claire! I think you should and you can discuss your idea with Eva after dinner, my dear," encouraged Gertrude.

Sarah can't help but laugh as she can divine some interesting social cross-currents.

Lisa was surprised to see Farrah Benson, but she covered it well as she bent to hug and kiss her while still holding Vidal's hand. She does the same with Mr Benson. A few minutes later, Rose announced that the Collins were here and that dinner is ready.

Nathan and Tia were by the pool when Chance greeted them and introduced Yolanda. Nathan thought, "Oh, yeah! This is going to be an interesting weekend!"

Aloud, he said to Chance, "I see you can't put my Baby down."

"Oh, Daddy! Chance has been doing lines with me. He knows how to do the double back flip too just like you, Daddy. Isn't he the coolest, Daddy?" Jayzel beamed.

"I hope your boyfriend knows my Baby can't date until she is forty," Nathan tells Yolanda.

Chance chuckles and sits back down with Jayzel. Vidal walks hand-in-hand with Lisa onto the deck of the pool. He sees Chance with Jayzel on his lap and thinks, "Fuck! This can't be happening."

Nevertheless, they exchange pleasantries and smile at each other. Lisa's heart skips a beat and flashes him a smile. "Come on, Baby! Let's go say hello," Lisa pulls Vidal. Lisa does her best to take away some of the awkwardness by making a joke about Jayzel.

"My brother is not going to be very happy that you are with his baby girl. I see you got the Jayzel Blues, too, eh?" Lisa warns Chance with a sexy smile that excellerates his heart rate as well as Vidal's.

"Hello, Princess. Mr Collins? How are you, sir?" Chance extends his hand to greet Vidal. They shake hands, smiling politely.

Nathan approaches the group to tell Lisa that Tia is in the study, that she may have found the edge they need for their magazine and they want to run it by Lisa.

"Would you excuse me, fellas?" asks Lisa.

"Oh! Are you starting up a magazine?" asks Chance.

Vidal says proudly, "Yes, indeed, she is. The first issue is almost done."

Jayzel has gone off somewhere with Yolanda. Jason and Jaden, too, have joined Nathan, Vidal and Chance by the pool side. They also expected it to be an interesting weekend. The mansion was already divided with all of the young men by the pool having their dinner without their wives and girlfriends. Jason suggested that Rose bring their food into the guest house so they could watch football on the TV. The championship games have begun and they want to watch while they eat.

"Brilliant!" exclaims Jaden.

The older women were in the dining room off the kitchen, eating with the children and Yolanda. Their husbands, just like the young men, were watching football in the living room. The younger women are in the kitchen, some sitting on bar stools at the island, and others standing next to the counter-top nibbling from their plates and keeping an eye on their youngsters behavior in the dining room.

Claire couldn't wait until after dinner like her grandmother suggested to propose her ideas. Of course, Tia has already heard the idea and loves it. It is much better than what she and Naana contrived. Claire begins by saying that the magazine is boring, and suggests they move the story about

Lisa and Vidal's wedding to the next issue along side Lock and Ashton's article introducing the film *Hope Lives*.

"No. That will leave a huge gap in the story about love and romance," Eva points out.

"No, it won't! I read all kinds of different magazines each week just to get creative ideas. The stories always have intrigue, passion and romance. Our magazine doesn't! No one cares about a super model and how she and her family live. You can see that on TV every day after the six o'clock news!"

Eva is offended by Claire's suggestions, so the two women begin to butt heads. Lisa tells them both to be quiet and asks Claire, "What have you got that has passion and intrigue that's better than my wedding?"

In response, Claire puts her laptop on the desk and explains how the idea came to her when she arrived home and saw the Bensons in the living room.

"We can't put the Bensons along side us. They live a very different lifestyle from us," Eva objects.

"But that is exactly why we should! Their story has intrigue, romance, and they also happen to be one of the most powerful families in Ghana. With the Ghanian elections coming next month, and with Chance's grandfather running for President, we can draw in people from our culture, too. My sisters and I know very little about that half of our heritage. Our mom's company in Ghana is one of Chance's grandfather's main sponsors. It will also introduce Mummy and Daddy in advance of when we do next month's issue with Lisa's wedding," Claire explains.

"I'm the editor, and I don't like it. The magazine stays the way it is," says Eva.

"Too bad! You said I would be the Creative Director and that overrules you. Your story is too dull. It's been done before so many times, Mrs Collins. Readers like to read about new stuff, not old stuff. The story we want to put out is just gonna show people that we have money and we have perfect lives. Boo hoo! No one cares! Readers will shy away from our magazine and we'll be out of a job! I'm not going to lose my job for you!" Claire screams at Eva.

"That's enough, Claire! You'll not speak to Mrs Collins in this manner. What do you think, Lisa?" Tia prompts her sister.

"I agree. Our story is a little dull. You heard me say that earlier. We are going to finish with all of the photo shoots as planned," Lisa says.

Eva smiles. Claire begins to yell and shriek. Lisa asked her to settle down and let her finish.

"Tia and I will discuss this with Mother first and then with the Bensons. Kojo can take some photographs for us while they are here. Eva can work on her ideas, too. Tia and I will make our final decision once our staffing issues are solved next week. Oh, Claire . . . Good job! But the next time your cross the line like you did a minute ago with your rudeness toward Mrs Collins, you'll be fired. We don't talk like that to each other in this company. Being a Creative Director or an Editor doesn't mean either one of you owns this magazine. The same goes for you, Eva. Tia and I own this magazine. We won't tolerate disruptions from either one of you. Your positions on this venture are still probationary and won't be finalized until we have sorted out our staffing needs," Lisa says.

Claire runs out of the meeting room with tears in her eyes, so does Eva. Brooke and Kate were there, so Lisa decides to ask their opinions.

"Brooke, you read fashion magazines. What really attracts you?"

"Claire does have a point. I think Mrs Collins head is getting big enough already. You need a strong chief editor, one who can negotiate competing interests. I don't think your soon-to-be mother-in-law is right for the position you have given her. Other than wearing fabulous clothes and spending her husband's money, what the hell does she know about business? I doubt if she even reads the stories in the magazine other than looking at the pictures," Brooke says bluntly. Kate and Tia laugh heartily, and Lisa joins in, too.

"I agree. Tia and I have had this conversation already."

The younger women finally join the rest of the women in the dining room.

Meanwhile, Claire is upstairs crying. She lights up a joint in her bathroom and takes a comforting drag. Lisa and Tia want to be sure that she is alright, so they have followed her upstairs. When she sees them, Claire tries to hide the joint.

"Oh! Claire, you go right ahead and smoke that doobie. Why hide it? You paid a lot of money for it, so don't let it go to waste," Tia says.

"Tia's right, you know?" Lisa comments.

Claire rolls her eyes impatiently and throws the joint in the toilet. Suddenly, Lisa begins to beat the shit out of Claire. Chance and Yolanda are passing by Claire's door and happen to witness Lisa slapping Claire while Tia sits on the bed frowning. Chance decides to intervene. He pulls

Lisa away from Claire. The aroma of marijuana still lingers in the air, so there's no guesswork needed to conclude why Claire is being punished so severely.

"Would you ladies excuse Claire and I for a moment? I want to talk privately with her."

Without addressing Chance, Tia and Lisa both leave, taking the opportunity to give Claire one more smack on the head as they leave the room.

"Why don't you go get me the rest of your joints?" Chance asks Claire.

Claire ignores him. She sits on her bed and begins to draw on a sketch pad. Chance decides to wait, so he sits on the bed, too, and watches Claire draw.

"You know, Princess, many great artists like yourself experiment with drugs, alcohol and sex, but the brilliant ones like Grandmother Gertrude don't fall for the stereotypical role of an artist."

Claire has stopped crying long enough to say, "Leave me alone, Chance."

Chance leans back on her bed and crosses his legs. He would like to hold Claire and tell her not to cry, but that would only work until the next time she got into trouble with Lisa, and what then?

"I will leave you alone, Princess, but first I want you to hear me out for a second, okay?"

Claire becomes child-like, ready to receive a scolding. She nods and wipes her face.

"Princess, it's not easy growing up with a family like those you and I come from, with everyone so perfect. I think you are perfect without the drugs and drinking. I'm looking at the beautiful sketch you just drew of Lisa and I. You were not even looking at me, but it's perfect. The resemblance is remarkable. I don't know if Tia can draw as well as you do, but I know Lisa can't draw to save her life," Chance chuckles. Claire thought it was funny, too.

"My sisters are perfect in everything they do. I'm just not like them," Claire cried.

"No, they are not. They have studied to become successful business people. They took courses, and they had lots of support and mentoring from your Mom and Dad. They have special training just like you do with your art. But you are right. You and your sisters are perfect. Drugs and alcohol destroy lives. Don't let it destroy yours, Princess. Everyone is so very proud of what you have been doing on your sister's magazine. That is the talk downstairs, Princess, and it's all about how brilliant you are. You know . . . Lisa is good in everything and she is a big bully, too." Claire laughs. "Shhhh! You don't want her to hear us! The walls have ears!" Chance says.

Tia, Lisa and Yolanda huddle in the hallway listening to the conversation between Chance and Claire. They hear Claire admit that she gets stressed and fears that she is not as good as her sisters.

"Actually, Chance, I don't really like drugs or wine, but they help relax me."

"Well, there are better ways to do that. I can show you a new way to relax yourself. I promised Jayzel I'd show her, too. We can do it in the morning after breakfast, okay?"

"Sure," agrees Claire, then a thought occurs to her, "Jayzel is a cute kid, but what does she know about stress?"

"Jayzel is also an artist and she tells me that she and Trey are going to be doctors. She gets nervous when she forgets her lines for her TV show and when Trey knows more about the human body than she does, she feels foolish. I promised to show her how to meditate and do some breathing techniques my Dad showed me and my sister. Please, don't tell Yolanda that I have a huge crush on Jayzel," Chance says.

Claire slaps his knee, "My brother will put you in jail, you sick pervert!" Claire says laughing. She goes and throws all her drugs in the loo and flushes it. "I think Lisa is making a mistake marrying that meat-head Vidal instead of you. You will make a better brother than that Mamma's boy," Claire says sharply.

"I think I'm going to marry Jayzel if her parents don't put me in jail first," laughs Chance as he puts his arms around Claire and gives her a big hug. When they appeared in the hall, they discovered Lisa, Tia and Yolanda waiting for them. Lisa shakes her head, turns away and heads downstairs. Tia whispers "thank you" to Chance and puts her arms around Claire as they walk downstairs together to eat.

Chapter 34

Yolanda thinks it is very sweet of Chance to talk to Claire. For Chance, being in the same house as Lisa has made him more horny. He make loves to Yolanda as soon as he closes their door and massages her to sleep. He wonders what Lisa and Vidal are doing. It is after mid-night. He can hear classical music coming from down the hall. He is not able to sleep and remembers that Lisa's mother has a gym in the mansion. As he pads down the hall, Chance notices that Lisa and Tia are still awake and talking in their grandfather's study. Nathan has come and is carrying Tia to bed in his arms. Chance closes the study door behind them.

"I thought you would be at the Collins home," Chance says.

Lisa is sitting on the sofa with her laptop on her lap. She wears a Nike track suit with slouchy socks. She smiles, though she feels nervous. "Are you in love with her?" she asks softly, never taking her eyes off him. Chance sits himself down on the far end of the sofa. He has Lisa's foot in his lap with his own on top of the glass center table.

"I fell in love with a beautiful Princess when I was eleven. She hurt me. I promised myself never to fall in love again. Are you in love with Mr Collins, or is it just sex?"

Lisa does not immediately respond to Chance's question as she returns her attention to her laptop and begins typing. "I would not know about sex. I have not had sex with him or with any man, if you must know."

Chance wishes that he has not asked that question. He realizes that just as he could not forgive her for sleeping with other women, Lisa also cannot forgive him for his own infidelities. It is written all over Lisa's face. His heart beats faster and faster now as he tries to frame the words to ask why Lisa and Vidal have not made love. He and Lisa never had sex. She claimed she wanted to wait until they were married. Chance tells himself he has been a fool all these years. Lisa didn't cause this separation, he did. Chance has difficulty accepting that girls sometimes experiment with other girls, discovering their sexuality. He has always thought, because of Lisa's penchant for girls, that Lisa is gay and never going to change. Finally, he makes eye-contact with her. He wants to say that he has missed her and thought about her everyday, but the words will not come out. Lisa wants to move her laptop and reach for Chance, tell him how much she misses him, but the words won't come, either. He rubs his hands on the arm where he has had a tattoo of her face. Chance recalls the day he got it done, how painful it was and the long slow French kiss they shared afterward on the street in London's West End. All eyes were on them. That day was also the very first time Chance saw Lisa fully naked. They went skinny dipping in the hot tub and had oral sex. They would have made love if his auntie had not showed up in the country home with her sons and her partner. Everything went south about three weeks later. Lisa is also thinking about that time. It was the first time Lisa ever saw two women kiss. Watching Chance's Aunt Lucy kiss her partner Mandy was the most beautiful thing Lisa has ever seen in her life. She liked Priscilla Gates, and when Lisa found out that Priscilla also liked girls, it was a match made in heaven for Lisa. Since that afternoon, Lisa has had countless oral sex, but it's never been the same as it was with Chance.

Lisa didn't want to cry. She closes her eyes and leans her head down as Chance rubs her feet with his own eyes closed, lost in his thoughts. This is the most privacy they've had in four years. Why can't he tell her how he feels about her, that he doesn't want her to marry Vidal, that he wants her to be his wife, that he wants her to be his everything just like they were when they were young?

"Princess, we need to talk, but not here. I feel like there is something we need to clear up between us. I'm still . . . very much in love with you. I've been a fool. I can't stand by and watch you marry . . ." he pauses.

Lisa gets up and heads for the door in tears. "Damn it!" Chance punches the sofa and runs after her to the guest house. He puts his foot down just as Lisa closes the door. Meanwhile, Farrah, Naana and BJ are gathered in the kitchen. BJ drinks milk while the two older women chat.

"Why is Lisa crying? And why are Lisa and Chance running toward the guest house?" asks BJ.

Farrah immediately expresses her concern, but Naana reassures everyone with her practical approach to family life.

"Lisa is going to be alright, BJ. Now, drink up your milk and get yourself to bed."

Farrah apologizes for Chance's behavior and Naana replies, "There is no need. They need to face whatever it is that has kept them apart. Lisa is not as happy as she claims. Believe me! This is the best way for them."

Farrah and Naana glance at the guest house before they, too, go upstairs each offering a silent prayer that all will be well.

Chance exhales, "Princess, please!"

"Not tonight! You're not to worry. Vidal and I will not be getting married. Priscilla died of a drug overdose five days ago."

Chance feels like he has been kicked in the gut. He would like to ask whether that is the real reason why Lisa has called off her wedding.

"Her death made me realize how much I love you, and I told Vidal. He thinks I'm in shock, but I just want to be left alone."

"Princess, please listen to me."

"No! You listen to me! Your girlfriend is upstairs in your bed waiting for you. I suggest you go to her. Four years! Four years I've been waiting for you to forgive me. I just don't care any more. You didn't come to Holland for me, so let's not make this about me."

"I would have, Princess. I've made mistakes, too. I don't want to intrude on your pain. I just don't know how to walk away from you knowing how much pain you must be feeling right now. I want to hold you and make it all go away, Princess," Chance declares.

"Of course! Tell me something, then. Since you love me so much, did you think of me when you brought your girlfriend with you on this trip?"

"Princess, that's not fair!" Chance is almost in tears.

"You're right! It's not. Was it fair making love to her before you came downstairs to tell me how much you still love me?" Lisa is shouting so loudly that probably everyone in the mansion can hear her. Chance collapses into the nearest chair. His father warned him about this eventuality. He can hear Lisa in her bedroom, crying. He almost opens the bedroom door, but decided he should not, so he sat on the floor outside the bedroom door instead.

"Princess ... please ... I've been wrong about us. I've been wrong about us on so many levels I can't begin to explain or ask you for forgiveness. I never meant to be with any woman other than you. I promise, I'll make things right. Oh, Princess, you have no idea how much my life will not be a whole life without you." Chance wipes the tears from his face.

Lisa hates crying, but whenever she thinks of Chance, she cries. Why should she believe him? She could not recall how she and Priscilla began their relationship. It just did. She also tried her very best to end things with her after their very first kiss on her sixteenth birthday, but it was already too late. She had lost Chance. It hurts very much to end things with Vidal, but Lisa knows in her heart that she can't be with Chance. She doesn't feel able to live up to his expectations and she's not sure that she will ever be able to measure up. She wishes that he would go away and leave her alone. Inside the guest house bedroom she is able to breathe and relax a little bit as she closes her eyes and tries not to think of anything or anyone. But it is no use. Knowing Chance is outside her door makes Lisa feel hunted. She comes out of the bedroom, "If you're not going to leave, then I will!"

"This might not be the best time for us to talk, but I'm not gonna give up on us like I did the last time. I'm gonna end things with . . . You don't have to leave, but we will talk. Soon. Can I hold you, just for a second? Please, Princess. Don't make me beg anymore."

"No. I can't. I can't be in your arms and watch you go and . . . I just can't," Lisa says.

"I love you! Please, don't lose faith in us like I did. Good-night, Princess. I promise you, I will make all the pain go away. I will." Chance leaves and retreats to the family room. Mrs Sharp finds him sobbing and goes to console him.

"Oh, Mrs Sharp! I've made a mess of everything. Life was so simple when Lisa and I were kids."

Mrs Sharp smiles, "I promise it will be alright again if that is what you and Lisa want." She hugs him and wishes him good-night. Chance feels able to breathe again after his little talk with Lisa's mom. Upstairs in his room, Yolanda is sound asleep. Chance hesitates for a second before slipping into bed next to her and putting his arms around her. His heart breaks for Lisa, all alone in the guest house, but Chance knows Lisa will keep Priscilla's death inside just like she did Dana's. Chance thinks, "I have to find a way to help her deal with Priscilla's death," and he closes his eyes thinking that is what he will do for her.

Claire awakens the next morning with a whole new attitude. Her father is surprised that he doesn't have to bang on her door like he normally does. BJ is in the kitchen barking orders at Rose not to give his father any fried eggs and bacon. The poor maid feels bad for Bobby, but as BJ instructs, she makes oatmeal and orange juice for all of them. Claire also asks for oatmeal and OJ. After breakfast, she goes in search of Jayzel and Chance, who are waiting by the pool. After yoga, Chance shows the girls how to use their diaphragms to breathe in and out. Jayzel loves the technique and Claire agrees that she also feels on top of the world. Then, without badgering from Bobby, Claire goes to her grandmother's studio and begins work before Kojo arrives for the next photo shoot. Claire also takes some candid shots. Most of the time, her subjects are not even aware she is taking pictures. Although Naana is not able to get Chance and Lisa in one place for more than a minute, she is more than a little hopeful that Lisa has called off her wedding to Vidal. Naana thinks Lisa seems to be coping well with Priscilla's death, a good thing since the launch of the magazine is proving to be extra-stressful. Finally, Naana is relieved that the house will be a little quieter next week since the Bensons intend to leave on Sunday after lunch. Chance informs his parents that he will not leave without his Princess. Chance Senior thinks his son's behavior is inappropriate and says so loudly. Gertrude overhears the conversation and adds, "What's a man to do? Lisa is known to make a grown man cry!" They all laugh in agreement with Gertrude's observation.

"Would it be too inappropriate if I say that by Valentine's Day I will be your new grand-son-in-law?" Chance asks with a straight face.

With a wink, Gertrude replies, "I'd say romance is in the air! Good luck winning back your Princess! I think your father is going to take his belt to you!" Gertrude chuckles and kisses Chance.

Naana shakes her head seeing her mother flirting with all the young men. Everyone thinks Gertrude is charming. Her husband claims it is the artist in her. "I thank God that Gerty is old," he says aloud.

"Being around young people and their exuberant spirits has taken forty years off me, darling," Gertrude says. "So, look out!" Gertrude kisses the backs of her husband's hands and gives them a squeeze.

Although everyone is happy to see Chance and Lisa's roller-coaster relationship coming to a stop, they can't help but feel their heartstrings vibrating for Vidal and what he must be feeling. Since Lisa called off their wedding, Vidal has done nothing but sleep with every beautiful women he meets. Most of the time, he doesn't even remember their names. It's not like Vidal is heart-broken about his loss. He did see it coming long before Chance showed up in Holland. He sees Chance's girlfriend, Yolanda, getting into the car and Guntar helping with her luggage. It's not hard to guess that Chance has unceremoniously dumped her. Vidal has stopped by the mansion to see how Lisa is doing, but decides to offer to drive Yolanda to the airport. She readily agrees and Guntar helps shift her luggage to Vidal's car. On the way to the airport, Vidal asks Yolanda to stay in Holland so he can show her the city. She accepts, so Vidal turns the car around and takes her home to his parents guest house where he and Lisa used to stay.

Eva and Eric want to invite Vidal and Lisa to the club for lunch, so they stroll out to the guest house and open the door. They walk in to discover their son with a beautiful blonde, having sex on the floor. Gingerly, Eva closes the door before Vidal knows they are there. Upset, extremely disappointed in her son, Eric reassures Eva it is all for the best. Vidal is too young. Lisa is too serious about life and Vidal ought to enjoy life a little. Eva agrees, but she loves Lisa and thinks they make a cute couple.

Chapter 35

Lisa could not sleep after her fight with Chance. She slips out of the mansion early the next morning with some files, taking one of her grandparents vehicles and leaving for their cottage in Utrecht, outside Amsterdam. Lisa has always loved the little Dutch town and the privacy the cottage offers. She feels nothing but pain—physical and emotional pain. The last twenty-four hours alone have brought tremendous anxiety about her personal life. She needs to breathe and cannot stay among all of her well-meaning, inquisitive relatives at the mansion. She calls Tia to let her know where she is. Tia tells her not to run away from true love and she will see her on Monday. Lisa throws her bag and her files down on the table next to her cellphone. Unable to relax, she puts on a track suit and goes outside for a long run. The idea of battling depression horrifies Lisa more than anything. After her run, Lisa drives to the street market to stock up on fish, fruits and vegetables. She picks up some take-out food from a nearby Greek restaurant and returns to the cottage. While munching on her Greek salad, she works on her laptop, looking at some of the recent loan applications that she needs her mother to approve. While she eats, she thinks of calling Gina, but does not since sleep is coming and Lisa is trying to fight it off. Sleep won and Lisa fell into a deep slumber that lasted the night. In the morning, she woke up feeling tired. She made herself some orange juice and went for a jog. Her cellphone rang just before she reached the cottage. It was Chance calling to ask where she is. She says, "I'm in Utrecht, at the cottage."

"So am I, Princess, but you're not. Where are you now?" Chance asks.

"Right out side."

Chance opens the door and smiles with relief and happiness. He is glad to see Lisa.

"Well, I don't have time to play house. I came here to be alone," says Lisa curtly.

Chance smiles and follows her indoors to the hot tub. She can see that he has prepared the tub. Every twist of Lisa's body, every toss of her hair, makes Chance's heart skip a beat.

Pointing at the tub, Lisa says, "I'll not get into that."

Chance begins helping Lisa undress. She intends to change and settle down to some work. He intends to get her into the tub, and then . . . well, who knows what possibilities may present themselves? Chance lifts up Lisa as she wriggles out of her track pants, but he doesn't set her back down. Instead, he puts her into the hot tub. Lisa pins up her hair and closes her eyes as the steam from the hot water begins to work its magic on her.

"Are you okay?" asks Chance.

"Uh-huh. And you?"

"I am now. I just couldn't stay away any longer, Princess. I couldn't leave Holland not knowing . . . I was hoping we could go out to lunch and talk, but then I thought this would be much more romantic."

"It is. I have not been in a hot tub since we split up. It feels good," Lisa whispers, gazing at Chance, smiling contentedly.

Chance cannot wait to get into the tub himself. Lisa watches him as he quickly strips and gets into the tub behind her. Chance is dying for Lisa to touch him, to feel the softness of her lips. He slips both arms around her. Lisa closes her eyes and relaxes against his chest. The temperature of the water is warm, but suddenly Chance's body has become ice cold. Intuitively, Lisa understands why. She recalls the moment they both knew they belonged to each other, and she knows that a part of each of them has died since they have been apart. She knows Chance is feeling her pain. As he incorporates her pain, his body begins to warm up, and she notices that Chance is not as cold anymore. Lisa puts back her head, resting it on his chest. He kisses the top of her head.

"Priscilla was a big part of you, Princess. Embrace her memory with the good and the not so good . . . It will get better each day, Princess. Don't let pain and sorrow tear you—us—apart again. I'm not letting go this time. I have missed you terribly, Princess."

Lisa cries openly because she has missed Chance so much. Priscilla is all she thinks about these days, and she can't seem to get the girl off her mind. It's amazing how Chance just knows her thoughts.

"I know that you feel all alone and probably think I will not understand, but I do. Priscilla never came between us. We just—we just weren't strong and stubborn enough to fight for us. We are older, wiser and so damn stubborn to face and deal with our fears and our pain, together, Princess. Priscilla and Dana loved you. They would not want you to grieve excessively for them. If Dana was here she would tell you, Lisa, for bloody sake, give the lad a good snog and grab his ass, will you?'" Chance mimics with a straight face.

Lisa elbows him in the ribs and starts to laugh. She wipes her face and places her hands over his.

"I miss you, Princess," Chance repeats.

Chance reaches for a bath towel from the chair beside the tub and jumps out, wrapping it around his waist. He takes Lisa by the hand and helps her out too, wrapping a towel around her. Lisa is a little more relaxed, but Chance asks whether she has been sleeping okay.

"Not very well, no."

They walk hand-in-hand to the bedroom where she sees that he has lit more candles and has been burning incense. Her yoga mat is on the floor. Chance guide her to the mat and they sit on it.

"I'm not trying to seduce you—well, what the hell?—yeah, I am," he says as he kisses the back of her neck.

Lisa shakes her head in amusement.

"I miss meditation with you," confesses Chance. "I figure we could both do with a little relaxing before I beg and plead with you to give us another chance. Yolanda and I broke up. She went home yesterday. I've been out of my mind with worry about you. I had a date with Claire and Jayzel and found I couldn't tear myself from them. I've been thinking of ways to seduce you, like forever."

"If this is a seduction, then it's not a very good one," Lisa observes. "I could use some meditation right now, even if it's with a jerk of a Prince."

"I'm still . . . your Prince?"

She sighs. "Yes, you're still my Prince, but any seduction ideas you have in mind, you have to put somewhere else. I do the seducing, not the other way around!"

Chance feels relieved that Lisa is finally able to talk to him about Priscilla's death.

"I didn't give Priscilla the help she needed to stay clean. That hurts me—a lot. I should have reached out to her, to Dana, too. That is my greatest regret, but with the demands of work and school, I found it difficult to find enough time for them. We grew apart."

"Princess, you loved them both. They chose drugs. You chose life. Don't let their deaths hunt you."

"They are all I think about—and you, too, of course. What we once shared, how I—"she gasps. Still wearing the towel, Lisa leaves the bedroom and goes to the kitchen to make herself a tofu sandwich. Chance follows her a few minutes later and finds Lisa sitting on the counter top near the sink, washing some fruit. He stands between her legs, rubbing her thighs.

"I leave for Hong Kong on Friday for two weeks. I want to, em . . ." he stops, removes the pins from her hair, letting it fall down.

"I don't wanna be a jerk of a Prince, but if I wait for you to kiss me, I'll die," he says softly as he places his lips on hers. Lisa pushes him away.

"What's the matter?"

"Here! Take your sandwiches, eat and go!"

"I'm not going anywhere, Princess. Don't you want me to kiss you?"

Lisa throws her plate of sandwiches and almost hits him. She lashes out at him, "We've been apart for six fucking years. I've made numerous attempts to talk to you! I've tried to make sense of why or what happened with us. You didn't want to know! Now that Priscilla is dead, all of a sudden you want me? Well, too bad!"

"You know that's not true. You have to accept responsibility for our split-up."

"Oh, I do. Every day."

"Princess, after your sixteenth birthday, I tried. For more than a year. Priscilla told me you didn't want to be with me, that you're gay. I wasn't going to wait around for you not to be gay. I didn't want you doing to me what my Auntie Lucy did to her partner. I couldn't wait."

"Well, isn't that sweet! I may not have been sleeping with Priscilla the past two years or so, but I'm sorry to tell you that I have fucked quite a few women after her. Now, do you still want to be with me?"

Lisa attempts to leave the kitchen, but Chance grabs hold of her wrist where she wears their promise bond. He says, "I don't give a rat's ass how many women you've been with. It stops now. I'm not going to lose you to anyone, especially a woman, Lisa. Do you hear me?" He raises his voice as if to drive home his point. His eyes are darker and dead-locked with Lisa's eyes.

"Lisa, if you don't want the future we planned when we were kids, then you should take that bracelet off your wrist."

Lisa frowns. Chance tries to remove it himself.

"Let me help you, so that you can go and do as you please. I'm sure Gina Read is keeping the bed warm for you at the penthouse."

Lisa slaps him and slaps again. She makes an attempt to kiss Chance, but he pushes her away. Lisa is crying now. "I never told Priscilla anything about breaking up with you. In fact, I was going to end things with her before you went to college in the States."

Chance has moved to the sink and does not want to make eye contact with her.

"I don't want to hear it, Lisa. You are my partner and we both have done things out of spite to hurt each other and our families. I can't be apart from you," he says softly.

Lisa stands behind him, running her hands in his wavy hair and privately confessing to herself that although she enjoyed being with Priscilla, it was like she knew how much she hurt him and simultaneously knew what was lost when he refused to have anything to do with her. Curtis, she recalls, has told her often how angry and jealous Chance becomes when he hears others talk about her, especially when gossip focuses on the sexy women she has had in her bed. She has gotten away with it until now. Lisa expects that Chance is too jealous to forbid her from being with any girl again. He never did. As if reading her thoughts, Chance says, "Well, I'm forbidding you now."

Lisa tried to slap him again, but Chance grabs her wrists and holds back her hands. She tries with the other hand, but he grabs it too. Chance knows how stubborn Lisa can be, but her heart always melts when he forbids her not to do something. It's been like that since they were kids. His reluctance to forbid Lisa from having a relationship with Priscilla has brought them to this point. He wishes now that he had been able to foresee the immense emotional pain Lisa would feel. Chance lets go of Lisa's hands and envelopes her in a hug, holding her for the longest time. When they finally drew apart, they were both in tears.

"I am sorry for all the hurt, Princess. I love you and I miss you. I won't share you with anyone. I want you to come to Hong Kong with me on Friday, please. I want . . ."

Lisa didn't let him finish, as she kisses him passionately. He lifts her off her feet and they kiss and kiss and kiss. They end up in bed with Lisa on top of him, still kissing. When they surface, Chance suggests going into town for lunch and a visit to the sex shop. He promises to buy Lisa all kinds of sex toys to satisfy her until they go to Hong Kong.

"You're unbelievable! We are not back together for one second and you are already thinking about sex. No wonder I'm so horny all the time! Being in love with you is a curse! I'm not going to Hong Kong with you. My mother is just about going to have a conniption, thanks to you."

"Every time you think of me, you get horny, eh? Wow!"

They begun laughing and feeling each other up. He slips his hands between her legs, and discovers she is wet.

"God! Your fanny is so tight. I can't wait to do all the things to you that vibrators can't!" he blurts out.

"Excuse me?" demands Lisa as she rolls off Chance. "I would never impose any rules on us. Sex is a healthy part of life and of relationships. I can show you what I mean now, if you want. Then again, I always did love our visit to the sex shop together," says Chance as he grabs his pants.

Lisa can see his dick standing up. He slips on his pants without his boxers and proceeds to put on socks. Lisa watches him dress and realizes that Chance is completely unlike anyone else she has ever loved. Lisa is usually the naughty one, but with Chance, she is usually shy. Chance grabs her ass and tells her to get dressed.

In no time at all, Lisa puts on a pair of jeans, a plain white T-shirt, high-heeled pumps and sunglasses with no make-up.

"Let's go!" she says.

"Oooo, Baby! You look hot!" says Chance, admiring her at arm's length.

Lisa pushes him away from her, but he takes her hands and slowly kisses her. Lisa melts every time they kiss and finds herself wanting more of him. He stops kissing her and opens the front door for her. In a few minutes, they end up in a small cafe. Chance pulls Lisa on his lap. She is still wearing the dark sunglasses. They order iced green tea, cheese and broccoli omelet, and keep their options open for dessert. Lisa is hungry, but food is not first on her mind. Chance feeds her while she sits on his lap. Their server thinks they are a very cute, romantic couple.

After lunch, Lisa feels relaxed, and they walk hand-in-hand to their car. A movement catches Lisa's eyes.

"Everything all right, Princess?" asks Chance.

"Isn't this ironic?" says Lisa as she points to Vidal and Yolanda openly kissing by Vidal's car.

"What the hell? How? Is he stalking us?" Chance asks.

"No . . . Just rebound sex. Who would have thought? My ex-boyfriend with your ex-girlfriend?" Lisa is amused.

"I don't care. Let's go find out what they are playing at," suggests Chance.

"Hmmm. No, let's not. He lives not too far from here. Unless you are jealous?"

"I am very happy. Now we can both move on without any guilt. I'm where I belong and that is all that matters. Come on, Princess. Stop looking at your ex locking lips with another woman. Let's go." Chance hurries Lisa into the car and takes a quick look at Vidal and Yolanda still kissing.

Lisa feels nervous about going into the sex shop and suggests that Chance should just go in and choose something for them while she stays in the car and makes a few phone calls.

"No, this is a two-person job," he says, laughing as he shuts her cell phone in the glove box.

Inside the store, Chance protectively puts his arm around Lisa, points to some sexy underwear, and tells the salesgirl that he and his wife want to spice up their sex life, but that his wife is very shy. The salesgirl suggests some massage oil and shows Chance several products with different scents.

"What does your lady like?" she asks. Lisa blushes crimson.

"Oh, she loves everything that I do to her in bed," Chance says with a grin, winking at Lisa. Her heart almost stopped with shock. The woman was more than happy to find several items for Chance to consider and took her time explaining each of them. There was a silver ring which he especially liked, so he asked, "Do you have a smaller size? I want to buy one like this for my wife, maybe a size five?" Lisa and the saleswoman take one look at each other and begin to laugh.

"Mr Horny, that," says Lisa, pointing to the silver ring, "is a penis ring." She can not contain her laughter, and burst out in gales of laughter once more.

"Oh! I knew that! I just wanted to make an ass of myself, so you'd loosen up a little." He grins, asks for more candles, some incense and a vibrator. "That pink one will do. My wife likes pink." Lisa covers her face with her hands, feeling her embarrassment as Chance pays for the toys.

It is now early evening, and already getting dark. They have spent quite a long time in the sex shop, so Chance asks if they should have dinner in town before going back to the cottage. Lisa says that she will make dinner for them at the cottage. It has begun to rain heavily, so they get soaked running from the parked car to the front door. Lisa gets some towels and spread them on the floor. Chance removes his soaked shoes and socks, bending to place them neatly on the towel. As he straightens up, he sees Lisa's nipples hardening under her wet T-shirt. Dropping his car keys and the bags of sex toys on the floor, he reaches for her and begins to nibble her breasts and nipples, cupping each breast in his hands. He peels off the wet shirt and adds it to the pile of clothes of the floor. He kisses her neck, slips his tongue into her mouth, which she gladly accepts. He grabs her butt cheeks and lifts her on top of the wooden dining table. He tugs off her jeans and is pleasantly surprised to see she is not wearing panties. Kneeling before her, he nibbles between her legs while rubbing her clitoris. Lisa clutches the edge of the table, enjoying the pleasure, feeling she might tip over the edge into madness. He sucks on her clitoris while his index finger attempts to explore her vagina. Having never been penetrated, Lisa's vagina is very tight, but her wetness and excitement allows his finger to find all of her pleasure zones. Standing up, Chance unzips his pants and lets them drop to his knees. He lifts both of Lisa's legs up in the air and rests them on his chest. Stepping forward a little bit, he rubs the head of his penis against her clitoris, encouraging her juices to flow, before penetrating her. Moaning, she closes her eyes, grabs his butt cheeks and squeezes them while Chance gently rides her, thrusting his cock ever deeper into her willing vagina.

"Open your eyes, Princess," he whispers.

Lisa will not open her eyes.

"Do you want me to stop?"

"No!" she moans, not able to gather enough words together to form a complete thought.

Supporting her back with one hand, Chance re-positions Lisa's legs so that they are wrapped around his waist. Then he presses her closer to him so that she must put her arms around his shoulders. Carefully, lifting Lisa off the table, he kicks off his pants.

"Open your eyes, Princess. Please," he whispers.

This time she does open her eyes. He kisses her eyelids as he negotiates his way through the cottage to the bedroom. He gently lays her down on the bed. Lisa digs her fingers into his back as he rides her very slowly, very gently, whispering into her ear how much he loves her fanny. Lisa's whole being is centered on the sensations in her vagina,. The sensation of Chance's penis inside her is very different from that of the vibrator and the other sex toys she customarily uses. Also, she is not in control, and she likes feeling his need of her in every thrust of his penis. He has his whole penis inside her when she begins to come. Wave after wave of sensations pulse over her body, hardening her nipples, making her vagina slippery, contracting her vagina in one sweet orgasm after another. Chance nibbles her ears as Lisa feels the flush of multiple orgasms, the weakness in her limbs. He begins to ride her faster, harder, more desperately. She digs her fingers into his back, scratching the skin. Suddenly, he stops, out of breath, cock detumescent, and lays on top of her.

"What happened?" she asks.

Chance lifts his head to ask, "What do you mean?"

"Why did you stop?"

"Princess, I just came. I didn't want to stop. You did . . . um, enjoy it?"

"I did! It was a little rough at times . . . Did you enjoy it? I mean, how was it?"

Chance chuckles as he caresses her back. "It was your first time. That's why it felt rough. Don't worry, though. It will get better every time we do it. The more we do it the more you will enjoy it." He pauses to kiss her again, softly, lingeringly. "I know you wanted to wait until we are married, but I just could not wait any longer."

"I don't think I wanted to wait any longer, either," says Lisa. "I think this was also the first time I've had multiple orgasms."

"Well, then! I have a standard to maintain!" jokes Chance. "You'll have them every time we make love."

Chance and Lisa lay in each other's arms as they fall asleep. Lisa's last conscious thought as she drifts off to sleep is that Diamond and Bella were right: men do taste different. "I like that taste," she thinks, and falls deeply, happily, into her dreams.

Chapter 36

On Monday, the Sharp sisters got the biggest surprise of their lives when they arrived at the office. There was a line-up out the front doors, through the parking lot and out onto the street for the open interviews. Tia could not believe how young and talented these people were as she put the few chosen ones through a grueling two-day interview process. They all fought hard for each of the positions. Lisa is impressed with her big sister's methods. They have agreed on twenty-five people in various creative and administrative positions. Eva said she would need two personal assistants, but for Tia, that was the last straw. She told her no, flat out.

"Mrs Collins, in a year or two, when I know that you can do this job, you may have two personal assistants, and when you are a full-fledged editor-in-chief, you may have as many assistants as you like. Right now, you have to settle for sharing one assistant with Claire and Lisa." Then, turning to everyone present, Tia said, "I want to make it perfectly clear to each and everyone in this room: we are going to work hard each day. If anyone here feels that they are not happy with what's on the table, then by all means, use the door."

Lisa added, "This is a great opportunity for all of us to be part of something unique here. We will be going head-to-head with all of the world's biggest fashion magazines, who have already established themselves. Let's not make mistakes here people. *No one* is a celebrity here. Everyone gets to be treated in the same way."

The conference room was quiet as Tia went on to describe routine expected of the staff: there would be monthly issues distributed at the middle of the month; contents would be developed at weekly conference call meetings which would take place every Wednesday at noon (Dutch time); nothing would be published in the magazine without Tia's prior approval; all of the banking and financial matters would be handled by Lisa, while the legal and contractual matters would be handled by Tia. Tia also introduced a new editor, a former University English professor, which triggered a tantrum from Eva. Lisa took her outside the conference room and put her in her place. Three more people were hired to help Kojo, and everyone seemed happy that the first issue was going to hit the newsstands in less than three weeks. The enthusiasm in the room was palpable.

Tia was staying in Amsterdam until a week before Lisa's wedding, when she and her family planned to leave to go back to Canada on Valentine's Day evening. Claire had already returned to England with her parents and her half-brother. She had exams to write, but everyday she submitted something spectacular. Eva, however, was having trouble settling into her job. She could not see eye-to-eye with anyone, especially when the new editor, Mrs Tyra Mercer, said that they should go with Claire's idea and that the second issue should feature Lisa's wedding. Eva was becoming argumentative, especially once the photos Claire had taken were available for perusal. It was clear to Mrs Mercer that Claire's photos were more natural than the posed ones Eva had had Kojo take. Tia's frustration with Eva escalated, primarily because she wanted to be able to leave Holland knowing the day-to-day operation of the magazine was in capable hands. She shared her sentiments with Lisa, who suggested moving Eva to the position of Fashion Editor. It proved to be a good business decision as Eva seemed to thrive on fashion. She landed an exclusive interview with former African super-model, Imam, and her rock 'n roll husband, David Bowie. The article and accompanying photo spread would appear in the next issue. Happy in her role as Fashion Editor, Eva was becoming more productive and less a diva each day. She also suggested to Tia that Lock Washington and her husband should be in the following issue as there was a rumor floating around that Tia might be making a movie about Lock and Ashton. Eva thought having Lock in the magazine would help keep things interesting. Eventually, Tia rewarded Eva with her very own assistants. She was also getting along better with Mrs Mercer, too. In the early days of the magazine, Tia and Lisa had to terminate two of their employees when one visited a porn web site and another leaked information to one of their competitors. Tia had no choice but to press charges. It sent the message to the rest of the staff that confidentiality was important, and that the confidentiality clause in their contracts would be enforced.

Lisa could not find the time to go to Hong Kong with Chance, so she enjoyed their remaining time together at the cottage. They soon settled into a kind of routine. Chance would drive her to Amsterdam each morning to work at the magazine with her sisters while Chance worked in her grandfather's study at the mansion. He would pick up Lisa in the evening and they would drive to the cottage, where they would make love before eating supper. Chance was right: making love does get better every time. Talking about sex still makes Lisa feel very shy, but she discovered that Chance behaves toward her in the same manner she used to do with her female lovers. Both of their families are very pleased that the two young people have found their way back to each other. Even though they will see each other at the end of the day, they talk on the phone everyday. When Chance left for Hong Kong, Lisa returned to England, where she has done nothing but work. Gina called and asked how she was doing, having heard from Mrs Sharp that Lisa was more-or-less hiding in her work.

Lisa Sharp is not one to dwell on past mistakes, but it has been extremely difficult to deal with Priscilla's death because it also brought back painful memories of the death of her one-time best friend, Dana Read. Chance has helped Lisa cope with the pain of her grief, and each day seems to get a little better.

When Lisa goes to work, she is usually the last to leave the building. Today, her father stops by and demands that she leave early, declaring they ought to have dinner together. Laughing, Lisa says, "I'm not going to say no, Papa, since you're paying for it."

Bobby Sharp loves his daughter's sense of humor. Lisa fixes her father's tie, and tells him he looks handsome. Bobby flashes her a smile as Lisa follows him to her car. They decide on Club Vibe. It's not the place where Lisa wants to be because she hasn't yet told Gina about Chance. And explaining her intimate relationship with Gina to her father smacks of a migraine about to happen. They are seated in the private dining room. Corey immediately comes to greet them.

"I couldn't think of anywhere to take you, darling," her father confesses. Lisa reaches over and pats his hand, reassuring him his choice is fine.

"I know why you brought me here, Papa. I'm dealing with things the best way that I know," she says fighting back tears.

"I know, my darling. Mummy and I wish you would come home so we can all spend some time together before you get married. We are so proud of you, you know? Princess never shuts up about 'her girls' and especially the way you have motivated Claire into taking her life seriously. You look out for all of us, Lisa. We just don't want you to forget about Lisa."

It is overwhelming to hear her father talk so intimately about the family. He usually detaches himself from them and lets Naana deal with emotional stuff. This is a new Bobby, and Lisa thinks she likes him this way.

"You are a good Papa," she says reassuringly. "I love you. Why don't we order our food to go? We can all have dinner as a family. I can check on Claire's work and I can spend some time with BJ, too."

"That's a brilliant idea! I'll call Princess and the kids."

"I'll be right back," says Lisa, getting up from the table. "Be ready to have a dance before we leave, Papa." She walks down the hall toward Gina's office, knocks and waits. She has not spoken to Gina since the day she broke the news about Priscilla's death. Lisa has been back in England for more than two weeks and has not called Gina, even though Gina has been on her mind. Gina finally opens the door, her hair disheveled.

"I'm having dinner with my father. I thought I would say hello. I can see you're busy . . . working hard," Lisa smiles as their eyes meet and hold. Gina can see the pain in Lisa's eyes. Gina gasps and says "Everything is going well."

Lisa leans over and kisses her on the cheek, turns, and walks back to the private dining room. Gina closes her eyes, sighs, then shuts the office door. Gina isn't sure how to help Lisa. She understands that it is a difficult time for her. Corey enters the office with some files for Gina.

"Corey, did you know that Lisa was here?" Gina turns to him and asks.

"Yes, she was having dinner with her old man." Corey points to the monitor above and says, "It looks like they will not be staying. Well . . . I guess we'll see her here tomorrow for the meeting. It's also my last day here."

Gina has been procrastinating about a lot of things in her life. Lisa's offer to manage the club makes one of those things possible for her. When she accepted the offer, Lisa instructed Gina to decide on a salary for herself.

"So, are you going back to the force?"

"Yes, I've been promoted, so no more undercover work for me. I enjoy being a cop," Corey smiles.

"I can tell. I'm gonna miss you, Corey."

"There is no reason why you can't go out with me since I'm not going to be working for Lisa anymore. Unless . . . you have a man and you were just trying to let me down gently?" he suggests playfully.

Gina finds herself agreeing to go out with Corey. She has not dated a man in five years. Corey could not believe it.

"You're a very sexy woman . . . You do like men, don't you?"

"Of course, I like men!" Gina throws a bunch of napkins at him. "There are a lot of weirdos out there. Being an undercover policewoman is a lot harder than it is for you men, you know. Women cops usually don't have time to think about relationships. With me personally, it is an occupational hazard. I love my work, but it has also made it difficult for me to establish a close relationship, until now."

"I agree on that one. It's more or less the same with me," says Corey.

Their eyes hold on to each other until Gina says she needs to go and check on things in the kitchen.

"I'll be going home early today," she says. Before she leaves the office, she agrees to go on a date with Corey. He asks a second time just to be certain she really meant "yes". Gina knows that Lisa needs her, but she doesn't know what is best for Lisa right now. She is certain that Lisa is not spending the night at her parents home, at least Gina hopes she is not. She reaches for the phone to call Lisa, but then suddenly disconnects the call. She decides to call her grandmother, instead. Gina and her grandmother are very close now. They spend hours discussing Lisa's upcoming wedding. They examine each detail minutely. Both fans of celebrity gossip, it is a game they like to play when they talk on the phone. Afterward, Gina decides to take a drive and try to figure out a way to reach Lisa.

After awhile on the streets, Gina finds herself pulling into the parking lot of her favorite gym. As she works out, her only thoughts are of Lisa, Priscilla and Dana. Gina ponders the three girls. It is ironic, she thinks, how Priscilla and Dana are physically dead, and Lisa is emotionally so. Though Priscilla and Dana are alive in their friends and relatives memories, Lisa's inability to experience her emotions leaves her in an emotional limbo, not fully alive, but not dead either. Gina suddenly broke down in tears and began to sob. Somehow, Gina manages to shower and dress, leave the gym, and drive her car to Lisa's loft. Still, she is afraid to leave her car. She is only dimly aware that another car has pulled into the spot next to her vehicle. The car door opens and Lisa steps out, flashing a warm smile at Gina before grabbing her files on the back seat of her car.

Lisa taps on Gina's window and Gina rolls down the window. "Are you coming up for a visit?" asks Lisa. Just then, Lisa's cell phone rings, "Wait a sec, it's Chance. Excuse me, Gina."

"Where are you?" asks Chance.

"I'm in the parking lot of my loft with Gina."

"I just got into London. Will you meet me at your parents home for dinner?"

"Yeah, sure!" responds Lisa, ending the call. Turning to Gina, she says, "Sorry for keeping you waiting!"

"I should have called first, Lisa," says Gina with a smile.

"I love surprises! You look good. I've missed you, Gina. I should have called you and let you know that I've been thinking about you," Lisa says softly. She pulls Gina into her arms and gives her a big hug. As Lisa kisses the backs of her hands, Gina feels hypnotized by Lisa, a feeling she always experiences around Lisa. Gina knows it is a difficult time for Lisa, so she has tried to stay away to give her some space to deal with her loss and to sort out her feelings for Chance. Gina thinks Lisa seemed to be disoriented when she came to the club with her father and wonders whether Lisa might have some unresolved feelings related to the shooting at the club. It is not difficult to see Lisa's immense loneliness as well as the extraordinary burden she carries. Gina just could not stay away after seeing Lisa at the club today. She looks so sad, it breaks Gina's heart to see her in this state. They go up to the loft together, arm-in-arm. Lisa opens the loft door and throws the files down on the table at the entry. Lisa would like very much to hold Gina, but knows she should not. She will not be able to let go of Gina if she does. Lisa strides across the loft to her office and grabs what she came for, and the two women return downstairs. Oddly enough, Chance is just pulling into the parking lot as the women exit the building.

Gina calls out, "I'll see you at the staff meeting tomorrow afternoon!"

Chance gets out of his car, sees them and smiles. He wears no jacket though the weather is chilly. Lisa smiles back at him. Gina waves and leaves. Lisa tosses her bag and files into the back seat of her car before throwing herself into Chance's arms. Gina can see them in her rear-view mirror, kissing passionately beside Lisa's car. "Well, at least that's one thing going right for Miss Lisa," thinks Gina.

They arrive at the Sharp home at the same time as her mother, in the company of her two younger siblings, returns from kick-boxing lessons. BJ runs down the stairs, through the doors into the kitchen, trying to beat his father to set the table for his mother. Unhappily for BJ, Bobby has already set the table and is making tea for his wife. BJ looks at his father with utter contempt.

"It's my job to set the table for my sisters and my mummy!" he asserts, frowning. Naana and the girls giggle.

"I see some things never change in this house," Lisa comments, deadpan.

"Son, Princess is my wife, and you are one of my children, and I can overrule any job in this house."

"Papa! Papa! Would it kill you to let your little boy win once or twice?" Lisa asks.

"Yes, it would!" their father assures her, winking.

Lisa brushes her brother's hair away from his face, patting him on the shoulder, she bends down and whispers in his ear, "Papa is old. He won't be able to win all the time. You are way handsomer than Papa, you know?" BJ smiles. Lisa has missed all the excitement of her family and their chronic competition to please their mother. It's what makes them a family. To think Lisa could have lost her mother at the hands of a woman whom she once loved made Lisa increasingly disappointed in her life choices. "Never again," thinks Lisa, vehemently.

"Lisa, dear. Jackie called to let us know she will be arriving in London tomorrow morning."

"Oh, that's too bad. We'll be leaving first thing in the morning to go to Rotterdam," Lisa announces. Leaving the clean-up of the dinner mess to BJ and Claire, Lisa and her mother retreat to Naana's study to talk.

"I thought you were going to stay in England until after your wedding?" Naana asks.

Lisa sighs. "I need to keep my head on things. There have been too many disruptions in my personal life, Mother. It's time to grow up. I just need this time to clear my head . . . alone time at the cottage with Chance is what we both need, right now."

Naana Konadu-Sharp has never forgotten the night she saw her daughter and Jackie Carter kissing and rubbing against each other. She feels relief to know that Lisa is beginning to take her personal life very seriously, but also recognizes that Lisa is running away from Jackie for whatever reason.

"Can you leave for Holland the day after tomorrow? I really do need you at the office."

"Of course, Mother. I know you don't need me at the office, but whatever you need me to stay and do, you know that I will."

"True enough, Lisa. A mother also has a right to want to spend some time alone with her children without everyone being so suspicious about it."

"Okay, the suspense is killing me! Why do you really not want me to leave town tomorrow? Don't give me a lie about spending time together. We work down the hall from each other and in some countries it would be considered as too much time for a mother and daughter to spend together. So . . . what's up, Mother?"

"If you insist."

"I do, Mother. Yes, please, I do insist." Lisa makes a please continue hand gesture.

Mrs Sharp gets up and closes the door of her study. She pauses, hesitant to broach the topic while knowing she must do so for her own peace of mind. "I saw you and Jackie."

"You saw me and Jackie where? Mother, you're not making sense," Lisa leans back in her chair and frowns. "You are still spying on me? You know that Jackie and I were sleeping together, don't you, Mother?" demands Lisa.

"I was not spying on you!" exclaims Naana defensively. "I was minding my own business when you two kids almost gave me a heart attack!" She swings in her chair. "For God's sake! Lisa, must you always be like your father, all the time?" Lisa wants to tell her mother there is nothing wrong with her father.

"It was a mistake, Mother. What can I say? I'm irresistibly charming to women," Lisa chuckles. "I know where you are coming from, Mother. I feel the same way, but that is not why I'm leaving tomorrow. My whole life changed that night, you know. I realized how much I love Chance. What I feel for him is a lot more than physical lust. Nothing can compare to it, Mother. I'll not trade that for anything or anyone. Jackie is not coming to

London to see me. She and Patrick are engaged to be married very soon. I'm not that stupid to get messed up in something too close to home. A lot of things . . . have changed for me in the past few weeks. Chance and I need time to ourselves before we make certain changes in our lives. I have a meeting at the club in the morning. If you still want to hang out with me, then lets all do it as a family. Claire, and maybe BJ can miss school, and we can all hang out and do something fun with Papa."

"Sure? Lisa, do I need to be worrying about you?"

Lisa's eyes held her mother's for a few minutes. "No . . . Mother, I'm fine. You're my mother. Worrying about me is what you do. I promise, I'm fine. I've got to run. Love you!"

"Okay, darling. I'm here if you need me for anything. I'll call you! Hey, Lisa! I'm so very proud of you, you know? Not just me. We all are."

Lisa hugs her mother. Chance is laughing with Claire about something on her laptop when Lisa and Naana join them in the kitchen. Claire asks whether they can stay the night, and Lisa replies, "Not tonight, Sweetie. I'll be here tomorrow before Chance and I leave, okay?"

"Cool!" Claire hugs them.

Lisa smiles, thinking of her mother's obvious embarrassment when she admitted to seeing Lisa and Jackie together.

Chance asks, "A penny for your thoughts?"

"Oh! Nothing, really. I am just glad you're home early!" replies Lisa. "I wasn't expecting you until tomorrow morning."

Chance grins. "Actually, I arrived early this morning. I couldn't keep my eyes open because of the time difference, so I had a nap. I woke up after lunch and thought I could go into the office to finish up some work. I want to be able to relax with you." He leans over and kisses her, grabs his overnight bag from the car and they walk into the loft apartment building together.

Right away, Chance notices that Lisa has bought a new bed. He asks, "What's wrong with the bed that you went and got a new one?"

Lisa replies, "Well, so many people have slept on that bed that I thought it would be nice to have a bed that has only had us on it."

Chance thinks it's a cute idea, and he pulls Lisa into his arms. They kiss and dance toward the new bed.

"Have you been sleeping, okay?"

"I find it hard to sleep without you beside me."

"I'm happy to hear that!" Chance opens his tote-bag. He has brought Lisa all kinds of sexy underwear from Hong Kong.

Lisa says, "I'm not very surprised about the gifts. I'm just surprised there are so many!" She undresses Chance, pushing him on to the bed and laying on top of him. "I miss you and the sex," she says.

"I miss you and the sex, too," he chuckles, grabbing her butt and giving it a playful slap. They press their foreheads together and kiss again. Chance wants to make love, but Lisa looks tired and on the verge of falling asleep. He holds her in his arms until she sleeps.

Chapter 37

Jackie's plane arrives on time. Naana and Claire meet her at the airport. Naana was busy reading the Financial Times newspaper when Claire runs to hug Jackie. She stashes her newspaper in her bag and hugs Jackie, too.

"How was your flight?" inquires Naana.

"Ugh! I was sick the whole flight," Jackie says.

"You look flushed. I'm going to take you to see Dr Washington before we go home. Lisa is in a meeting and will meet us for lunch."

"No, no. There is no need," protests Jackie. "I think I have just exhausted myself. You know, studies and exams and stuff . . ."

"Well, you're in my house now, and I'm not taking any chances with your health while you're my guest. It won't take long," says Naana with her famous no-nonsense tone. Naana calls Lisa to advise her of their change in plans, and Lisa agrees to meet them at the walk-in clinic, later.

At the club, Lisa is just finished her de-briefing meeting with Corey. It is his last day as he is returning to the police force.

"Jackie just arrived and she is not feeling well," Lisa says to Corey.

"Oh, no! I hope it's nothing serious?" Corey asks.

"Yeah, me too. My Mom is taking her to see a doctor. I'm on my way to meet them at the clinic," Lisa says, a worried frown creasing her brow.

"I'll tell you what . . . why don't you go and see her, and we can finish our talk later," Corey offers.

"Thanks! I'm gonna miss you, Corey. You've been like the big brother I always wanted. You may not know it, but my chef over there has a huge crush on you," Lisa says as they walk to her car. Corey has come to adore all the members of the Sharp family. Corey asks Gina to make up some take-out meals for him for lunch.

"I didn't know you were having a going away party."

"Oh, no. Um . . . I want it for the Sharp family. Mrs Sharp was going to take her kids out for the day, but Jackie has arrived from LA feeling sick. I thought it would be nice to take lunch to them. Maybe you can come with me, and afterward perhaps we can do something together."

"No, thank you. Didn't you and Jackie date at one time?" asks Gina.

Corey smiles. "Why? You jealous?" Gina doesn't respond. "I like that! It means you care and you won't hurt me," concludes Corey.

"Don't flatter yourself!" snaps Gina, then more calmly she says, "I'd love to, but I'm going out of town this evening and I have a ton of stuff to do first."

"Jackie's boyfriend is arriving tomorrow. I am more interested in you. Please, come with me," Corey pleads.

"Why not? I'd better go and make sure that the meals are done properly. Lisa is still my boss and I can't afford any more screw-ups," Gina says.

"Fantastic! So . . . are you going anywhere special?"

Gina does not reply right away. Instead, she nervously runs her hands through her hair. Corey is disappointed that Gina is going out of town. He follows her to the kitchen, dogging her steps. Corey muses, "Lisa was right when she said that Gina is passionate about cooking. Gina seems to be more relaxed and the staff has really taken a liking to her as the new club manager."

In no time at all, the lunch for the Sharp family was done, packaged in take-out cartons and bagged. Gina helps Corey take the food to his car.

"Would you excuse me for a minute? I need to run upstairs to change," Gina asks.

Corey nods agreement and sighs. He hates dating people from work, though he thinks Gina is really in a different class because they are friends and because he was on assignment when they met. Corey hopes they can spend more time together once she returns from her trip.

Dr Freedom Washington is a close, personal friend of Sarah Williams and also of the Sharp family. The nurse asks Jackie for a urine sample and Dr Washington checks Jackie's temperature. Jackie has a slight fever. Recalling her own hospital experience with a fever, Lisa calls Patrick right away. She is still on the phone, talking to Patrick, when the doctor says that

Jackie is a few weeks pregnant. Of course, Patrick overhears the diagnosis and screams for joy. Lisa's ear experiences a ringing sensation for a few minutes and Jackie faints upon hearing the news. Patrick tells Lisa to look after 'his girl' and says he will be in England tomorrow. Lisa looks at her mother and says sardonically, "Well! We can rule me out as the father!"

"That's not very funny, Lisa. Does Tony know about Patrick?"

"Mother, it will be alright. Jacks is going to have a baby. She's not going to jail!"

"Lisa, this is serious, darling. Jackie is only in her second year at medical school. I'm sure Tony has bigger dreams for Jackie than dropping out to care for a baby!"

Jackie regains consciousness and asks what's happening. Lisa kisses her on the cheek and says, "You are going to have a baby, Jacks."

"Holy crap! How can this happen?" Jackie asks. She runs her hands through her hair. Naana hugs her and tells her it will all work out, don't worry.

"But it won't be alright! I hardly even know Patrick. My Dad and my brothers are going to have a fit about this."

"No, they won't! Jackie, we all love you, and there is one thing that the Carter and Sharp families are known for: we all love babies. We are going to love this one just as much, Sweetheart," Naana reassures her.

"Mother is right, you know! You should have heard how loudly Patrick screamed when I told him you are going to have a baby. One would think he had just won the lottery."

Jackie is quiet, contemplating the news she has just received. She sincerely wishes Lisa had not told Patrick about the baby. She twists a lock of hair around her index finger and wishes she were alone in Lisa's loft so she can have a good cry. Naana senses that Jackie is not thrilled about the baby, so she suggests they go home and maybe Jackie will want a rest.

Claire drives to Kingsdale Secondary School to pick up BJ after she drops off her mother and Jackie at the doctor's office. BJ is holding a classmate's backpack and insists that Claire give the girl a ride home. When Naana and Lisa get home with Jackie, Claire and BJ still have not returned. Bobby says Claire has called and says BJ needs new clothes.

"They are up to something," declares Naana. "Vidal and Lisa took him shopping just last week with Trey and Jayzel. What could he possibly need?"

"Yeah, well, you know kids these days," says Bobby with a shrug. "Oh, Gina and Corey are here. They brought lunch to welcome Jackie home."

"That's very nice of them, darling. Can you put the kettle on? I want to call Tony and let him know that Jackie is home safe."

Corey gives Jackie a hug and asks if she is alright. Jackie thinks it is sweet of him to be so concerned about her. She hugs Gina and thanks her for the lovely meal. Jackie wishes she could be alone with Lisa. She has not realized until now how much she has missed Lisa. The news that she was going to have a baby—and with Patrick, too—had hardly begun to sink into her mind.

Naana broke the news to Tony, who asked her advice on the situation.

"I think it is safe to say that Patrick is head over heels in love with Jackie. Jackie, however, may have been caught up in the moment. She does love him, but the baby is a little overwhelming for her. I'll keep my eye on her."

"Do you think she wants the child?" asks Tony, thinking of contingencies.

"It's hard to say now. She is more worried about the reaction she'll get from you and the boys. I was thinking you could break the news to them—quietly, you know, man-to-man sort of thing—and calm them down before she tells them herself. She doesn't need upset right now. She needs understanding and support. Patrick will arrive tomorrow. Bobby and I are hoping they will want to stay here with us, instead of at the loft, so we can keep our eyes on them."

"Thank you. I'm taking Gertrude and Evelyn for lunch. Evelyn will be in England with us on the weekend."

"Give them my love! Tell Mother I'll call her tonight. Do take care, Tony."

Naana smiles to herself and sighs before she joins the rest of her family in the dining room. Gina and Corey did not stay for lunch. Lisa walked them to Corey's car and thanked them profusely for their thoughtfulness. She stood and watched them drive away. At that moment, Claire and BJ arrived home. BJ sports a new hair cut and has his ears pierced. Lisa takes one look at her baby brother and asks, "Did you get a tattoo?"

"No! Do you think I should get a tattoo?" asks BJ anxiously.

"Oh *yeah*, little brother. You should," Lisa encourages.

"Claire never said anything about a tattoo!" begins BJ defensively. "My ears still hurt. I have to ask Mummy first before I get a tattoo. I got my very own Hugo Boss perfume. Claire says it will help India to like me more."

"Who is India, Sweetie?"

"She's only the prettiest girl in Year Seven. Claire said I should ask her on a date."

"Over my dead body, Bobby Sharp Junior!" intervenes Naana. "What in God's name are you wearing, Sweetie?" As Naana comes down the stairs, she sees her son dressed like a thug. His father, Jackie and Lisa think BJ's new gangster look is enough to make a depressed person laugh. He looks a bit like the rapper Slim Shandy-Eminem with the white chains and bracelets to go with it. BJ looks so screamingly funny that Jackie forgets all about her own troubles and joins in the laughter.

"I'm happy that the four of you can laugh. My son is wearing clothes that would fit his father and you think it's funny?"

"I don't really like the clothes either, Mummy, but Claire said I have to step up my game if I'm going to ask India out on a date." His mother raises her eyebrows.

"Sweetie, you don't have to change how you dress for a girl to like you. You just have to be yourself."

"I told Claire that's what you said, Mummy, but Claire says you and Daddy are too old and don't know much about romance like she does." Naana glances at her husband, who suddenly stops laughing. Lisa chuckles gleefully, enjoying how this scene is playing out.

Lisa decides to stir it up a bit. "BJ, why don't you tell Mother about the tattoo?" Lisa prompts BJ.

"Oh, no! I don't want a tattoo. My ears hurt too much, a tattoo will hurt way more. I don't think I'll get one. I'll go change into my old clothes now, Mummy. Can I use the phone to call India, please?"

"Yes, Sweetie," his mother says.

Lisa and Jackie were still laughing when Naana shot them a look that unmistakably said to put a sock in it. Jackie is suddenly extremely quiet. She can see that Lisa has changed since they last saw each other and she doesn't want to push things. There has been a lot of emotional ups and downs for both girls, lately, a lot to deal with.

Lisa goes to the kitchen to call Tia. Jackie retreats to Lisa's bedroom to use her computer to chat with Patrick on-line, and then takes a nap.

About an hour later, Lisa goes into the bedroom to check on Jackie. She pulls the cover up over Jackie's shoulders and quietly leaves the room. As Lisa is pulling the door closed, Jackie says, "How could you not miss me? I've missed you like crazy, Lisa."

Lisa stops, closes her eyes as she leans against the door frame. She turns toward Jackie and says, "I've missed you too, Jacks. How are you feeling, Jacks?"

"I'd feel a lot better if you could hold me," comes the reply. Lisa smiles and her heart beats faster as she walks toward the bed. Jackie's heartbeat quickens, too. Lisa slips under the covers and holds Jackie. They are both in tears as they draw apart and begin kissing. Lisa is the first to pull away.

"We can't, Jacks."

Jackie whispers, "We can. This may be the last time we get to make love. Please, don't say we shouldn't."

Lisa kisses and caresses Jackie's hair. She pauses to ask how Jackie feels about being pregnant.

"I'm not sure," she sighs. "I wish you had not asked me that."

"Well, I guess it's safe to say I'm not the father!" exclaims Lisa.

Jackie chuckles and smiles. "I've missed your smile and the sound of your voice the most."

Lisa is still caressing her hair. "Can I ask you something, Jacks?"

"Anything."

"Do you love him, or did you just get caught up in the moment?"

"I do love him. I also did get caught up in the moment. He proposed to me in bed, in the middle of making love. It was *so* romantic. I cannot describe the euphoria I felt when he slipped the ring on my hand. It made perfect sense." Jackie kisses the ring on her finger.

"Does it still make perfect sense?"

"Yes," sighs Jackie.

"I'm heading out of town tonight, Jacks. Why did you leave him and come to England alone?"

"I didn't want you to be alone when I heard that Pris—" she stopped mid-sentence. "I just needed to be with you before you got married."

"You didn't want me to be alone when Priscilla died. I'm so sorry, Jacks."

Jackie did not get the chance to respond since Claire and BJ burst into the room upset that they were in trouble for buying new clothes.

"Too bad," says Lisa sarcastically. "Get lost! Beat it, you two!"

Jackie says, "No, no! It's okay. Really! Come on, you guys," as she pats the bed. Claire and BJ jump onto the bed with Lisa and Jackie. Lisa turns on the TV and selects MTV.

She says to BJ, "If you are going to be a gangster, then you must learn how to do it well. Maybe I should buy you a gun, tomorrow," she says winking at Claire.

BJ runs off to his mother crying, while his sisters have a good laugh. Jackie goes after him.

"I'm sorry your sisters tease you, BJ. Please come back," Jackie apologizes.

"I won't! They will laugh at me again!"

"You know, my brothers used to tease me, too. Maybe I can teach you a trick so that when your sisters laugh at you it won't hurt so much. They will get fed up and stop, okay?"

BJ looks up at his mother and Naana tells him it's okay to go back to Lisa's room.

"I'll talk to your sisters later, okay?" his mother promises. Naana thinks it is very nice of Jackie to talk to BJ. The girls do like to tease him endlessly. She wishes they would give him a break.

Jackie slept right after dinner, so Lisa and Claire both worked on the final draft of the magazine that Tia has sent them. They could not believe that in less than two weeks it would be all over the news agents stands around the world. Lisa is more nervous about the magazine since the whole thing was her idea. She hates to fail. She is in her parents study when her mother comes downstairs to make herself some tea. Lisa has her elbow on the desk, looking like she is in deep thought about something. She swings the chair and sees her mother, so she lifts up the magazine to show her. As a result of the Priscilla fiasco, the Vidal-Chance switch-up, and the launch of the magazine, mother and daughter have become closer than ever in the last few weeks.

"Are you all right?" asks Naana.

"Yes, Mother. Just a little nervous. I'm getting married in less than a week."

Naana knows how she feels. "Your magazine will do well. You and Chance are going to be very happy together, darling."

Lisa giggles, "Chance and I just got off the phone with Father Thomas. We'll be getting married at the church."

Naana pulls out a chair and sits down. She smiles. Lisa asks what's she thinking.

"You and Chance have a lot of faith. I was surprised you wanted to get married at the loft."

"I think that was out of fear and desperation. This is something we both want. I've been thinking . . . Instead of buying gifts, we can make a donation to the out-reach program that our church runs."

"That sounds like a good idea. What exactly do they do?"

"It's a shelter for young kids—young mothers, drug abusers, mostly run-aways. We are hoping to build a bigger shelter next year. Maybe bigger than the one that Dean Madison built in honor of Margaret Benson. They have made a big difference in many young people's lives. Chance and I want to continue that tradition. Mrs Benson was big on charity. Chance has always wanted to find something to keep his grandmother's memory alive. I like the idea, too."

"Father Thomas mentioned that. Sarah and I have been wanting to go see him about it."

"Do you think that Mrs Williams company will sponsor the church fundraiser next month?"

"She might. We didn't know about the fundraiser, but Brooke wants the twins to be baptized."

"That's a good idea, to baptize the twins. I was on the phone with Lock Washington. She tells me that Ashton and the whole Chelsea FC teammates will be donating money to the youth shelter as well as volunteering their time next month. We also ran into Dr Parker and Dr Appiah having lunch at The Vibe with Dr Washington. They agreed to volunteer their time, too."

"That sound good. Do you need anything else for the fundraiser?"

"We need more sponsorships and donations. Papa says he will canvass the folks at work for me."

Naana asks about the wedding and what is left to do that she can work on while Lisa is away.

"Everything is almost done, now. We will have the wedding reception at The Vibe. Claire and Tia will help me turn the place into something magical. Gina sent me the menu that Grandmother gave her for me to approve. It came today. Everything looks scrumptious. I have to fax a copy to Farrah and Maria Benson—just in case they want to add or delete anything."

Naana is relieved to see Lisa looking less sad. She wonders whether Jackie coming home may have had something to do with the sudden change in Lisa's mood. She hopes that Lisa will not carry on her affair with Jackie after she's married.

"So, are you and Chance going to Rotterdam, or should I not ask?"

"We both love the cottage, Mother. I have . . . um . . . been dealing with Priscilla's death as well as I can. It's been difficult, but Chance has been wonderful. We just want to have a pre-honey moon."

"I know, darling. I wish you would let us help you, Lisa. I know how much she meant to you. What is a pre-honey moon? On second-thought, I don't want to know! I'm happy to see that someone is looking after you," her mother says softly. Lisa leans back in her chair and sighs deeply.

"I'll be all right, Mother."

"Oh . . . Lisa, it's okay not to be the strongest. Your father and I are . . . Darling, we are here if you need us."

"I know, Mom. I was wondering if you'd mind, um . . . when I get back, if . . . I can come and stay here until I get married?"

Naana has tears in her eyes. She is so proud of Lisa. "No! You can't stay here until you marry unless you promise you will come home and spend more time with us *after* you marry!"

Lisa runs into her mother's arms, then goes to check on Jackie before she leaves.

Chapter 38

Tyra and Tia are very pleased with the first issue of Urban Style Magazine going to print in a week. Their budget is just below target, fulfilling Lisa's expectations. No one is prouder than Eva, Fashion Editor. When everyone else returns to Holland after Lisa's wedding, Eva plans to stay behind so she and Claire can set up their London office. Lisa has been scouting the commercial real estate already and has found a suitable location for them. Meanwhile, Tia gets a call from Amy, who informs her that the City of Hamilton has not approved one of their building permits. She says Chase is working on the problem, but it could take up to forty days before the approval can be granted.

"Damn! That's not good!" exclaims Tia. "What now?"

"Well, Steven has an idea, but he wants to run it by your father-in-law first."

Tia snaps, "I need a studio to shoot my TV movie in less than three weeks. Amy, if my father-in-law had a studio, I think he would have told me. I'm on my way home. I'll call you with an alternative location once I know it. I will need a couple of days before we put the word out that Sunlight Studio is in trouble. Tell Chase."

"Okay, hon! I'll wait for your call."

The Sharp and the Carter families are blessed with talents in everything they do whether it is business or personal matters. Although they have dealt with tragedy in the past and have come out of it relatively unharmed, there is a new threat they face that could rip apart the Sharp and Carter dynasty in such a way the whole world will take notice.

In show business, image is everything. Kelly Powers, model turned actress, has been working steadily as an actress for twenty years. She is by no means an A-list actress, but unlike some of her modeling peers, she has made the transition from modeling to acting comparatively smoothly. Miraculously, she has avoided any hint of scandal—until now. LAX has always been a paparazzi hang-out. You never know when you might get the photograph that will make the cover of a tabloid. Kelly Powers is seen at LAX with a much younger man, hugging and kissing him. It looks like she is being dumped by him, and that is what the photographer thinks from his vantage point as he snaps a series of photos. He follows her to her car. As Kelly opens her car door, he gets her attention and suggests, "I'm free tonight. I'd like to take you to dinner." Kelly ignores him, jumps into her car and drives off. The photograph makes the cover of *The National Enquirer*: *KELLY POWERS DUMPED BY YOUNG STUD AT LAX.* Kelly's attorney files a law suit against the tabloid giant. One would think that they would have printed an apology after it was confirmed that the young stud at LAX was, in fact, not a boyfriend but Kelly's son, Patrick. The tabloids then spin the story and run with it: the affair with Nick Collins, their break-up, the secret son. It is just too juicy to pass up. Kelly is interviewed on a local entertainment program. Her interviewer wants to know why she kept her son secret, and why she and Nick Collins are not married, even though everyone could tell that they were passionately in love, at the time. Kelly reputedly tells her interviewer that she simply does not believe in the whole black-white mixed-marriage thing. Of course, the audience gasps with the shock of the statement, as do audiences world-wide since the clip from the show is uploaded to YouTube and Twitter, quickly becoming a popular download. But this is the twenty-first century. Mixed marriages are not new. In fact, such marriages are more common in show biz than in any other social strata. Even though her statement seems disingenuous, it is actually a topic about which Kelly Powers has very strong opinions. Even though she shares a child with a Caucasian man, she tells *The National Enquirer* that she believes black men should date their own kind and that white men should date their own women.

Amy Hall is fascinated with celebrities, their lives, their peccadilloes, and the gossip that continually surrounds them. She reads, with a great deal of interest, the interview with Kelly Powers. She sits back in her chair, mulling over the problem. She has to tell Tia, but Amy wants to be ready with some solutions of her own before making the call. Feeling satisfied with her own ideas, Amy makes the call even though it is the early hours of the morning in England. Nathan answers the phone and tells Amy he will not disturb Tia as she has just gotten to sleep.

"Go get yourself laid, Amy," says Nathan rudely. "There must be better things for you to be doing at this hour than bugging my wife."

"I promise, you will want to wake up Tia for this one."

Reluctantly, Nathan calls Tia to the phone. Listening to Amy's description of Kelly's interview, Tia was unimpressed. She instructs Amy to cancel Kelly's contract and to ensure that Sunlight Studio has nothing further to do with Miss Powers.

"What if the tabloids agree to print a retraction?"

"No deal. The damage has been done already. I want her off our payroll immediately! I will review her contract with us on *Forever Never Dies*, but we may have to look for a replacement." Pacing up and down the kitchen like a steam engine, Tia brings Nathan up to date. Tia could not believe the woman could not be more careful talking to the press. "Surely, she knows how the press love to misconstrue what people say," fumes Tia.

"Baby, calm down! This could all be over by lunch time," Nathan tries to reassure Tia.

"Nathan! It will not be over for me. My father is a white man. Your mother was a white woman. I'll not have racists working for me!" Tia runs to the bathroom and locks herself inside, sobbing with frustration over the sheer stupidity of it all.

Nathan calls Amy to tell her to proceed carefully. "My sister is engaged to Kelly Powers's son. I need some time to talk to Tia before she calls Kelly's agent and fires her."

Amy replies, "Okay, Nathan. You have one day to try to talk sense into your wife."

Nathan agrees and disconnects the call. He pauses for a moment, collecting his thoughts, then dials the number of the Sharp residence in London. He wants his mother-in-law's advice. Naana Konadu-Sharp has always stood by Nathan through all of the ups and downs of his first marriage to Tia. When everyone else thought Nathan Carter was a cad, only Naana kept telling him to stay true to himself and to work his way back to Tia. Nathan has always valued Naana's advice since those hard times.

"Patrick's here with us," says Naana, "and so are the paparazzi. The curb is just peppered with them."

"What's the best way to keep business and family life separate, Mother?" asks Nathan.

"I don't see how you can. If Tia fires Kelly, Jackie and Patrick's relationship may not last and you could lose Jackie over it."

"Well, what then?"

"Is there something she can do that is less visible? Something that will keep her out of the eye of the press for awhile?" suggests Naana.

"Hmmm . . . that's an idea. I'll see what Tia thinks. Thanks, Mother." Nathan says as he ends the call.

Tia is still ferocious by the time she returns to bed.

Nathan sits on the side of the bed and motions for Tia to come sit beside him. "Don't you think you're overreacting on this one? Kelly Powers is not just one of your two-bit actresses that works for you for a few weeks and then moves on to something else. Her son and my sister are going to have a child together."

Tia laughs hysterically. "Isn't that ironic? Oh! That's just too rich!"

Suddenly becoming serious, Tia says tartly, "I love your romanticism, Sweetie, but this is business. I'm sick of people going around hurting me and my family—and getting away with it!"

Nathan realizes that Tia's sentiments have nothing to do with Kelly Powers or with the tabloids. He takes his wife in his arms and tells her it will all work out. Tia struggles to free herself, yelling, "It will never be alright! I'm sick of you saying that all the time!"

Anthony hears the commotion in Tia and Nathan's room. He feels deeply concerned for Tia and would like to go to their room to comfort her, whatever it is upsetting her. She has stopped yelling, but Anthony can hear her crying and Nathan talking to her. He knows that Tia has never really dealt with what Kevin Peters did to her. Anthony has warned Nathan that if they are not careful, Tia will exact her rage on innocent people.

"I guess father was right," thinks Nathan privately. Nathan holds Tia, gently rocking her while she cries. He looks at his wife with sympathy. He hates seeing her feel so vulnerable and scared.

"I'm sorry, Sweetie. You were right about Kelly."

"It's okay, Baby. It's okay. I'm here and no one is going to hurt you like that evar again. I promise." Tia sleeps through the night without any nightmares.

Anthony advises Nathan to stay strong for his wife. "Tia has been under a lot of stress and so have you. Perhaps her reaction to Miss Powers and the tabloids was a way for Tia to reveal her vulnerability to everything that has happened. Nate, you look unbearably sad. Angel needs your strength now more than ever. Naana is right: this could tear us all apart if we let it."

"I know, Dad. I just wish Tia could see that too. This is one man's greed interpreting a mother saying good-bye to her son at the airport as something else entirely, something despicable. It's disgusting, really. Kelly is very much in love with her son's father. This blow-up has nothing to do with race relations."

Tia awakens to the sound of male voices. Nathan and Anthony are talking in the ensuite bathroom and she can't help overhear their conversation. Nathan is standing by the bedroom windows by the time Tia re-appears all dolled up in her gym clothes.

"Good morning, Sweetie!" exclaims Tia. Nathan smiles and kisses her.

"Good morning! How are you feeling today?" he asks softly.

"Sweetie, I'm fine. I'm ready to play the tabloids games."

"How do you mean?"

"I'm facing problems at Sunlight with my building permits. Shooting begins next week and I have no studio in which to shoot my TV movie. I'm sorry about last night. It is difficult for me to separate my emotions from what Kelly may, or may not, have said."

"Do you believe that Kelly made those statements about race relationships?"

"No! Come on! She would never say such a thing in a million years! I was mad because everything seems to be falling apart at the last minute. I needed someone to . . . I'm sorry. I have to run downstairs and call Amy. I'll talk to you later!" Tia hugs Nathan and assures him that she's fine. They meet Anthony with their children down the hall. She kisses and hugs them, saying she will join them at breakfast in a few minutes.

The Sharps and the Carters are not only wealthy, they are also celebrities in their own right. Tia and Nathan Carter are not strangers to celebrity gossip. After all, their divorce made the tabloid newspapers for awhile, too. Celebrity gossip is a huge market in today's entertainment industry. Celebrity lifestyle information is communicated instantly around the world via the internet, TV, blackberries and by clicking on a computer mouse. The tabloids are well-known for having no boundaries, especially since the death of Princess Diana and her companion Dodi el-Fayed. Sometimes celebrities are their own worst enemies, gossiping about their friends to paparazzi. Tia makes this point to Amy.

"Hon, I know. For awhile I thought you had forgotten that. I take it Kelly Powers still works for the studio? And . . . you'll find a way to use it to our advantage, of course?"

"Are you kidding? You bet I will!" exclaims Tia.

"Thank God! Welcome back to the game! Hon, good news! We got our permit, but we are pushing for time here, Tia."

"I'll be home this weekend. Rehearsals begin first thing Monday morning. Lunch is at my house on Sunday." Tia hangs up the phone and joins her family for breakfast. Nathan tells his children that they will be returning to Canada on the weekend. Trey did not understand. He knows they are going to see BJ tonight and can't wait. Jayzel is happy.

"Cool, Daddy. I know all my lines for Uncle Steven's movie. Grandma Gertrude helped me. She said she can't wait to see me on TV again," Jayzel exclaims.

"Being on TV is for girls. I'm going to play football with BJ everyday!" Trey announces.

"You can't play football with BJ everyday. We are going to our home! Silly baby," Jayzel says scornfully.

"I don't like our home. I want to stay with BJ and do cool stuff!" Trey cries.

Tia picks up her son. She has forgotten how close he has become with BJ. Tia glances over at her husband and father-in-law as she hugs her son and rubs his back. They all know how much Trey loves BJ. "Oh, Baby, I was thinking you and I could do some cool stuff. When we go home, you see, Daddy will be busy with his work, and Jayzel will have her movie. I was hoping you could teach me how to play video games and then, in the summer, when BJ and his mother come to visit, I can play on the boys team with you guys."

"Girls can't play football, Mummy. You will make your clothes dirty," observes Trey. Jayzel giggles. Nathan and his father both sigh and join in the laughter with Tia and the children. Jayzel has more clothes again. Tia and Nathan need to buy another suitcase for her before they fly to England for their last week in Europe and Lisa's wedding. They take that time alone to talk and enjoy some time with each other before returning to the mansion.

Chapter 39

Lisa and Chance arrive in Rotterdam after seven and rent a car. They go to a comedy club and enjoy a late supper before driving to the cottage. Chance smiles and says how much he loves the cottage. Lisa gives him a long hug before they go inside. Chance immediately makes a fire in the family room before going into the kitchen and making tea for Lisa.

"Don't tell me you are going to wait on me hand and foot?" Lisa asks.

"Is there any other way?" Chance replies.

"Yes! We should both relax and enjoy our time together."

Lisa smiles and puts her head in Chance's lap. She confesses that she has not been able to relax for some time now. Chance knows what she means, but he doesn't feel ready to talk about Priscilla. He knows that Lisa loved her very much, that she has tried to push Priscilla out of her mind, but still feels tremendous guilt for her death.

"It will get better. Try not to push Priscilla out of your mind. Lisa, you loved her for a long time and she loved you too. It's okay to feel this way about her death. Don't force it . . . please."

"I think about her more now than I did when she was alive. Chance, you are so beautiful—inside and out. There is no one like you." Lisa gazes into his eyes. Her words touch his heart and he spontaneously kisses her on the cheek. It does break his heart to see Lisa so perturbed by Priscilla's death. He reassures her that it will be alright. Chance would like to do something to take Lisa's mind off Priscilla, but he is not sure what to do or say.

"Why are you so quiet?"

"I'm just thinking about how peaceful it is here and the last time I was alone here with you."

Lisa replies, "I've not stopped thinking about the last time we were here, either. I meant everything that I promised. Things are going to be better and nothing is going to come between us. I almost followed you to Hong Kong. It was difficult without you. Having someone to share each day, someone who is crazy in love with me makes each day better. You know me better than I know myself, Chance. You have a way of seeing things the same way I do. I don't know how I survived all these years without you."

It warms Chance's heart to hear Lisa describe how much she misses him. He misses her, too. "I'll make it all up to you with every kiss," Chance kisses her . . ., "and with every touch," he removes her top and kisses between her breasts, "and all the things that I should have done last night and this morning that I didn't do, and more!" He holds her hands and leads her to the shower. They enjoy bathing each other as the water pelts their bodies. Afterward, the only light in the bedroom is the glow from the fireplace. Chance cuddles behind Lisa and watches her sleeping. "She looks beautiful," he thinks. He tries to move his arm, but Lisa gently holds him close and whispers "Hold me." She has her eyes closed when she kisses Chance, saying, "I forgot to give you a good-night kiss."

Chance smiles, "I love you, Lisa."

"I know, Sweetheart, and I love you . . . more than you know," Lisa says, half asleep.

Lisa awakened late in the night, exhausted by nightmares about Priscilla and Dana. Chance is not by her side, so she buries her face in the pillow, shivering as she weeps. She asks herself why the dreams are still happening. "How am I going to get through these nightmares? They're tearing me up!" she thinks. The sadness that Lisa feels translates into everything she does lately. It's like she is not the same person anymore. Suddenly, the silhouette of Chance appears in the doorway to the bedroom. He is so handsome. And he is real. He is shirtless, holding a coffee mug. His lips taste like honey . . . warm . . . a quiet ecstasy. Lisa moans as Chance kisses and nibbles her ears. She pulls him close, running her fingers through his hair. Her lips find his lips much more delicious, more than any other time. It's different this time. They are not so anxious. They know each other's bodies now. Chance and Lisa snuggle close together and look into each other's eyes. They caress each other. He tells her to roll over so he can rub her back. Lisa complies, enjoying his touch on her body. Chance slowly rubs her back, helping each taught muscle to relax. He pushes his hips close to her buttocks, pressing his hard penis against her butt-crack. In such close proximity to her vagina, the member stiffens. Chance is always amazed at how hard he gets when he and Lisa make love. He keeps caressing her back, feeling Lisa gradually relax as her muscles loosen, and rocking his hips against her bum every so slightly. The heat of his penis against her buttocks makes Lisa's vagina slippery. When Chance judges that Lisa is completely relaxed, he pulls her hips closer and slips his penis inside. She is so wet with anticipation that they rock themselves to a speedy climax. The intensity of the orgasm, the sensation of taking him from behind, is new to Lisa and thrilling in a thoroughly naughty way. Though it has been a slow, subtle sex, the chill of the cottage is off their skin and they are cozily warmed up. Chance has been burning for Lisa's touch since the last time they were together. He confesses it has been a tantalizing two weeks. Lisa agrees as it has been the same for her. Two weeks apart has just been too long. Work wasn't fixing any of her problems, either.

"What? Did it fix everything? I mean, did making love fix it?" Chance teases.

"No, silly! You fix it! Chance, when you didn't let me hide myself in my work. Talking about things with you helps a great deal. Making love to you is something that I think about each time. I'm not sure how to make you understand, but you mean more to me than you think. I don't have to sleep with you to make love to you, Chance."

"How do you mean?"

"Gazing into your eyes is making love. The way that you take my sadness away makes me love you even more. Making love for me is different. It's not just the physical stuff. Thinking about you is making love. It sounds crazy, right?"

Chance smiles and kisses the back of her hands. "I made breakfast. Do you fancy something to eat?"

"You did, eh? I fancy you!" Lisa says impishly.

Chance lays back and enjoys every bit of pleasure Lisa gives him. They sleep throughout the day until the sound of Lisa's cellphone wakes them. Chance runs into the bathroom and when he reappears, he finds Lisa still in bed. Her phone is still ringing.

"Are you going to answer that?"

Lisa grunts, for an answer.

"You must be hungry, eh? I've not slept this well for a long time. I didn't realize we've been sleeping the whole day." He kisses the back of Lisa's neck as he puts his arms around her and pulls her close. The phone rings again, so Chance places the phone close to Lisa's ears and whispers, "it could be important." Lisa smiles.

The time away with Chance has done Lisa some good. She is better able to cope with Priscilla's death. They spend the first night back at the loft with Jackie and Patrick. Lisa also invites Corey and Gina to join them for dinner. After Cory and Gina leave, Lisa sends Gina a text message saying she misses her already and wants to spend the night with her. Despite sexual preoccupations, Lisa has her hands in everything to do with her wedding, which keeps her very busy in the week prior to the big day.

Patrick is enjoying his stay at the Sharp's home and Jackie is happy to have him with her. The paparazzi have moved on to new victims, Prince William and Prince Harry, and Patrick is happy about that, too. His father has also arrived in London to meet Jackie, another happy event since Patrick and Nick Collins don't see each other enough. Jackie has moved to the apartment that Vidal and Patrick keep, situated on the riverside across from Tower Bridge. Nick is delighted to see his son settling down. They tell him they have decided to move to Toronto in two months, where Jackie will finish her internship at the Children's Hospital, just like her father did years ago. Collins Enterprise has a branch in Toronto, so Patrick has arranged a transfer there. They will be getting married at Nathan and Tia's home in Binbrook, just before Easter.

They are all excited about Chance and Lisa's wedding. Lisa has planned a fabulous bachelor party for Chance. One of Lisa's many associates owns one of the biggest spas in London. She has four huge hot tubs put side by side in one of her night clubs. Lisa was there early in the morning putting things together with the help of her sisters, Jackie, Naana, Sarah Williams, Brooke and Kate. Lisa even works in the kitchen helping with the meals. By six o'clock, four huge limousines pull up in front of the club carrying London's finest strippers, all girls. They hug and kiss Lisa. Her family and friends stand there, astonished expressions on their faces, watching Lisa welcome the women to her club. A short while after, two more limousines arrive, prompting Corey to ask Lisa whether she's ready. Over the P-A system, Lisa tells Corey to bring them in, and asks Gina to dim the lights, then on second thought asks Gina to put the lights back on. Half of the strippers are already naked and in the hot tubs. The rest have taken up positions around the club wearing their sexiest underwear and high-heels. Some of them carry trays of food, while others stand at the bar. Chance, Curtis, Meg and his parents are the first to arrive followed by Dr Doyle, Anthony and Bobby. Jaden arrives with Jason and Nathan. Patrick and his father enter the club with Vidal and Eric, the last to arrive at the party. Lisa jumps onto the stage and takes the microphone in hand: "As you all know, Chance and I are getting married in two days." There are a few cat-calls and some hooting, in response. "Come on up here, Sweetie," says Lisa to Chance. He joins her on the stage. He is wearing Levi's jeans and a white T-shirt with a sports jacket.

"Doesn't my Baby look handsome tonight?" They all laugh. "I want you to help him enjoy his bachelor party." She replaces the microphone on its stand, kisses Chance on the cheek and leaves. Corey escorts Lisa's sisters, her mother, Sarah, Brooke, Kate, and Vidal's mother out of the club. He is about to close the door when Jackie asks him, "What the hell are you doing, Corey?"

"I'm sorry, Jackie, but you ladies cannot stay around the club tonight," Corey replies nervously.

"We are not leaving our husbands in there with those tarts!" Brooke asserts.

"I'm sorry, Ma'am. This is Lisa's party. I work for the lady, and she left specific instructions to charge anyone with trespass who was not specifically invited to this shin-dig." Corey closes the door on them. Lisa stands next to her car with Gina, who is putting food into the trunk. When Lisa sees the expressions of anger on the faces of her female relatives, she tells Gina to get into the car quickly. She rolls down her window and shouts, "I'll see you all at home! Grandmother and the kids are waiting for dinner!" She drives away, laughing. As Lisa pulls into her parents driveway, she leans over and kisses Gina.

"Hey, Lisa! Don't you think your mother is going to have a cow?"

"I hope so, Sweetheart," Lisa smiles. "Come help me with dinner."

There girls are all in one limousine, heading back to the Sharp home. They are full of speculation about Lisa's plans for them.

"Lisa had better have strippers up in your home or else you will have one less daughter," Brooke tells Naana.

"Brooke is right, Mother. I don't want Nathan around women who are way hotter than me," Tia objects. Sarah thinks that it is a very nice gesture for Lisa to plan this party for Chance.

"It shows how much she trusts him," comments Sarah. They all look at Sarah in various stages of incredulity.

"Darling, I speak for our kids and for Eva . . . those tarts can teach our husbands and your boyfriend things none of us knows. Ah-huh!" Naana said making her dismissive hand-gesture.

"I second Brooke's idea. Lisa better have equally hot men for us, or else!" Eva says.

They are laughing as they go into the Sharp's dining room and see Lisa with her grandparents casually eating dinner with Gina Read. Lisa puts down her fork and pulls out a chair for her mother.

"What took you so long?" asks Lisa. She knows Naana will not dare to mention the word strippers in front of her own parents.

"Come on, ladies! Do you think I would leave my father and Chance in a room full of tarts? Do you? Come on, don't be mad at me. I'm getting married in two days. A girl's got to have fun and we are all going to learn about the men we love tonight. Ladies, please, let's eat. I'll tell you what I'm up to later." Lisa winks at them.

"If my husband gets into anything smarmy . . .," Tia says doubtfully. Then heaving an exasperated sigh, she says, "I'm going to check on my children."

On her return, Tia sees Claire in the family room laughing hysterically, so she investigates what Claire is doing. Claire is watching TV, and the program is ludicrously funny. Tia calls Brooke and Kate to come and look. They also join in the laughter. For a moment, Brooke and Kate both forget their feud and begin laughing as they watch their husbands with all of the beautiful ladies. All of them have their heads down on the tables. Tia yells for her mother to come watch TV. Naana brings Eva, Farrah, Maria and Sarah, too.

"Well, I almost feel sorry for them," Naana chuckles. They cannot hear what's going on in the club, but the picture quality is very good. Two of the strippers try to sit on Nathan's lap, but he jumps up and sits on top of his father's lap. The women will not leave him alone.

"I don't know about you, but I'm going to get my Eric before he has a heart attack," says Eva.

"Oh, no, you will not do that!" says Lisa, coming down the hall with Jackie.

Brooke says, "I see I am going to have to educate you ladies about men. They always have this perverted fantasy about tarts. Hell, they sneak off behind our backs with cheap tarts any day of the week, but look at them! They don't even know we are spying on them and they are hiding from them! I say we leave them there and go have ourselves a bloody good night! They will come home feeling all guilty and give in to whatever we want."

The women raise their glasses in a cheer to Brooke's suggestion. Lisa tells them that Chance is throwing a Victoria's Secret party for her at her other night club. "Would you like to start there, this evening?"

Eva puts her arm around Lisa and remarks, "You know, I was not happy when you called off your wedding to my son, but there is no way he would have thought of throwing an underwear party for you. I love Chance! Let's go, ladies!"

Jackie says she will pass on the party because she is feeling too tired. She offers to stay behind with Claire and Meg, watching movies.

At the Empire night club, the ladies could not believe their eyes. Young models walk around the club wearing the latest lingerie fashions from Victoria's Secret. Eva feels like she's watching her past life flash before her eyes. In the middle of the room there is a huge round table at which one of the models demonstrates an assortment of sex toys. Blushing, Sarah clears her throat. Naana giggles and tells her to relax.

"After all, it's not every day that we get to see what our kids get up to without having to spy on them!"

Eva chuckles, "I love your parenting methods, Naana!"

Chance's Aunt Lucy is already there with her partner Mandy, looking at the tickle toys and aphrodisiac powders. Lucy comes and greets her mother. Maria is glad that Lucy has come to the party. The ladies enjoyed themselves enthusiastically, and by the time Lisa put them into the back of the limo, not only were all of them drunk, but they had also purchased a vast assortment of sex toys, massage oils, and sexy underwear. Farrah, Maria, Sarah, Eva and Naana also realize that modern young women are very comfortable talking about sex and sharing stories about their sexual encounters with their peers, more so than most middle-aged women. Tia, Brooke and Kate enjoyed themselves, too. They all love Lisa's energy and the lifestyle she lives. They agree that hanging around with Lisa makes them all feel like old farts, a disparaging name they used to call their mothers. Farrah and Maria left in the same limo as Lucy and Mandy. They went to the Benson home in South Kensington. Chance, Curtis, and some of their cousins all plan to spend the night together. Lisa left her sisters at the loft to go and spend the night with Gina at the penthouse. She loves what Gina has done to the penthouse. It looks different.

When Lisa arrives at the penthouse, Gina does not waste any time blindfolding her friend and leading her into the bedroom where she undresses Lisa, knowing that Lisa prefers being the seducer. This time, the tables are turned. They have shared many desires together, and Gina knows this will be the very last time for them. She puts her police handcuffs on Lisa's wrists and slowly rubs an ice cube over her lips. Gina begins to suck each breast while caressing Lisa's body. She knows Lisa's needs very well, so it is easy to find her most sensitive places between her thighs. Gina removes the handcuffs so Lisa can sit on the side of the bed. Kneeling between Lisa's legs, Gina sucks her breasts and kisses her belly down to the navel. Then, gently pushing Lisa back, Gina slowly licks and sucks Lisa's clitoris until it is swollen, hard, and pulsing. Lisa's moans, tugging on Gina's hair, and cries out as she has her orgasm. She has no idea how she is going to live without Gina, especially as she is by far the best lover she has ever had. Gina pulls herself on top of the bed and can see the tears rolling down Lisa's face. They embrace, feeling each other's quick heart-beat. Gina wants to cry, too. She has fallen madly in love with Lisa. She rolls Lisa on top of her, saying, "It's a beginning for us, not the end. You're stronger than you know." They hug again and Gina tells Lisa not to cry, fighting back her own tears.

"I love you, Gina. I didn't think it would be this difficult. It's not the intimacy between us. With you, I can be myself, the part of myself that . . ." Lisa presses her face against Gina's.

"Lisa, it will be okay. I wanna hold you, Lisa."

"I don't know how I'm gonna . . ." Gina didn't let her finish what she was going to say. It was heart-breaking for Gina, too. She wants to say she feels the same way, but it would only prolong the heartbreak. Instead, Gina wants to make sure she caters to every sexual fantasy of Lisa's before she goes off and gets married. Gina is the first to fall asleep. Lisa gets out of bed, dresses, and softly kisses Gina on the lips, whispering, "I love you." Lisa is not able to fight back her tears. As she walks to the door, she looks back to see Gina sound asleep. Lisa chokes back a sob as she returns to kiss Gina once more. Gina opens her eyes and tears well up. She knows she should not follow Lisa to the door, but she does anyway. She should let Lisa go. Gina can hear Lisa weeping in the hallway. As Gina opens the door, Lisa has already left the building. She only saw a glimpse of Lisa as she closed the door. Lisa runs back up the stairs and opens the penthouse door. Gina is in the bedroom sitting on the bed, dazed. Lisa throws her keys and cell phone on the bedside table as she cuddles up with Gina. They could not sleep, but they could not let go of each other, either.

"I planned a surprise for the ladies at the loft. I was about to drive off when it hit me that I may never get to do this with you two days from now." Lisa kisses Gina and admits she is not ready to let go.

"You mean everything to me, Gina."

They hold each other as they both finally sleep soundly. In the morning, Lisa takes Gina to a spa where they enjoy a massage, then a romantic lunch at the Penthouse in bed. Gina confesses that this is the best Valentine's Day she has ever spent. She loves all the gifts Lisa has bought for her. She feels badly that she didn't get anything for Lisa, but it is not so difficult saying good-bye, now that they have had this time together.

"So, I think this will be the time to dump me with a kiss, don't you think?" Lisa says sardonically.

"I will miss you terribly, too, Lisa."

"I must say, you're truly breaking my heart, Miss Read."

Gina gasps and holds Lisa one last time before they both let go.

Chapter 40

The next day, all of the ladies have hangovers when they awaken at Lisa's loft. After lunch, Lisa has more surprises in store for them. They easily forget about their husbands and children. Meanwhile, at the Sharp residence, Nathan asks Jackie to tell him where Lisa has hidden his wife and mother-in-law. Jaden and Jason, too, come by the Sharp home looking for their wives. When Jason calls Brooke's cellphone, Gertrude answers it. She is in the living room with her husband and Jayzel. Apparently, all of the girls had left their cellphones at home last night.

Jason harrumphs, "Well! If they want to play silly games, that's fine with me! I'm going to take the twins to my parents. If Brooke comes here, tell her to call me, please."

"I know where they are! I just don't know how to get there," Nathan tells everyone.

"Of course! Why didn't I think of it! Come on!" Jason says.

The loft door is not locked, so the boys let themselves in. They couldn't see the girls, but they could hear them talking and laughing. Nathan says, "I bet they're in the hot tub."

He is right. Tia and her mother are being given a massage by two sexy guys. The other ladies are in the hot tub drinking wine.

Jason says, "We should leave before they see us."

Nathan whispers, "I'm not leaving without my wife and my mother-in-law."

"If it was just the girls alone, I'd say let's go and break up their stupid little party and drag them home. Let's ignore them and do something fun with the kids. When they come home, they will feel guilty, not us," suggests Jaden. Nathan reluctantly agrees to leave with Jaden and Jason.

Tia confesses to the other women that she half hopes Nathan will come and barge into the apartment and drag her home. She calls the house, and when Nathan answers, he doesn't ask where she is. He simply says the children are fine, that Father is making dinner, and he wonders whether Tia and Naana will be joining them. Tia says they won't since they have already had dinner. Indeed, Lisa has surprised them all with a lavish dinner prepared by Gina in the kitchen of Club Vibe. By the time Brooke, Sarah and Kate leave, it is close to nine o'clock at night. Lisa drives her mother, Tia and Eva home. They drop off Eva before heading to the Sharp house. Nathan and Bobby are waiting in the driveway when she pulls up.

"I see someone misses you two," Lisa remarks to her mother and to Tia.

Gertrude asks Naana why she is crying.

"It's just dawned on me that two of my kids will be leaving home tomorrow, Mother."

"My dear, we are all going to see Nathan, Tia and the children in six weeks," Gertrude says soothingly.

Naana wipes her face. "In six weeks? Bobby and I will be in Ghana, Mother."

"Jackie and Nick's boy are having their wedding in six weeks, my dear."

Naana sighs.

Everyone is asleep except Tia and Lisa who are still in the study working.

"So what did you get up to last night?" Tia asks.

Lisa chuckles. "I think you should be asking him that," she says pointing to Nathan who is standing by the door.

Nathan says nastily, "She was with the chef person up in her penthouse. For your information, I did not get up to anything." Nathan pauses for dramatic effect, then continues, "When Chance finds out about your cheating ways, he will leave you."

"Lisa! What are you doing? You told mother that it is over between you and Gina. Are you sure you're ready to get married?" whispers Tia.

Lisa throws down her pen and picks up her glass of juice. As she leaves the room, she kisses her sister and winks at her brother-in-law. Tia cannot believe the nerve of her sister.

"I've got to pack, Baby."

"We are all packed up and ready to go home. I don't want to leave, Baby," says Nathan.

Tia sighs and smiles. "I miss sleeping in our own bed, Sweetie. I want to spend Valentine's Day evening with my husband in our home, so I can tell you how much I love you."

"You can tell me how much you love me, right now, upstairs." He pulls her gently towards him. "I want to take off your clothes and massage you so that you can forget about those nasty men who gave you and mother massages at the loft this afternoon."

"You came to drag me home, didn't you?" Tia chuckles.

"You damn right, Baby! I missed you. I wanted to take you and Mother home. The guys made me leave."

Tia kisses him softly and again on the full lips.

"For God's sake, take it to your room!" Lisa yells at them.

"Good-night to you, too, Lisa!" Nathan yells back at her.

"You know, you are going to miss her the most," Tia says.

"Yeah, but she's too damn much like me," he muses. Nathan carries Tia upstairs to bed.

As it turns out, Brooke is right about the men. Jason leaves the twins with his parents, and by the time she returns home, he has a bubble bath and a bottle of wine waiting for her. He could not keep his hands off her. Michael has also missed Sarah. She could hear Mozart playing in their bedroom. She finds him sitting on the bed, and as she enters the room, he puts out his hands for her to come to him. They embrace for a long time as he slowly undresses her, then massages her body with a rich hot oil before making love to her. Sarah enjoys their love-making a lot more now, too. She massages him and they talk about their evening and laugh until they fall asleep in each other's arms.

Jaden has not shared a bed with Kate since New Year's Eve. The more he misses her, the more he can't get Brendon Chan out of his head. Jaden is not able to sleep, so he takes a shower, and wrapping a towel around his waist, he goes to check on his boys. They are both sound asleep. He can see that Kate has laid out their suits and shoes for the wedding tomorrow. He quietly closes the door and heads to the kitchen to get a glass of milk. Jaden does not hear her coming in behind him. Kate slips her hands under the towel and kisses his back. Jaden closes his eyes, wanting to tell her to stop, but can't get the words out. It's been a long time now, since Kate has done that to him. He turns slowly to face her, biting one side of his lips, not wanting to look at her. He can see through the white silk robe she wears that she has nothing on underneath. She slips the towel off his waist and takes him in her mouth. He is tempted to bring his hands up to touch her hair, but puts them down again. He looks up at the ceiling and closes his eyes, then giving in to the temptation, gently runs his hands through her hair. He lifts her up and places her on the counter top. As they kiss passionately, Kate's mouth is warm and wet. She brushes his hair off his face and kisses him on the forehead. She whispers, "Fuck me." Offended, Jaden lets go of Kate, feeling lightheaded and sad. He can't hold back his feelings any longer.

"You've got the wrong bloke for the job, Love! If I wanted a fuck, I could get it from any cheap tart that I want. Thanks for the fucking blow job. Call Brendon Chan to come and fucking fuck you. You are my fucking wife, Kate!"

Jaden runs off. Kate, in tears, has no idea what has just happened. Jaden is dressed and almost out of the house, when Kate picks up her courage to say, "You leave now, don't think I'll be here with the boys when you come back!"

Her words cut through Jaden and go straight to his heart. His body begins to shiver as he asks Kate, "What did you just say?"

"You heard me loud and clear, Jay. I'm your wife. I'm done with your abuse and your anger. I'll not live this way with my boys."

"You want to take away my children?" Jaden asks with an even tone.

"Jay, I made one mistake. You have made plenty. I always forgive you. Always! I am in love with you. I've always been in love with you. I made a mistake. Can't you forgive me?"

Jaden is furious. He wants to respond by calling her a mixture of disgusting names like his father used to call his mum when he was a lad. He remembers the last time when Kate told him about Brendon, and recalls the scene when he slapped her open-handed across her face. It's a scene that has replayed in his head over and over. Tears roll down his face as his heart beats rapidly. He throws his jacket on the floor. The screaming has awakened their oldest child. He comes into the living room asking if they are fighting. Kate immediately wipes her face and says, "No, we're not fighting." She takes her son back to his bedroom. By the time she returns to the living room, Jaden is not there. Thinking he has left, Kate begins to cry softly as she walks to their bedroom. She closes the door and flicks on the lights. Jaden is sitting on the bed also crying. He knows much of this is his fault. After all, Kate still doesn't know that he worked as a male escort when he was in Holland. She runs to him and puts her arms around him.

"I love you, Jaden. I'm sorry. Please, Jay, don't leave me. I'm so sorry about everything. Please?"

Jaden puts his arms around her, "I'm sorry too. I'm sorry that I hit you. I'm sorry for everything. From now on I will make an effort."

For the first time in weeks, they sleep in the same bed. Jaden holds Kate close to him, each of them in their own private thoughts as they drift off to sleep. In the morning, they make love and talk afterward like old times. Jaden promises never to raise his hands against Kate, not ever again. She promises to talk to him about her feelings. They are still in bed making love when Kate's mother arrives to take the boys to the Sharp home.

Chapter 41

At the Sharp home, everyone is up and having breakfast, except Lisa. She is still sleeping in her parents bed. Unable to sleep last night, she went to her parents room and found Claire and BJ in their king-sized bed, so Lisa jumped in, too. Naana is working on her laptop when Tia comes into the bedroom.

"Don't you think your children are a little old to be sleeping with you in your bed?" asks Tia.

"Next time you come home, you can come and sleep in our bed," Naana teases.

"BJ was going to bring you tea, but I begged him to let me do it for you. We will be leaving at the same time as Chance and Lisa, so I was hoping I could spend some time alone with you and thank you for having us. Mother, it means a lot to me and Nathan that you can have us all here all this time."

"We are family and that's what we do. I'm gonna miss you all very much, darling."

Both Tia and her mother are almost in tears when Nathan knocks on the door. He, too, hopes to spend some time alone with his mother-in-law thanking her for her kind hospitality. He asks her the same questions when he sees Lisa sleeping in their bed.

"I just told Tia, next time, she can sleep in our bed, too."

Lisa wakes up and throws a pillow at Nathan. "What time is it?"

"Time for you to get up," says Nathan.

Lisa throws another pillow at Nathan, "Why did you guys let me sleep this late? I have a lot of work to do." Lisa kisses her mother and her sister good morning.

"Relax! I drove to the club with Papa to make sure everything is to your liking. Oh! I told your chef-girlfriend that if she wants to keep her job, she'd better keep her hands off you!"

"I don't believe you," Lisa says as she turns to Tia and asks, "did you really have to marry him again? One would think I'm the only person in this family who can't keep her hands to herself! It's my wedding day today . . . you can talk to me about my cheating ways when you see me do that after I'm married. I hate you, Nathan!" Lisa throws one more pillow at him before she leaves.

Tia and her mother laugh. "This house is going to be quiet come tomorrow morning," Naana observes.

"I wouldn't be too surprised if we all come back soon. Trey and Dad don't want to go home now. I'm not too crazy about going home and working all the time either, Mother," says Nathan.

"Oh, it can't be that bad! Once you walk back into the courtroom, you'll feel right at home. Trey will see BJ sooner than he thinks, darling."

"I wish I could stay home and get my wife pregnant," Nathan blurts out.

Naana looks at Tia. "Okay! It's time I leave you and your son-in-law to have your alone-time, Mother," Tia says.

"No, Baby. You stay and talk to Mother. I want to go and talk to Jackie."

"Oh, no, you don't! You leave her alone! Maybe you and your wife should go and talk about your next baby, eh?" says Naana.

"Are you pregnant, Tia?" asks Nathan.

"No! I'm not!"

"Why would Mother say that, then?"

"Mother did not say anything. Baby, let's go get ready for the church." Tia shakes her head in disbelief at her mother who is giggling at her son-in-law's expression. As Tia and Nathan left to get ready for church, Naana sighs and smiles as she looks out her windows. She can't believe Lisa is actually getting married this afternoon.

Jackie is not coping well with morning sickness. Lisa discovers her vomiting in the bathroom and runs back to her mother's room to get some help, almost giving everyone a heart attack.

"Where the hell is Patrick? I though he was here with you?" Nathan asks.

"Vidal needed him. I'm fine. I wish you all would stop worrying. I'm not the first woman to have a baby, you know. Now, get out of here. I have to get ready."

"Are you sure you're fine, Jacks?" asks Lisa.

Jackie sighs, smiles, "Yes, I'm fine. You should have seen your face, Lisa." Jackie and Naana are laughing, but, of course, Nathan and Lisa don't think it is funny. They think that Patrick should have been there looking after Jackie.

"Wait until I get my hands on him!" Lisa says threateningly.

"Not if I get my hands on him first," Nathan adds.

"Nobody is going to get their hands on anyone! You two are a pair of bad pennies! Damn it! Nate, I'm not a baby anymore. Why don't you go bother Tia? Maybe you and Lisa ought to find something competitive."

"Fine! I know when I'm not wanted! We're just trying to look out for you, Jacks. I guess loving someone in this family is a crime these days. I will see you all at the church!" Lisa leaves.

Jackie feels badly for hurting Lisa's feelings, but she really isn't as delicate as they all seem to think.

The Sharp household is dead quiet once they all leave for the church. Only Lisa and her parents are still at home. Her hair is done, but she is not dressed. Lisa is in the study on the phone, drinking milk while her father paces up and down the hallway. Naana comes downstairs dressed in a white pants suit, her hair in a pony tail. Bobby helps her with her jacket as she asks whether Lisa is ready.

"Last time I checked, she was still on the phone."

Bobby and Naana exchange a glance when they saw her standing by the window looking grave. Her father asks, "Are you ready to get married?"

"I will be, Papa," she sighs. "This has always been my favorite room in the house." She looks up and around the study. Smiling, Lisa tells her father, "You look very handsome in that tuxedo."

Bobby feels he ought to give his middle daughter some advice as he sits with her. He feels awkward because it is usually Naana who does all the talking and all the disciplining in the family. He begins by telling Lisa, "I am so proud of you, my girl. You are more like me than your sisters—and your brother, for that matter. I hope you will take what is good in me with you today when you get married, my Sweetheart. Not so much of my womanizing ways . . . behavior like that destroys a marriage. Not many people have the heart of gold to forgive like my wife. Sweetheart, it is so easy to be seduced by temptation. My only advice to you is always make the right choice with your marriage and don't give in to temptation. I love you, Lisa." Bobby is teary-eyed as he kisses the backs of Lisa's hands. Naana walks over to her and hugs her daughter. Bobby's words have moved her to tears, too.

"I am excited and nervous, both," remarks Lisa as they leave the house to go to church. Lisa doesn't talk much on the way to the church, but when they get there, she strikes a pose and asks her parents whether her gown is sexy enough. They both smile. She takes their hands and says, "I want to thank you. I love you both very much." They all hug one more time before Naana helps Lisa put on her veil. The usher leads Naana to her seat at the front of the church and Lisa takes her father's arm, preparing to walk down the aisle.

Chance has been nervous since he woke up this morning. He asks Curtis, his best man, "What if she don't show up?" Curtis tells Chance to relax.

"Lisa is crazy about you. Why wouldn't she show up?"

Naana walks into the church sanctuary. Before taking her seat next to her own parents, she walks over to Father Thomas and thanks him. Chance nervously walks to the alter with his father and grandfather. All of the men wear the same tuxedo, except Chance who wears a white Gucci suit that Lisa chose for him. The wedding is not as grand as Tia and Nathan's wedding. There are fewer guests and the setting is more intimate. Claire and Jayzel walk to the altar, followed by Jackie and Tia. The girls are all wearing gowns in a white textured fabric trimmed with fur. They hold candles. Lisa walks down the aisle with her father and BJ, each holding her hands. BJ waves to his mother when they pass her. Lisa's gown is also designed by Gucci—silk with lace overlay—and her veil is lace with diamond and pearl accents that sparkle and reflect the light.

Chance shivers as he takes Lisa's hand. The bridesmaids light the candles and Father Thomas runs through the service as quick as he can. When the final "I do's" are over, Chance feels relieved. They have made it through the service without incident. Chance has brought a new 13-carat diamond engagement ring for Lisa, which he asks Father Thomas to bless for her. Naana is weeping openly when Lisa comes down the aisle to hug her and her grandparents.

Lisa rides in the same limousines with Tia and Nathan. Suddenly, Lisa tells Chance to take off his jacket and shirt.

Nathan glances at Tia, "Okay . . . if you kids want to get your freak on, my wife and I will leave the limo for you." Nathan laughs.

Frowning, Lisa slaps Nathan and demands again that Chance take off his shirt. It dawns on Chance that perhaps Lisa knows that he cheated on her with Yolanda. How could she know? He tries to act cool and asks Lisa what is the matter? Lisa becomes increasingly agitated and yells at him.

Mystified, Tia asks, "What is it? What's going on?"

"That's why Nathan cheats on you and gets away with it every time. Can't you see all the love bites she made on his neck?" Tears are rolling down Lisa's cheeks.

Chance closes his eyes, fighting back tears and embarrassment. He begins talking to Lisa in Twi. Nathan looks at Tia and she shakes her head.

"What? She everything I'm not?" Lisa asks.

Chance tries to touch Lisa's hands to calm her down. Lisa tells the limo driver to drop her off at her parents home. Chance is out of the limo first. He tries one more time to hold her hands, but Lisa runs into the house. Chance kicks the limo and Nathan tells him to take it easy. Chance loosens his tie and runs after Lisa into the house. Tia falls into Nathan's arms, crying. Nathan assures her that her sister and Chance will work things out. Inside the Sharp home, Chance finds Lisa taking off her wedding dress. He doesn't know what to say to Lisa, but he's certain she won't believe him if he says it wasn't something he planned. Last night, Chance went to apologize to Yolanda for dumping her the way he did, and one thing lead to another and they ended up having sex. She doesn't want Vidal to know, and of course, Chance is not about to lose Lisa a second time. Lisa cannot calm herself down. She tells Chance that unless he wants a big scene at the reception, he should leave her alone to get changed.

"Princess, I'm sorry. It's not what you think. I will explain everything to you later . . . I love you and I will not lose you a second time. You are my wife, Lisa. Our destiny is for . . ." They are both in tears now, but Chance is all choked up and can't get his words out. Lisa pushes him out the door and closes it behind him. Turning, Chance sees Tia and Nathan in the hallway, but he is so ashamed he can't make eye contact with them. He tells them that Lisa is getting changed and he will see them at the reception. Tia nods at Nathan to go with Chance, and she will follow with Lisa in Lisa's car.

Tia and Lisa change into mini shirt dresses and drive to the reception together.

"You look gorgeous! It's a good thing I'm married and you are my sister!" Lisa jokes.

"You are one sick kid, Lisa, but thanks for the compliment anyway. Nathan's ego is big enough," Tia giggles. She turns toward her sister and asks, "Are you okay?"

Lisa laughs. "No! I dunno. I'm scared. There was something that Papa said about cheating today. I can't believe it! Two days apart and he goes and does this!"

"It's a conspiracy, you know! The men we love, cheat on us," Tia observes.

Both Lisa and Tia laugh. "Conspiracy, eh? Well, that's not good enough for me. I cannot live with a cheating husband."

"Oh, no, Lisa! You can't be thinking about divorce?"

Lisa puts the car into park at the reception hall. "I can't get a divorce—period. That is the irony of all this mess."

"What are you talking about?" Tia asks.

"Tia, marriage for me is forever. At the church in the presence of God, I meant everything that I said. One cannot make a promise in church and change one's mind later. It's not that simple. I know you think I do things to please Mother. Yes, somethings. But never on the things that I believe in. Mother has always thought of us as right and wrong. I'm who I am because of my faith. It is also something Chance and I have shared since we were kids."

Tia's heart broke for her little sisters. She asks if they can sit in the car and talk for a little while longer. She, too, is going to miss Lisa very much. Lisa says they will talk on the phone each day.

"We've kept everyone waiting long enough. Grandmother probably has been waiting for Mr Irresistible over there. I'm going to miss you very much. Hopefully, the next time I'm in Canada, I can wipe the smile off Nathan's face."

"Dream on, Baby sister! I'm still the man," says Nathan as he barges into their conversation. He stands next to the car with Chance by his side.

Chance has been waiting outside the reception hall for Lisa. The four of them make a grand entrance into the party.

They feast on chicken, steak, roasted portobello mushrooms stuffed with smoked trout and sun-dried tomatoes with a seven-foot red velvet cake. Lisa and Chance danced to "I wanna Know" by Joe. Chance held her while they danced and cried. He did his very best to make small talk with Lisa, but it was no use. He asks whether Lisa has canceled their honeymoon like they discussed and she replies that she has not yet told her father that he is taking Naana for a much needed rest before they go to Ghana. Her mother overhears them and asks what is going on.

"Chance and I will be taking you and Papa to the airport in an hour. I suggest you spend time with your parents and with Tia and her family, Mother," Lisa tells her mother.

"Lisa! That is not what I asked."

"Mother, you and Papa need this time alone. I need to be here with my husband to work on some things and to take care of other things in your absence. It's that simple, Mother." Lisa walks away with Chance.

"Tia, is Lisa okay? Has anything happened today?" asks Naana.

Tia and Nathan lie, saying that Lisa is fine. "This is what they both want, Mother."

"I can't just leave in an hour!" wails Naana.

"Why not?" Chance asks.

"I have a little boy who needs me. He is not happy that I'm going to Ghana, leaving him for a whole month. I can't do this to BJ."

"Yes, you can Mummy. Lisa knows how to make fish and chips. I get to sleep in her room and I can go to the office, too, and learn the business on weekends. I'll still miss you, Princess." BJ runs and hugs his mother. He has cake all over his face. Naana cleans his face. Their mother knows Lisa was looking forward to going away with Chance to Cuba. Something must have happened to make Lisa want to give it all up. But she looks so happy dancing with her father, and also with her grandfather . . .

Chapter 42

On Valentine's Day, Nathan and his family arrive back in Canada just before midnight. He puts the children to bed and by the time he returns to his wife's office, Tia was not there. He sees a light through the patio doors, and thought Chase must still be awake, but it is, instead, the fireplace light from the pool area. Enrique Inglesias is playing on the sound system. He dips his hands into the pool, enjoying the cold water, then walks over to the hot tub to see whether it has been turned on. Tia is nowhere to be seen. In the kitchen, Tia searches for wine glasses. She has put up her hair in a pony tail and is wearing one of Nathan's shirts. She heads back to the enclosed patio and finds Nathan in the hot tub.

"Great minds think alike, Baby." Tia hands Nathan a glass of wine and kisses him on the cheek.

"Happy Valentine's Day, Goddess. I do have a gift for you. It's upstairs in our bedroom along side your birthday gift."

"My birthday is in six more days."

"I know. It's not everyday that a very handsome man like myself meets a very beautiful teenager at the airport, falls in love, lives to watch the very beautiful teenager grow into a sexy, twenty-seven-year-old woman, and still feels crazy about her."

"Oh, Sweetie! You're so bad when you talk romance. I love you! Amy, Mrs Hall and Chase will be joining us for dinner tomorrow." Tia puts down her glass of wine and moves away from Nathan as he tries to pull her toward him.

"I want you very close, so I can do naughty things to you under the water. There is something I've been contemplating. In fact, I was discussing it with Mother and Grandmother today."

"You want us to have another child?"

Nathan turns a mock-astonished face to her, "Were you eaves-dropping?"

Tia giggles, "No, Sweetie. I was with you in Mother's bedroom when you blurted out 'I'd like to stay home and make babies with my wife, like a cave man. Mother thought I was pregnant."

"Are you?"

"No. I want us to have another child, too."

"Can we have three more?"

"Now you are pushing it. You want to have a whole African village?"

"That would be awesome! Baby, I was thinking three more boys."

Tia laughs. "I see . . . you've got it all worked out, eh?"

"Baby, you know something? With Jayzel and Trey, I was not a good husband when you were pregnant with them. This time, I'll take classes. Hell, Baby, if I could, I'd give birth for you!"

Tia is laughing as she steps out of the hot tub. "You're nuts! But I love you anyway. Why don't I put our drinks back in the fridge and you can meet me upstairs so we can practice making babies?"

"A whole African village?" Nathan smiles.

Tia is the first to awaken the next day. She calls her family in Europe and chats with everyone while sipping her morning tea. Later, she empties her fridge and freezer, goes grocery shopping, bakes, and does the prep for her dinner. When all of those chores are finished, she picks up Amy and they go to Sunlight Studios. The facility is a lot bigger than Tia expected. She could not believe how much work the builders have accomplished in two and a half months. The builders were especially happy to see her because she had brought them all Tim Horton's coffee and donuts to warm them up in the—28°C wind chills. Chase is on-site too, and he shows Tia and Amy around the set of *Forever Never Dies*. It was just like Claire's design, and how Tia has envisioned it.

"This looks beautiful, Chase," Tia compliments the work. "Steven will be here on Tuesday. I know he will be pleased with everything you and the guys have done."

"Hear, hear!" seconds Amy.

Chase asks, "Any ideas what to do with the rest of the land?"

Tia sighs, "We wanted to wait until all the snow has melted so we can have a really good look, but Amy and I could not resist coming by today. We will drive around and decide. We like the huge wall you have built around the property. Too bad the city will not let us raise it higher. How long will it be before our main office will be finished?"

"Well, with a building this size, you are look at seven more months, give or take nine months. In the mean time, I can show you your temporary offices. They are now doing the flooring on the first floor. Amy was saying that your furniture will be arriving tomorrow. Come this way, please."

Tia and Amy follow Chase as he continues the tour of their temporary offices. "This is only 45,000 square feet. As you said, you will use this space later for your magazine and photo studio, so we incorporated your list of needs and specs into the building. There are sixteen good-sized offices and two big ones on each corner for you and Miss Hall to use. There are two bathrooms and two conference rooms. As you can see we couldn't find the flooring that you wanted with the budget we had, so we went with a cheaper one." Chase opens one of the small offices to show them. He tells them that all of the smaller offices are all the same size. They walk down the hall and he shows them the ladies bathroom and one of the larger offices. He is right about it being big.

"Hon, this is bigger than my whole damn condo!" exclaims Amy.

"It also has its own private bathroom," says Chase.

"Oh, Hon! I need a good excuse to stay late at work now! This is very nice, very nice indeed." Amy applauds Chase's work.

Tia smiles. "So the office is to your liking, Miss Hall?"

"Tia Sharp, God blessed the day I read your script! Hon, I love it! *Love it!*"

"I need to take some pictures. By the time I come back tomorrow, I will know where everyone and everything will go. We will have people here starting on Tuesday. Amy, which one is going to be your office?"

"I will take the one closest to the stairs, so I can hear all the gossip."

Tia throws her arms around her and says, "We did it, Amy! Now we need to make money! By the way, this is for you. Our first issue of Urban Style Magazine. It hits all the newsstands first thing tomorrow. I told the editor that the studio head of Sunlight will be on the center page of the next issue to introduce Sunlight to the world. We need to glam you up, Miss Hall!" Tia winks.

"Hon, like I said, it couldn't get any better than this," Amy shrieks.

Tia loves the offices too, but can't show how much without seeming inappropriate. She wishes Nathan could be here to see the offices with her. She smiles and thanks Chase again.

The next day, Tia is out of the house by seven in the morning with boxes and paintings to decorate her new office. First, she stops at Tim Horton's and picks up assorted teas, coffees and donuts. Then she heads to Wal-Mart for a kettle, a huge coffee maker, mugs, a microwave oven, a toaster, plates and dish soap. Her next stop is Sunlight Studios. She hands the security guard coffee and tells him there are more coffees at the kitchen in the main office. The man thanks her. She is wearing a Nike track suit with a baseball cap and running shoes. Some of the builders come to assist her with moving the stuff from her car. They all love her already, and some of them already know her as Nate's wife since they helped to build the Carter home and have remained friends with Nathan. They play hockey together and sometimes they come to the house after a game and eat, or they just hang out and watch a game on the big-screen TV. On these occasions, Tia would usually make them all kinds of snack foods and bring them beers. One of the builders remarked, "Hell, she waits on all of us like we're kings when we go to their house. My bitch of a wife could learn a thing of two from Mrs Carter."

While the men were carting Tia's shopping into the staff room Tia busied herself organizing the cupboards and unpacking the new coffee maker and getting it started. She set out a basket of snacks and told the workmen to help themselves to coffee, pop, food.

One of the younger workers helped Tia carry all of the huge photographs of the cast members of *The Saga*. She also had a hand-painted photograph of Amy Hall positioned on the reception room wall so that it would be the first visual when one comes through the doors. Underneath Amy's photo is a plaque with her name and the title Studio Head. "Amy will like that," muses Tia.

When the staff room and the reception area are organized, Tia takes the rest of the boxes to her office and lines them up against the wall. The telephone technician from Bell Canada has been in the building since 8:30 am, and has the telephone system wired and set up by lunch-time.

Amy arrives after lunch with Nathan and the children. Anthony has tagged along, too. Trey and Nathan high-five the workmen and introduce themselves to the new guys. Nathan tells the men he can't play football this week because "it's Tia's birthday. She will kill me if I leave the house." They all laugh. Someone murmurs something about Nathan being hen-pecked.

Suddenly, Amy screams and everyone runs into the main office thinking something terrible has just happened, but it is only that Amy has seen the painting Gertrude has done of her. Tia stands on the stairs, shaking her head, smiling. She knew Amy would scream like that.

"No! No! This will not do!" says Amy forcefully.

Tia asks, "What's wrong?"

Amy replies, "There are no photos of you, Tia."

"Miss Hall, you are the dick of this place. I'm simply the testicles." Tia winks. All the guys laugh. Tia comes down the stairs and kisses her family. They accompany her back upstairs to see her new office. Trey loves his mother's corner office. She has a large, flat-screen TV on the wall and video games. There is an office for Anthony, as the studio medical consultant, one for Steven just two doors down the hall from Tia and all the furniture is in place.

"Mummy! I saw a huge satellite dish on the roof, Mummy," Jayzel exclaims.

"Wow! Come, let's go see the set and then we can go home," Tia suggests.

Some of the producers for *The Saga* come to visit Sunlight Studio and they are all impressed with the site and the amenities of the building. Amy reminds them to be punctual tomorrow as filming will begin at ten o'clock sharp. They have just five episodes of *The Saga* left in the season. Afterward, Tia leaves with her family.

The next day a huge snow storm hits the Hamilton-Niagara area, so filming and rehearsals are canceled until the weather abates. Nathan and Anthony take Jayzel and Trey outside where they build two huge snowmen. Tia uses the down-time from the studio to sleep. Nathan notices that she seems to be sleeping better lately. Deciding to leave Tia be, Nathan undertakes to keep the children occupied and as quiet as possible. They snuggle up together on the couch and watch "The Lady and the Tramp," a Disney favorite. When Tia awakened just before lunch, she could not believe how much snow had fallen in such a short time. When she came downstairs to join the family, Anthony told her that Steven had arrived safely, despite the snow storm, and that he and Nathan were in the study. Kelly Powers had also accompanied him, and Anthony expressed his worry that Tia might still be angry with her because of Kelly's run-in with the paparazzi. Tia put her arms around her father-in-law, "Don't worry, Daddy. Kelly and I will be fine. Just fine."

Anthony nodded his acceptance of the situation and returned to preparing lunch for all of them.

"By the way, Daddy," says Tia. "We are going to the cottage at Niagara Falls on the weekend. Evelyn is back from Ghana, and I was wondering whether it would be okay to bring her with us? What do you think?"

Focusing on the salad, Tony says, "Oh, I think Trey and I would like that. Are you okay with me seeing her?"

"Of course, Daddy! I can't keep you all to myself all the time. Besides, I think you are going to have your hands full keeping Evelyn away from Trey. God help us now that Nathan wants us to have three more boys!"

Anthony raises his eyebrow quizzically, "Are you—?"

"No, Daddy. I don't even know if I can still have children after all the chemo treatments. Three boys! As if we can just pick them from a store shelf. My husband is nuts!"

"You'll be fine. Three boys! Maybe you should have three boys and one more girl, just to keep them all in line," Anthony teases.

"Oh, Daddy! Not you, too!" Tia cries out. She puts her arm around her father-in-law's shoulders. "I'll go and make up guest rooms for Steven and Kelly, Daddy."

"Okay, Angel."

Tia has finished getting Steven's room ready, and she is making the bed in another room for Kelly when she hears Nathan calling her. She pops her head out in the hallway and sees him coming with Kelly Powers. Kelly looks even more beautiful than she did the last time they met. She is wearing Sean John jeans and high-heeled pumps. She holds Trey in her arms and gently puts him down to hug Tia. There were tears in her eyes when she finally let go of Tia.

"Oh, Sweetie! You had us all scared," says Kelly. "I'm so glad you're okay. Steven was worried about you too, you know?" Then holding Tia at arm's length, Kelly remarks, "You look good, Tia! Thank God!" They hug again.

"It's good of you to agree to do this project with us," Tia says noncommittally.

"I couldn't put the script down when I read it! I was going to come and see you when Steven told me you had written the part for me. I screamed like a teenage girl! You know your stuff! And Jayzel is adorable."

Kelly picks up Trey again and says, "I think I just met my Prince Charming!" She giggles with delight. They all walk back to the kitchen. Jayzel is sitting on Steven's lap and he is reading to her.

"Mummy, look what Uncle Steven bought for me. It's a story about Oliver Twist and Tom Sawyer. It's a classic, Mummy. Uncle Steven says maybe one day he will make a movie about them and I can be in it," Jayzel enthuses.

Tia kisses her brother-in-law and then pecks Jayzel on the cheek. Tia boils water for tea.

Kelly says, "Oh! I forgot to tell you! I couldn't get a copy of Urban Style Magazine because it sold out in LA by the time it hit the newsstands. Can you believe it?"

"Oh! That's great! I was just on the phone with my sister who says the sales in Europe are rather disappointing. Less than 10% has been sold."

"It's only the second day. The magazine got a great review, too," Kelly says. Tia chuckles.

"The European market is very fickle. We'll see. We still have three more weeks before our next issue. Who knows? By then it may have picked up. I have this new drama that Steven and I are developing. It's about a single father who has special needs twins. He meets a music teacher and they fall in love. I was hoping, Kelly,—and you too, Steven—maybe you could read it for us while you're in Canada?"

"Of course! You know, with everything to do with Patrick and the tabloids, I thought Sunlight Media Group might drop me as their artist," Kelly confesses.

"I wanted to," admits Tia.

Kelly glances at Steven and Nathan, who both have their poker faces on, revealing nothing. "Are you serious?" asks Kelly.

"Yes. I felt it was too close to home. I wasn't sure how to play the tabloids game."

"Are you okay now? I mean . . . is my job safe on this movie?"

"Of course! It will take me awhile to get used to the tabloids."

"Oh, Sweetie! You won't. I never have," says Kelly.

"Why do you still do it?" asks Nathan.

"Honey, it's like you and the law. I love show business, but it does come with a high price sometimes. Still . . . I love it!"

"She *is* nuts," says Steven, shaking his head.

Kelly and Tia head to Tia's office. Amy Hall arrives with bad news from the studio. The bad weather will definitely affect the rehearsal and shooting schedule. Furthermore, there has been a power failure and the heavy snowfall has made the grounds of the studio unsafe. Some downed hydro wires are live and the company has shut down the supply of electricity to the studio until they repair the damage and it is safe to go in.

"Any idea how long we have to wait for the hydro?" Tia asks.

"We may have our power back on by tonight, or it could be next week. They can't say," Amy says.

"Damn it!" says Tia, allowing the frustration to get to her. "Oh, Amy, Liz Star is in Toronto. I invited her and Parker Hudson to come to dinner tonight to meet Steven and Kelly. Oh, I'm sorry! Kelly, meet your boss, Miss Amy Hall. Amy is the studio head of Sunlight Studio and Sunlight Media Group."

"You made it, hon, you know. This will all work out very well for us," Amy exclaims.

"Amy, you've lost me. I'm going to fix you a margarita, then you can tell me how this is going to work out for us. By the way, Lock and Ashton called to say they loved the script of *Hope Lives*, and if everything goes well, I will fly to Africa before Thanksgiving to scout locations for the movie. I'm hoping that Kelly will read some of the script for us while she's in town."

"That sounds good," says Amy as she sits behind Tia's desk. She makes a few phone calls, brain-storms with Kelly about the challenges they face at the studio and how to solve them.

"Now, hon, I'm gonna need you to help me sell this to Mrs Carter and her handsome husband," says Amy to Kelly. It's not hard to see why Amy has the most powerful job at the studio, and Kelly already likes her very much.

As Amy and Kelly re-join Tia and Nathan, something about their entrance into the room causes Tia to look up. "Oh, no!" she exclaims.

Nathan knows that tone of voice. "What's Amy done now, Baby?"

"Baby, I cannot handle this much stress if I'm going to try to get pregnant." Nathan folds his newspapers and goes to hold his wife. He lifts her up and sits her on top of the island in the kitchen and puts his forehead against hers to calm her. Kelly is fascinated by Tia and Nathan's relationship. She pulls Amy aside for a second and says, "They're truly in love, ain't they?"

Amy isn't one to gossip, but makes this one exception. "Hon, *in love* isn't the word!"

Nathan sees Kelly and Amy approaching the kitchen. He wastes no time telling Amy he doesn't want his wife stressed.

"We're going to have a whole African village of children!"

Amy assumes Tia is already pregnant.

Nathan snaps at Amy, "Miss Hall, you are the head of Sunlight Studio. My wife's job is done, writing you that script. Find a solution to your problem! Canadian weather is always going to be what it is! Fix it, Miss Hall!"

Glancing at Kelly, Amy smirks, "Isn't he so sexy when he gets all manly about his wife?"

Nathan is still holding Tia, who has now put her head on his shoulder while he rubs her back.

"I have found a solution, Mr Carter. May I have your attention and that of your beautiful wife for a second?"

Amy goes to the fridge and takes out a Maria Christina red wine, two wine glasses and pours one for herself and one for Kelly. "Last month, when we were having problems with our permits at Sunlight, Steven had this brilliant idea about a location."

Tia leaves her husband's embrace, jumps off the island, and shouts, "No!" She waves her left hand in the air, shouting repeatedly, "No, no, no, no, no!"

Amy protests, "But you don't even know what I am going to say!"

Tia pulls a chair out and sits down, crossing her legs. "Miss Hall, I love your enthusiasm, but absolutely no. Amy, I'm trying to get pregnant here. I'll not have crazy show-business people turning my home into a movie set. Call the hydro company, and threaten them until they put the power back on," Tia orders.

"Hon, I will call them, but just in case, there's a Plan B. Your father-in-law, I'm told, has a beautiful cottage outside Ottawa; you and Mr Handsome here have a beautiful home in Ottawa and one in Stoney Creek, where we can shoot; and the rest can be done in the studio so that we meet our deadline. Hon, don't you two think you have too many children already?"

Kelly watches Amy, thinking, "This woman has guts, but she's also partially crazy."

"You know what Sweetie? I don't want a whole African village of babies, but I think we should, in honor of Miss Hall," says Tia, smiling. Amy puts her arms around Tia and says, "Well, you two make very beautiful babies. What the hell! I'll drink to that! I'm going to call the hydro company again and see where we are."

As Amy exited the room, Kelly asks Tia, "Is she for real?"

"Oh, yes! She's for real, all right!" Tia begins to laugh.

Chapter 43

In England, just like she promised her mother, Lisa and Chance are staying with BJ and Claire at the Sharp's house. Patrick and Jackie are keeping them company, too. The first night after the wedding, Lisa took them all out to dinner. Gertrude and Kofi left the next day to return to Holland, so it was a nice opportunity to have some time with them. Now that all of the wedding guests have departed, Lisa has developed a kind of routine. She is always home no later than four to help BJ with his homework. Jackie and Claire take him to his after-school activities while Lisa gets dinner started. She and Chance have not yet consummated the marriage. Neither one feels able to open a dialogue about Chance's involvement with Yolanda the day before their wedding. Of course, BJ cannot sleep in his own bed, so he crawls in with them, which does not help matters very much.

The excitement at work is waning. The sales of the first issue of Urban Style Magazine have declined, and are not as good as they were in the first two weeks of its launch. In the course of investigating why the magazine was doing so poorly, Lisa discovered that their promotional advertisement had not been placed as the marketing team had been instructed to do, several weeks before the launch. Fortunately, the entertainment news programs on television mentioned the magazine in their "what's new" segment, drawing attention to the magazine's North American success. Eva Collins also appeared on Holland RTLV and since then, the magazine's sales have improved markedly.

Naana and Bobby have returned from Cuba feeling very relaxed and happy. They are more like newly weds than Lisa and Chance are. A few days later, Naana finally got Lisa alone to talk about what's bothering her.

"Mum, Chance slept with Yolanda the day before our wedding, and I just can't get past it."

"You and Chance have to sort it out yourselves. Share your feelings with him, darling. Let him explain himself. Don't let it tear you apart."

Lisa thanked her mother for the advice, but didn't know how to broach the subject with Chance.

Patrick and Jackie will be leaving for Canada in two days, so Lisa and Chance have invited them to have dinner with them at the loft. They stop at Club Vibe to pick up some take-out meals. Gina is not in her office, so Lisa goes up to the penthouse apartment. Chance sees her going up, but he is talking on his cellphone and can't intervene. He has his suspicions about Lisa and her chef, but none he can prove. Nevertheless, he feel certain there is something going on between the two women. Chance knows he has hurt Lisa, but he is determined not to lose his wife to another woman. Angrily, he throws his cellphone across the street and runs inside. He puts his foot to the door before it closes. Inside, he loosens his tie and runs up the stairs. Through the wide-open door, Chance can see Lisa standing by the window. Gina comes into the room with a bottle of water for her.

"How are you?" asks Gina. "How's married life?"

Lisa turns around with tears in her eyes. It breaks Chance's heart to see Lisa so upset. Gina puts her arms around Lisa, telling her, "If you ever need someone to talk to, I'm a good listener."

Lisa smiles and sighs. "How about a big hug before you walk me out?" asks Lisa. As they hug Lisa whispers to Gina how much she misses her, then straightens herself before going downstairs. A moment later, Gina realizes that Lisa has left her purse behind. As she turns to retrieve it, Gina sees Chance in his hiding place and knows he has been spying on them. Gina takes the back stairs, which enter into the kitchen, and runs into Chance in the private dining room.

"Mr Benson, sir! Lisa stopped by to say hello and left her purse behind. Do you mind giving to her?"

"Thank you," Chance says coldly. "Um . . . Please, it's Chance. Call me Chance, Miss Read. Thank you." He turns and walks to his car. Lisa is already there waiting for him.

At the loft, Chance carried the take-out meals from the car to the apartment. He opens the door for Lisa, who steps into the foyer of the apartment. Chance puts the food in the kitchen and returns to help Lisa with her jacket. He hangs it up for her, then takes her by the hand, braiding his fingers into hers. She does not move away, but her heart is beating a little faster. Chance scoops Lisa into his arms and carries her into the living room, placing her gently on the sofa. He goes into the office and comes back with a gift-wrapped box, which he presents to her. Lisa takes the package and puts it on the floor. Needing something to do, Chance goes over to the stereo and selects a Michael Bolton CD. "Completely" begins to play as Chance pulls Lisa toward him and removed the hair clip from her hair. He massages the back of her neck with one hand while the other hand runs through her hair. Tension melts away as Lisa turns to face him. She slides her hands down his arms as their bodies rub against each other. They begin undressing each other, they braid their fingers together, they gaze into each other's eyes and slowly, sensuously kiss and caress each other with their tongues and fingers. While the Michael Bolton CD blasts through the sound system, they continue to kiss. "I said I love but I lie" plays as Chance carries Lisa into the bedroom. He puts her on the bed, covers her with the bedspread and leaves the room. He returns moments later with a single pink rose between his teeth, a bowl of fresh grapes and glass of orange juice for Lisa. She laughs as he presents her with the rose. Taking a foot in his hands, Chance begins to massage Lisa's feet with oil and works his way up to her breasts.

"Will you ever forgive me?" he begs.

Lisa takes the rose from him with one hand, while feeding him some of the grapes. She kisses his nose. Lisa's whole body melts as her husband rolls her on top of him, continuing to massage and kiss her all over as they make love again and again. Lisa is beginning to wonder how she was able to deny herself something this delicious all this time.

"Are you okay?" asks Chance.

"Yes, are you okay?" responds Lisa.

"Yes, Princess. I will never hurt you again. I thought I had lost you, you know? I wanted to kill myself for being so stupid. Nathan smacked me and threatened to have me killed if I ever did anything to hurt you again. Jaden and Jason said that they should tie me to the Limousine to bring me back to your parents house to apologize. Thank God Tia rang at that moment. Otherwise, I'm sure I'd be in hospital by now. I had too much to drink. I had no idea what I did until it was too late."

"I'm sorry, Chance. I have always loved you. I've just been afraid to let myself believe it. I thought being with Priscilla would help get rid of my feelings for you."

"Did it?"

"No . . . you are everything I've wanted and more. I was just hurt after we were married . . . when you told me you had slept with your ex . . . I was devastated. I wanted to take a plane and just leave, and never come back," Lisa gasps.

"Why didn't you?"

Lisa sighs, wiping the tears off her face. "I thought about everything that you are to me—all the romantic things that we've done, the way that we fight and make up, and how you always make me feel safe." She pauses, thinking how to say everything. "I couldn't break my promise to you and God, to love and cherish you till death do us part. I just can't break my promise to God and us. You are my husband. You have been my only friend since we were kids. I love you. You have no idea how lonely it was without you after Dana died. I haven't been able to talk to you. I can't share you any more than you can share me."

"I don't want you to share me. It will never happen again. I would have told you. I was waiting for the right time. I didn't want to begin our marriage with a lie between us. I didn't know Gina was Dana's sister. I thought you . . ."

"No. I didn't know Gina was Dana's sister, either. My mother did. Gina has been a very good friend to me. I love her, you know. I'm able to talk to her about things and be myself with her. She is the one who encouraged me to talk to you after Priscilla shot at us." Lisa smiles.

"I know. I can see that. I'm happy that you have someone you can trust around you. Lisa, we are husband and wife now. I want us to be able to talk and share things with each other. I promise you, we are going to have the life that we planned, and I will love you more each day," Chance tells her.

Of course, Chance and Lisa forgot they were having dinner with Patrick and Jackie. They let themselves into the loft and Jackie found them making love—again. She sighed and closed the door before gently knocking again.

"We're here! I see you got the dinner. I'll get everything ready," yelled Jackie.

Chance emerged from the bedroom first wearing Levi jeans and a polo shirt.

"You made the lady happy, I hope?" inquires Patrick.

"I'm trying, bro," Chance kisses Jackie on the cheek. "And how are you feeling?"

"I'm a lot better."

"Lisa has been worried about you. I'd not be surprised if you see us in Canada soon. She is going to miss you, you know?"

Jackie smiled, wondering what caused such friction between them. She's happy they are back being in love again. Lisa was taking so long getting dressed that Jackie decided to go check on her. When the two girls re-joined the boys, Patrick thought that Lisa and Chance were better suited than Lisa and Vidal had been.

"My mother is in Canada shooting a movie with Jackie's brother. She is also staying with them during the shoot, so I expect we will be seeing her more often. She tells me that she has a nice surprise for me there," Patrick chuckled.

"Jackie, when do you begin your internship?" asked Chance.

"In a week. This will give me a chance to show my Baby around Toronto," Jackie said proudly.

"Don't you go and spoil him, now!" said Lisa.

Jackie laughed. "I plan to everyday. Just like Chance spoils you." She smiles.

Nathan can't seem to give Tia a moment of peace, with all the gifts he buys and the endless love-making. "The man has lost it," Tia tells Brooke and Kate over the phone. He walks in and takes the phone from Tia to tell her friends, "I'm going to take my pregnant wife upstairs so I can rub her feet and make passionate love to her. I suggest you two get off the phone and go give Jason and Jaden some."

"What am I going to do with you, Mr Hot?" Tia wonders, shaking her head.

"Well, since you are going to have another son for me very soon, why don't you make me a smoothie? I was thinking that you and I should spend the weekend in Niagara Falls at the Falls view Hotel, in their best honeymoon suite with the biggest jacuzzi tub filled with your favorite bubble bath and oil, with me, your very sexy, hot husband in the tub doing all kinds of nasty romantic things to you. When we come home, you can call and tell your sisters what a bad, bad man I am." He winks.

"Mm . . . I like that, Mr Hot! You are one bad boy, Sweetie," Tia says as she kisses him softly. He asks her to tell him how much she loves him as he makes love to her. "It's forever, Sweetie. It will never die."

Epilogue

Back in Holland, Eva is relieved that the magazine is doing well. She has had her weekly over-the-phone meeting with Tia, who is also very happy with the success and they are all looking forward to their mid-March issue which has lots of exclusive photos of the stars of *Forever Never Dies*. Eva saw a preview of the movie on TV and told her husband that it is the movie Kelly did at Tia's studio. Kelly will be shooting another movie with Jayzel next month. Vidal has been enjoying his single lifestyle with a different woman on his arm every night. He still has strong feelings for Lisa, but is relieved every time he sees them being chased by photographers everywhere they go. He didn't want that for himself.

Kelly Powers and Nick Collins have re-kindled their romance after a breech of almost twenty-five years. Kelly has signed a six-year contract with Sunlight Media Group to do three more movies and a mini-series with them. She and Nick bought Tia's old house in Stoney Creek so they can be closer to their son and their grandchild. They, too, are very happy. They have become close to the whole Carter family and Kelly has also formed a friendship with Amy Hall. She introduced Amy to one of Nick's friends who works at Collins Enterprise in Toronto, and Amy couldn't be happier.

Kate and Brooke have made up over the Brendon Chan fiasco. They spend most of their weekends together as well as working in the same building. Their children have become the best of friends and they enjoy going to the Sharp home to play video games with BJ. It's often difficult to get them to come home after Bobby and Naana have spoiled them rotten.

Dr Michael Doyle and Sarah Williams have announced their engagement and plan to get married in the summer.

Bobby and Naana Konadu-Sharp are more in love now than they were thirty years ago. Bobby is less nervous around his in-laws, too, though he still fights with BJ over his wife.

That once-spoiled young lady, Claire Sharp, has taken her parents and sisters by surprise. She is now a workaholic just like her two older siblings. Her work with Sunlight Media Group and Urban Style Magazine has got people's attention in both the television and advertising industries in Europe and North America. She did not go to NYU as she had hoped, but she spends most of her time all over the world, working on one project after another. She has begun a romance with Michael Washington, the son of Dr Freedom Washington.

Lisa and Chance Benson have known since they were teenagers that they are soul mates. They are a power couple, regulars in the society magazines, and the press loves them, so they are often swamped by paparazzi everywhere they go. Just like Lisa predicted, the two of them have more money than their parents, put together.

Corey and Gina have married and are expecting their first child in four months. Gina and Lisa have managed to keep their affairs a secret from their husbands, and it's still going strong without anyone knowing.

Jackie and Patrick welcomed a baby girl—Heather Rose—and expect a second child in less than a month. They live in Toronto, which they love.

The Carters are also doing very well. Steven has always said that he will never date one of Nathan's ex-girlfriends, but he and Liz Starr found themselves drawn to one another during the filming of *Forever Never Dies*. They eloped to Las Vegas, just like in the movies, and were married at a road-side chapel. Steven now spends more time in Canada and Jayzel loves having her Uncle Steven around to read to her. Meanwhile, Anthony's romance with Evelyn has blossomed into something beautiful. They both enjoy watching Trey play hockey on weekends, and they love taking him to Tim Horton's afterward.

Tia now has two top-ten shows in Canada, both being filmed at Sunlight Studios. Their next movie is about Tia's good friend Lock Washington and her husband, Mr Ashton Wentworth, titled *Hope Lives*. It will be filmed in Africa next month. Things couldn't be better with Tia and Nathan, who has got his wish. Tia gave birth to their second son,

Rio. Tia is now pregnant with their third son and Nathan has become an over-bearing father and husband since they learned the news about the new addition to the Carter family.

With love and devotion, the Carter's and the Sharp's enthralling dynastic saga continues as the lives of the amazing Brooke, Kate, and Tia, and their husbands and lovers unfold. Love, sex and heartwarming fascinations with those who are allowed to be close to these two unusual families and their friends for whom forever never dies. In *Hope lives* . . .

The end